True Beauty

by Yaongyi

BOBBIE CHASE Executive Editor
MONIQUE NARBONETA ZOSA Cover Designer
NEIL ERICKSON English Language Lettering
PATRICK McCORMICK Production Manager

ARON LEVITZ President
ASHLEIGH GARDNER SVP, Head of Global Publishing
DEANNA McFADDEN Executive Publishing Director, Wattpad WEBTOON Book Group
DAVID MADDEN Global Head of Entertainment
TAYLOR GRANT VP, Head of Global Animation
LINDSEY RAMEY VP, Head of Global Film
SERA TABB VP, Head of Global Television
TINA McINTYRE VP, Marketing
CAITLIN O'HANLON Head of Content & Creators
DEXTER ONG Managing Director, International
RYAN PHILP SVP, Operations
MAXIMILIAN JO General Counsel
AUSTIN WONG Head of Legal and Business Affairs
COREY HOCK Director, Legal & Business Affairs
KEN KIM WEBTOON CEO

UN**S**CROLLED

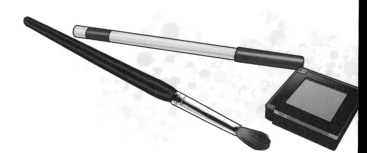

CONTENTS

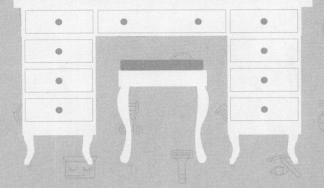

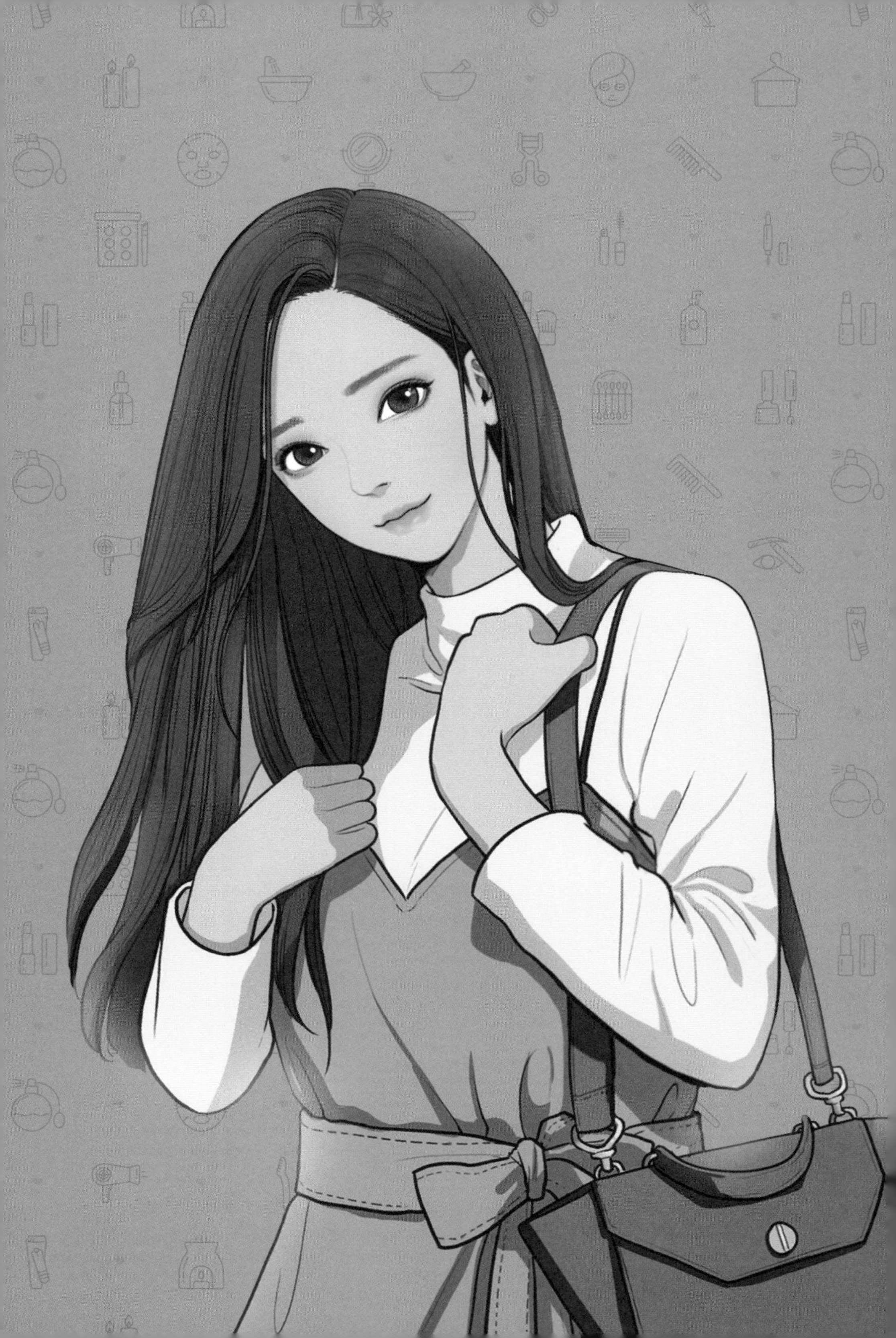

Prologue—
Episode 4

여신강림

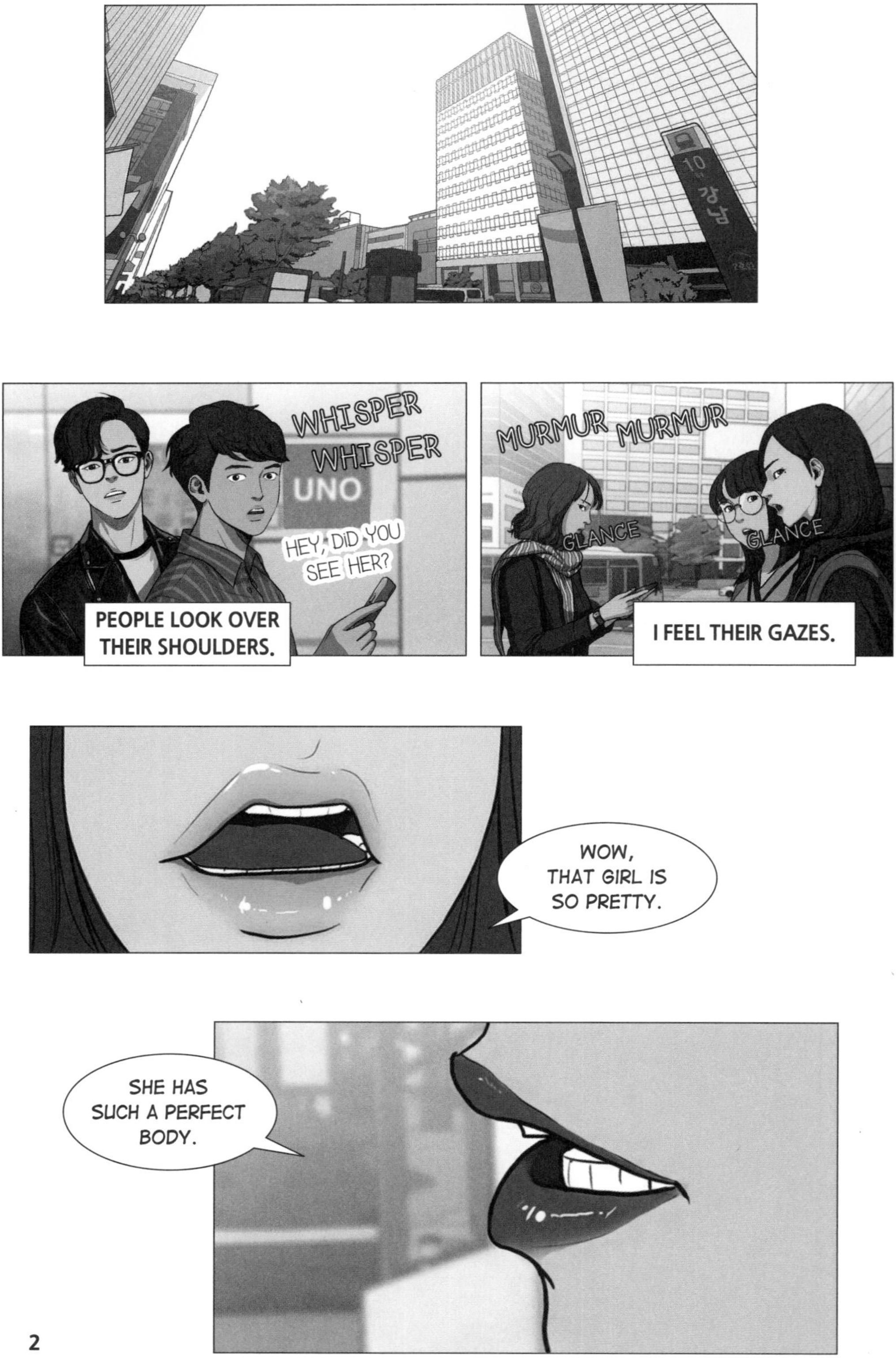
10
강남
WHISPER
WHISPER
UNO
HEY, DID YOU SEE HER?
PEOPLE LOOK OVER THEIR SHOULDERS.
MURMUR MURMUR
GLANCE
GLANCE
I FEEL THEIR GAZES.
WOW, THAT GIRL IS SO PRETTY.
SHE HAS SUCH A PERFECT BODY.

CLICK

CLICK

CLICK

I'M SO USED TO PEOPLE WHISPERING ABOUT ME.

CLICK

CLICK

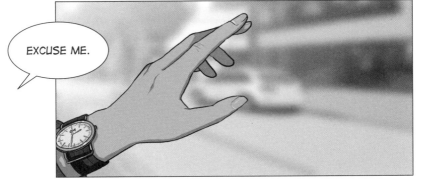

EXCUSE ME.

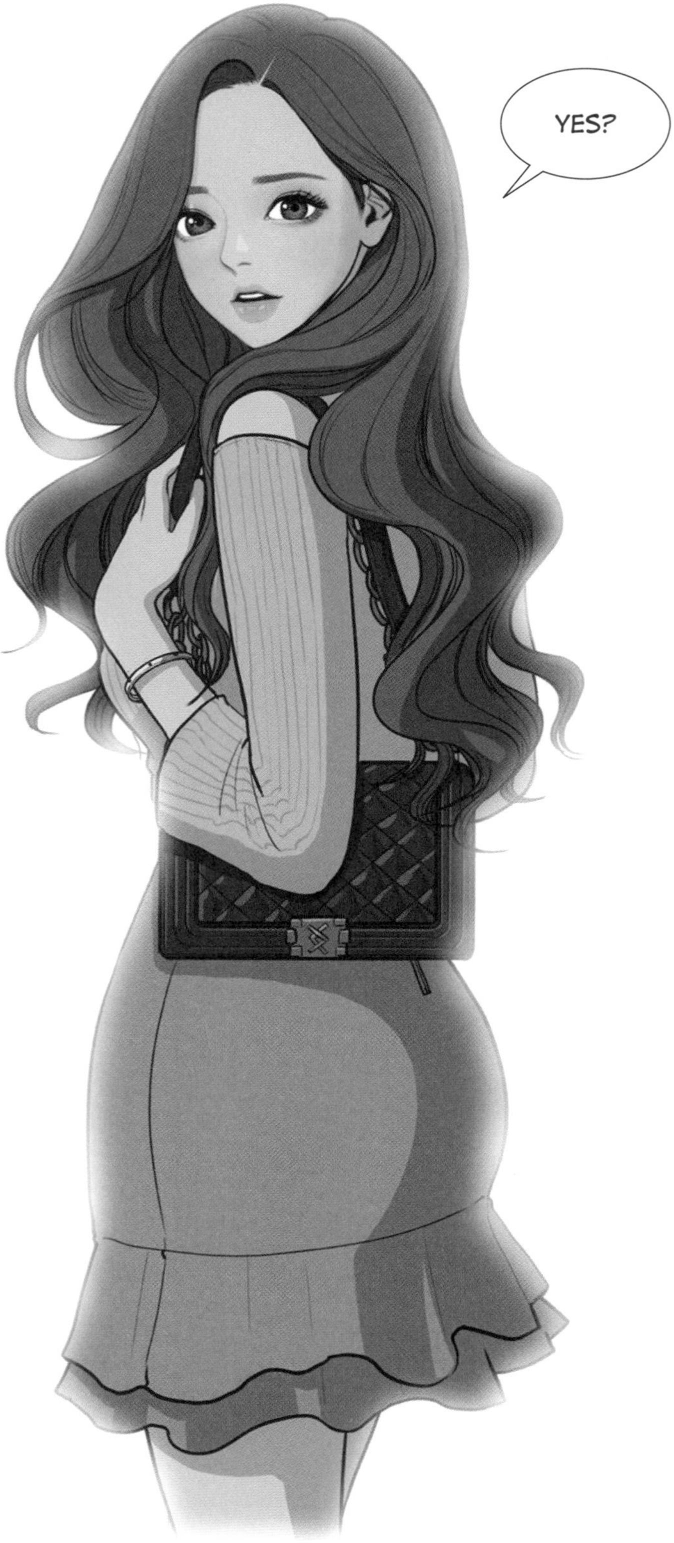
YES?

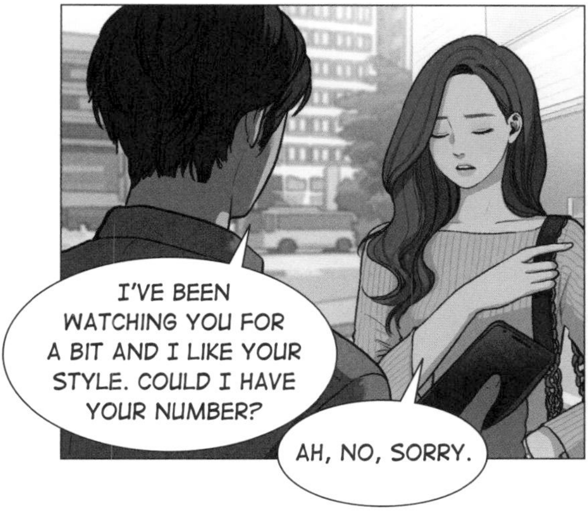
I'VE BEEN WATCHING YOU FOR A BIT AND I LIKE YOUR STYLE. COULD I HAVE YOUR NUMBER?
AH, NO, SORRY.

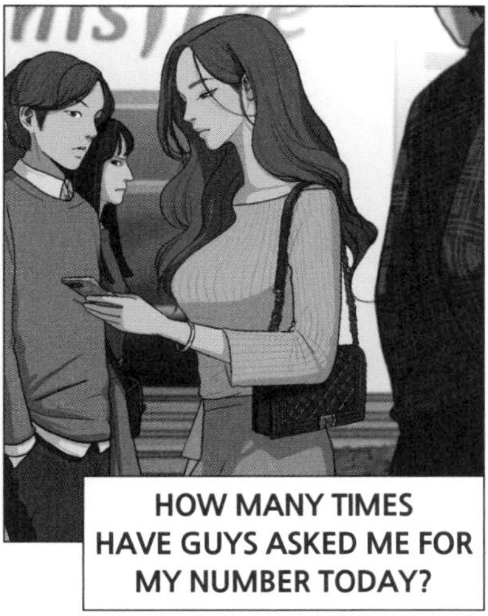
HOW MANY TIMES HAVE GUYS ASKED ME FOR MY NUMBER TODAY?

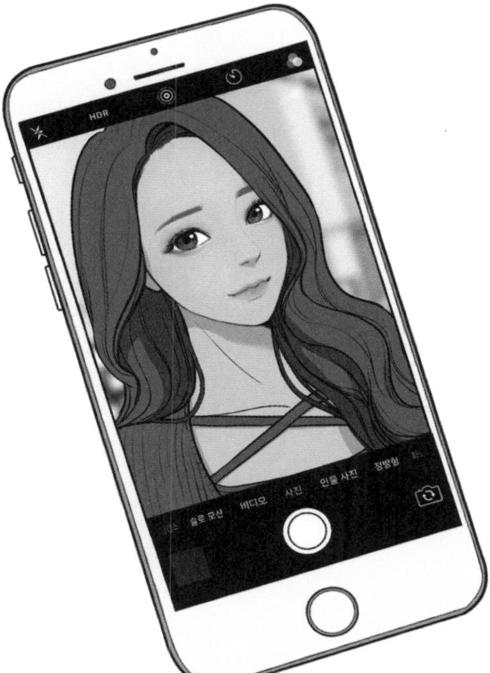
HDR
슬로 모션
비디오
사진
인물 사진
정방형

WHO AM I, YOU ASK?

A UNIVERSALLY RECOGNIZED

GODDESS!

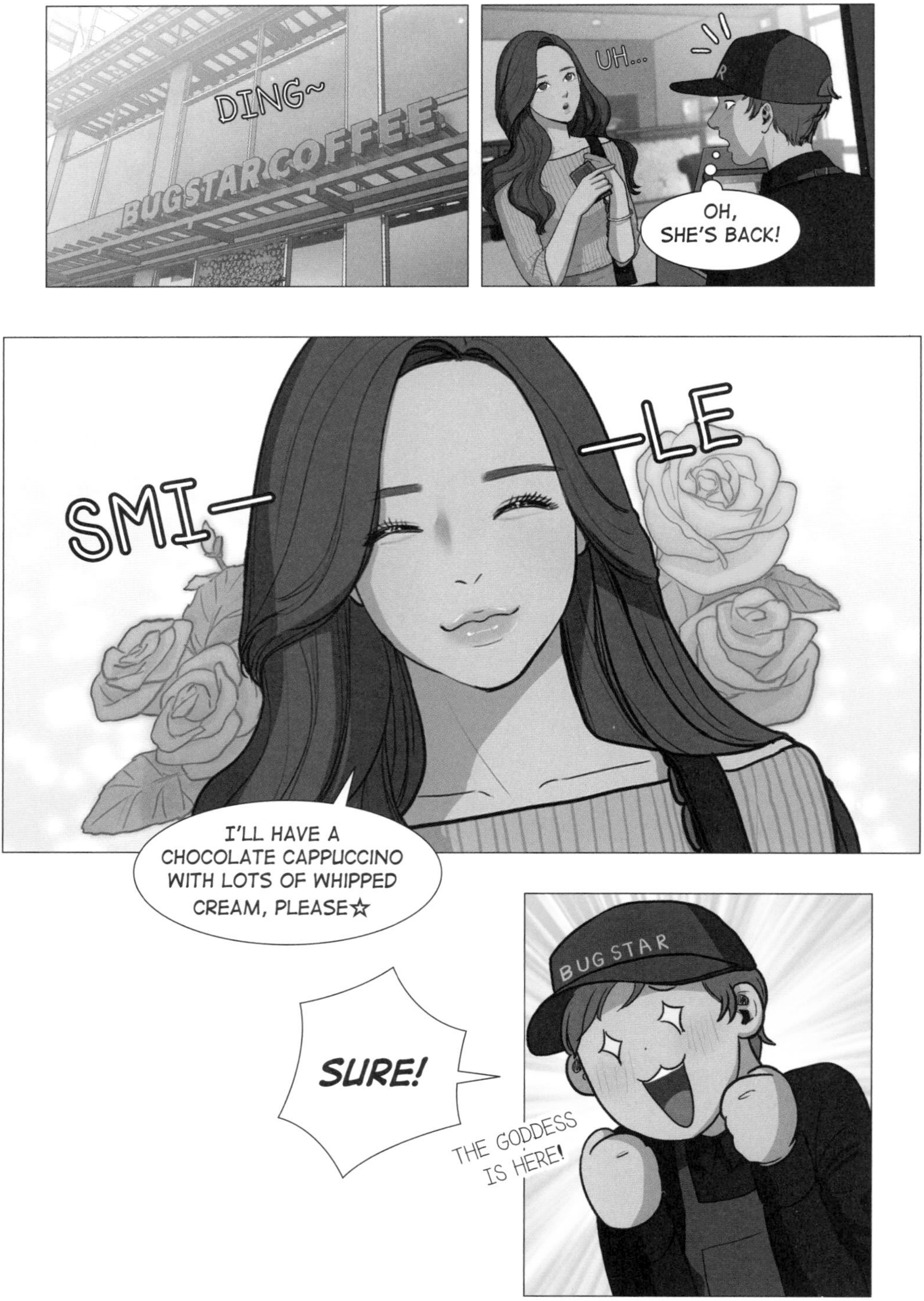
DING~
BUGSTAR COFFEE
UH...
OH, SHE'S BACK!
SMI— —LE
I'LL HAVE A CHOCOLATE CAPPUCCINO WITH LOTS OF WHIPPED CREAM, PLEASE☆
BUG STAR
SURE!
THE GODDESS IS HERE!

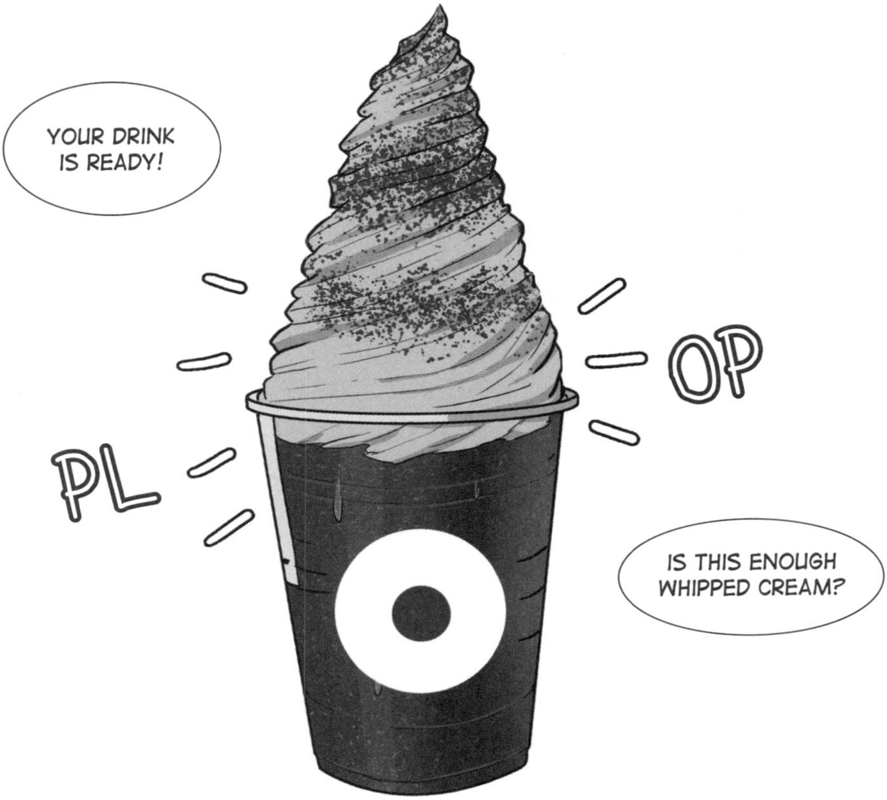
YOUR DRINK IS READY!
PL
OP
IS THIS ENOUGH WHIPPED CREAM?

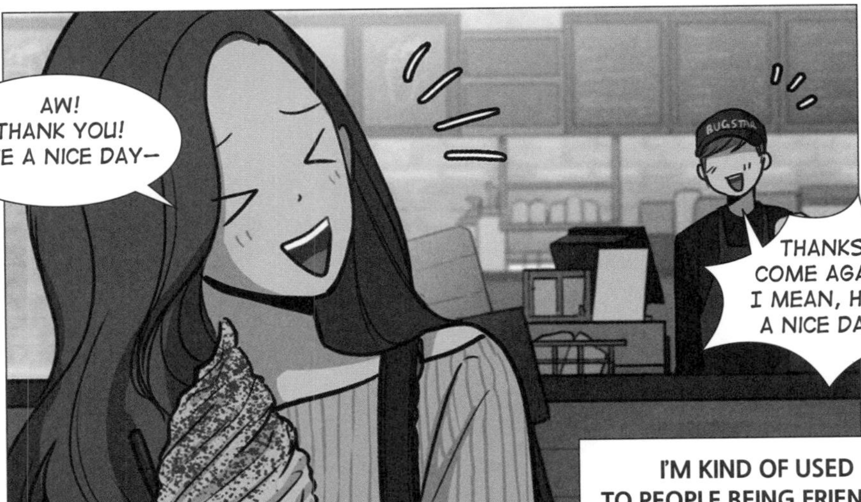
AW! THANK YOU! HAVE A NICE DAY–
THANKS! COME AGAIN! I MEAN, HAVE A NICE DAY!!
I'M KIND OF USED TO PEOPLE BEING FRIENDLY.

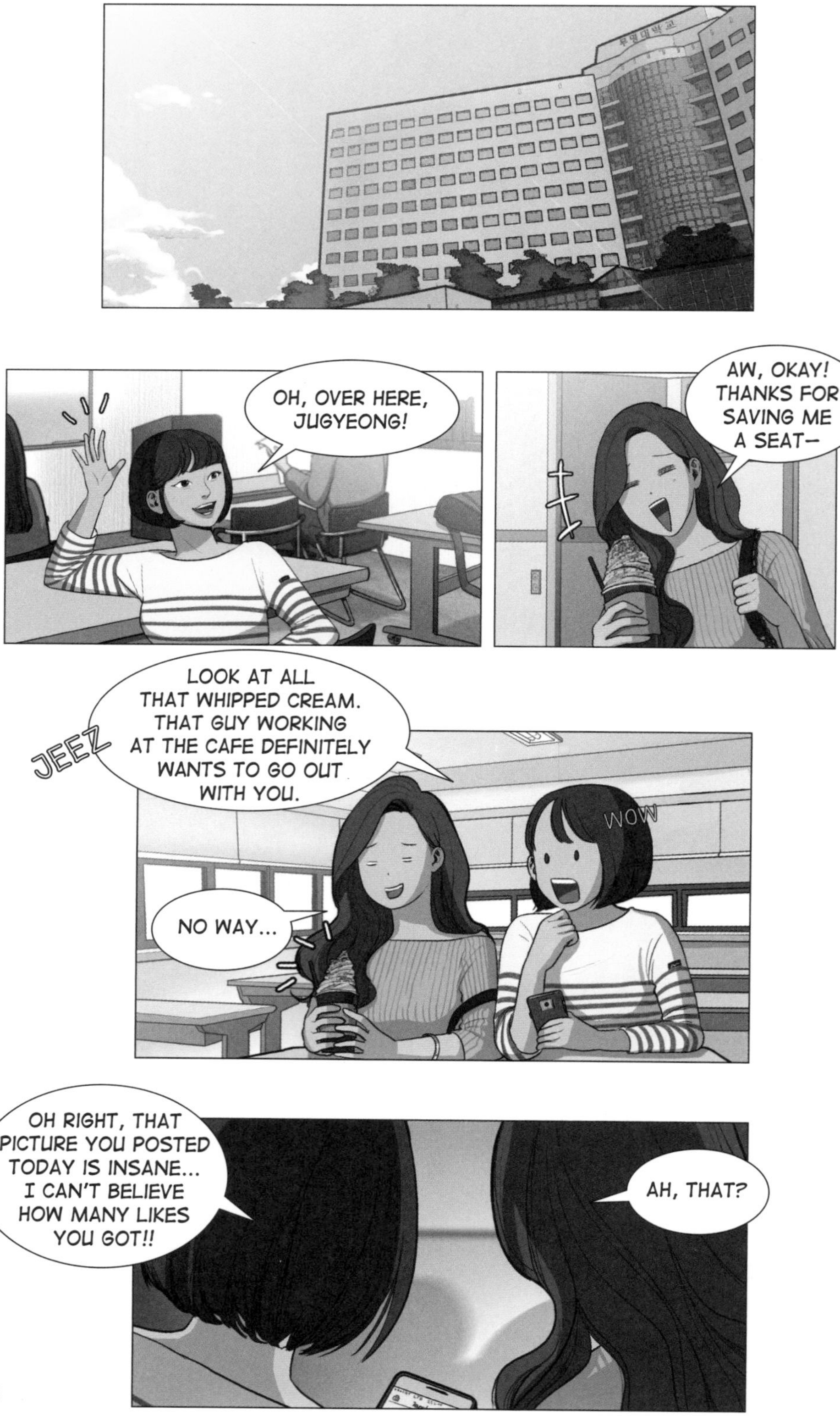
OH, OVER HERE, JUGYEONG!
AW, OKAY! THANKS FOR SAVING ME A SEAT—
JEEZ
LOOK AT ALL THAT WHIPPED CREAM. THAT GUY WORKING AT THE CAFE DEFINITELY WANTS TO GO OUT WITH YOU.
WOW
NO WAY...
OH RIGHT, THAT PICTURE YOU POSTED TODAY IS INSANE... I CAN'T BELIEVE HOW MANY LIKES YOU GOT!!
AH, THAT?

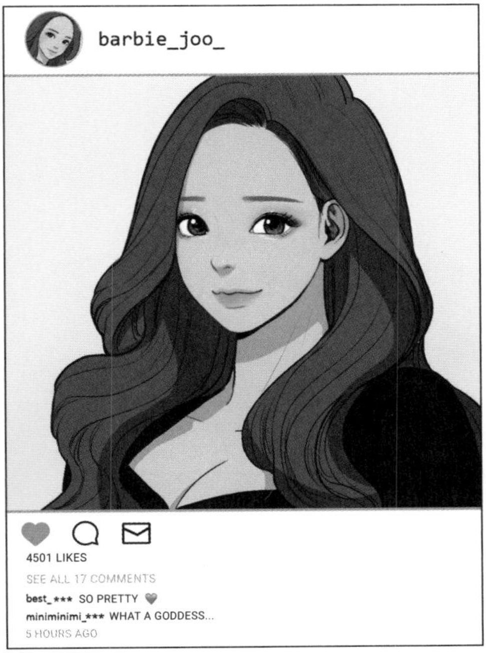
barbie_joo_
4501 LIKES
SEE ALL 17 COMMENTS
best_*** SO PRETTY
miniminimi_*** WHAT A GODDESS...
5 HOURS AGO

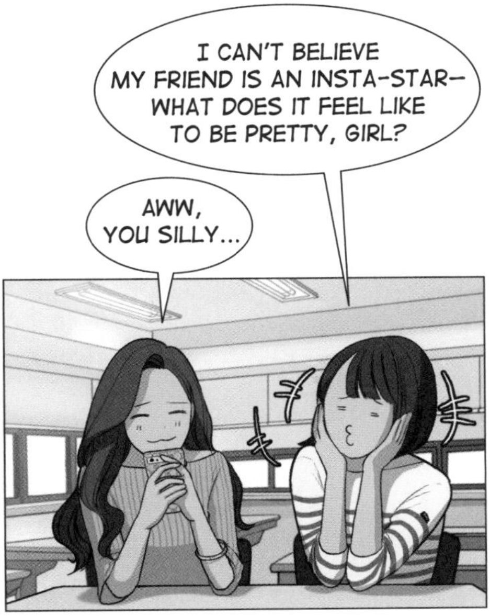
I CAN'T BELIEVE MY FRIEND IS AN INSTA-STAR— WHAT DOES IT FEEL LIKE TO BE PRETTY, GIRL?
AWW, YOU SILLY...

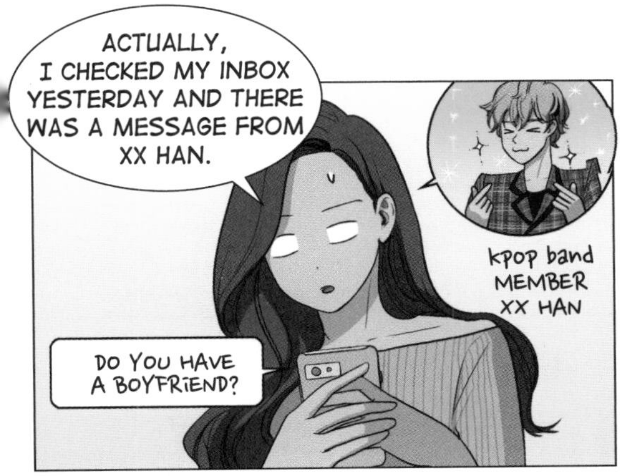
ACTUALLY, I CHECKED MY INBOX YESTERDAY AND THERE WAS A MESSAGE FROM XX HAN.
kpop band MEMBER XX HAN
DO YOU HAVE A BOYFRIEND?

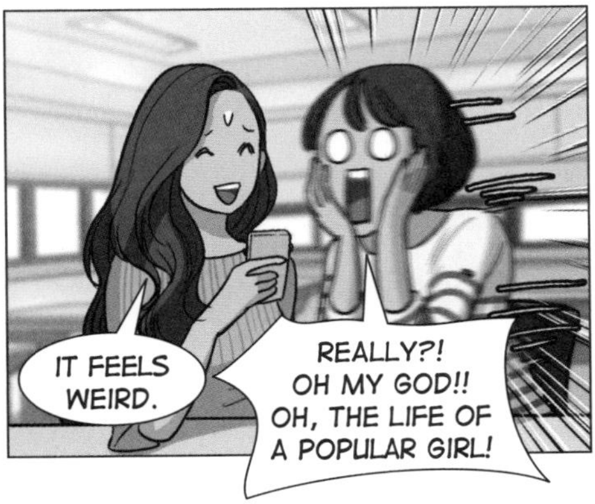
IT FEELS WEIRD.
REALLY?! OH MY GOD!! OH, THE LIFE OF A POPULAR GIRL!

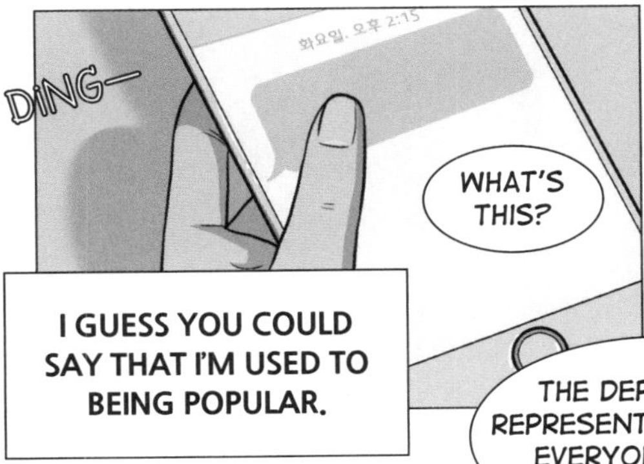
화요일. 오후 2:15
DING—
WHAT'S THIS?
I GUESS YOU COULD SAY THAT I'M USED TO BEING POPULAR.

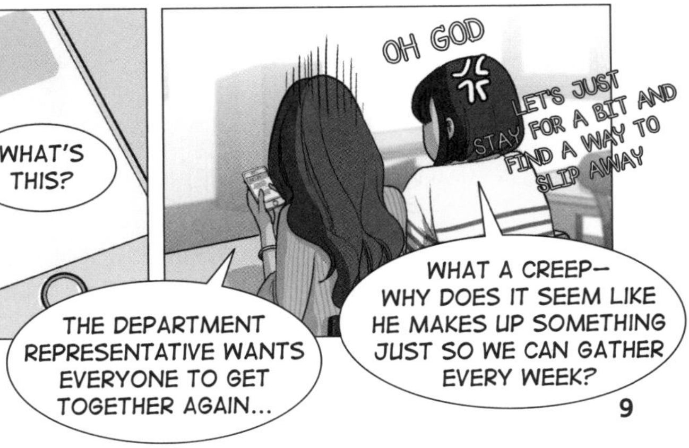
OH GOD
LET'S JUST STAY FOR A BIT AND FIND A WAY TO SLIP AWAY
THE DEPARTMENT REPRESENTATIVE WANTS EVERYONE TO GET TOGETHER AGAIN...
WHAT A CREEP— WHY DOES IT SEEM LIKE HE MAKES UP SOMETHING JUST SO WE CAN GATHER EVERY WEEK?

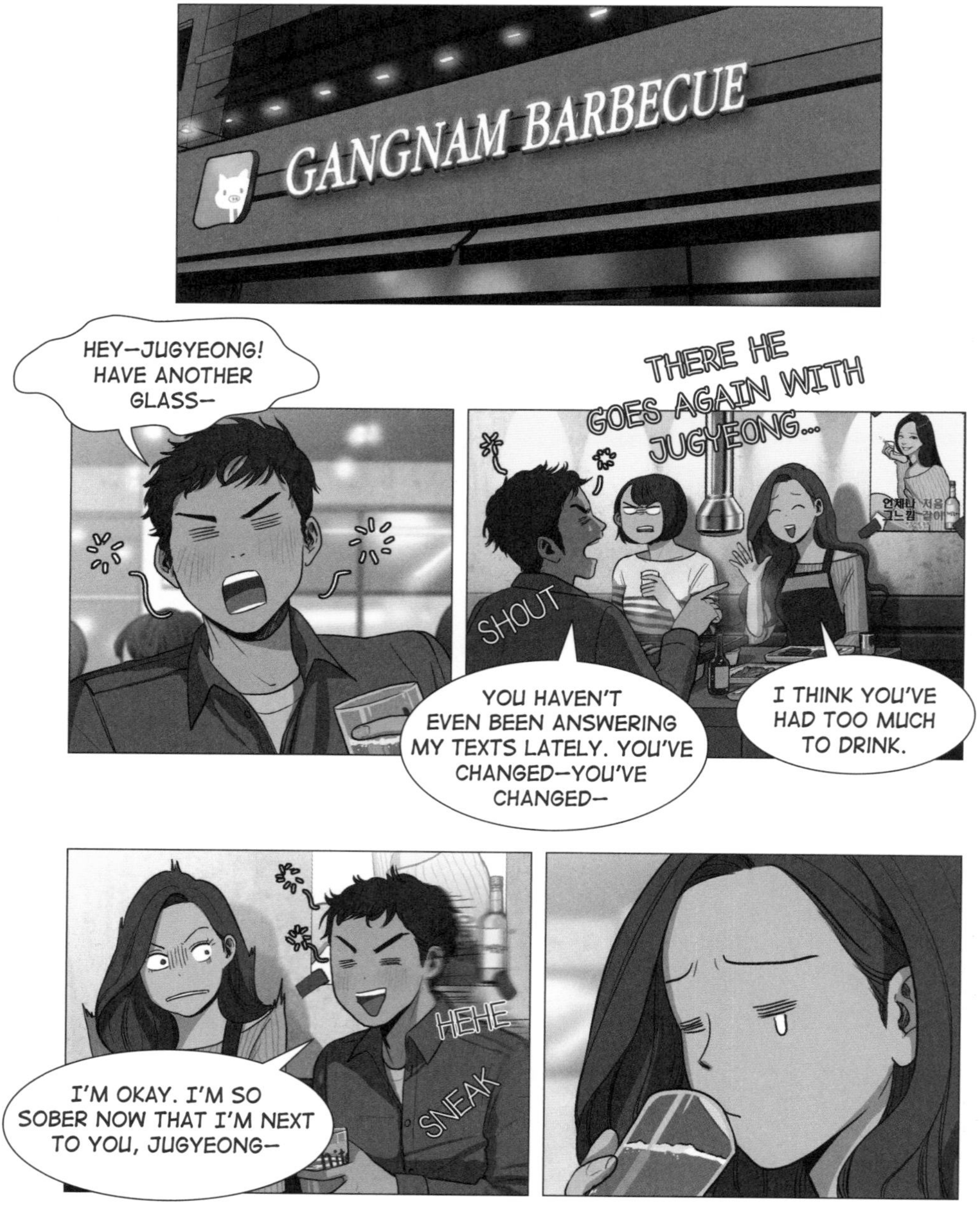
GANGNAM BARBECUE
HEY—JUGYEONG! HAVE ANOTHER GLASS—
THERE HE GOES AGAIN WITH JUGYEONG...
SHOUT
YOU HAVEN'T EVEN BEEN ANSWERING MY TEXTS LATELY. YOU'VE CHANGED—YOU'VE CHANGED—
I THINK YOU'VE HAD TOO MUCH TO DRINK.
HEHE
SNEAK
I'M OKAY. I'M SO SOBER NOW THAT I'M NEXT TO YOU, JUGYEONG—

OF COURSE, BEING PRETTY ISN'T ALWAYS NECESSARILY A GOOD THING.

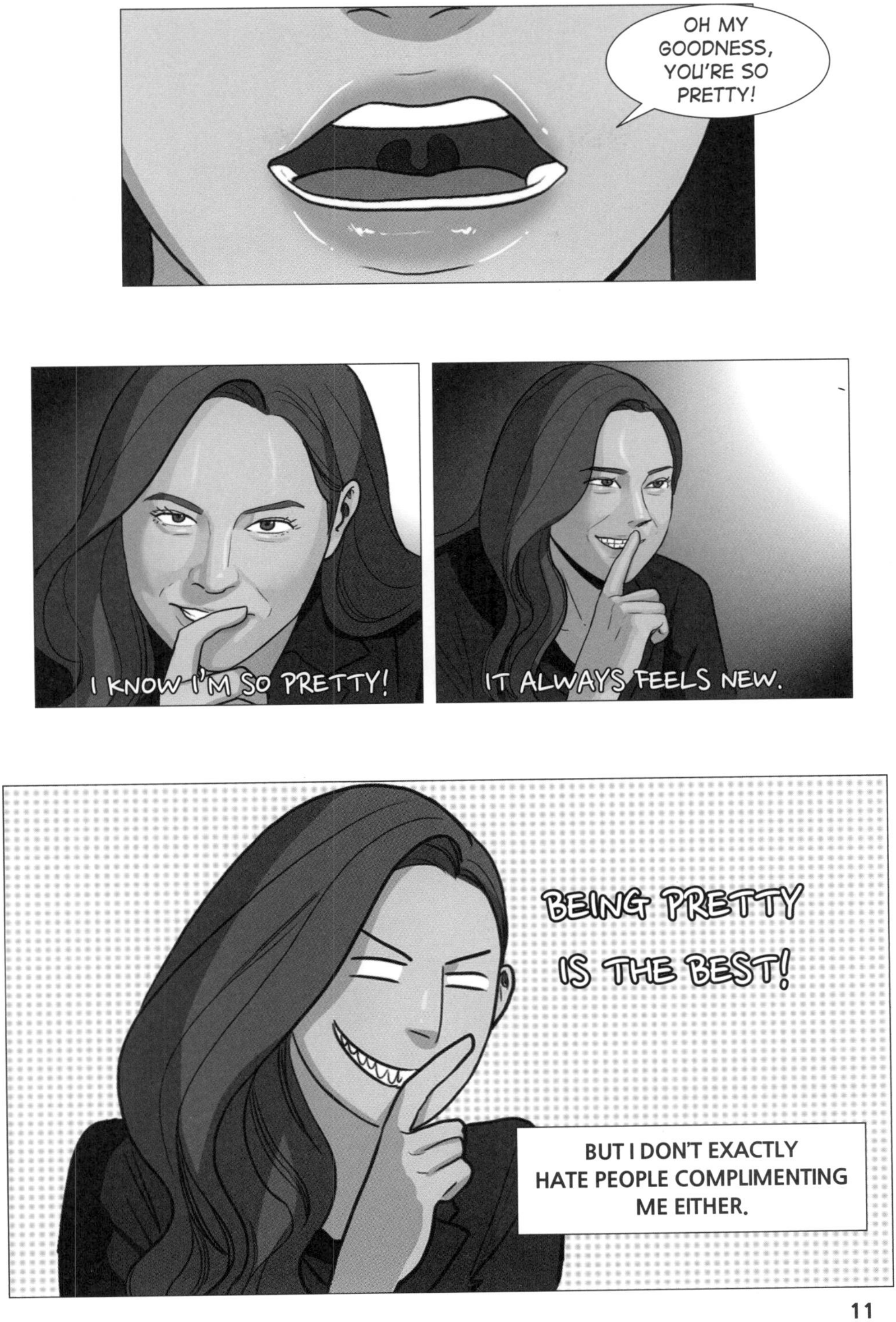
OH MY GOODNESS, YOU'RE SO PRETTY!
I KNOW I'M SO PRETTY!
IT ALWAYS FEELS NEW.
BEING PRETTY IS THE BEST!
BUT I DON'T EXACTLY HATE PEOPLE COMPLIMENTING ME EITHER.

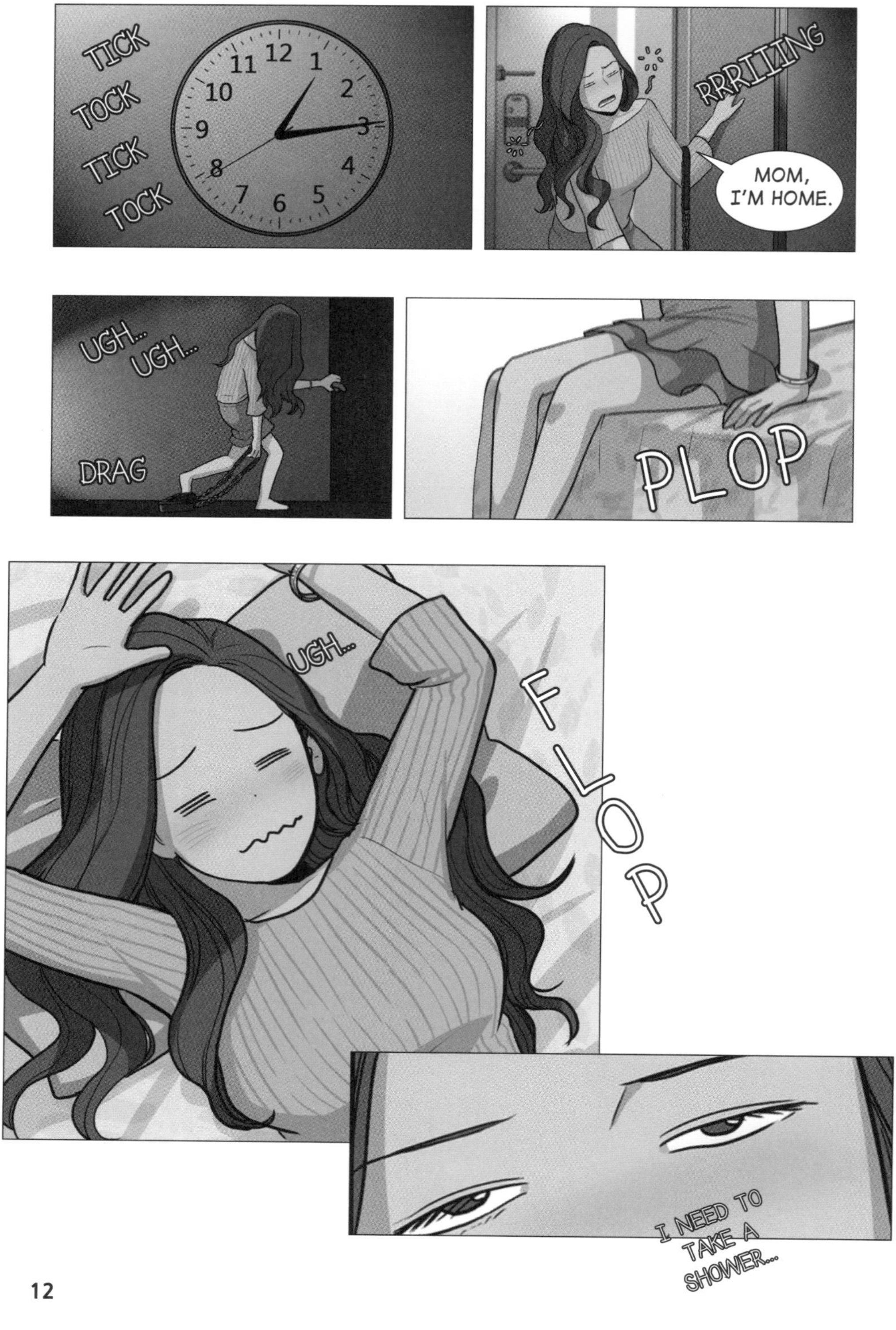
TICK
TOCK
TICK
TOCK
RRRIIING
MOM, I'M HOME.
UGH... UGH...
DRAG
PLOP
UGH...
FLOP
I NEED TO TAKE A SHOWER...

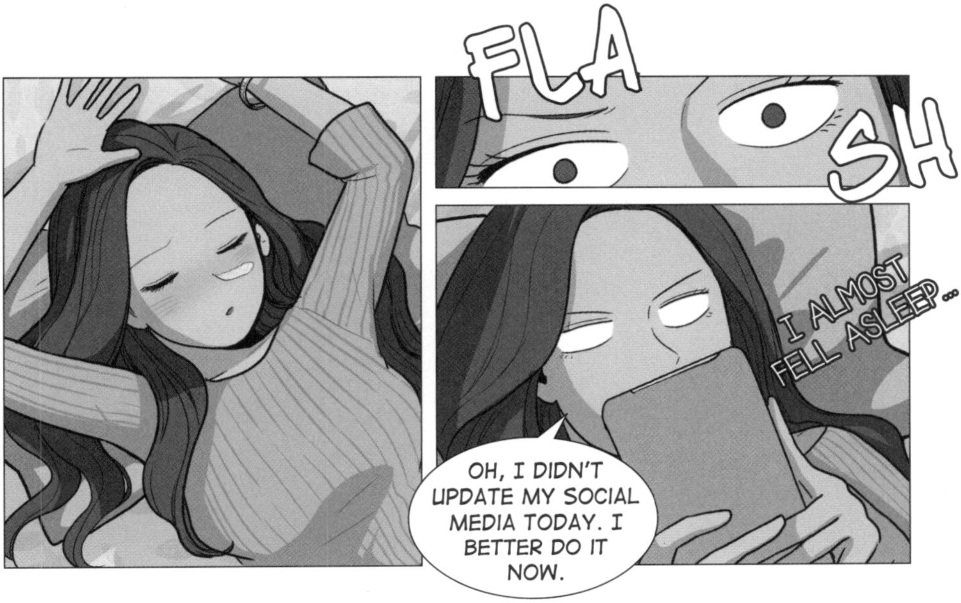
FLASH
I ALMOST FELL ASLEEP...
OH, I DIDN'T UPDATE MY SOCIAL MEDIA TODAY. I BETTER DO IT NOW.

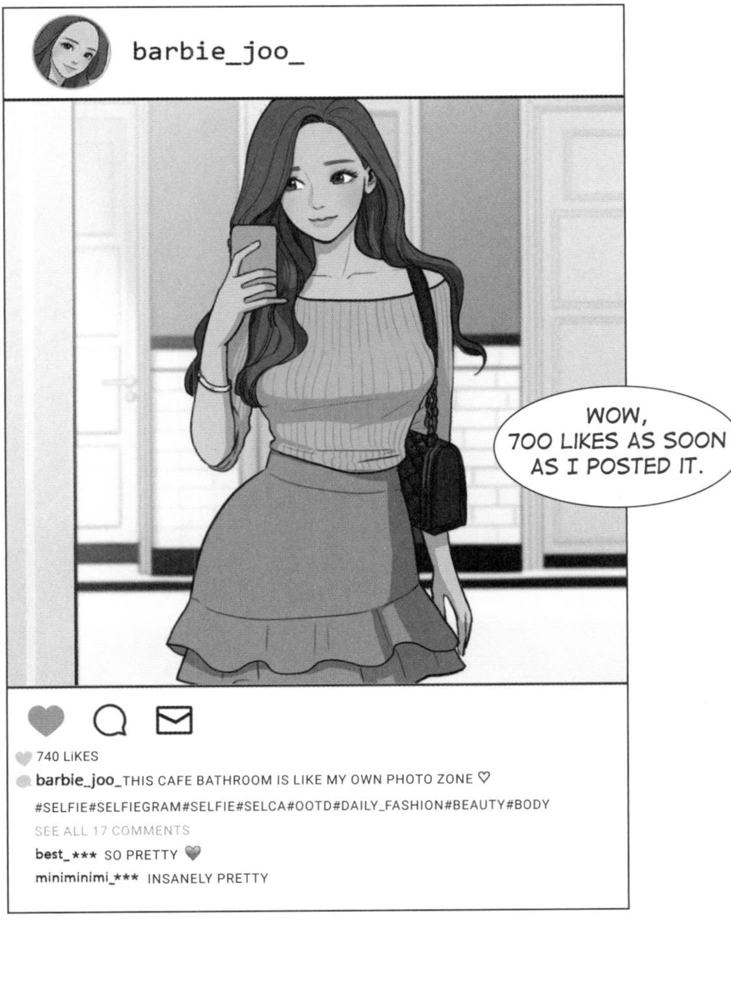
barbie_joo_
WOW, 700 LIKES AS SOON AS I POSTED IT.
740 LIKES
barbie_joo_ THIS CAFE BATHROOM IS LIKE MY OWN PHOTO ZONE ♡
#SELFIE#SELFIEGRAM#SELFIE#SELCA#OOTD#DAILY_FASHION#BEAUTY#BODY
SEE ALL 17 COMMENTS
best_*** SO PRETTY
miniminimi_*** INSANELY PRETTY

YOU KNOW, BEING ME ♥

OOH

IT'S PRETTY SWEET.

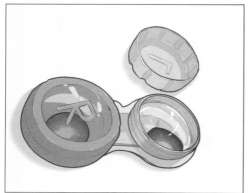

PSSHH~

WHEW~

BUT ONLY UNTIL
I WASH OFF MY MAKEUP ★

AHH~ THAT FEELS BETTER!

14

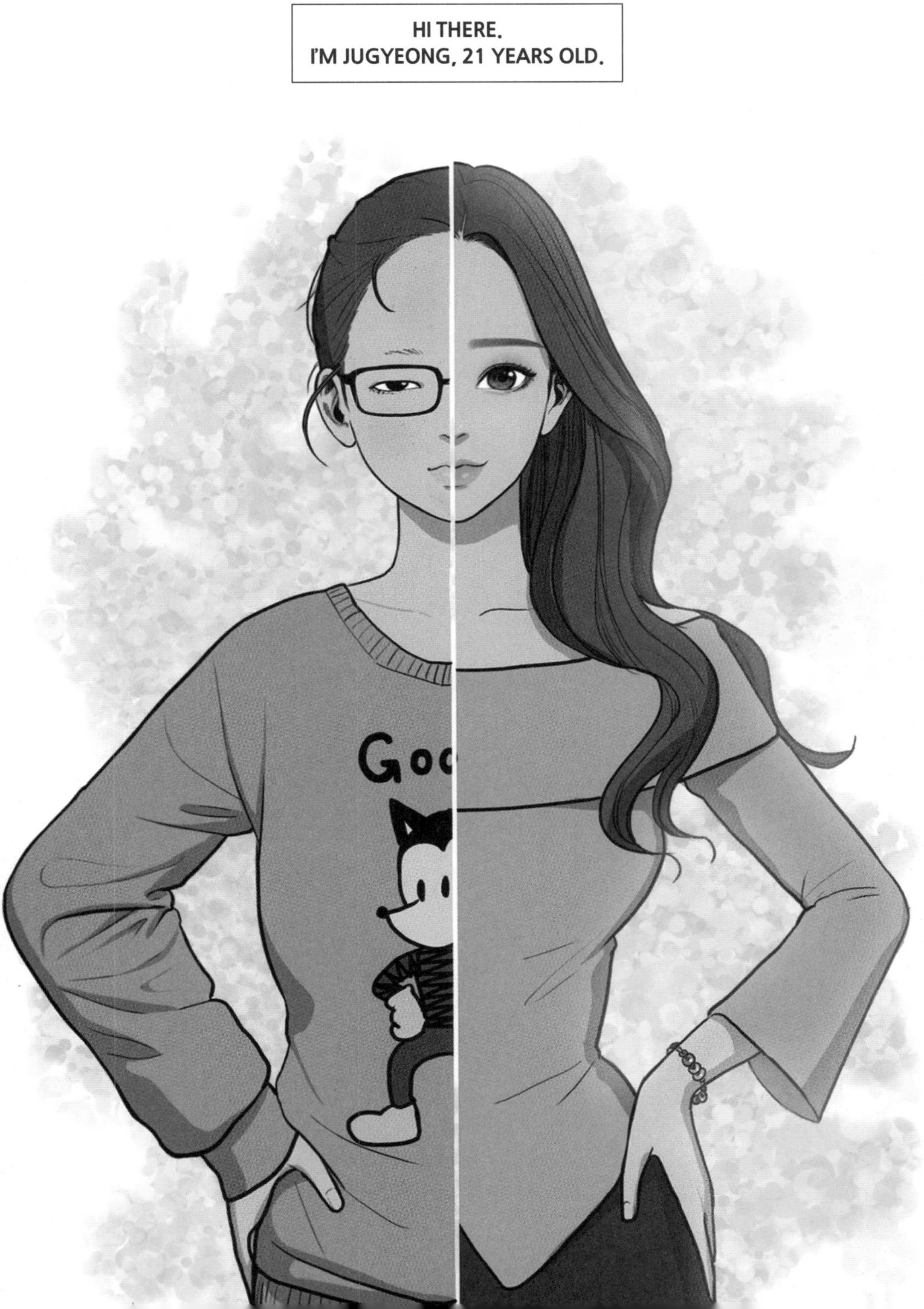
HI THERE.
I'M JUGYEONG, 21 YEARS OLD.

I don't like myself right now

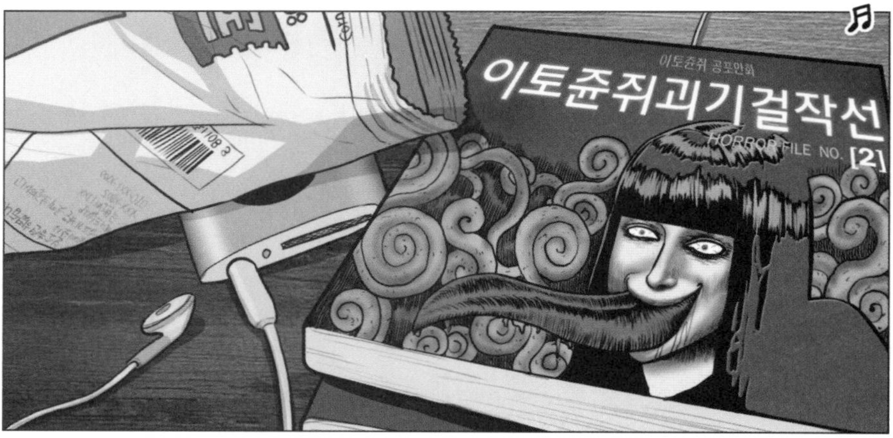
이토춘쥐 공포만화
이토쥰쥐괴기걸작선
HORROR FILE NO. [2]

And your comments are so unnecessary

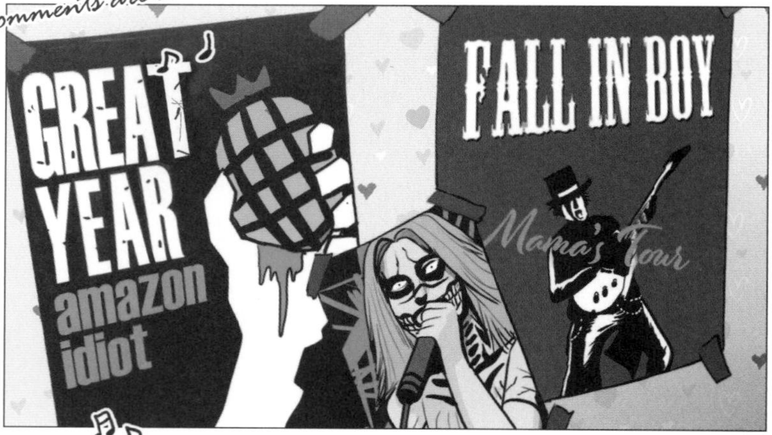
GREAT YEAR
amazon idiot
FALL IN BOY
Mama's Tour

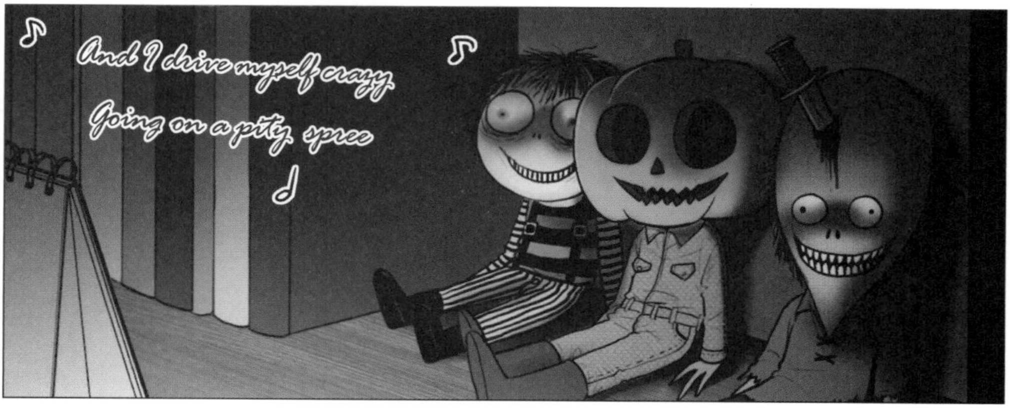
And I drive myself crazy
Going on a pity spree

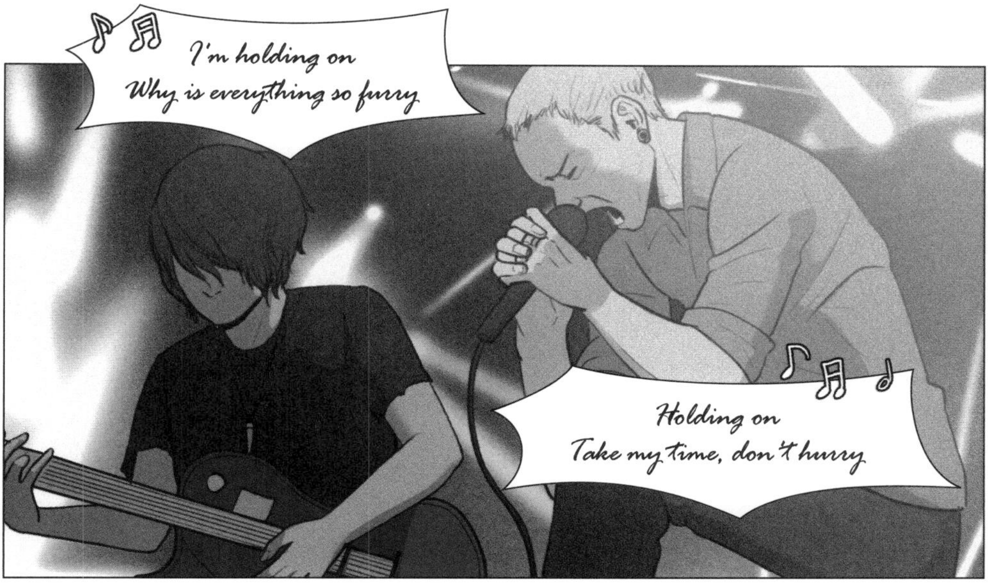
I'm holding on
Why is everything so furry
Holding on
Take my time, don't hurry

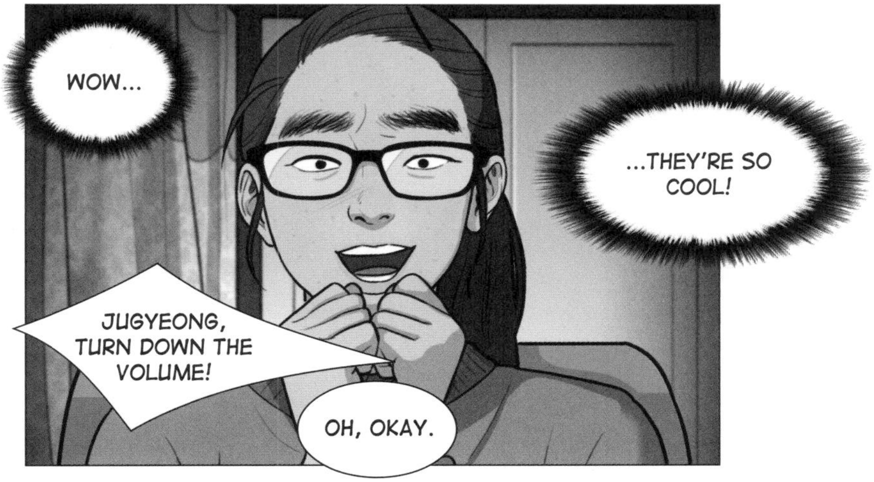
WOW...
...THEY'RE SO COOL!
JUGYEONG, TURN DOWN THE VOLUME!
OH, OKAY.

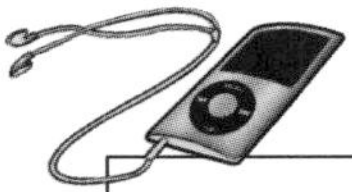

MY LIFE AS A SENIOR IN MIDDLE SCHOOL IS REALLY GOOD.

I CAN LISTEN TO WHATEVER MUSIC I LIKE.

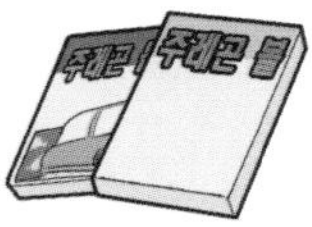

AND I CAN WATCH AS MANY CARTOONS AND MOVIES AS I WANT.

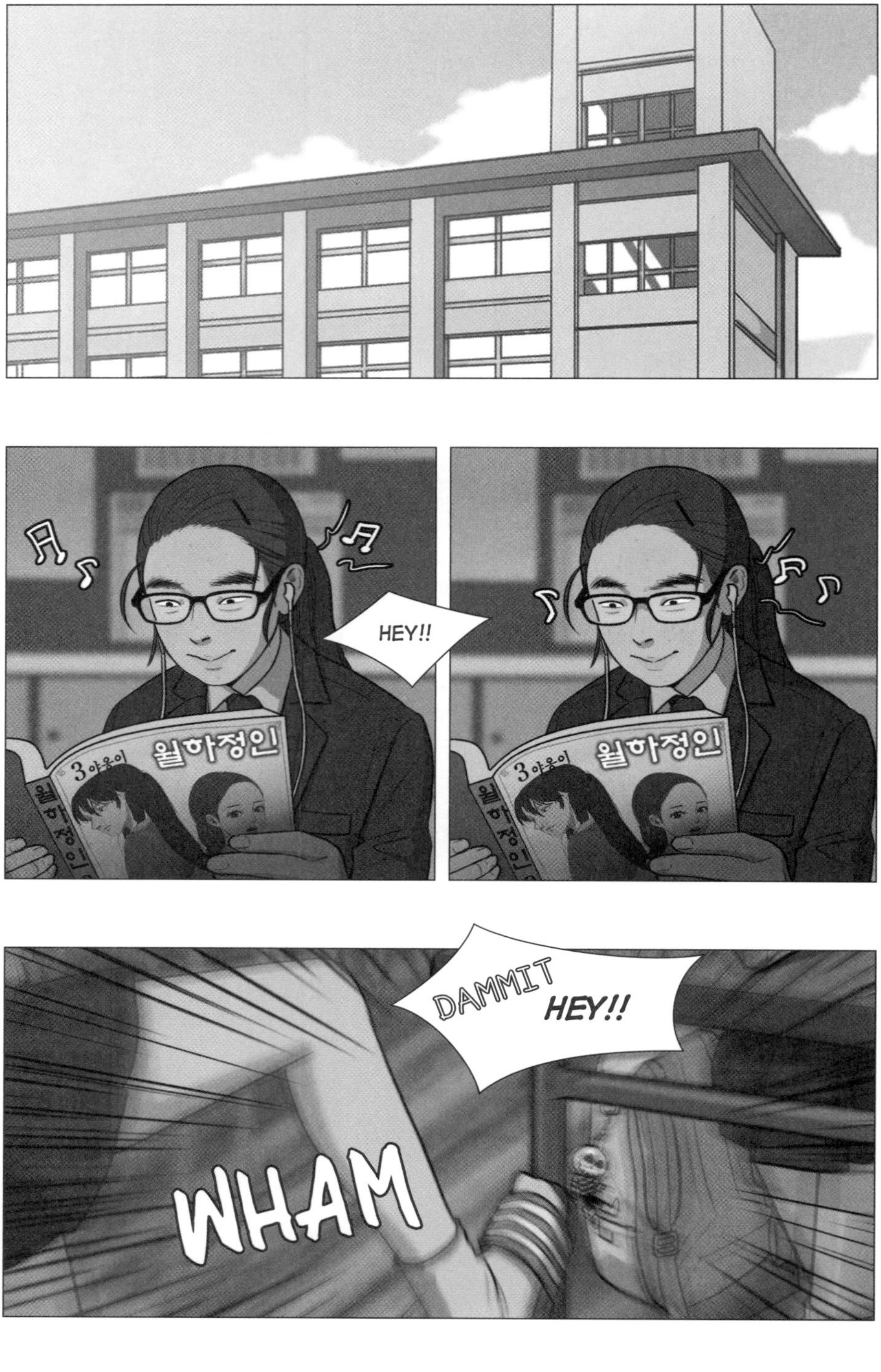
3야옹이
월하정인
HEY!!
3야옹이
월하정인
DAMMIT
HEY!!
WHAM

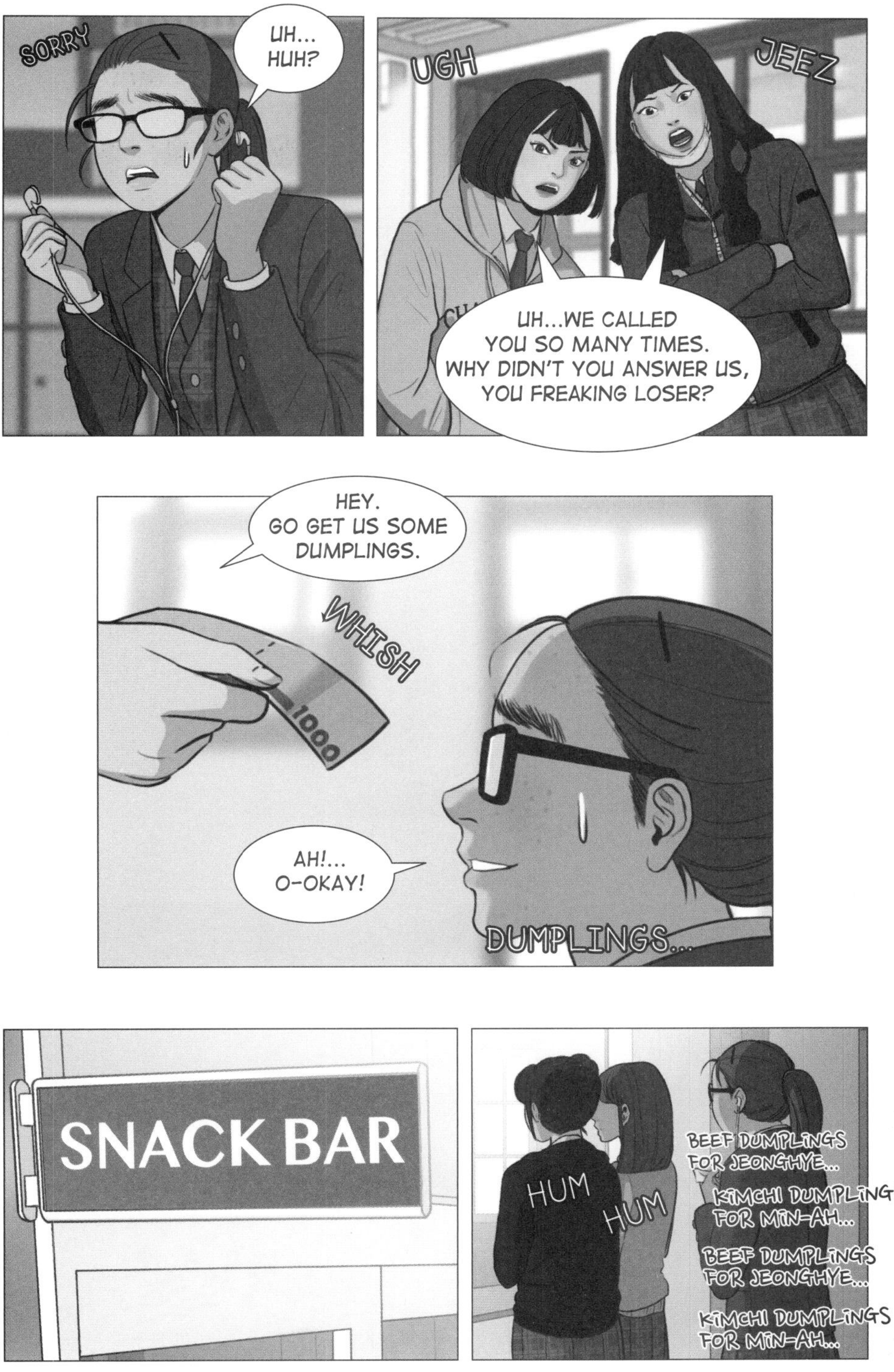
SORRY
UH... HUH?
UGH
JEEZ
UH...WE CALLED YOU SO MANY TIMES. WHY DIDN'T YOU ANSWER US, YOU FREAKING LOSER?
HEY. GO GET US SOME DUMPLINGS.
WHISH
1000
AH!... O-OKAY!
DUMPLINGS...
SNACK BAR
HUM
HUM
BEEF DUMPLINGS FOR JEONGHYE...
KIMCHI DUMPLINGS FOR MIN-AH...
BEEF DUMPLINGS FOR JEONGHYE...
KIMCHI DUMPLINGS FOR MIN-AH...

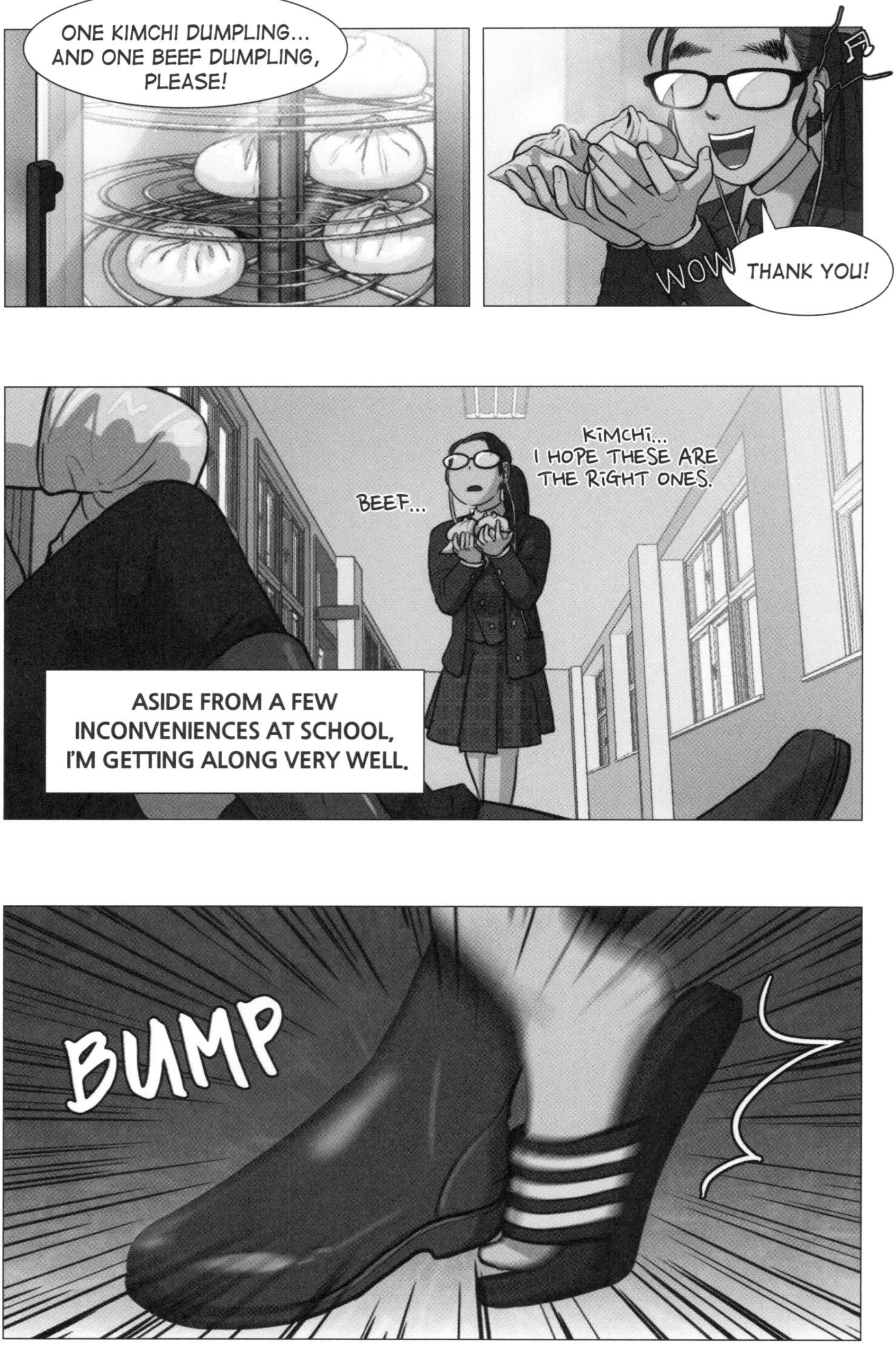

ONE KIMCHI DUMPLING...
AND ONE BEEF DUMPLING, PLEASE!
WOW
THANK YOU!
BEEF...
KIMCHI...
I HOPE THESE ARE THE RIGHT ONES.
ASIDE FROM A FEW INCONVENIENCES AT SCHOOL, I'M GETTING ALONG VERY WELL.
BUMP

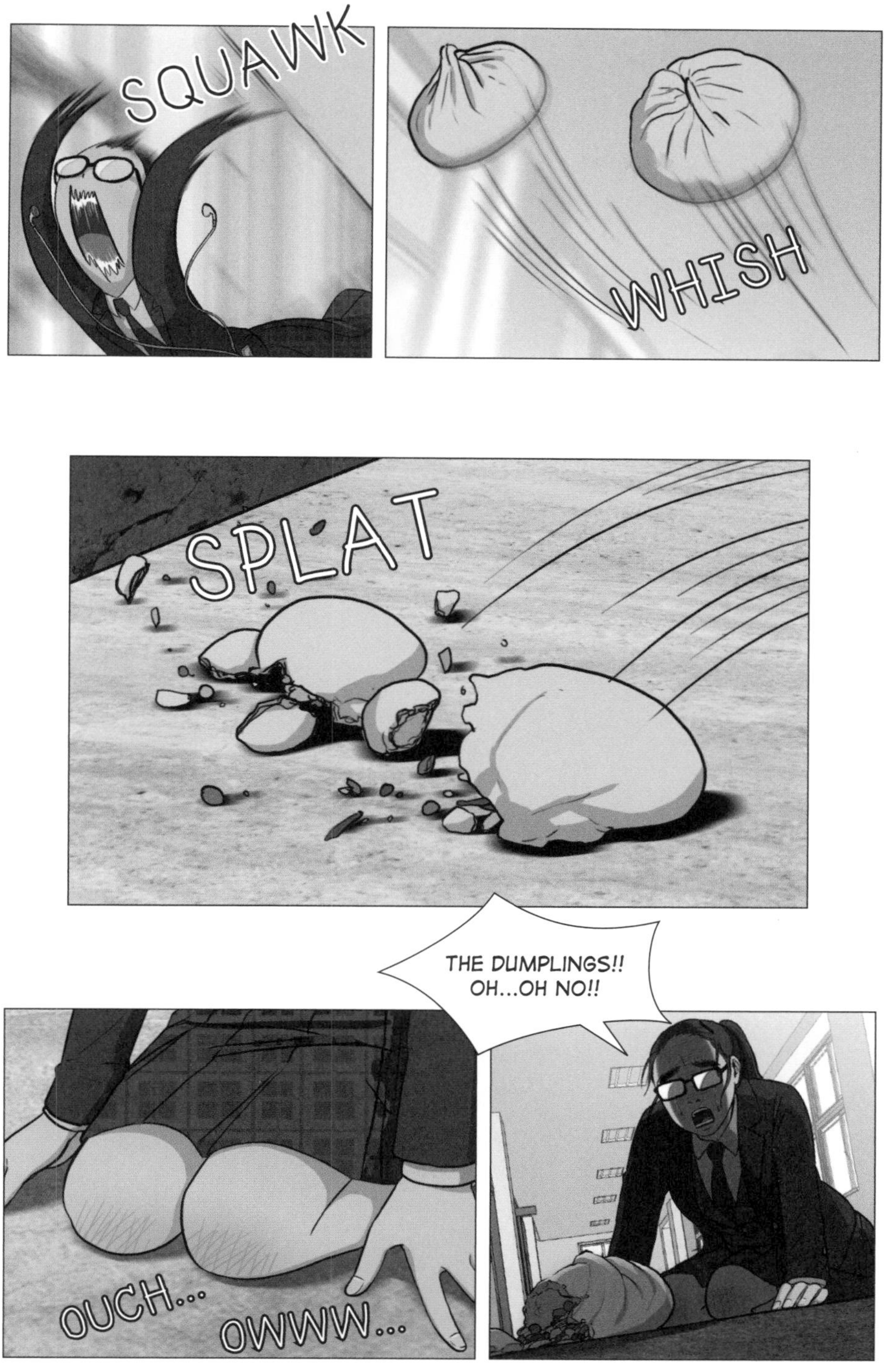

SQUAWK
WHISH
SPLAT
OUCH... OWWW...
THE DUMPLINGS!! OH...OH NO!!

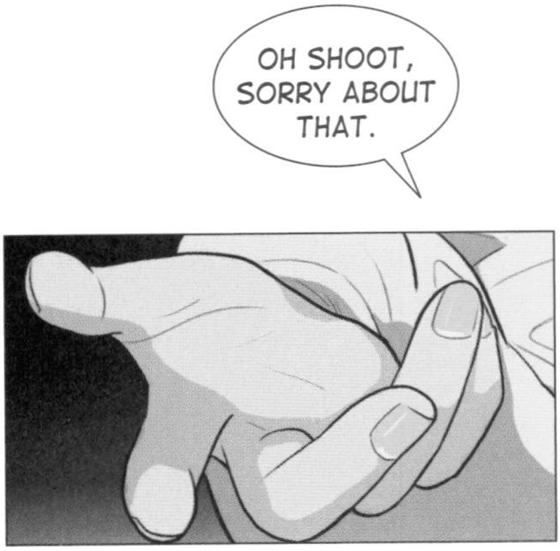
OH SHOOT, SORRY ABOUT THAT.

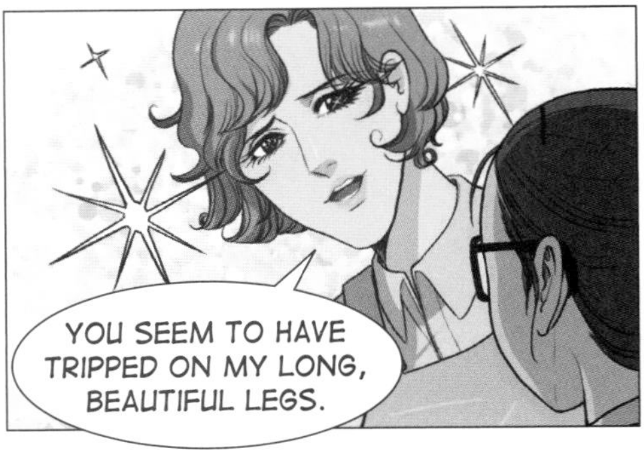
YOU SEEM TO HAVE TRIPPED ON MY LONG, BEAUTIFUL LEGS.

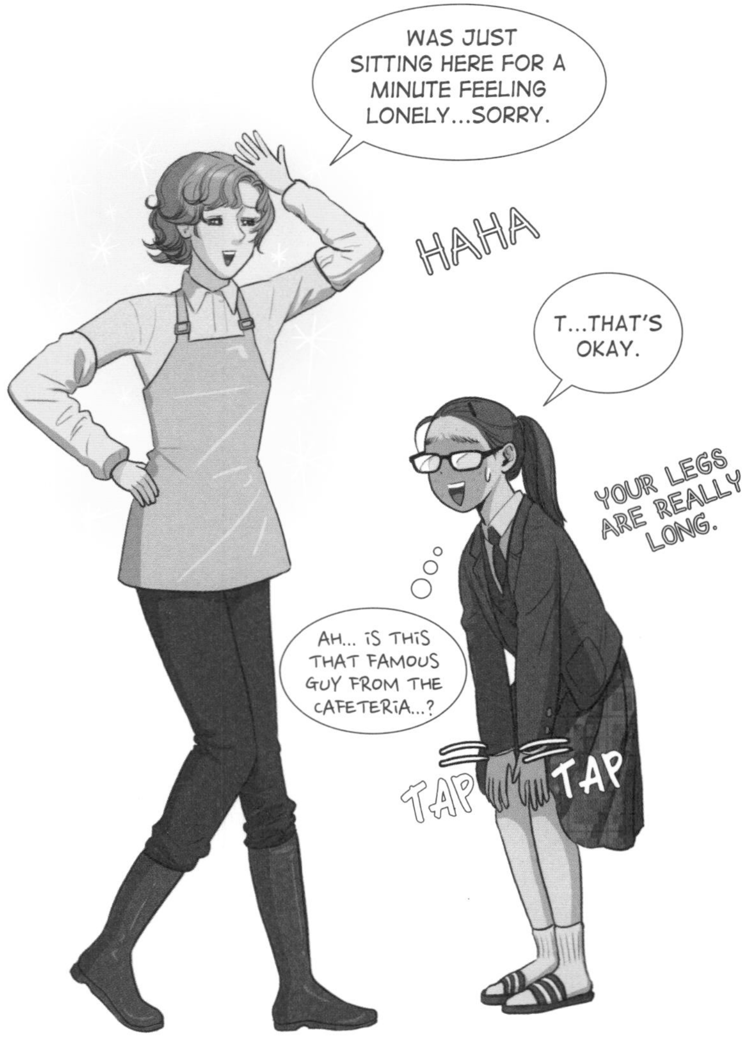
WAS JUST SITTING HERE FOR A MINUTE FEELING LONELY...SORRY.
HAHA
T...THAT'S OKAY.
YOUR LEGS ARE REALLY LONG.
AH... IS THIS THAT FAMOUS GUY FROM THE CAFETERIA...?
TAP
TAP

?!

WAIT, THAT MUSIC... IS THAT ROB... ZOMBOID...?

UH, HEY, THAT'S MY MP3 PLAYER...

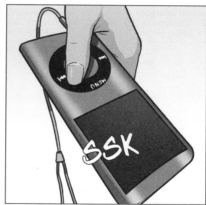

SSK

HAHA— YOU HAVE

SMILE

GREAT TASTE IN MUSIC☆

BLUSH

THANK YOU.

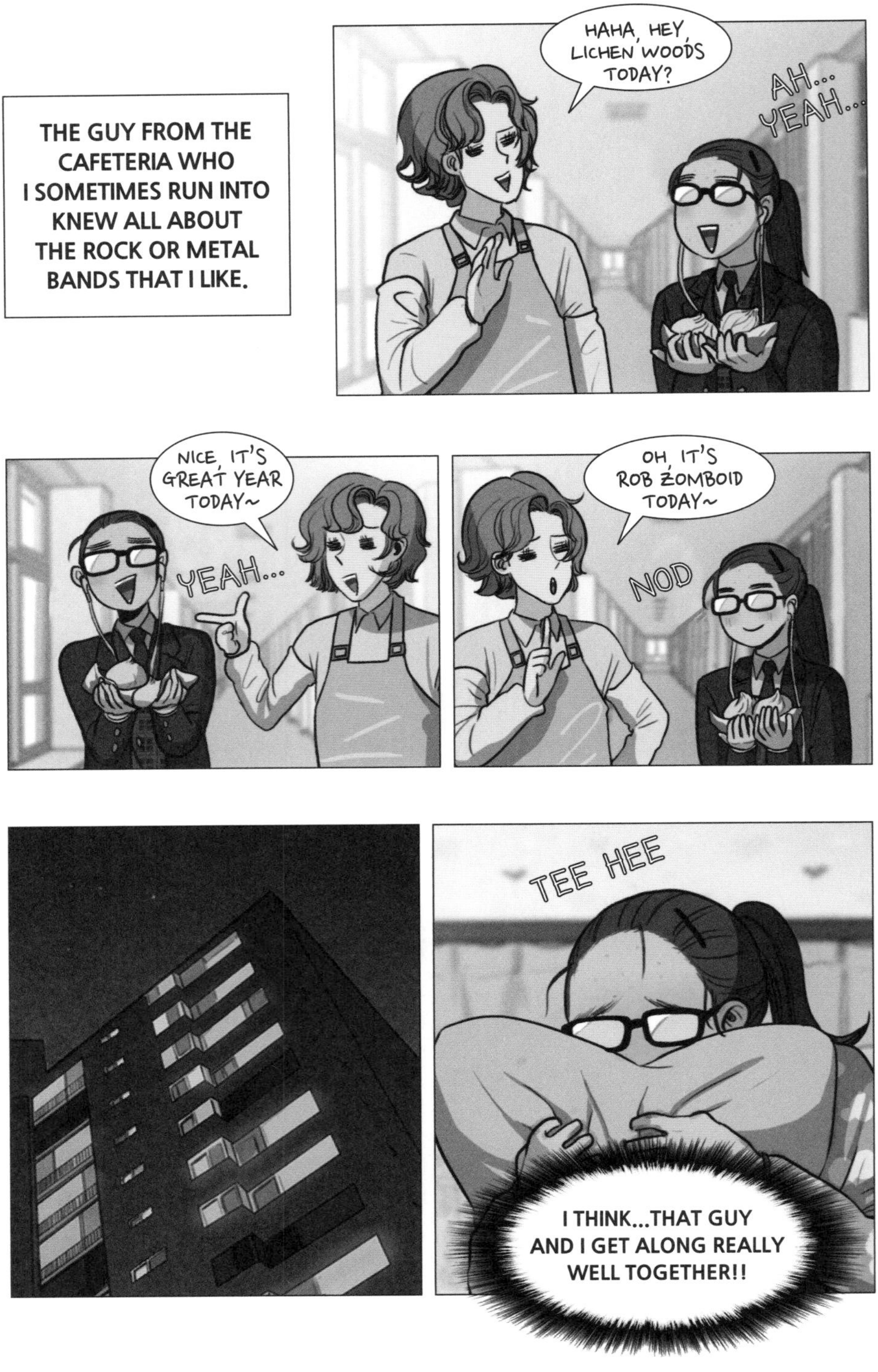
THE GUY FROM THE CAFETERIA WHO I SOMETIMES RUN INTO KNEW ALL ABOUT THE ROCK OR METAL BANDS THAT I LIKE.
HAHA, HEY, LICHEN WOODS TODAY?
AH... YEAH...
NICE, IT'S GREAT YEAR TODAY~
YEAH...
OH, IT'S ROB ZOMBOID TODAY~
NOD
TEE HEE
I THINK...THAT GUY AND I GET ALONG REALLY WELL TOGETHER!!

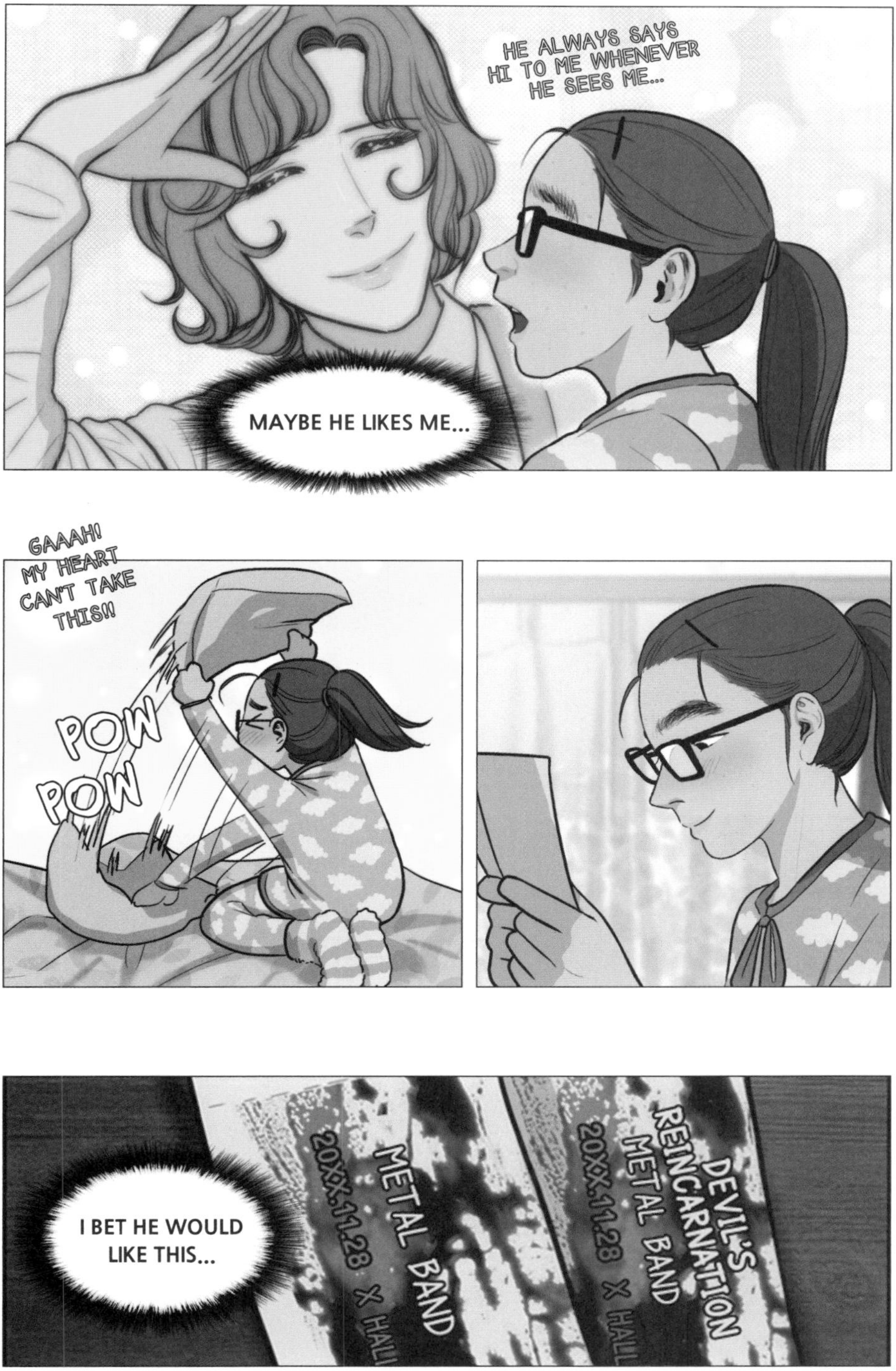
HE ALWAYS SAYS HI TO ME WHENEVER HE SEES ME...
MAYBE HE LIKES ME...
GAAAH! MY HEART CAN'T TAKE THIS!!
POW POW
I BET HE WOULD LIKE THIS...
METAL BAND
20XX.11.28 X HAL
DEVIL'S REINCARNATION
METAL BAND
20XX.11.28 X HAL

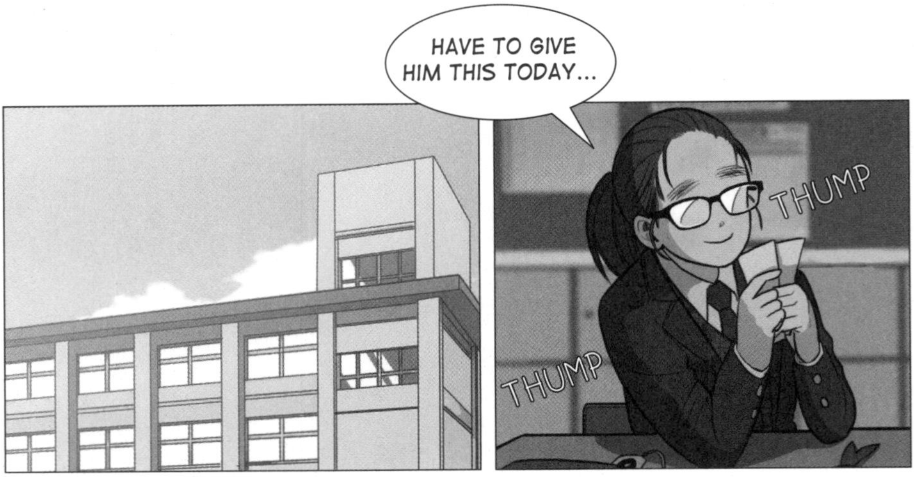
HAVE TO GIVE HIM THIS TODAY...
THUMP
THUMP

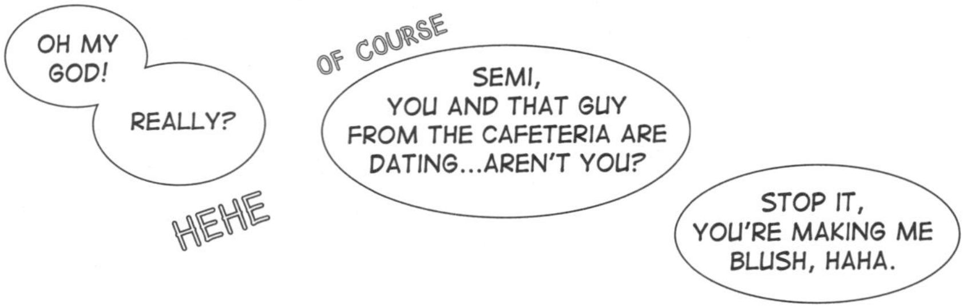
OH MY GOD!
REALLY?
HEHE
OF COURSE
SEMI, YOU AND THAT GUY FROM THE CAFETERIA ARE DATING...AREN'T YOU?
STOP IT, YOU'RE MAKING ME BLUSH, HAHA.

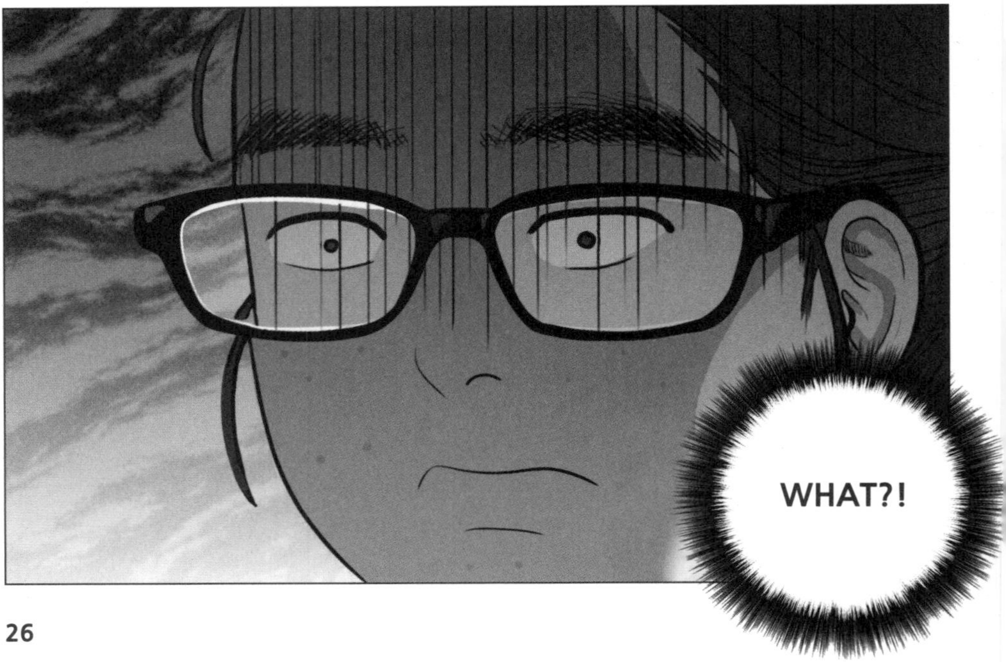
WHAT?!

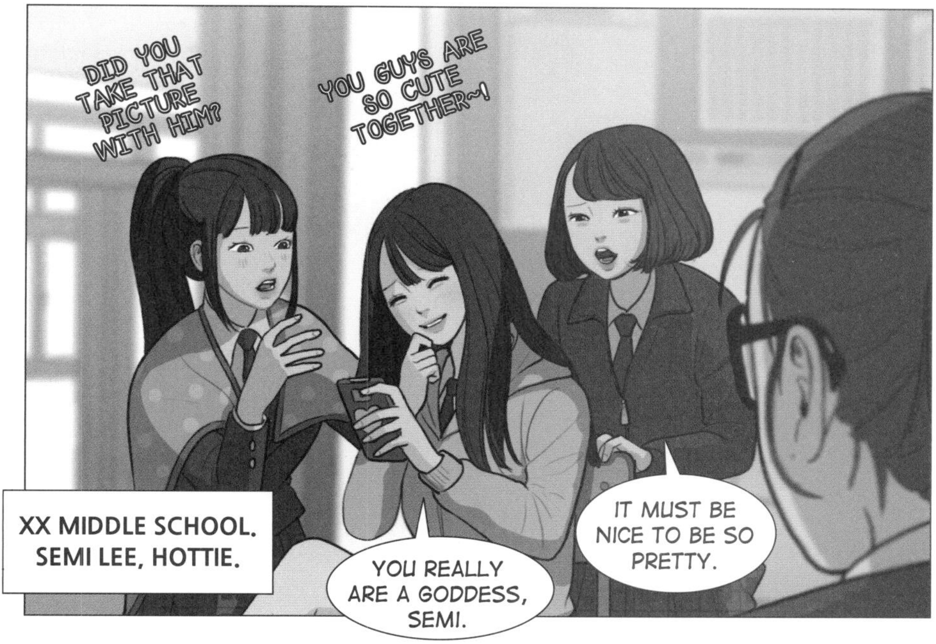
DID YOU TAKE THAT PICTURE WITH HIM?
YOU GUYS ARE SO CUTE TOGETHER~!
XX MIDDLE SCHOOL. SEMI LEE, HOTTIE.
YOU REALLY ARE A GODDESS, SEMI.
IT MUST BE NICE TO BE SO PRETTY.

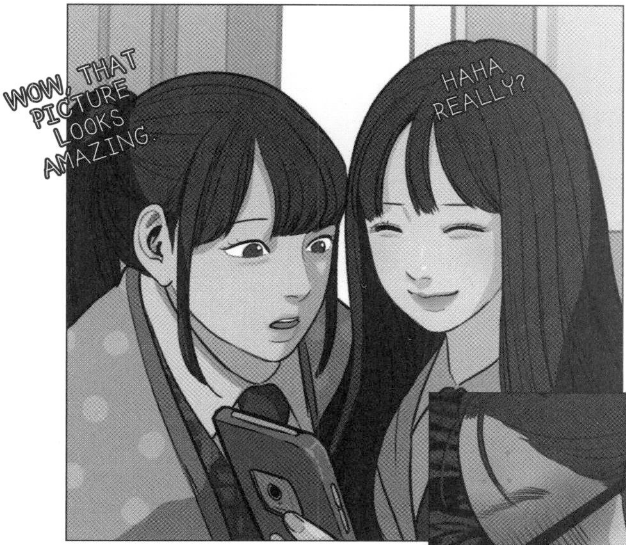
WOW, THAT PICTURE LOOKS AMAZING.
HAHA REALLY?

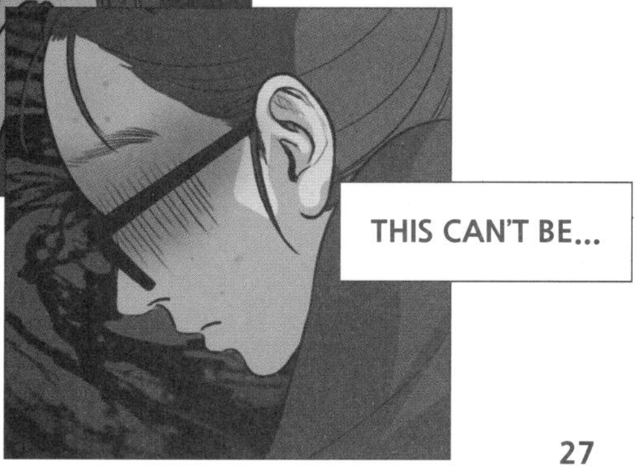
THIS CAN'T BE...

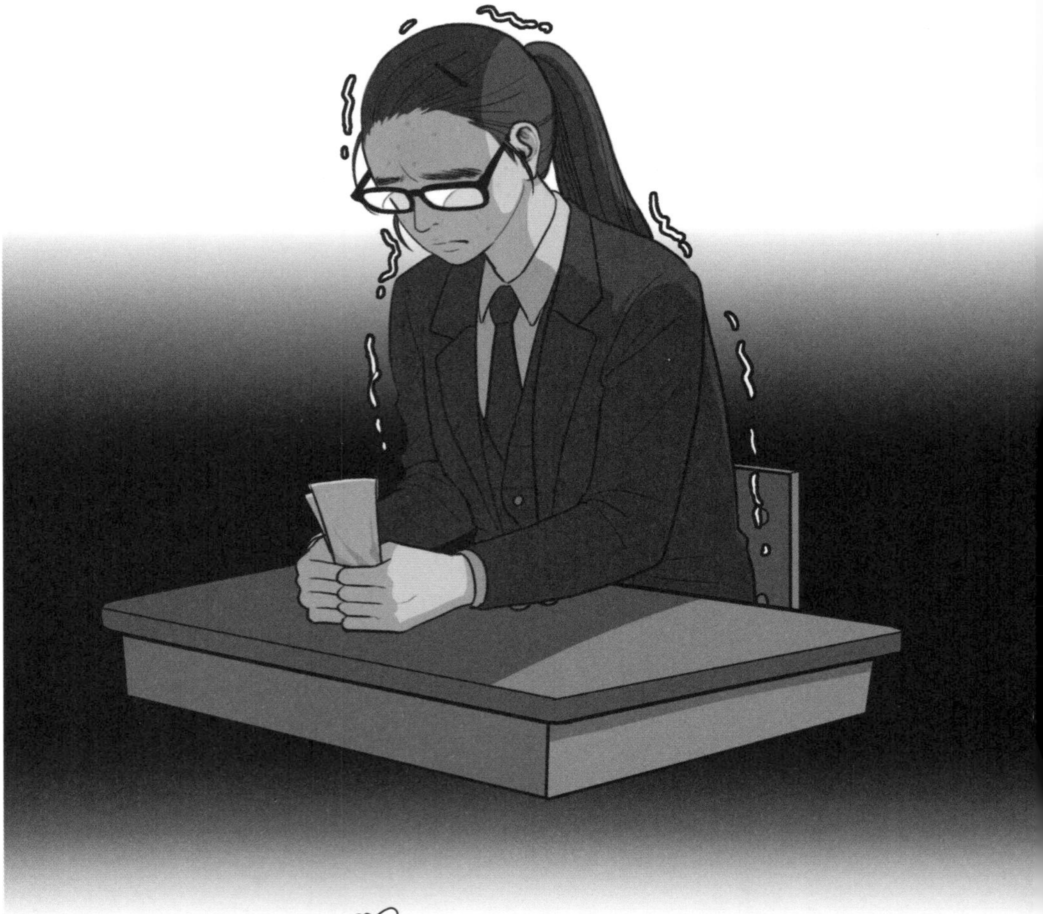

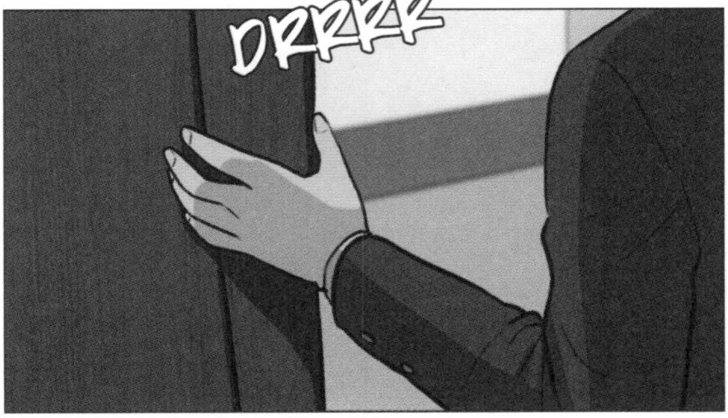
DRRRR

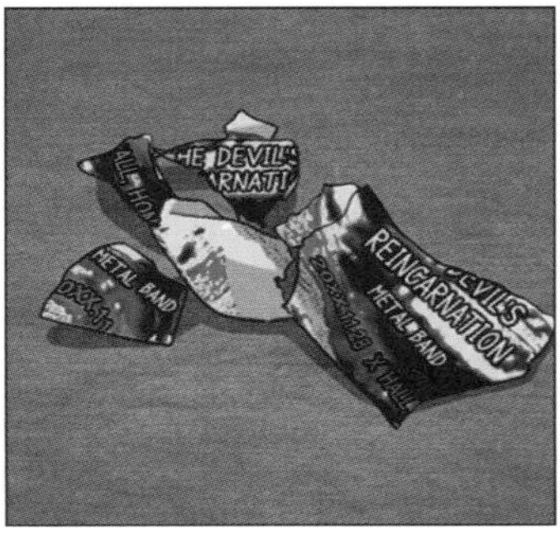
HE DEVIL'S
RNATI
METAL BAND
REINCARNATION
METAL BAND

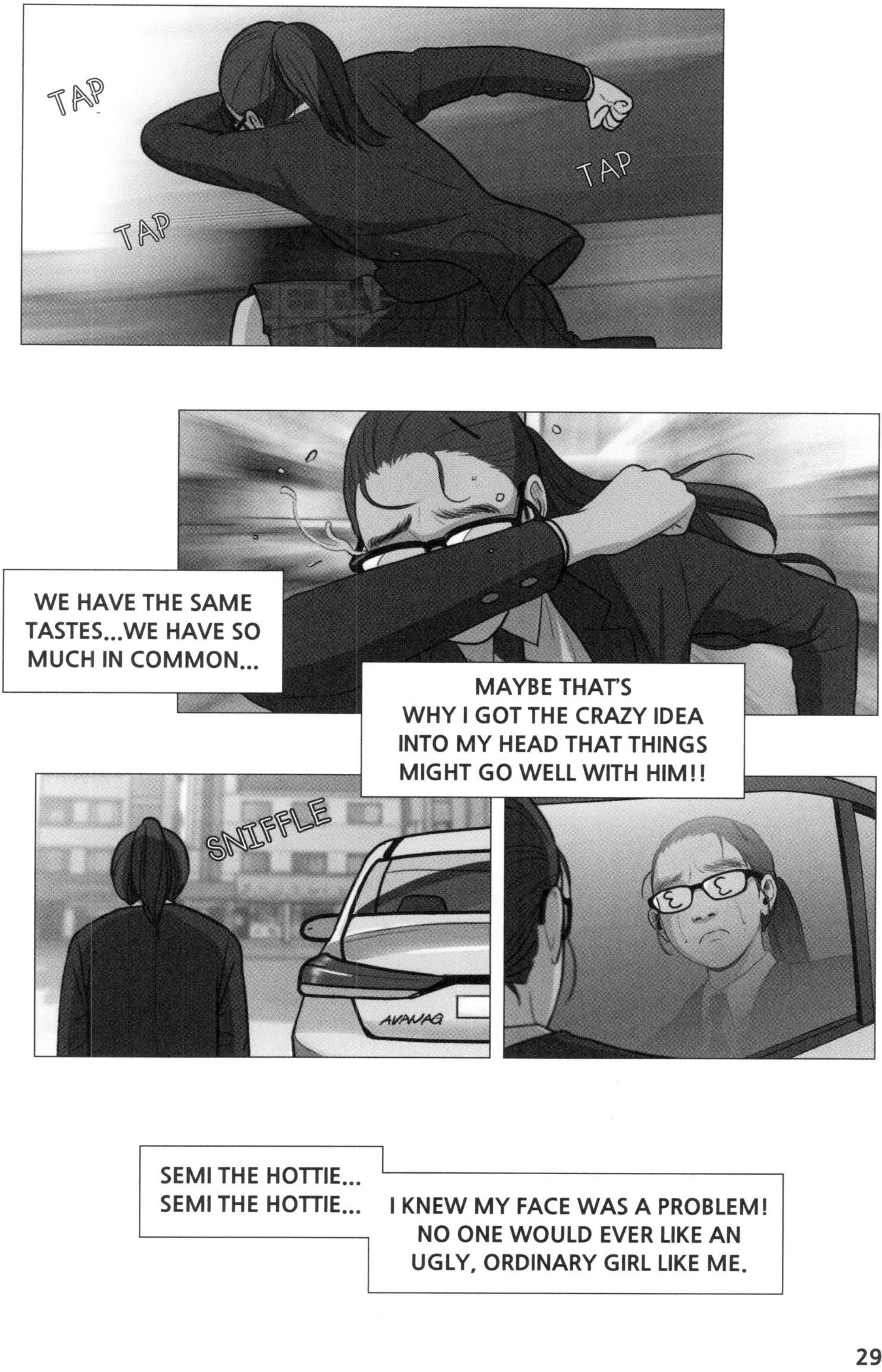
TAP
TAP
TAP
WE HAVE THE SAME TASTES...WE HAVE SO MUCH IN COMMON...
MAYBE THAT'S WHY I GOT THE CRAZY IDEA INTO MY HEAD THAT THINGS MIGHT GO WELL WITH HIM!!
SNIFFLE
AVANAG

SEMI THE HOTTIE...
SEMI THE HOTTIE...

I KNEW MY FACE WAS A PROBLEM!
NO ONE WOULD EVER LIKE AN UGLY, ORDINARY GIRL LIKE ME.

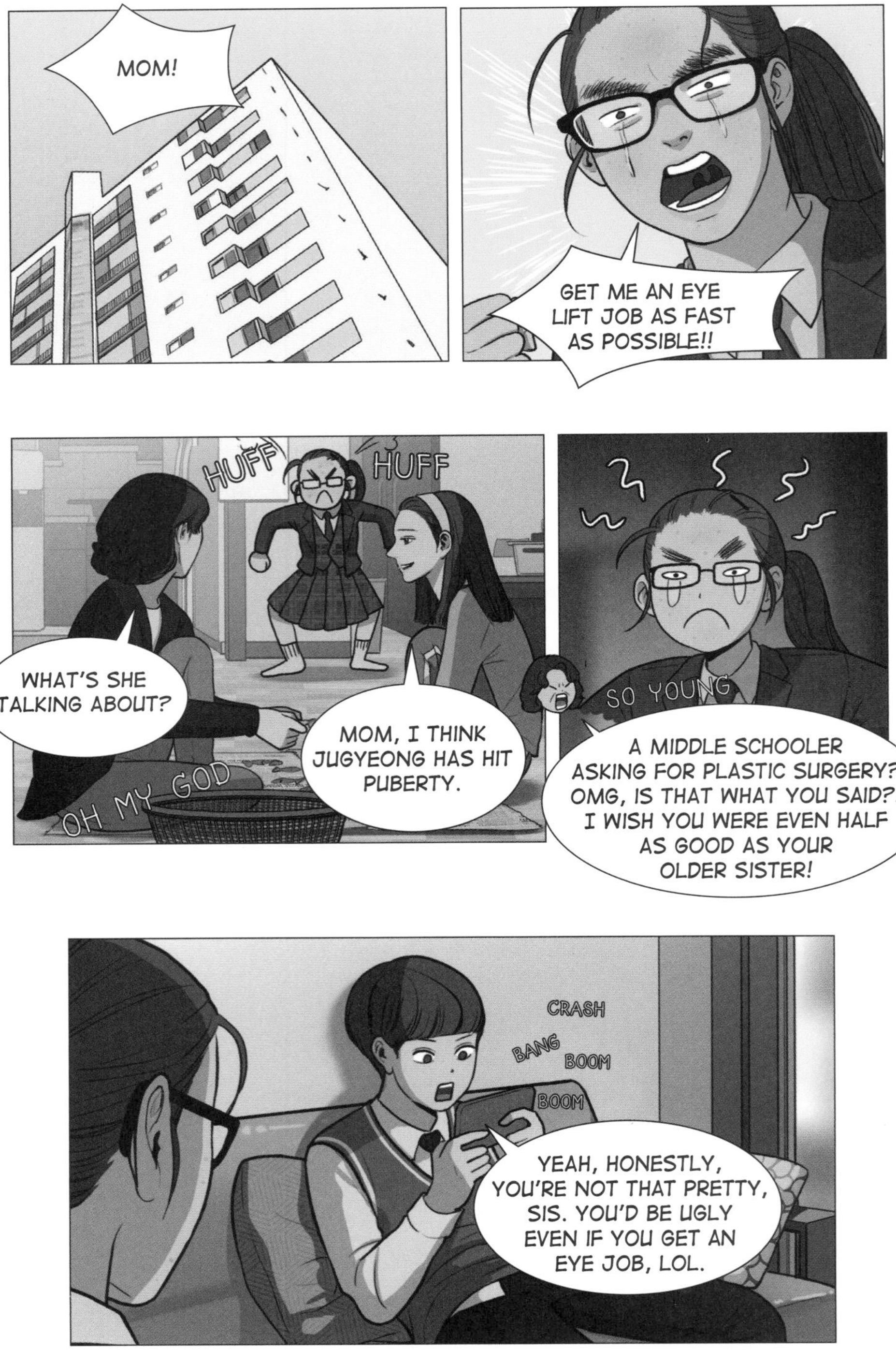
MOM!
GET ME AN EYE LIFT JOB AS FAST AS POSSIBLE!!
HUFF
HUFF
WHAT'S SHE TALKING ABOUT?
MOM, I THINK JUGYEONG HAS HIT PUBERTY.
OH MY GOD
SO YOUNG
A MIDDLE SCHOOLER ASKING FOR PLASTIC SURGERY? OMG, IS THAT WHAT YOU SAID?! I WISH YOU WERE EVEN HALF AS GOOD AS YOUR OLDER SISTER!
CRASH
BANG
BOOM
BOOM
YEAH, HONESTLY, YOU'RE NOT THAT PRETTY, SIS. YOU'D BE UGLY EVEN IF YOU GET AN EYE JOB, LOL.

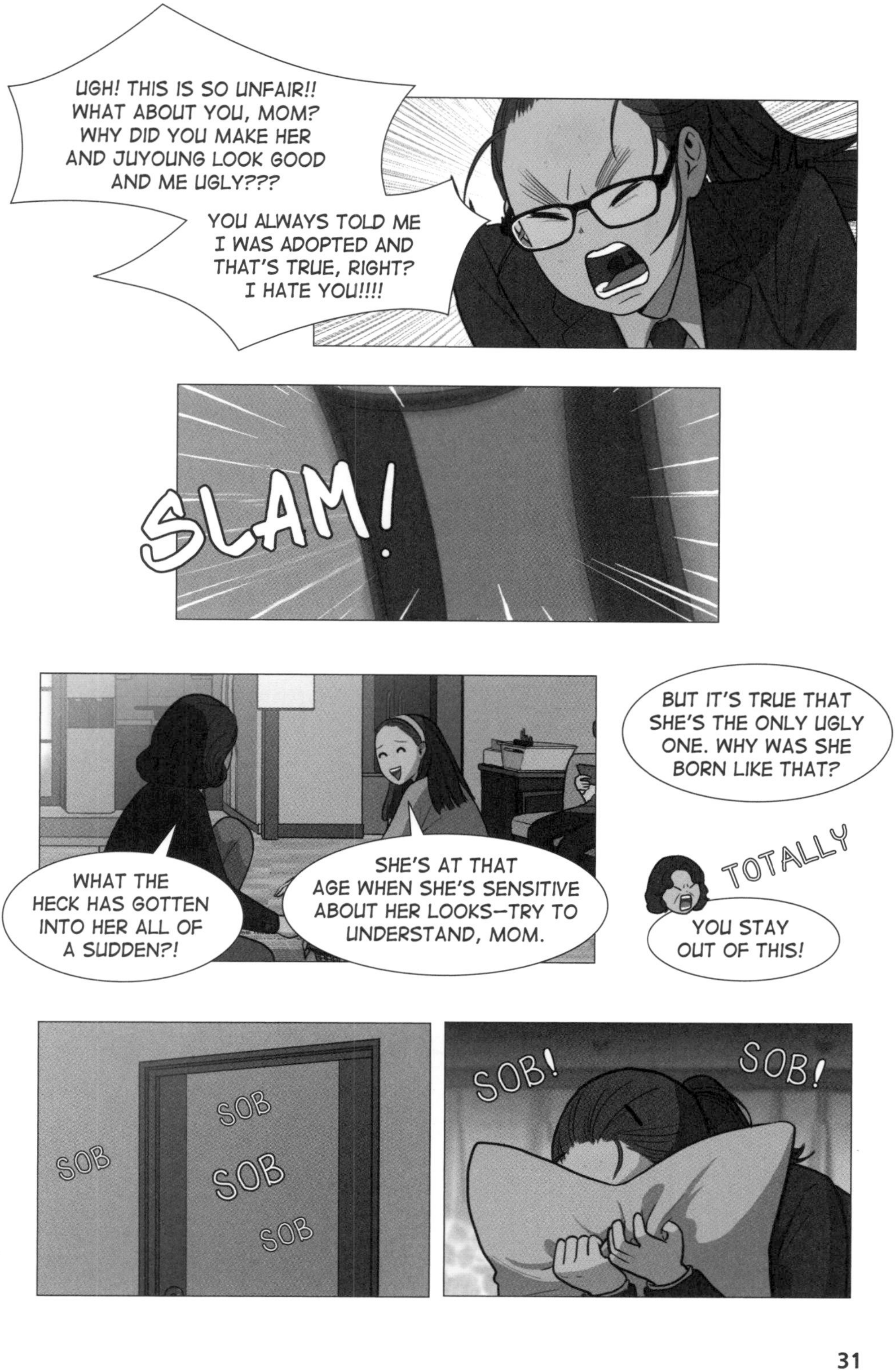
UGH! THIS IS SO UNFAIR!! WHAT ABOUT YOU, MOM? WHY DID YOU MAKE HER AND JUYOUNG LOOK GOOD AND ME UGLY???
YOU ALWAYS TOLD ME I WAS ADOPTED AND THAT'S TRUE, RIGHT? I HATE YOU!!!!
SLAM!
WHAT THE HECK HAS GOTTEN INTO HER ALL OF A SUDDEN?!
SHE'S AT THAT AGE WHEN SHE'S SENSITIVE ABOUT HER LOOKS—TRY TO UNDERSTAND, MOM.
BUT IT'S TRUE THAT SHE'S THE ONLY UGLY ONE. WHY WAS SHE BORN LIKE THAT?
TOTALLY
YOU STAY OUT OF THIS!
SOB
SOB
SOB
SOB
SOB!
SOB!

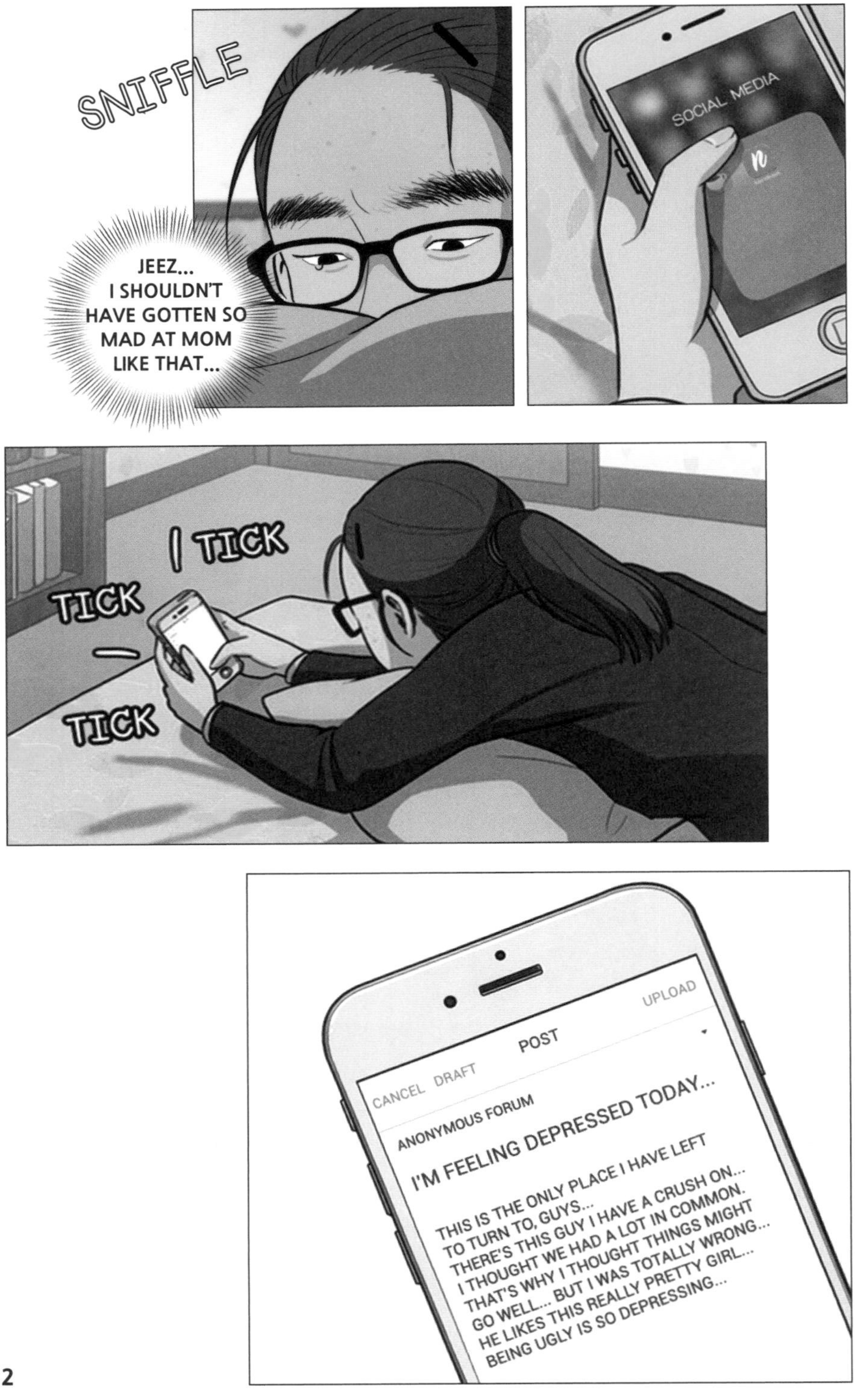
SNIFFLE
JEEZ... I SHOULDN'T HAVE GOTTEN SO MAD AT MOM LIKE THAT...
SOCIAL MEDIA
TICK
TICK
TICK
UPLOAD
POST
CANCEL DRAFT
ANONYMOUS FORUM
I'M FEELING DEPRESSED TODAY...
THIS IS THE ONLY PLACE I HAVE LEFT TO TURN TO, GUYS...
THERE'S THIS GUY I HAVE A CRUSH ON...
I THOUGHT WE HAD A LOT IN COMMON.
THAT'S WHY I THOUGHT THINGS MIGHT GO WELL... BUT I WAS TOTALLY WRONG...
HE LIKES THIS REALLY PRETTY GIRL...
BEING UGLY IS SO DEPRESSING...

30 MINUTES LATER.

ARE THERE ANY COMMENTS...?

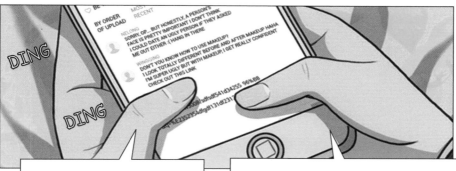

DING

DING

SORRY, BUT HONESTLY, A PERSON'S FACE IS PRETTY IMPORTANT.

DON'T YOU KNOW HOW TO USE MAKEUP? I LOOK TOTALLY DIFFERENT BEFORE AND AFTER MAKEUP HAHA. I'M SUPER UGLY BUT WITH MAKEUP, I GET REALLY CONFIDENT. CHECK OUT THIS LINK.

OKAY...

OH? IS THIS IT?

I WONDER WHAT IT IS...

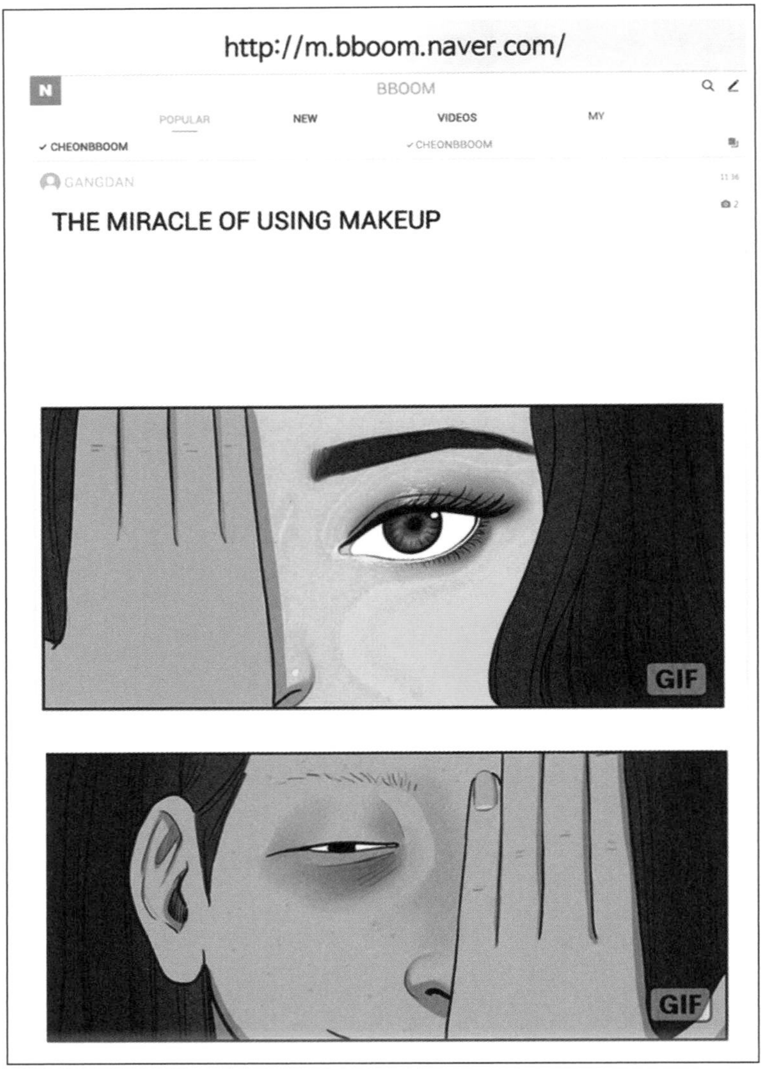
http://m.bboom.naver.com/
N
BBOOM
POPULAR
NEW
VIDEOS
MY
✓ CHEONBBOOM
✓ CHEONBBOOM
GANGDAN
THE MIRACLE OF USING MAKEUP
GIF
GIF

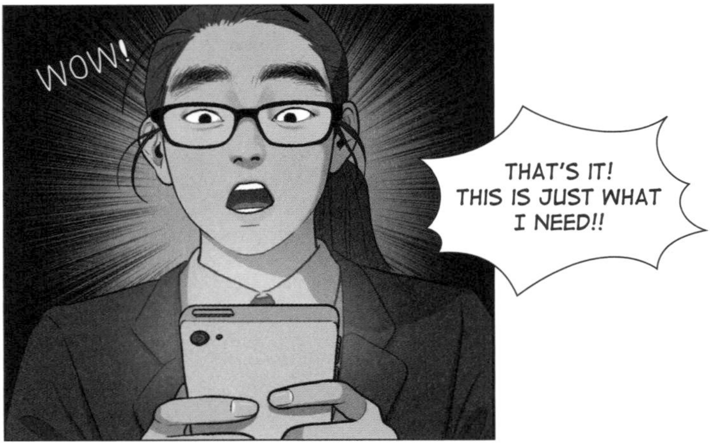
WOW!
THAT'S IT! THIS IS JUST WHAT I NEED!!

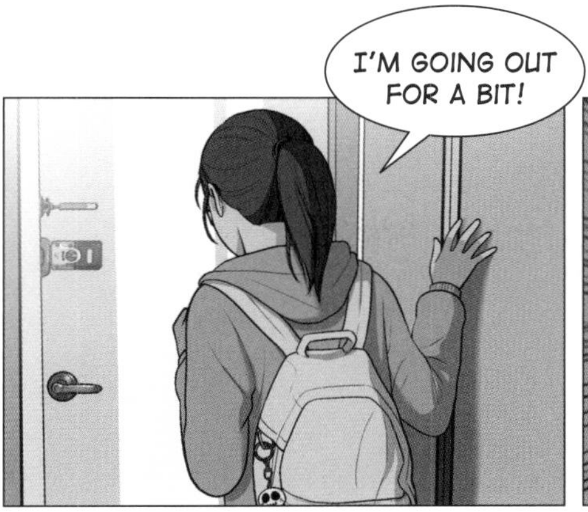
I'M GOING OUT FOR A BIT!

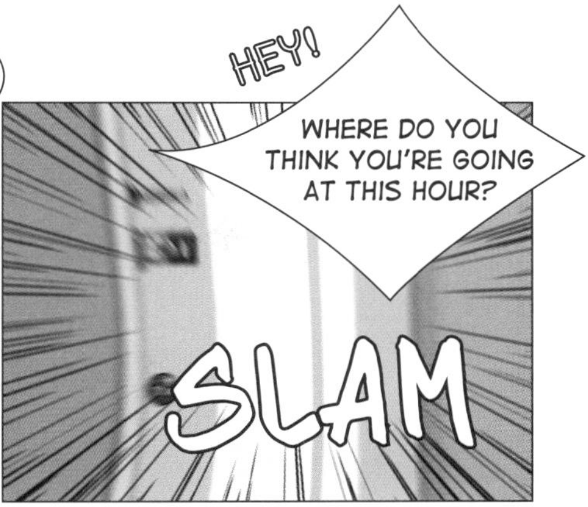
HEY!
WHERE DO YOU THINK YOU'RE GOING AT THIS HOUR?
SLAM

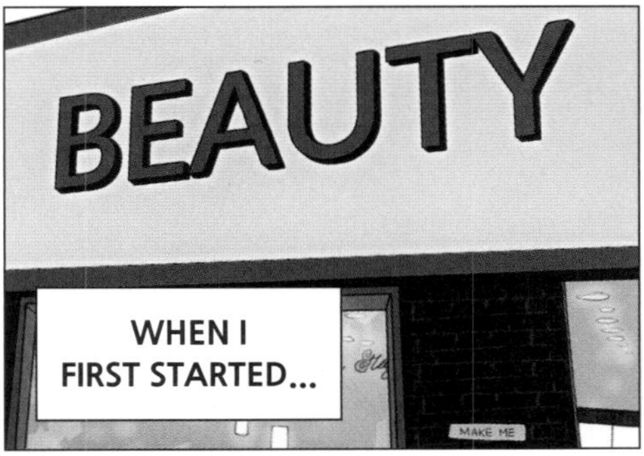
BEAUTY
WHEN I FIRST STARTED...
MAKE ME

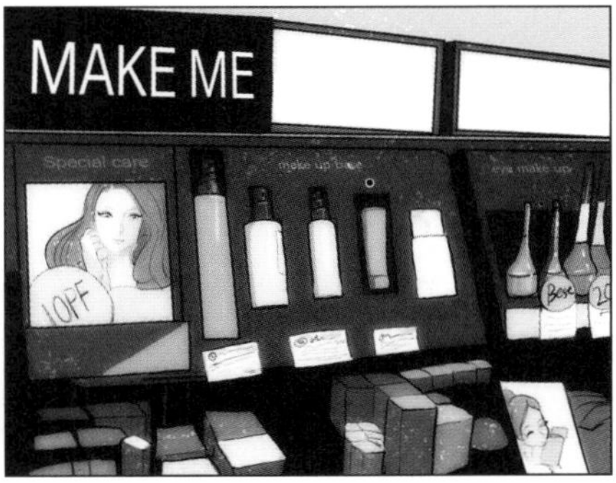
MAKE ME
Special care

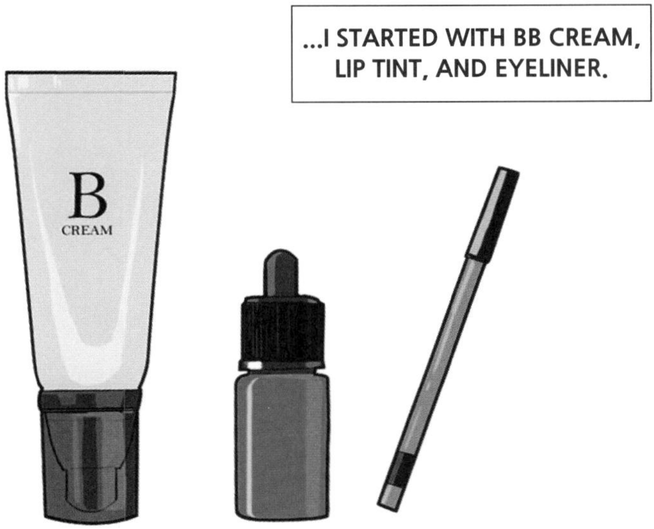
...I STARTED WITH BB CREAM, LIP TINT, AND EYELINER.
B
CREAM

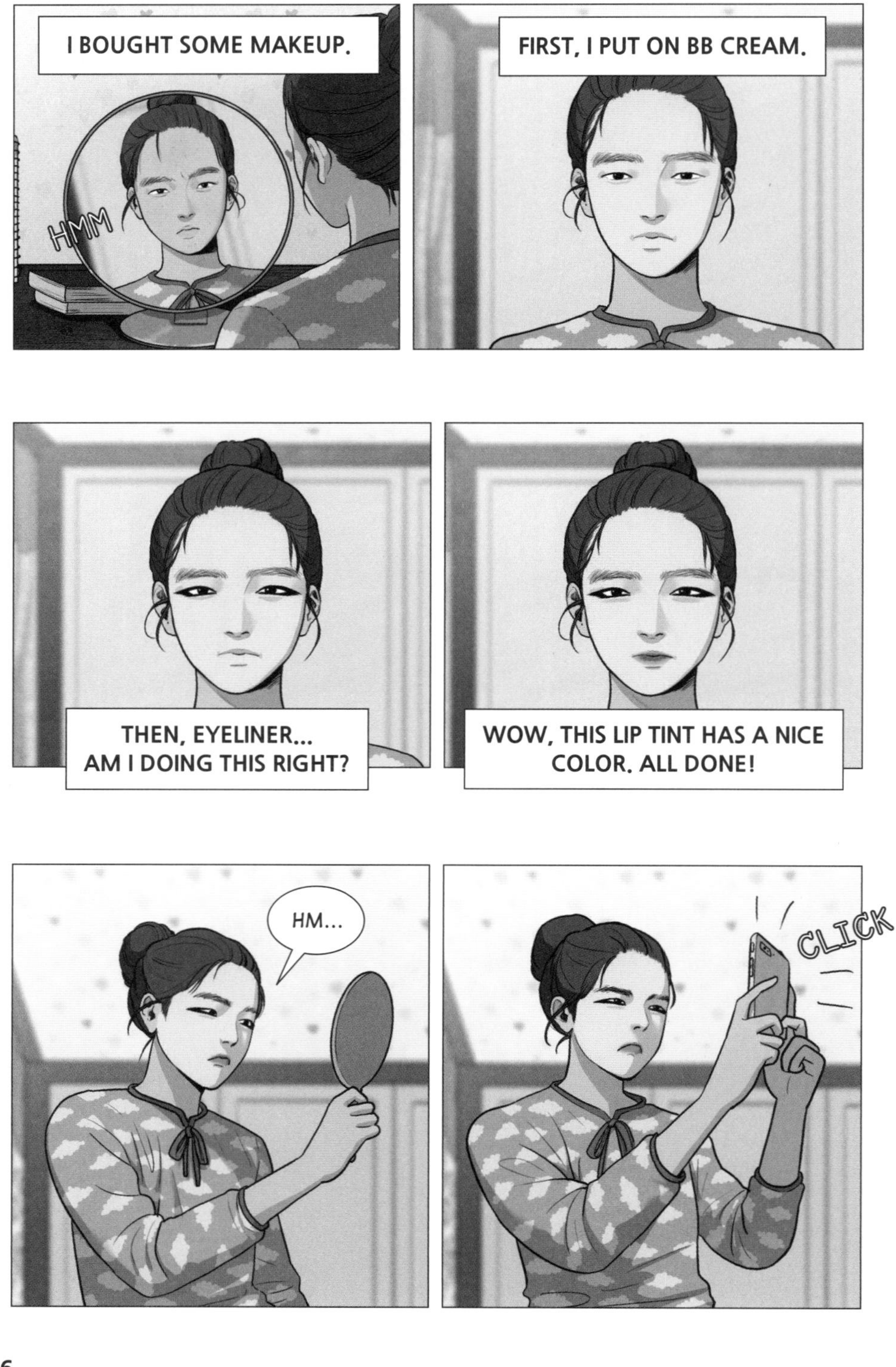
I BOUGHT SOME MAKEUP.
HMM
FIRST, I PUT ON BB CREAM.
THEN, EYELINER...
AM I DOING THIS RIGHT?
WOW, THIS LIP TINT HAS A NICE
COLOR. ALL DONE!
HM...
CLICK

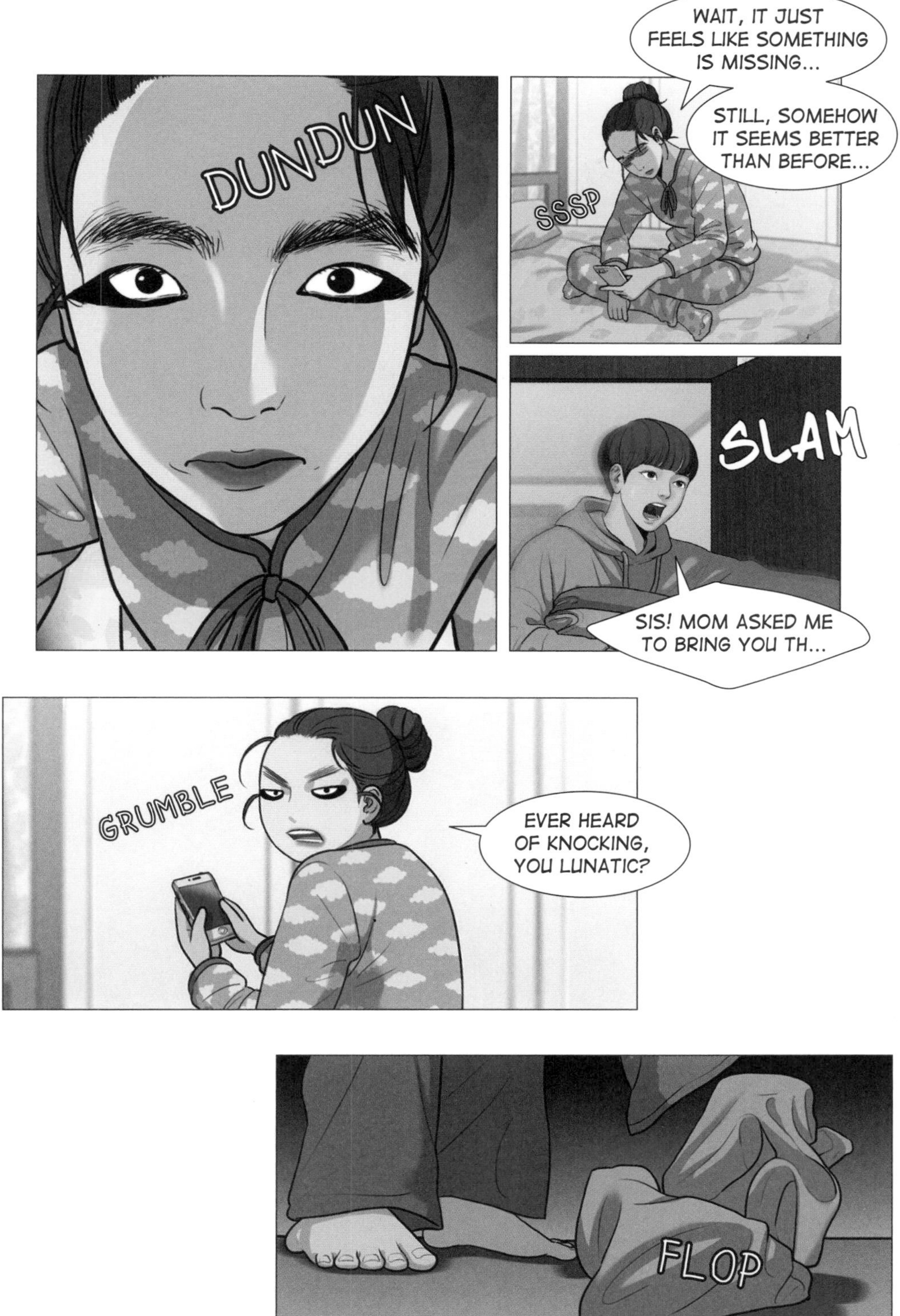
DUNDUN
WAIT, IT JUST FEELS LIKE SOMETHING IS MISSING...
STILL, SOMEHOW IT SEEMS BETTER THAN BEFORE...
SSSP
SLAM
SIS! MOM ASKED ME TO BRING YOU TH...
GRUMBLE
EVER HEARD OF KNOCKING, YOU LUNATIC?
FLOP

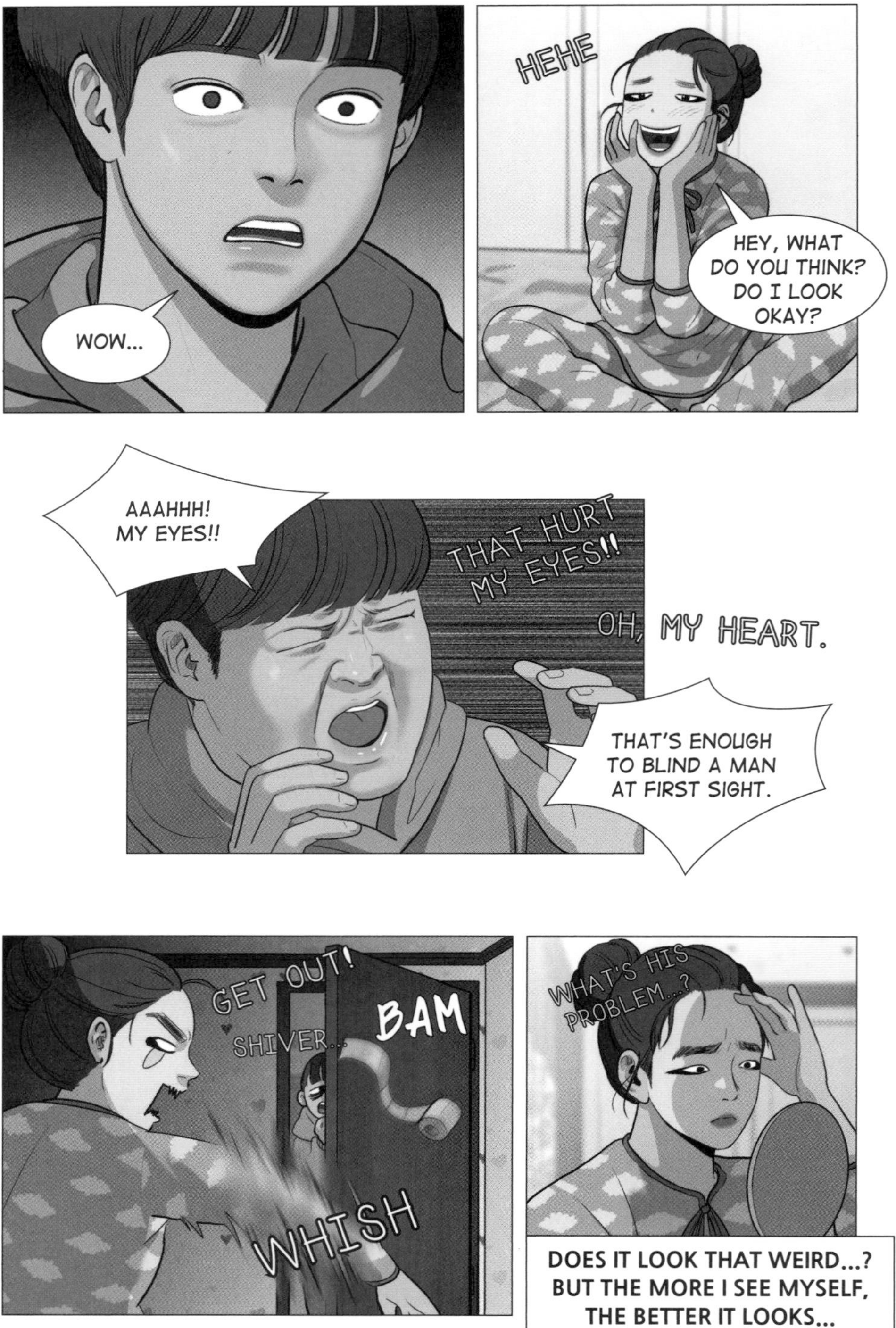
WOW...
HEHE
HEY, WHAT DO YOU THINK? DO I LOOK OKAY?
AAAHHH! MY EYES!!
THAT HURT MY EYES!!
OH, MY HEART.
THAT'S ENOUGH TO BLIND A MAN AT FIRST SIGHT.
GET OUT!
SHIVER...
BAM
WHISH
WHAT'S HIS PROBLEM...?
DOES IT LOOK THAT WEIRD...? BUT THE MORE I SEE MYSELF, THE BETTER IT LOOKS...

THE NEXT DAY.

GLANCE

MURMUR

GLANCE

MURMUR

THUMP

THUMP

THIS IS SO AWKWARD...
IS EVERYONE STARING AT ME?
THIS MUST BE HOW PRETTY GIRLS
FEEL EVERY DAY.

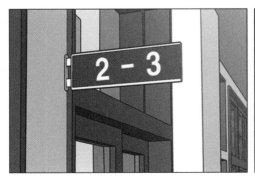

2 - 3

DRRRR

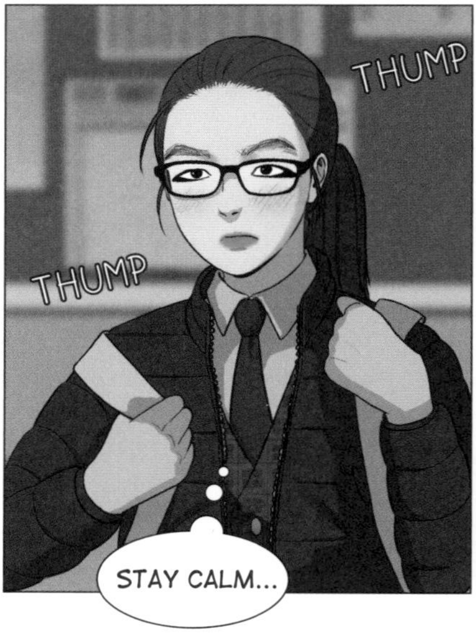
THUMP
THUMP
STAY CALM...
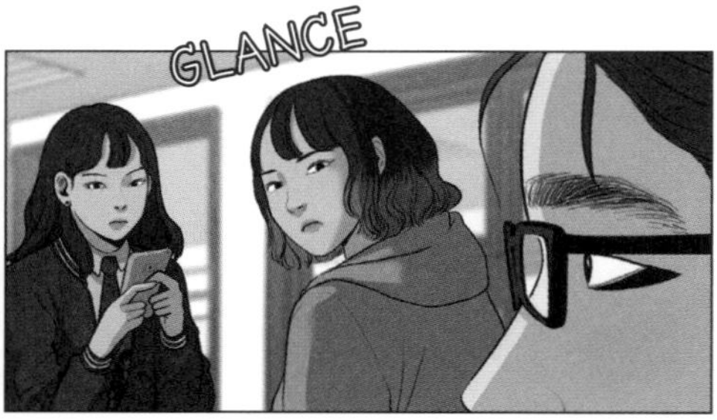
GLANCE
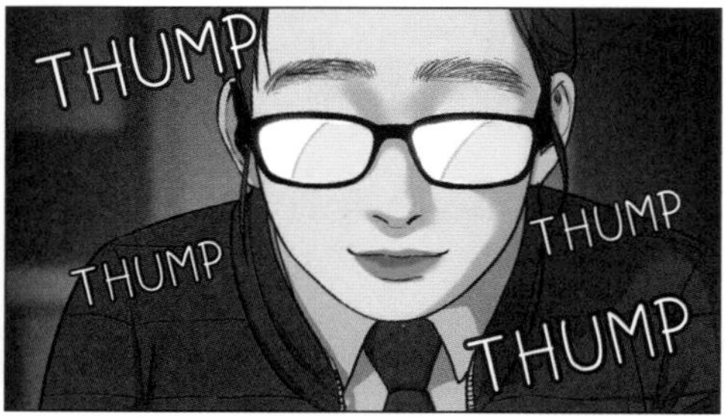
THUMP
THUMP
THUMP
THUMP

WHAT IS IT?
DO I LOOK A BIT
DIFFERENT TODAY?

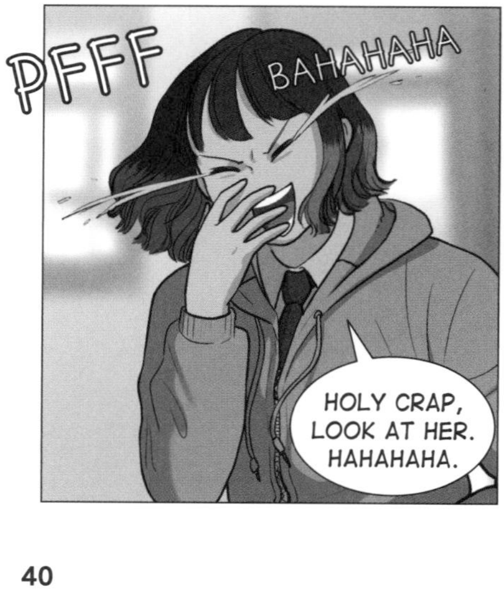
PFFF
BAHAHAHA
HOLY CRAP, LOOK AT HER. HAHAHAHA.
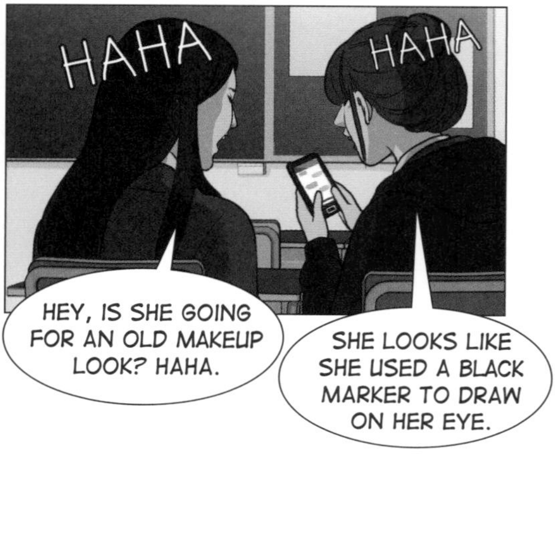
HAHA
HAHA
HEY, IS SHE GOING FOR AN OLD MAKEUP LOOK? HAHA.
SHE LOOKS LIKE SHE USED A BLACK MARKER TO DRAW ON HER EYE.

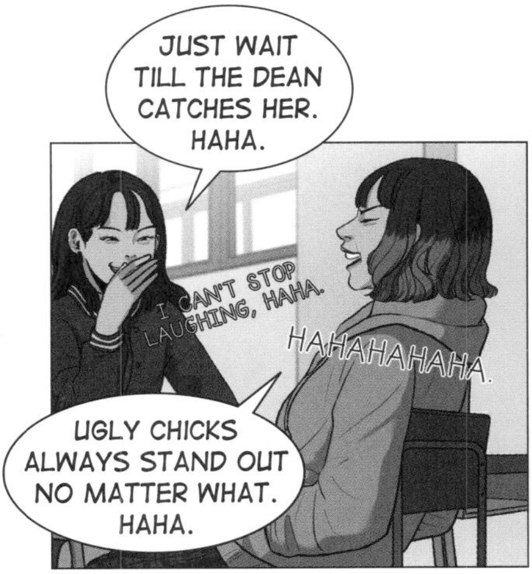
JUST WAIT TILL THE DEAN CATCHES HER. HAHA.
I CAN'T STOP LAUGHING, HAHA.
HAHAHAHAHA.
UGLY CHICKS ALWAYS STAND OUT NO MATTER WHAT. HAHA.
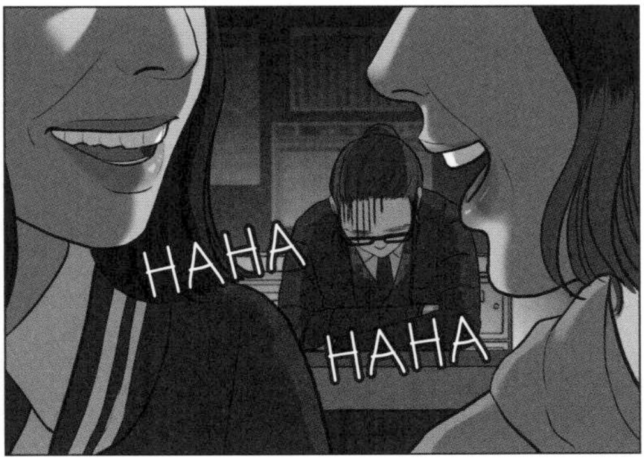
HAHA
HAHA

I KNEW IT...!!

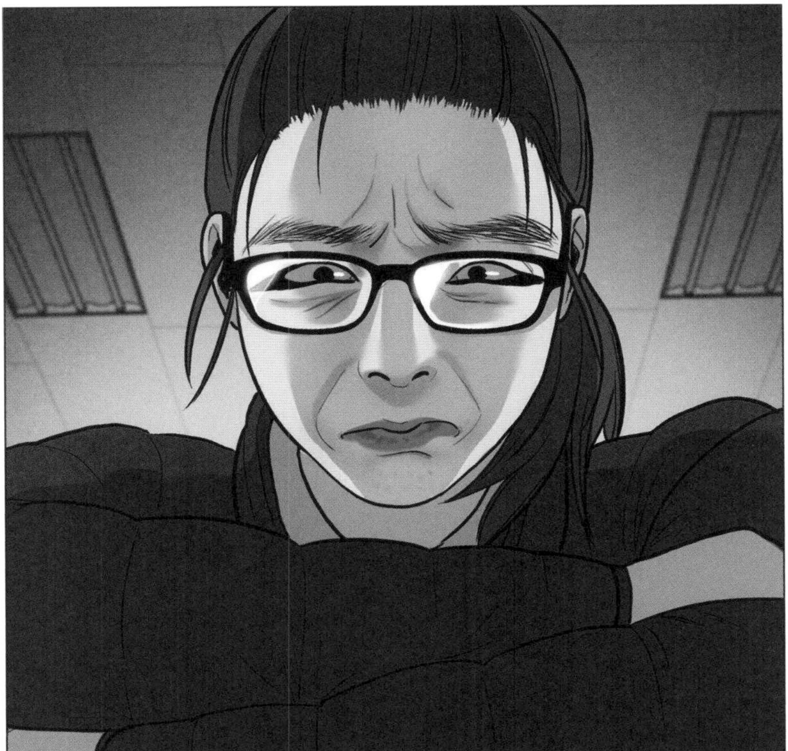

A GIRL LIKE ME IS UGLY
EVEN WITH MAKEUP!!

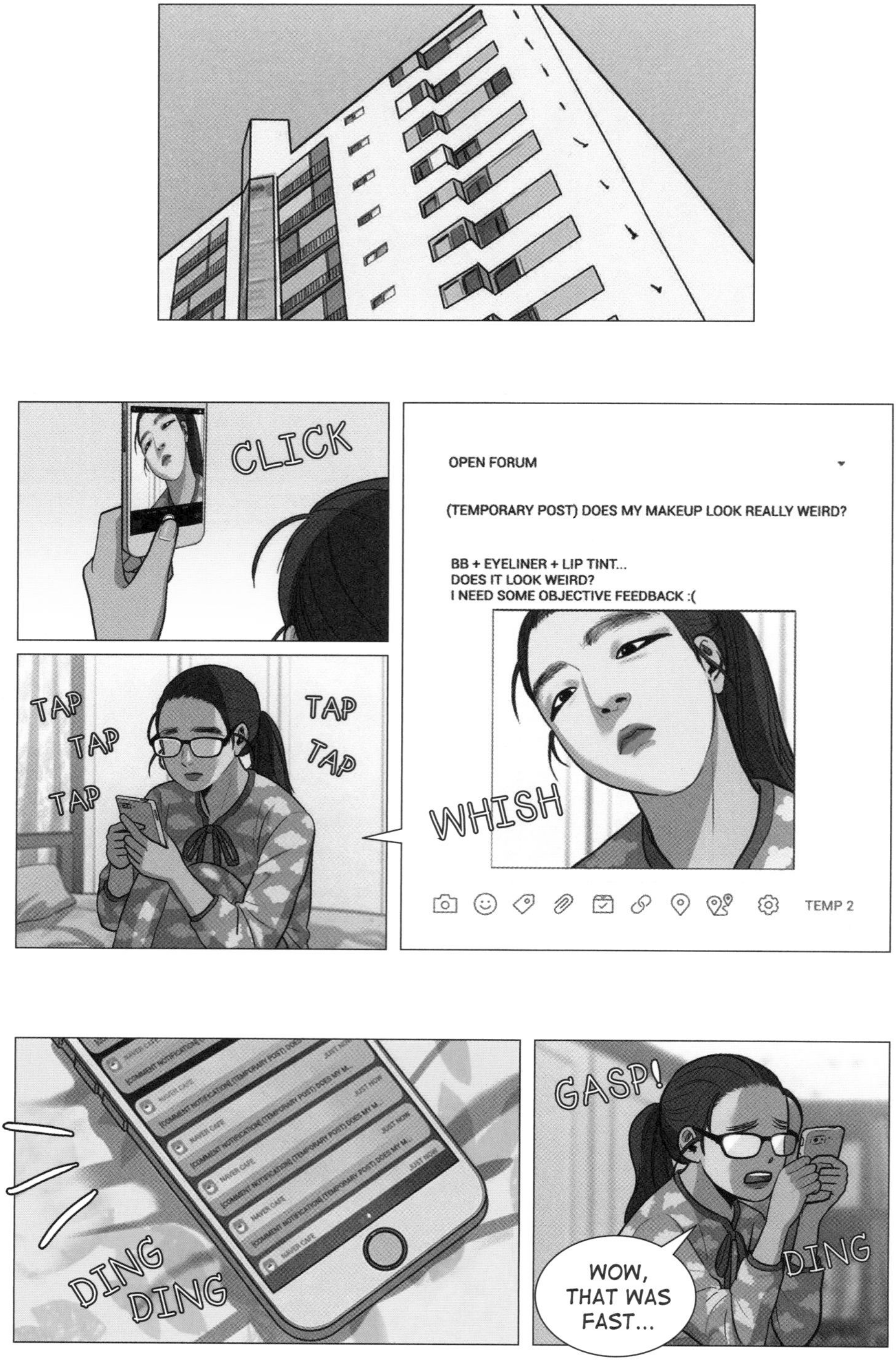
CLICK
TAP
TAP
TAP
TAP
TAP
OPEN FORUM
(TEMPORARY POST) DOES MY MAKEUP LOOK REALLY WEIRD?
BB + EYELINER + LIP TINT...
DOES IT LOOK WEIRD?
I NEED SOME OBJECTIVE FEEDBACK :(
WHISH
TEMP 2
DING
DING
GASP!
DING
WOW, THAT WAS FAST...

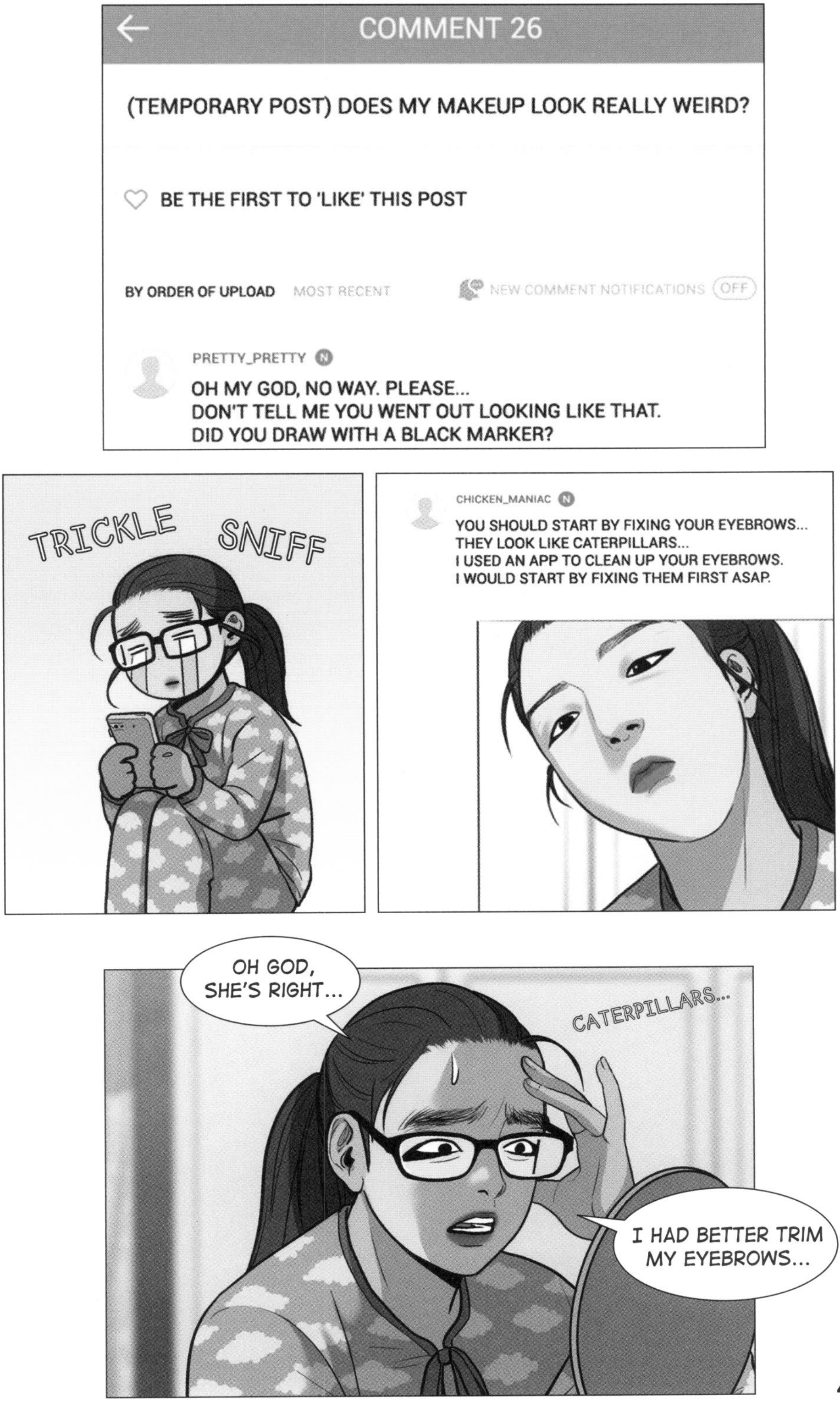
COMMENT 26
(TEMPORARY POST) DOES MY MAKEUP LOOK REALLY WEIRD?
BE THE FIRST TO 'LIKE' THIS POST
BY ORDER OF UPLOAD
MOST RECENT
NEW COMMENT NOTIFICATIONS
OFF
PRETTY_PRETTY
OH MY GOD, NO WAY. PLEASE...
DON'T TELL ME YOU WENT OUT LOOKING LIKE THAT.
DID YOU DRAW WITH A BLACK MARKER?
TRICKLE
SNIFF
CHICKEN_MANIAC
YOU SHOULD START BY FIXING YOUR EYEBROWS...
THEY LOOK LIKE CATERPILLARS...
I USED AN APP TO CLEAN UP YOUR EYEBROWS.
I WOULD START BY FIXING THEM FIRST ASAP.
OH GOD, SHE'S RIGHT...
CATERPILLARS...
I HAD BETTER TRIM MY EYEBROWS...

DING

PLAY_WITH_FIRE
HEY, READ THE THIRD 'BEST POST.'
I THINK IT WILL HELP YOU OUT.

BEST POST?

IS THIS WHAT
SHE MEANT...?

BEFORE AND AFTER
USING DOUBLE EYELID GLUE

HEY, GIRLS!
I'D LIKE TO GIVE YOU
SOME MAKEUP TIPS
AND SECRETS FOR USING
DOUBLE EYELID GLUE ^O^

 WANNABE IRING

 30 999+

HEY, GIRLS! I'D LIKE TO GIVE YOU SOME
MAKEUP TIPS AND SECRETS FOR USING
DOUBLE EYELID GLUE.

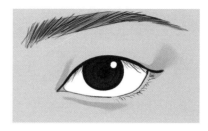

THIS IS HOW MY EYES USUALLY LOOK.

AND THIS IS HOW THEY LOOK WITH
DOUBLE EYELID GLUE + LENSES!
AMAZING, RIGHT?!

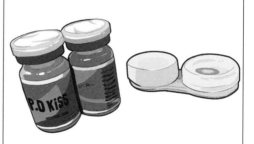

SINCE SOME PEOPLE HAVE ASKED
FOR INFO ABOUT THE LENSES, THEY'RE
BROWN "OPTICS KISS" LENSES
MADE BY XX MEDICAL~

44

GASP

W...WOW, HOW IS THAT EVEN POSSIBLE?!

I EMBARKED ON MY JOURNEY...

QINK!!

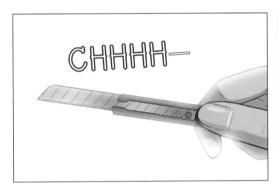

CHHHH—

SORRY

THE DAY HAS FINALLY COME TO OPEN YOU...

MOM!

I'M GOING OUT FOR A BIT!

...DOWN THAT PATH.

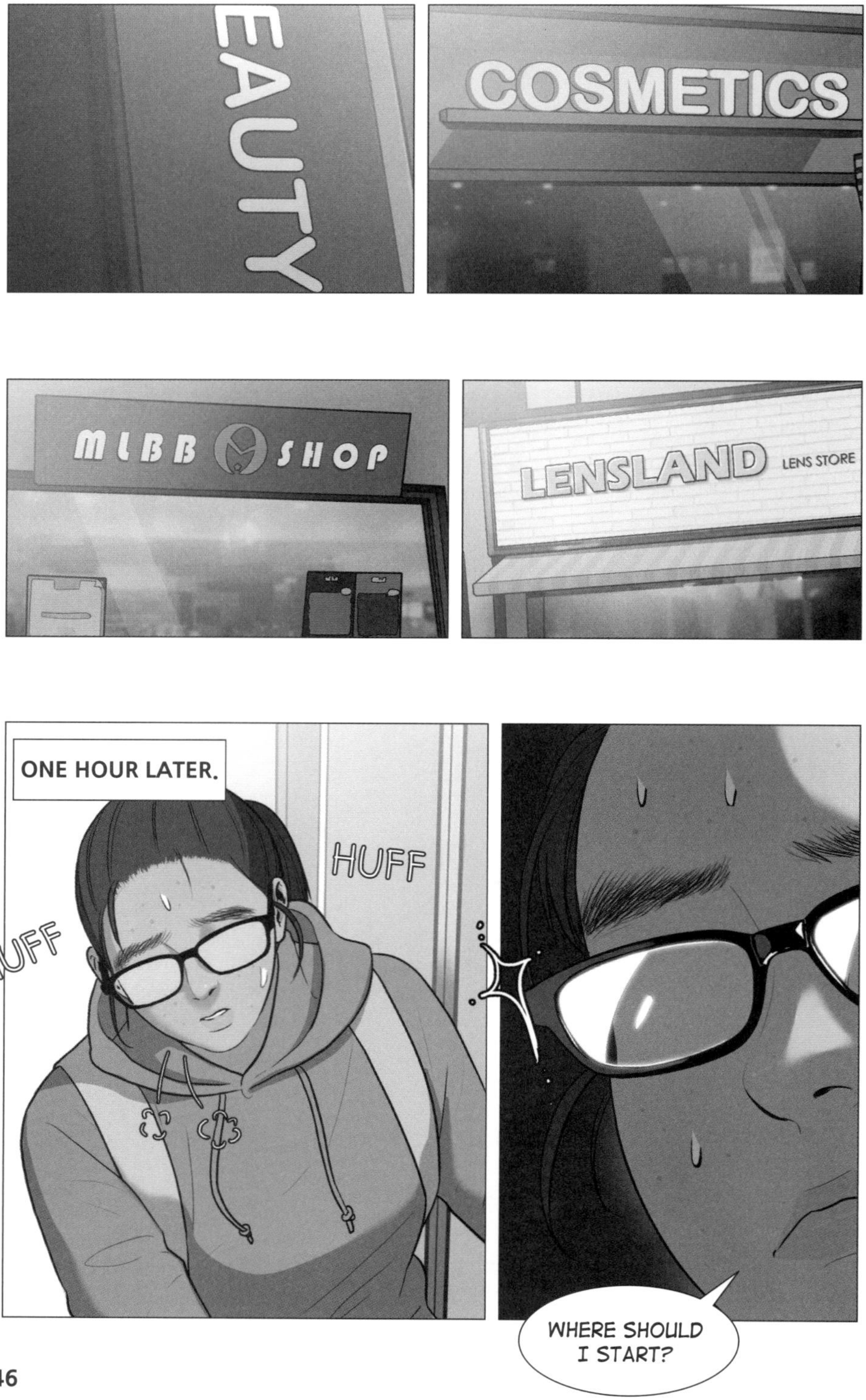
EAUTY
COSMETICS
MLBB SHOP
LENSLAND
LENS STORE
ONE HOUR LATER.
HUFF
HUFF
WHERE SHOULD I START?

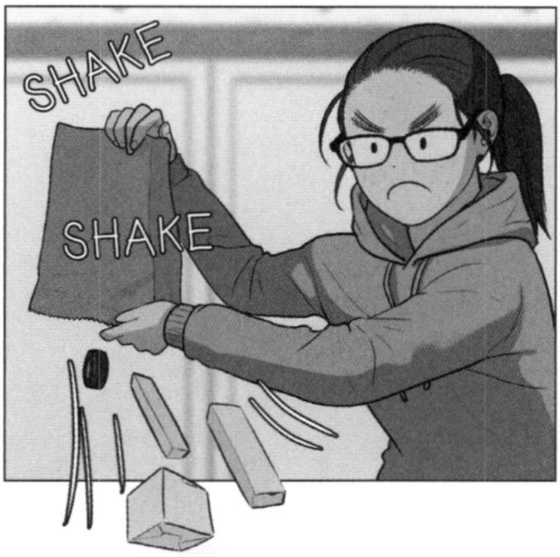
SHAKE
SHAKE

THE RESULTS OF MY EXPEDITION...

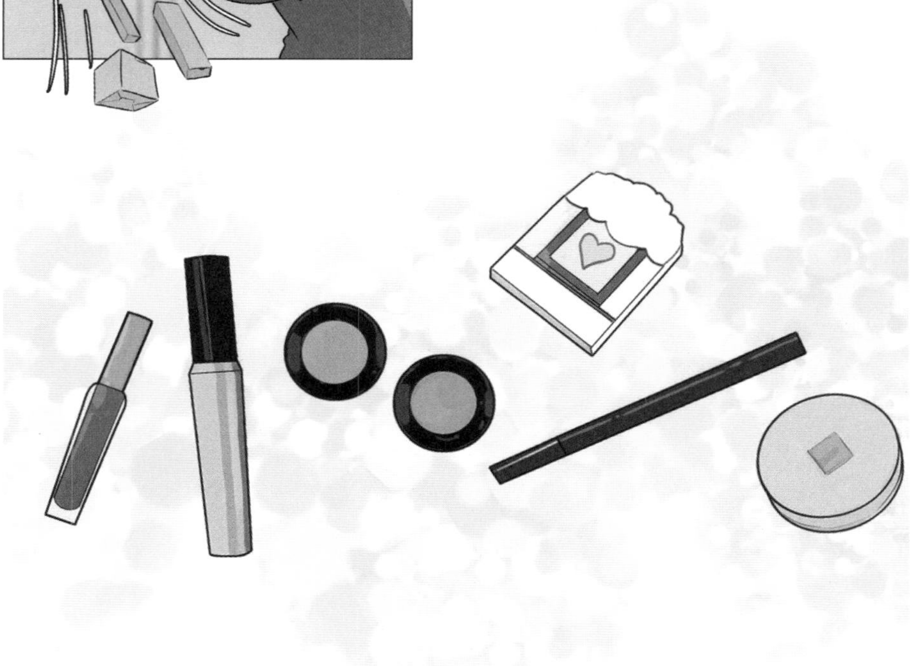

...WERE TREMENDOUS.

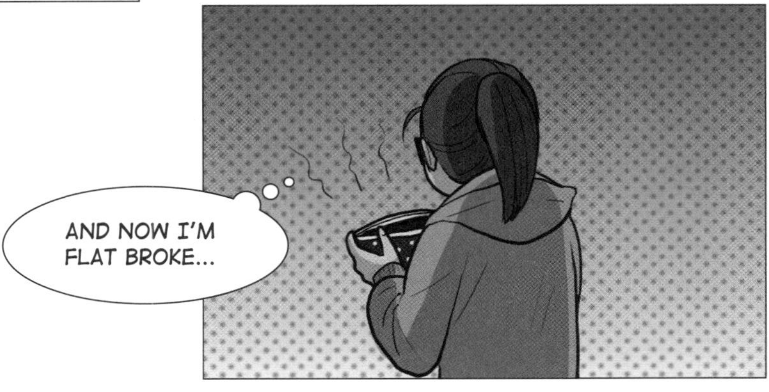
AND NOW I'M FLAT BROKE...

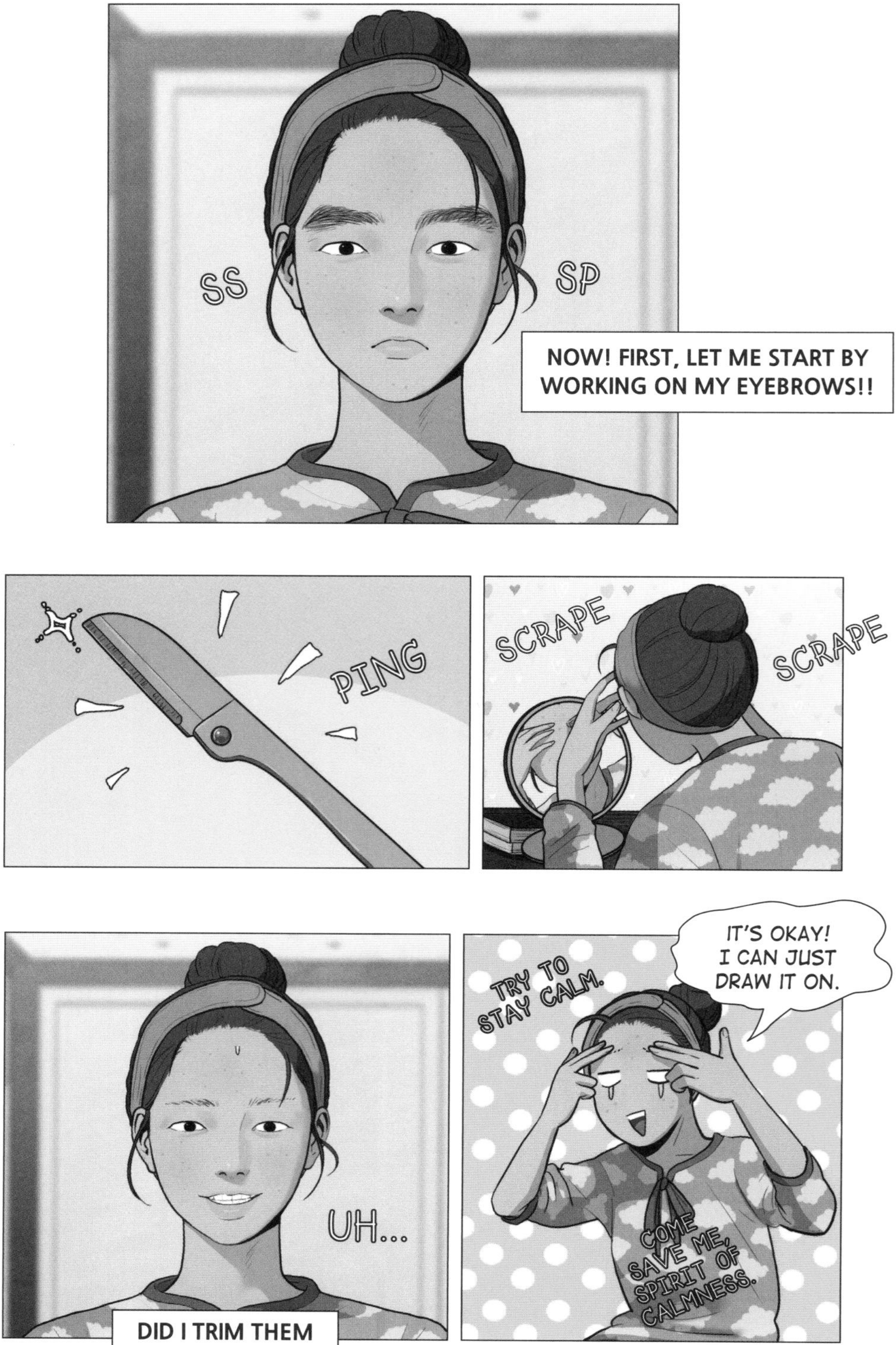
SS
SP
NOW! FIRST, LET ME START BY WORKING ON MY EYEBROWS!!
PING
SCRAPE
SCRAPE
UH...
DID I TRIM THEM TOO MUCH...?
TRY TO STAY CALM.
IT'S OKAY! I CAN JUST DRAW IT ON.
COME SAVE ME, SPIRIT OF CALMNESS.

I TRIMMED MY EYEBROWS...NOW IT'S TIME FOR DOUBLE EYELID GLUE!

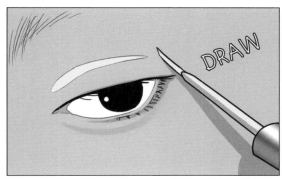

DRAW

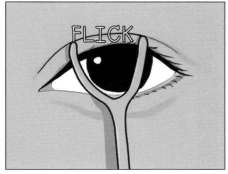

FLICK

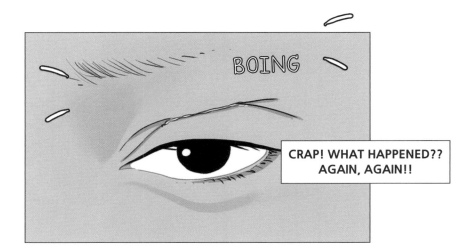

BOING

CRAP! WHAT HAPPENED?? AGAIN, AGAIN!!

49

DRAW

DRAW

UGH, THIS ISN'T RIGHT EITHER! AGAIN!!

HEY! THAT LOOKS PRETTY GOOD! MAN, DOUBLE EYELID GLUE IS HARD TO USE :(

NOW THE EYELASH CURLER...

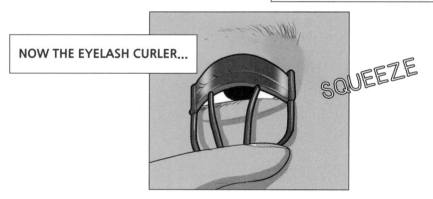

SQUEEZE

NEXT, LENSES...

FINALLY, MASCARA...

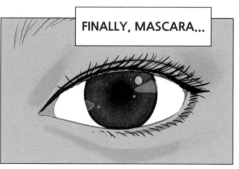

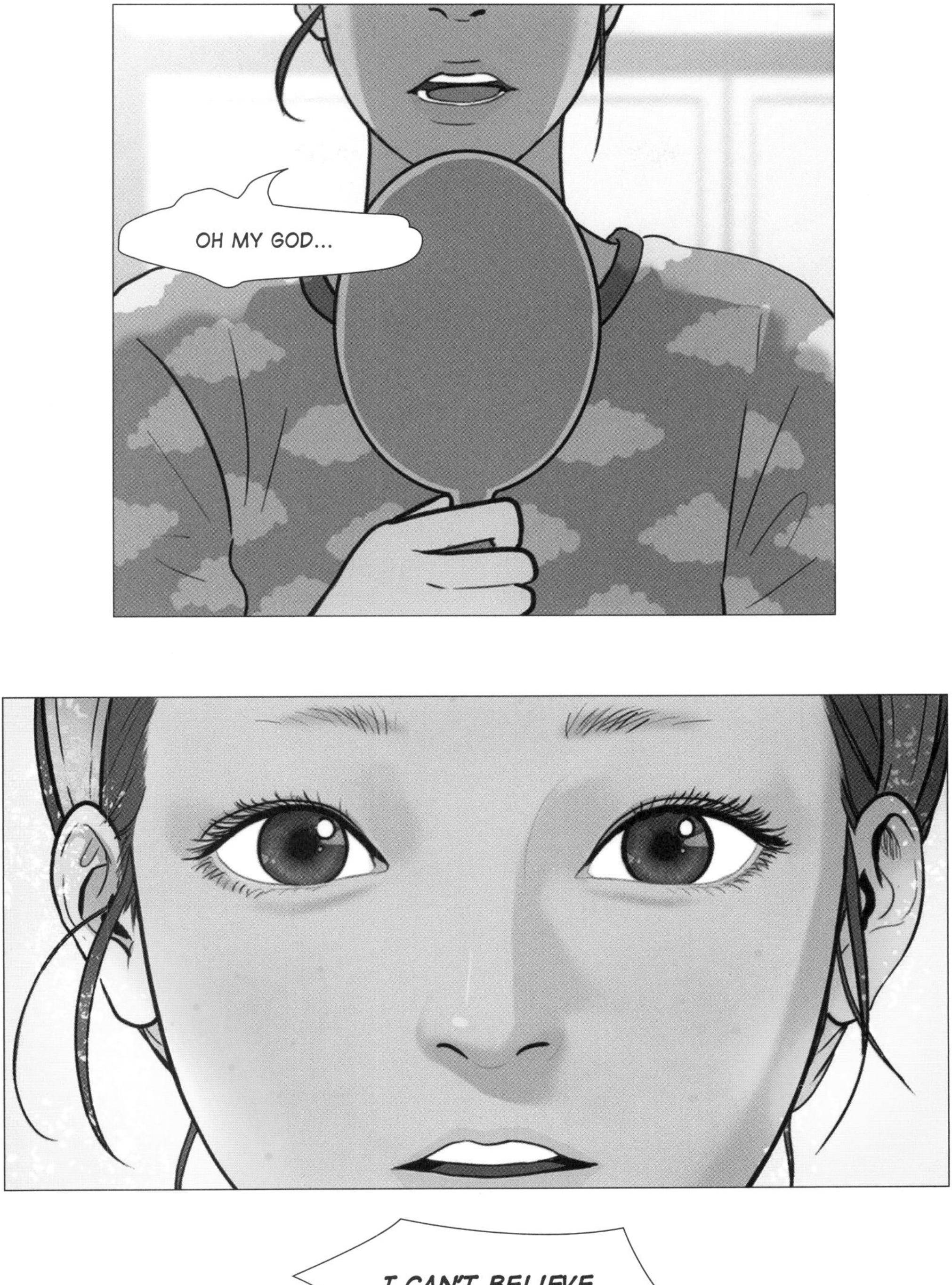
OH MY GOD...
I CAN'T BELIEVE THIS!!

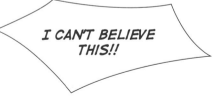

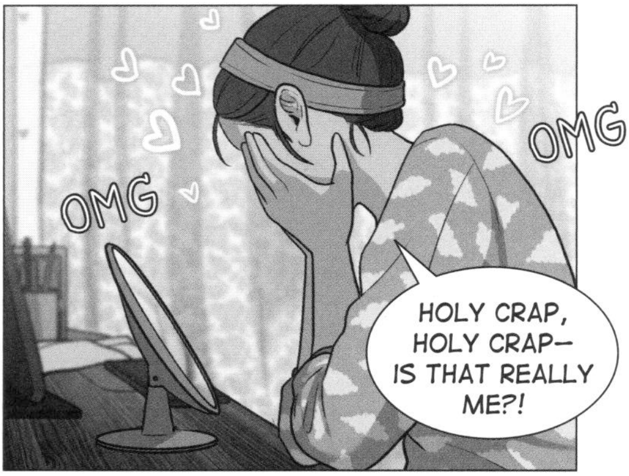
OMG
OMG
HOLY CRAP, HOLY CRAP— IS THAT REALLY ME?!

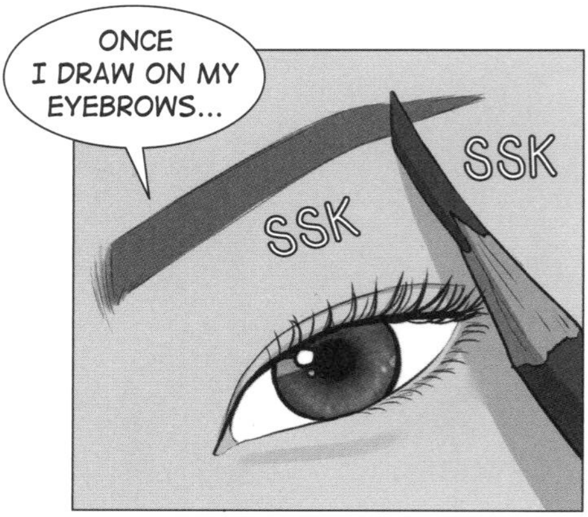
ONCE I DRAW ON MY EYEBROWS...
SSK
SSK

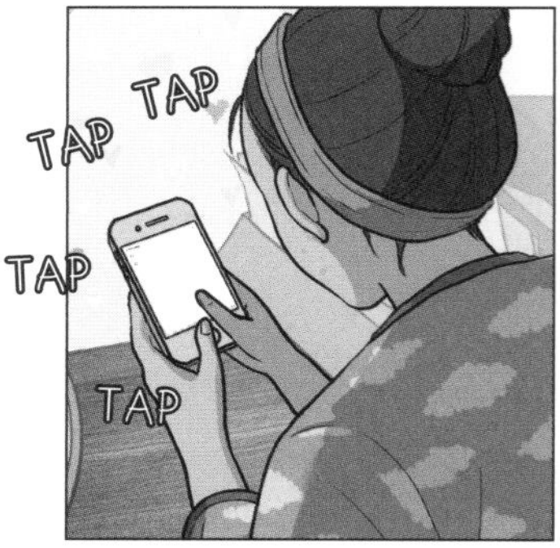
TAP TAP
TAP
TAP
TAP

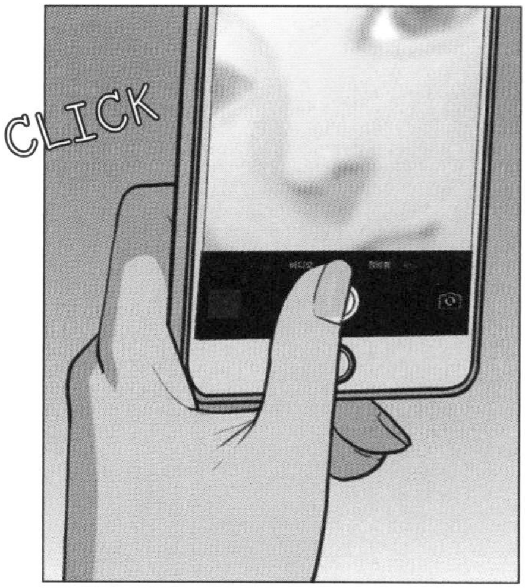
CLICK

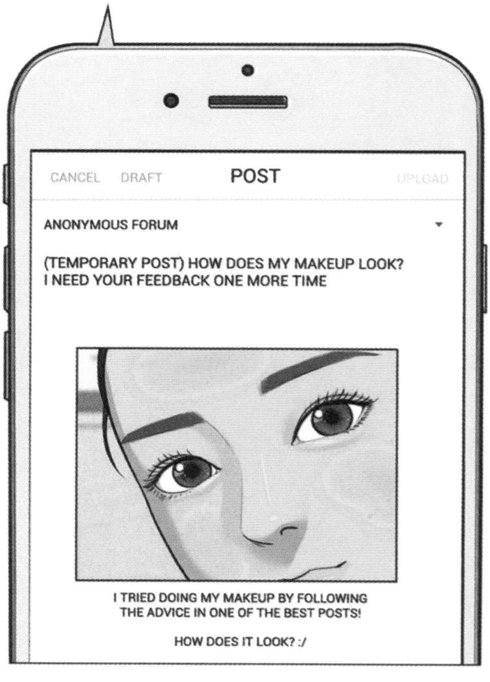
CANCEL
DRAFT
POST
UPLOAD
ANONYMOUS FORUM
(TEMPORARY POST) HOW DOES MY MAKEUP LOOK? I NEED YOUR FEEDBACK ONE MORE TIME
I TRIED DOING MY MAKEUP BY FOLLOWING THE ADVICE IN ONE OF THE BEST POSTS!
HOW DOES IT LOOK? :/

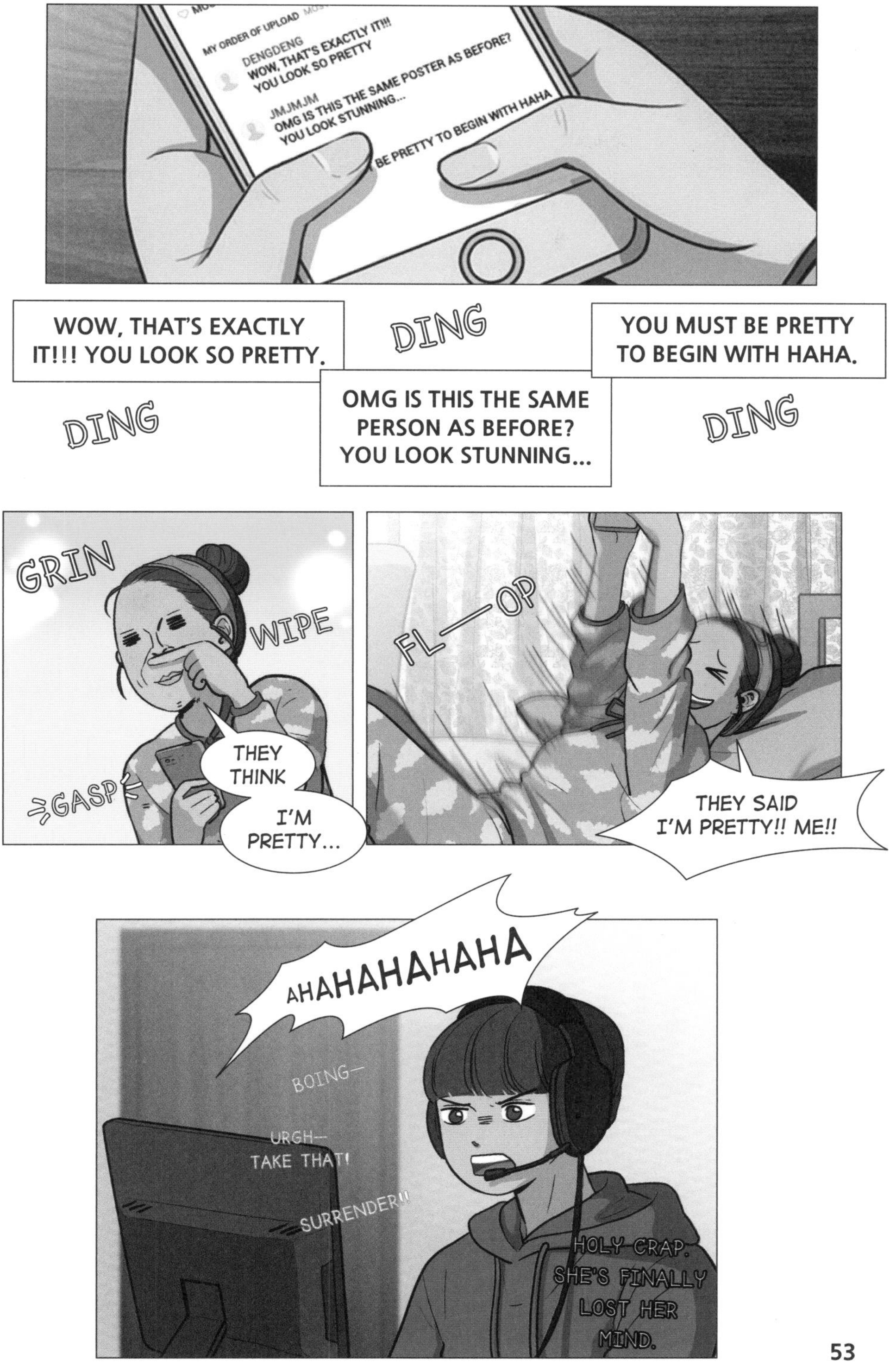
MY ORDER OF UPLOAD
DENGDENG
WOW, THAT'S EXACTLY IT!!! YOU LOOK SO PRETTY
JMJMJM
OMG IS THIS THE SAME POSTER AS BEFORE? YOU LOOK STUNNING...
BE PRETTY TO BEGIN WITH HAHA
WOW, THAT'S EXACTLY IT!!! YOU LOOK SO PRETTY.
DING
DING
OMG IS THIS THE SAME PERSON AS BEFORE? YOU LOOK STUNNING...
YOU MUST BE PRETTY TO BEGIN WITH HAHA.
DING
GRIN
WIPE
GASP
THEY THINK
I'M PRETTY...
FL—OP
THEY SAID I'M PRETTY!! ME!!
AHAHAHAHAHA
BOING—
URGH— TAKE THAT!
SURRENDER!!
HOLY CRAP. SHE'S FINALLY LOST HER MIND.

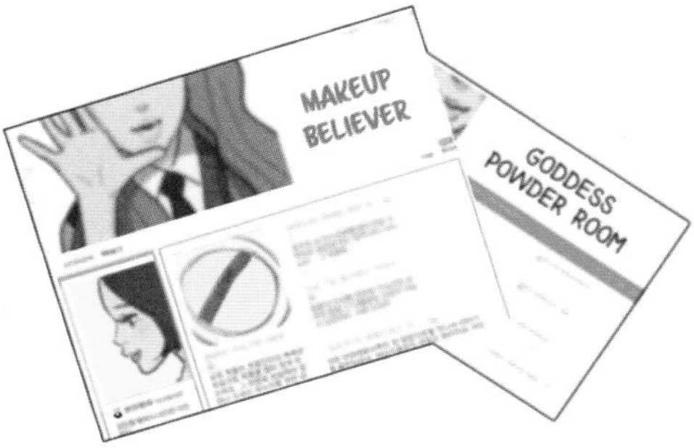
MAKEUP BELIEVER
GODDESS POWDER ROOM

FROM THAT DAY ON,
I STARTED READING
BEAUTY BLOGGERS...

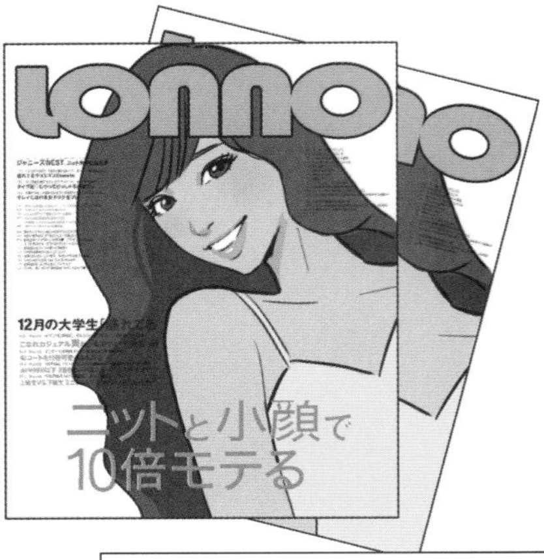
lonno
ニットと小顔で
10倍モテる

...AND MAKEUP MAGAZINES.

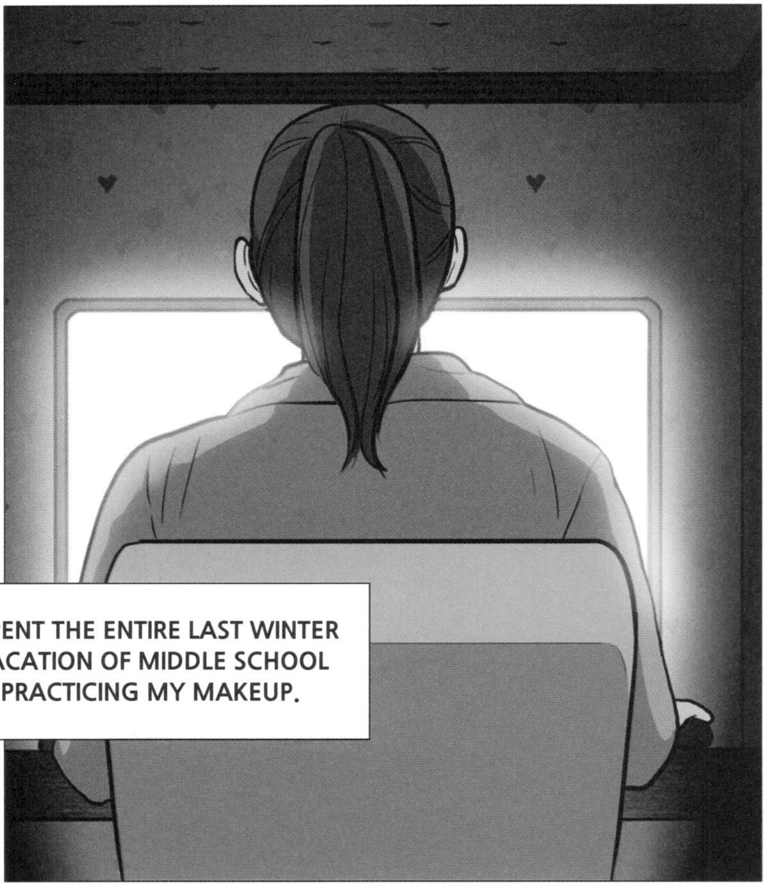
I SPENT THE ENTIRE LAST WINTER
VACATION OF MIDDLE SCHOOL
PRACTICING MY MAKEUP.

DECEMBER
Sun Mon Tue Wed Thu Fri Sat
1 2 3
4 5 6 7 8 9 10
11 12 13 14 15 16 17
18 19 20 21 22 23 24
25 26 27 28 29 30 31

JANUARY

환 신입생 여러분의 입학을 환영합니다 영
새 봄 고 등 학 교

FEBRUARY

MARCH

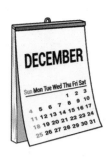

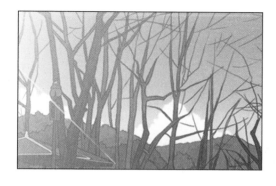

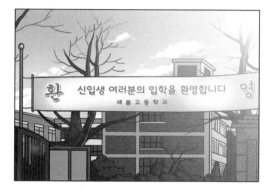

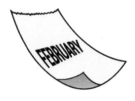

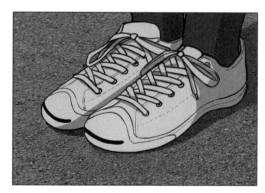

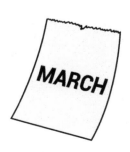

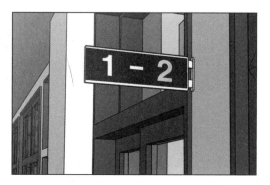

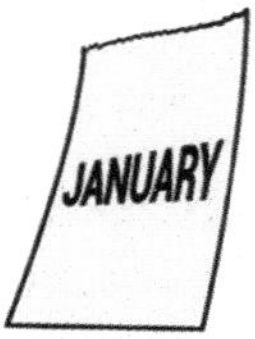

1 - 2

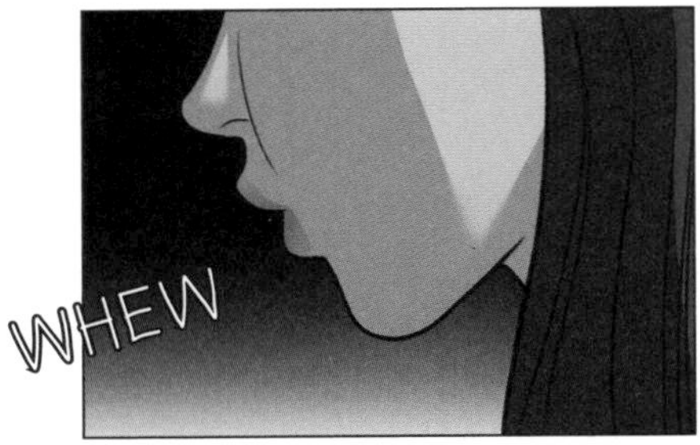
WHEW

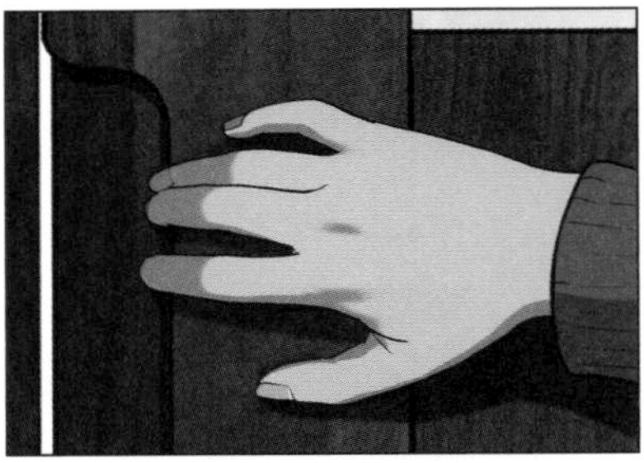

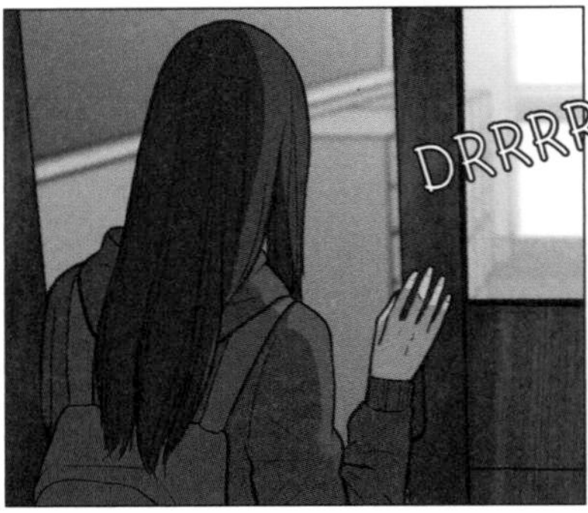
DRRRR

AND THEN
MY NEW LIFE BEGAN.

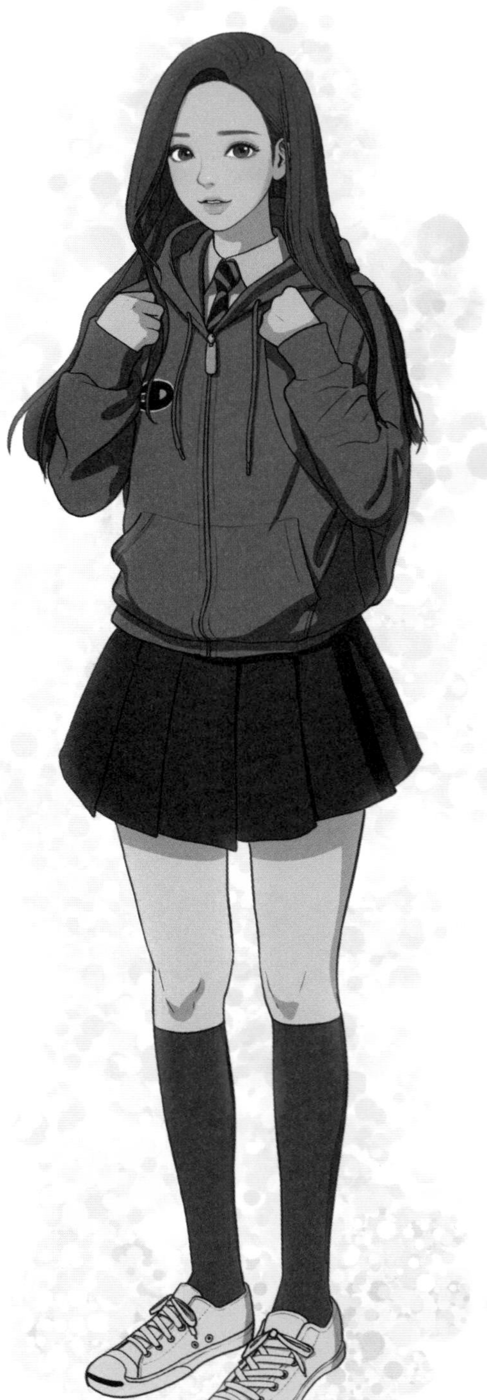

GLANCE

GLANCE

FRE EZE

RELAX, JUGYEONG LIM!

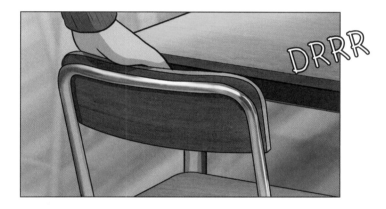

DRRR

HM 'MM

THANKFULLY I ENDED UP AT A SCHOOL THAT'S FAR AWAY, SO I HOPE NO ONE RECOGNIZES ME...

COME TO THINK OF IT, SINCE THIS SCHOOL IS SO FAR AWAY, I DON'T HAVE A SINGLE FRIEND HERE...

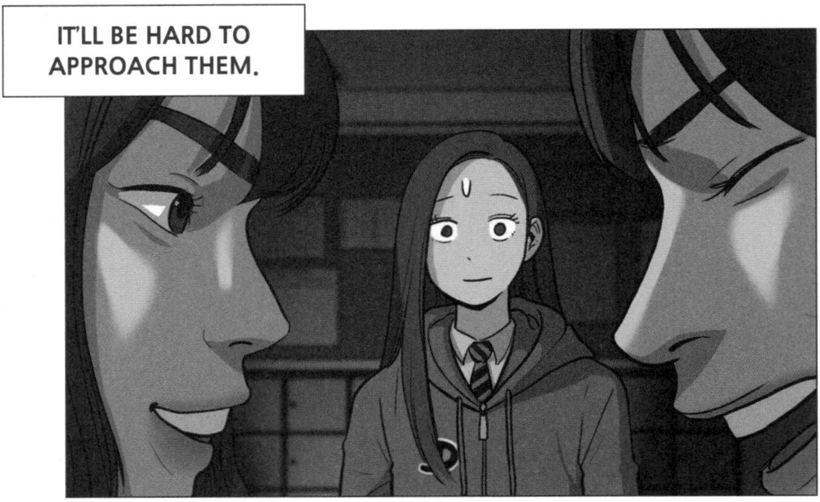
IT'LL BE HARD TO APPROACH THEM.

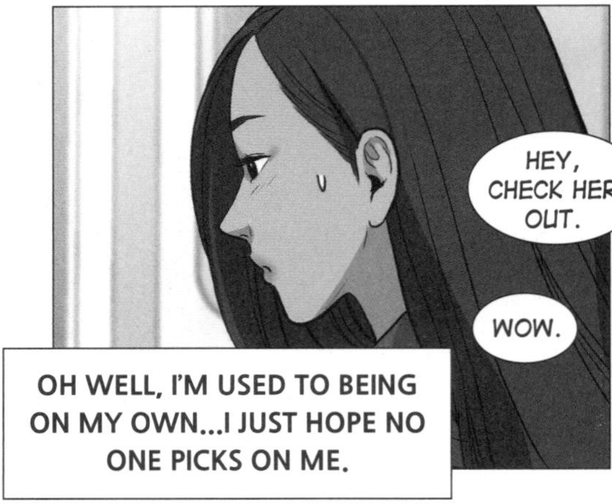
HEY, CHECK HER OUT.
WOW.
OH WELL, I'M USED TO BEING ON MY OWN...I JUST HOPE NO ONE PICKS ON ME.

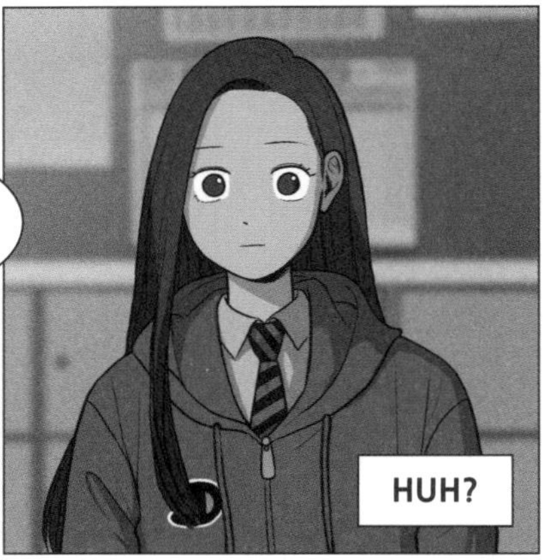
HUH?

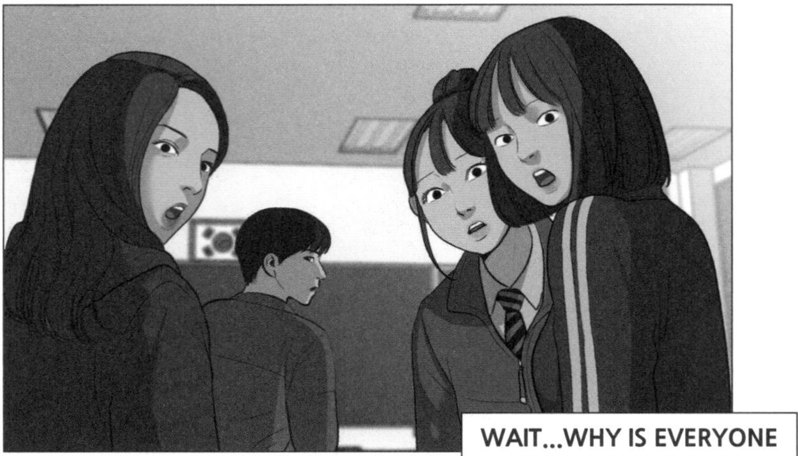
WAIT...WHY IS EVERYONE STARING AT ME...?

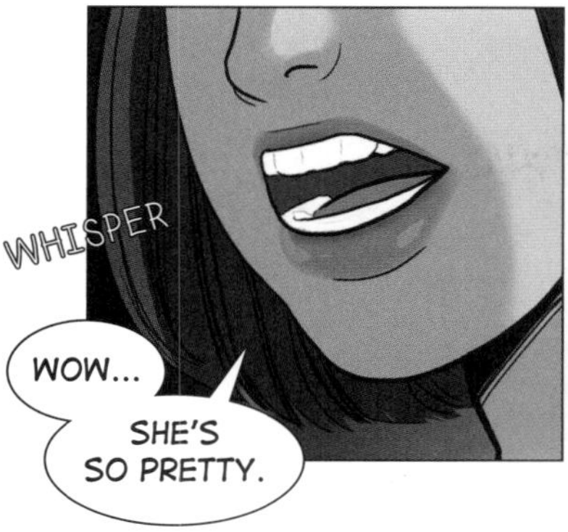
WHISPER
WOW...
SHE'S SO PRETTY.
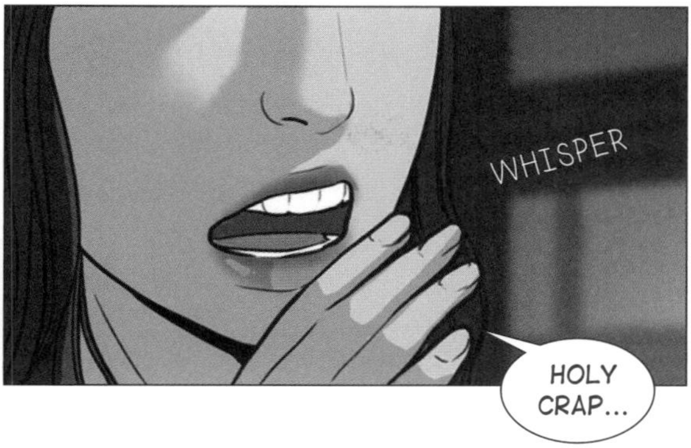
WHISPER
HOLY CRAP...
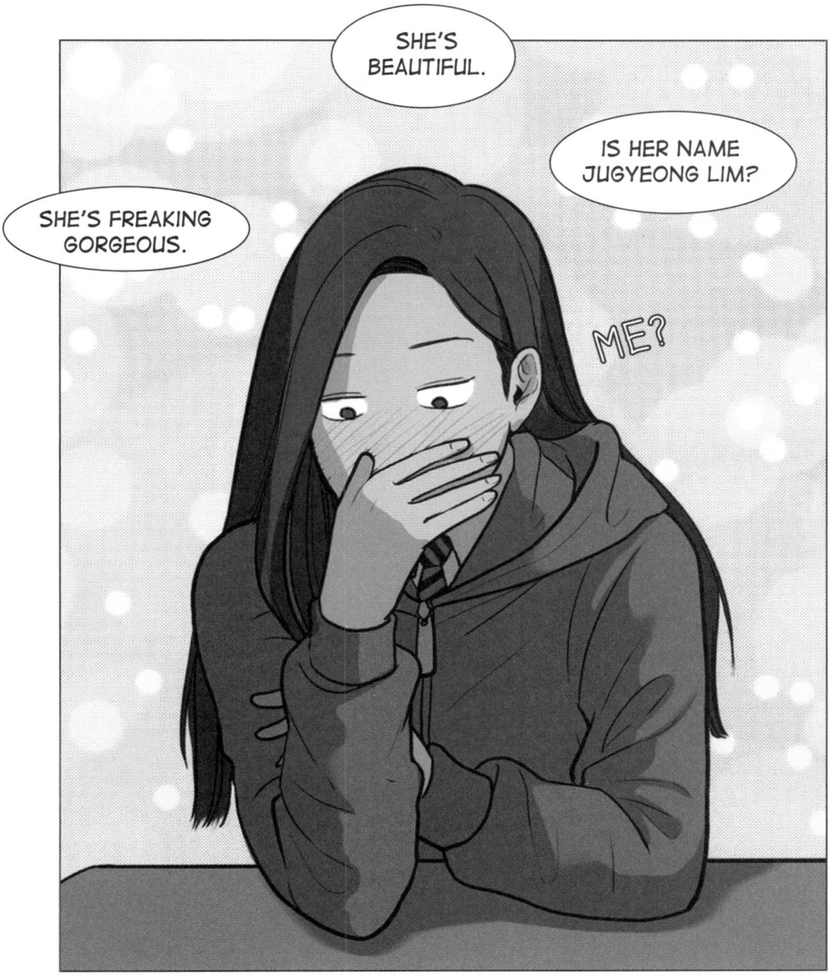
SHE'S BEAUTIFUL.
SHE'S FREAKING GORGEOUS.
IS HER NAME JUGYEONG LIM?
ME?

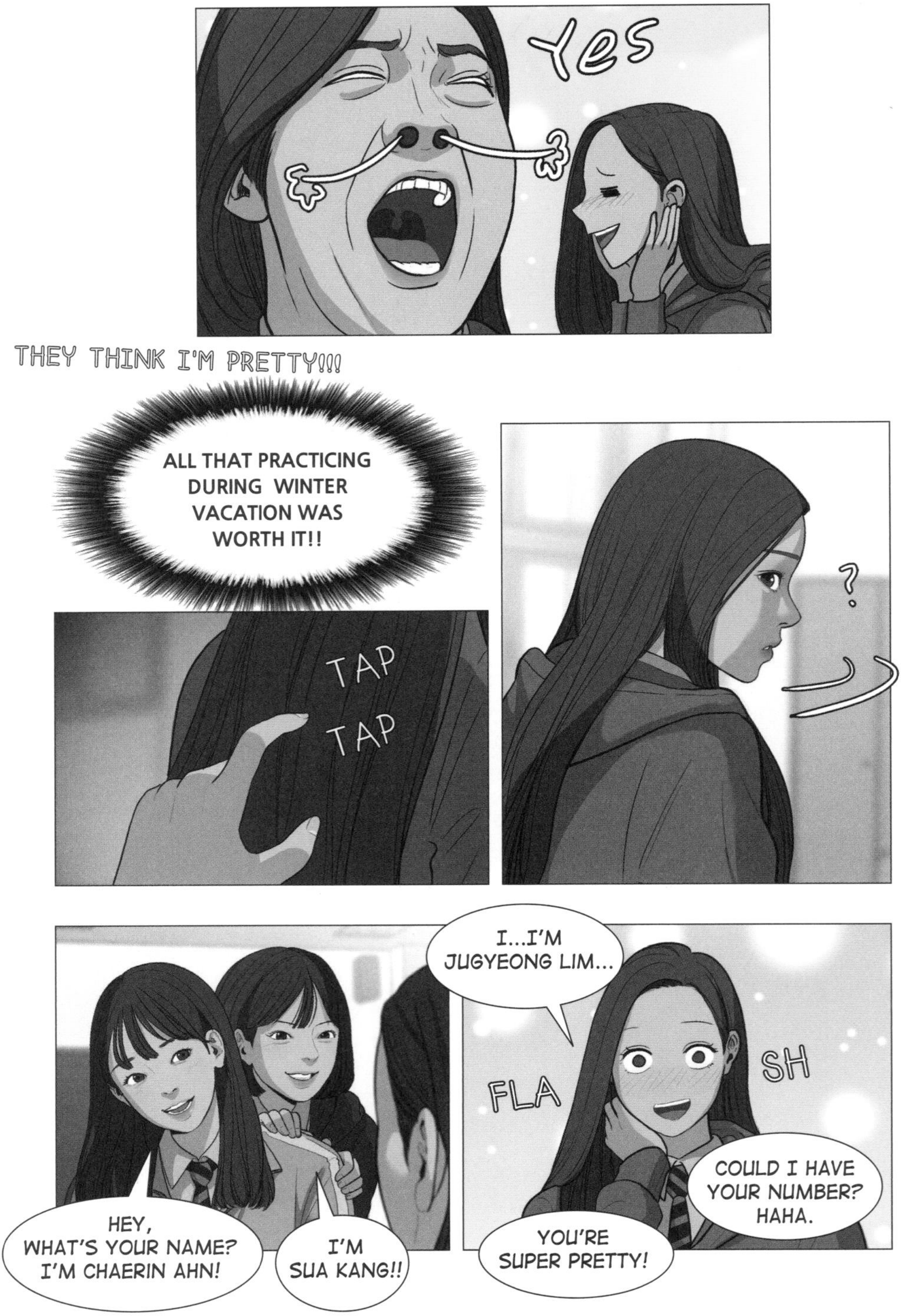
Yes
THEY THINK I'M PRETTY!!!
ALL THAT PRACTICING DURING WINTER VACATION WAS WORTH IT!!
TAP
TAP
?
HEY, WHAT'S YOUR NAME? I'M CHAERIN AHN!
I'M SUA KANG!!
I...I'M JUGYEONG LIM...
FLA
SH
YOU'RE SUPER PRETTY!
COULD I HAVE YOUR NUMBER? HAHA.

MAKING A BOND WITH THE KIDS WAS EASY.

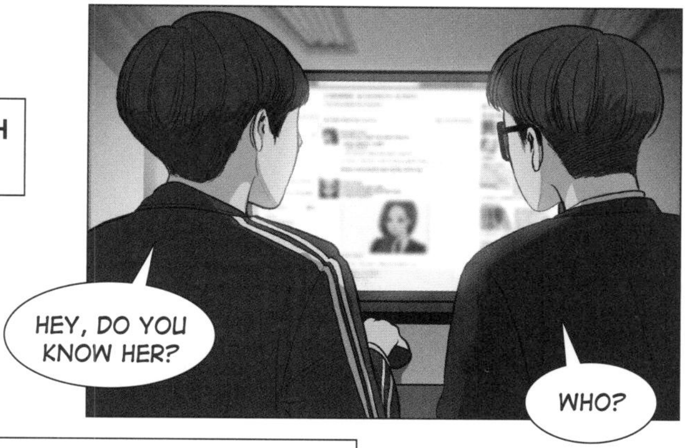

HEY, DO YOU KNOW HER?
WHO?

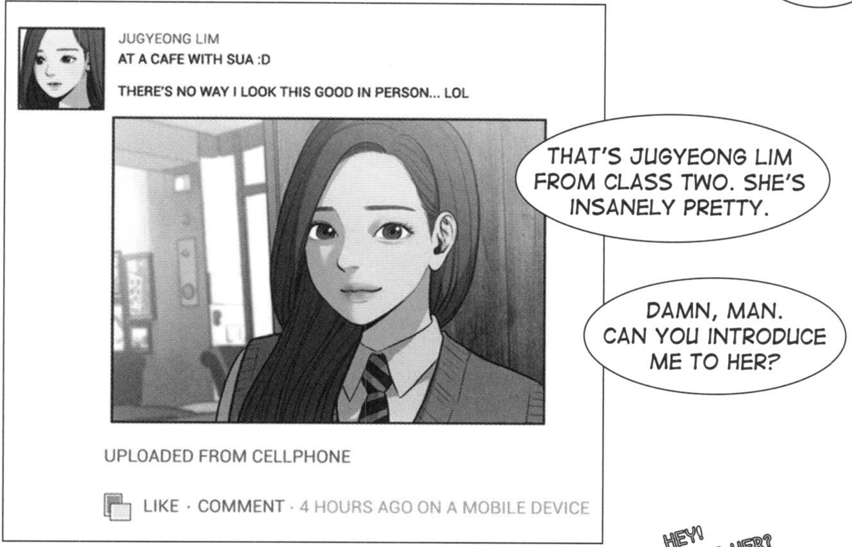

JUGYEONG LIM
AT A CAFE WITH SUA :D
THERE'S NO WAY I LOOK THIS GOOD IN PERSON... LOL
UPLOADED FROM CELLPHONE
LIKE · COMMENT · 4 HOURS AGO ON A MOBILE DEVICE
THAT'S JUGYEONG LIM FROM CLASS TWO. SHE'S INSANELY PRETTY.
DAMN, MAN. CAN YOU INTRODUCE ME TO HER?

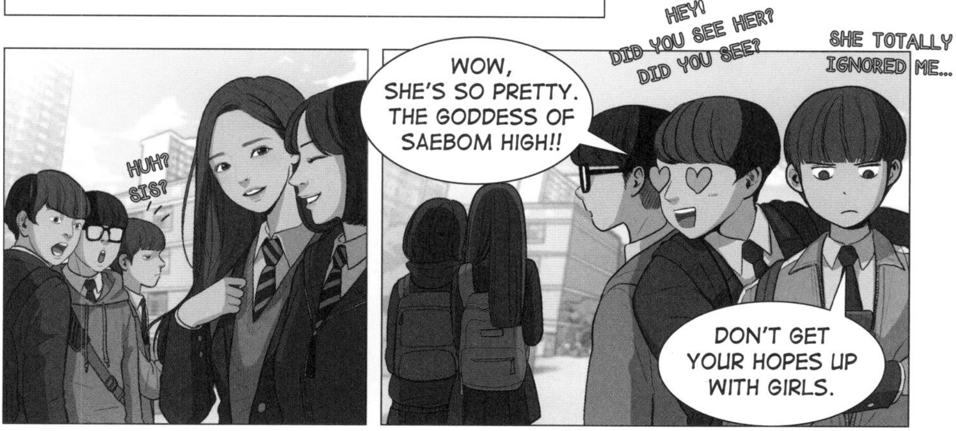

HUH? SIS?
WOW, SHE'S SO PRETTY. THE GODDESS OF SAEBOM HIGH!!
HEY! DID YOU SEE HER? DID YOU SEE?
SHE TOTALLY IGNORED ME...
DON'T GET YOUR HOPES UP WITH GIRLS.

I BECAME PRETTY WELL KNOWN.

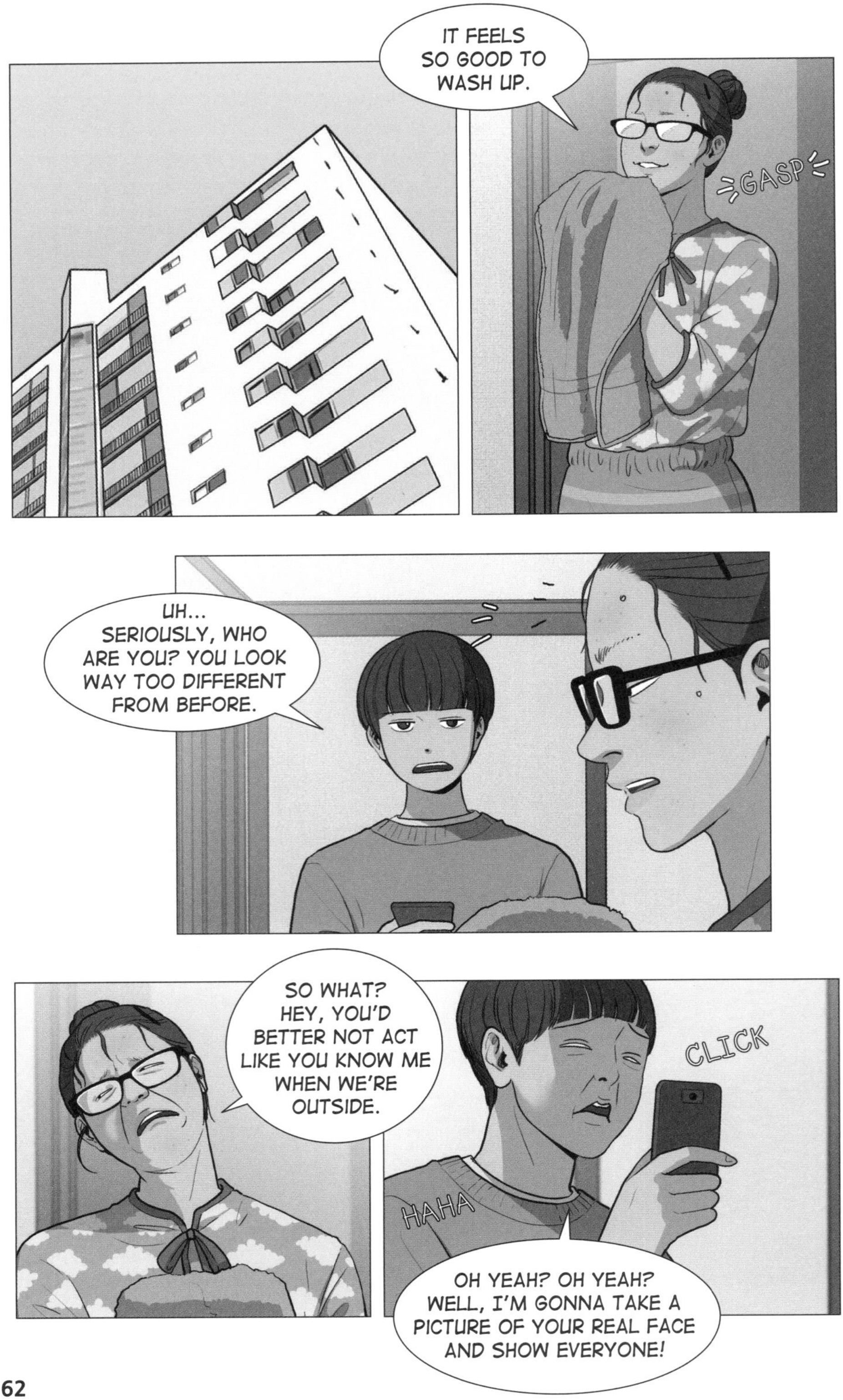
IT FEELS SO GOOD TO WASH UP.
GASP
UH... SERIOUSLY, WHO ARE YOU? YOU LOOK WAY TOO DIFFERENT FROM BEFORE.
SO WHAT? HEY, YOU'D BETTER NOT ACT LIKE YOU KNOW ME WHEN WE'RE OUTSIDE.
CLICK
HAHA
OH YEAH? OH YEAH? WELL, I'M GONNA TAKE A PICTURE OF YOUR REAL FACE AND SHOW EVERYONE!

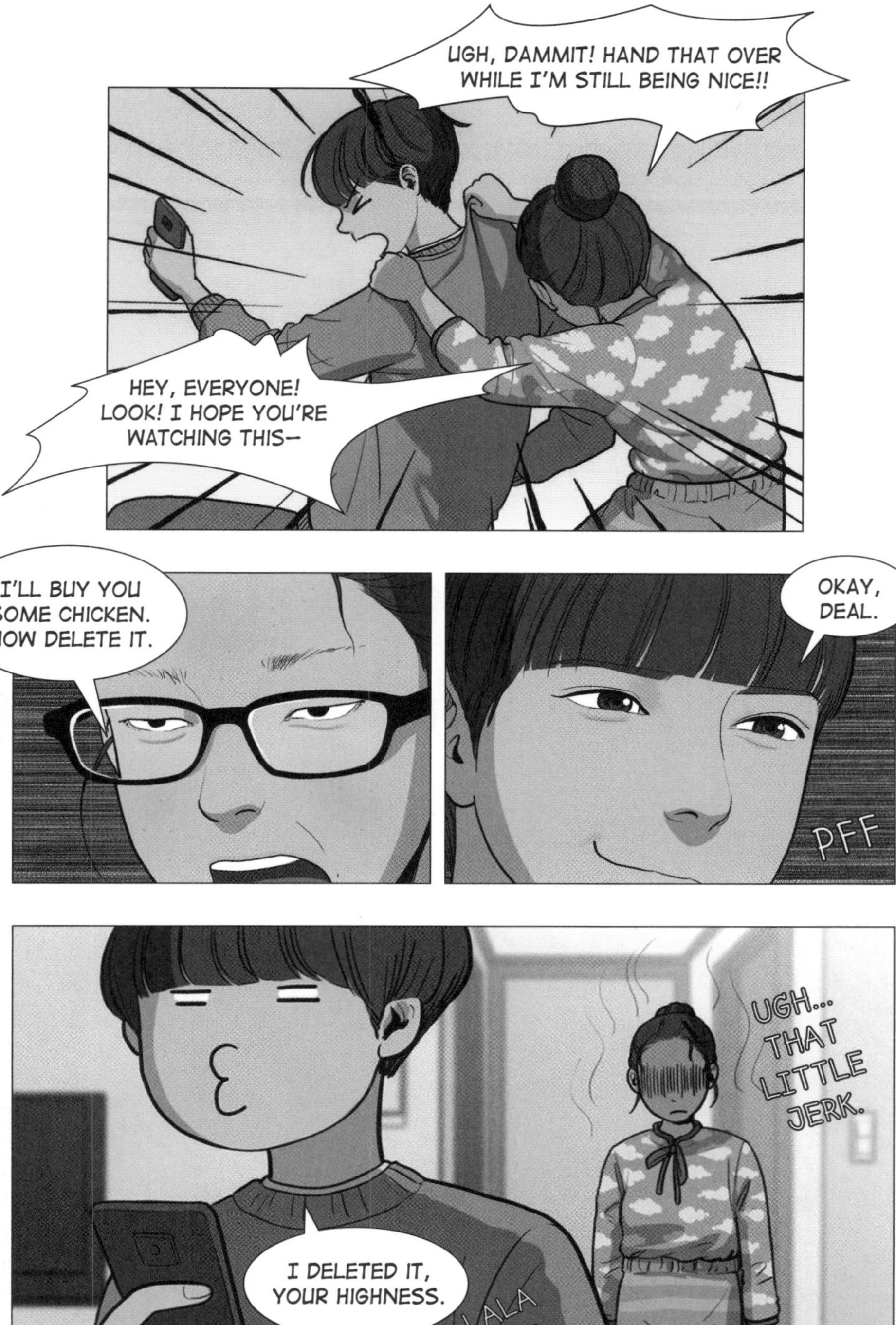
UGH, DAMMIT! HAND THAT OVER WHILE I'M STILL BEING NICE!!
HEY, EVERYONE! LOOK! I HOPE YOU'RE WATCHING THIS—
I'LL BUY YOU SOME CHICKEN. NOW DELETE IT.
OKAY, DEAL.
PFF
UGH... THAT LITTLE JERK.
I DELETED IT, YOUR HIGHNESS.
LALA

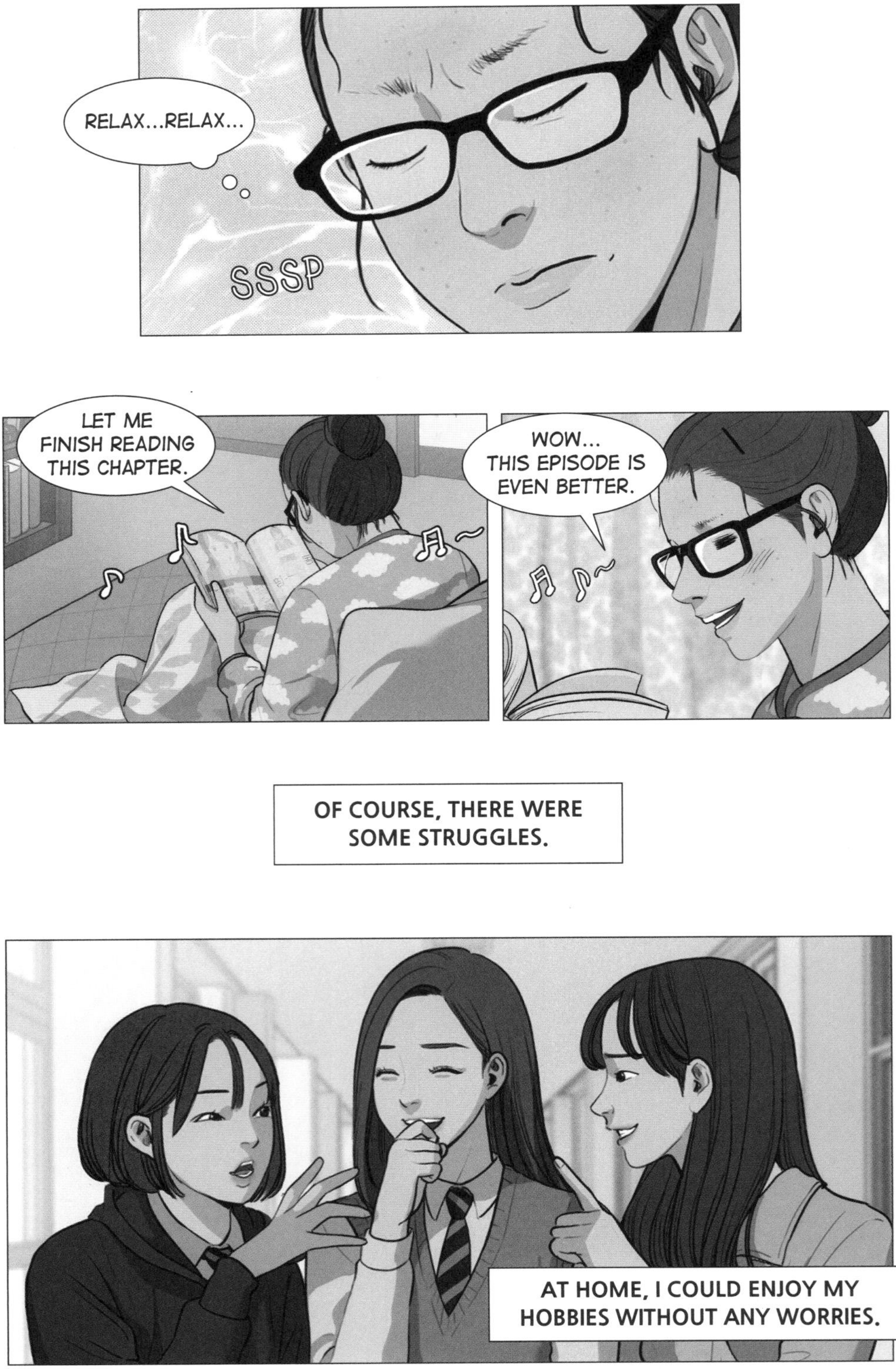
RELAX...RELAX...
SSSP
LET ME FINISH READING THIS CHAPTER.
WOW... THIS EPISODE IS EVEN BETTER.
OF COURSE, THERE WERE SOME STRUGGLES.
AT HOME, I COULD ENJOY MY HOBBIES WITHOUT ANY WORRIES.

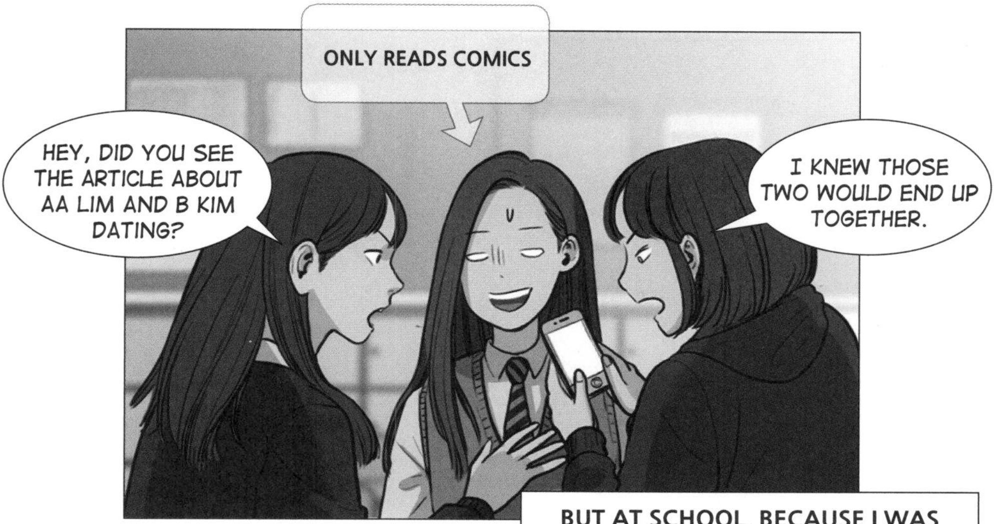
HEY, DID YOU SEE THE ARTICLE ABOUT AA LIM AND B KIM DATING?
ONLY READS COMICS
I KNEW THOSE TWO WOULD END UP TOGETHER.

BUT AT SCHOOL, BECAUSE I WAS LABELED AS THE "PRETTY GIRL"...

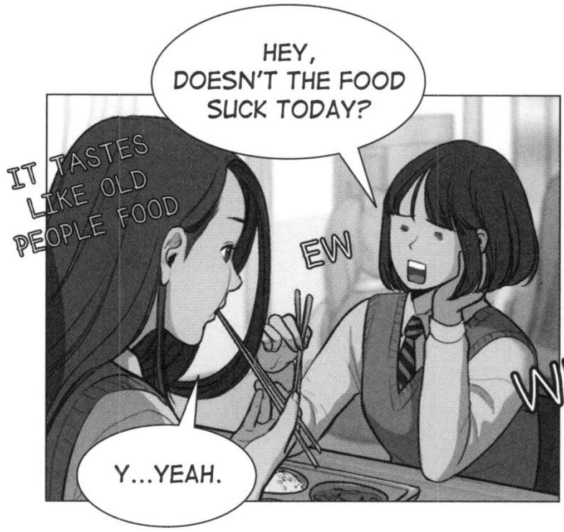
HEY, DOESN'T THE FOOD SUCK TODAY?
IT TASTES LIKE OLD PEOPLE FOOD
EW
Y...YEAH.

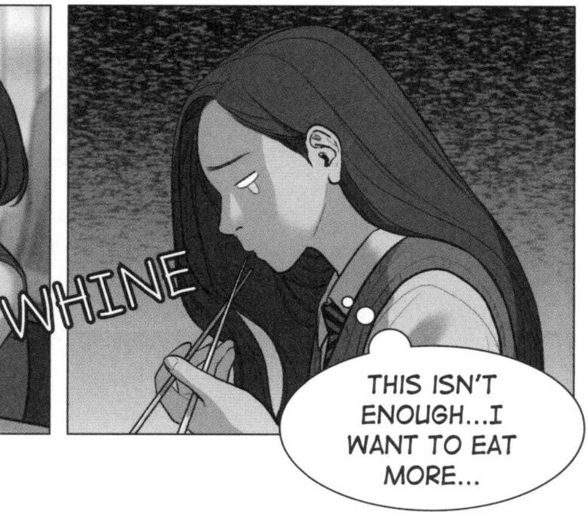
WHINE
THIS ISN'T ENOUGH...I WANT TO EAT MORE...

...HAVING TO MAINTAIN MY IMAGE WAS EXHAUSTING.

STILL, THANKS TO MY MAKEUP, IT SEEMED LIKE IT WOULD BE SMOOTH SAILING UNTIL THIRD YEAR OF HIGH SCHOOL...

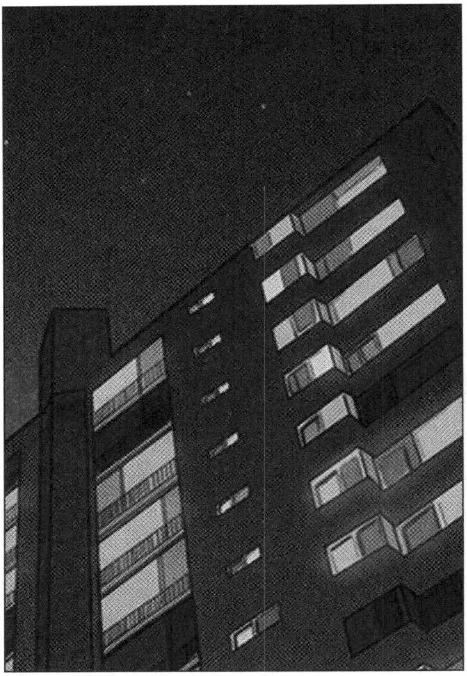

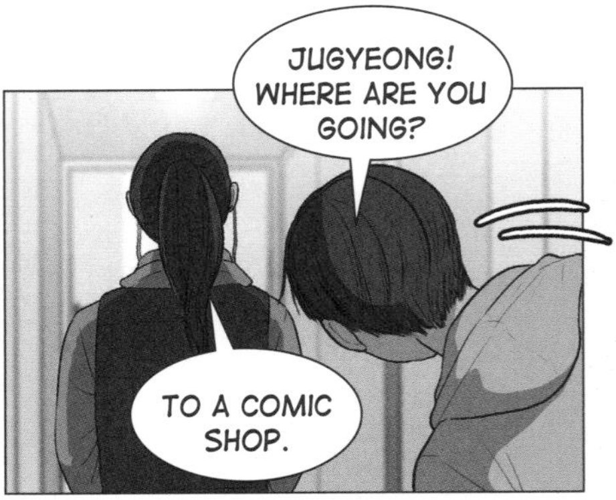
JUGYEONG! WHERE ARE YOU GOING?
TO A COMIC SHOP.

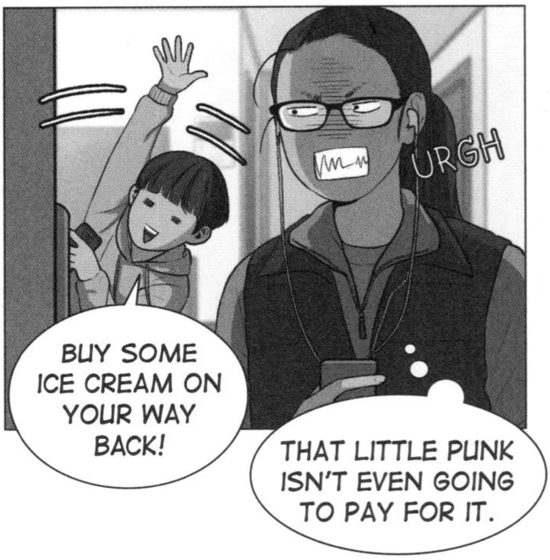
URGH
BUY SOME ICE CREAM ON YOUR WAY BACK!
THAT LITTLE PUNK ISN'T EVEN GOING TO PAY FOR IT.

...UNTIL I MET THAT JERK.

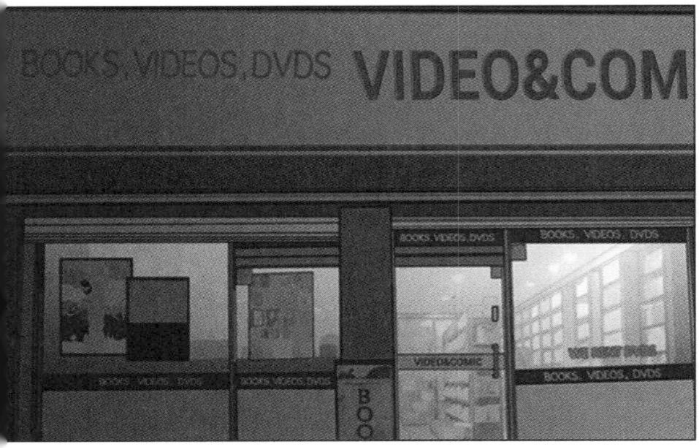
BOOKS, VIDEOS, DVDS
VIDEO&COM

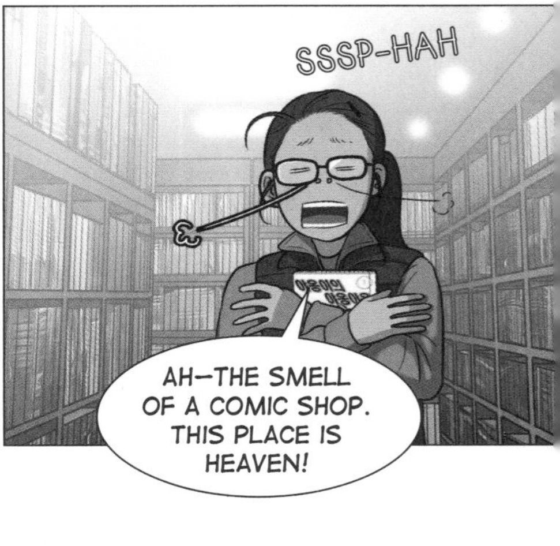
SSSP-HAH
AH—THE SMELL OF A COMIC SHOP. THIS PLACE IS HEAVEN!

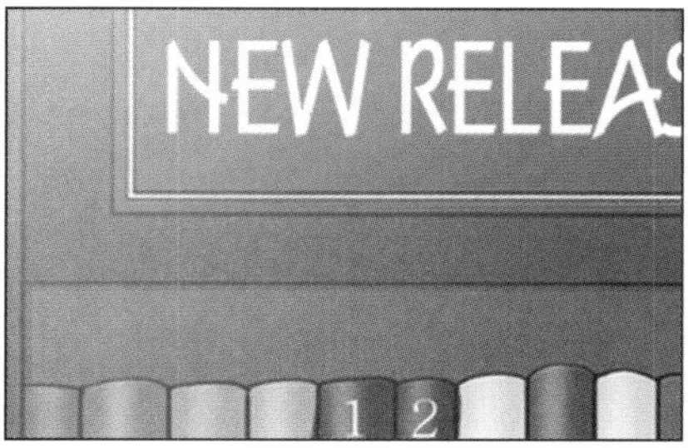
NEW RELEAS

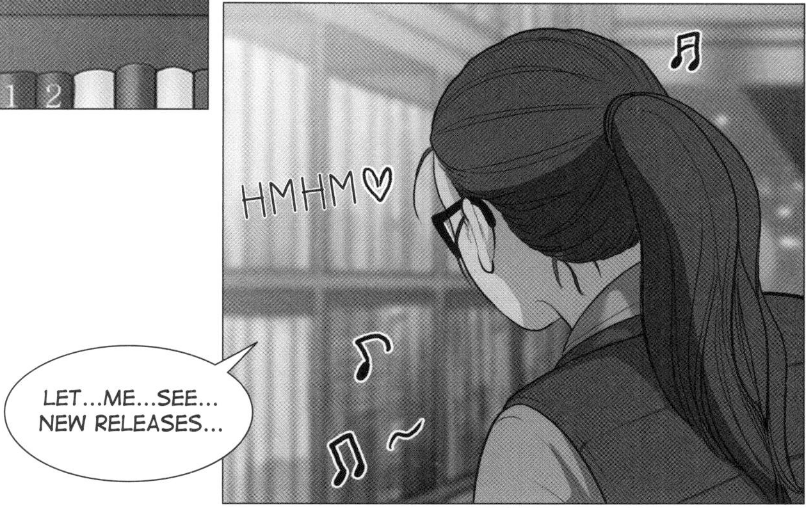
HMHM♥
LET...ME...SEE... NEW RELEASES...

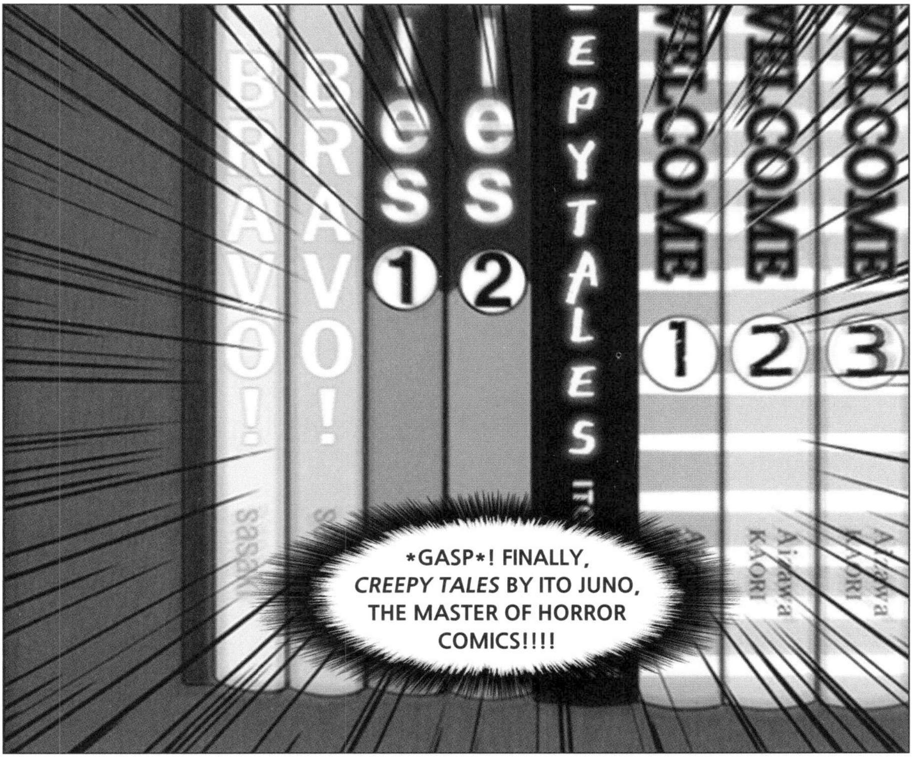
GASP! FINALLY, *CREEPY TALES* BY ITO JUNO, THE MASTER OF HORROR COMICS!!!!

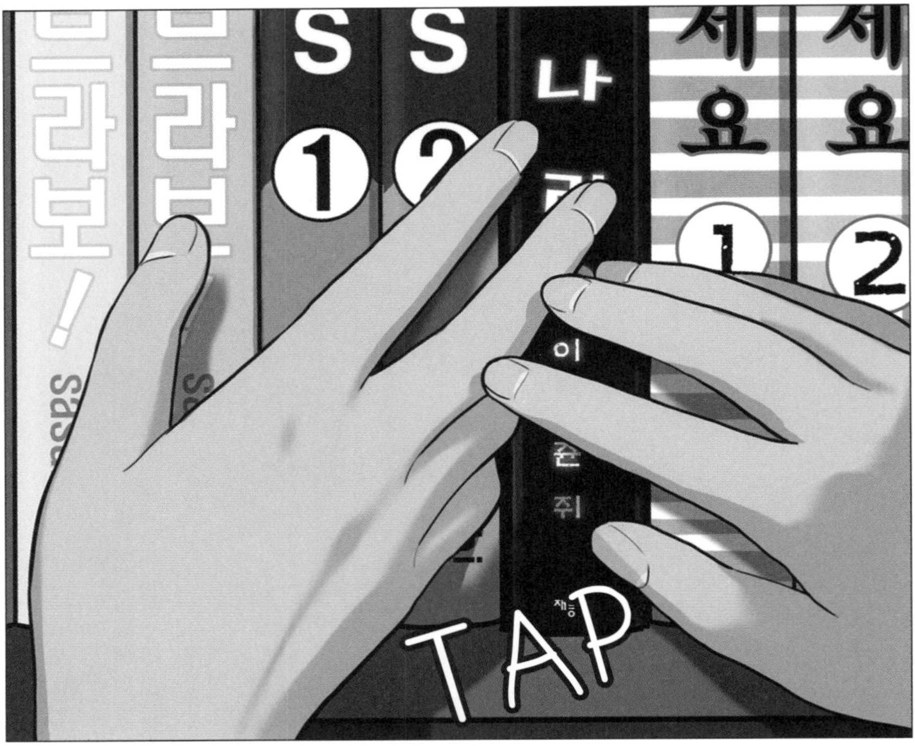
TAP

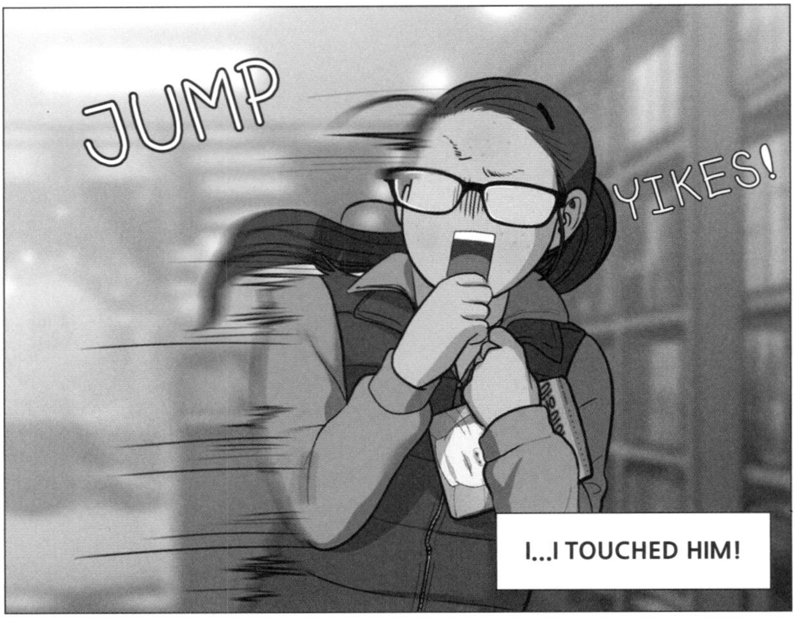
JUMP
YIKES!
I...I TOUCHED HIM!

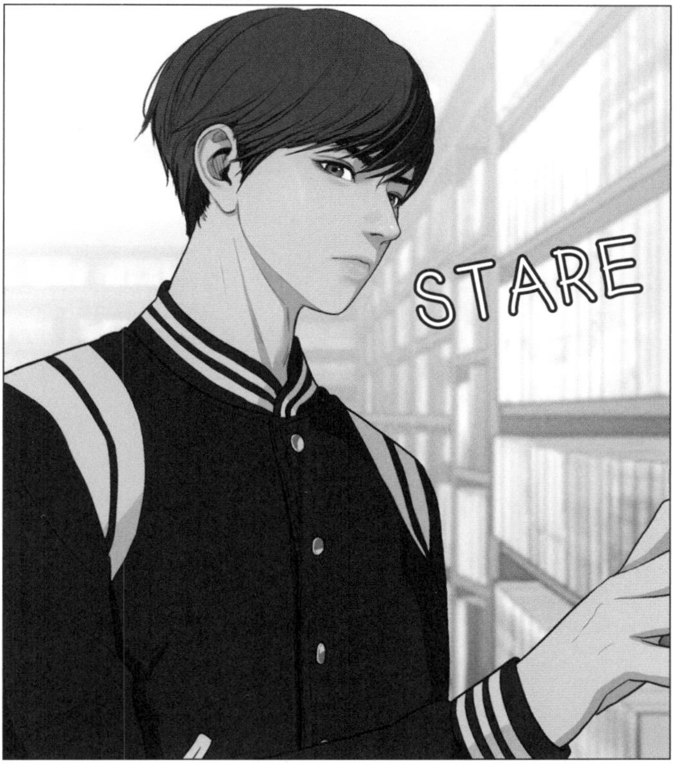
STARE

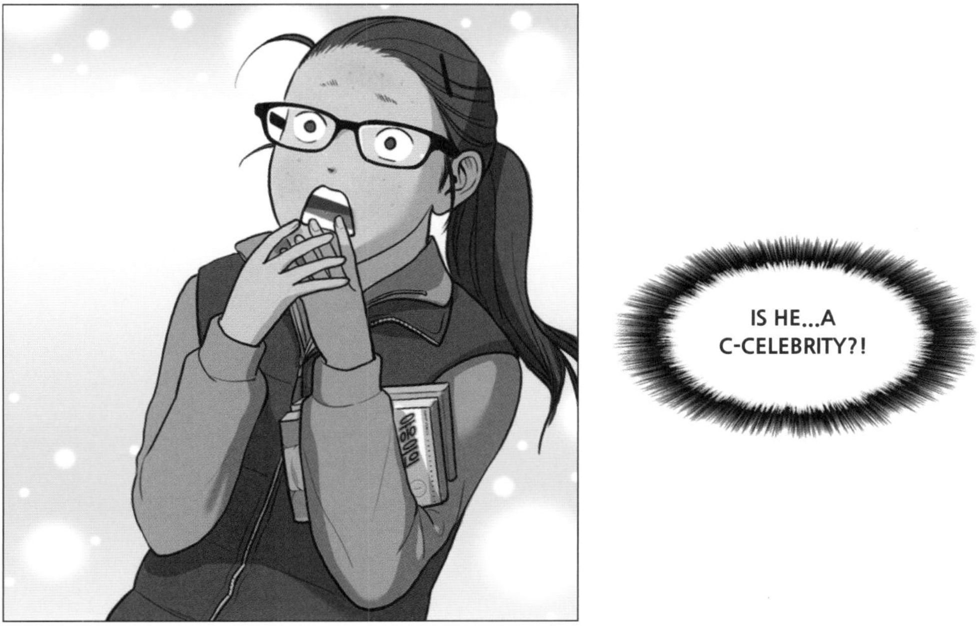
IS HE...A
C-CELEBRITY?!

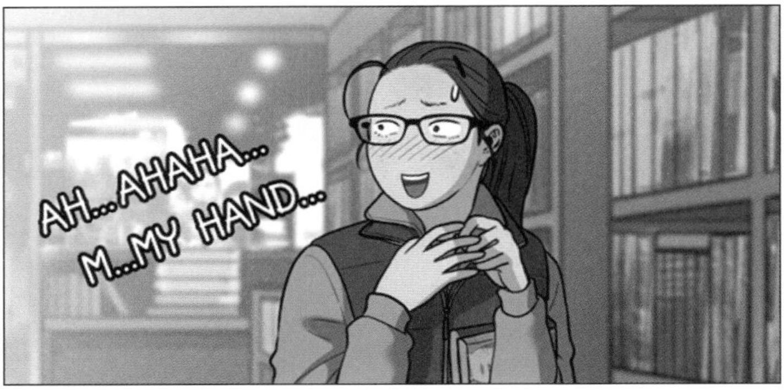
AH...AHAHA...
M...MY HAND...
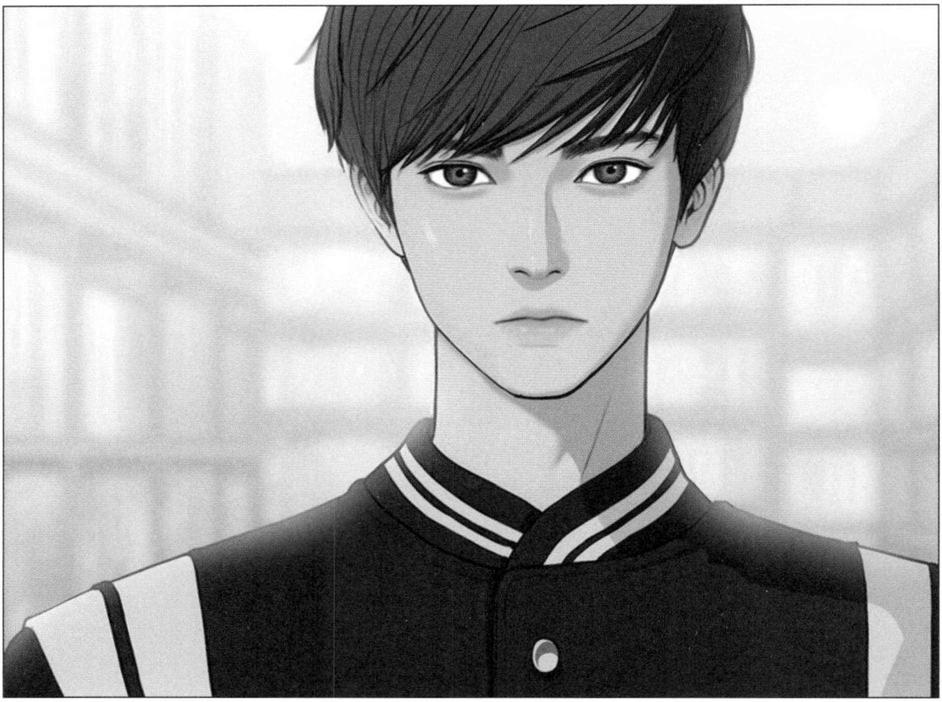
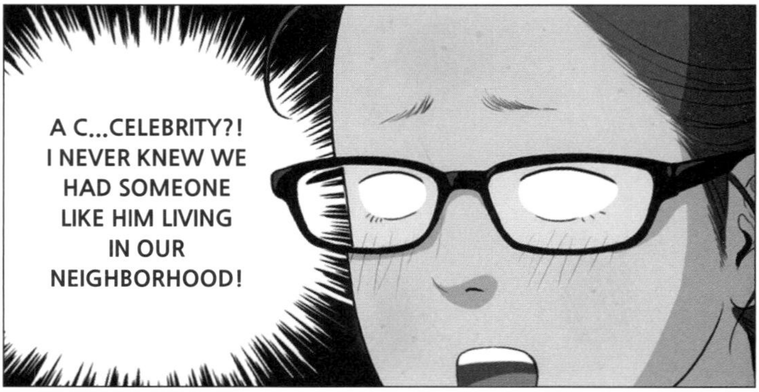
A C...CELEBRITY?! I NEVER KNEW WE HAD SOMEONE LIKE HIM LIVING IN OUR NEIGHBORHOOD!

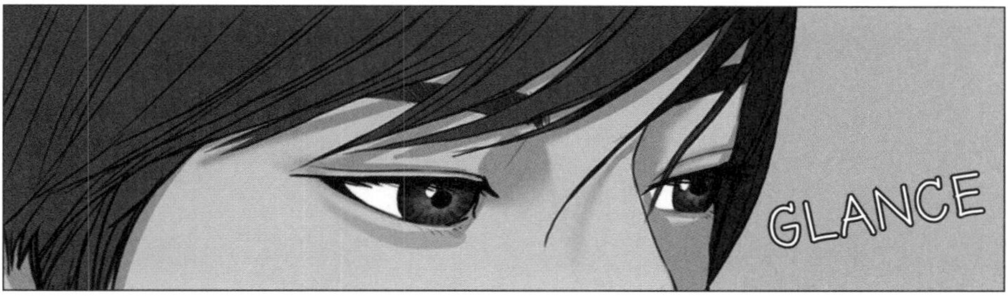
GLANCE

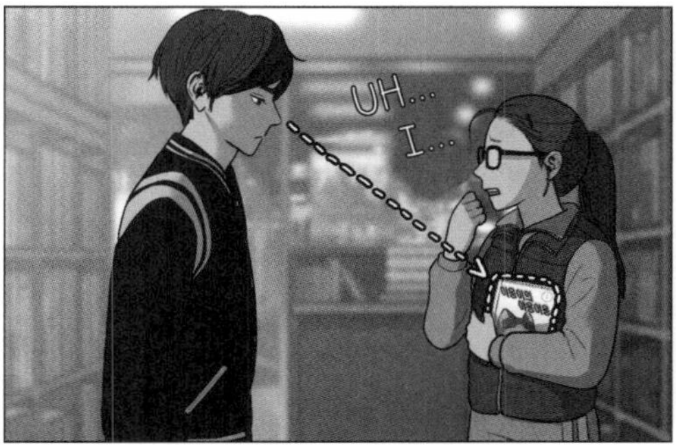
UH... I...

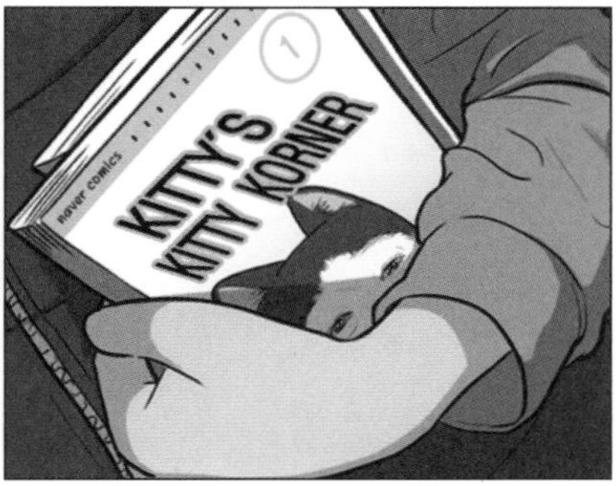
KITTY'S
KITTY KORNER

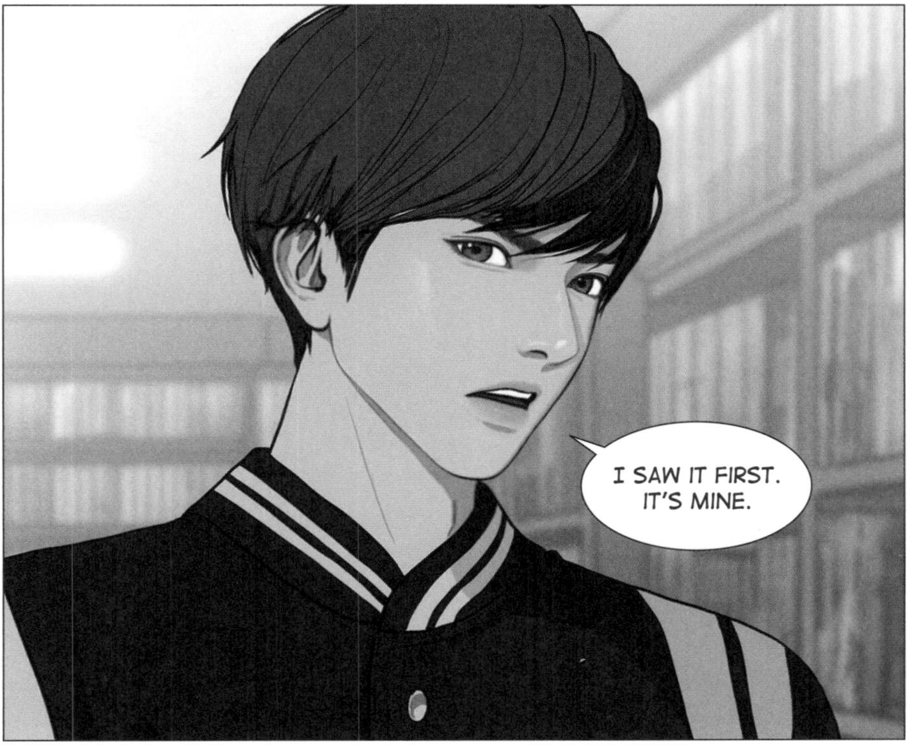
I SAW IT FIRST.
IT'S MINE.

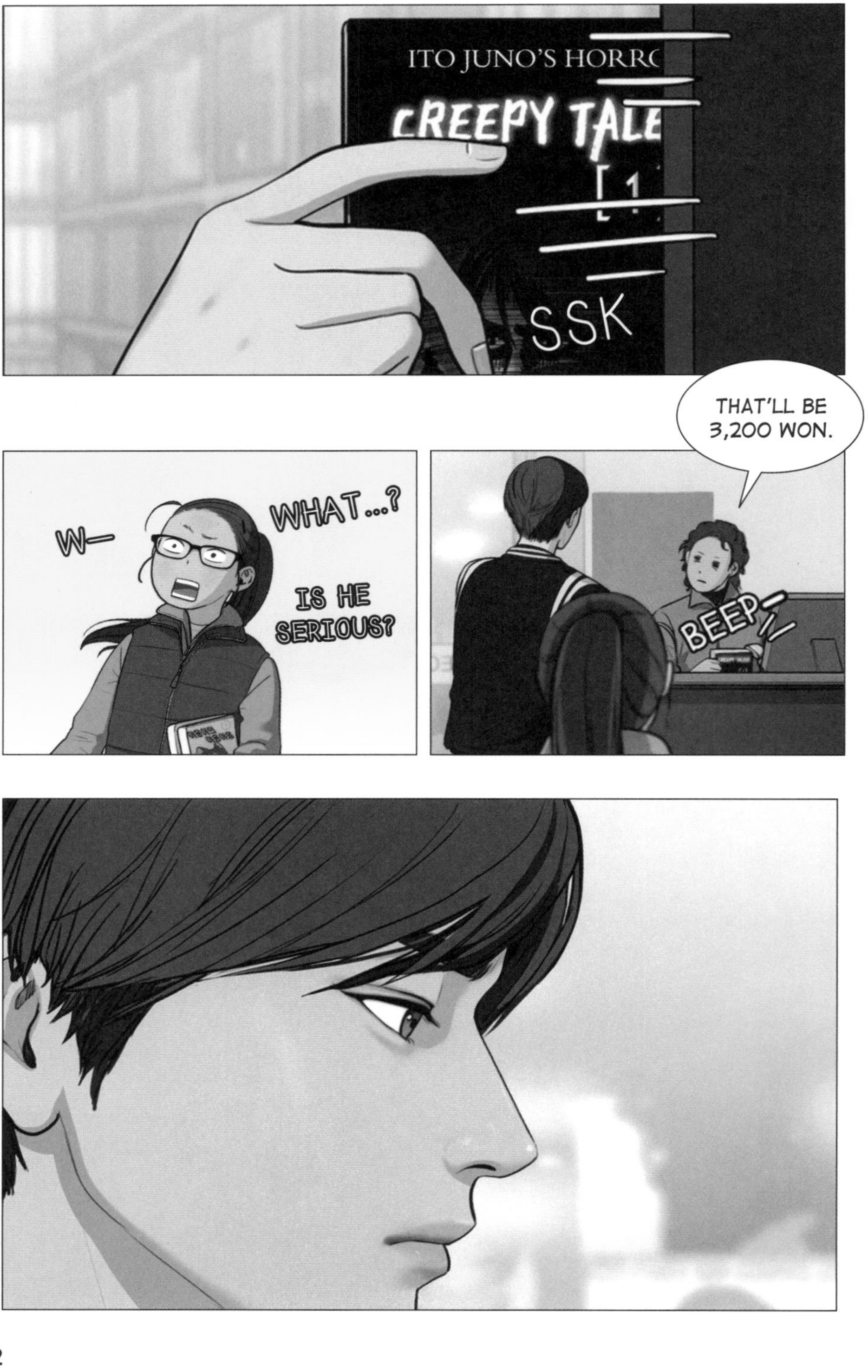
ITO JUNO'S HORRC
CREEPY TALE
SSK
W—
WHAT...?
IS HE SERIOUS?
THAT'LL BE 3,200 WON.
BEEP

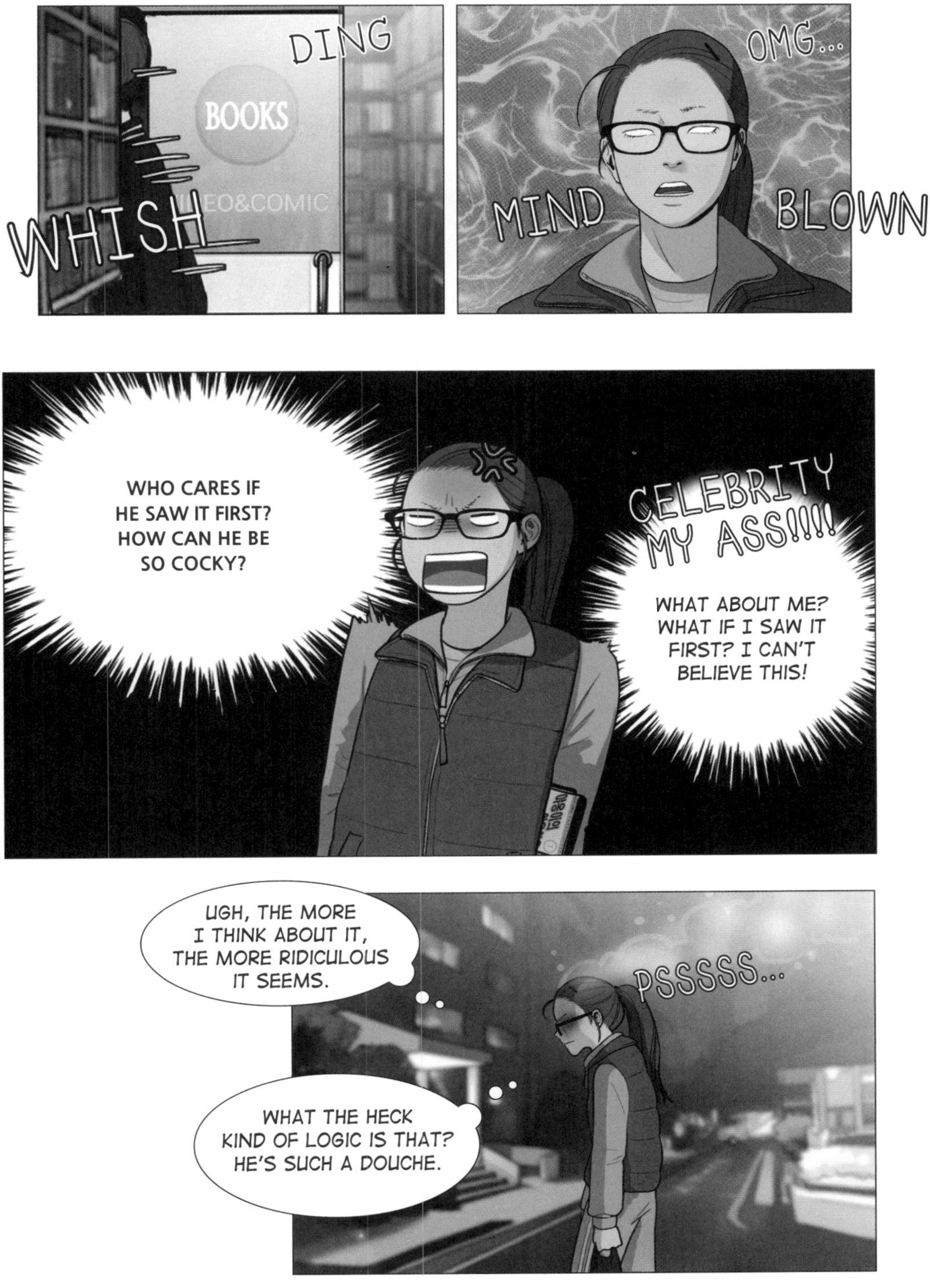
DING
BOOKS
WHISH
OMG...
MIND BLOWN
WHO CARES IF HE SAW IT FIRST? HOW CAN HE BE SO COCKY?
CELEBRITY MY ASS!!!!
WHAT ABOUT ME? WHAT IF I SAW IT FIRST? I CAN'T BELIEVE THIS!
UGH, THE MORE I THINK ABOUT IT, THE MORE RIDICULOUS IT SEEMS.
PSSSSS...
WHAT THE HECK KIND OF LOGIC IS THAT? HE'S SUCH A DOUCHE.

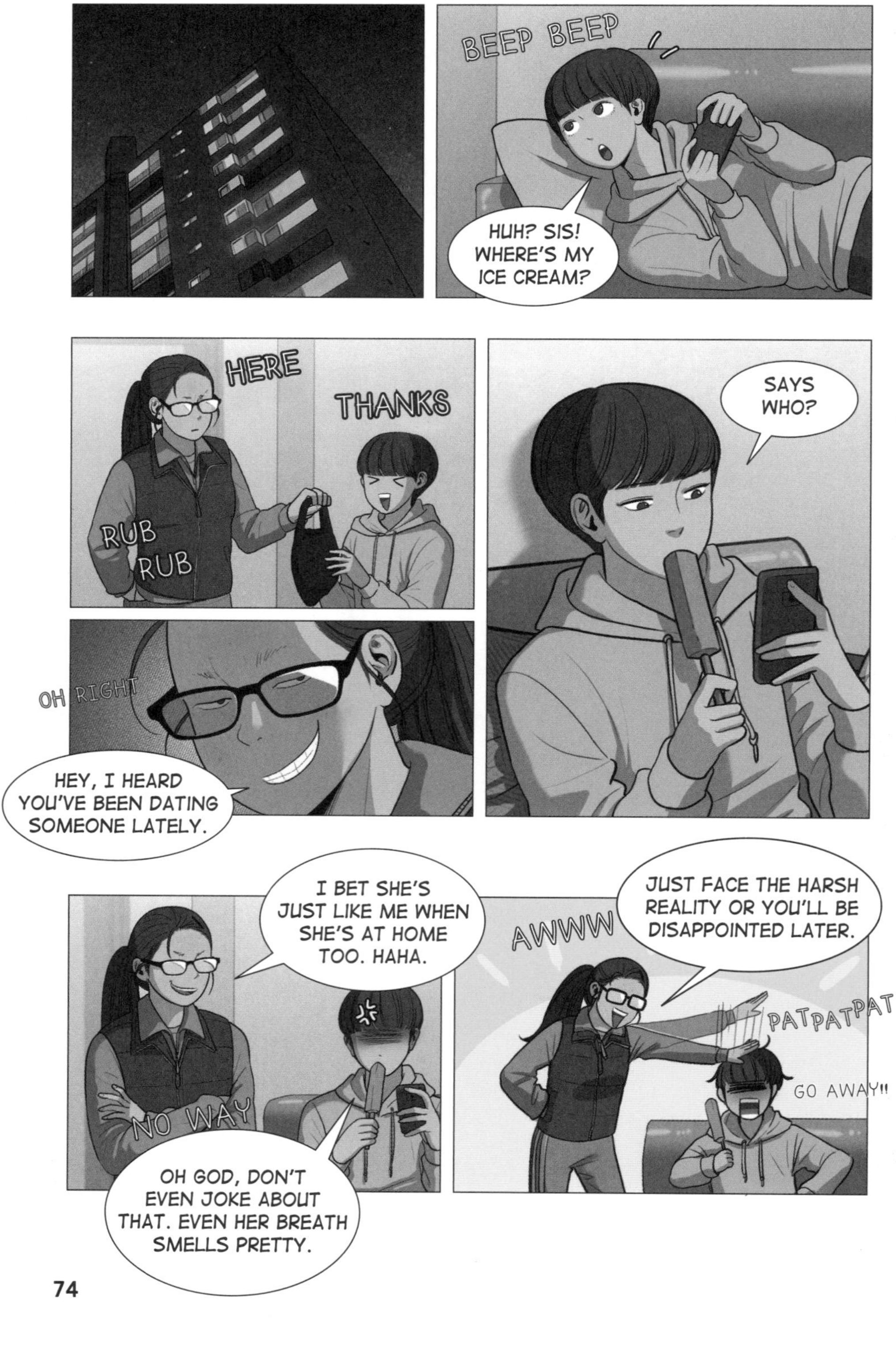
BEEP BEEP
HUH? SIS! WHERE'S MY ICE CREAM?
HERE
THANKS
RUB RUB
OH RIGHT
HEY, I HEARD YOU'VE BEEN DATING SOMEONE LATELY.
SAYS WHO?
I BET SHE'S JUST LIKE ME WHEN SHE'S AT HOME TOO. HAHA.
NO WAY
OH GOD, DON'T EVEN JOKE ABOUT THAT. EVEN HER BREATH SMELLS PRETTY.
AWWW
JUST FACE THE HARSH REALITY OR YOU'LL BE DISAPPOINTED LATER.
PATPATPAT
GO AWAY!!

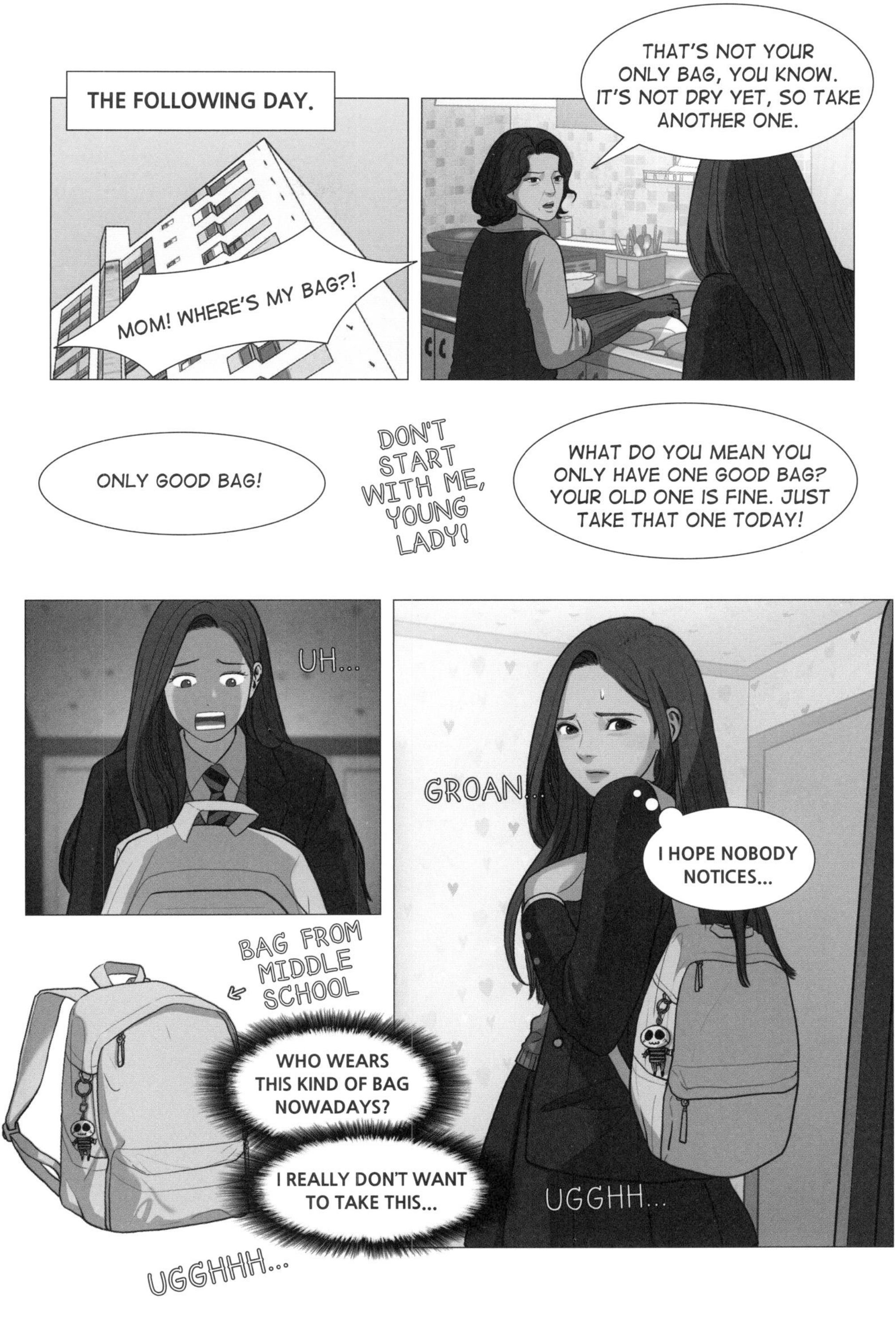
THE FOLLOWING DAY.
MOM! WHERE'S MY BAG?!
THAT'S NOT YOUR ONLY BAG, YOU KNOW. IT'S NOT DRY YET, SO TAKE ANOTHER ONE.
ONLY GOOD BAG!
DON'T START WITH ME, YOUNG LADY!
WHAT DO YOU MEAN YOU ONLY HAVE ONE GOOD BAG? YOUR OLD ONE IS FINE. JUST TAKE THAT ONE TODAY!
UH...
BAG FROM MIDDLE SCHOOL
WHO WEARS THIS KIND OF BAG NOWADAYS?
I REALLY DON'T WANT TO TAKE THIS...
UGGHHH...
GROAN...
I HOPE NOBODY NOTICES...
UGGHH...

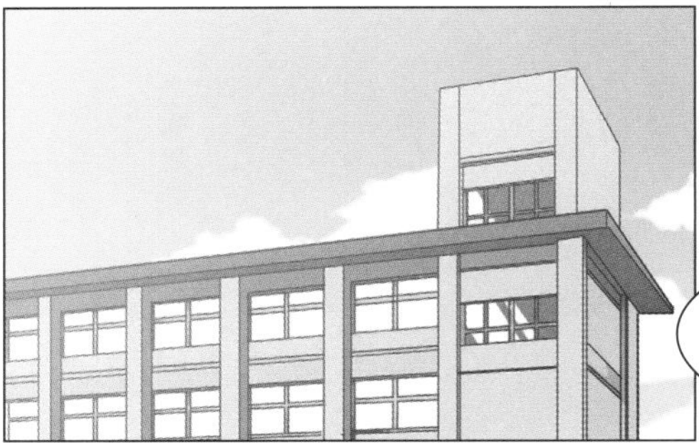

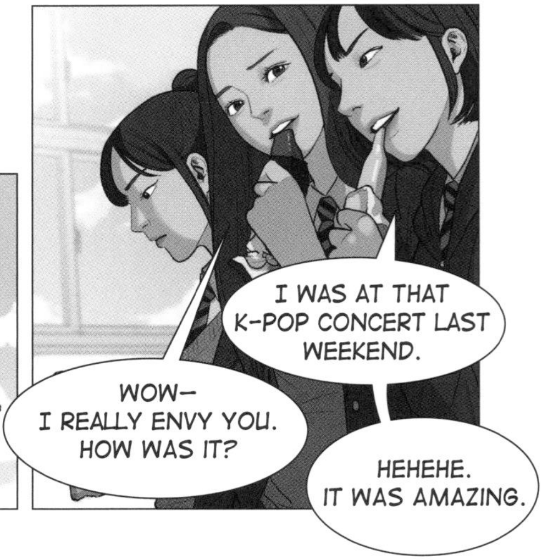
I WAS AT THAT K-POP CONCERT LAST WEEKEND.
WOW— I REALLY ENVY YOU. HOW WAS IT?
HEHEHE. IT WAS AMAZING.

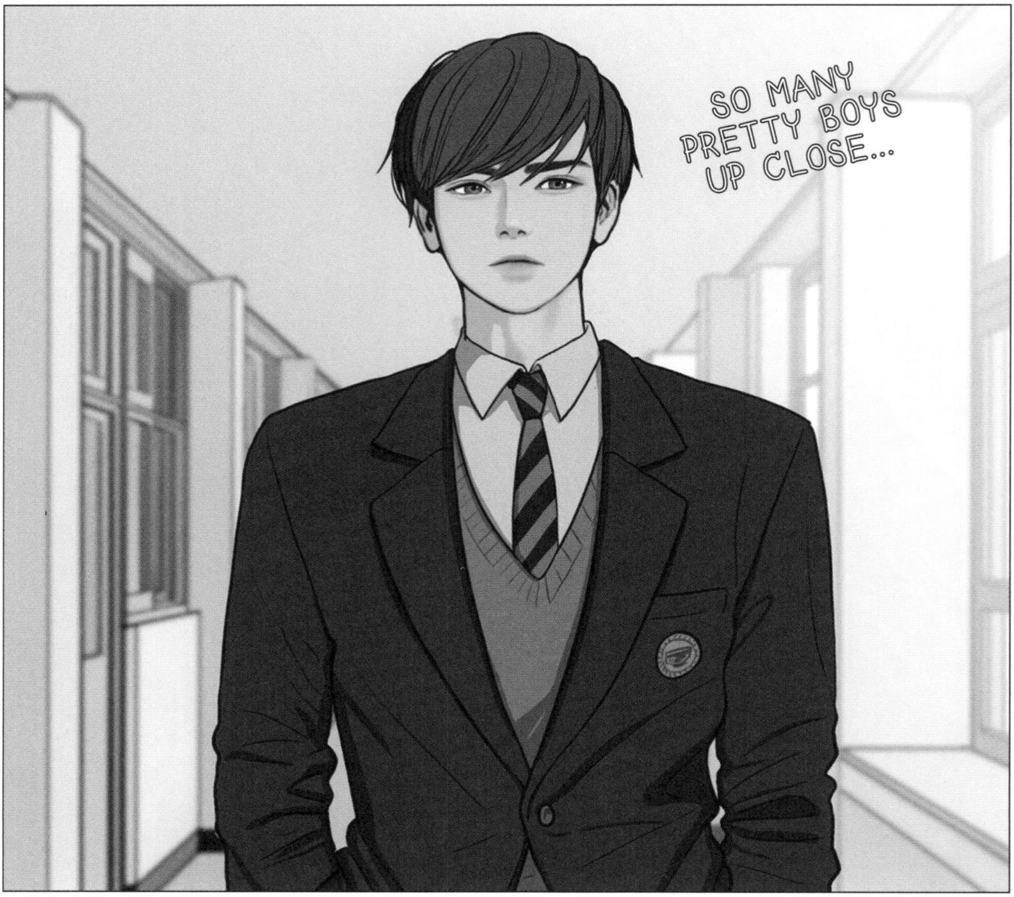
SO MANY PRETTY BOYS UP CLOSE...

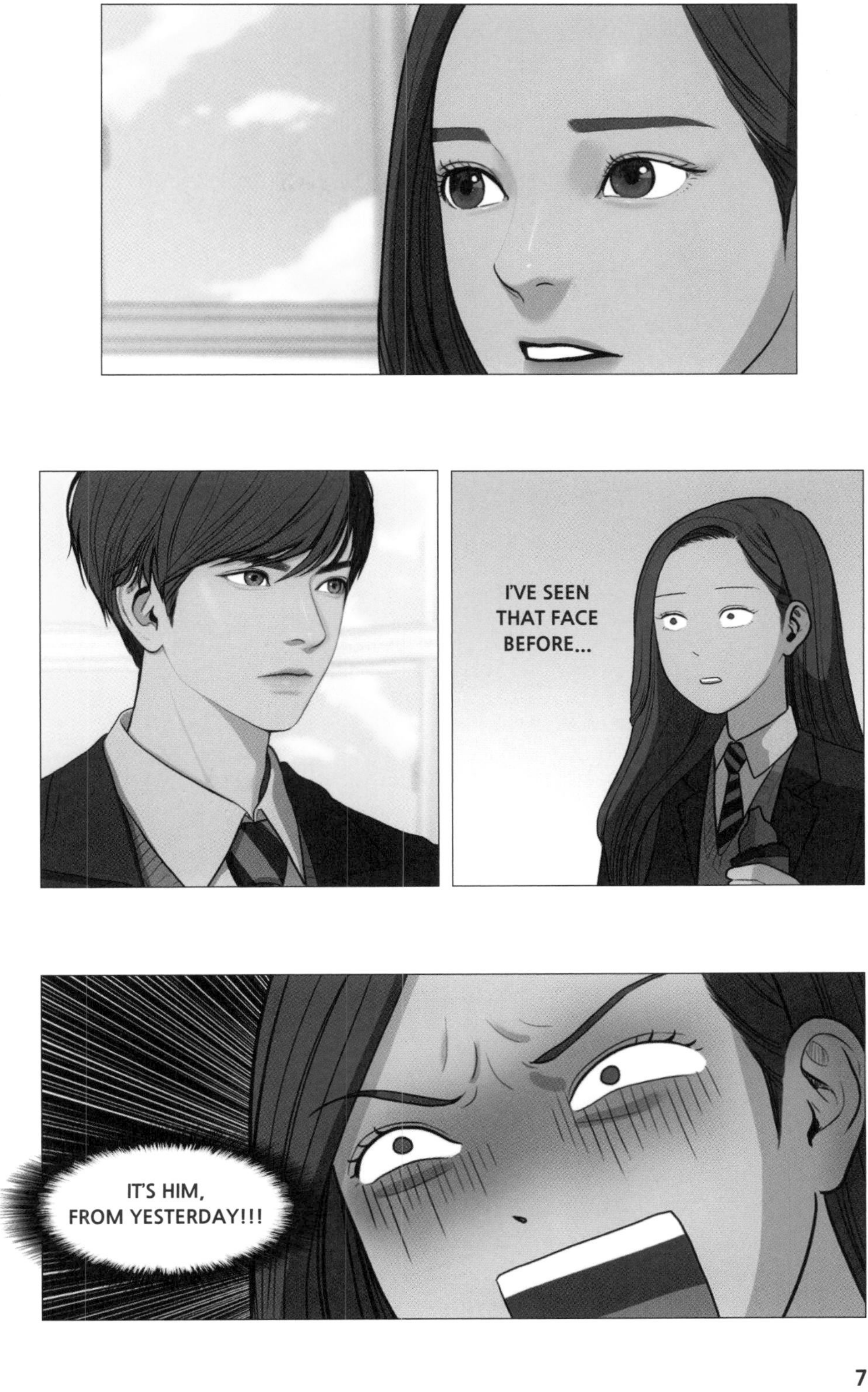
I'VE SEEN THAT FACE BEFORE...
IT'S HIM, FROM YESTERDAY!!!

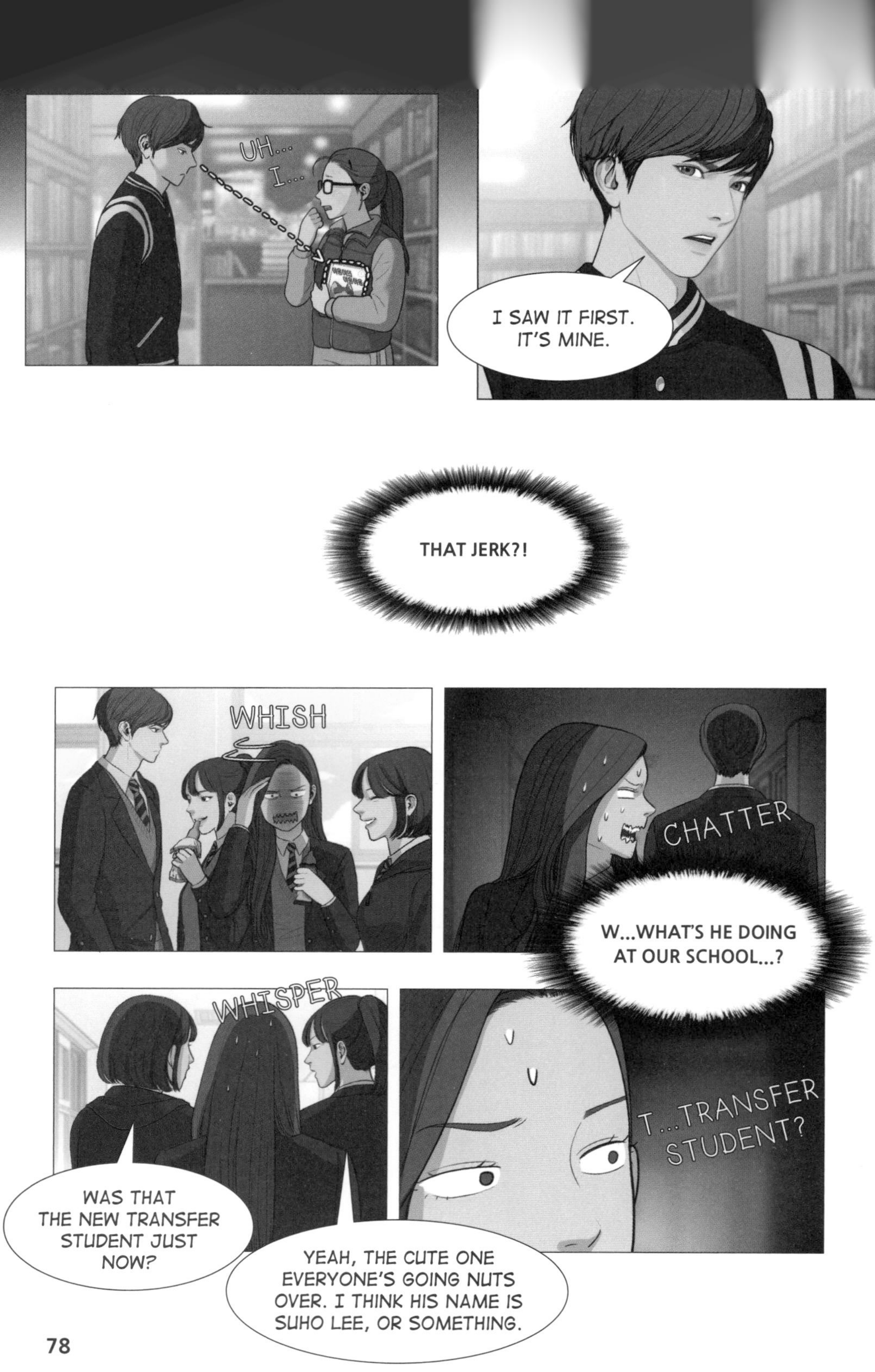
UH...
I...
I SAW IT FIRST. IT'S MINE.
THAT JERK?!
WHISH
CHATTER
W...WHAT'S HE DOING AT OUR SCHOOL...?
WHISPER
WAS THAT THE NEW TRANSFER STUDENT JUST NOW?
YEAH, THE CUTE ONE EVERYONE'S GOING NUTS OVER. I THINK HIS NAME IS SUHO LEE, OR SOMETHING.
T...TRANSFER STUDENT?

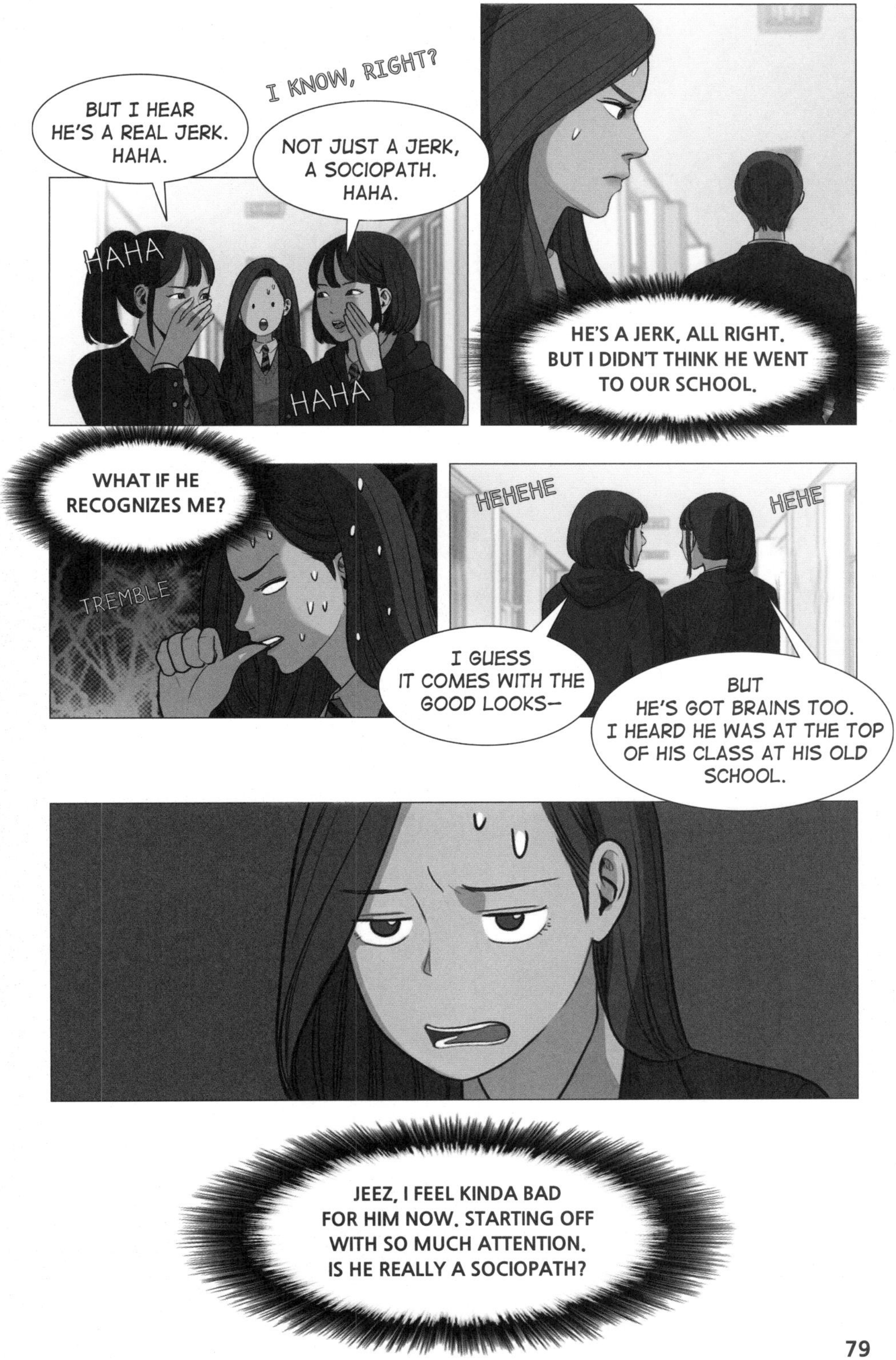

BUT I HEAR HE'S A REAL JERK. HAHA.
I KNOW, RIGHT?
NOT JUST A JERK, A SOCIOPATH. HAHA.
HAHA
HAHA
HE'S A JERK, ALL RIGHT. BUT I DIDN'T THINK HE WENT TO OUR SCHOOL.
WHAT IF HE RECOGNIZES ME?
TREMBLE
HEHEHE
HEHE
I GUESS IT COMES WITH THE GOOD LOOKS—
BUT HE'S GOT BRAINS TOO. I HEARD HE WAS AT THE TOP OF HIS CLASS AT HIS OLD SCHOOL.
JEEZ, I FEEL KINDA BAD FOR HIM NOW. STARTING OFF WITH SO MUCH ATTENTION. IS HE REALLY A SOCIOPATH?

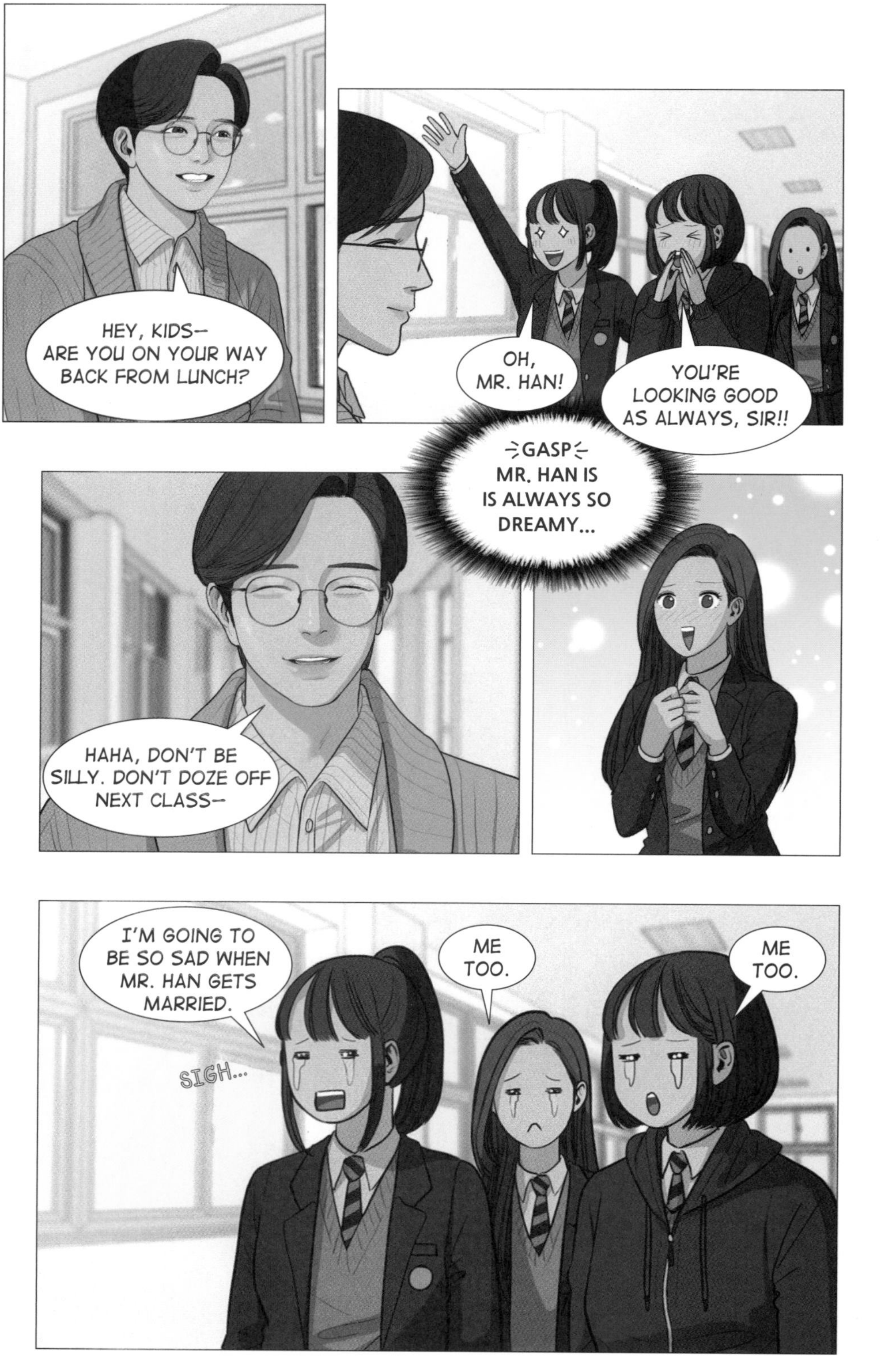
HEY, KIDS–
ARE YOU ON YOUR WAY BACK FROM LUNCH?
OH, MR. HAN!
YOU'RE LOOKING GOOD AS ALWAYS, SIR!!
HAHA, DON'T BE SILLY. DON'T DOZE OFF NEXT CLASS–
GASP
MR. HAN IS IS ALWAYS SO DREAMY...
I'M GOING TO BE SO SAD WHEN MR. HAN GETS MARRIED.
SIGH...
ME TOO.
ME TOO.

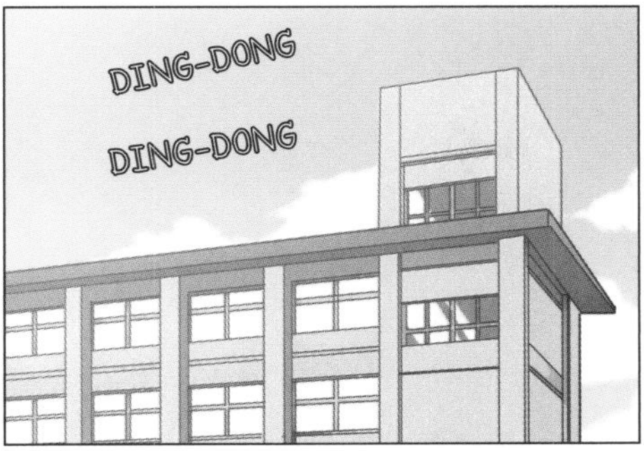
DING-DONG
DING-DONG
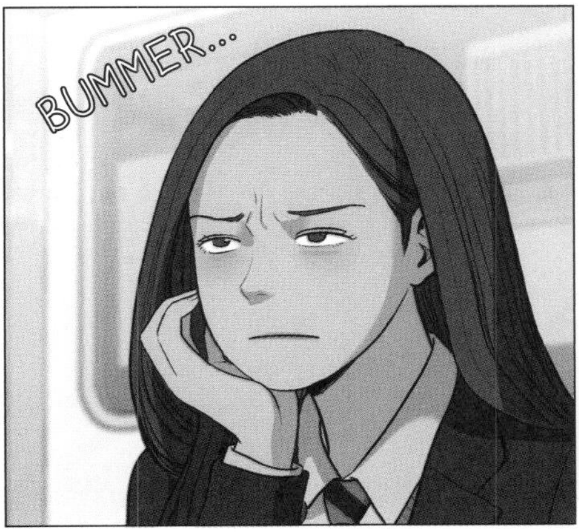
BUMMER...
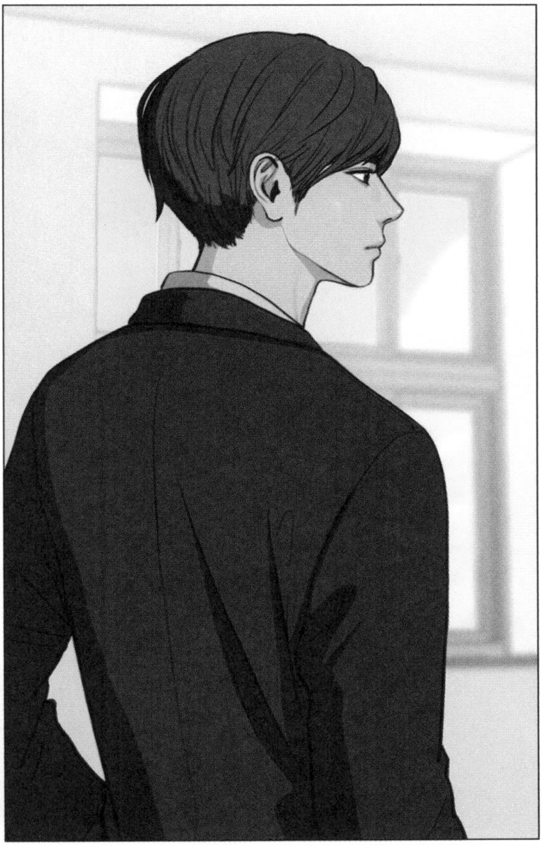
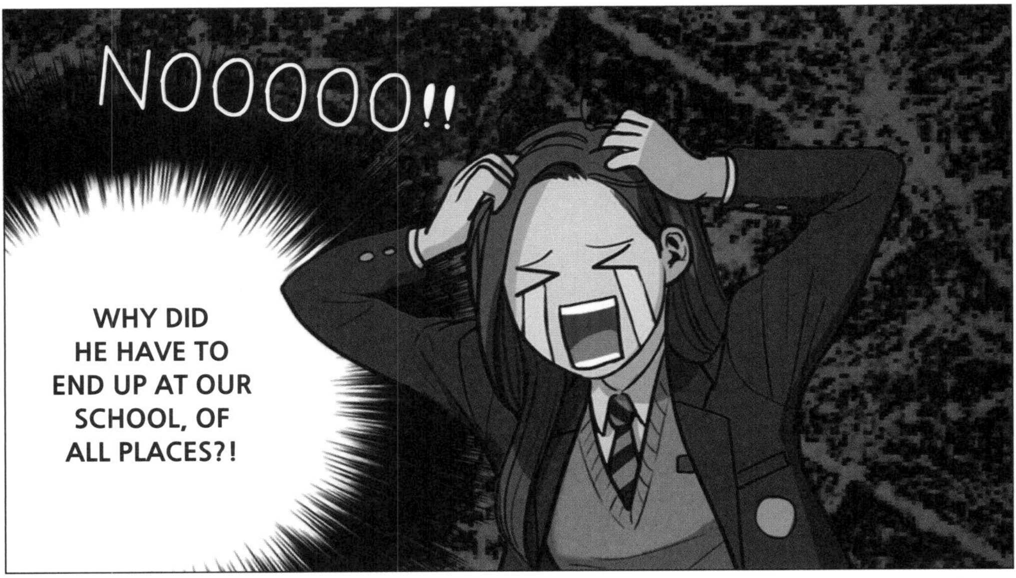
NOOOOO!!
WHY DID HE HAVE TO END UP AT OUR SCHOOL, OF ALL PLACES?!

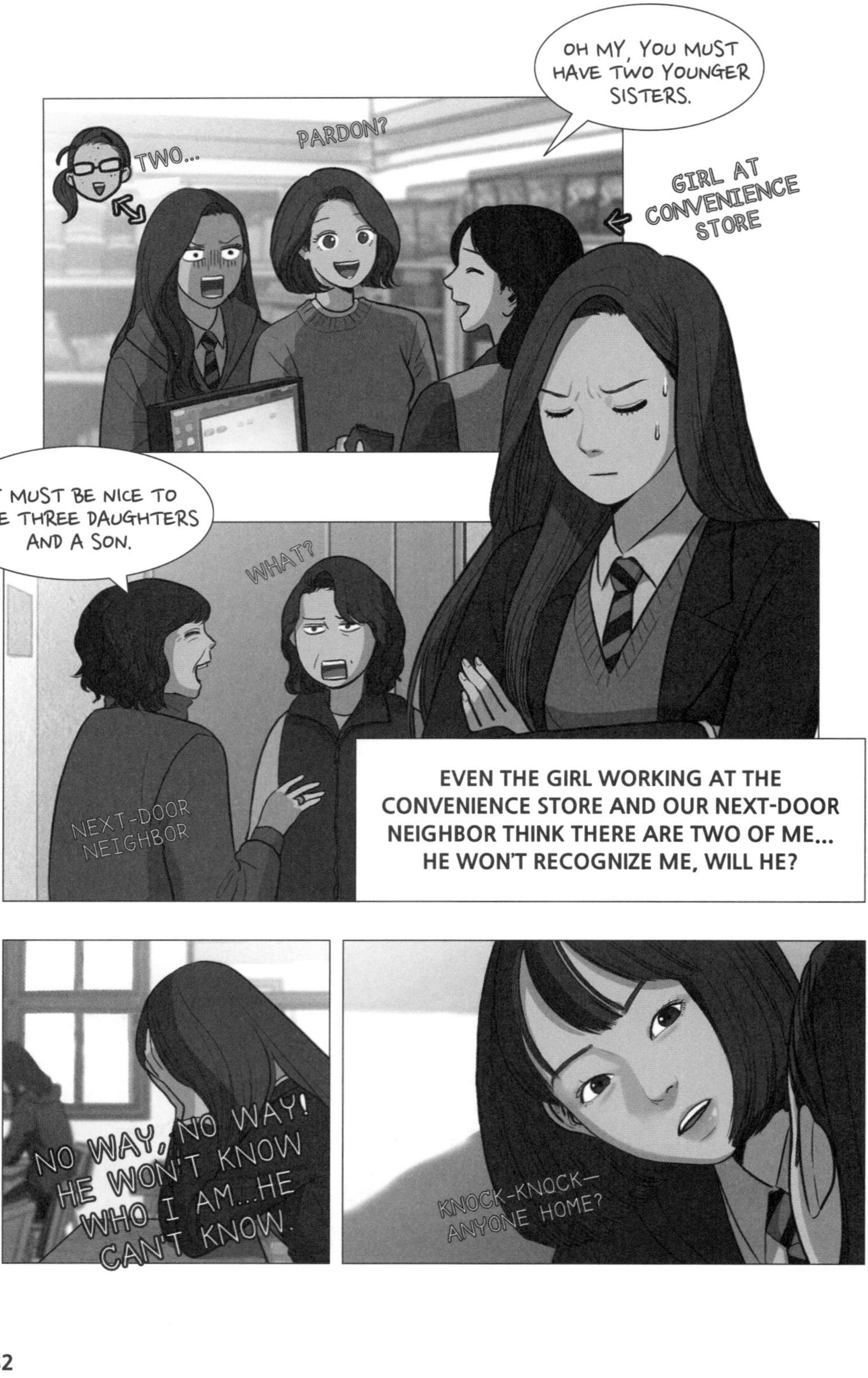
OH MY, YOU MUST HAVE TWO YOUNGER SISTERS.
TWO...
PARDON?
GIRL AT CONVENIENCE STORE
IT MUST BE NICE TO HAVE THREE DAUGHTERS AND A SON.
WHAT?
NEXT-DOOR NEIGHBOR
EVEN THE GIRL WORKING AT THE CONVENIENCE STORE AND OUR NEXT-DOOR NEIGHBOR THINK THERE ARE TWO OF ME... HE WON'T RECOGNIZE ME, WILL HE?
NO WAY, NO WAY! HE WON'T KNOW WHO I AM...HE CAN'T KNOW.
KNOCK-KNOCK— ANYONE HOME?

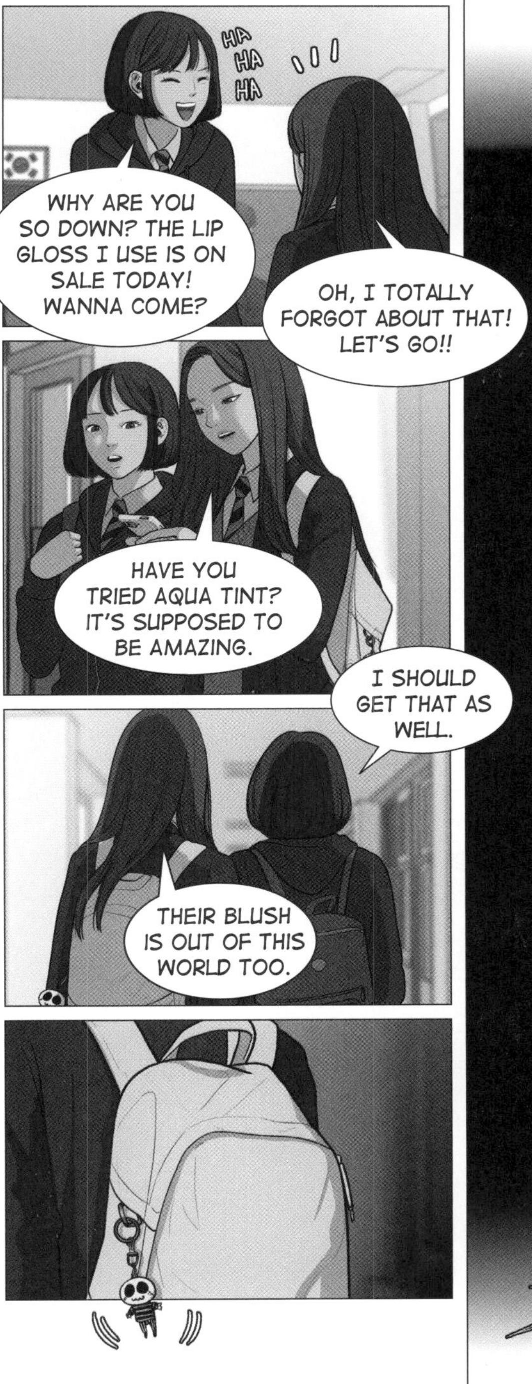
HA HA HA
WHY ARE YOU SO DOWN? THE LIP GLOSS I USE IS ON SALE TODAY! WANNA COME?
OH, I TOTALLY FORGOT ABOUT THAT! LET'S GO!!
HAVE YOU TRIED AQUA TINT? IT'S SUPPOSED TO BE AMAZING.
I SHOULD GET THAT AS WELL.
THEIR BLUSH IS OUT OF THIS WORLD TOO.

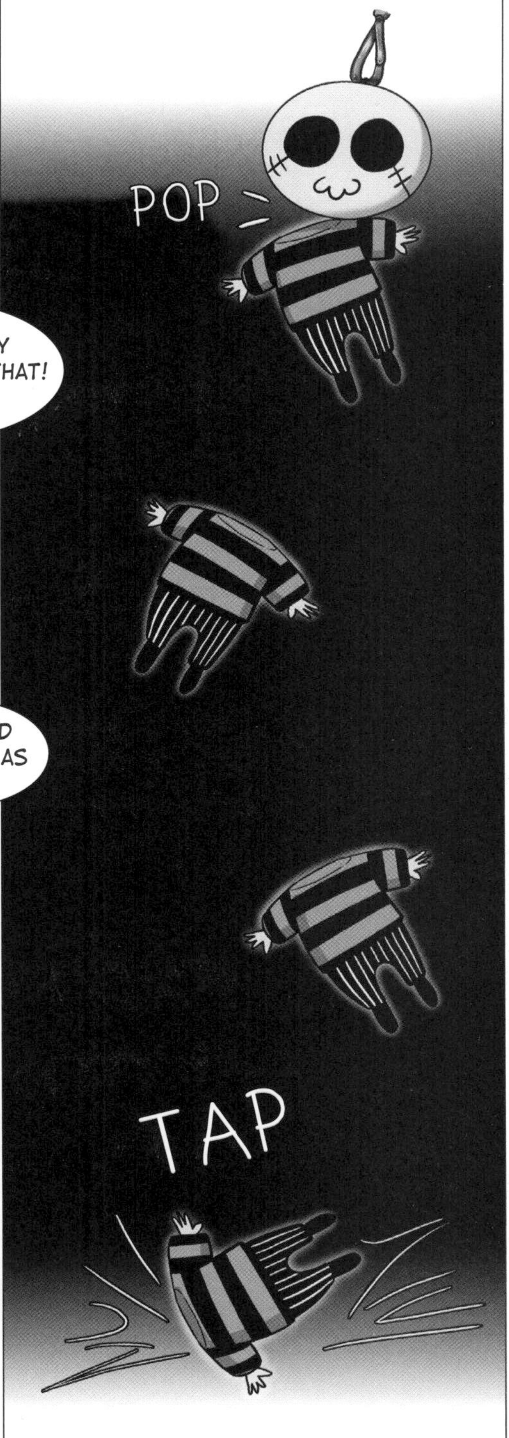
POP
TAP

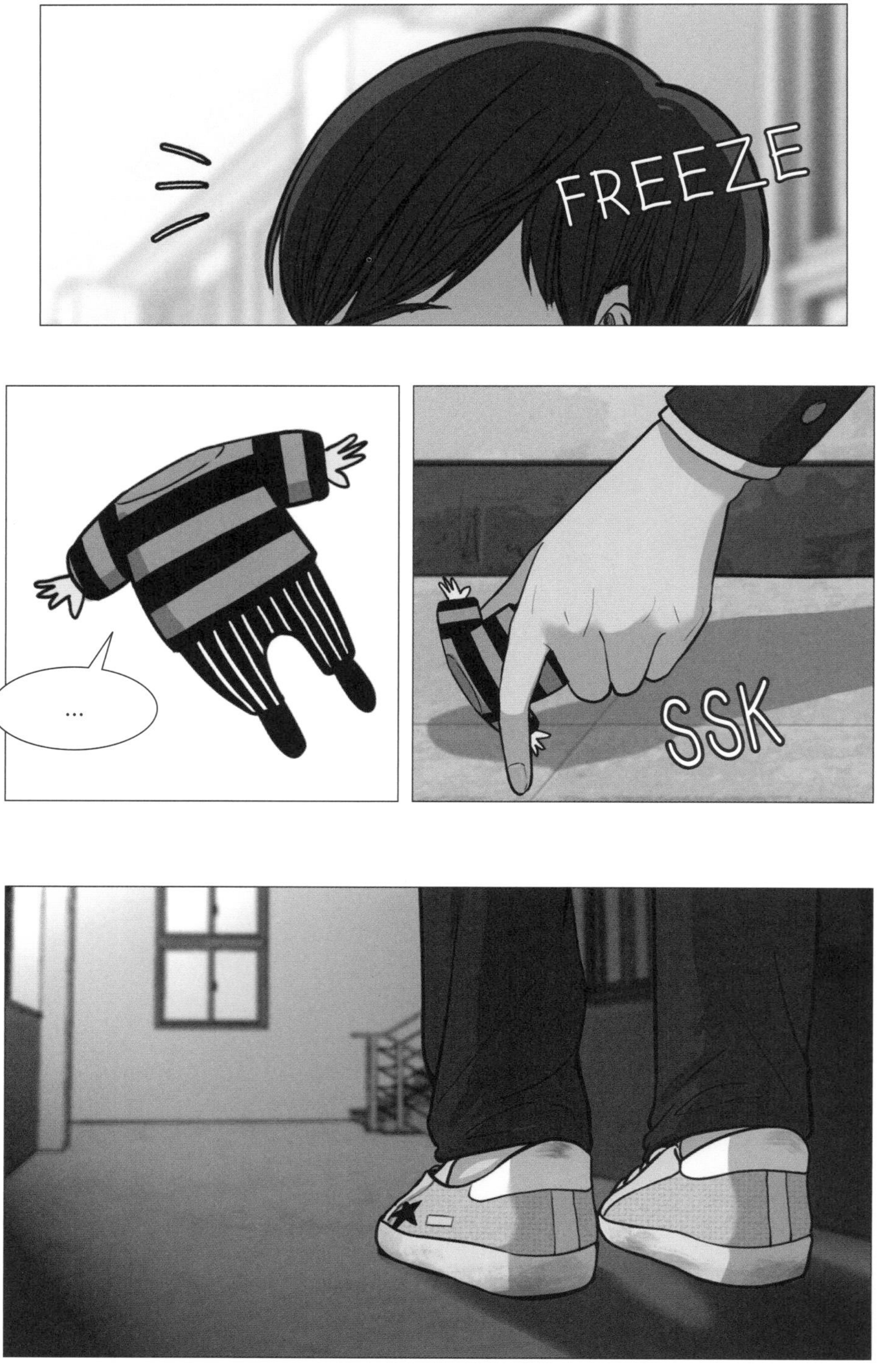
FREEZE
...
SSK

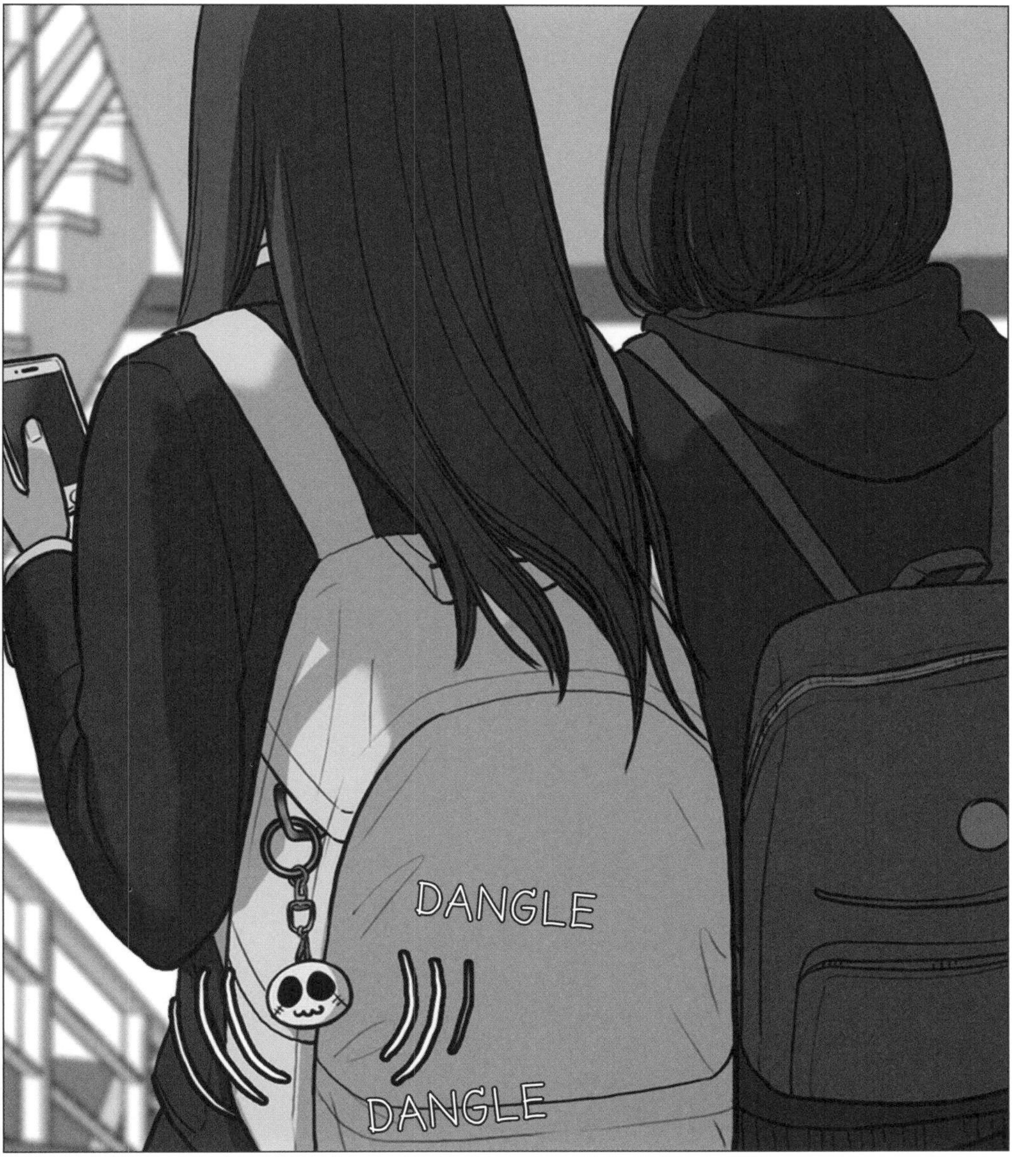
DANGLE
DANGLE

I SHOULDN'T
HAVE WORN THAT BAG
TO SCHOOL THAT DAY.

Episodes
5–9

여신강림

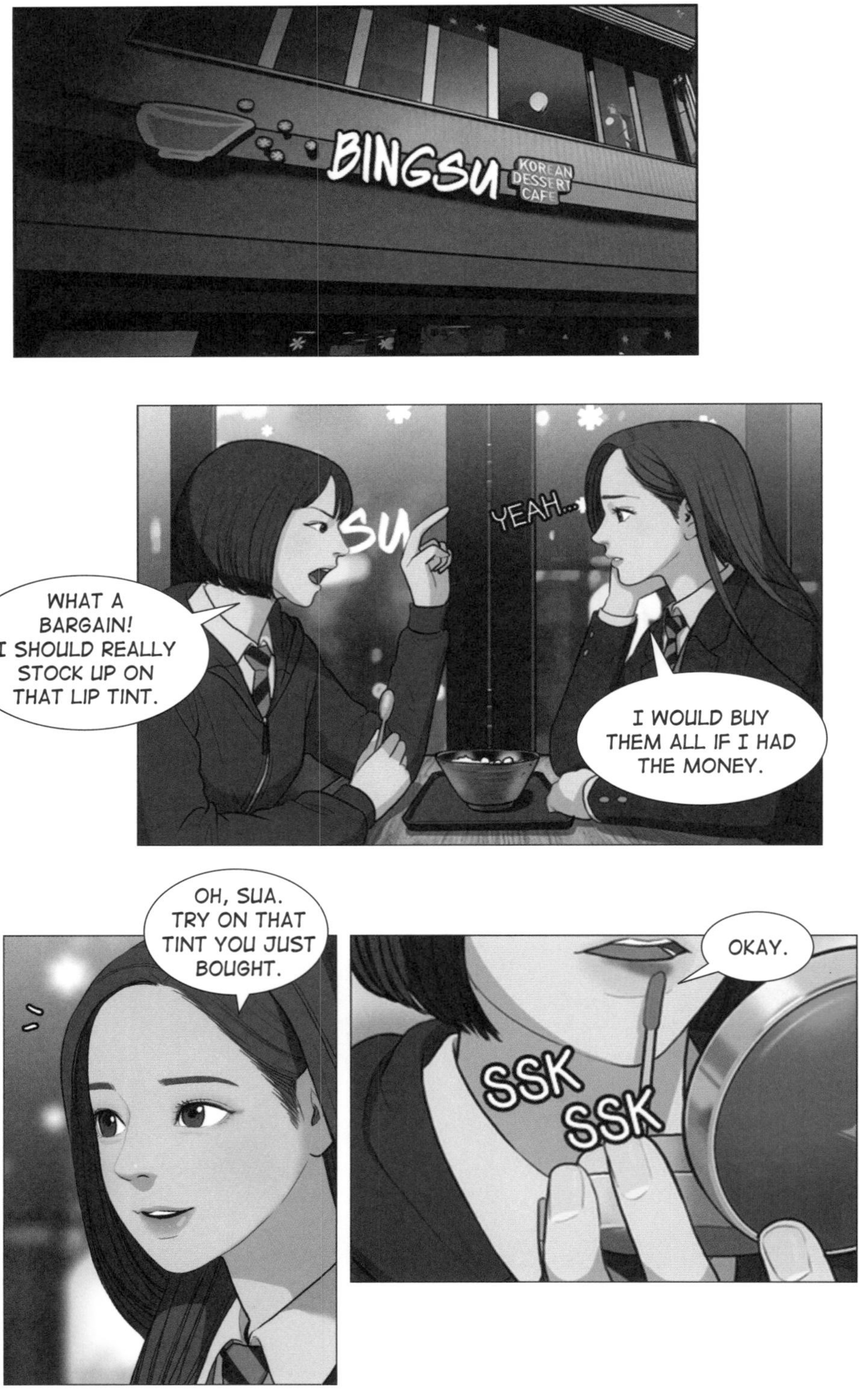
BINGSU
KOREAN DESSERT CAFE
SU
YEAH...
WHAT A BARGAIN! I SHOULD REALLY STOCK UP ON THAT LIP TINT.
I WOULD BUY THEM ALL IF I HAD THE MONEY.
OH, SUA. TRY ON THAT TINT YOU JUST BOUGHT.
OKAY.
SSK SSK

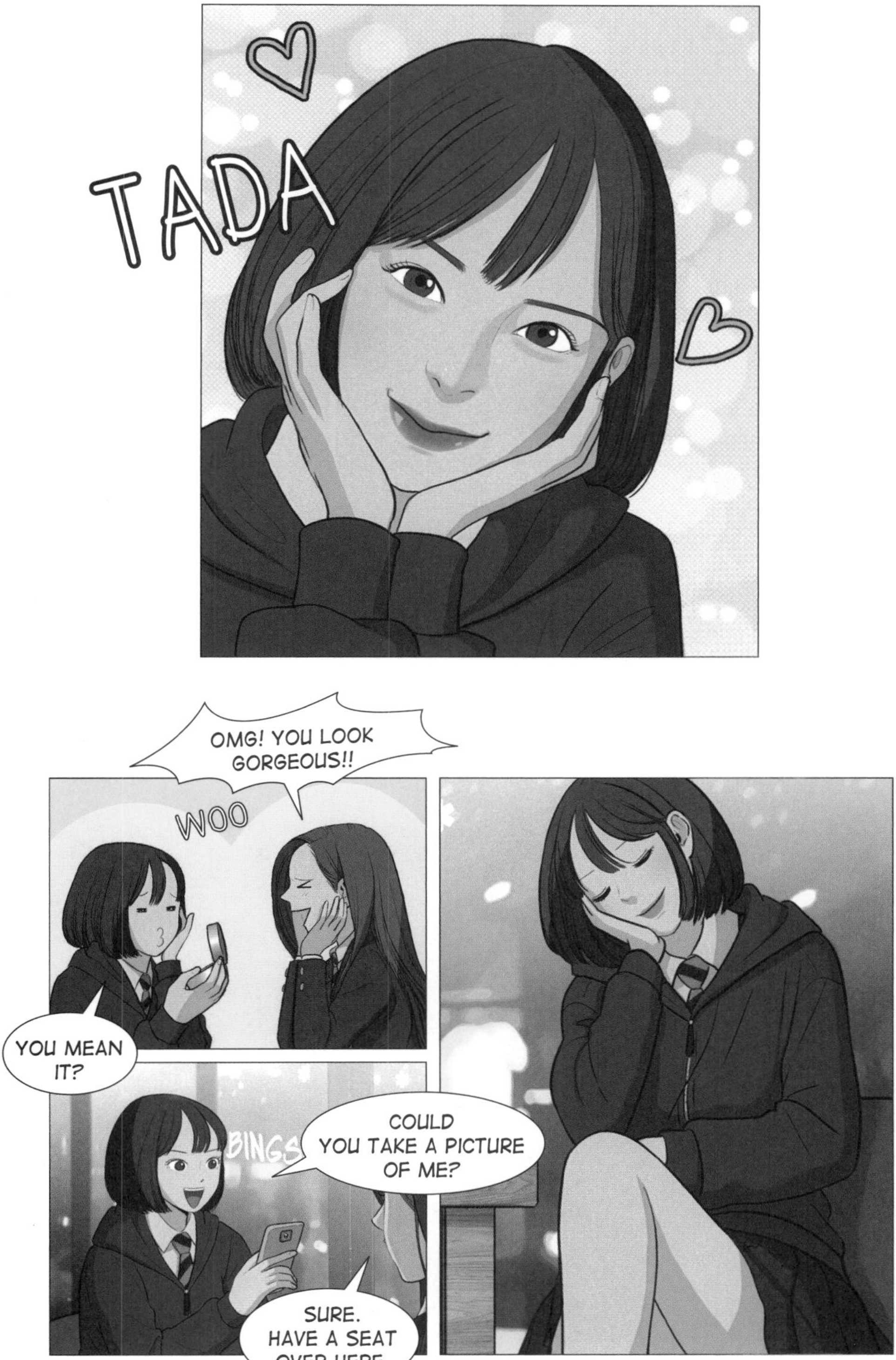
TADA
OMG! YOU LOOK GORGEOUS!!
WOO
YOU MEAN IT?
COULD YOU TAKE A PICTURE OF ME?
SURE. HAVE A SEAT OVER HERE.

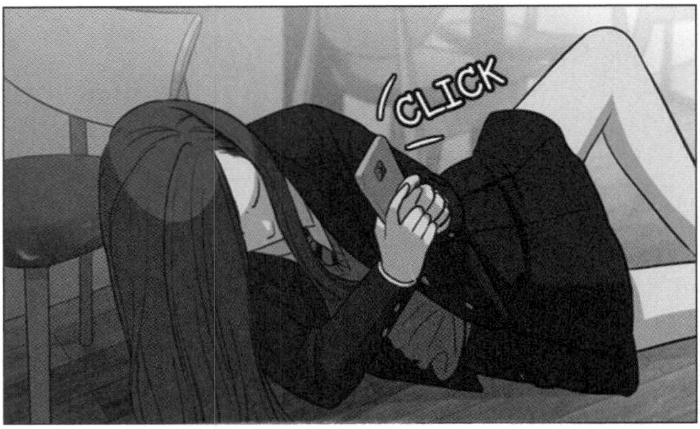
CLICK

HOW_U_CASUALLY_TAKE_PICTURES.JPG

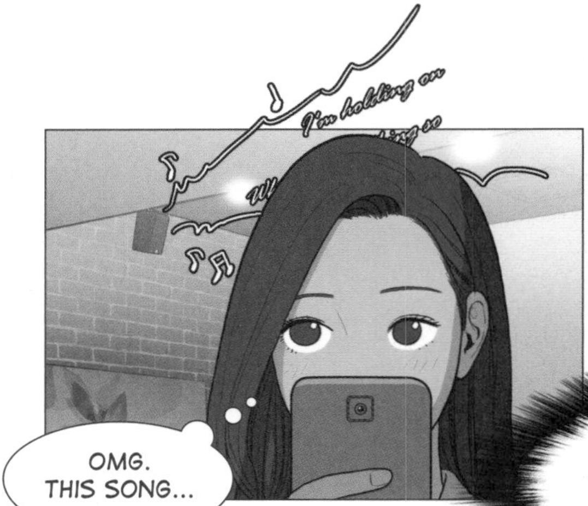
I'm holding on
OMG.
THIS SONG...

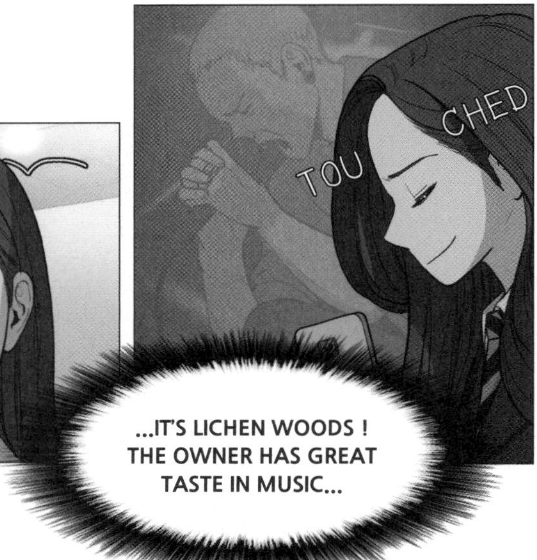
TOU
CHED
...IT'S LICHEN WOODS !
THE OWNER HAS GREAT
TASTE IN MUSIC...

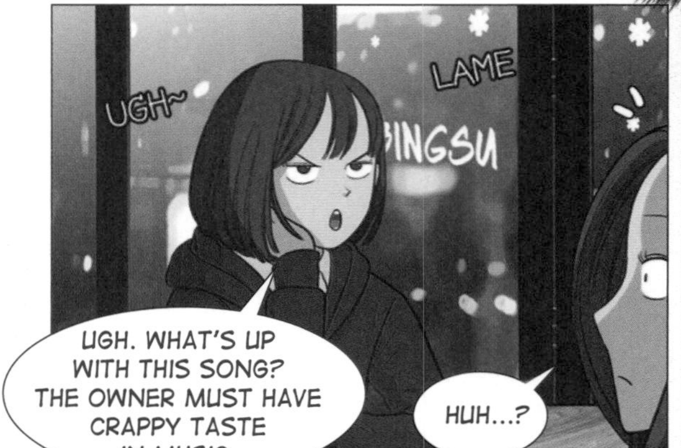
UGH~
LAME
BINGSU
UGH. WHAT'S UP
WITH THIS SONG?
THE OWNER MUST HAVE
CRAPPY TASTE
IN MUSIC.
HUH...?

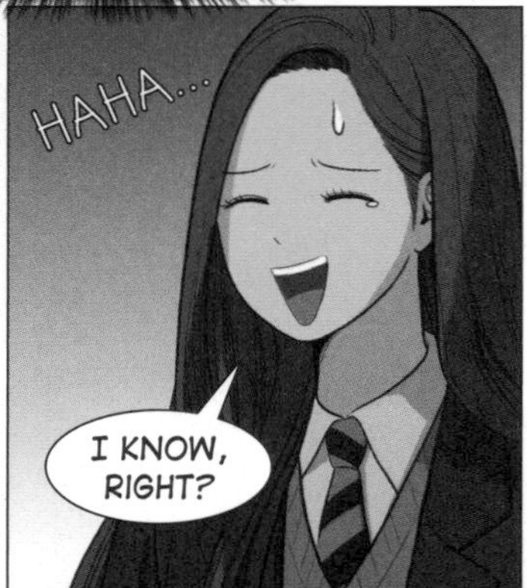
HAHA...
I KNOW,
RIGHT?

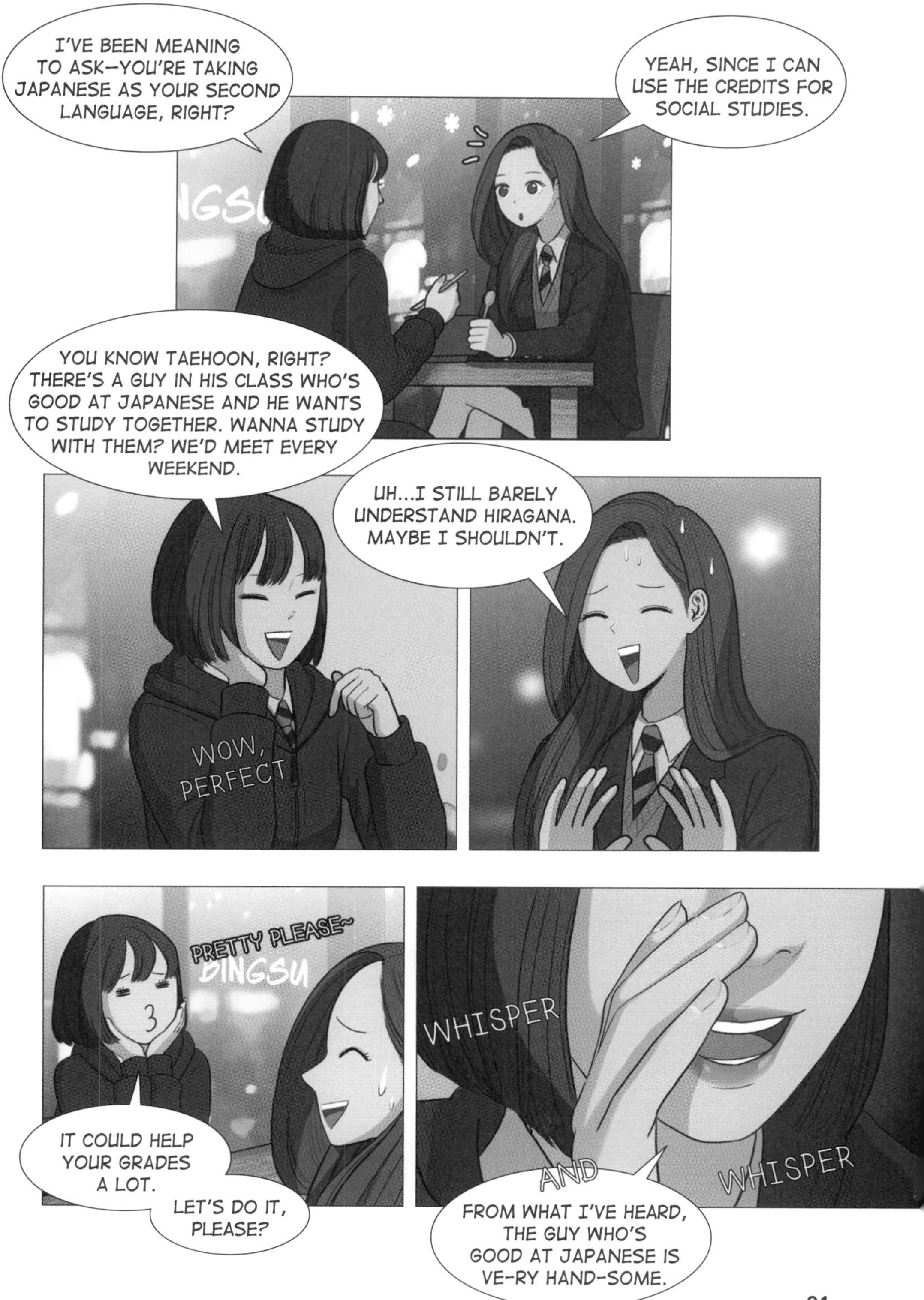
I'VE BEEN MEANING TO ASK—YOU'RE TAKING JAPANESE AS YOUR SECOND LANGUAGE, RIGHT?
YEAH, SINCE I CAN USE THE CREDITS FOR SOCIAL STUDIES.
YOU KNOW TAEHOON, RIGHT? THERE'S A GUY IN HIS CLASS WHO'S GOOD AT JAPANESE AND HE WANTS TO STUDY TOGETHER. WANNA STUDY WITH THEM? WE'D MEET EVERY WEEKEND.
WOW, PERFECT
UH...I STILL BARELY UNDERSTAND HIRAGANA. MAYBE I SHOULDN'T.
PRETTY PLEASE~
BINGSU
IT COULD HELP YOUR GRADES A LOT.
LET'S DO IT, PLEASE?
WHISPER
AND
WHISPER
FROM WHAT I'VE HEARD, THE GUY WHO'S GOOD AT JAPANESE IS VE-RY HAND-SOME.

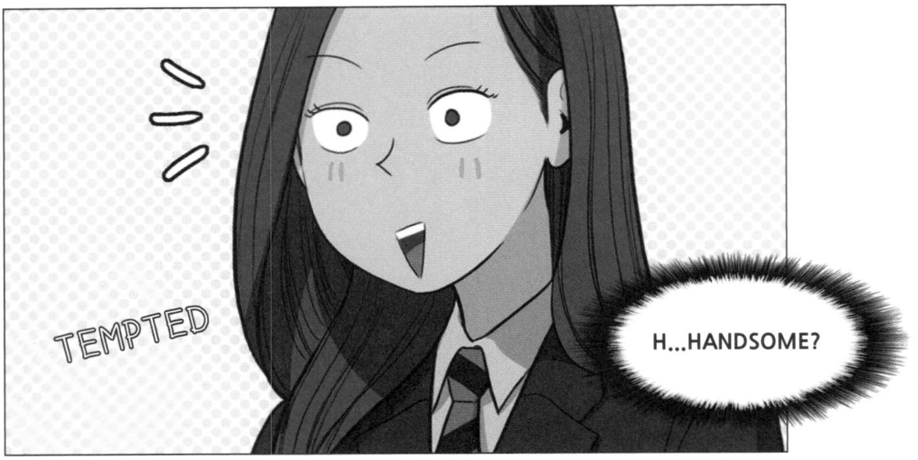
TEMPTED
H...HANDSOME?

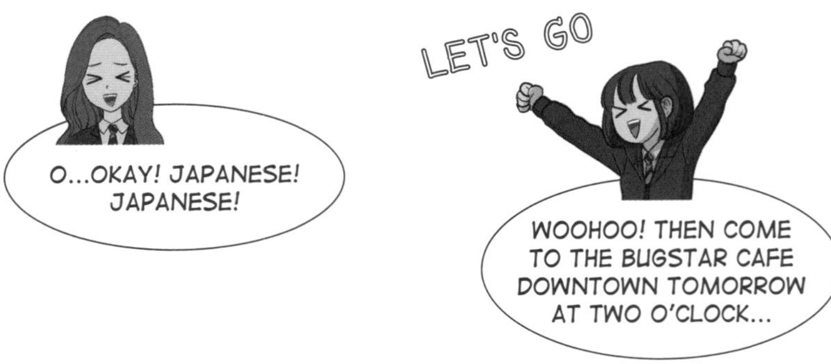
O...OKAY! JAPANESE! JAPANESE!
LET'S GO
WOOHOO! THEN COME TO THE BUGSTAR CAFE DOWNTOWN TOMORROW AT TWO O'CLOCK...

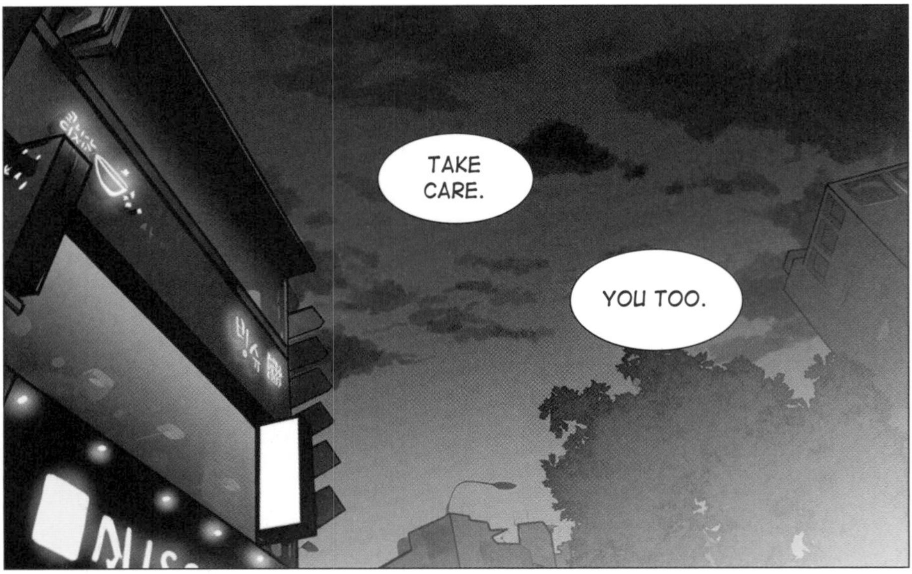
TAKE CARE.
YOU TOO.

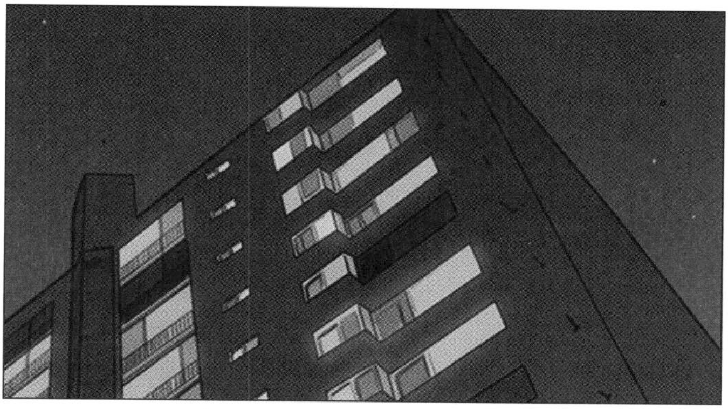

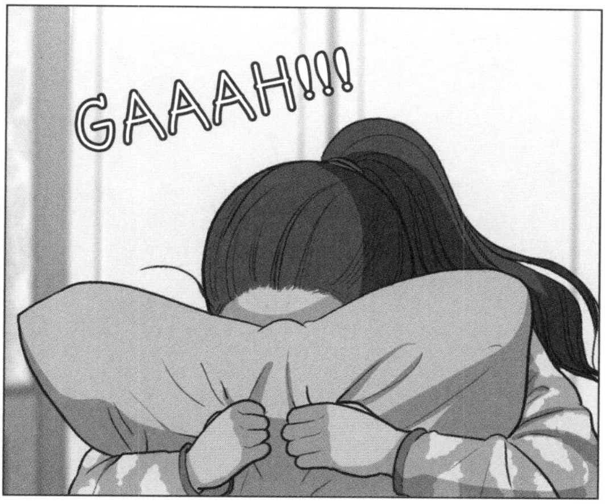
GAAAH!!!

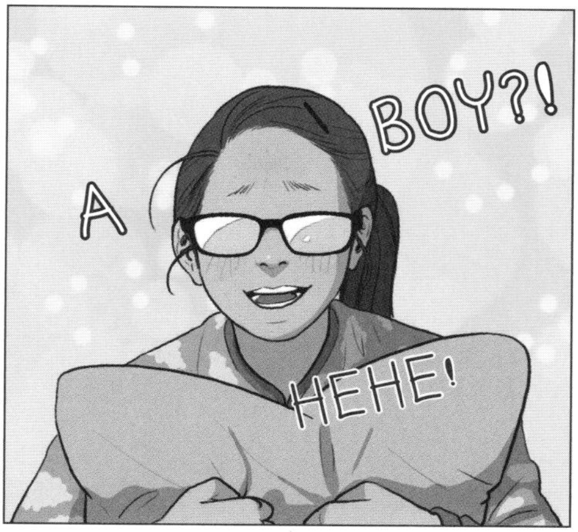
A BOY?!
HEHE!

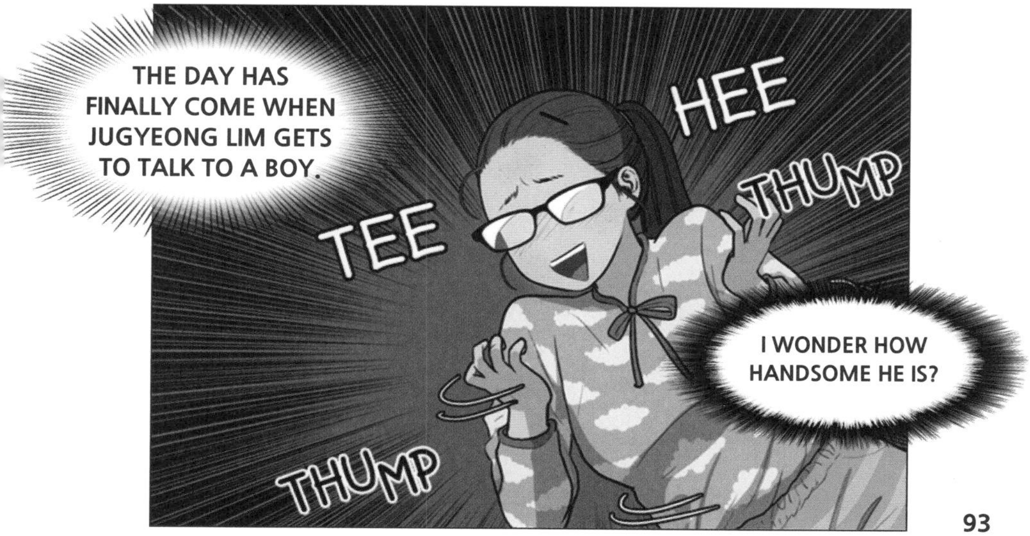
THE DAY HAS FINALLY COME WHEN JUGYEONG LIM GETS TO TALK TO A BOY.
HEE
THUMP
TEE
I WONDER HOW HANDSOME HE IS?
THUMP

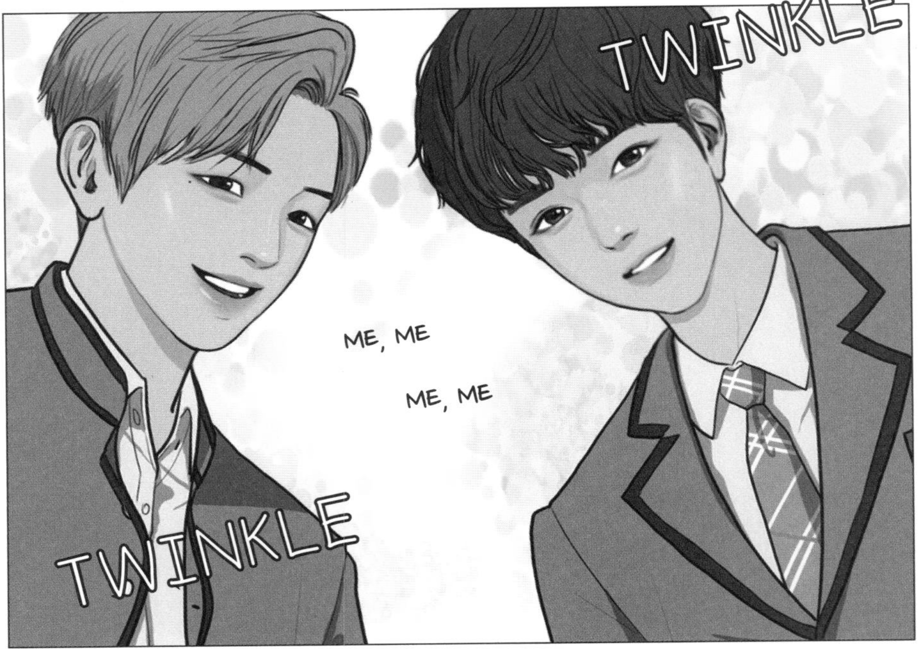
TWINKLE
ME, ME
ME, ME
TWINKLE

*DREAM VERSION OF "JAPANESE GUY"

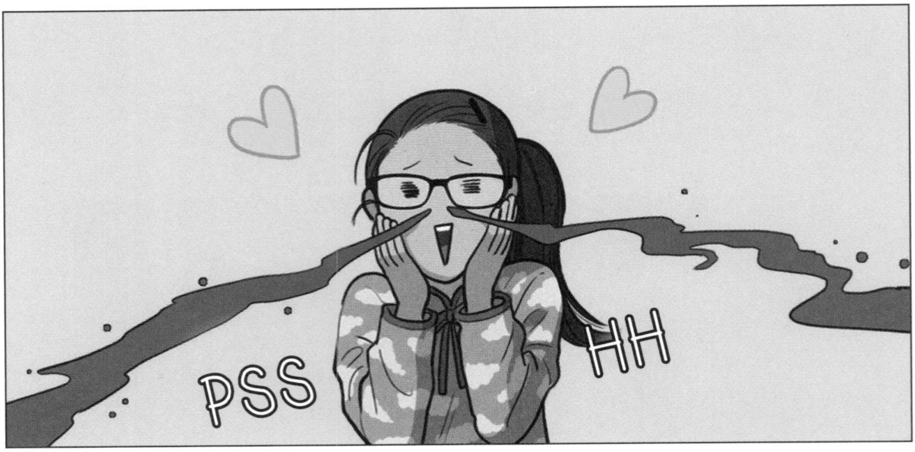
PSS
HH

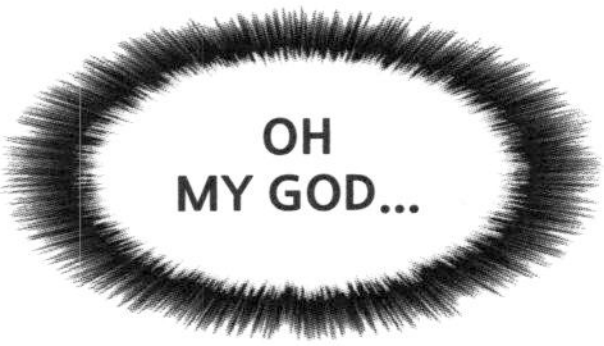
OH
MY GOD...

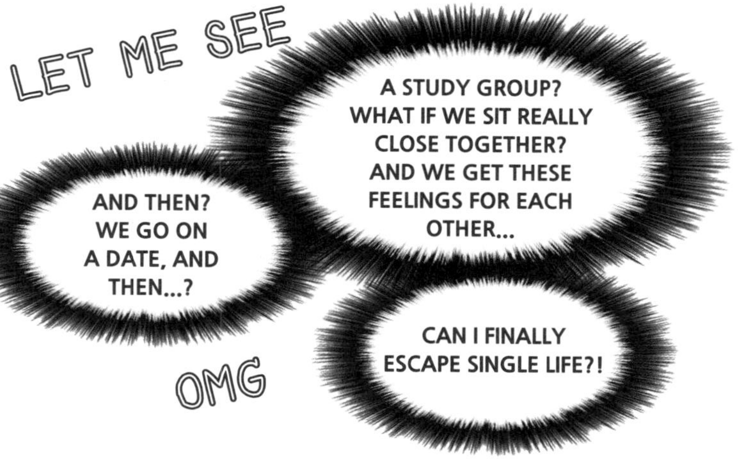
LET ME SEE
A STUDY GROUP? WHAT IF WE SIT REALLY CLOSE TOGETHER? AND WE GET THESE FEELINGS FOR EACH OTHER...
AND THEN? WE GO ON A DATE, AND THEN...?
CAN I FINALLY ESCAPE SINGLE LIFE?!
OMG

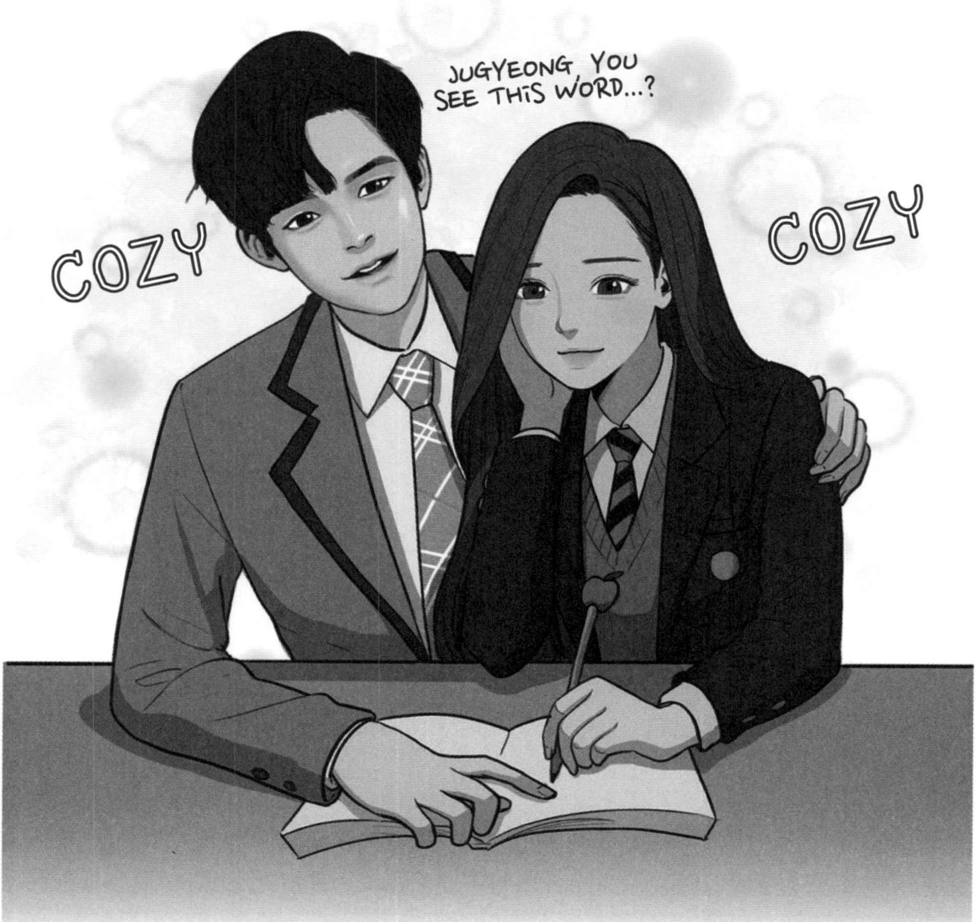
JUGYEONG YOU SEE THIS WORD...?
COZY
COZY

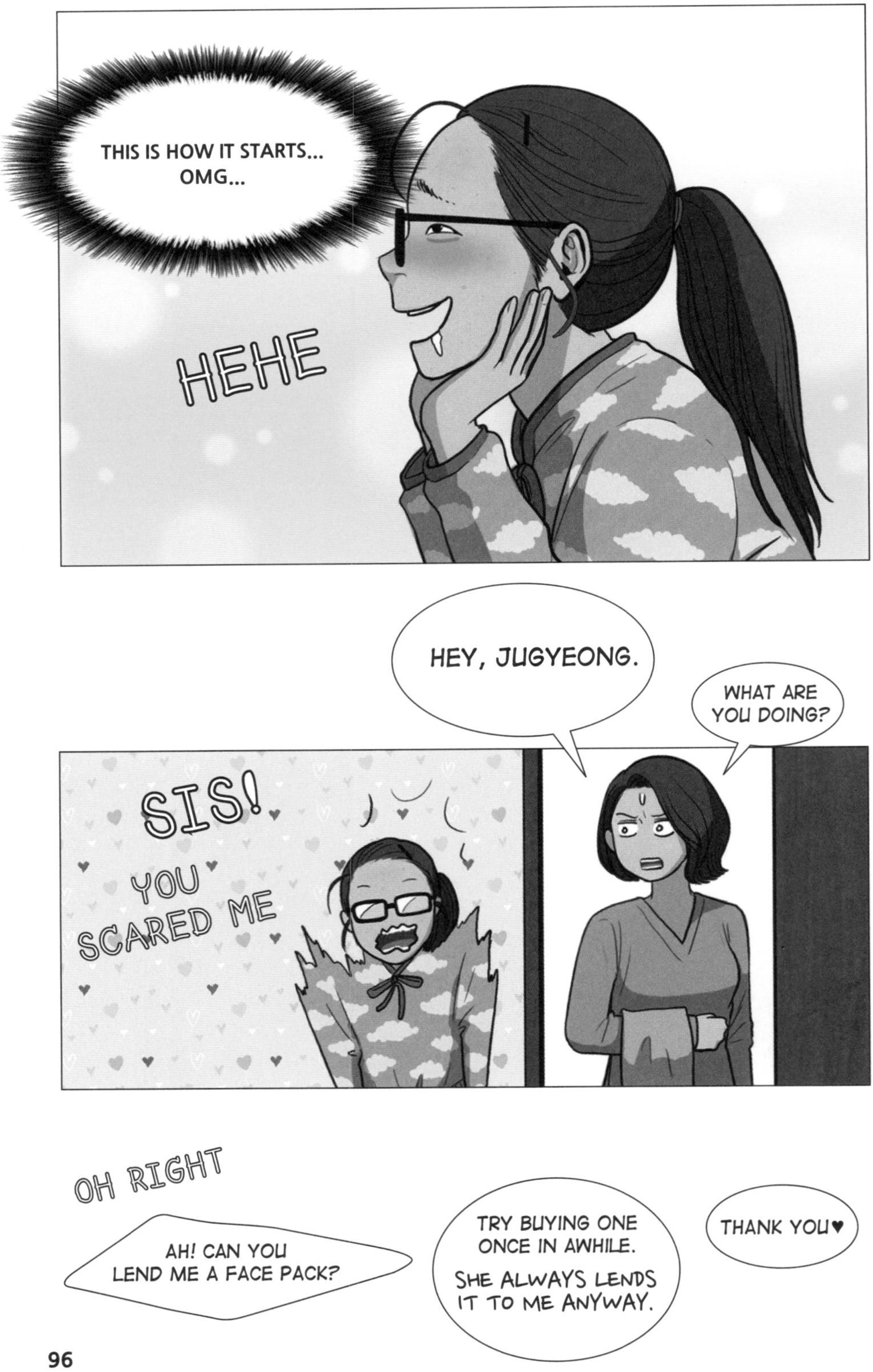
THIS IS HOW IT STARTS... OMG...
HEHE
SIS!
YOU SCARED ME
HEY, JUGYEONG.
WHAT ARE YOU DOING?
OH RIGHT
AH! CAN YOU LEND ME A FACE PACK?
TRY BUYING ONE ONCE IN AWHILE.
SHE ALWAYS LENDS IT TO ME ANYWAY.
THANK YOU♥

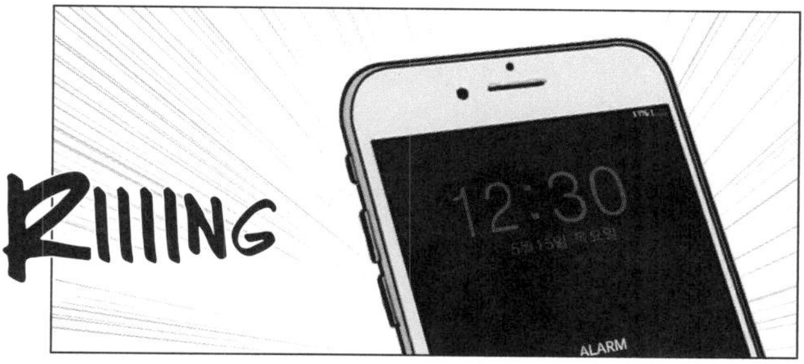
RIIIING
12:30
ALARM

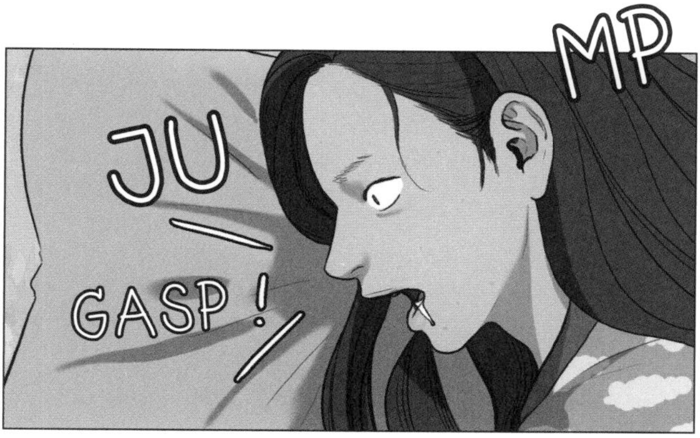
JU
MP
GASP!

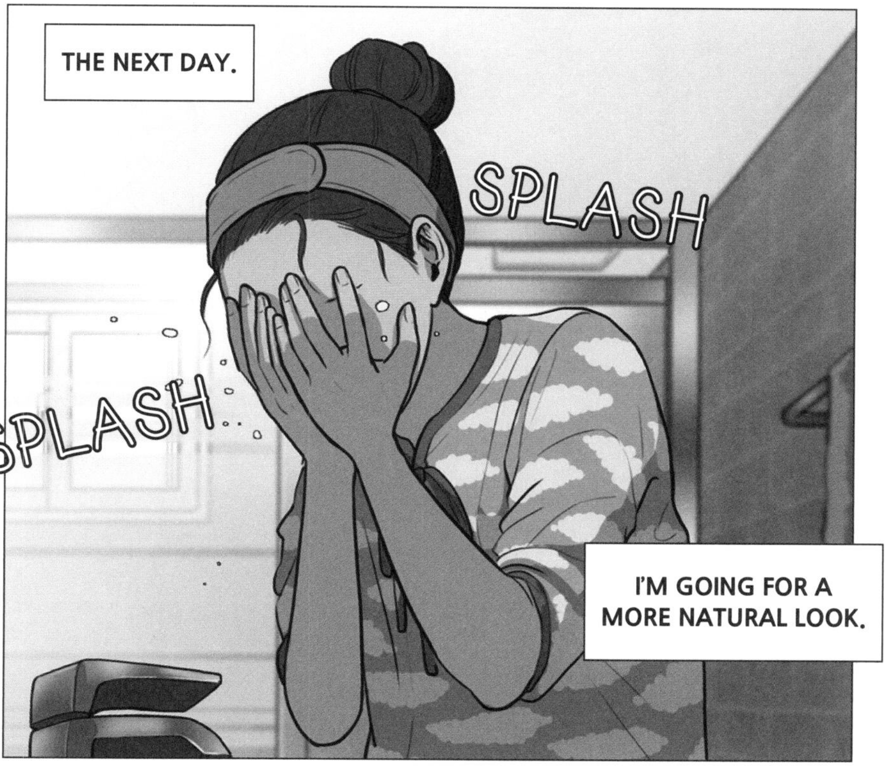
THE NEXT DAY.
SPLASH
SPLASH
I'M GOING FOR A MORE NATURAL LOOK.

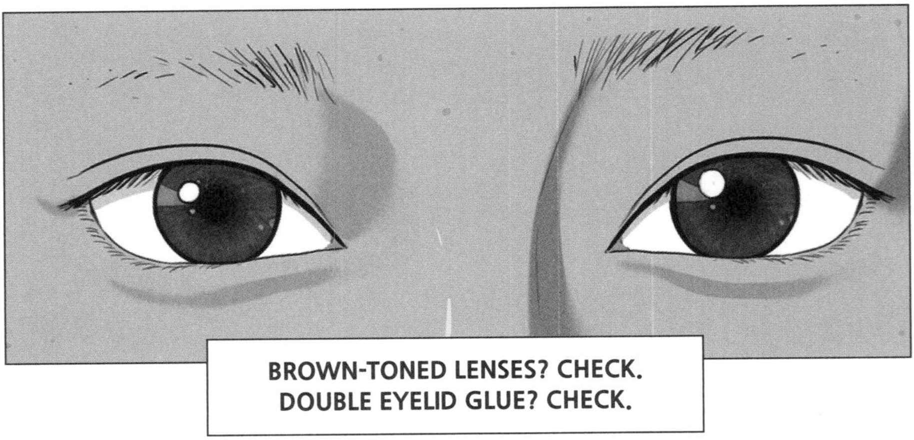
BROWN-TONED LENSES? CHECK.
DOUBLE EYELID GLUE? CHECK.

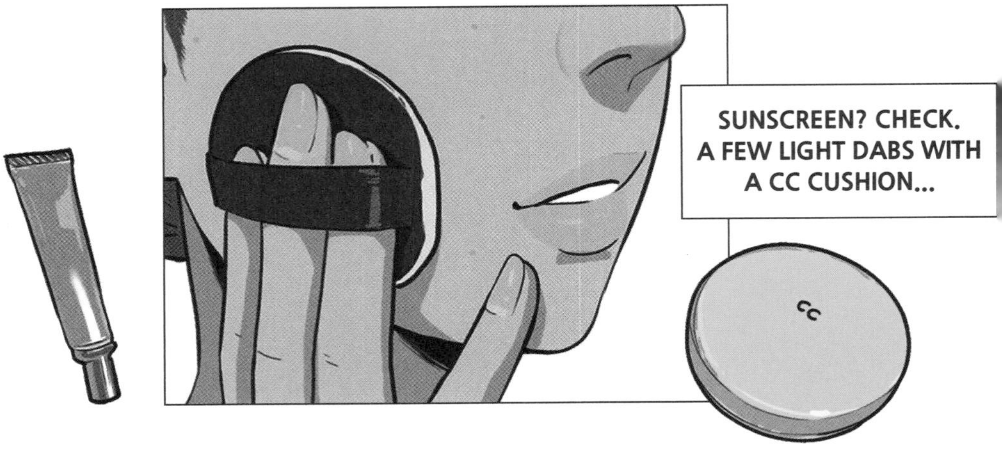
SUNSCREEN? CHECK.
A FEW LIGHT DABS WITH
A CC CUSHION...
CC

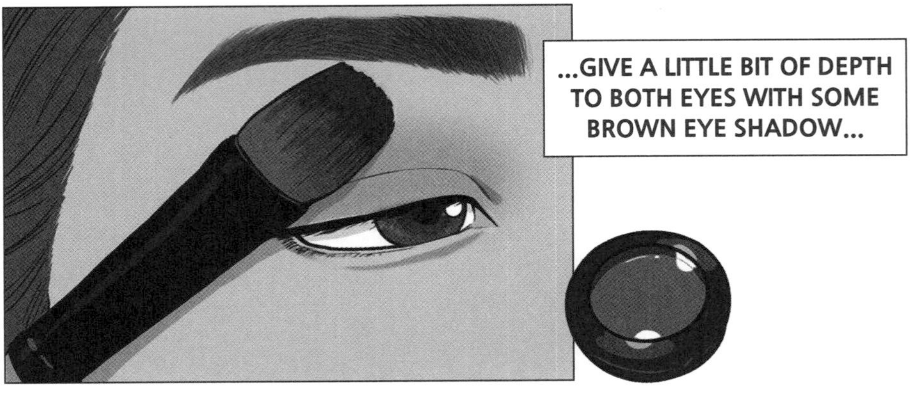
...GIVE A LITTLE BIT OF DEPTH
TO BOTH EYES WITH SOME
BROWN EYE SHADOW...

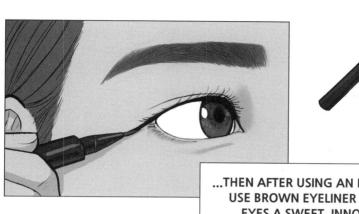

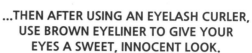

...THEN AFTER USING AN EYELASH CURLER, USE BROWN EYELINER TO GIVE YOUR EYES A SWEET, INNOCENT LOOK.

DAB WITH PEACH-COLORED BLUSH.

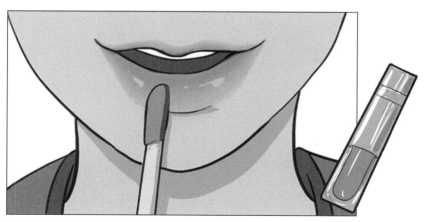

FINALLY, FINISH IT OFF WITH SOME GLOSSY CORAL LIP TINT...

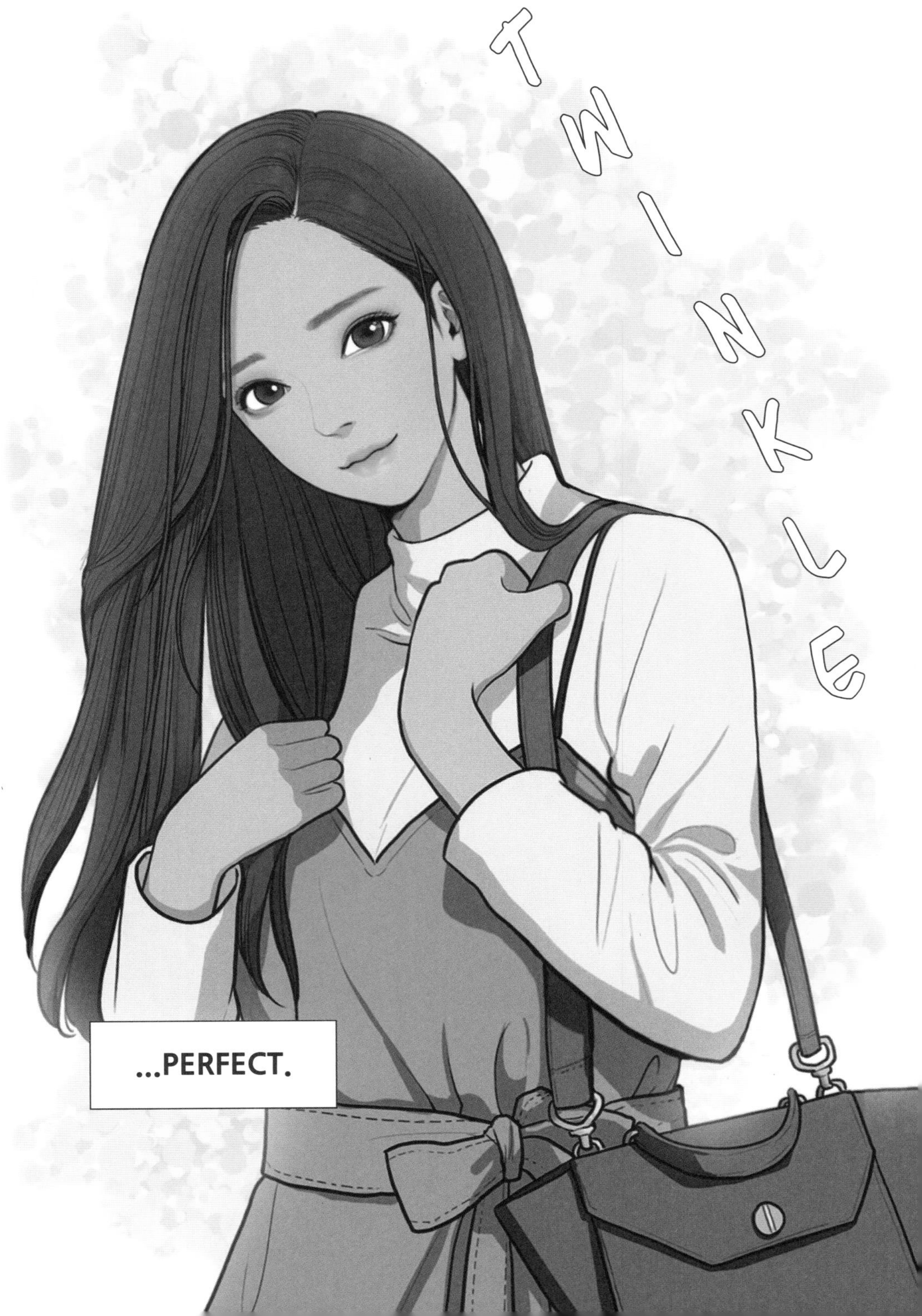
TWINKLE
...PERFECT.

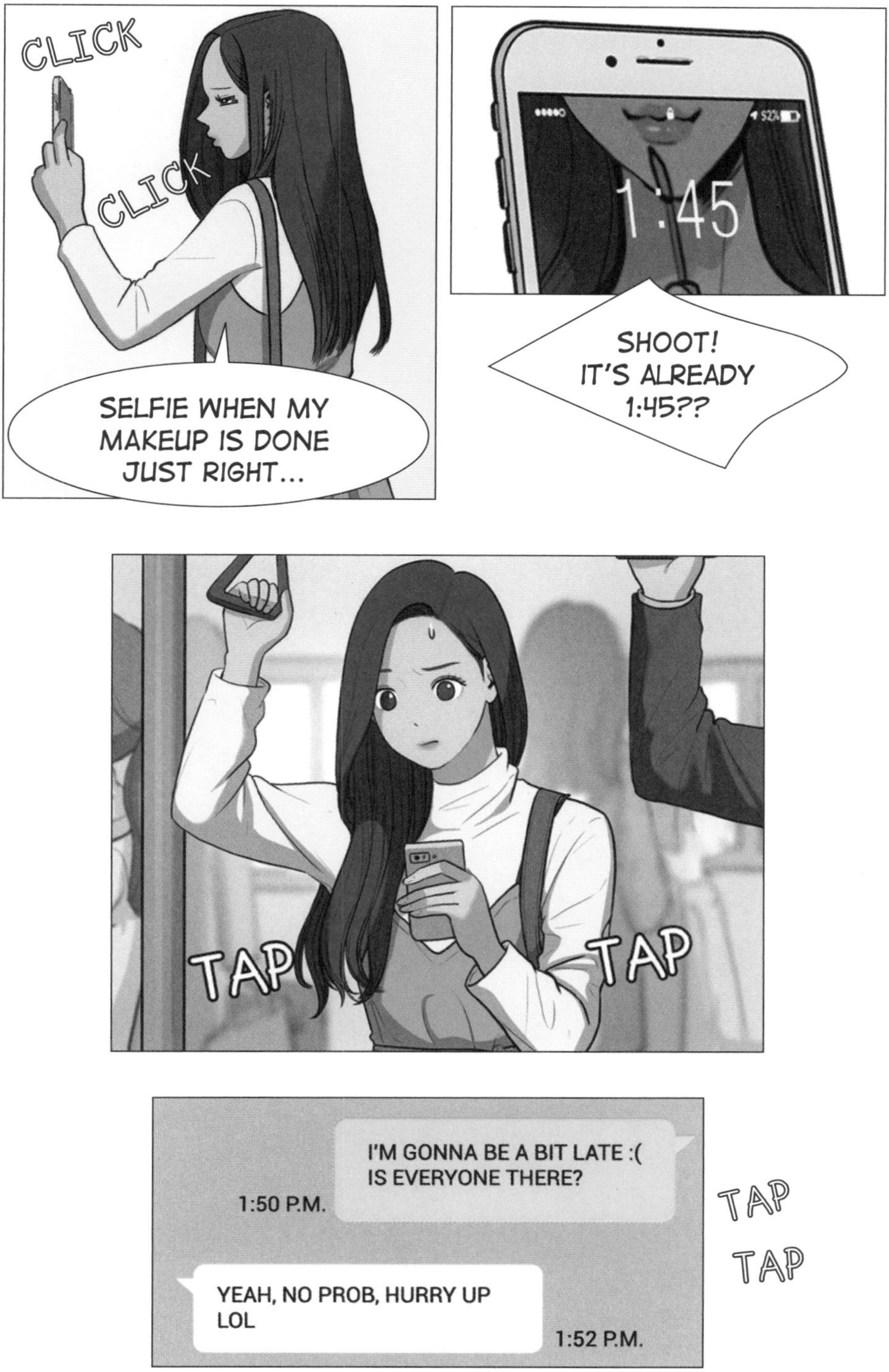
CLICK
CLICK
SELFIE WHEN MY MAKEUP IS DONE JUST RIGHT...
1:45
SHOOT! IT'S ALREADY 1:45??
TAP
TAP
I'M GONNA BE A BIT LATE :(IS EVERYONE THERE?
1:50 P.M.
TAP
TAP
YEAH, NO PROB, HURRY UP LOL
1:52 P.M.

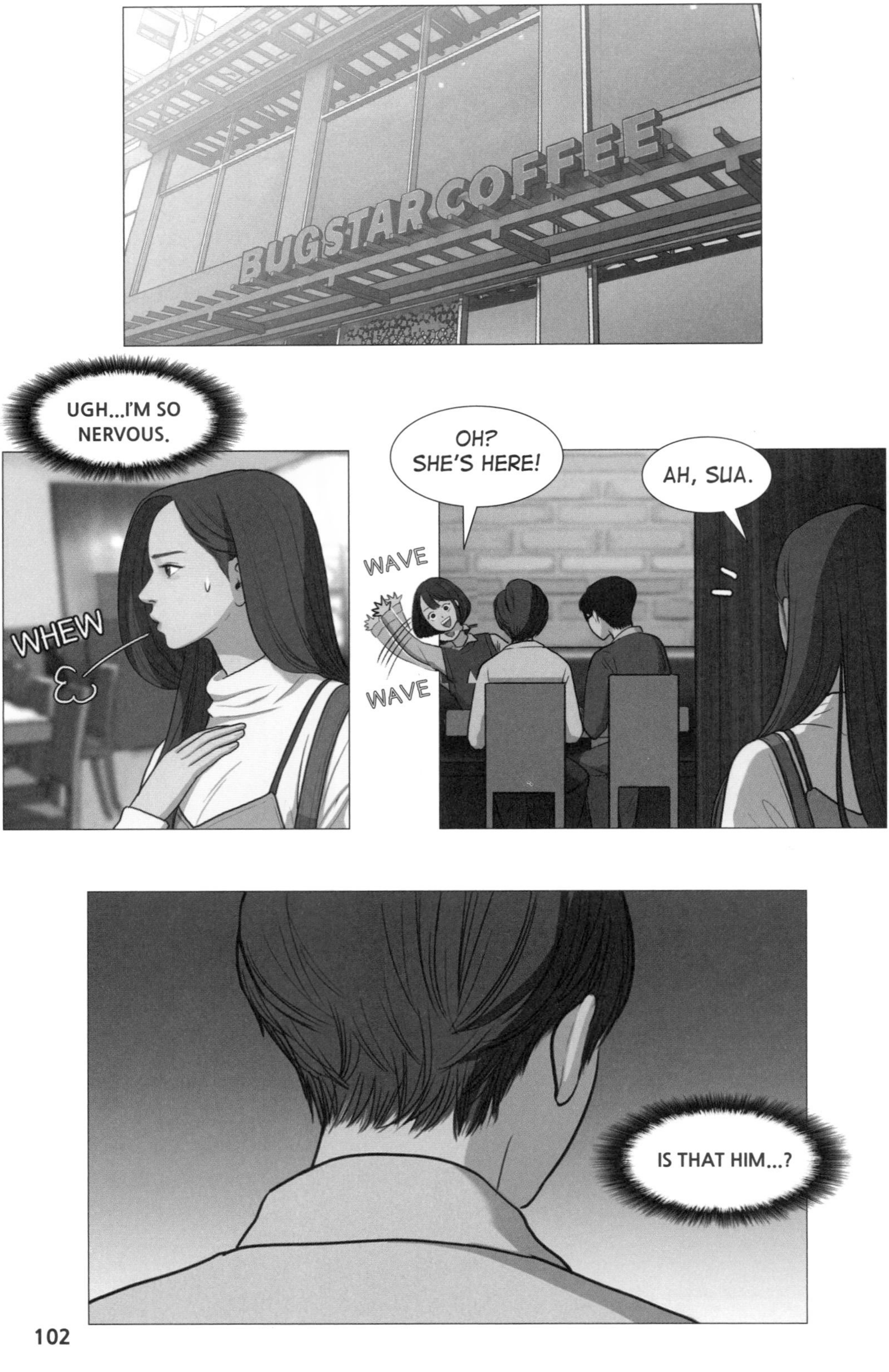
BUGSTAR COFFEE
UGH...I'M SO NERVOUS.
WHEW
OH? SHE'S HERE!
WAVE
WAVE
AH, SUA.
IS THAT HIM...?

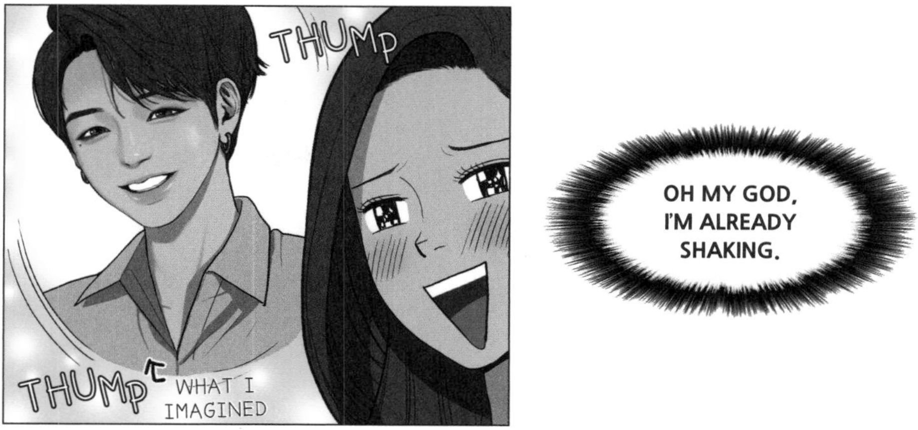
THUMP
THUMP
WHAT I IMAGINED
OH MY GOD, I'M ALREADY SHAKING.

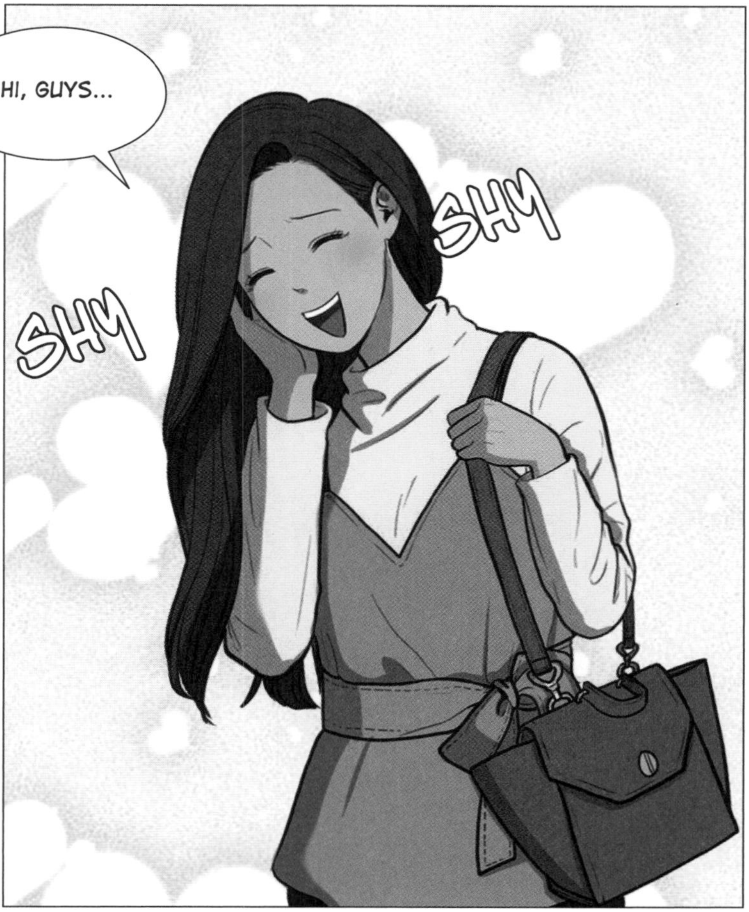
HI, GUYS...
SHY
SHY

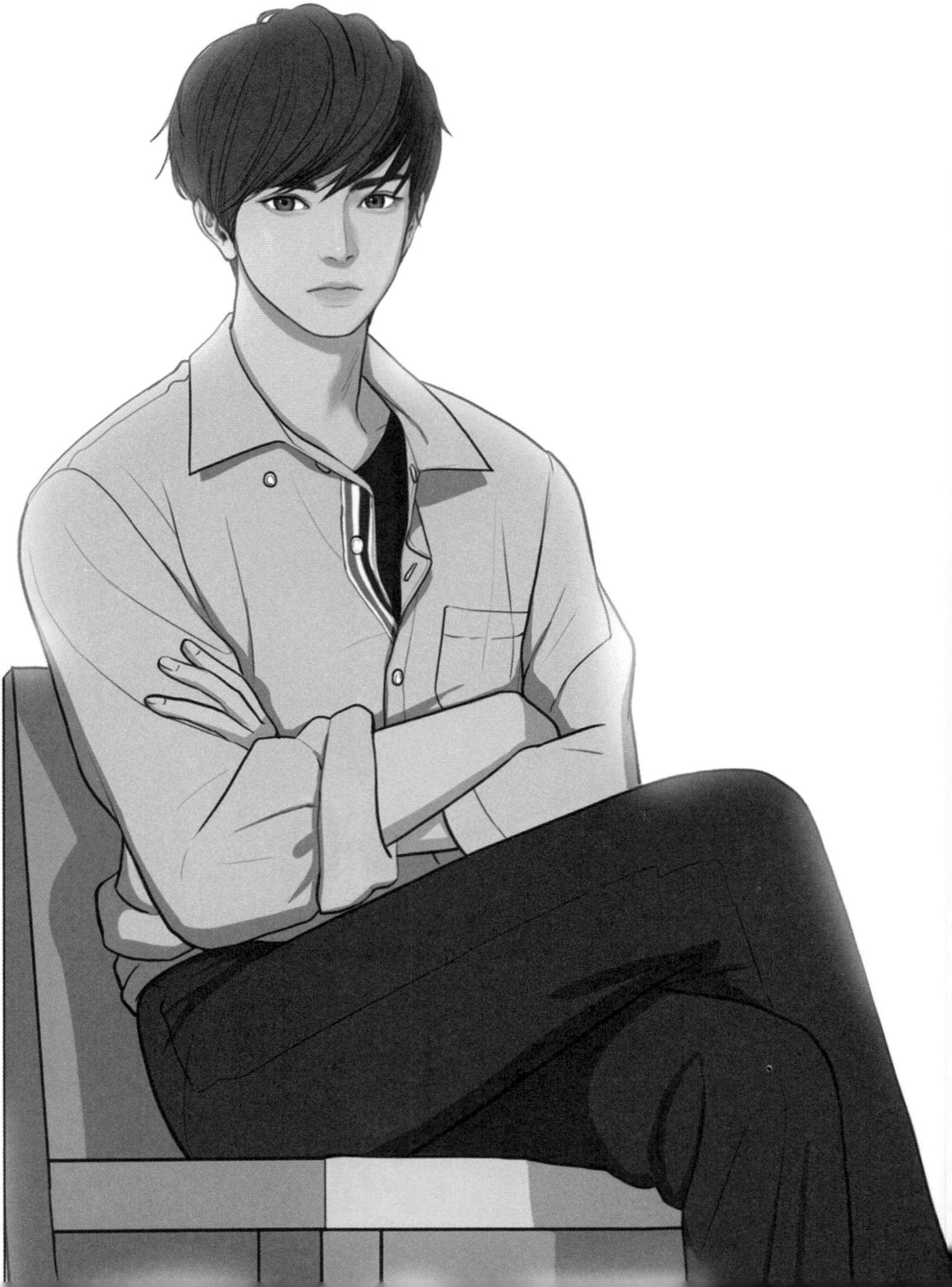

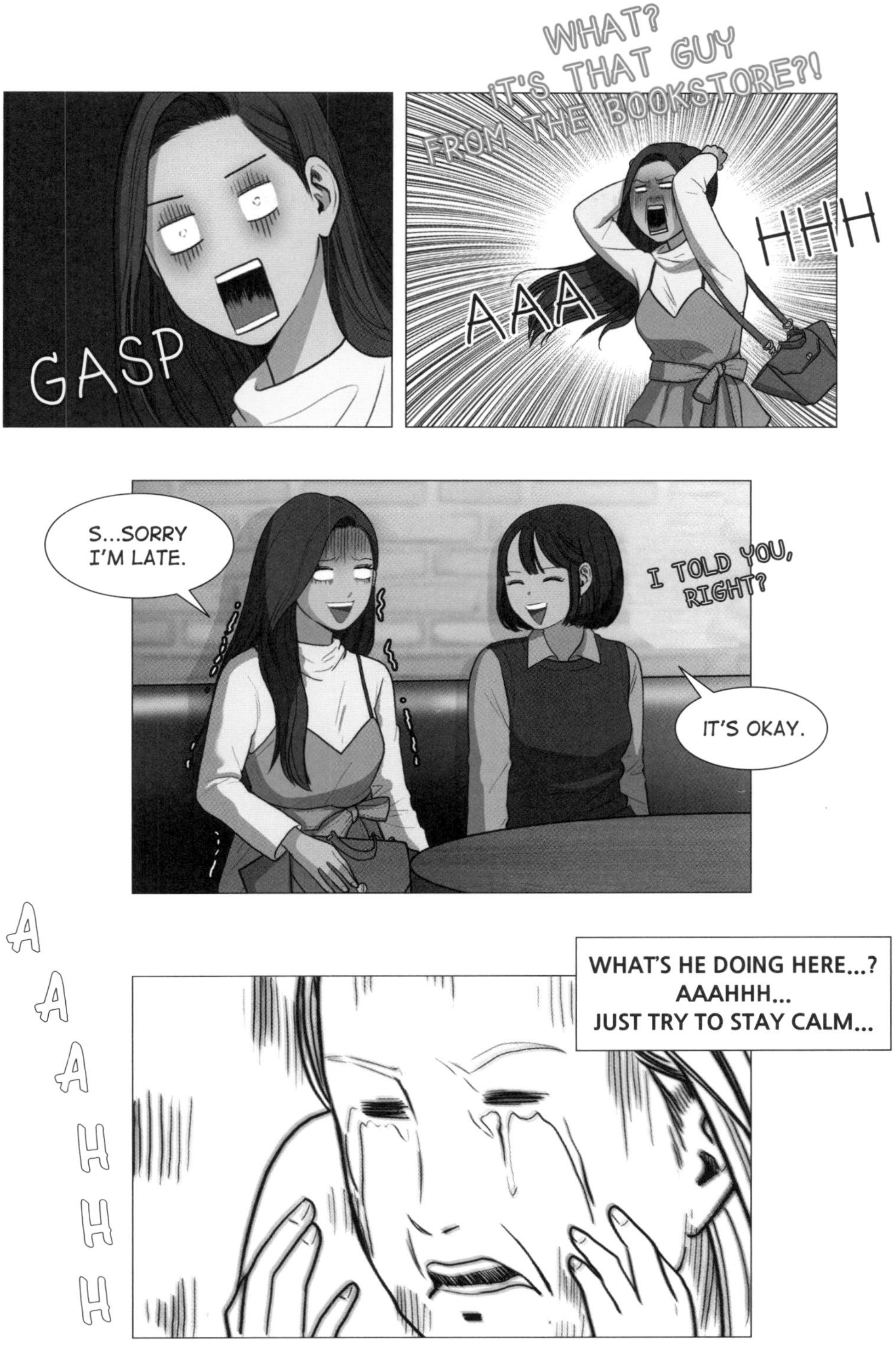
GASP
WHAT? IT'S THAT GUY FROM THE BOOKSTORE?!
AAA
HHH
S...SORRY I'M LATE.
I TOLD YOU, RIGHT?
IT'S OKAY.
AAAHHHH
WHAT'S HE DOING HERE...? AAAHHH... JUST TRY TO STAY CALM...

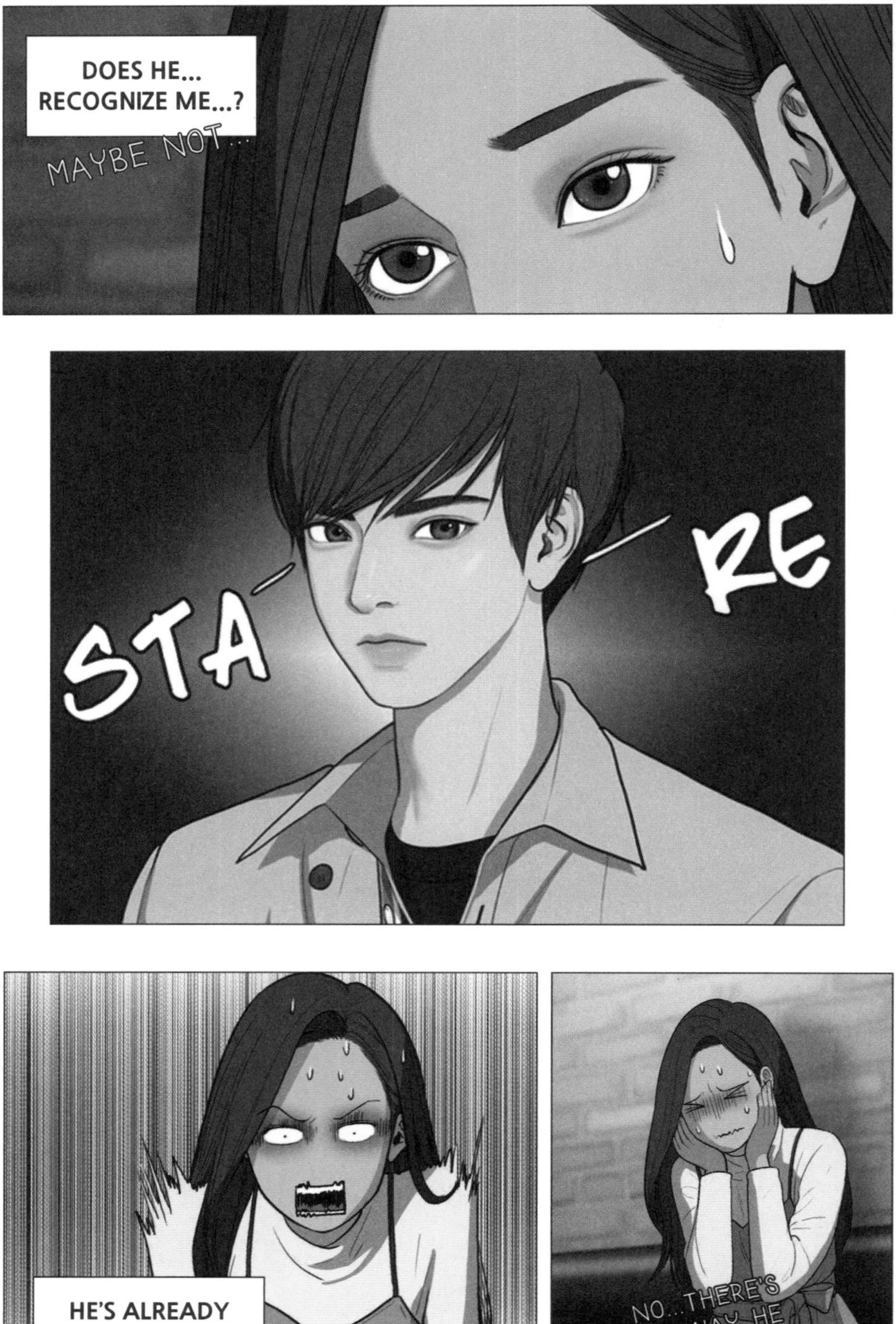
DOES HE... RECOGNIZE ME...?
MAYBE NOT...
STA—
—RE
HE'S ALREADY STARING AT ME!!
NO... THERE'S NO WAY HE RECOGNIZES ME.

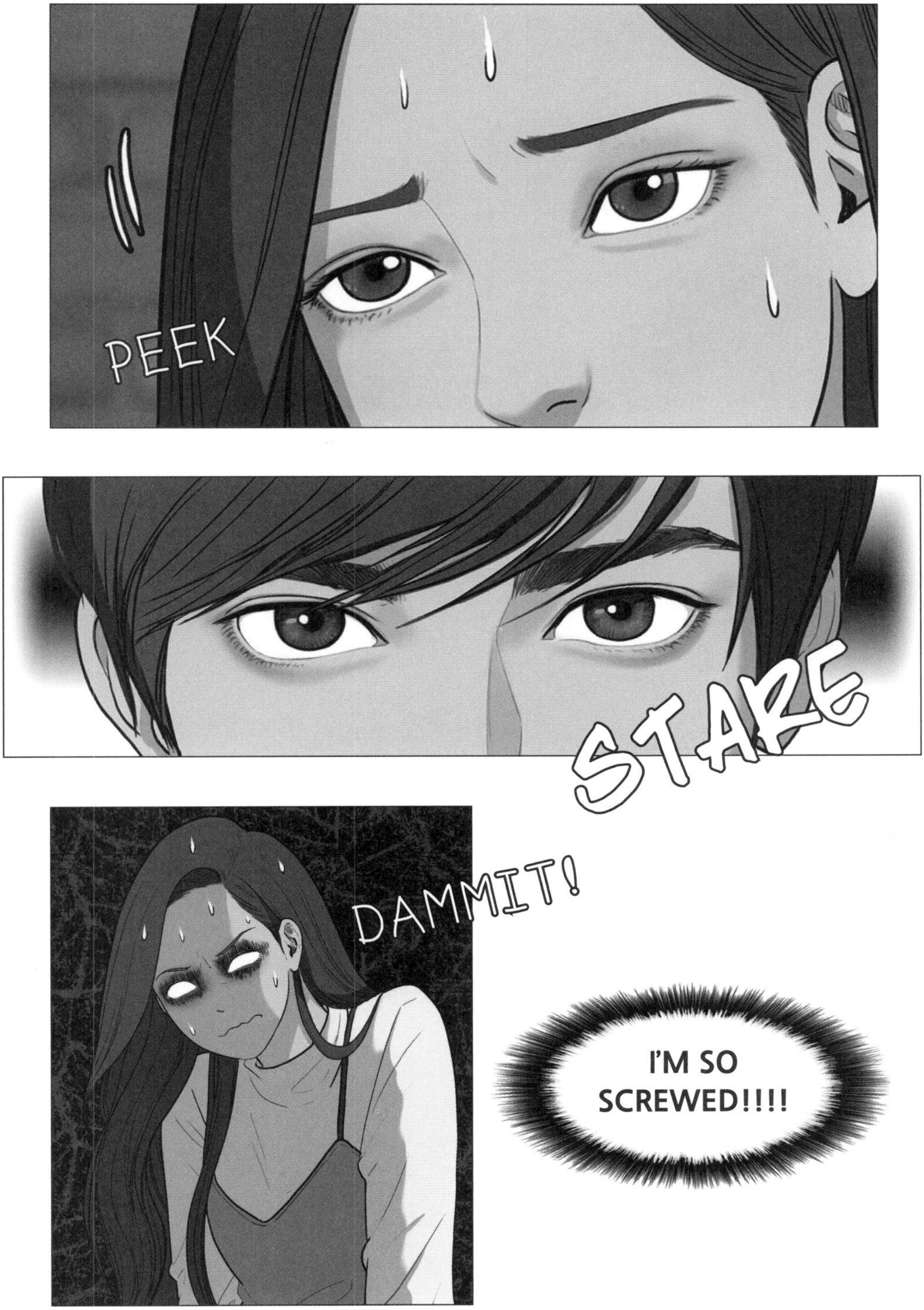
PEEK
STARE
DAMMIT!
I'M SO SCREWED!!!!

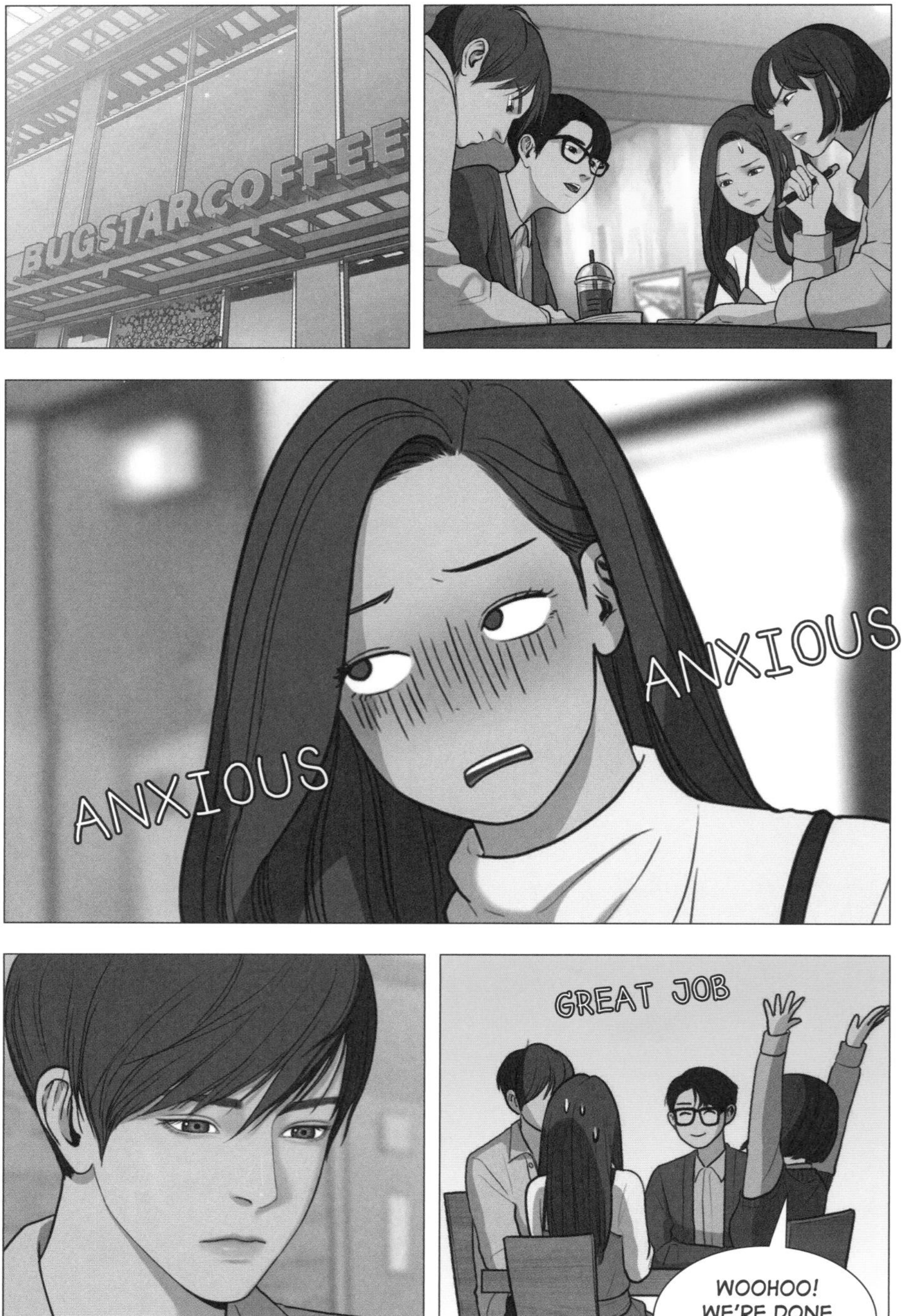
BUGSTAR COFFEE
ANXIOUS
ANXIOUS
GREAT JOB
WOOHOO! WE'RE DONE FOR TODAY!♥

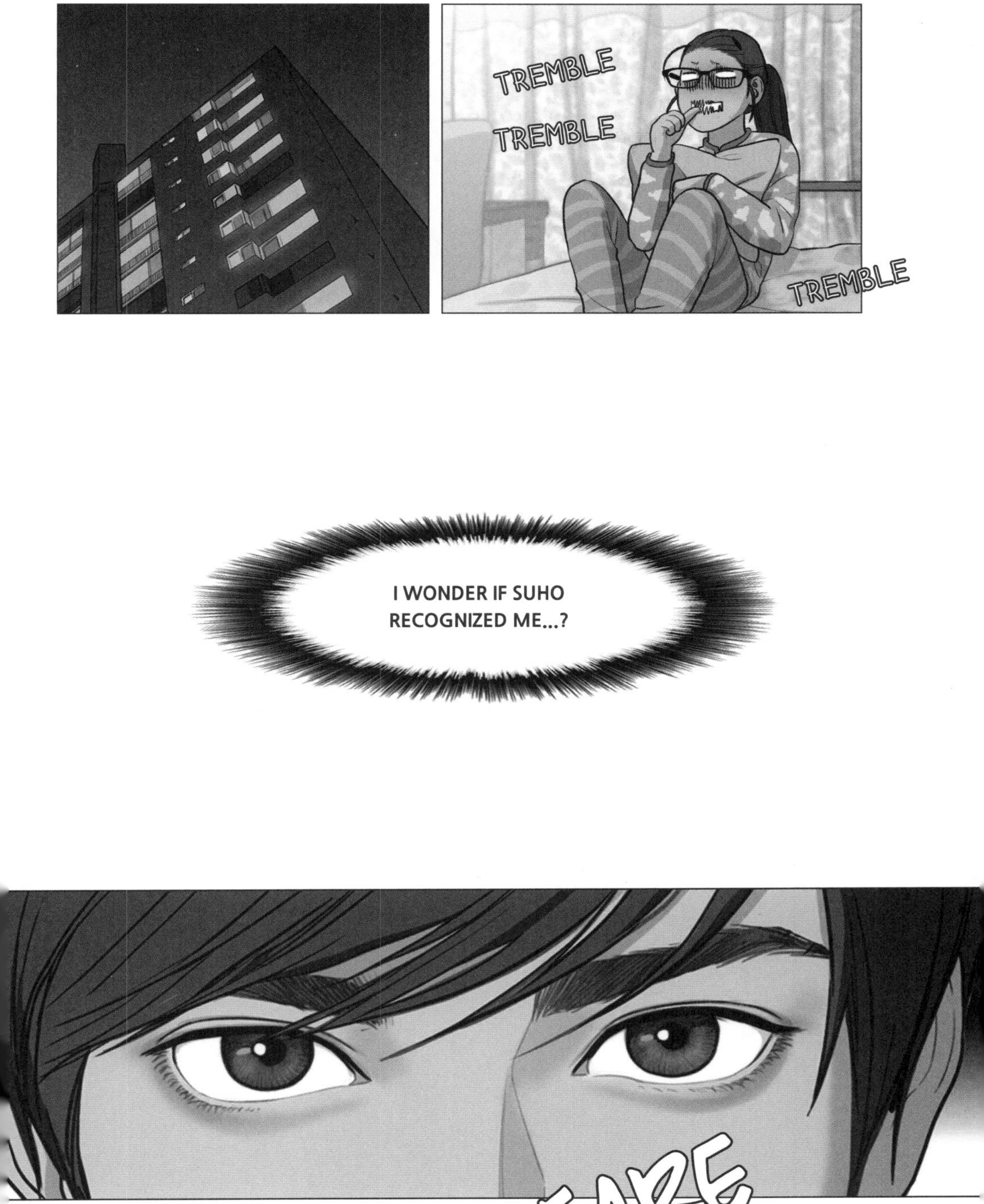
TREMBLE
TREMBLE
TREMBLE
I WONDER IF SUHO RECOGNIZED ME...?
STARE

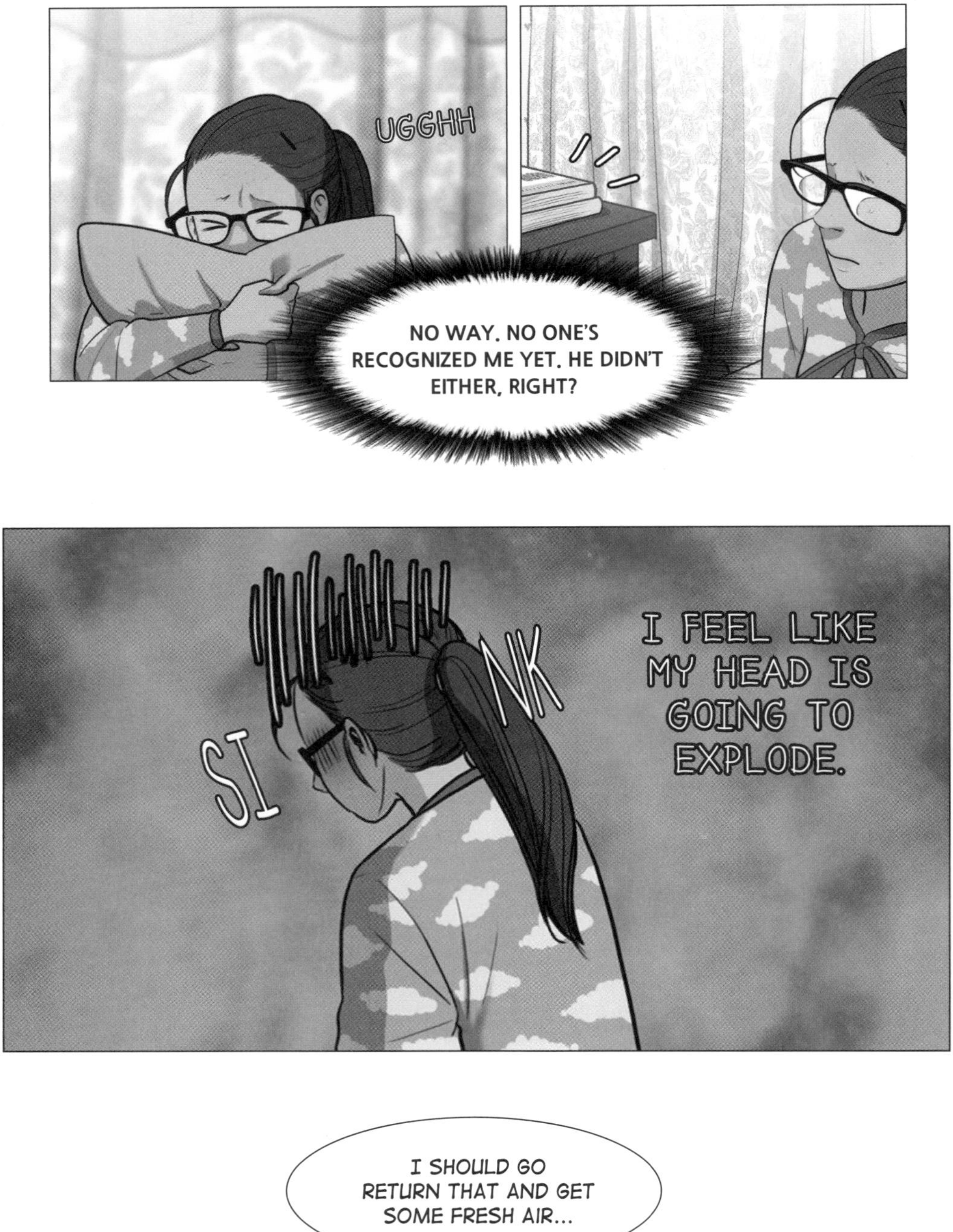
UGGHH
NO WAY. NO ONE'S RECOGNIZED ME YET. HE DIDN'T EITHER, RIGHT?
SI
NK
I FEEL LIKE MY HEAD IS GOING TO EXPLODE.
I SHOULD GO RETURN THAT AND GET SOME FRESH AIR...

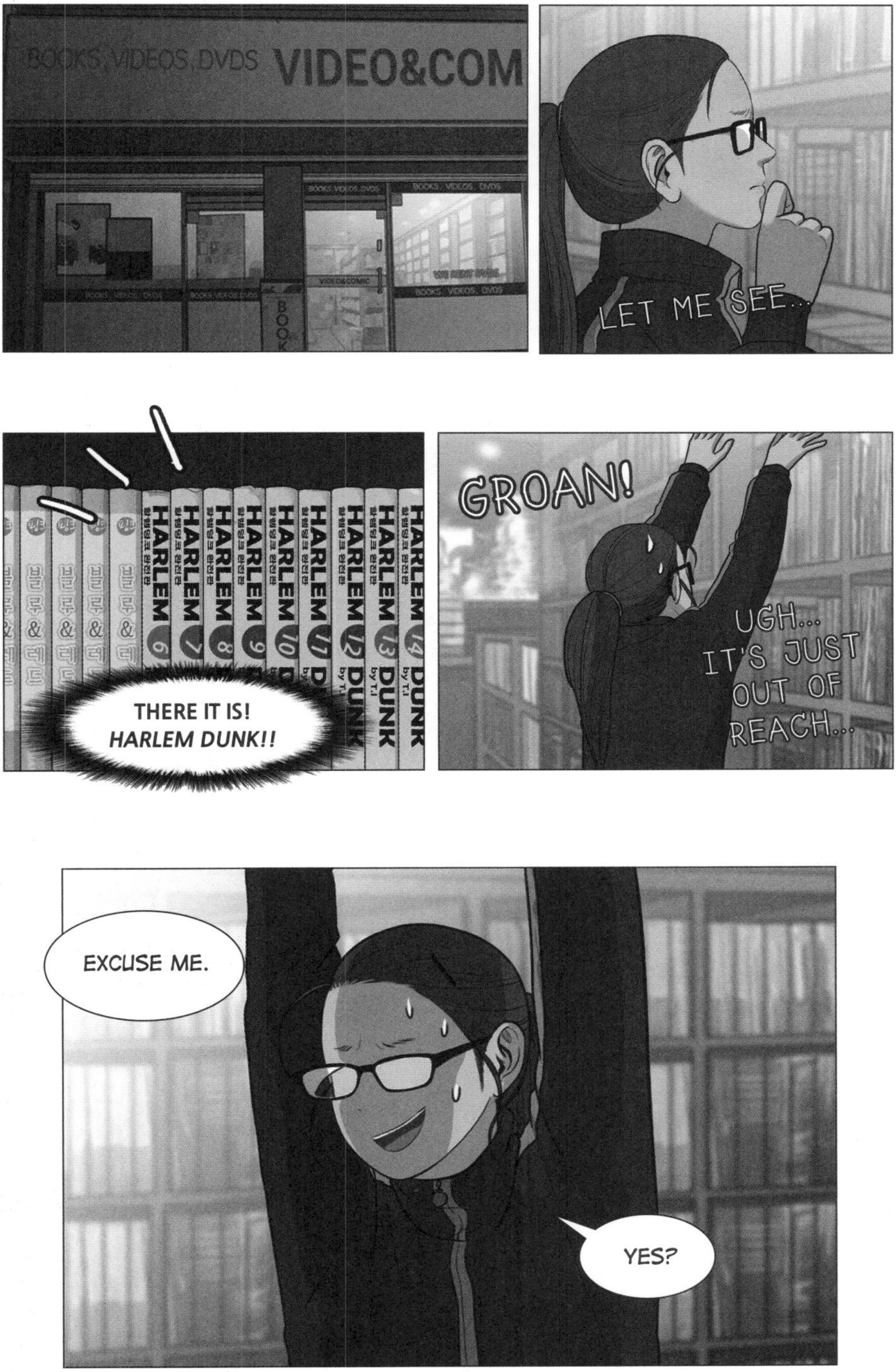
BOOKS, VIDEOS, DVDS VIDEO&COM
LET ME SEE...
THERE IT IS! *HARLEM DUNK!!*
GROAN!
UGH... IT'S JUST OUT OF REACH...
EXCUSE ME.
YES?

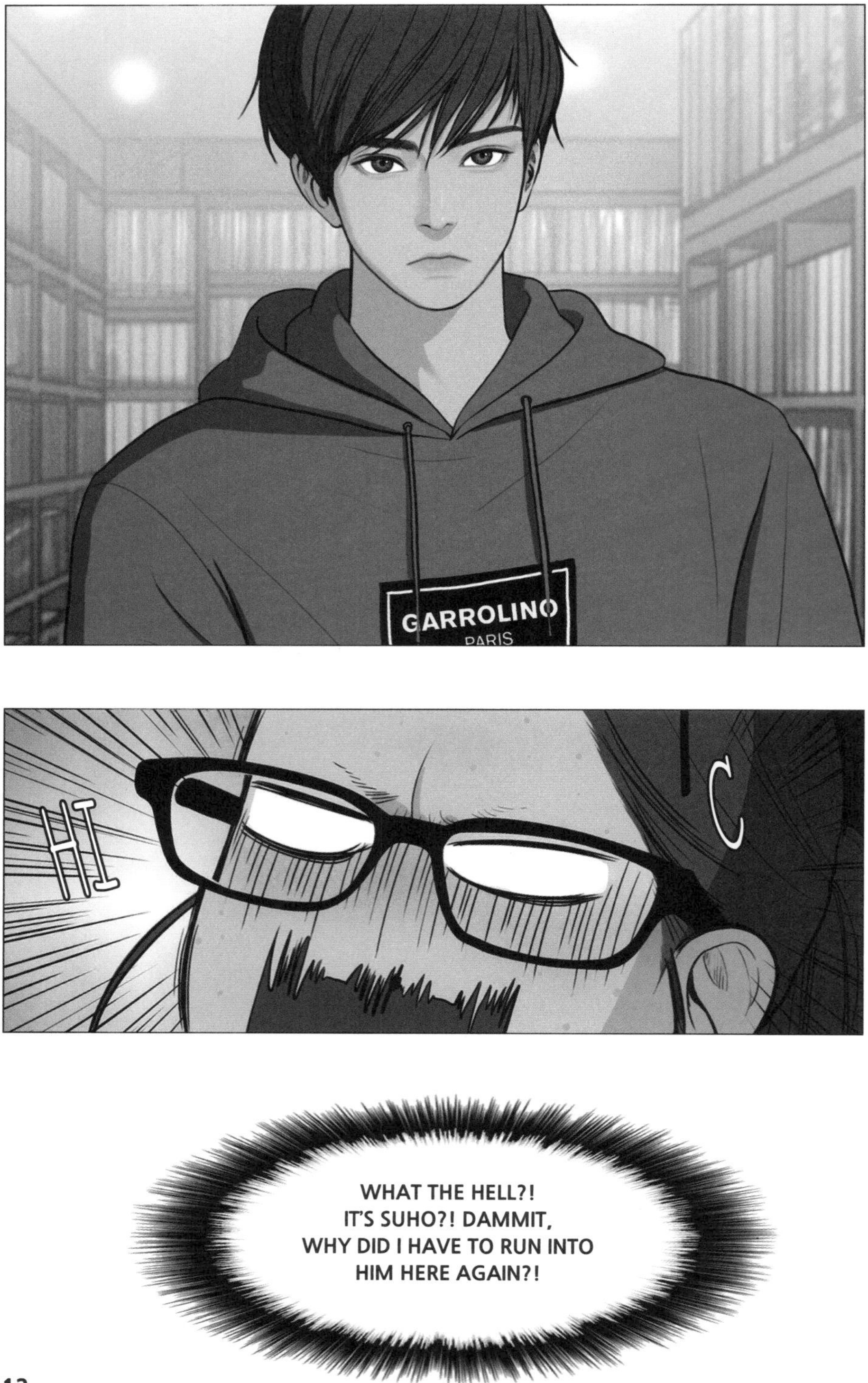
GARROLINO
PARIS
HI
C
WHAT THE HELL?! IT'S SUHO?! DAMMIT, WHY DID I HAVE TO RUN INTO HIM HERE AGAIN?!

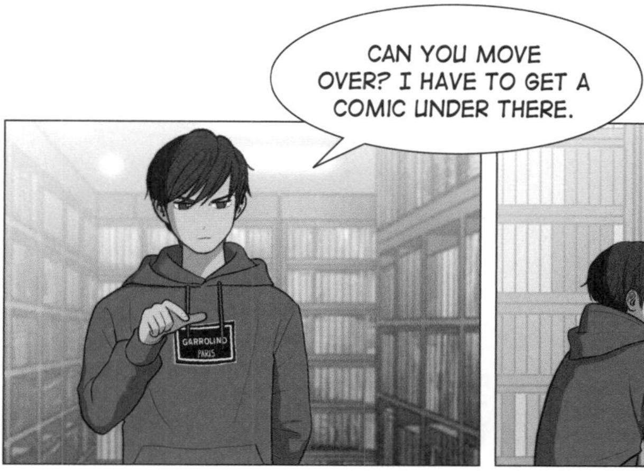
CAN YOU MOVE OVER? I HAVE TO GET A COMIC UNDER THERE.
GARROLIND PARIS

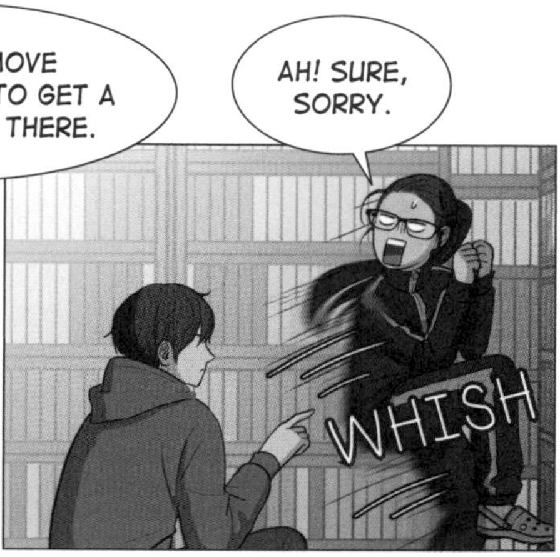
AH! SURE, SORRY.
WHISH

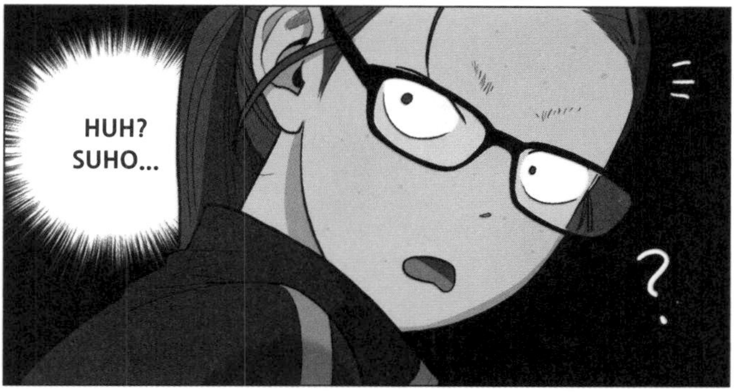
HUH? SUHO...
?

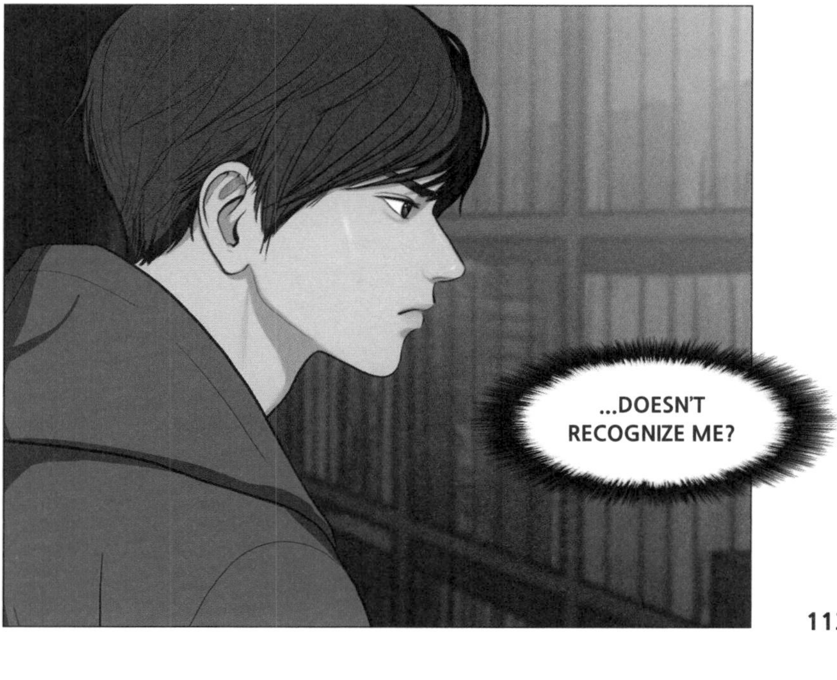
...DOESN'T RECOGNIZE ME?

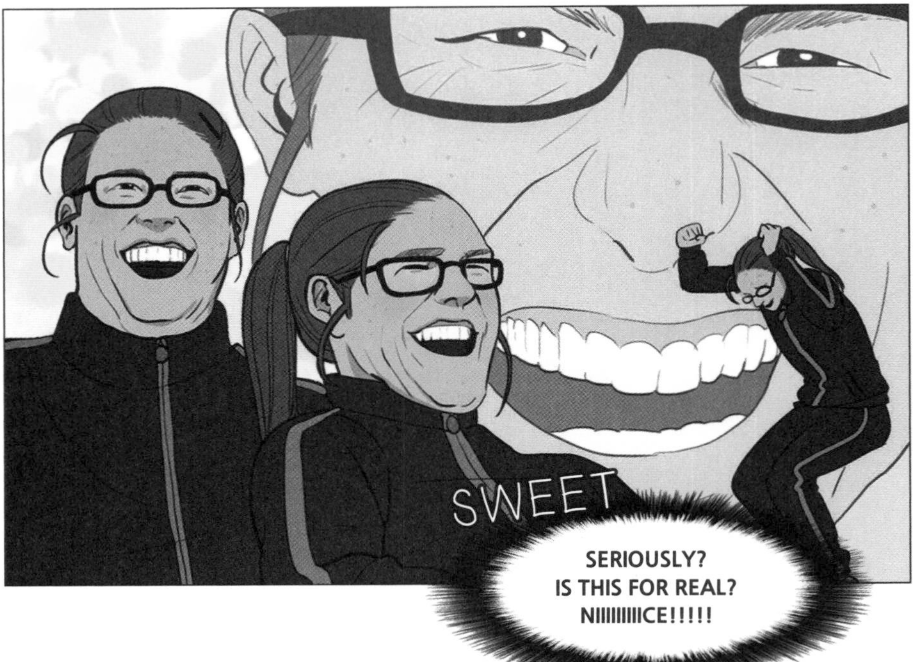
SWEET
SERIOUSLY? IS THIS FOR REAL? NIIIIIIIICE!!!!!

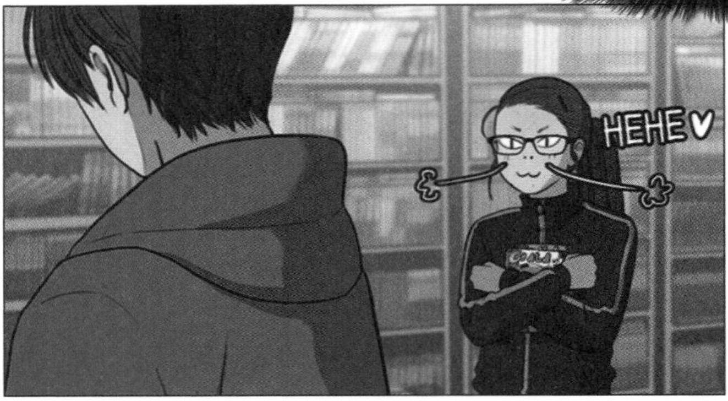
HEHE♥

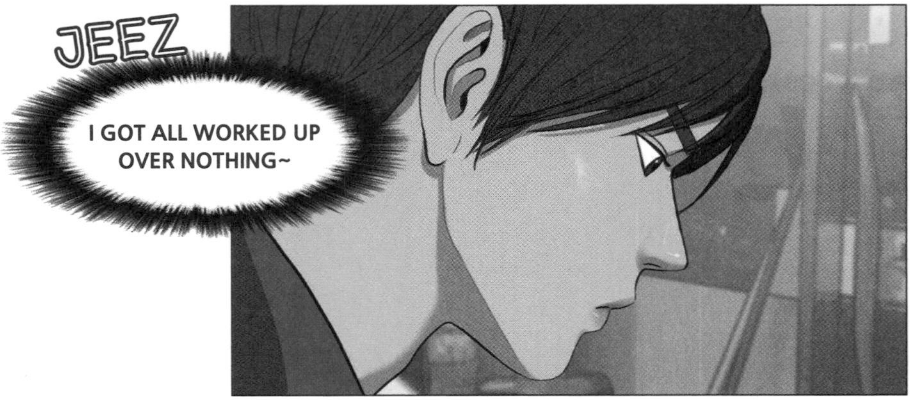
JEEZ
I GOT ALL WORKED UP OVER NOTHING~

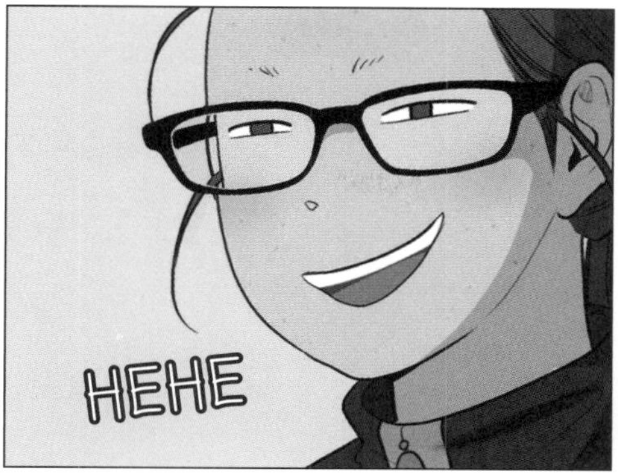
HEHE

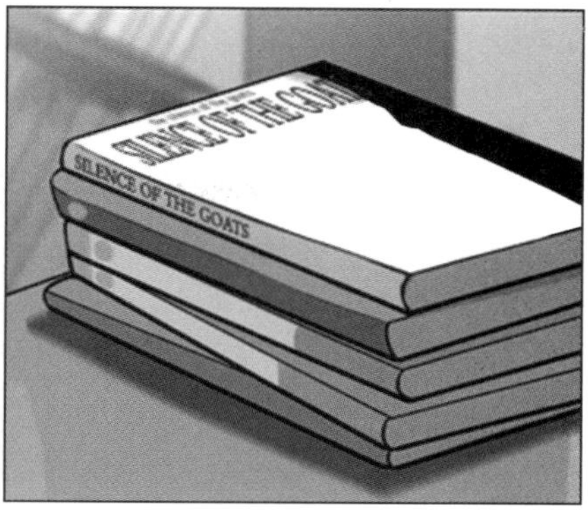
SILENCE OF THE GOATS
SILENCE OF THE GOATS

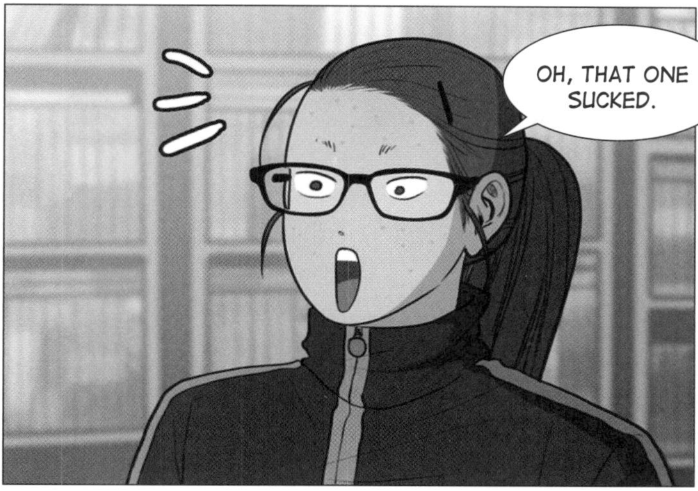
OH, THAT ONE SUCKED.

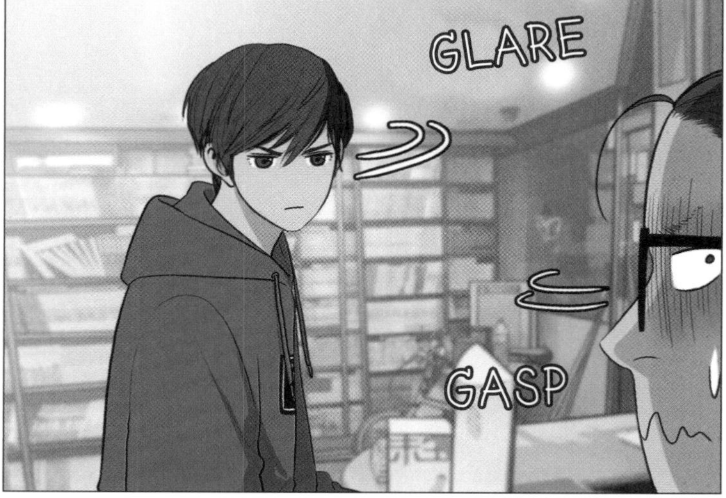
GLARE
GASP

I...I MEAN...IT WAS GOOD AT THE BEGINNING, BUT IT GOES DOWNHILL HALFWAY THROUGH... IF I WERE YOU, I'D READ SOMETHING ELSE...

SSK

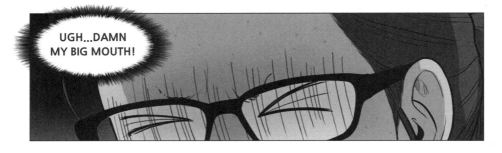

UGH...DAMN MY BIG MOUTH!

THEN...

WHAT WOULD YOU RECOMMEND?

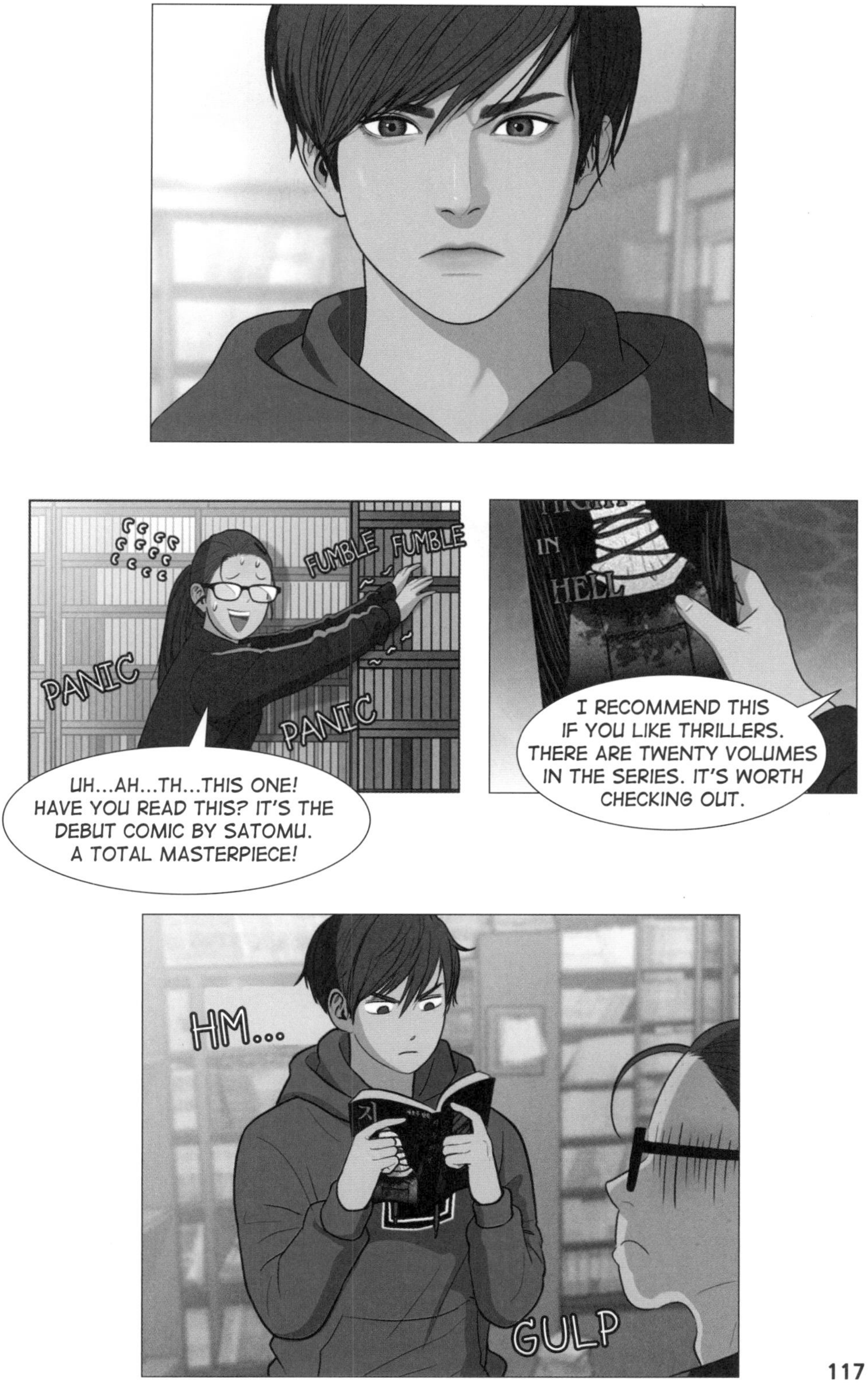
FUMBLE FUMBLE
PANIC
PANIC
UH...AH...TH...THIS ONE! HAVE YOU READ THIS? IT'S THE DEBUT COMIC BY SATOMU. A TOTAL MASTERPIECE!
IN HELL
I RECOMMEND THIS IF YOU LIKE THRILLERS. THERE ARE TWENTY VOLUMES IN THE SERIES. IT'S WORTH CHECKING OUT.
HM...
GULP

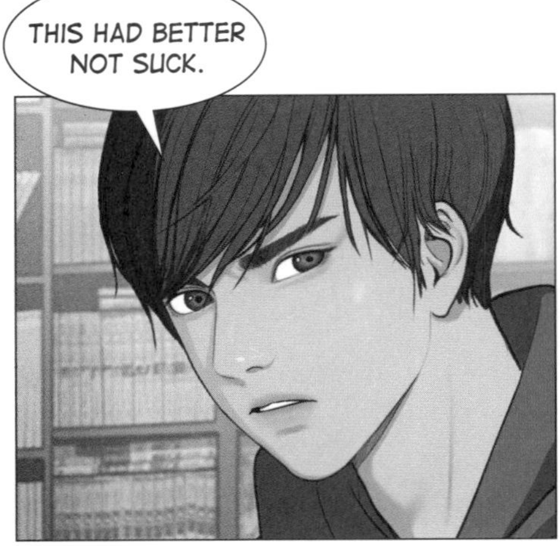
THIS HAD BETTER NOT SUCK.
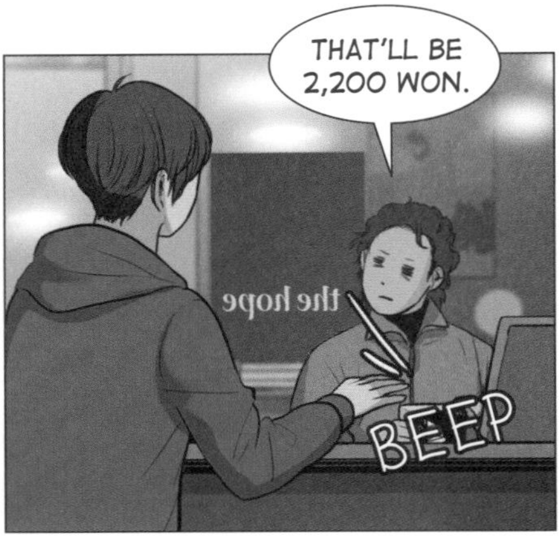
THAT'LL BE 2,200 WON.
the hope
BEEP
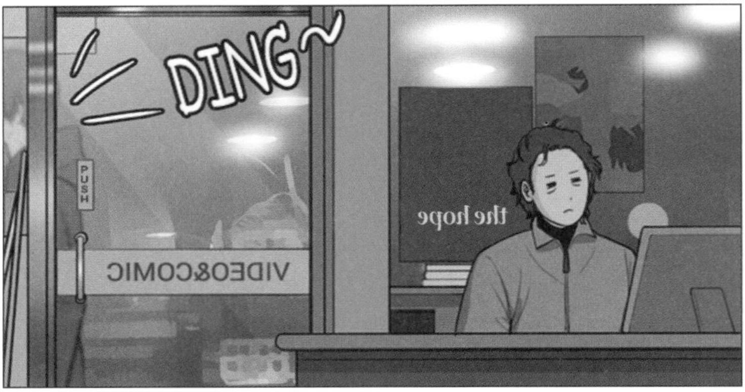
DING~
PUSH
VIDEO&COMIC
the hope
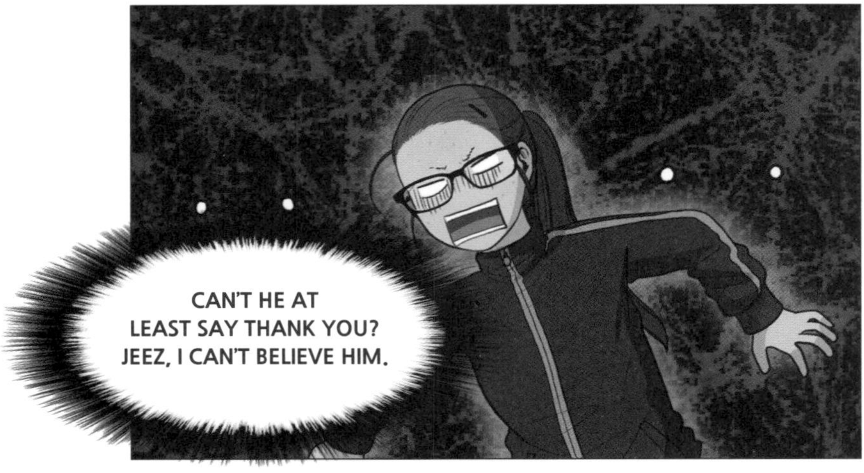
CAN'T HE AT LEAST SAY THANK YOU? JEEZ, I CAN'T BELIEVE HIM.

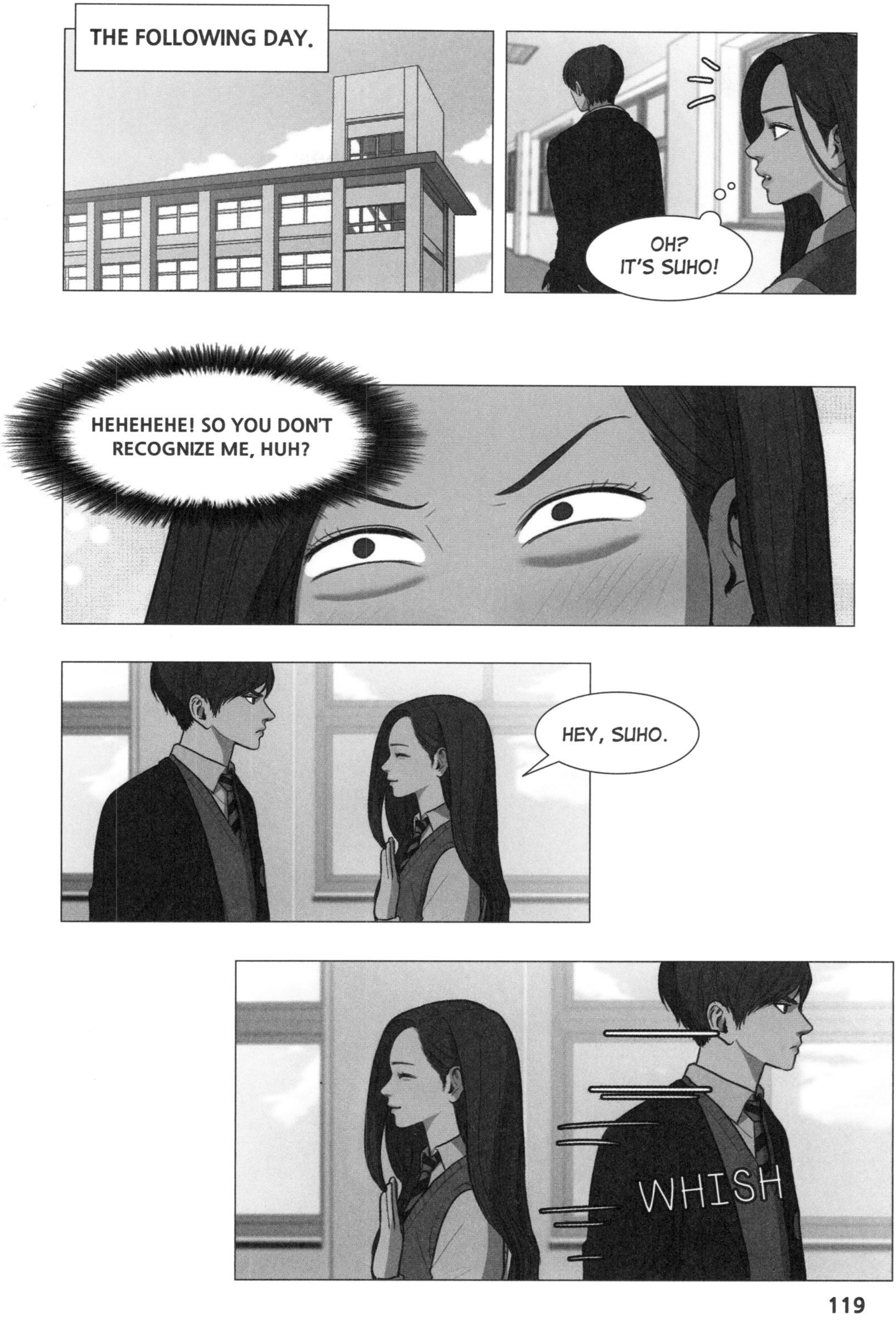
THE FOLLOWING DAY.
OH? IT'S SUHO!
HEHEHEHE! SO YOU DON'T RECOGNIZE ME, HUH?
HEY, SUHO.
WHISH

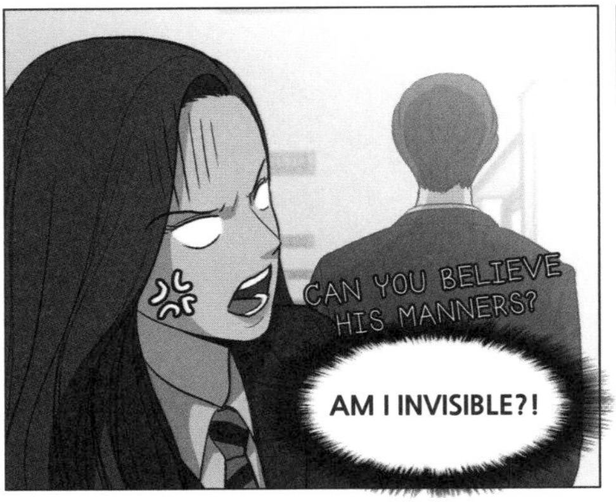
CAN YOU BELIEVE HIS MANNERS?
AM I INVISIBLE?!
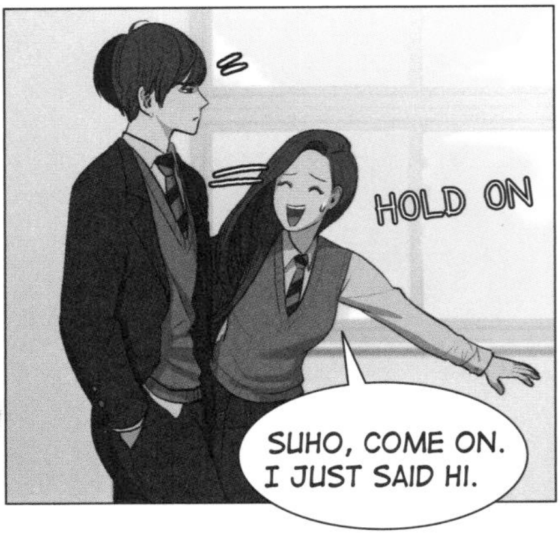
HOLD ON
SUHO, COME ON. I JUST SAID HI.
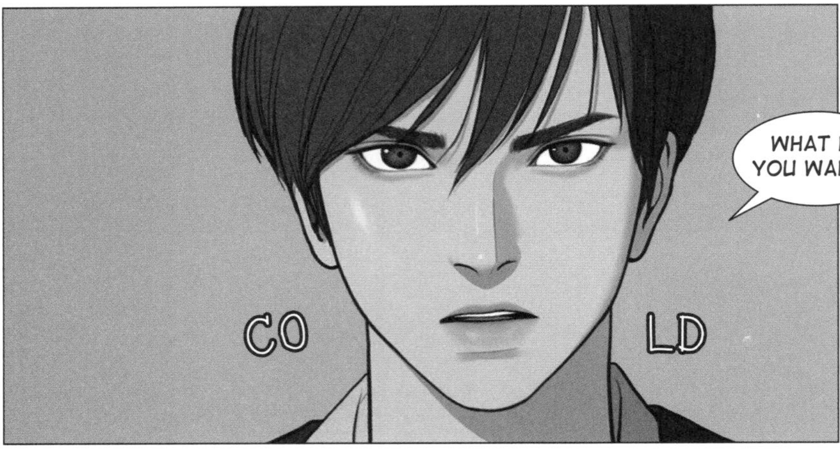
WHAT DO YOU WANT?
CO
LD
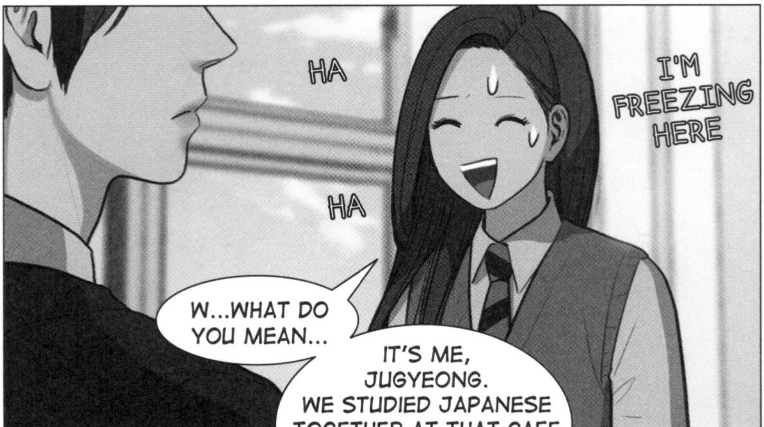
HA
HA
I'M FREEZING HERE
W...WHAT DO YOU MEAN...
IT'S ME, JUGYEONG. WE STUDIED JAPANESE TOGETHER AT THAT CAFE LAST WEEK. DON'T YOU REMEMBER?

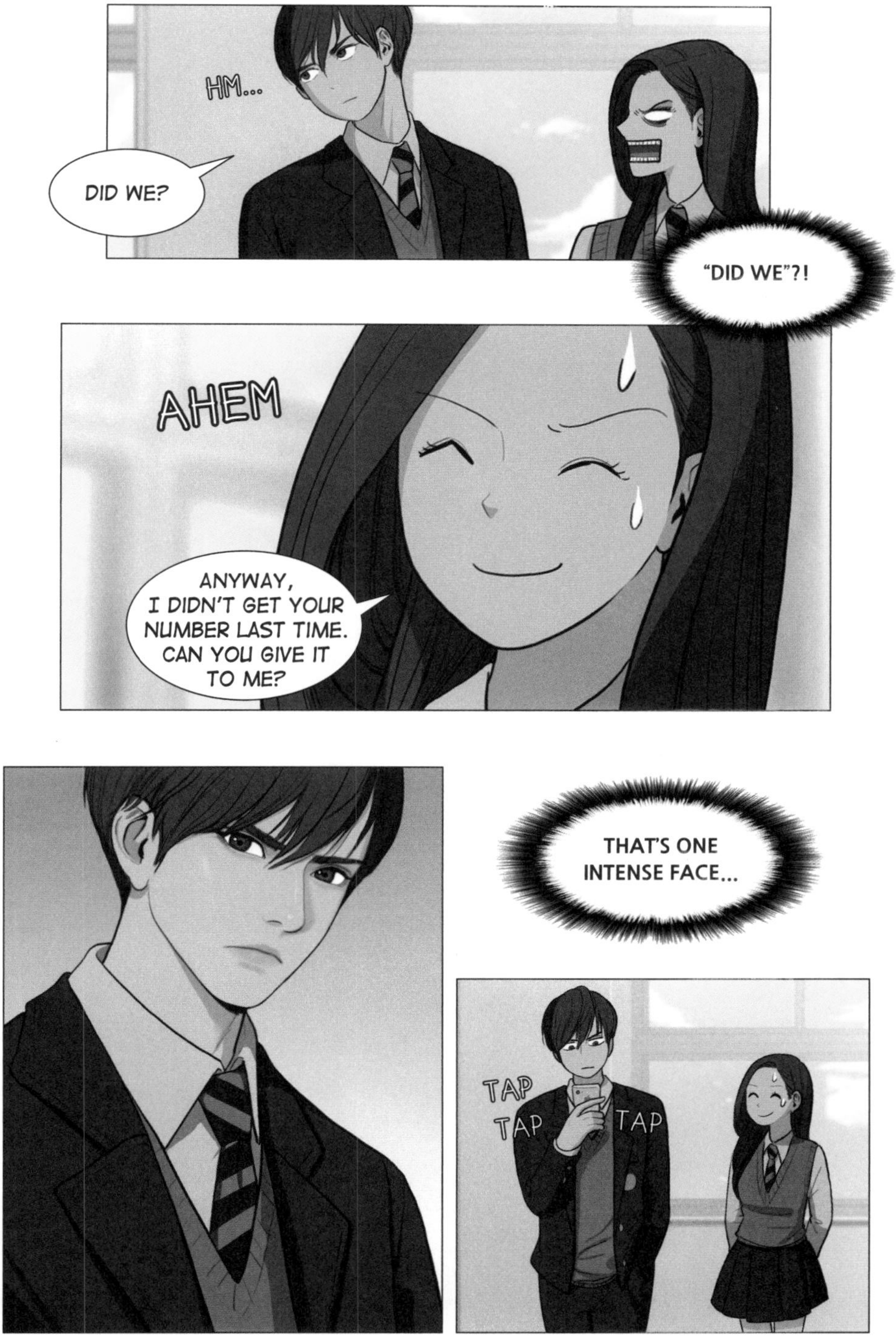
HM...
DID WE?
"DID WE"?!
AHEM
ANYWAY, I DIDN'T GET YOUR NUMBER LAST TIME. CAN YOU GIVE IT TO ME?
THAT'S ONE INTENSE FACE...
TAP
TAP
TAP

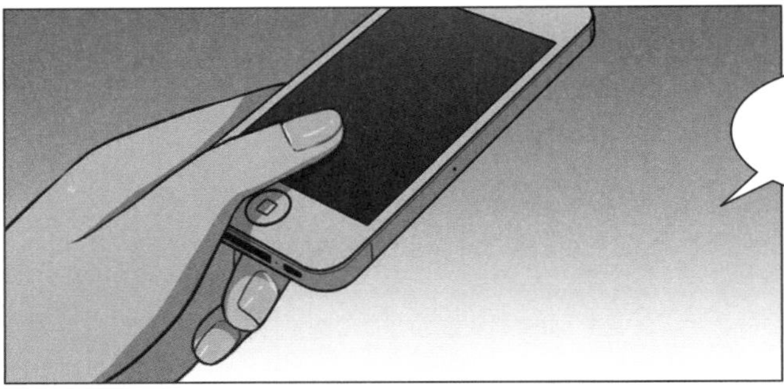
HERE–
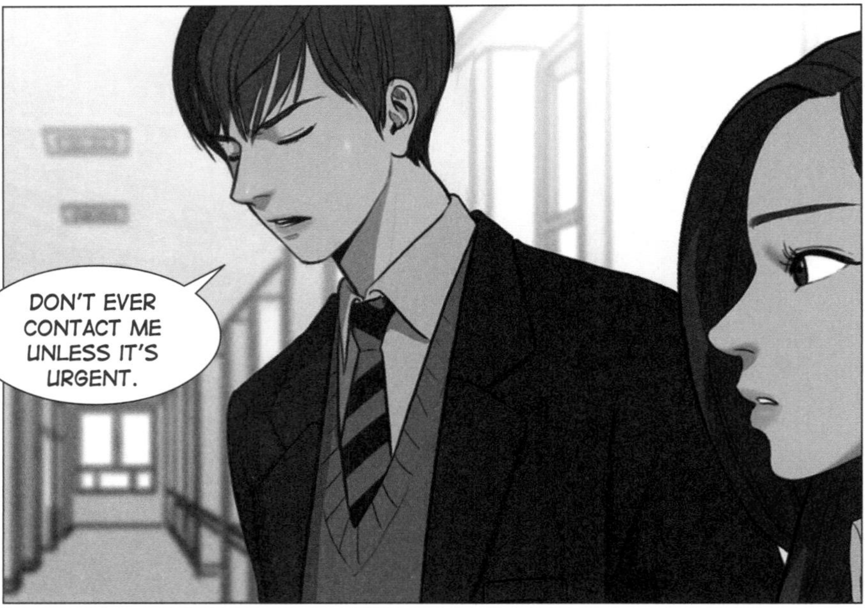
DON'T EVER CONTACT ME UNLESS IT'S URGENT.
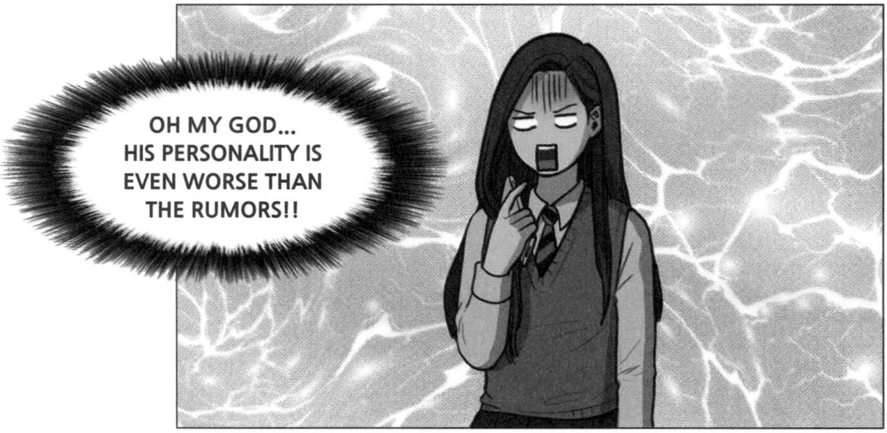
OH MY GOD...
HIS PERSONALITY IS EVEN WORSE THAN THE RUMORS!!

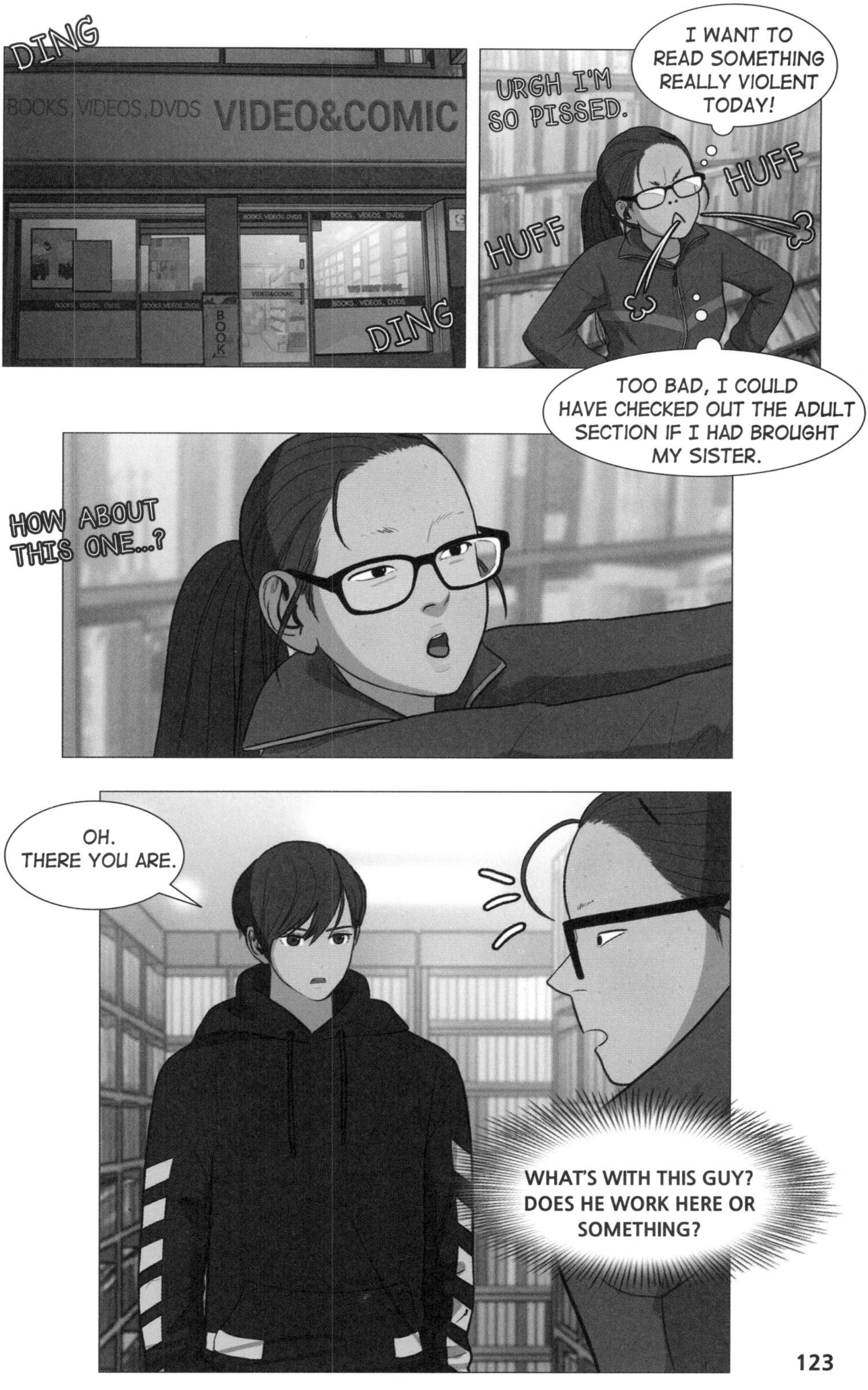
DING
BOOKS, VIDEOS, DVDS
VIDEO&COMIC
BOOK
DING
URGH I'M SO PISSED.
I WANT TO READ SOMETHING REALLY VIOLENT TODAY!
HUFF
HUFF
TOO BAD, I COULD HAVE CHECKED OUT THE ADULT SECTION IF I HAD BROUGHT MY SISTER.
HOW ABOUT THIS ONE...?
OH. THERE YOU ARE.
WHAT'S WITH THIS GUY? DOES HE WORK HERE OR SOMETHING?

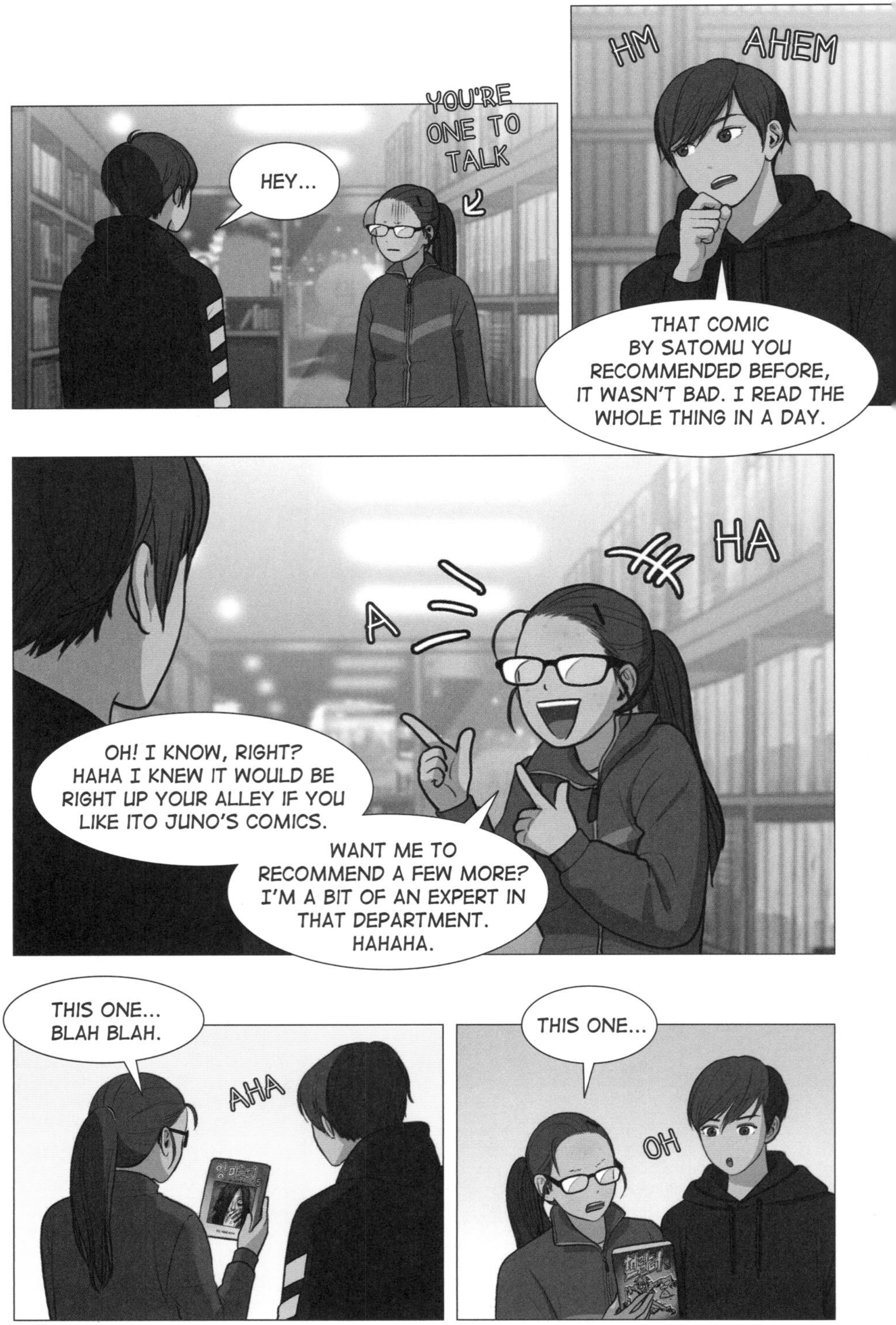
HEY...
YOU'RE ONE TO TALK
HM
AHEM
THAT COMIC BY SATOMU YOU RECOMMENDED BEFORE, IT WASN'T BAD. I READ THE WHOLE THING IN A DAY.
A
HA
OH! I KNOW, RIGHT? HAHA I KNEW IT WOULD BE RIGHT UP YOUR ALLEY IF YOU LIKE ITO JUNO'S COMICS.
WANT ME TO RECOMMEND A FEW MORE? I'M A BIT OF AN EXPERT IN THAT DEPARTMENT. HAHAHA.
THIS ONE... BLAH BLAH.
AHA
THIS ONE...
OH

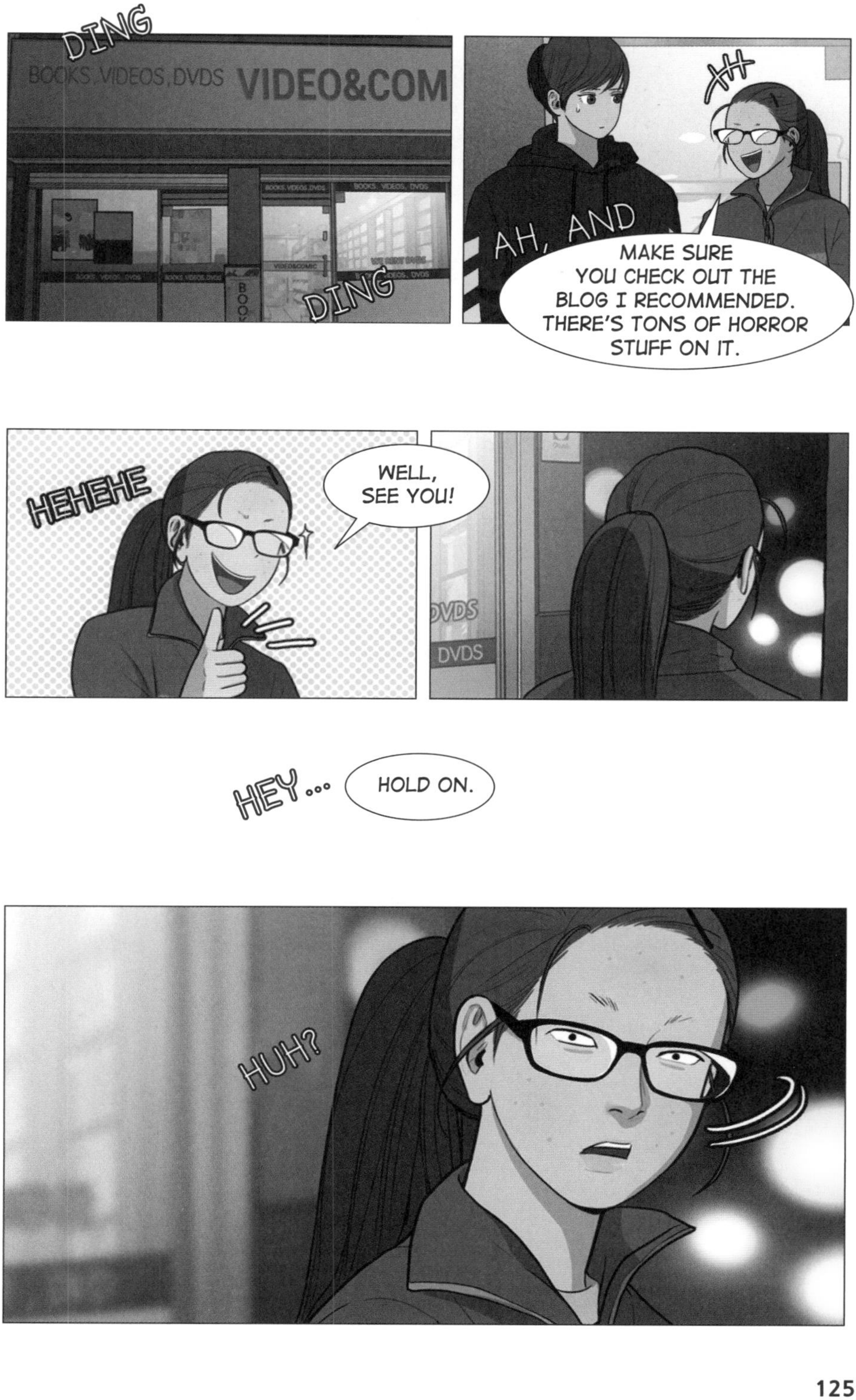
DING
BOOKS, VIDEOS, DVDS VIDEO&COM
DING
AH
AH, AND
MAKE SURE YOU CHECK OUT THE BLOG I RECOMMENDED. THERE'S TONS OF HORROR STUFF ON IT.
HEHEHE
WELL, SEE YOU!
DVDS
DVDS
HEY...
HOLD ON.
HUH?

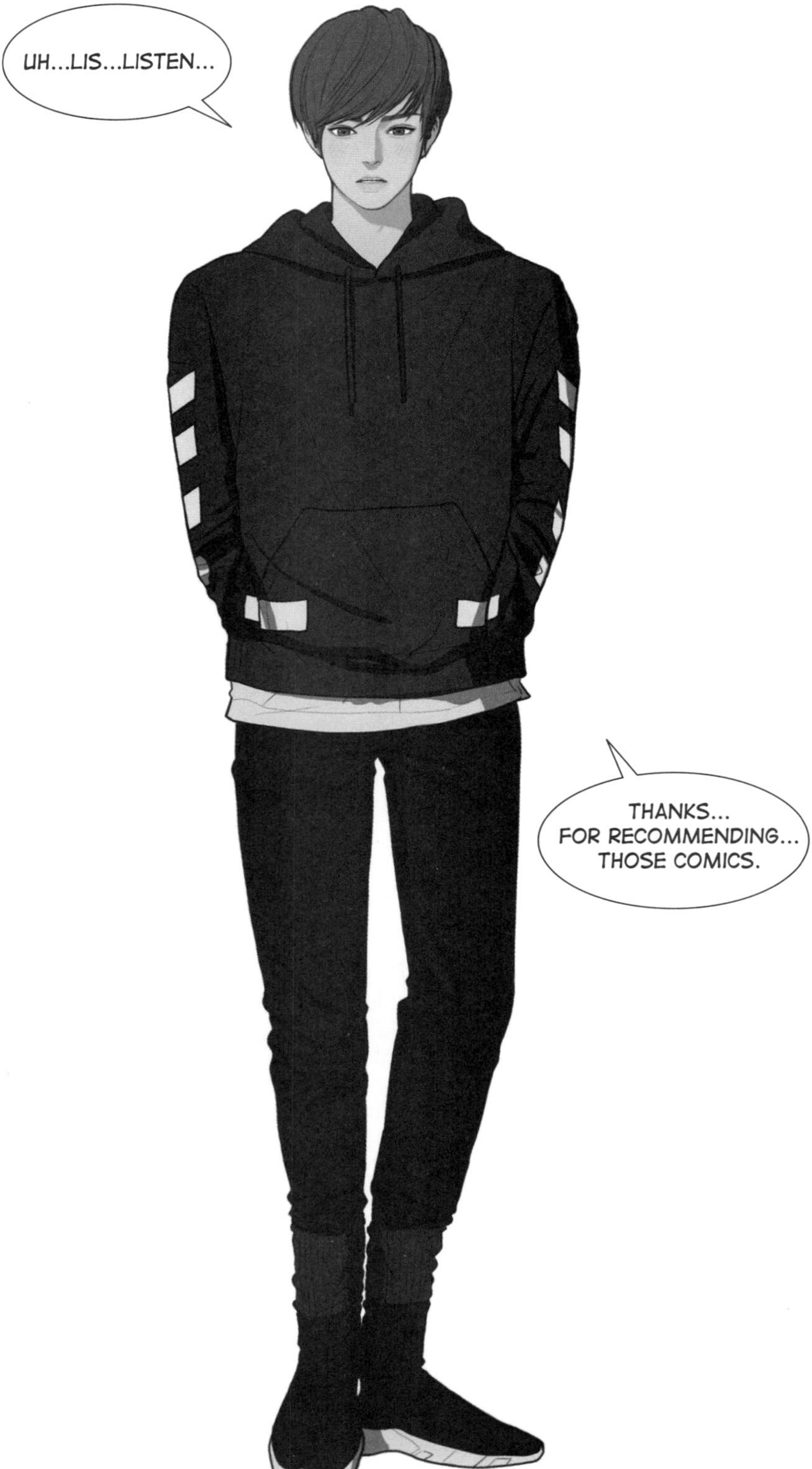
UH...LIS...LISTEN...
THANKS... FOR RECOMMENDING... THOSE COMICS.

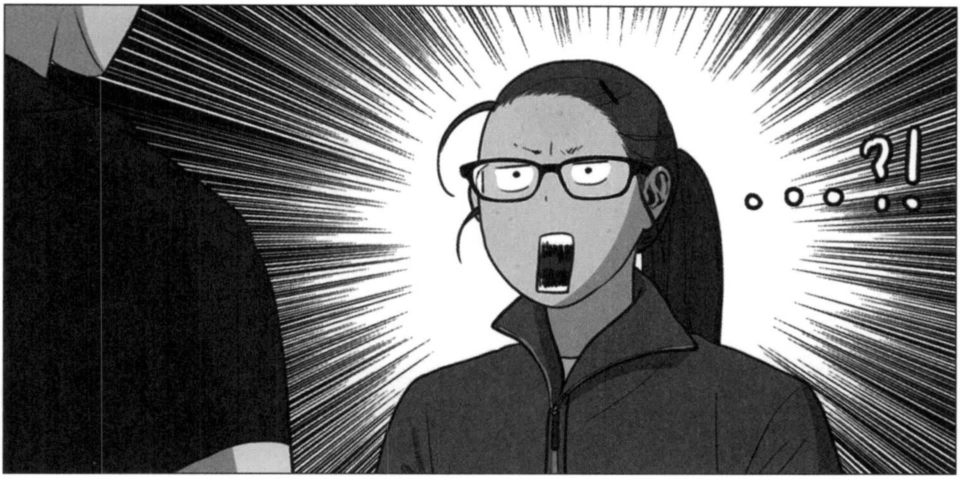
...?!

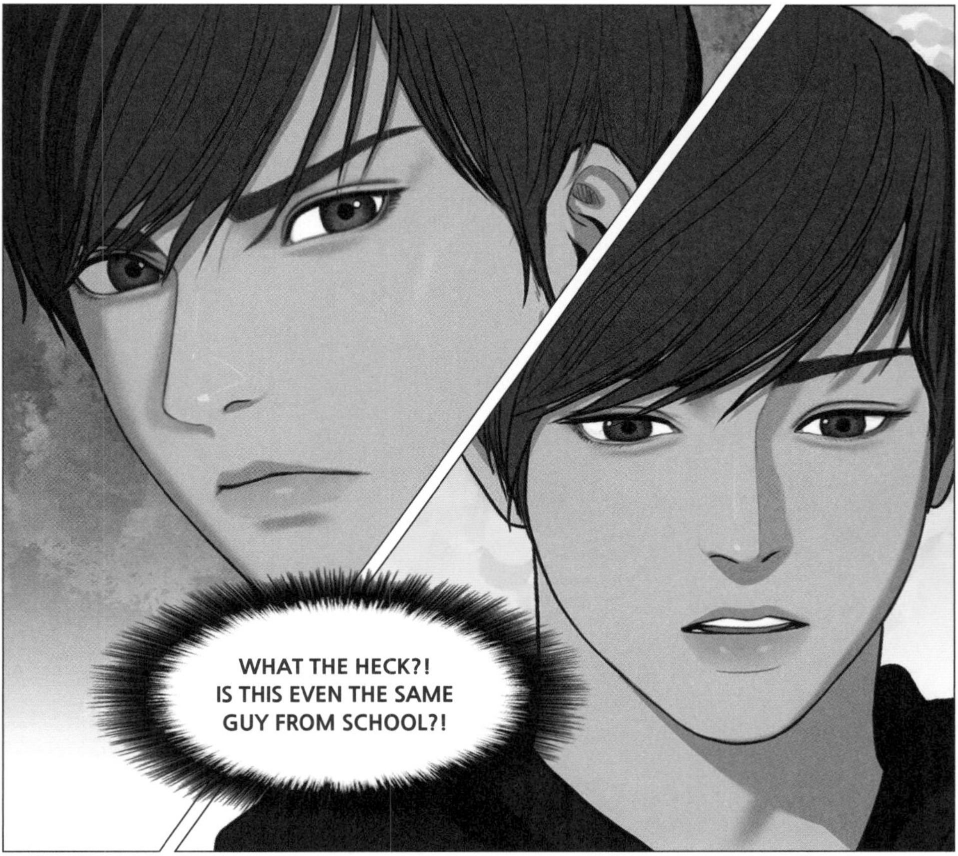
WHAT THE HECK?!
IS THIS EVEN THE SAME
GUY FROM SCHOOL?!

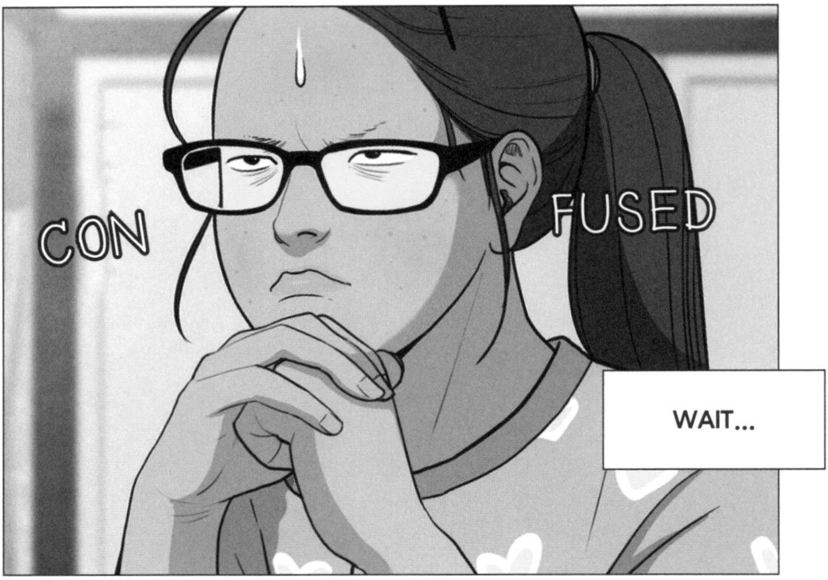
CON
FUSED
WAIT...

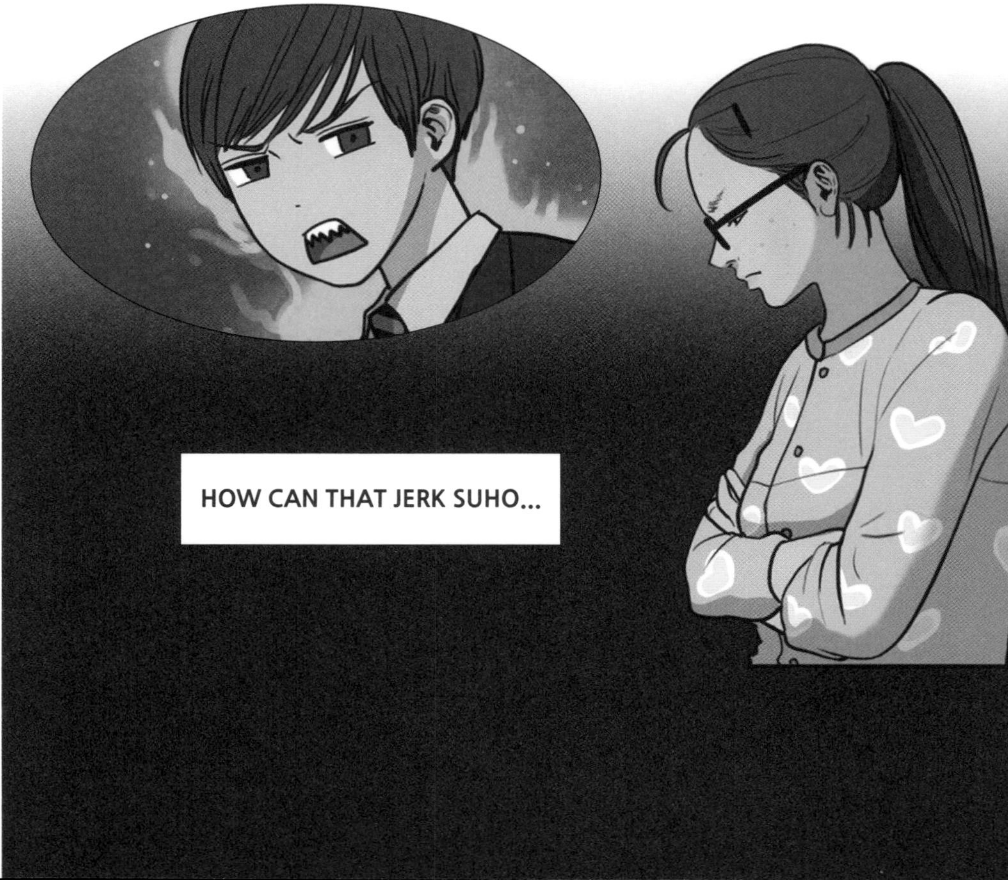
HOW CAN THAT JERK SUHO...

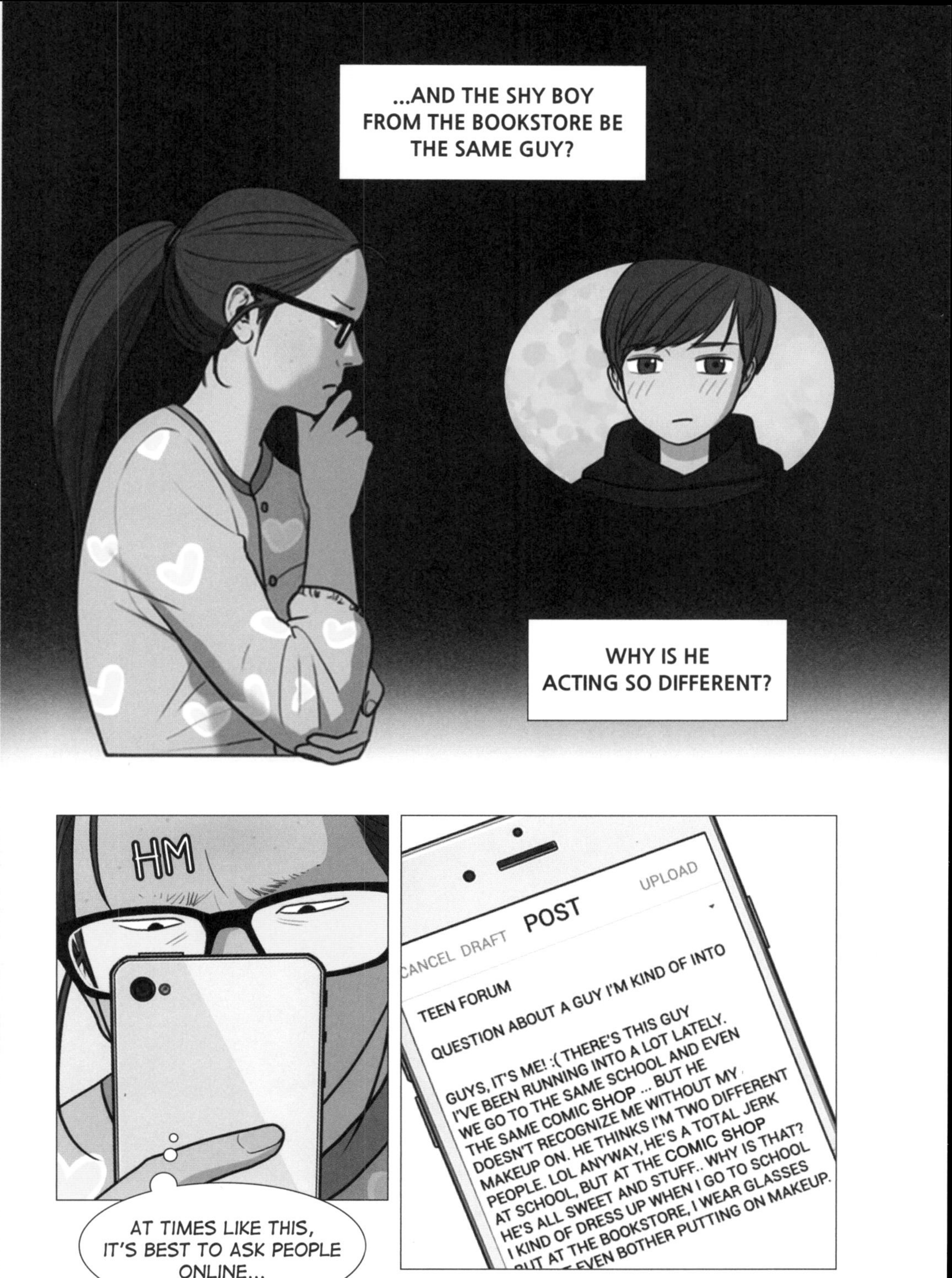
...AND THE SHY BOY FROM THE BOOKSTORE BE THE SAME GUY?
WHY IS HE ACTING SO DIFFERENT?
HM
UPLOAD
CANCEL DRAFT
POST
TEEN FORUM
QUESTION ABOUT A GUY I'M KIND OF INTO
GUYS, IT'S ME! :(THERE'S THIS GUY
I'VE BEEN RUNNING INTO A LOT LATELY.
WE GO TO THE SAME SCHOOL AND EVEN
THE SAME COMIC SHOP ... BUT HE
DOESN'T RECOGNIZE ME WITHOUT MY
MAKEUP ON. HE THINKS I'M TWO DIFFERENT
PEOPLE. LOL ANYWAY, HE'S A TOTAL JERK
AT SCHOOL, BUT AT THE COMIC SHOP
HE'S ALL SWEET AND STUFF.. WHY IS THAT?
I KIND OF DRESS UP WHEN I GO TO SCHOOL
BUT AT THE BOOKSTORE, I WEAR GLASSES
EVEN BOTHER PUTTING ON MAKEUP.
AT TIMES LIKE THIS, IT'S BEST TO ASK PEOPLE ONLINE...

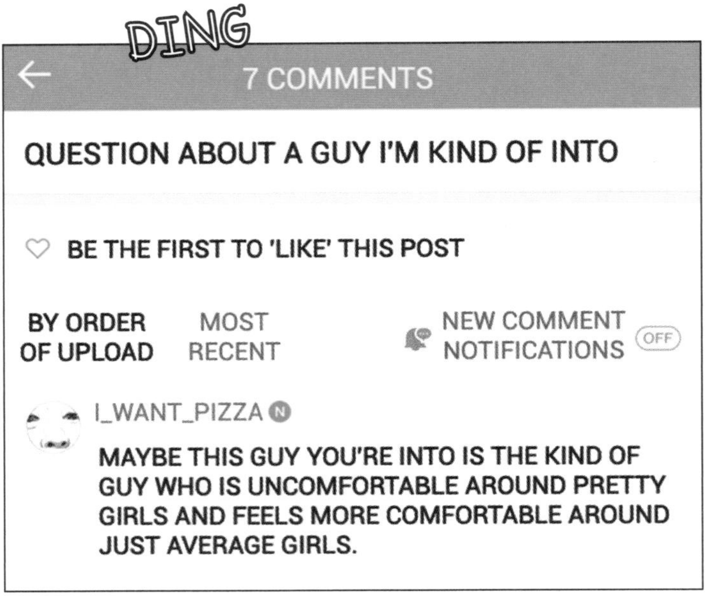
DING
7 COMMENTS
QUESTION ABOUT A GUY I'M KIND OF INTO
BE THE FIRST TO 'LIKE' THIS POST
BY ORDER OF UPLOAD
MOST RECENT
NEW COMMENT NOTIFICATIONS
OFF
I_WANT_PIZZA
MAYBE THIS GUY YOU'RE INTO IS THE KIND OF GUY WHO IS UNCOMFORTABLE AROUND PRETTY GIRLS AND FEELS MORE COMFORTABLE AROUND JUST AVERAGE GIRLS.

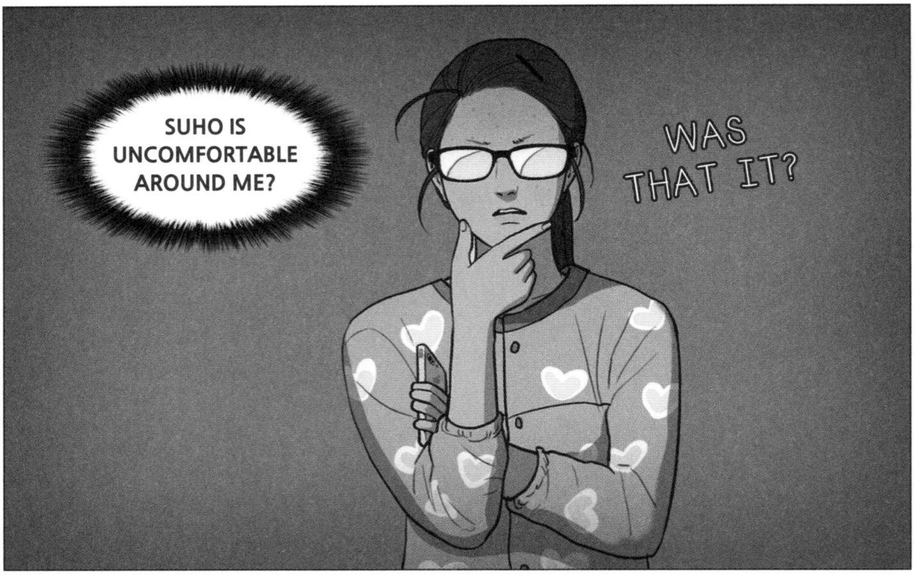
SUHO IS UNCOMFORTABLE AROUND ME?
WAS THAT IT?

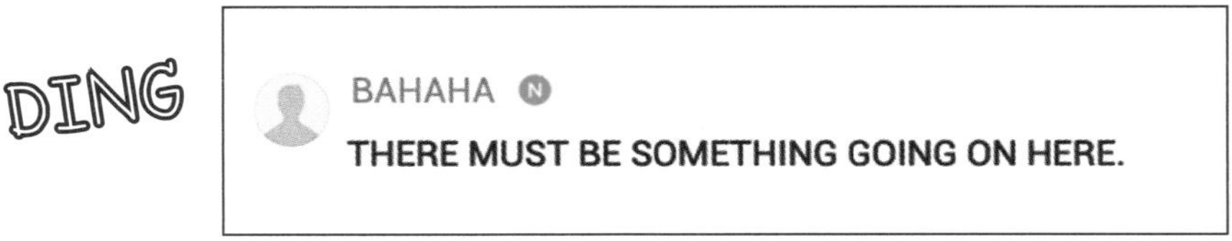
DING
BAHAHA
THERE MUST BE SOMETHING GOING ON HERE.

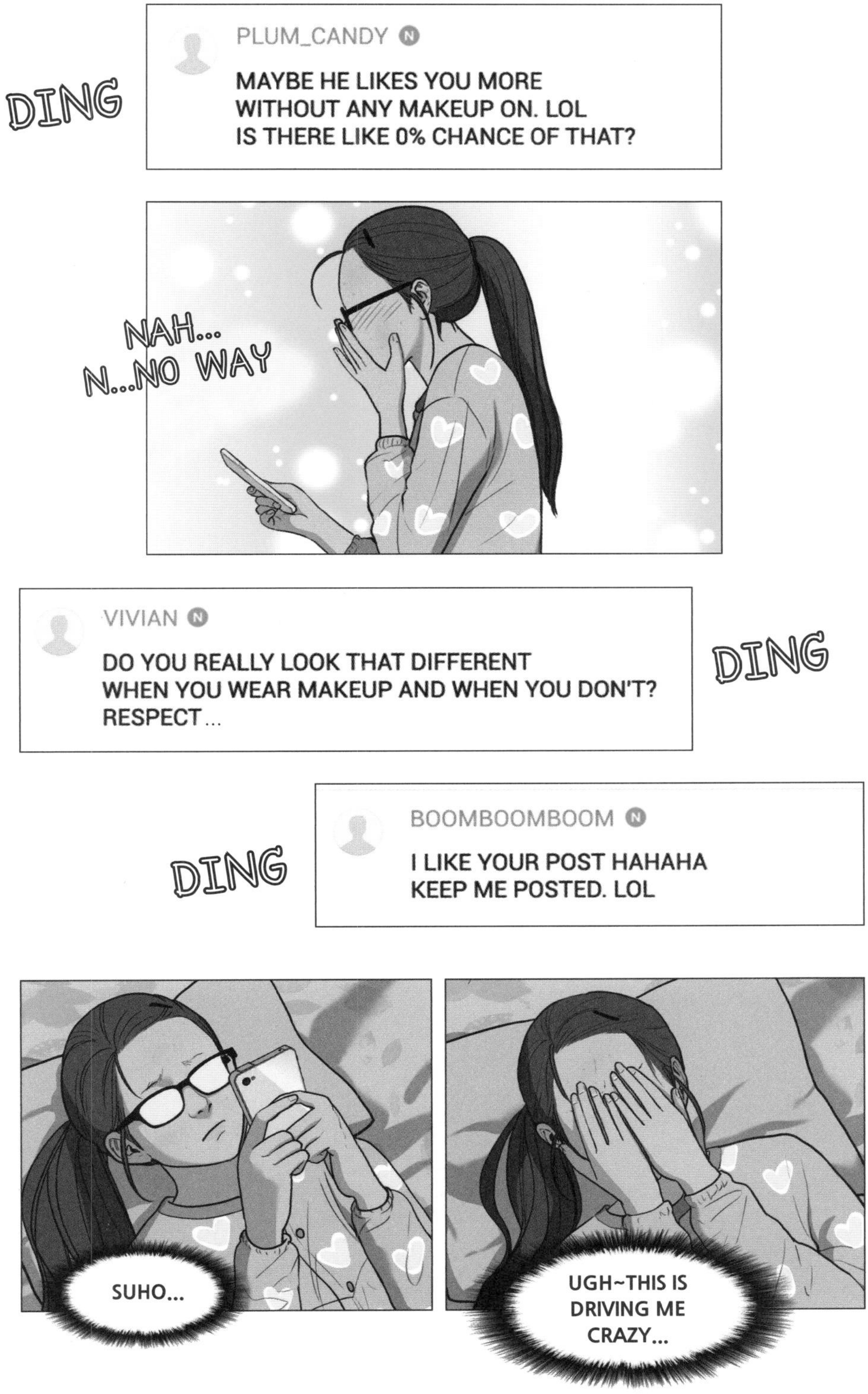
PLUM_CANDY
DING
MAYBE HE LIKES YOU MORE
WITHOUT ANY MAKEUP ON. LOL
IS THERE LIKE 0% CHANCE OF THAT?
NAH...
N...NO WAY
VIVIAN
DO YOU REALLY LOOK THAT DIFFERENT
WHEN YOU WEAR MAKEUP AND WHEN YOU DON'T?
RESPECT...
DING
DING
BOOMBOOMBOOM
I LIKE YOUR POST HAHAHA
KEEP ME POSTED. LOL
SUHO...
UGH~THIS IS DRIVING ME CRAZY...

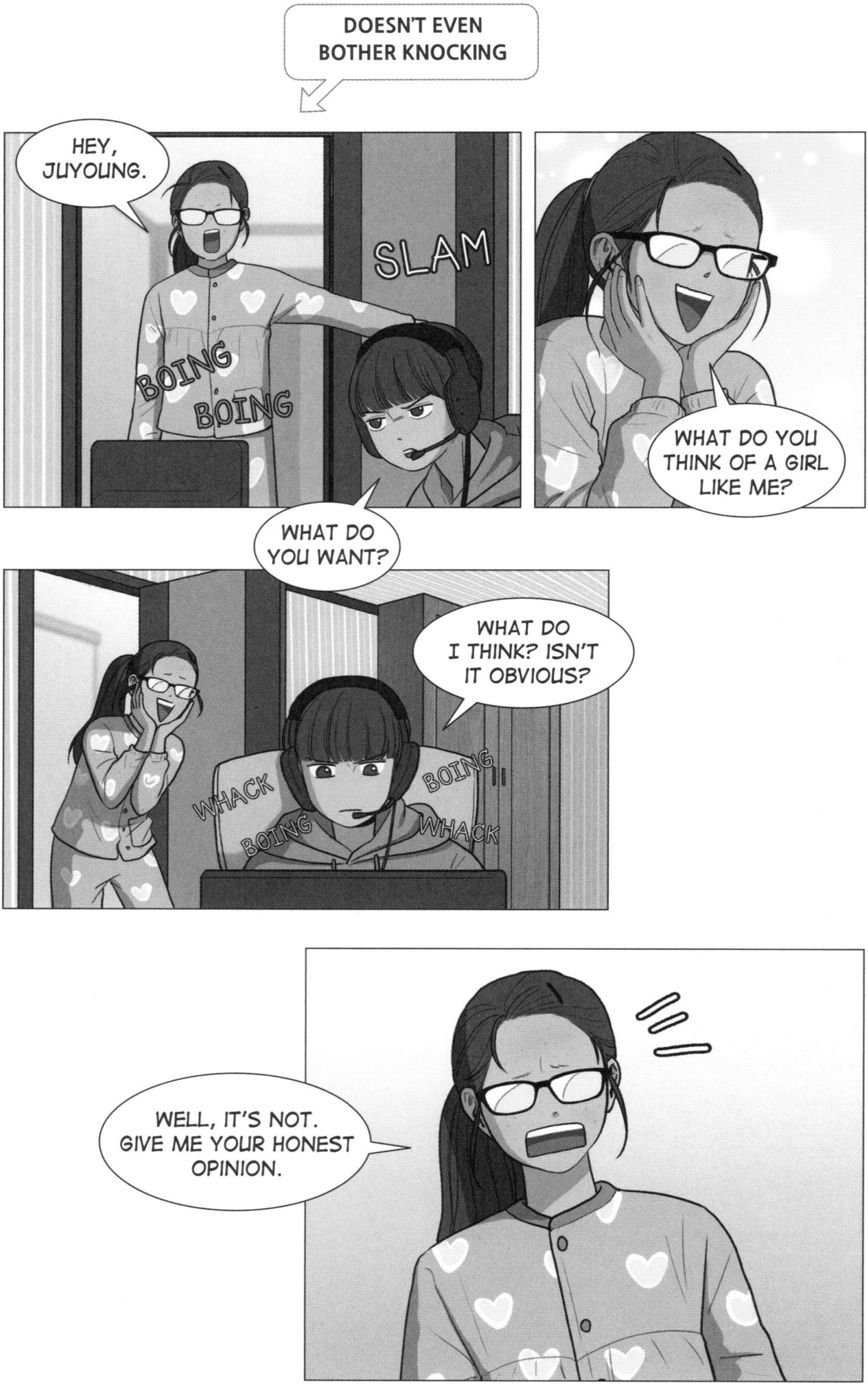
DOESN'T EVEN BOTHER KNOCKING
HEY, JUYOUNG.
SLAM
BOING
BOING
WHAT DO YOU WANT?
WHAT DO YOU THINK OF A GIRL LIKE ME?
WHAT DO I THINK? ISN'T IT OBVIOUS?
WHACK
BOING
BOING
WHACK
WELL, IT'S NOT. GIVE ME YOUR HONEST OPINION.

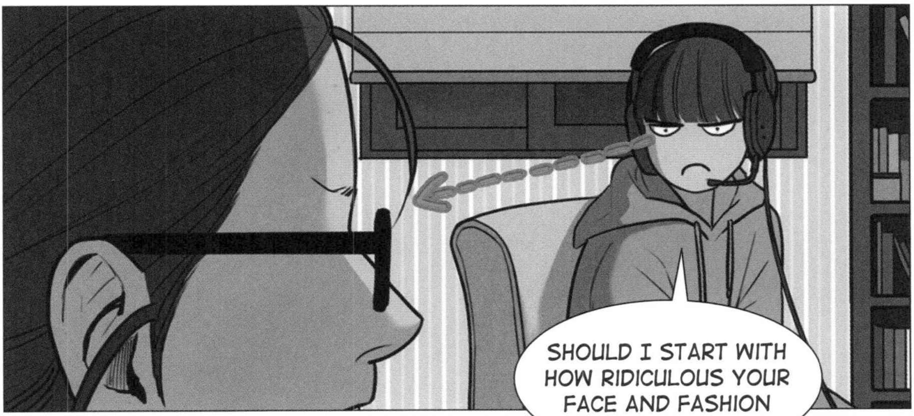
SHOULD I START WITH HOW RIDICULOUS YOUR FACE AND FASHION SENSE ARE?
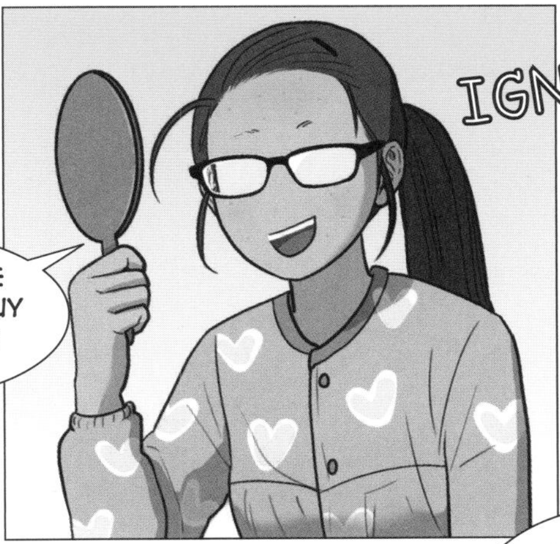
IGNORED
THERE MUST BE AT LEAST ONE GUY WHO FINDS ME ATTRACTIVE.
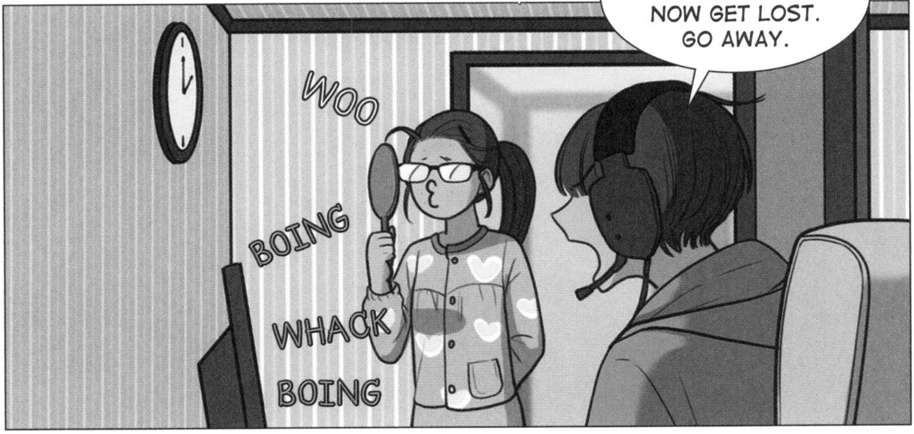
NOPE. NOT IN A MILLION YEARS. NOW GET LOST. GO AWAY.
WOO
BOING
WHACK
BOING

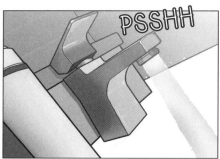

AS ANNOYING AS IT MAY BE,
JUYOUNG IS RIGHT.

WIPE

THINKING THAT
SOMEONE MIGHT ACTUALLY
LIKE ME LOOKING LIKE THIS...

DAMN THIS ACNE.

...IT REMINDS ME OF EVERYTHING
I'VE BEEN THROUGH.

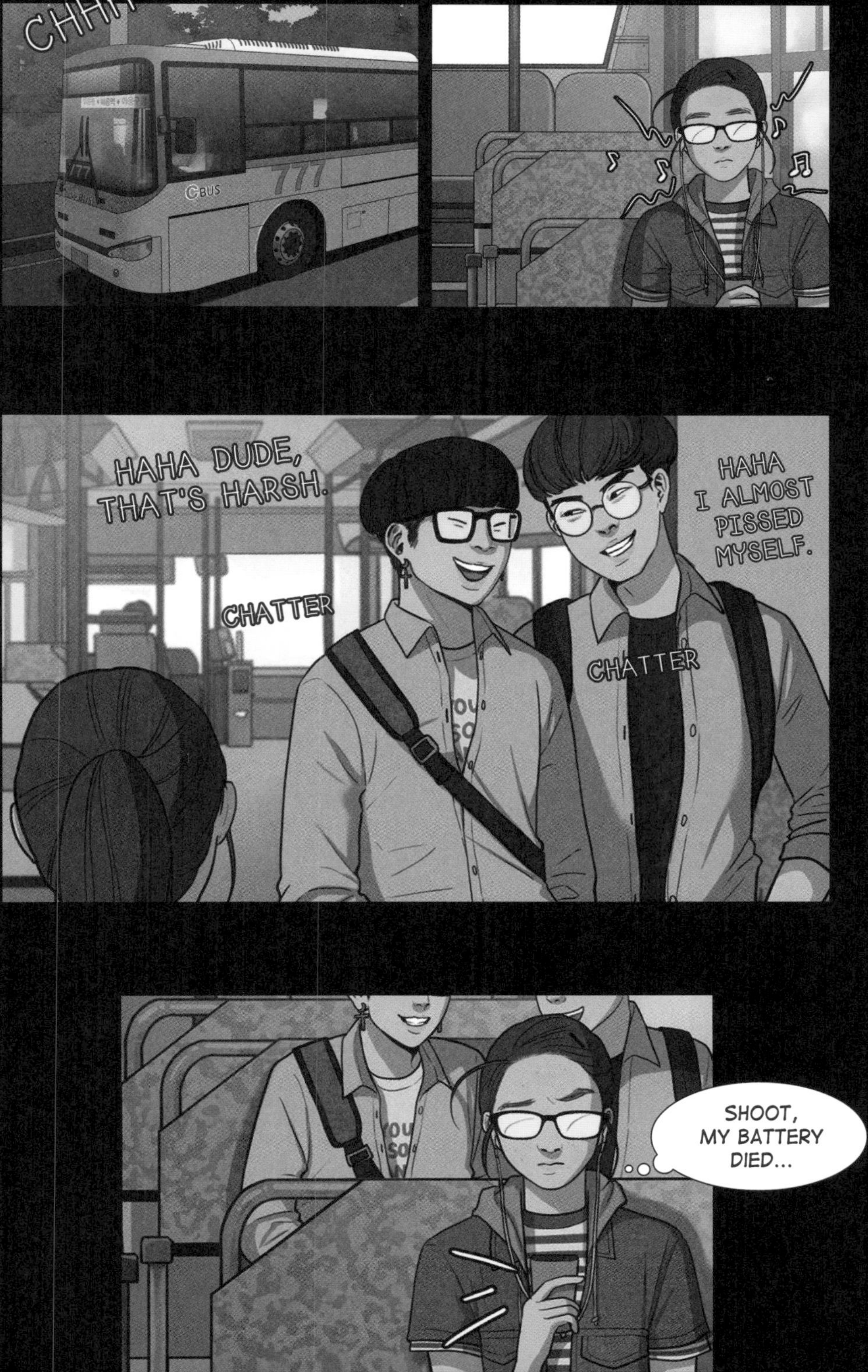

CHHH
777
HAHA DUDE, THAT'S HARSH.
CHATTER
CHATTER
HAHA I ALMOST PISSED MYSELF.
SHOOT, MY BATTERY DIED...

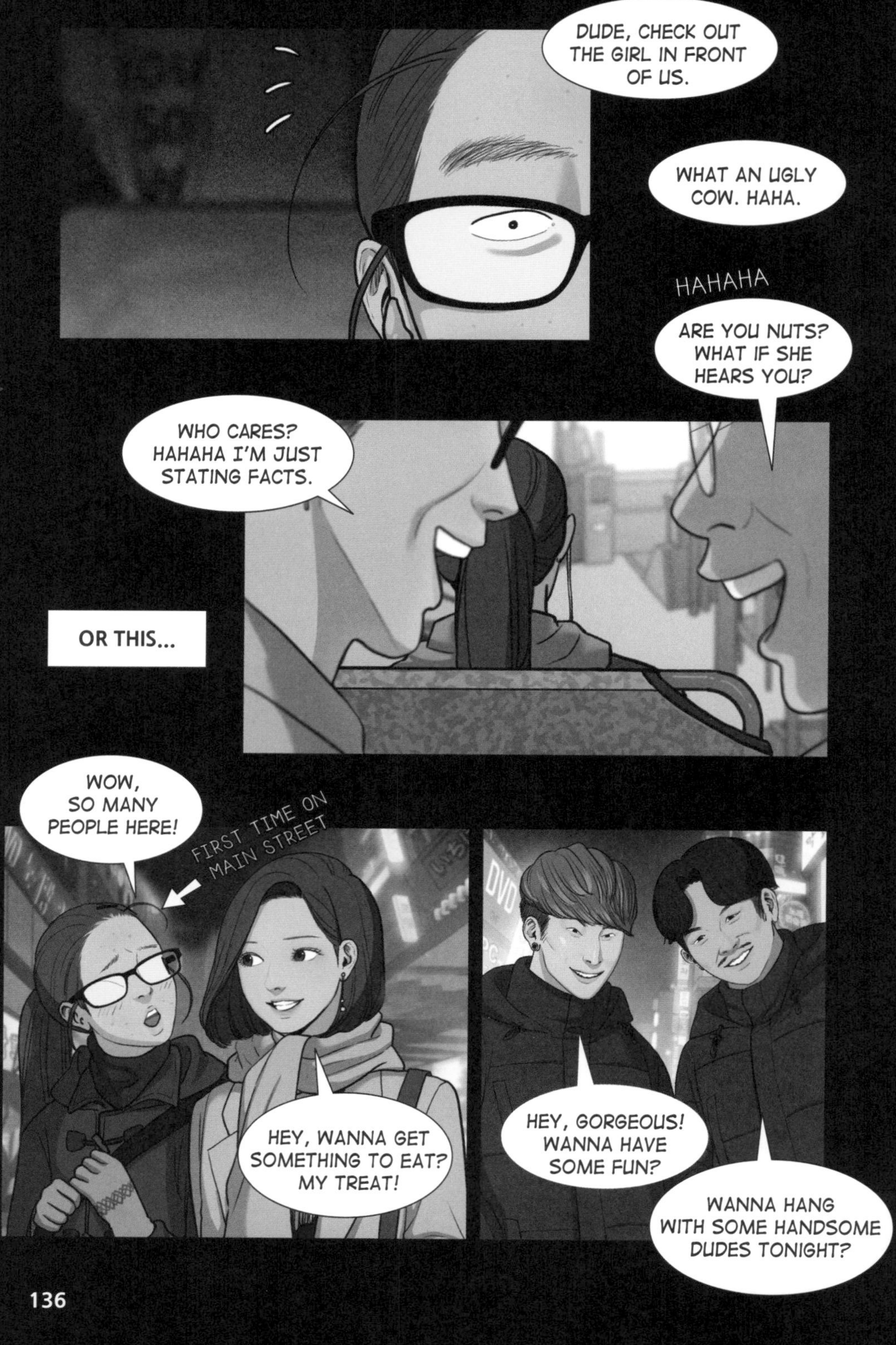
DUDE, CHECK OUT THE GIRL IN FRONT OF US.
WHAT AN UGLY COW. HAHA.
HAHAHA
ARE YOU NUTS? WHAT IF SHE HEARS YOU?
WHO CARES? HAHAHA I'M JUST STATING FACTS.
OR THIS...
WOW, SO MANY PEOPLE HERE!
FIRST TIME ON MAIN STREET
HEY, WANNA GET SOMETHING TO EAT? MY TREAT!
HEY, GORGEOUS! WANNA HAVE SOME FUN?
WANNA HANG WITH SOME HANDSOME DUDES TONIGHT?

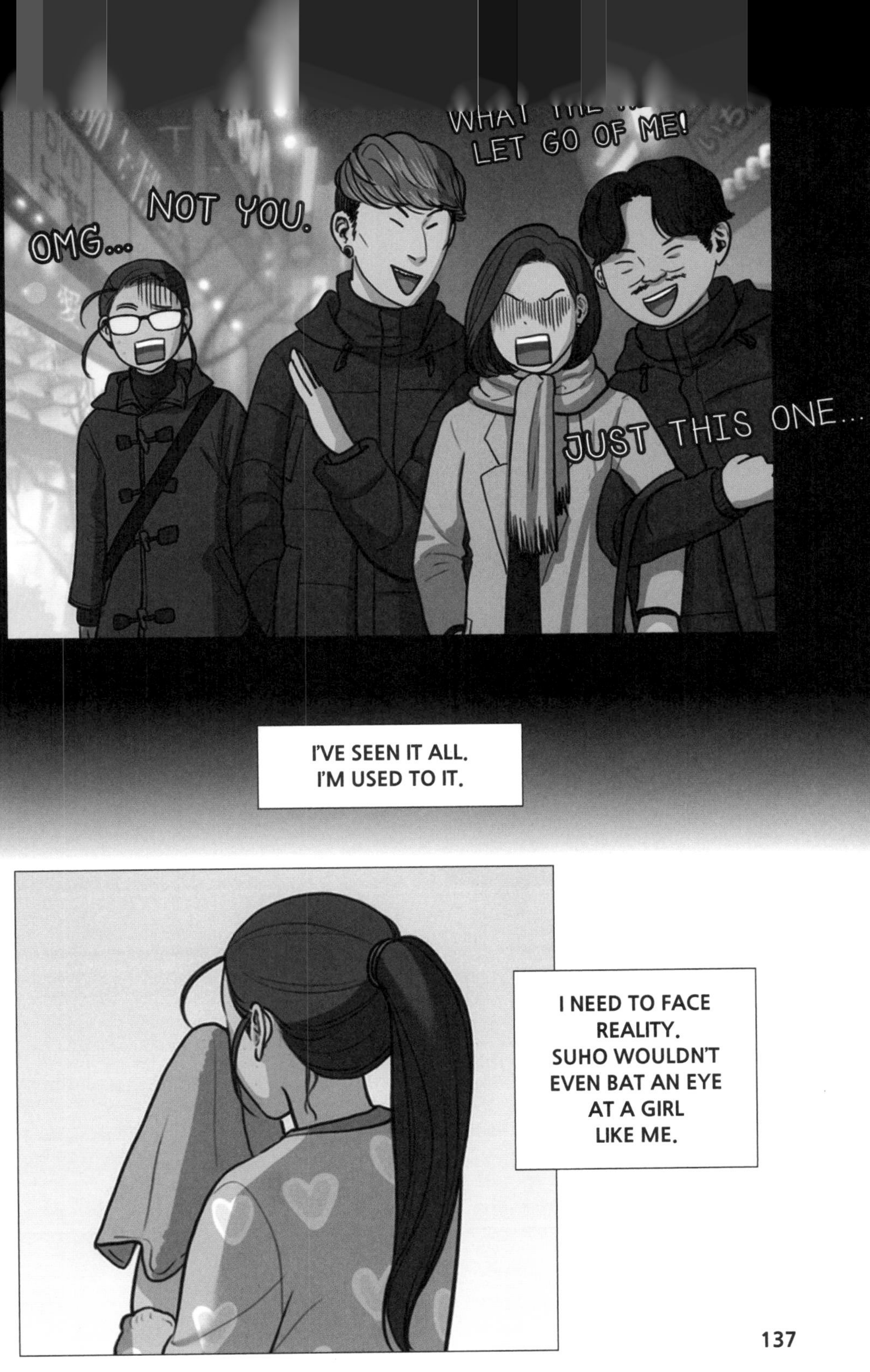
OMG...
NOT YOU.
LET GO OF ME!
JUST THIS ONE...
I'VE SEEN IT ALL.
I'M USED TO IT.
I NEED TO FACE REALITY.
SUHO WOULDN'T EVEN BAT AN EYE AT A GIRL LIKE ME.

BOOKS, VIDEOS, DVDS VIDEO&COM
WHAT?!?!
GASP
TH...THIS IS FOR ME??
YEAH.
YOU KNOW THAT TALL,
FOREIGN-LOOKING KID?
HE TOLD ME TO
GIVE THIS TO THE "PIMPLY
GIRL IN GLASSES AND A
SWEAT SUIT" WHO COMES
HERE EVERY DAY. YOU FIT
THE DESCRIPTION.

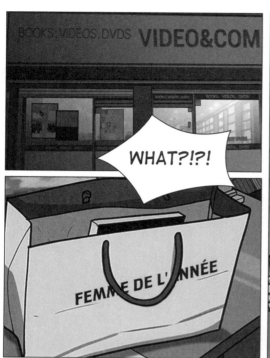

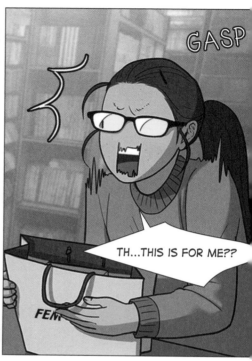

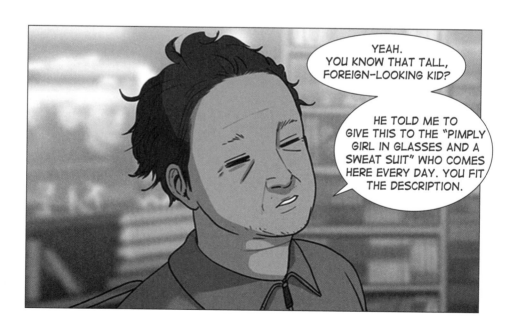

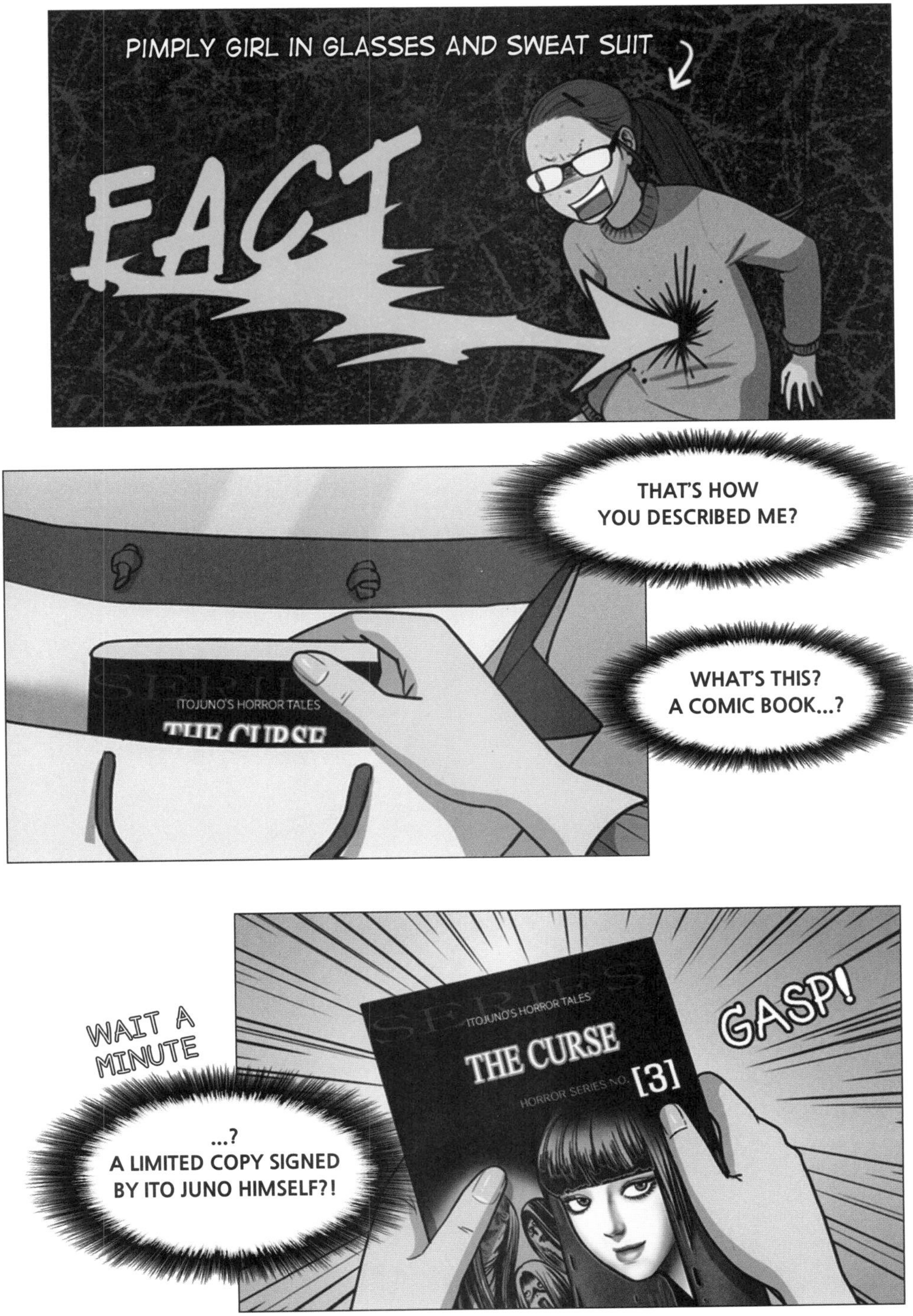
PIMPLY GIRL IN GLASSES AND SWEAT SUIT
FACT
THAT'S HOW YOU DESCRIBED ME?
ITOJUNO'S HORROR TALES
WHAT'S THIS? A COMIC BOOK...?
WAIT A MINUTE
...? A LIMITED COPY SIGNED BY ITO JUNO HIMSELF?!
ITOJUNO'S HORROR TALES
THE CURSE
HORROR SERIES NO. [3]
GASP!

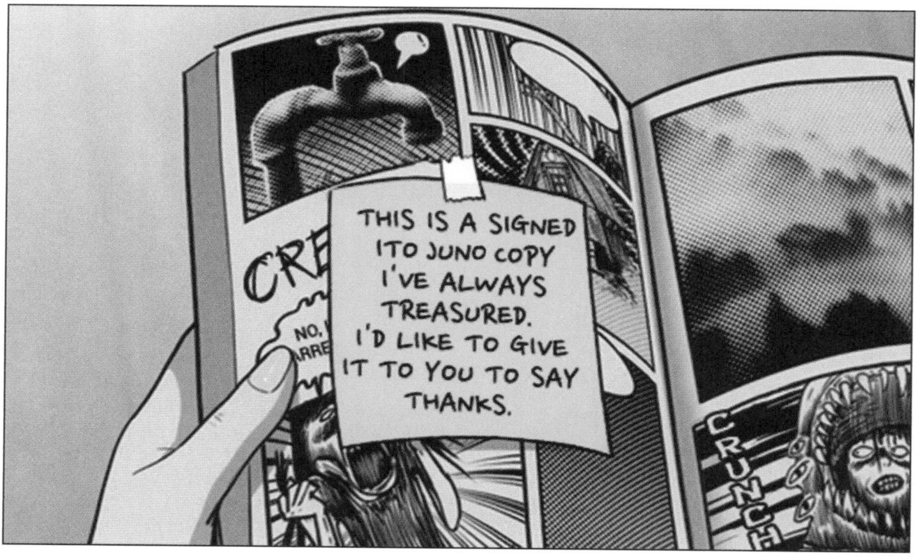
THIS IS A SIGNED ITO JUNO COPY I'VE ALWAYS TREASURED. I'D LIKE TO GIVE IT TO YOU TO SAY THANKS.
CRUNCH

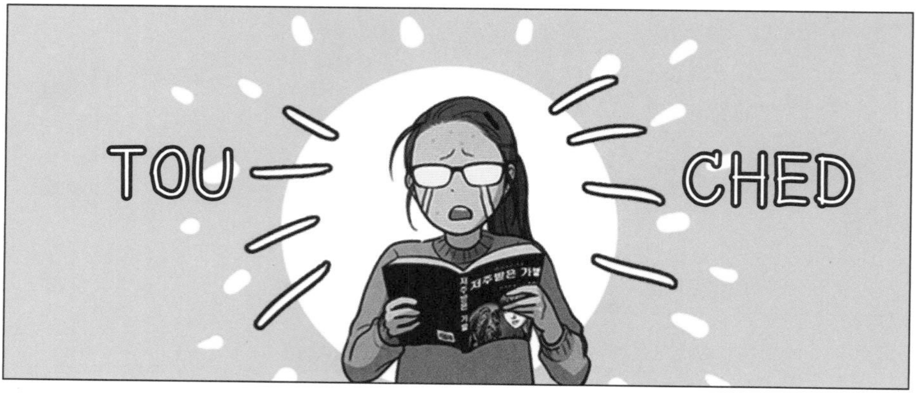
TOU
CHED
저주받은 거울

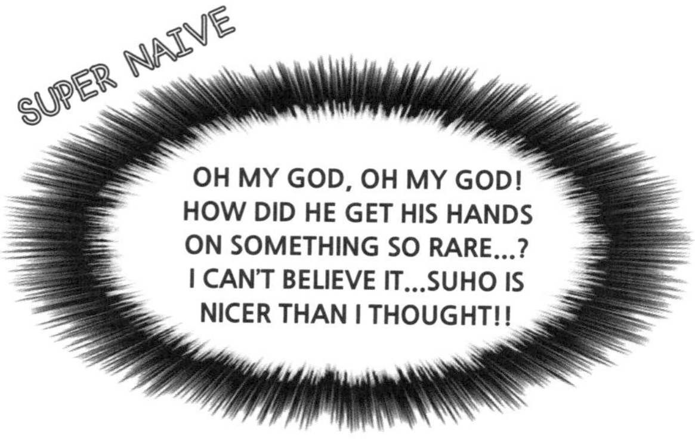
SUPER NAIVE
OH MY GOD, OH MY GOD! HOW DID HE GET HIS HANDS ON SOMETHING SO RARE...? I CAN'T BELIEVE IT...SUHO IS NICER THAN I THOUGHT!!

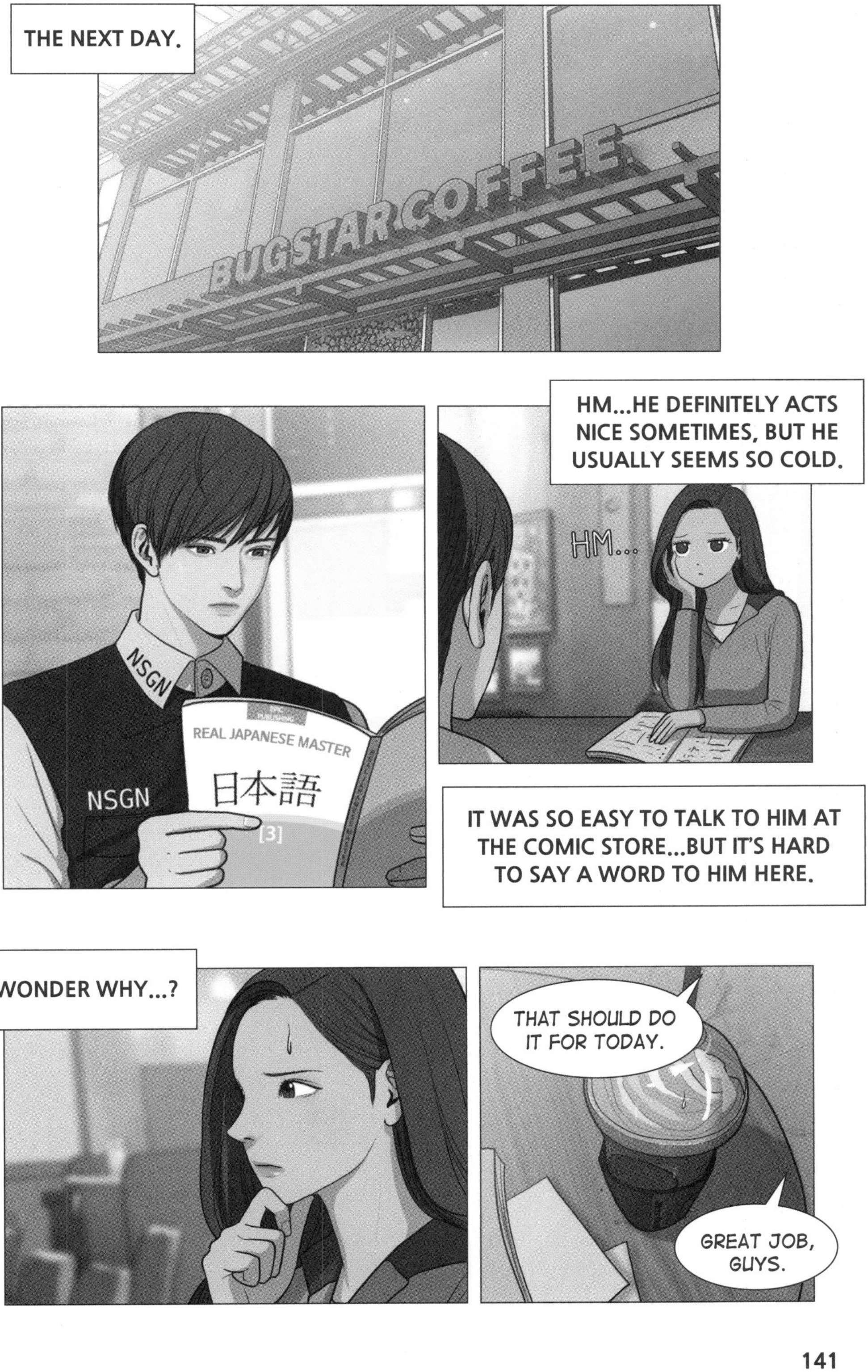
THE NEXT DAY.
BUGSTAR COFFEE
NSGN
REAL JAPANESE MASTER
日本語
[3]
NSGN
HM...HE DEFINITELY ACTS NICE SOMETIMES, BUT HE USUALLY SEEMS SO COLD.
HM...
IT WAS SO EASY TO TALK TO HIM AT THE COMIC STORE...BUT IT'S HARD TO SAY A WORD TO HIM HERE.
I WONDER WHY...?
THAT SHOULD DO IT FOR TODAY.
GREAT JOB, GUYS.

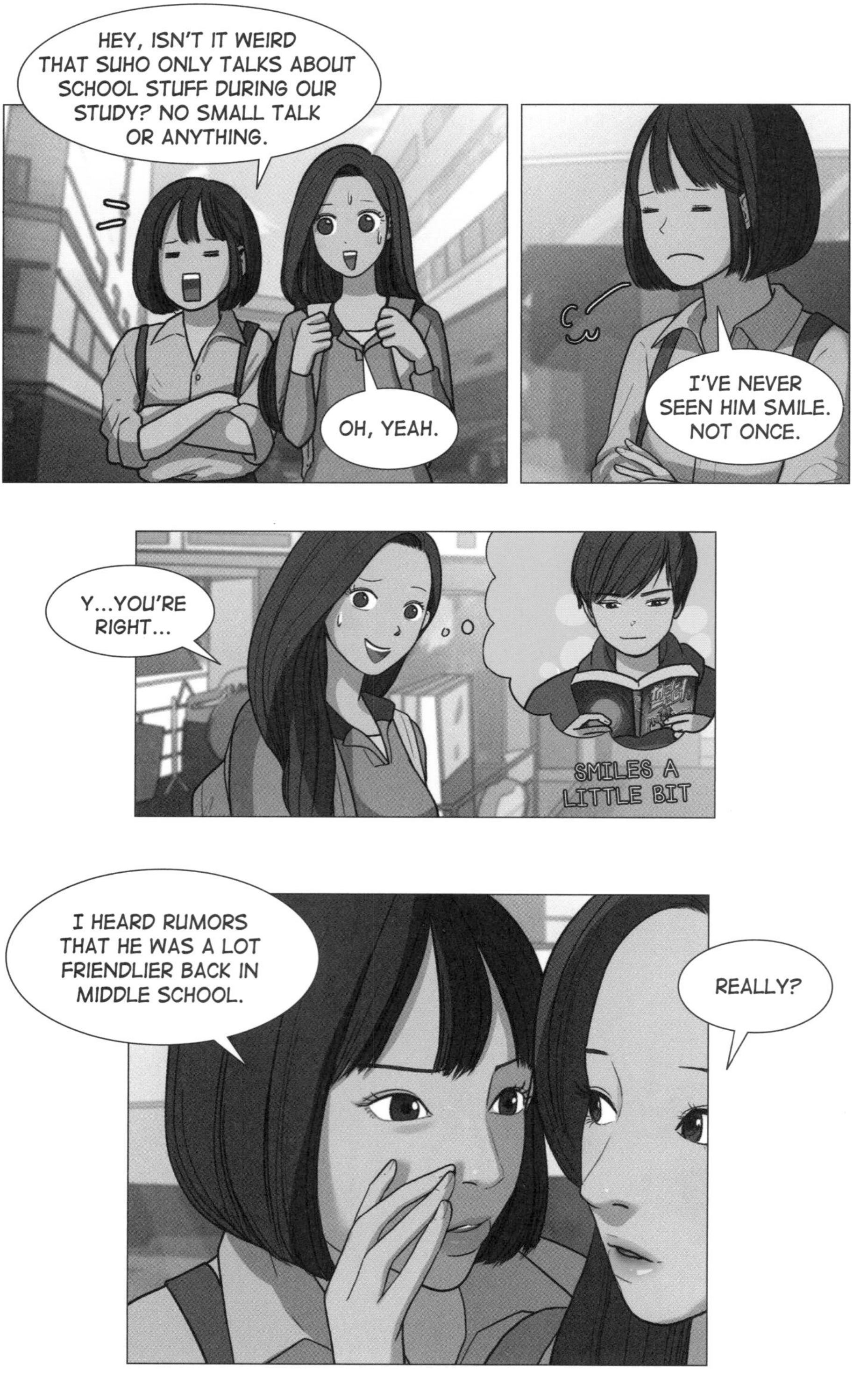
HEY, ISN'T IT WEIRD THAT SUHO ONLY TALKS ABOUT SCHOOL STUFF DURING OUR STUDY? NO SMALL TALK OR ANYTHING.
OH, YEAH.
I'VE NEVER SEEN HIM SMILE. NOT ONCE.
Y...YOU'RE RIGHT...
SMILES A LITTLE BIT
I HEARD RUMORS THAT HE WAS A LOT FRIENDLIER BACK IN MIDDLE SCHOOL.
REALLY?

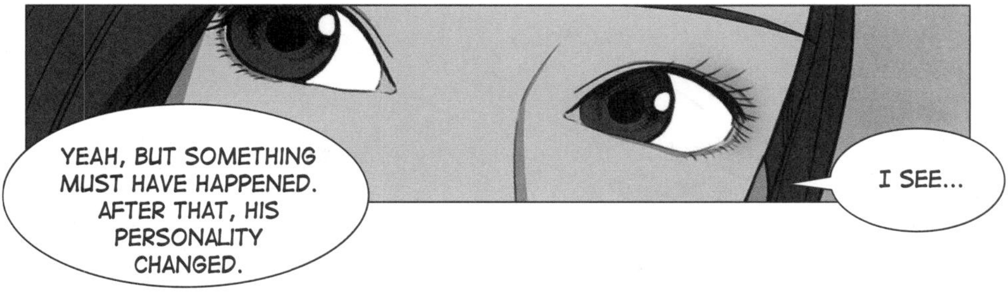
YEAH, BUT SOMETHING MUST HAVE HAPPENED. AFTER THAT, HIS PERSONALITY CHANGED.
I SEE...

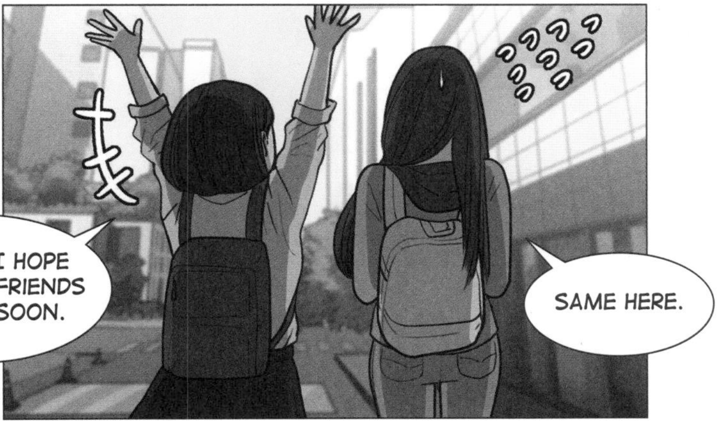
ANYWAY, I HOPE WE CAN BE FRIENDS WITH HIM SOON.
SAME HERE.

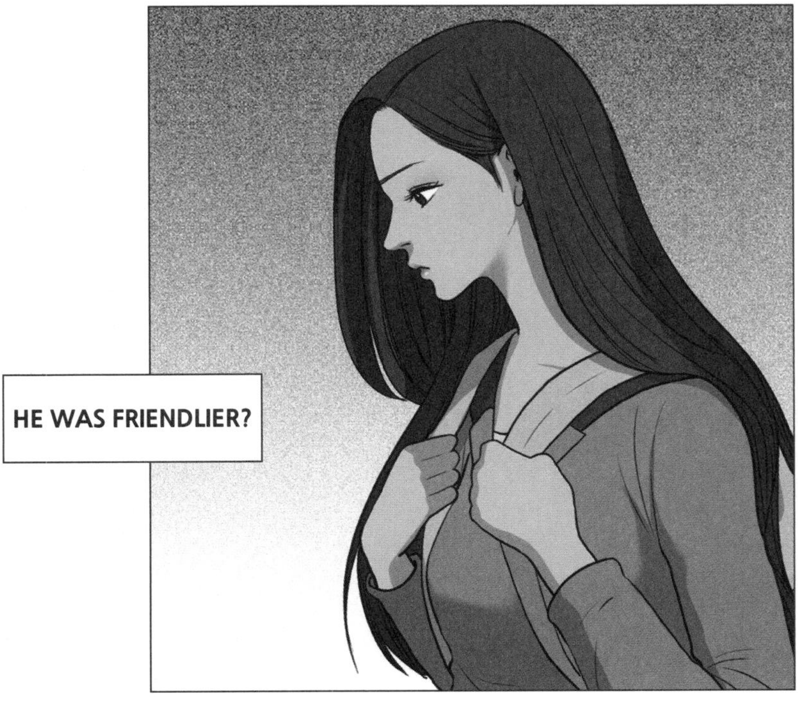
HE WAS FRIENDLIER?

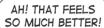
AH! THAT FEELS SO MUCH BETTER!

RIIIING

HUH?
AN ALARM?

5:00

SALE AT BEAUTY X

REMIND ME LATER

OH RIGHT! TODAY'S THE ANNUAL SALE!

I CAN'T MISS IT!!

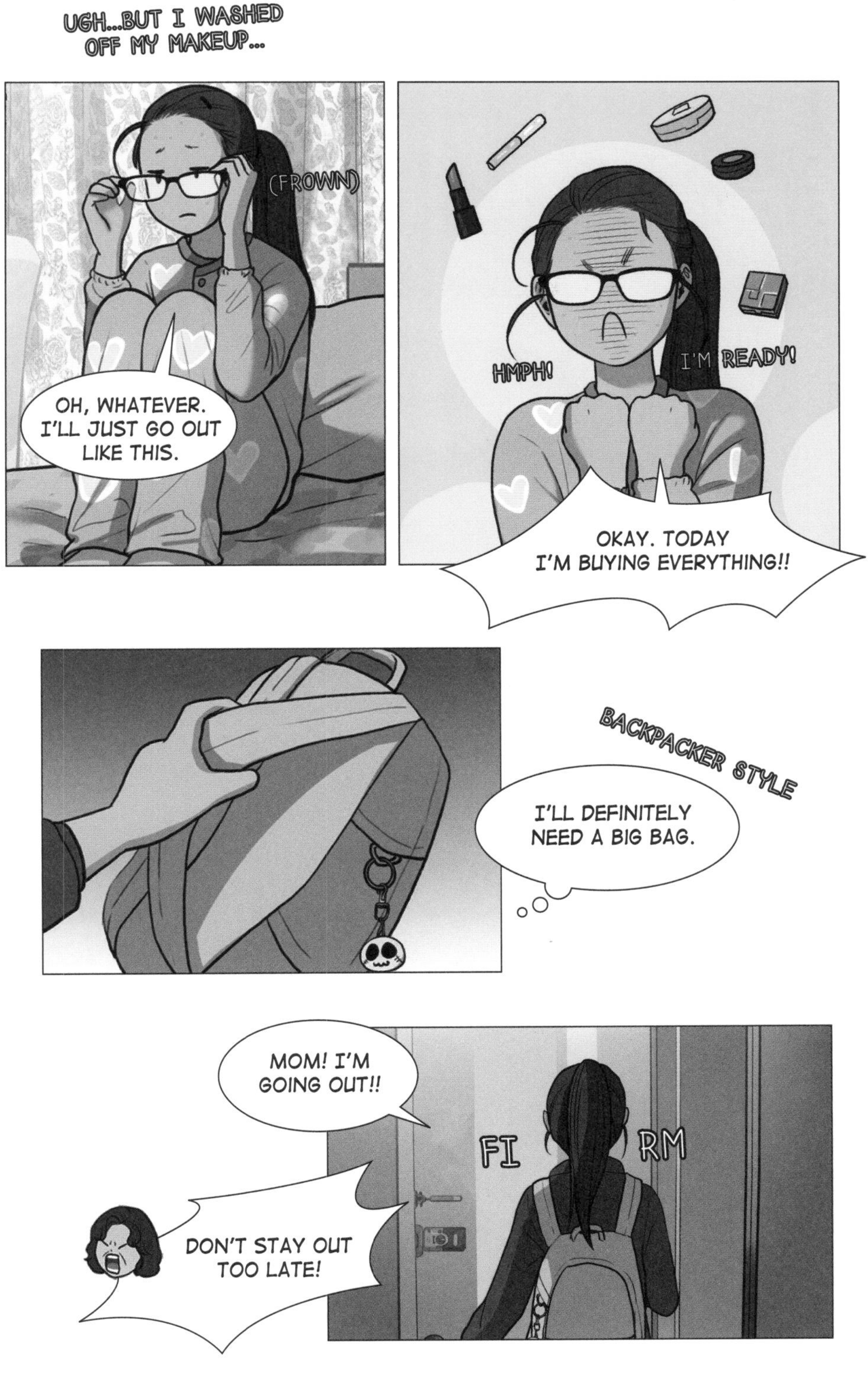
UGH...BUT I WASHED OFF MY MAKEUP...
(FROWN)
OH, WHATEVER. I'LL JUST GO OUT LIKE THIS.
HMPH!
I'M READY!
OKAY. TODAY I'M BUYING EVERYTHING!!
BACKPACKER STYLE
I'LL DEFINITELY NEED A BIG BAG.
MOM! I'M GOING OUT!!
FI RM
DON'T STAY OUT TOO LATE!

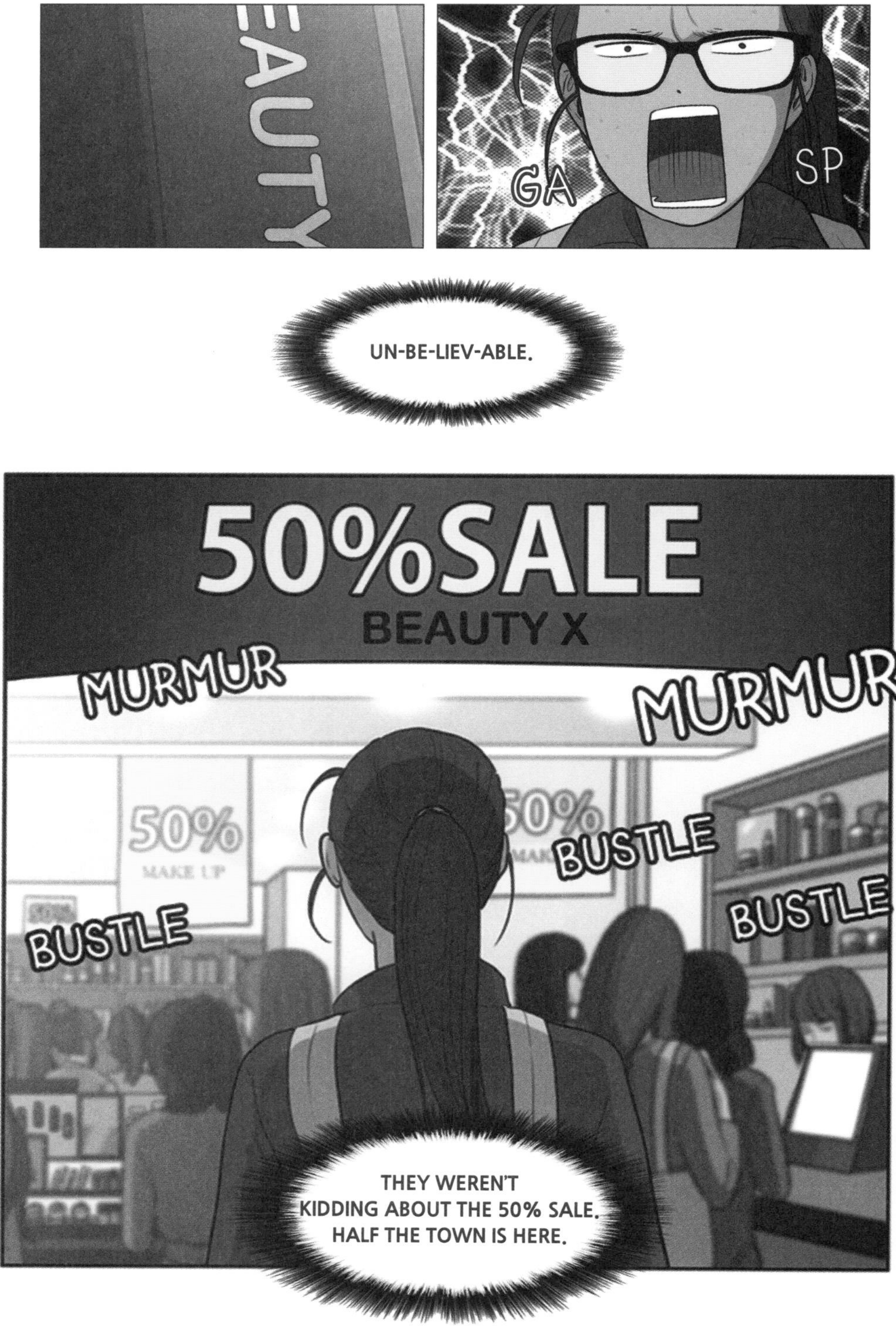
EAUTY
GA
SP
UN-BE-LIEV-ABLE.
50%SALE
BEAUTY X
MURMUR
MURMUR
50%
MAKE UP
BUSTLE
BUSTLE
BUSTLE
THEY WEREN'T
KIDDING ABOUT THE 50% SALE.
HALF THE TOWN IS HERE.

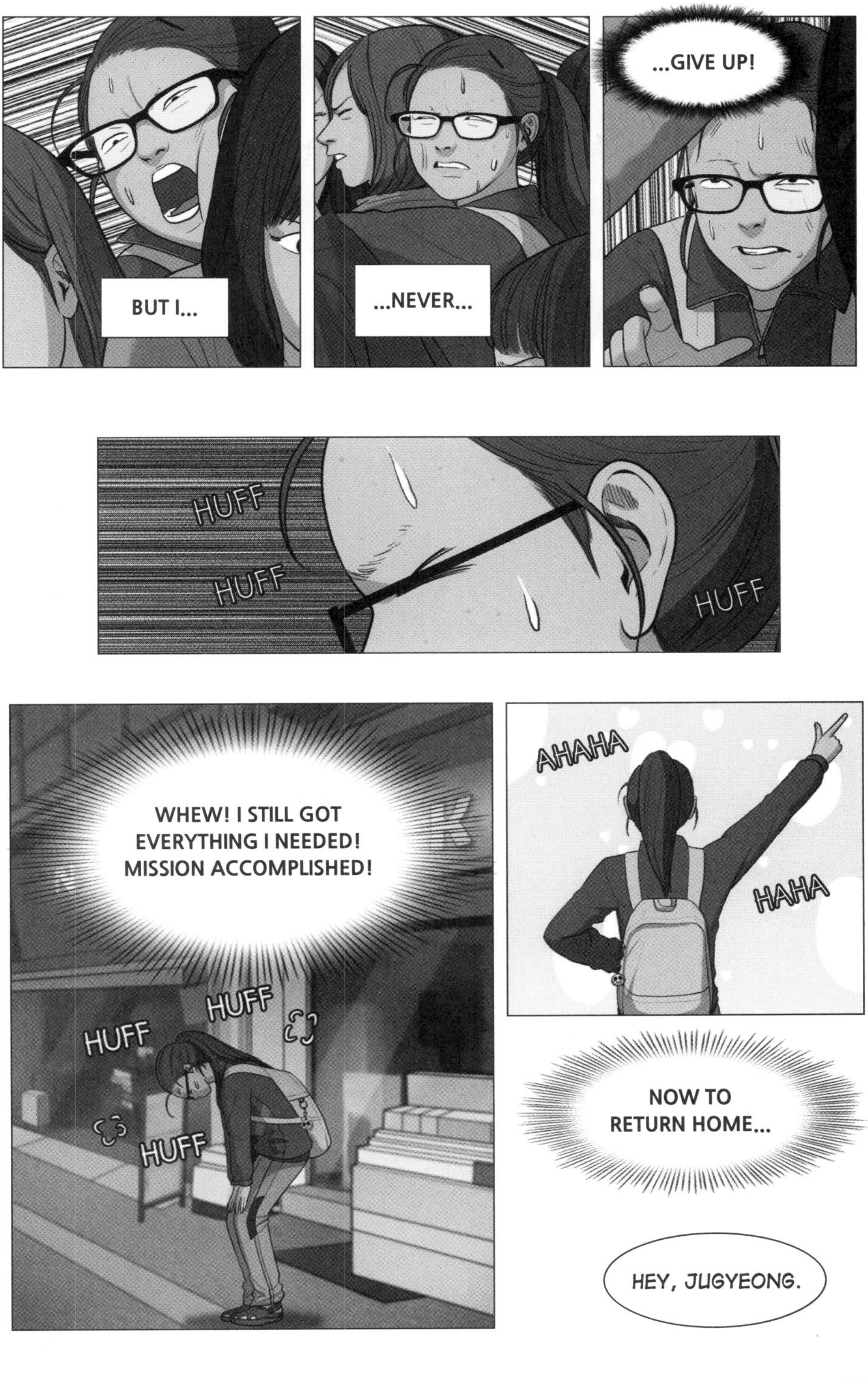
BUT I...
...NEVER...
...GIVE UP!
HUFF
HUFF
HUFF
WHEW! I STILL GOT EVERYTHING I NEEDED! MISSION ACCOMPLISHED!
HUFF
HUFF
HUFF
AHAHA
HAHA
NOW TO RETURN HOME...
HEY, JUGYEONG.

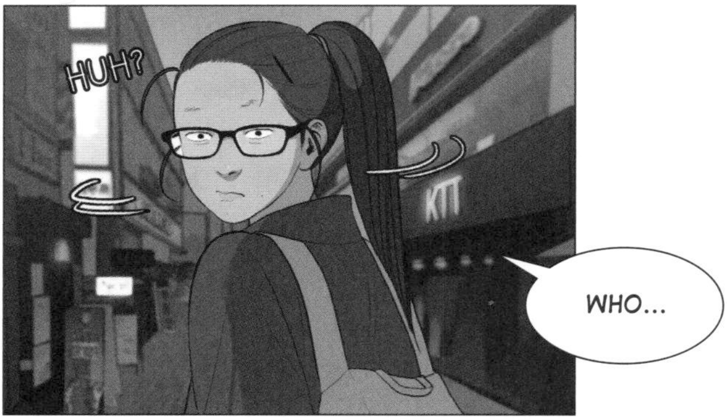
HUH?
WHO...

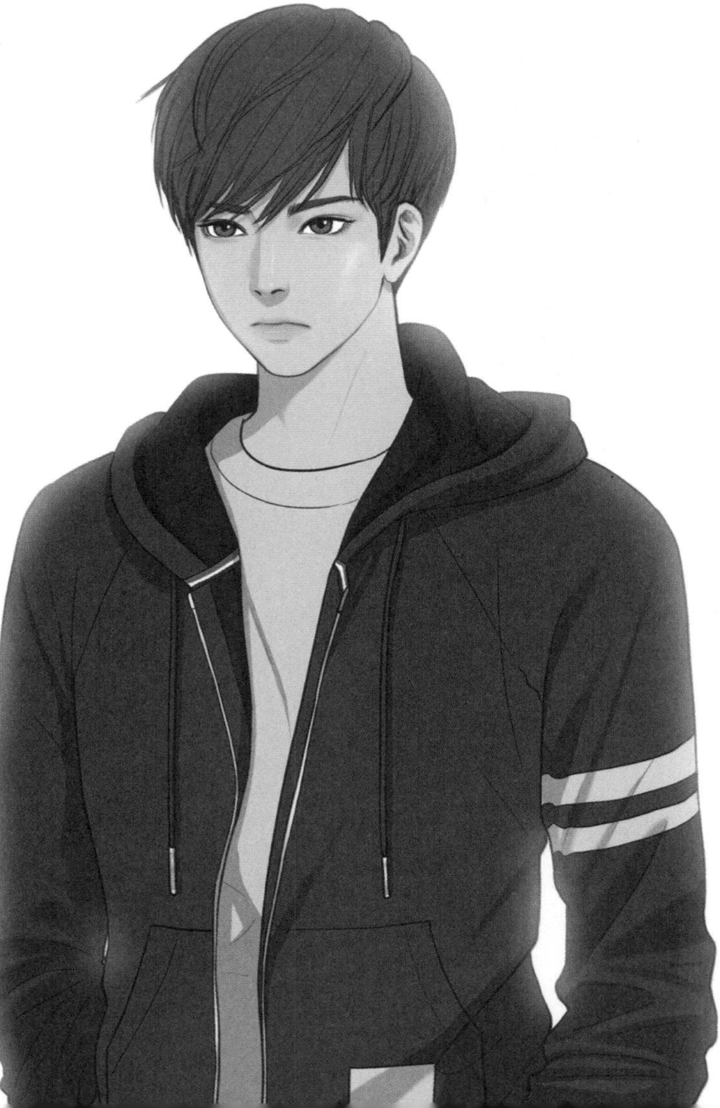

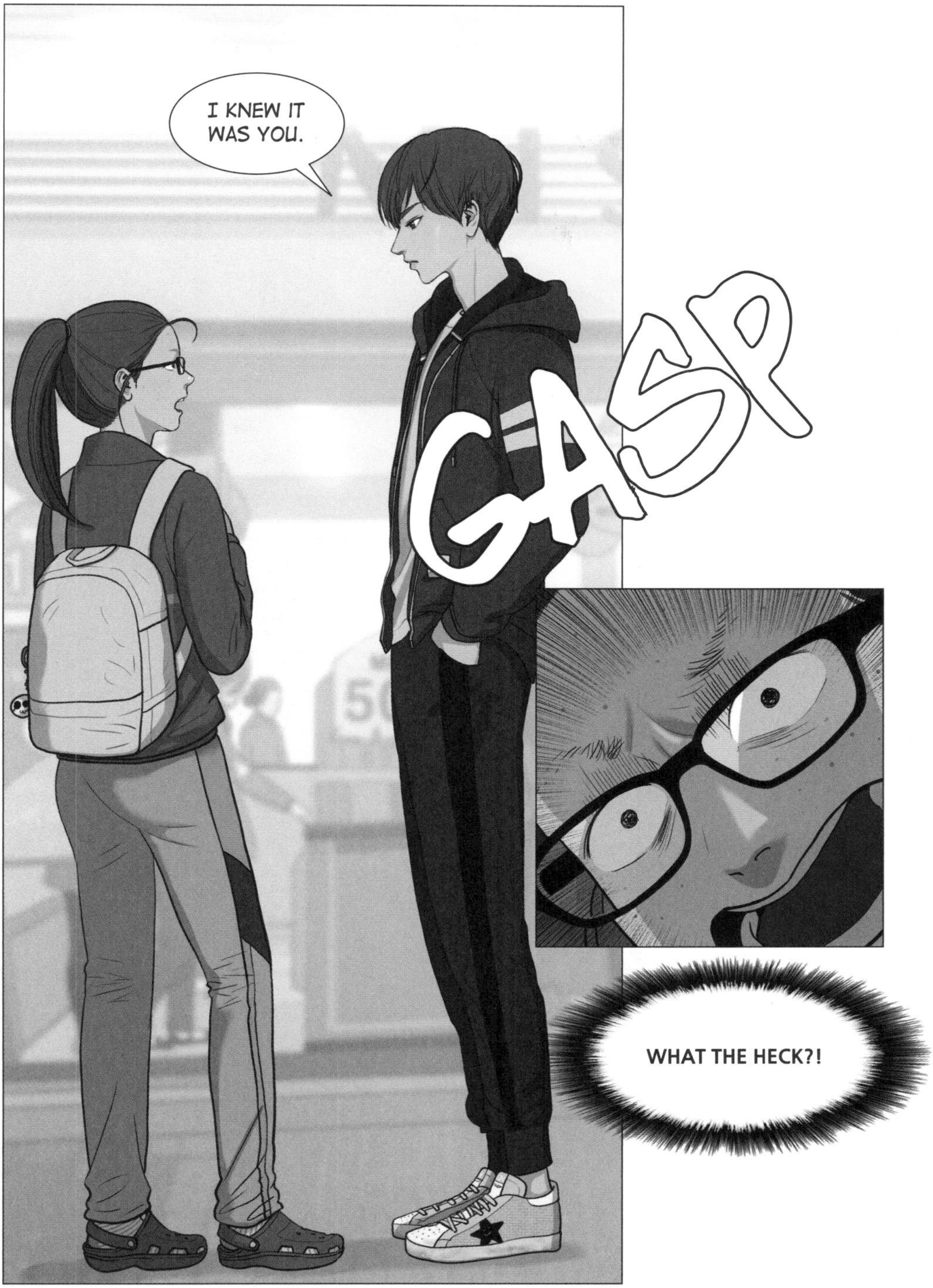
I KNEW IT WAS YOU.
GASP
WHAT THE HECK?!

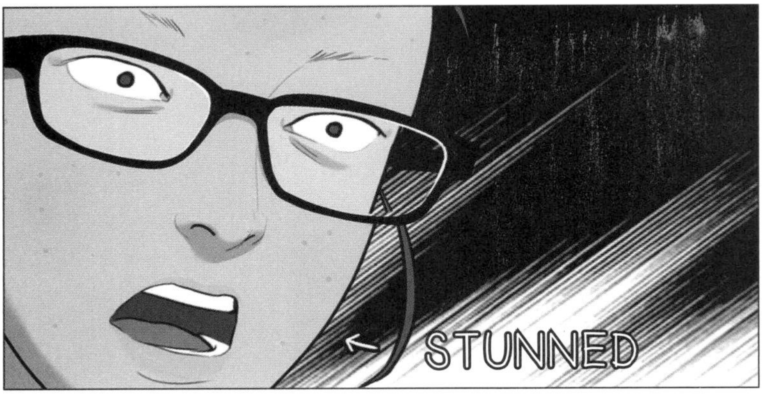
STUNNED

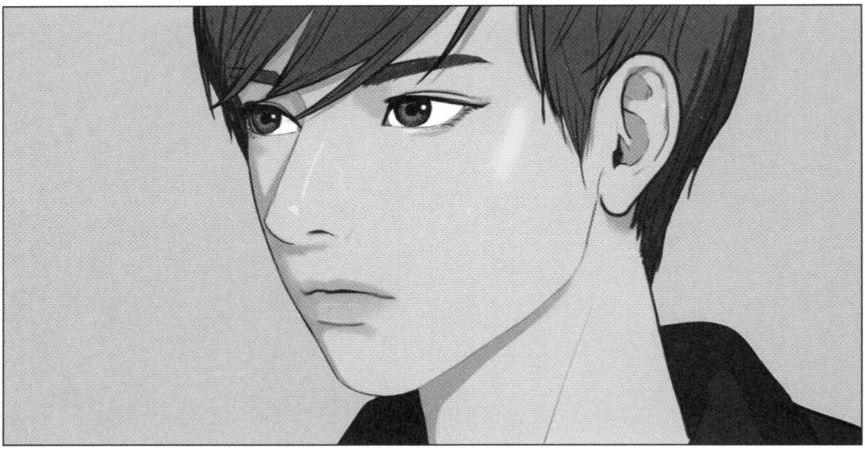

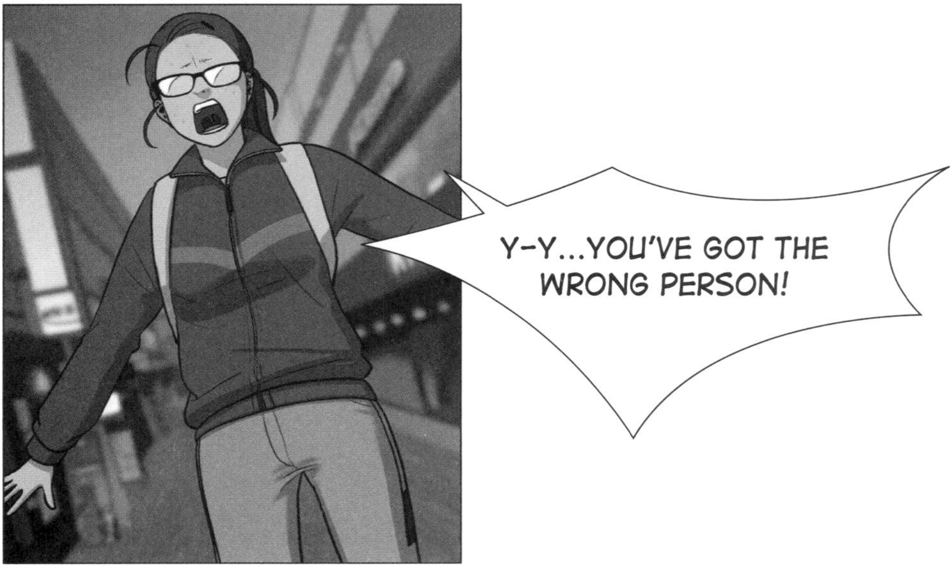
Y-Y...YOU'VE GOT THE WRONG PERSON!

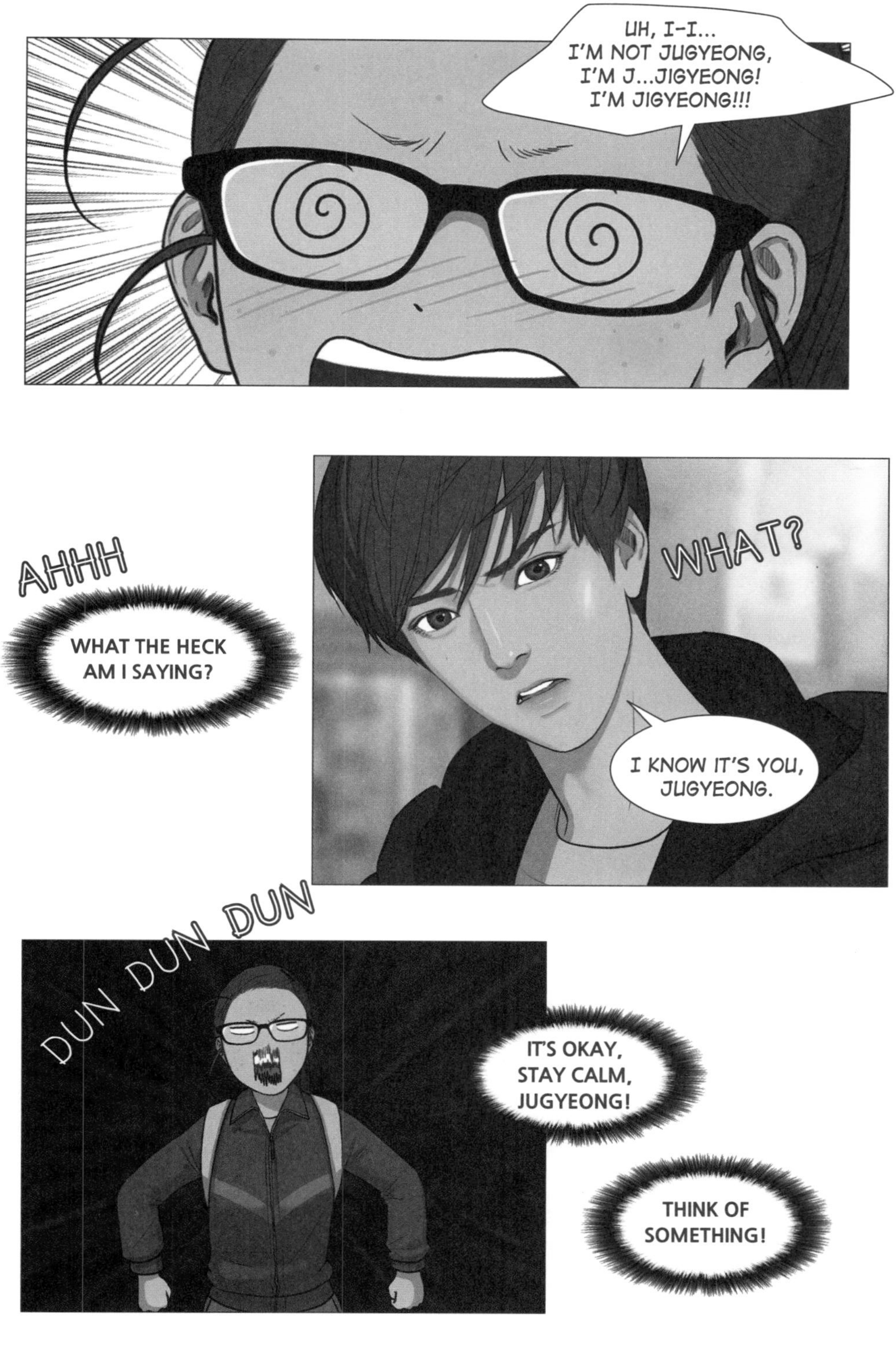
UH, I-I...
I'M NOT JUGYEONG,
I'M J...JIGYEONG!
I'M JIGYEONG!!!
AHHH
WHAT THE HECK
AM I SAYING?
WHAT?
I KNOW IT'S YOU,
JUGYEONG.
DUN DUN DUN
IT'S OKAY,
STAY CALM,
JUGYEONG!
THINK OF
SOMETHING!

AHHH
HEY! WHERE ARE YOU GOING?

#1 JUST RUN

REJECTED

UM, W...WHO ARE YOU? I DON'T REMEMBER...
GOSH, I MUST BE GETTING OLD...
HA

#2 SUDDEN ALZHEIMER'S

REJECTED

YEAH, THIS IS MY NATURAL FACE.
DIDN'T FEEL LIKE PUTTING ON MY MAKEUP TODAY.
YEAH, SO I HAVE ACNE, SO WHAT?
...?

#3 ADMIT IT

REJECTED

NO, NO!

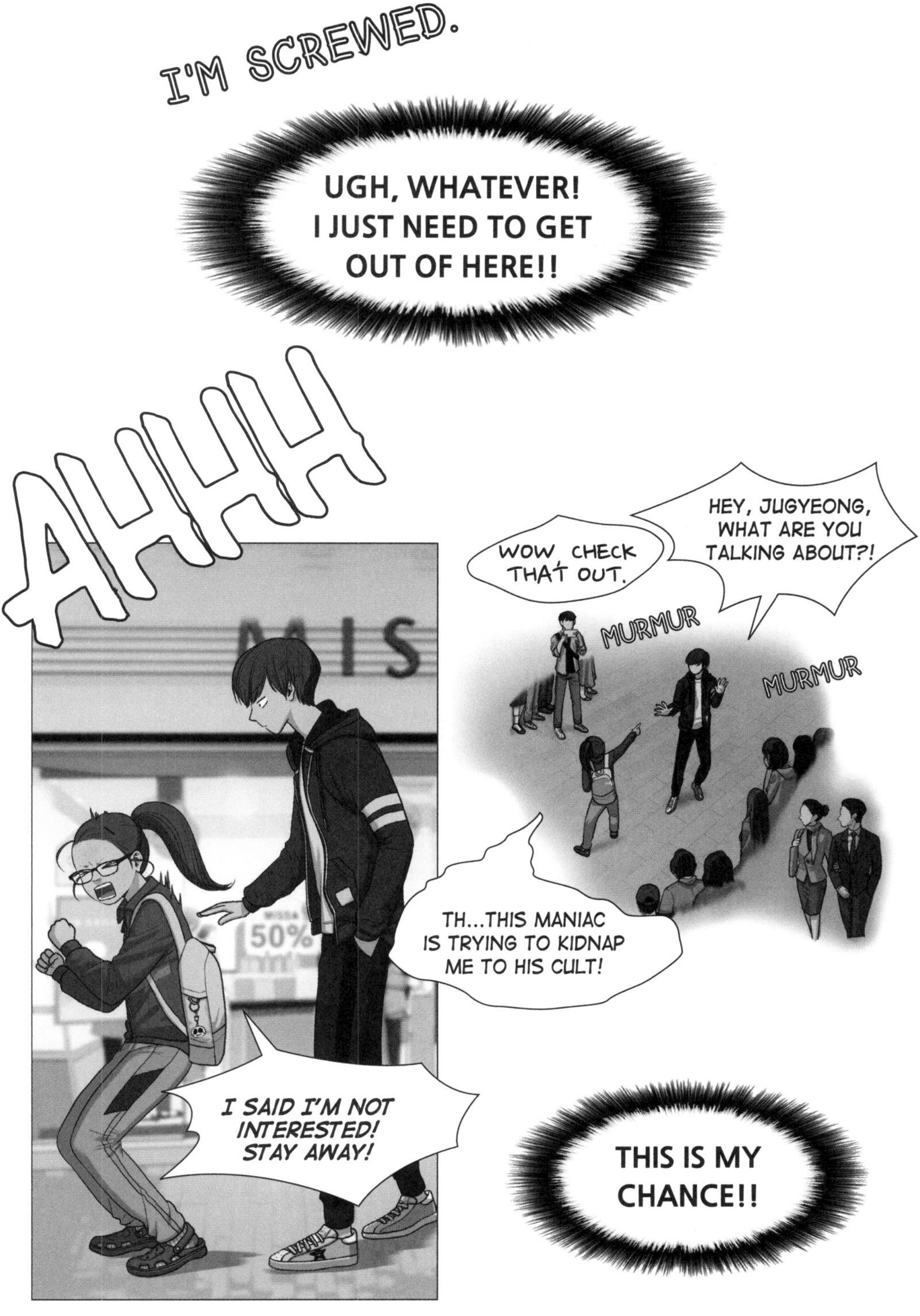
I'M SCREWED.
UGH, WHATEVER! I JUST NEED TO GET OUT OF HERE!!
AHHH
I SAID I'M NOT INTERESTED! STAY AWAY!
TH...THIS MANIAC IS TRYING TO KIDNAP ME TO HIS CULT!
WOW, CHECK THAT OUT.
HEY, JUGYEONG, WHAT ARE YOU TALKING ABOUT?!
MURMUR
MURMUR
THIS IS MY CHANCE!!

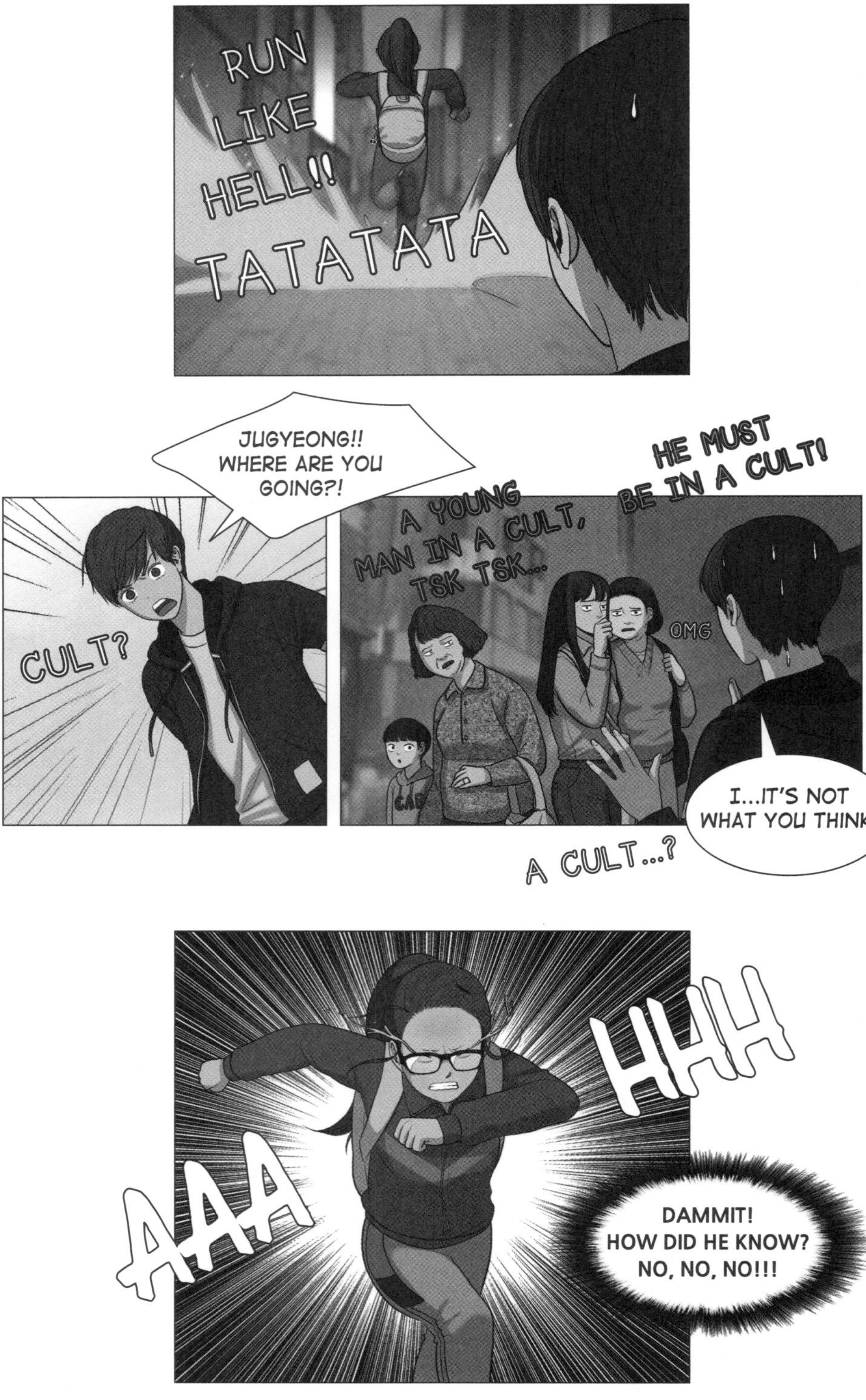
RUN LIKE HELL!!
TATATATA
JUGYEONG!! WHERE ARE YOU GOING?!
CULT?
A YOUNG MAN IN A CULT, TSK TSK...
HE MUST BE IN A CULT!
OMG
I...IT'S NOT WHAT YOU THINK.
A CULT...?
AAAHHH
DAMMIT! HOW DID HE KNOW? NO, NO, NO!!!

WOBBLE
WOBBLE
PLOP

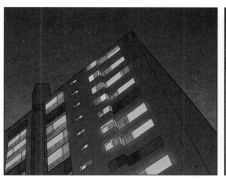

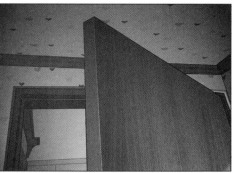

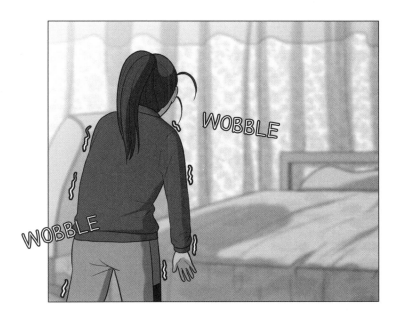

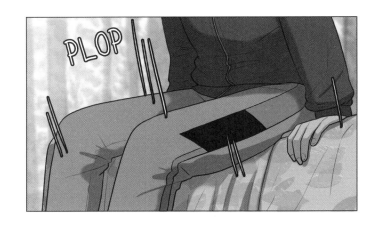

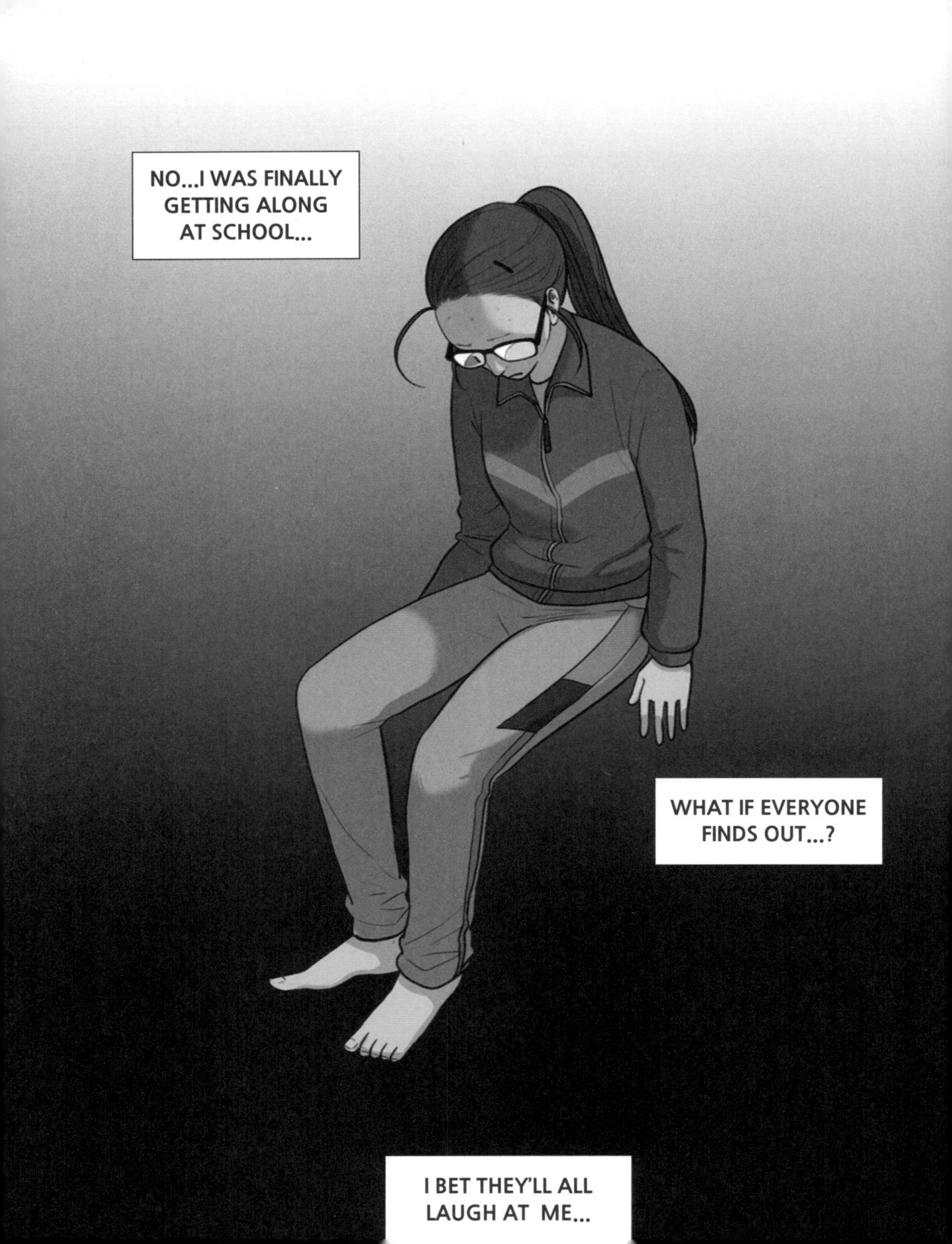
NO...I WAS FINALLY GETTING ALONG AT SCHOOL...
WHAT IF EVERYONE FINDS OUT...?
I BET THEY'LL ALL LAUGH AT ME...

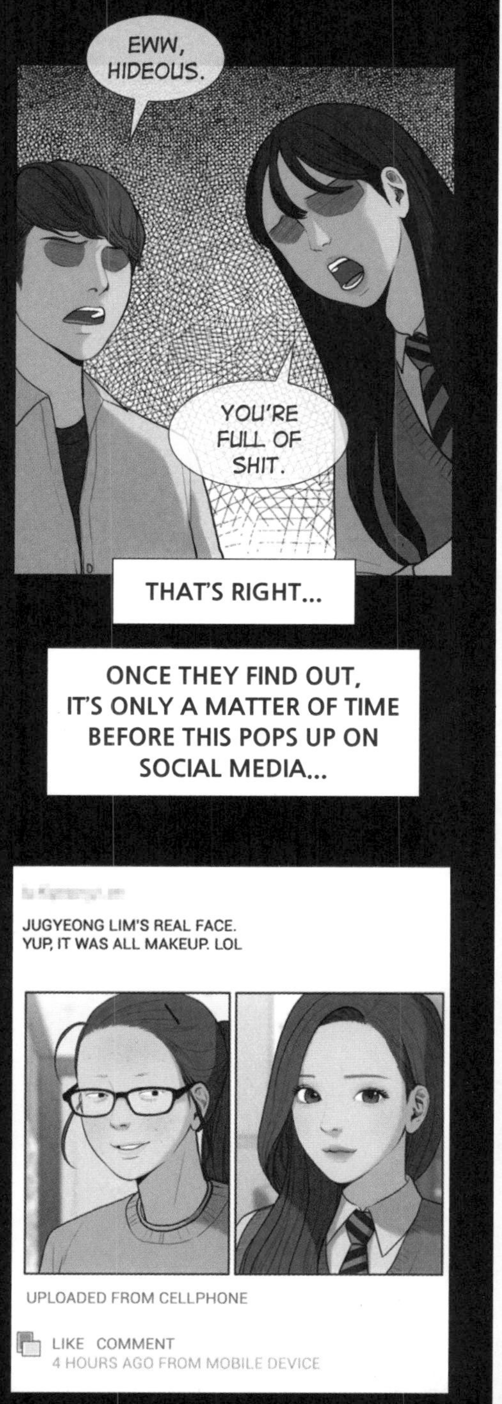
EWW, HIDEOUS.
YOU'RE FULL OF SHIT.
THAT'S RIGHT...
ONCE THEY FIND OUT, IT'S ONLY A MATTER OF TIME BEFORE THIS POPS UP ON SOCIAL MEDIA...
JUGYEONG LIM'S REAL FACE.
YUP, IT WAS ALL MAKEUP. LOL
UPLOADED FROM CELLPHONE
LIKE COMMENT
4 HOURS AGO FROM MOBILE DEVICE

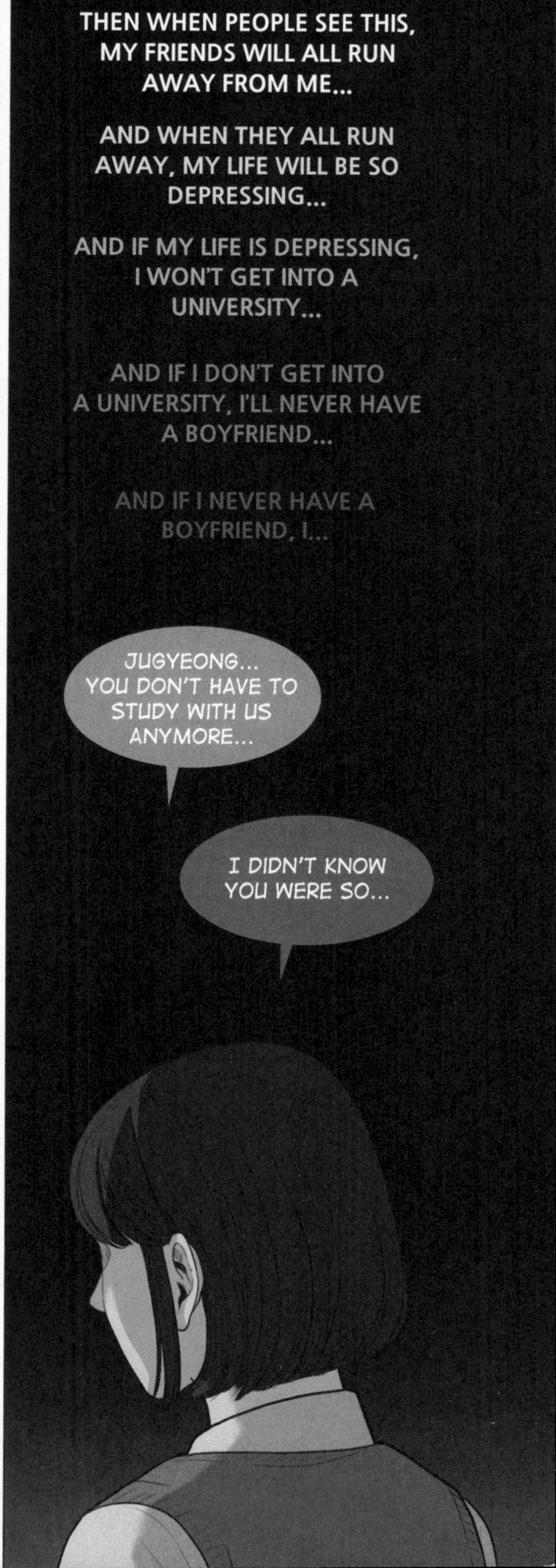
THEN WHEN PEOPLE SEE THIS, MY FRIENDS WILL ALL RUN AWAY FROM ME...
AND WHEN THEY ALL RUN AWAY, MY LIFE WILL BE SO DEPRESSING...
AND IF MY LIFE IS DEPRESSING, I WON'T GET INTO A UNIVERSITY...
AND IF I DON'T GET INTO A UNIVERSITY, I'LL NEVER HAVE A BOYFRIEND...
AND IF I NEVER HAVE A BOYFRIEND, I...
JUGYEONG... YOU DON'T HAVE TO STUDY WITH US ANYMORE...
I DIDN'T KNOW YOU WERE SO...

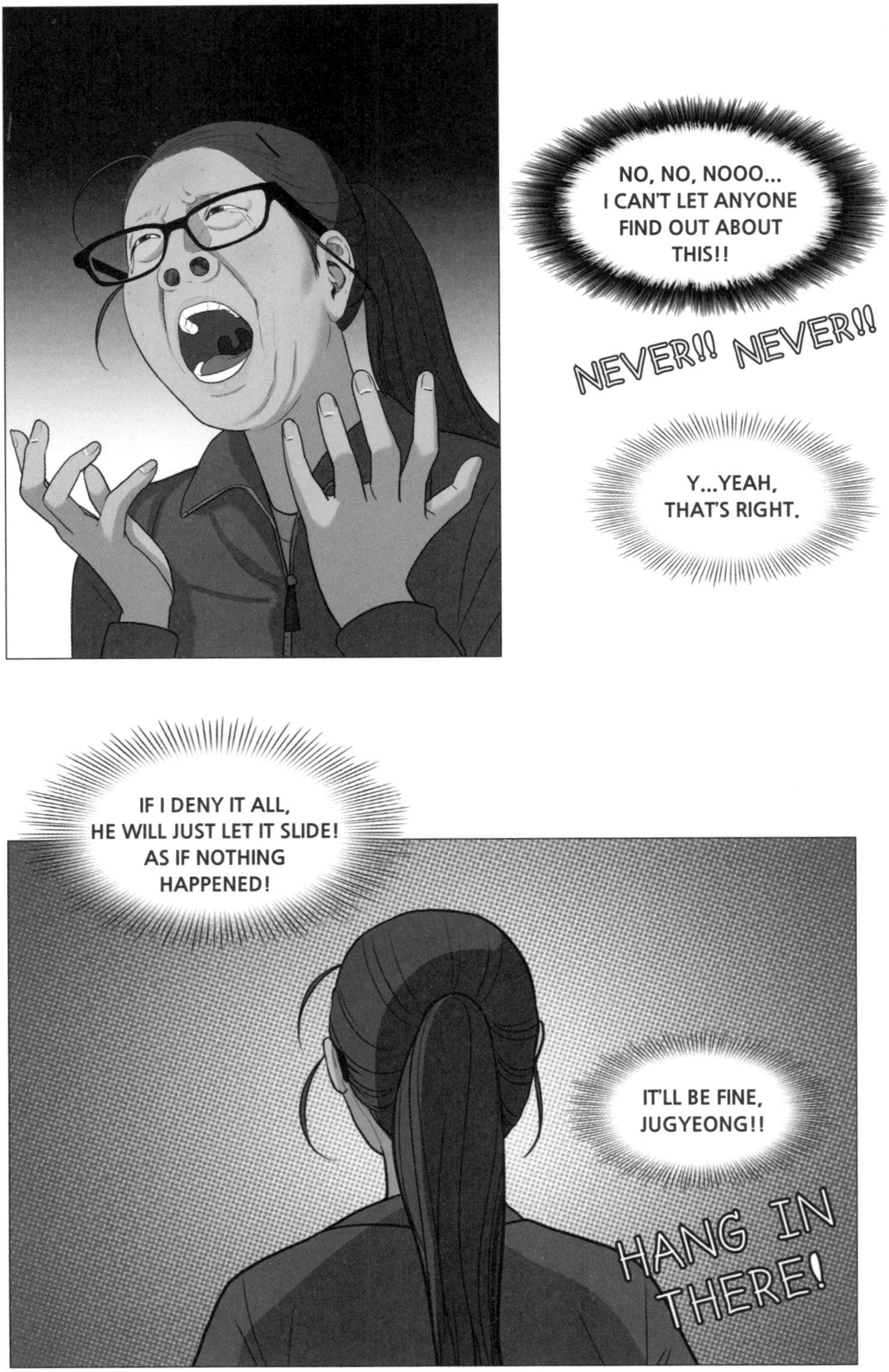
NO, NO, NOOO...
I CAN'T LET ANYONE
FIND OUT ABOUT
THIS!!
NEVER!! NEVER!!
Y...YEAH,
THAT'S RIGHT.
IF I DENY IT ALL,
HE WILL JUST LET IT SLIDE!
AS IF NOTHING
HAPPENED!
IT'LL BE FINE,
JUGYEONG!!
HANG IN
THERE!

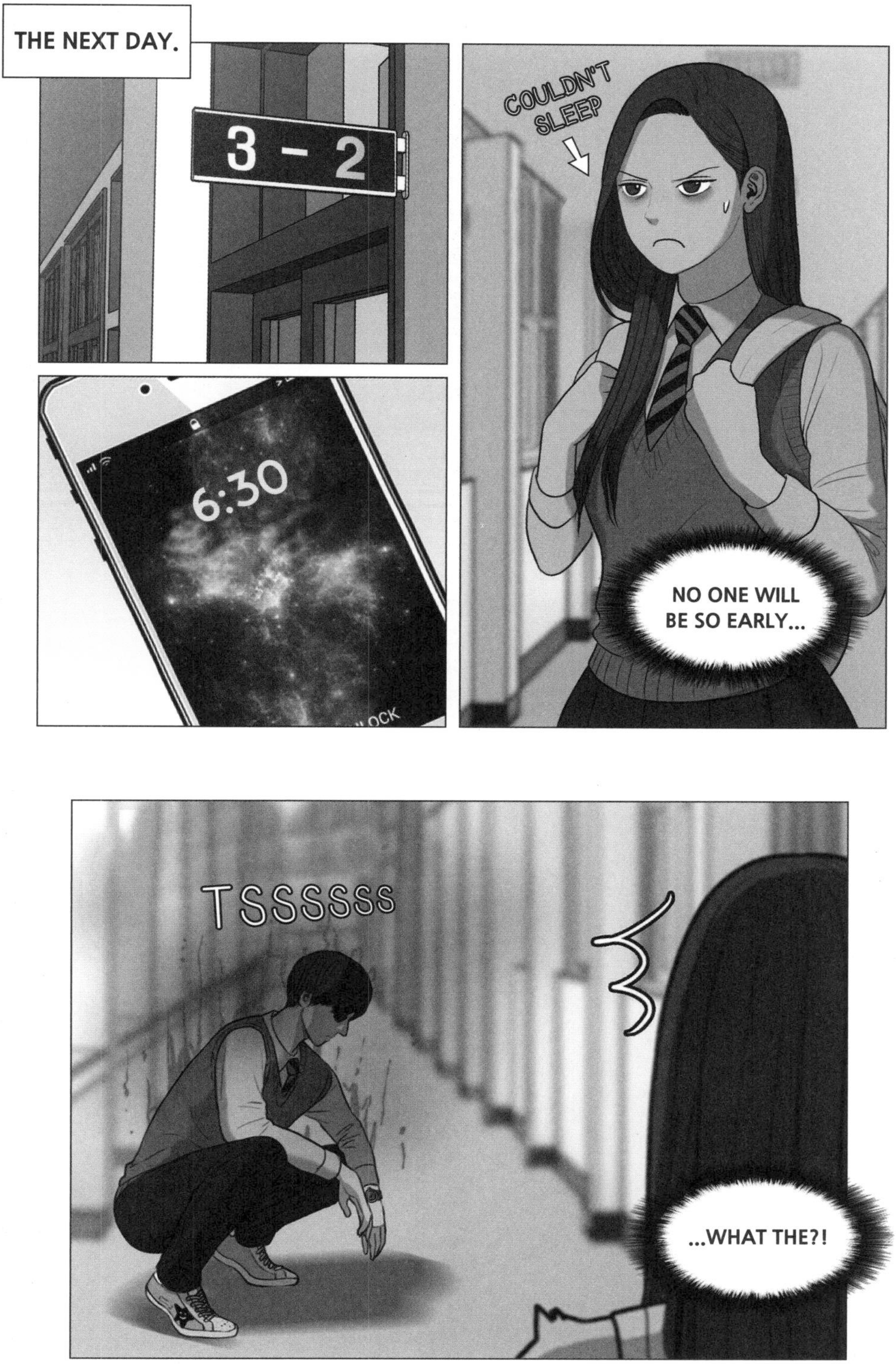
THE NEXT DAY.
3 - 2
6:30
COULDN'T SLEEP
NO ONE WILL BE SO EARLY...
TSSSSSS
...WHAT THE?!

IT'S 6:30
IN THE MORNING.

ARE YOU SERIOUSLY
IN MY CLASSROOM TOO?
THIS EARLY?

OH?

SNEAK

SNEAK

HEY,
JUGYEONG.

GASP!

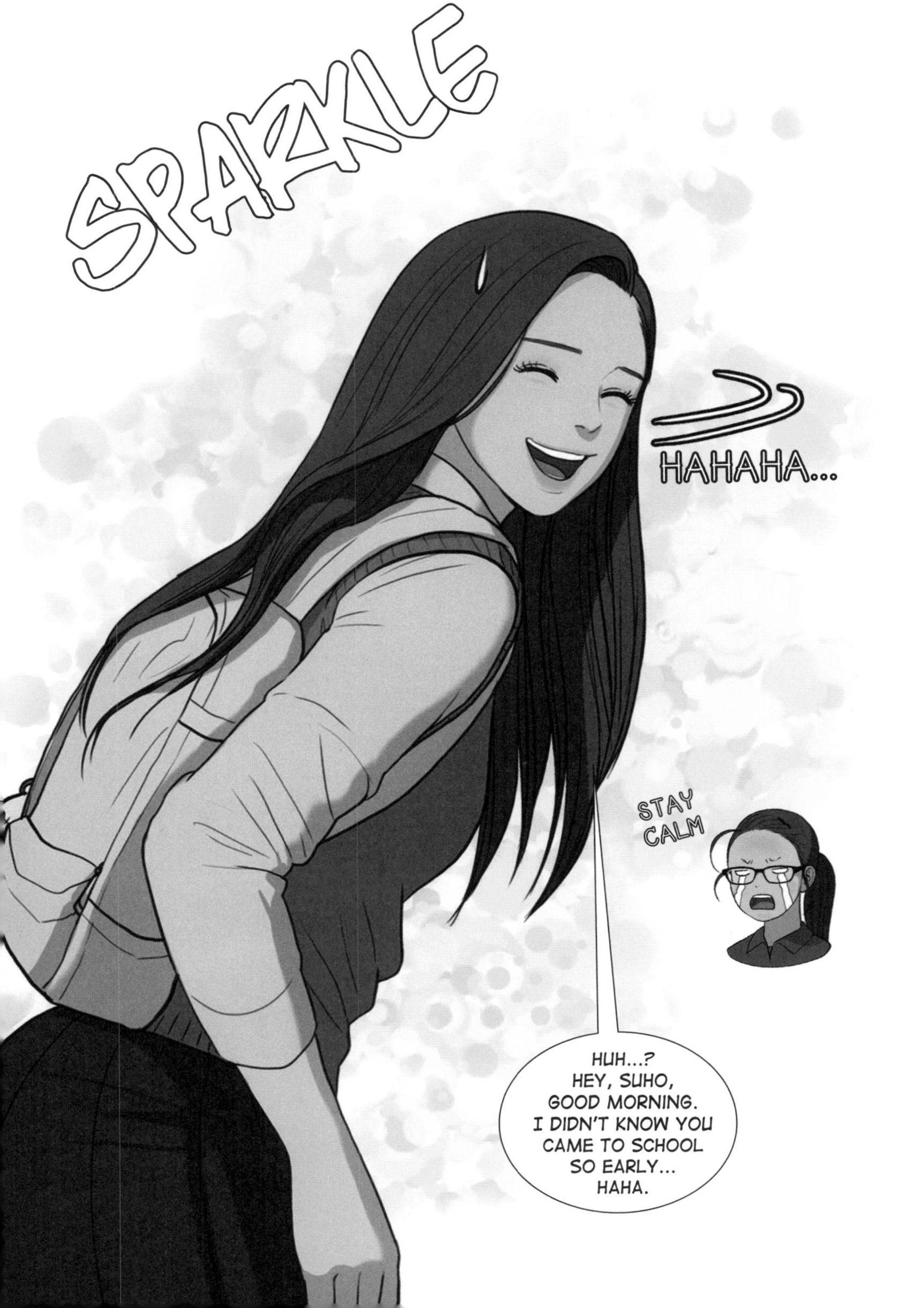
SPARKLE
HAHAHA...
STAY CALM
HUH...? HEY, SUHO, GOOD MORNING. I DIDN'T KNOW YOU CAME TO SCHOOL SO EARLY... HAHA.

IS THIS SOME KIND OF JOKE?

WHAT COULD BE ON YOUR MIND?

HUH?

W...WHAT DO YOU MEAN, SUHO?

JUGYEONG, I SAW YOU YESTERDAY...

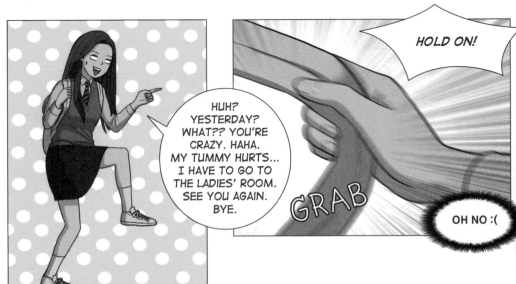

HUH? YESTERDAY? WHAT?? YOU'RE CRAZY. HAHA. MY TUMMY HURTS... I HAVE TO GO TO THE LADIES' ROOM. SEE YOU AGAIN. BYE.

HOLD ON!

GRAB

OH NO :(

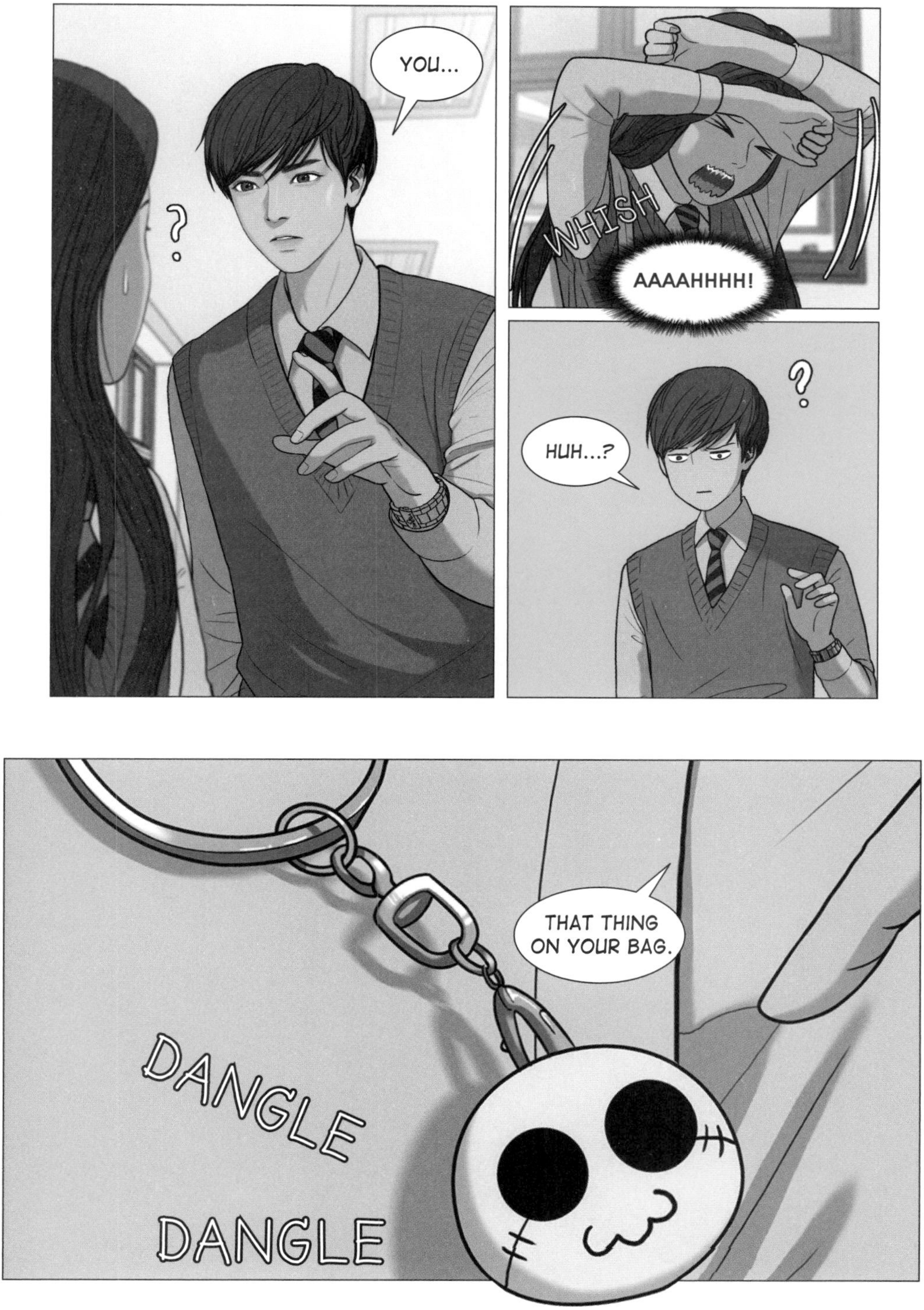
YOU...
WHISH
AAAAHHHH!
HUH...?
THAT THING ON YOUR BAG.
DANGLE
DANGLE

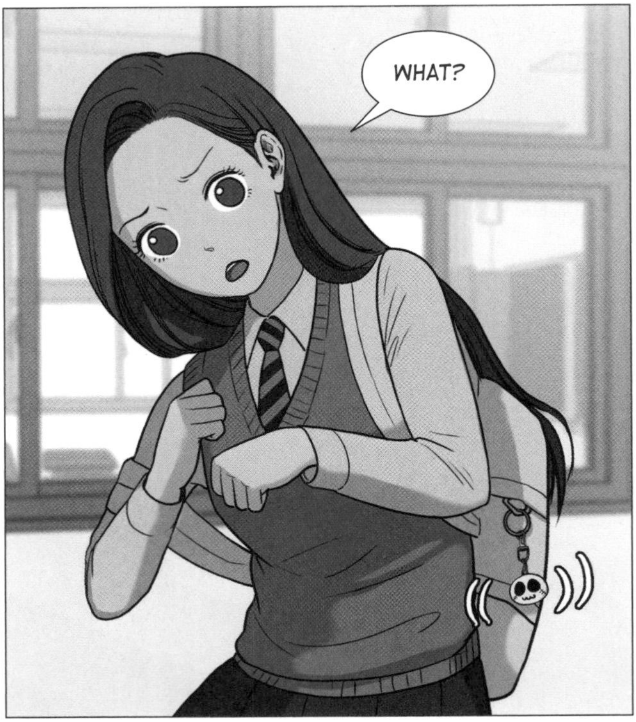
WHAT?

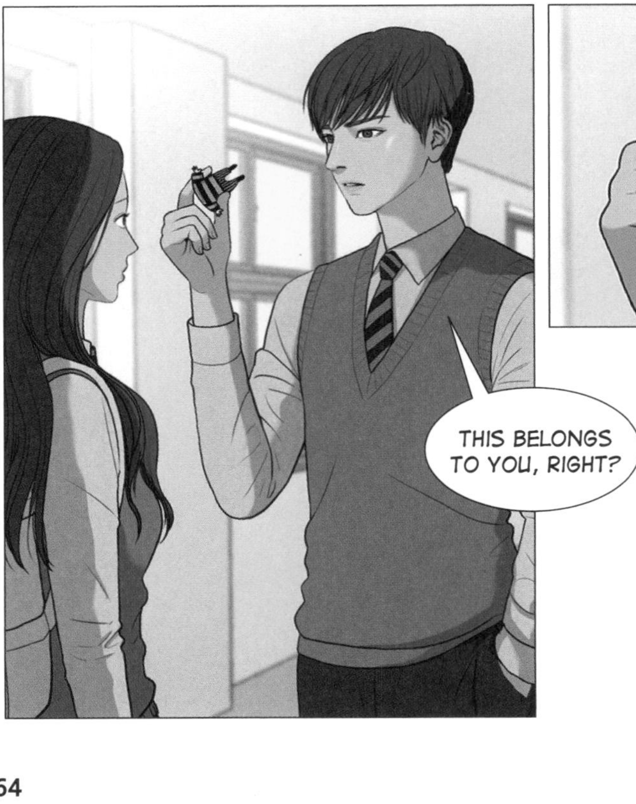
THIS BELONGS
TO YOU, RIGHT?

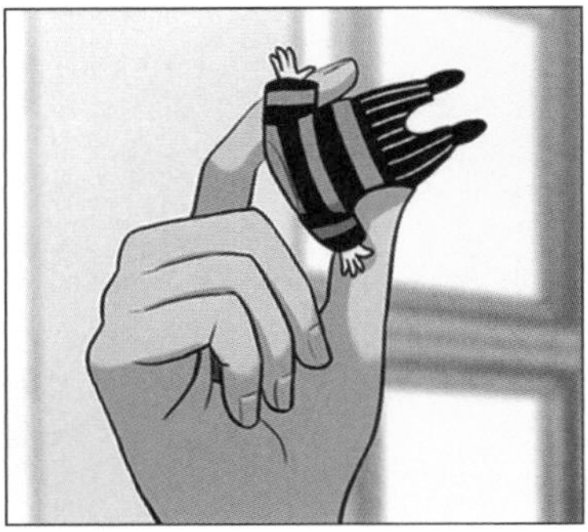

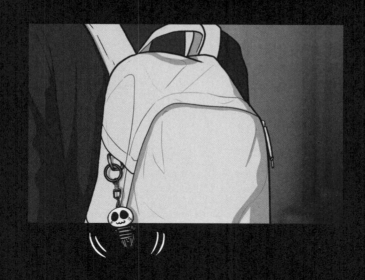

POP

SSK

TAP

SCR EECH

AAAHHH!
WHY DO YOU HAVE
THAT?!?

CRAP

THE BODY'S
REALLY GONE!!

I'M ALL OUT OF
EXCUSES NOW!!

BUT IF
THIS IS YOURS...

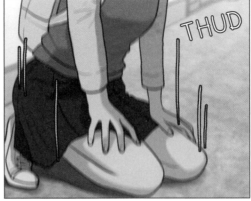

THUD

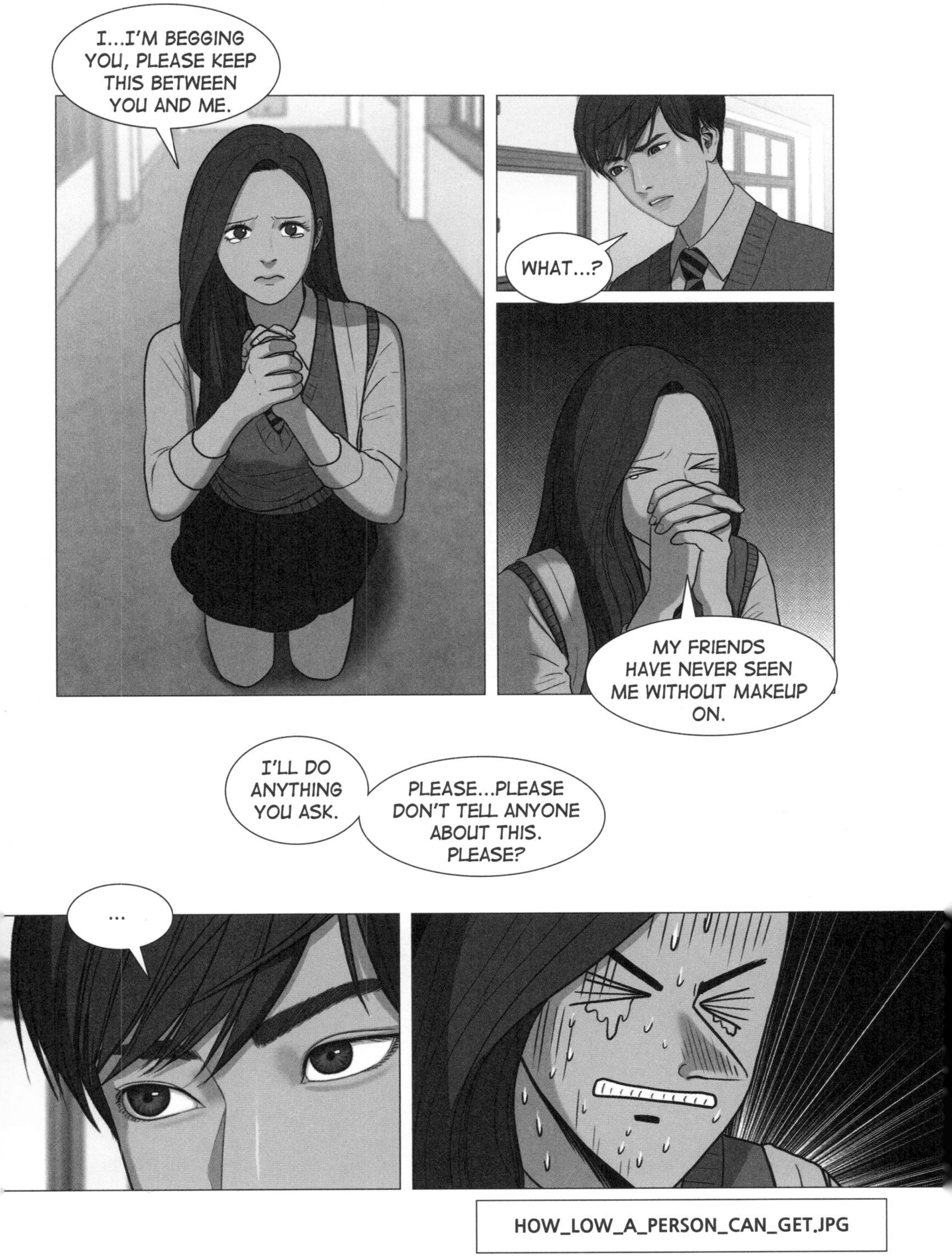

I...I'M BEGGING YOU, PLEASE KEEP THIS BETWEEN YOU AND ME.
WHAT...?
MY FRIENDS HAVE NEVER SEEN ME WITHOUT MAKEUP ON.
I'LL DO ANYTHING YOU ASK.
PLEASE...PLEASE DON'T TELL ANYONE ABOUT THIS. PLEASE?
...
HOW_LOW_A_PERSON_CAN_GET.JPG

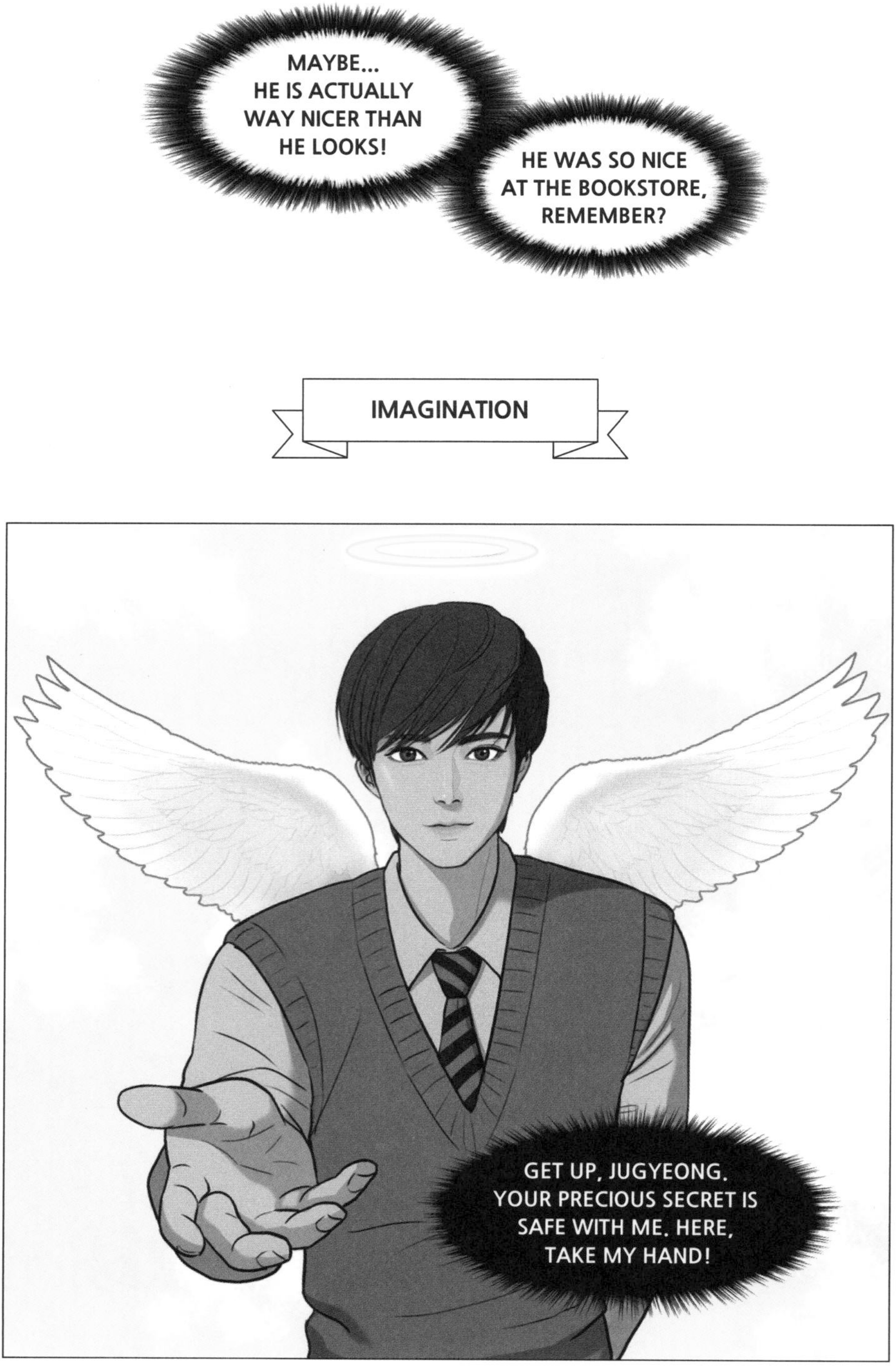
MAYBE... HE IS ACTUALLY WAY NICER THAN HE LOOKS!
HE WAS SO NICE AT THE BOOKSTORE, REMEMBER?
IMAGINATION
GET UP, JUGYEONG. YOUR PRECIOUS SECRET IS SAFE WITH ME. HERE, TAKE MY HAND!

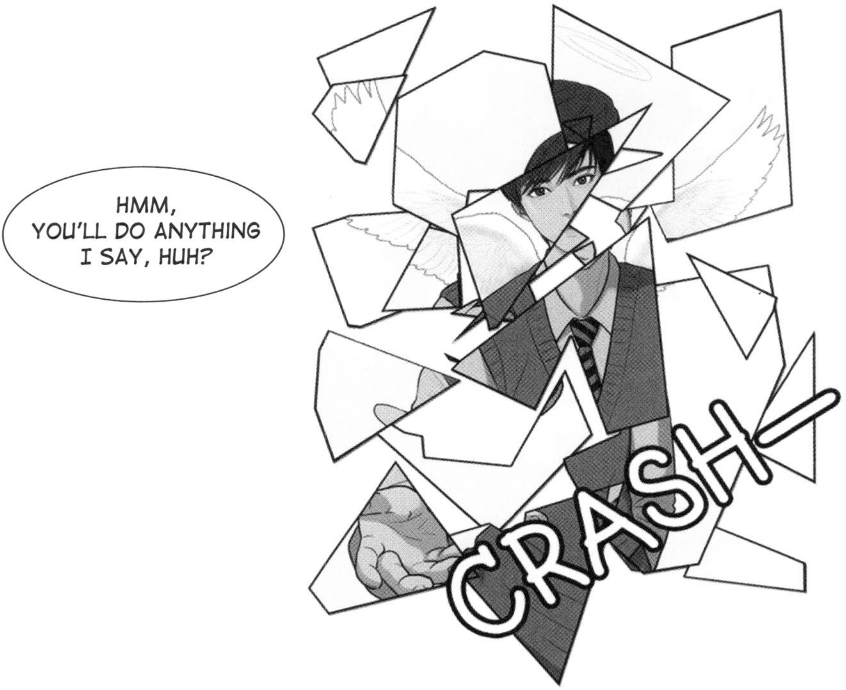
HMM, YOU'LL DO ANYTHING I SAY, HUH?
CRASH-

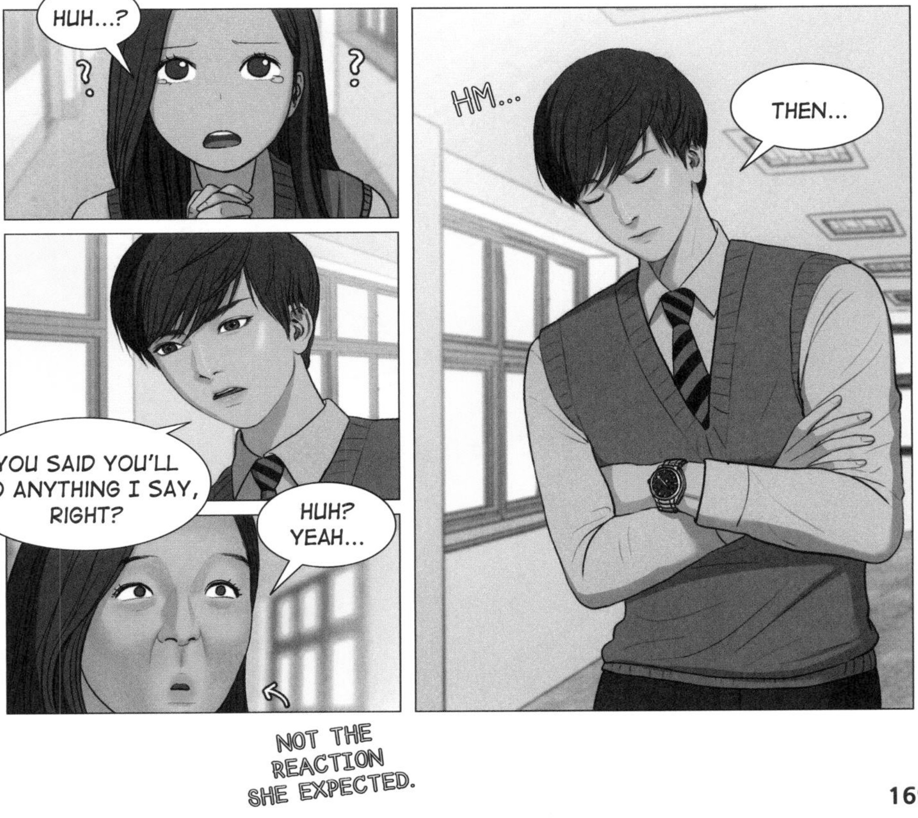
HUH...?
?
?
YOU SAID YOU'LL DO ANYTHING I SAY, RIGHT?
HUH? YEAH...
NOT THE REACTION SHE EXPECTED.
HM...
THEN...

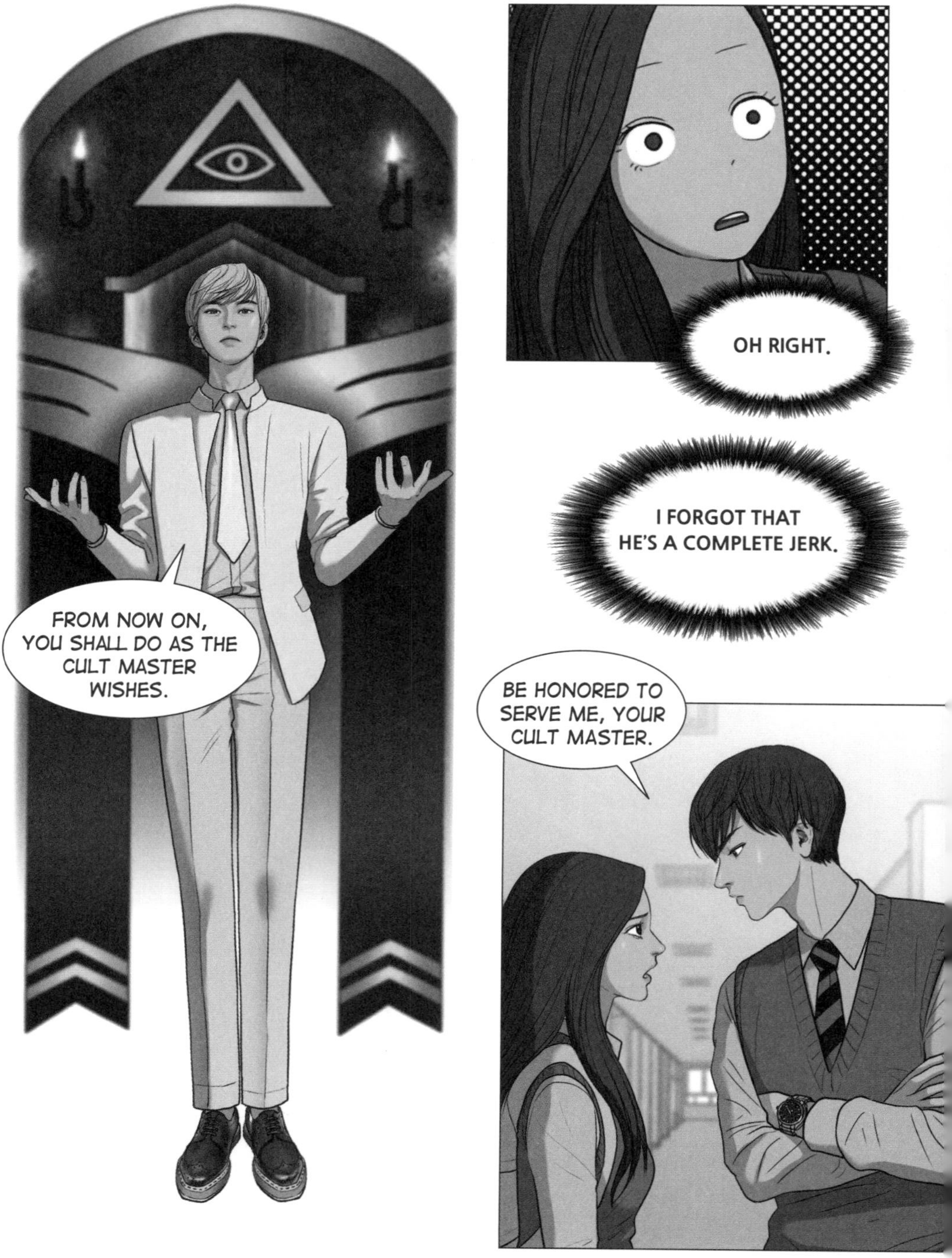
FROM NOW ON, YOU SHALL DO AS THE CULT MASTER WISHES.
OH RIGHT.
I FORGOT THAT HE'S A COMPLETE JERK.
BE HONORED TO SERVE ME, YOUR CULT MASTER.

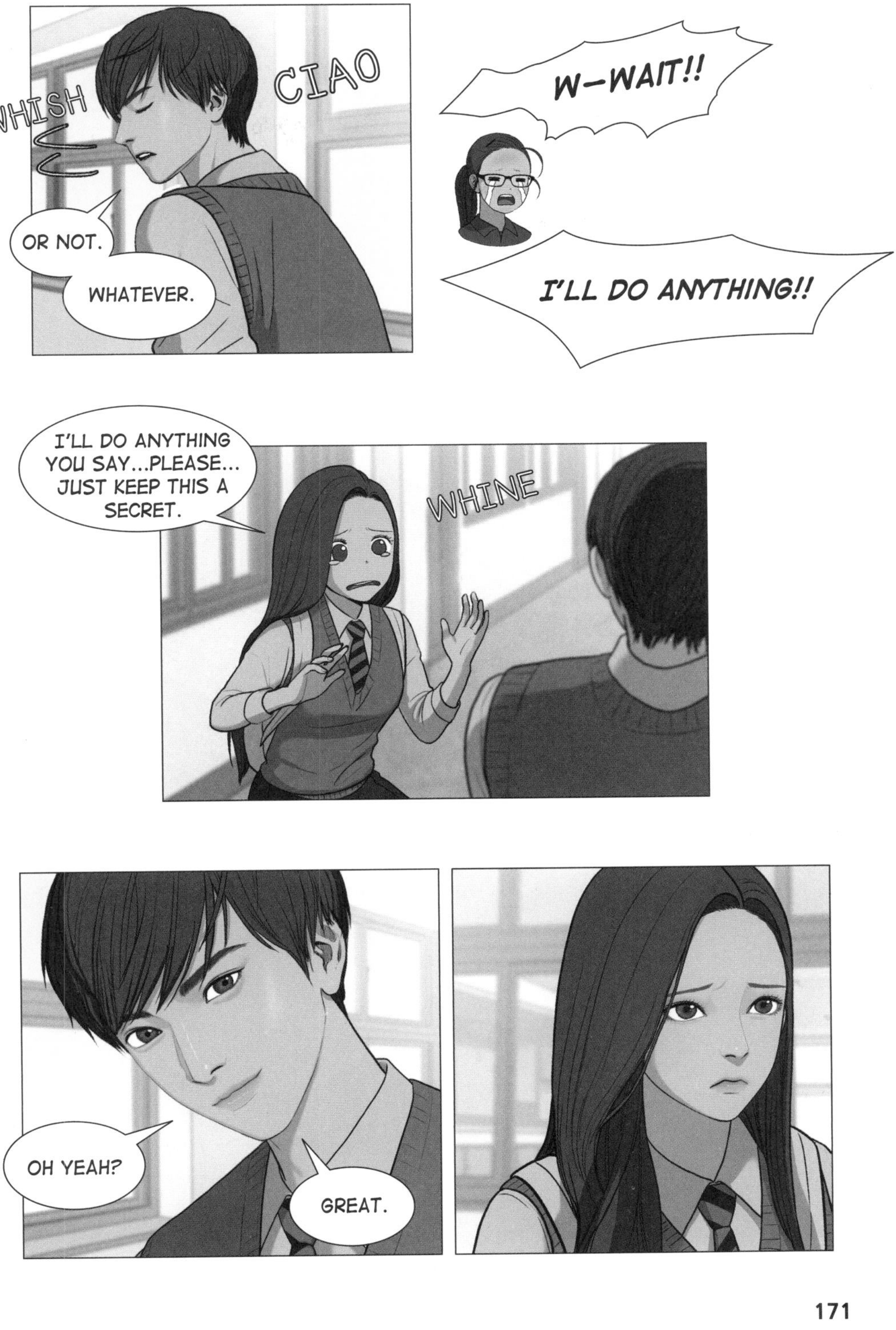
WHISH
CIAO
OR NOT.
WHATEVER.
W-WAIT!!
I'LL DO ANYTHING!!
I'LL DO ANYTHING YOU SAY...PLEASE... JUST KEEP THIS A SECRET.
WHINE
OH YEAH?
GREAT.

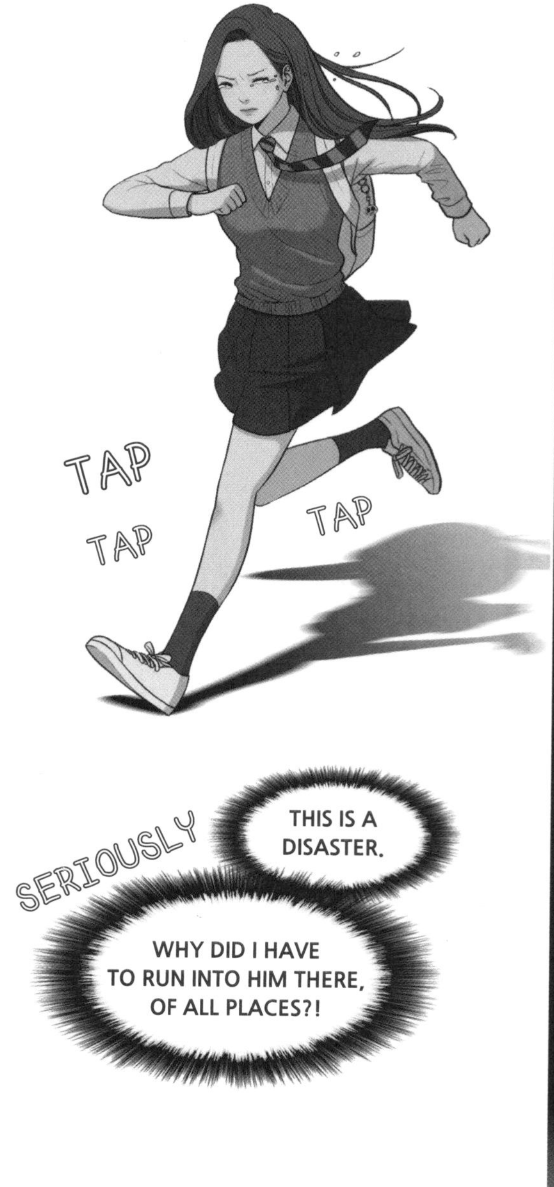
TAP
TAP
TAP
SERIOUSLY
THIS IS A DISASTER.
WHY DID I HAVE TO RUN INTO HIM THERE, OF ALL PLACES?!

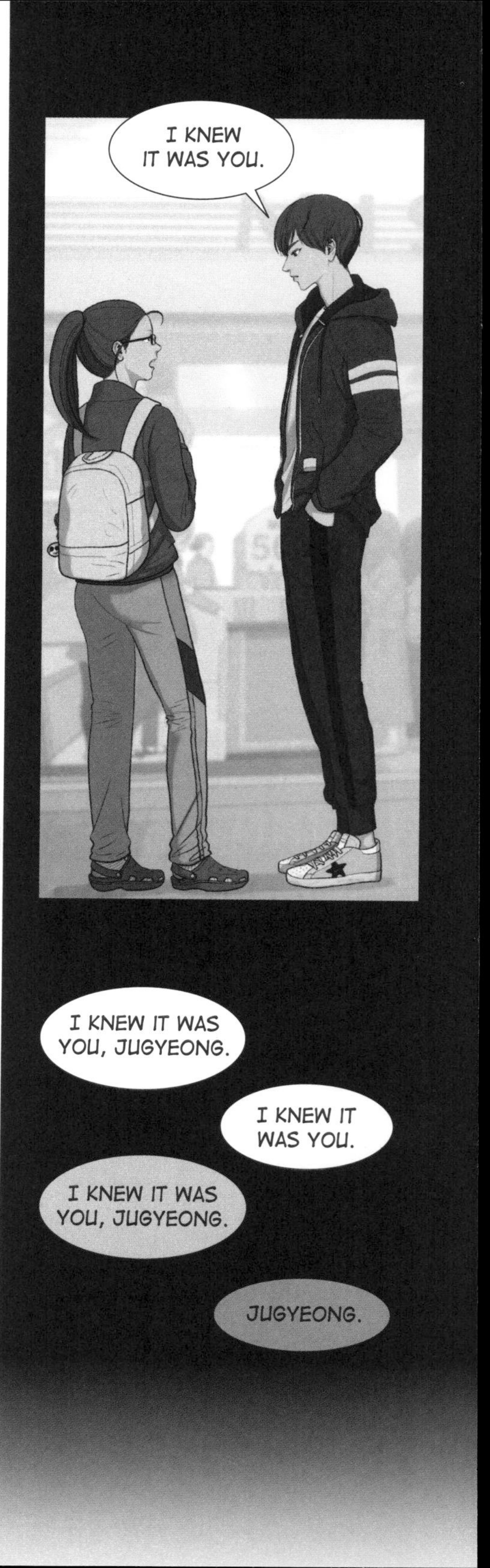
I KNEW IT WAS YOU.
I KNEW IT WAS YOU, JUGYEONG.
I KNEW IT WAS YOU.
I KNEW IT WAS YOU, JUGYEONG.
JUGYEONG.

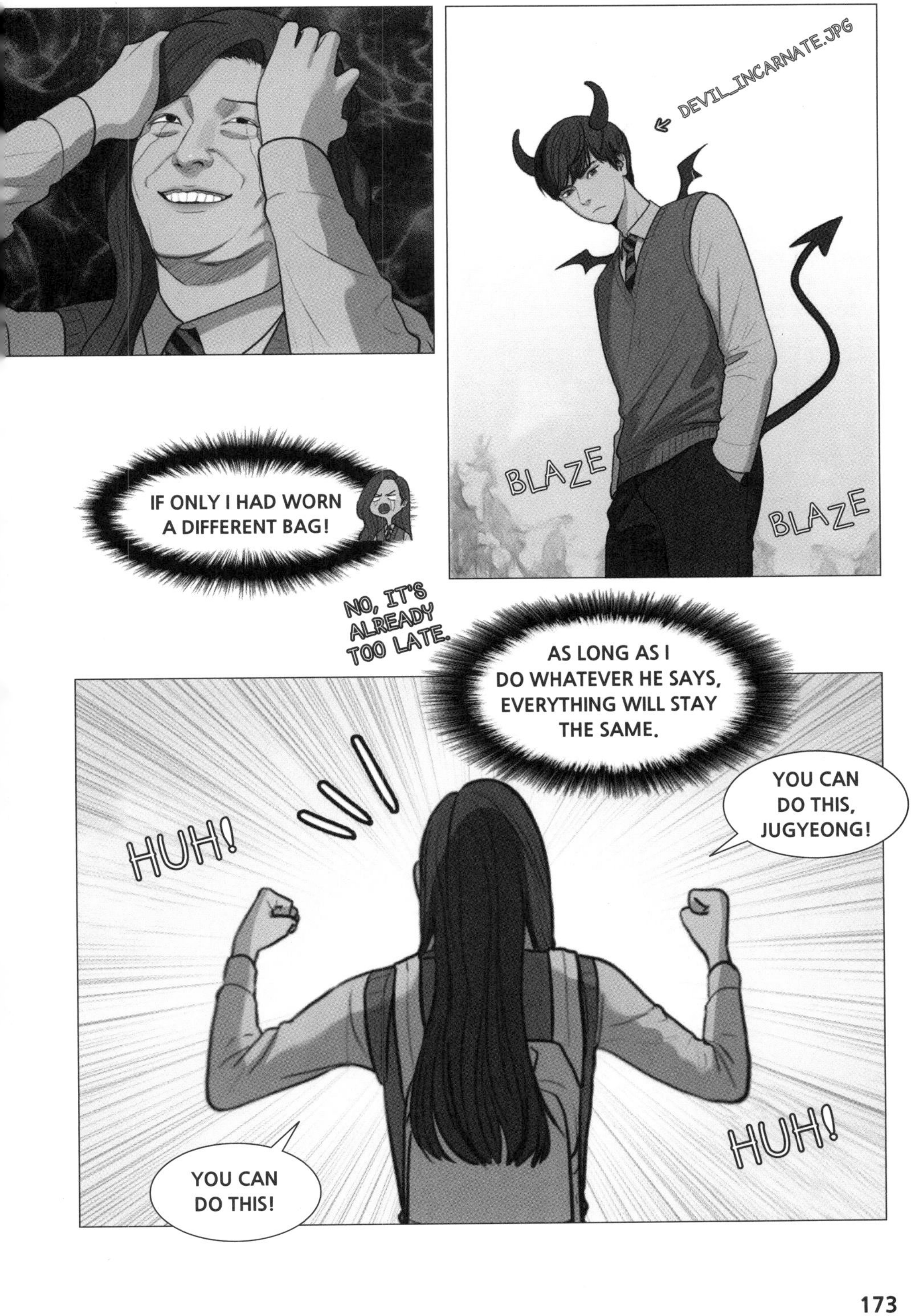
IF ONLY I HAD WORN A DIFFERENT BAG!
DEVIL_INCARNATE.JPG
BLAZE
BLAZE
NO, IT'S ALREADY TOO LATE.
AS LONG AS I DO WHATEVER HE SAYS, EVERYTHING WILL STAY THE SAME.
HUH!
YOU CAN DO THIS, JUGYEONG!
HUH!
YOU CAN DO THIS!

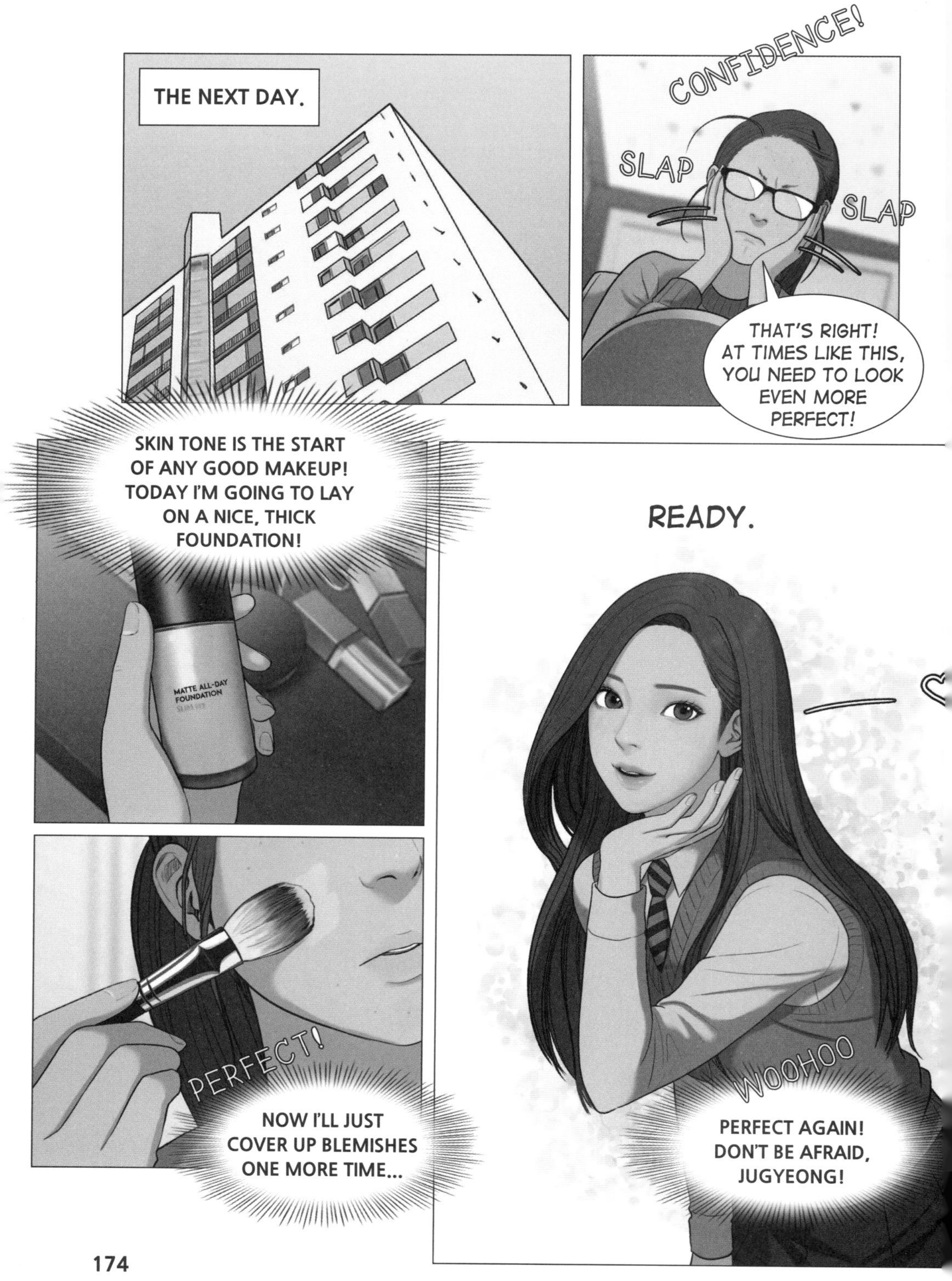
THE NEXT DAY.
CONFIDENCE!
SLAP
SLAP
THAT'S RIGHT! AT TIMES LIKE THIS, YOU NEED TO LOOK EVEN MORE PERFECT!
SKIN TONE IS THE START OF ANY GOOD MAKEUP! TODAY I'M GOING TO LAY ON A NICE, THICK FOUNDATION!
MATTE ALL-DAY FOUNDATION
PERFECT!
NOW I'LL JUST COVER UP BLEMISHES ONE MORE TIME...
READY.
WOOHOO
PERFECT AGAIN! DON'T BE AFRAID, JUGYEONG!

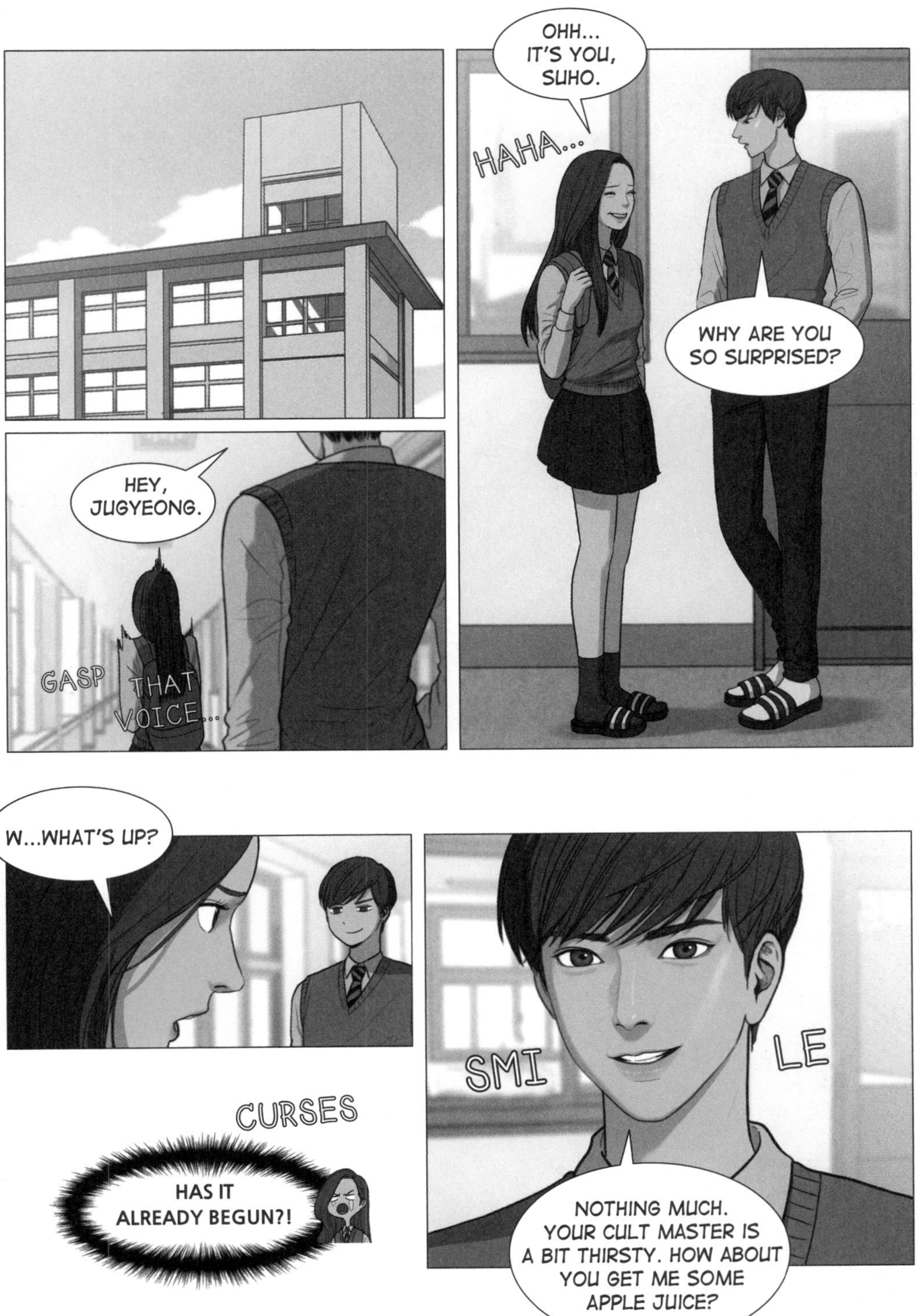
HEY, JUGYEONG.
GASP
THAT VOICE...
OHH... IT'S YOU, SUHO.
HAHA...
WHY ARE YOU SO SURPRISED?
W...WHAT'S UP?
CURSES
HAS IT ALREADY BEGUN?!
SMI LE
NOTHING MUCH. YOUR CULT MASTER IS A BIT THIRSTY. HOW ABOUT YOU GET ME SOME APPLE JUICE?

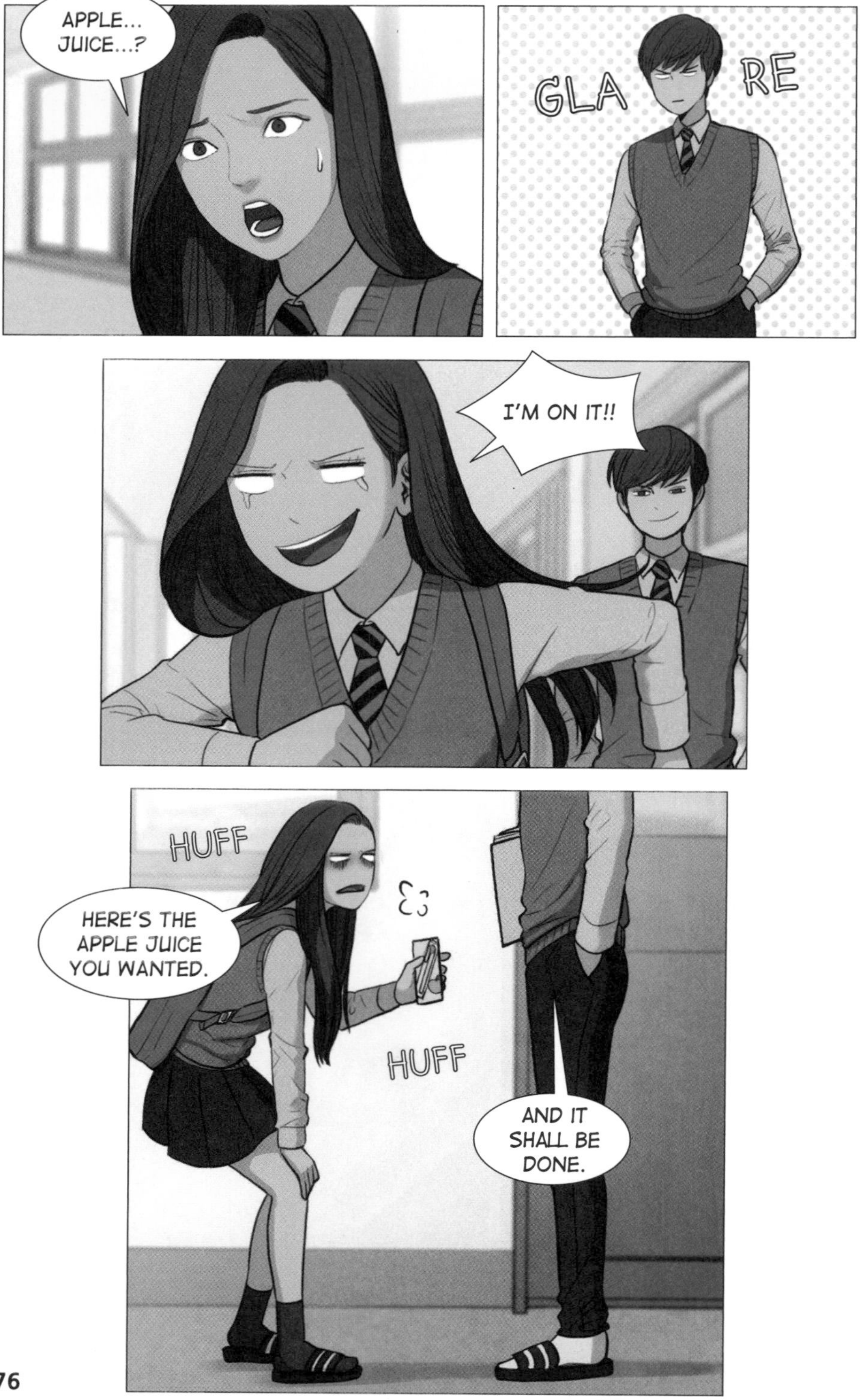
APPLE... JUICE...?
GLA RE
I'M ON IT!!
HUFF
HERE'S THE APPLE JUICE YOU WANTED.
HUFF
AND IT SHALL BE DONE.

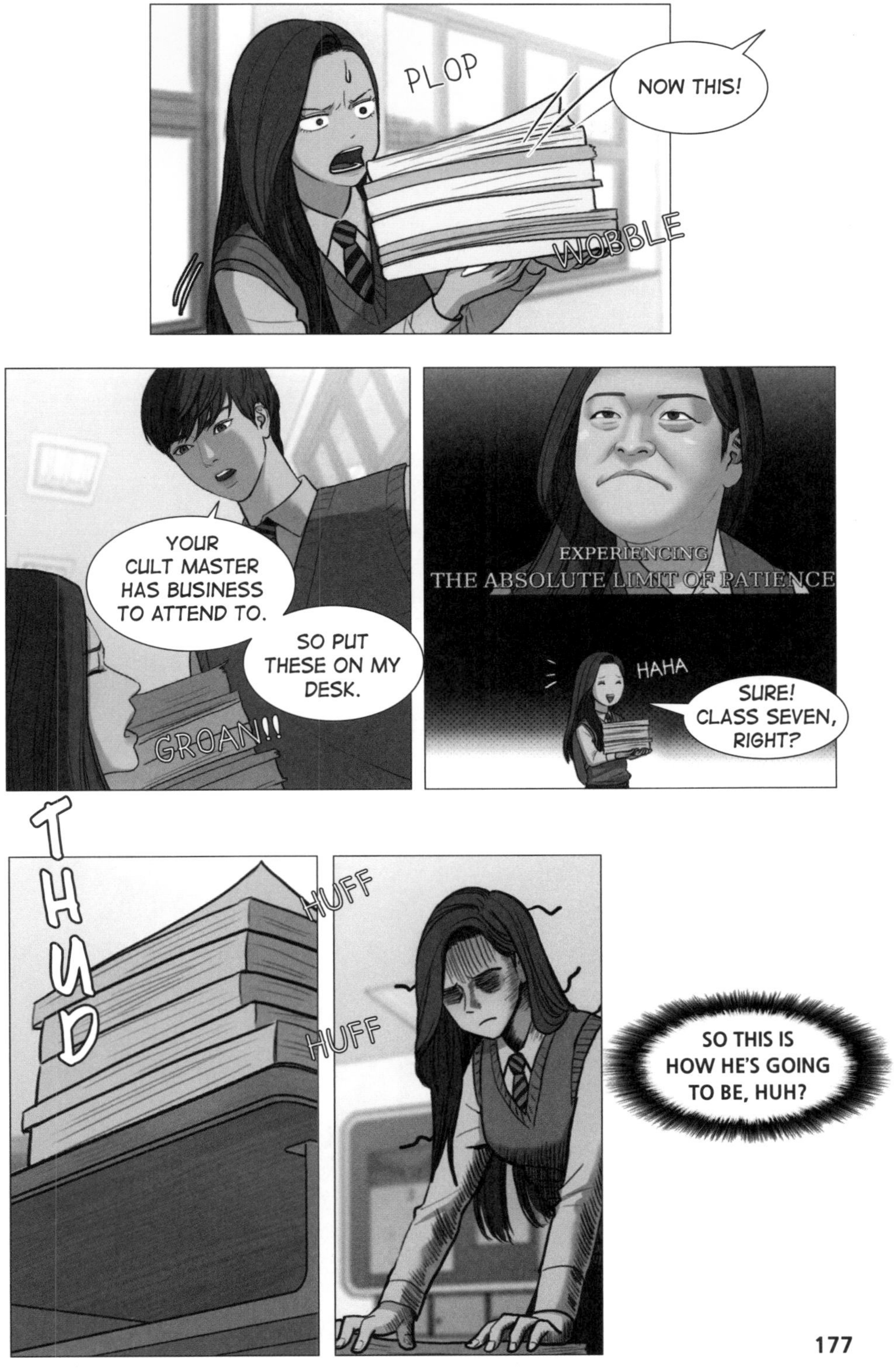
PLOP
NOW THIS!
WOBBLE
YOUR CULT MASTER HAS BUSINESS TO ATTEND TO.
SO PUT THESE ON MY DESK.
GROAN!!
EXPERIENCING THE ABSOLUTE LIMIT OF PATIENCE
HAHA
SURE! CLASS SEVEN, RIGHT?
THUD
HUFF
HUFF
SO THIS IS HOW HE'S GOING TO BE, HUH?

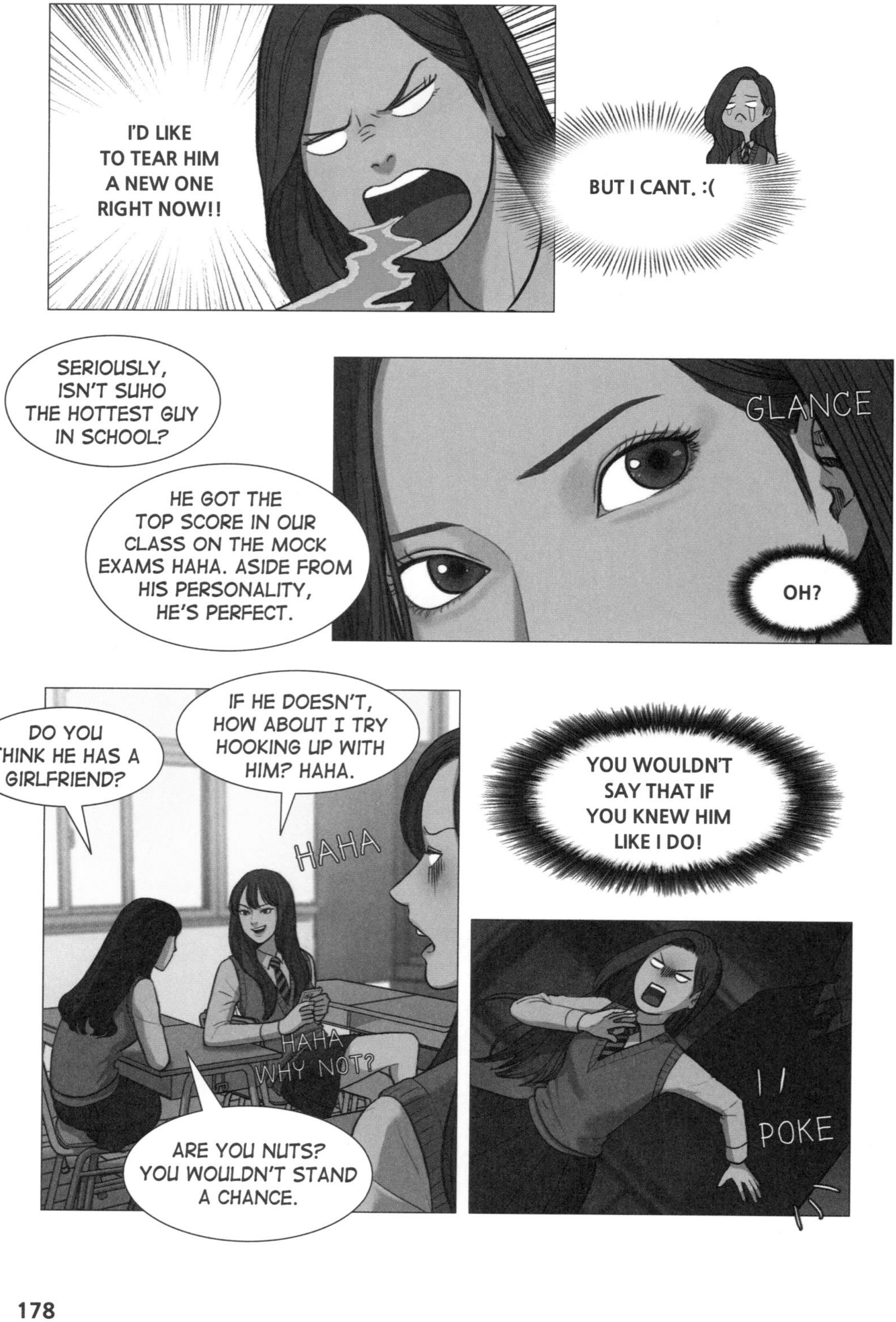
I'D LIKE TO TEAR HIM A NEW ONE RIGHT NOW!!
BUT I CANT. :(
SERIOUSLY, ISN'T SUHO THE HOTTEST GUY IN SCHOOL?
HE GOT THE TOP SCORE IN OUR CLASS ON THE MOCK EXAMS HAHA. ASIDE FROM HIS PERSONALITY, HE'S PERFECT.
GLANCE
OH?
DO YOU THINK HE HAS A GIRLFRIEND?
IF HE DOESN'T, HOW ABOUT I TRY HOOKING UP WITH HIM? HAHA.
HAHA
HAHA WHY NOT?
ARE YOU NUTS? YOU WOULDN'T STAND A CHANCE.
YOU WOULDN'T SAY THAT IF YOU KNEW HIM LIKE I DO!
POKE

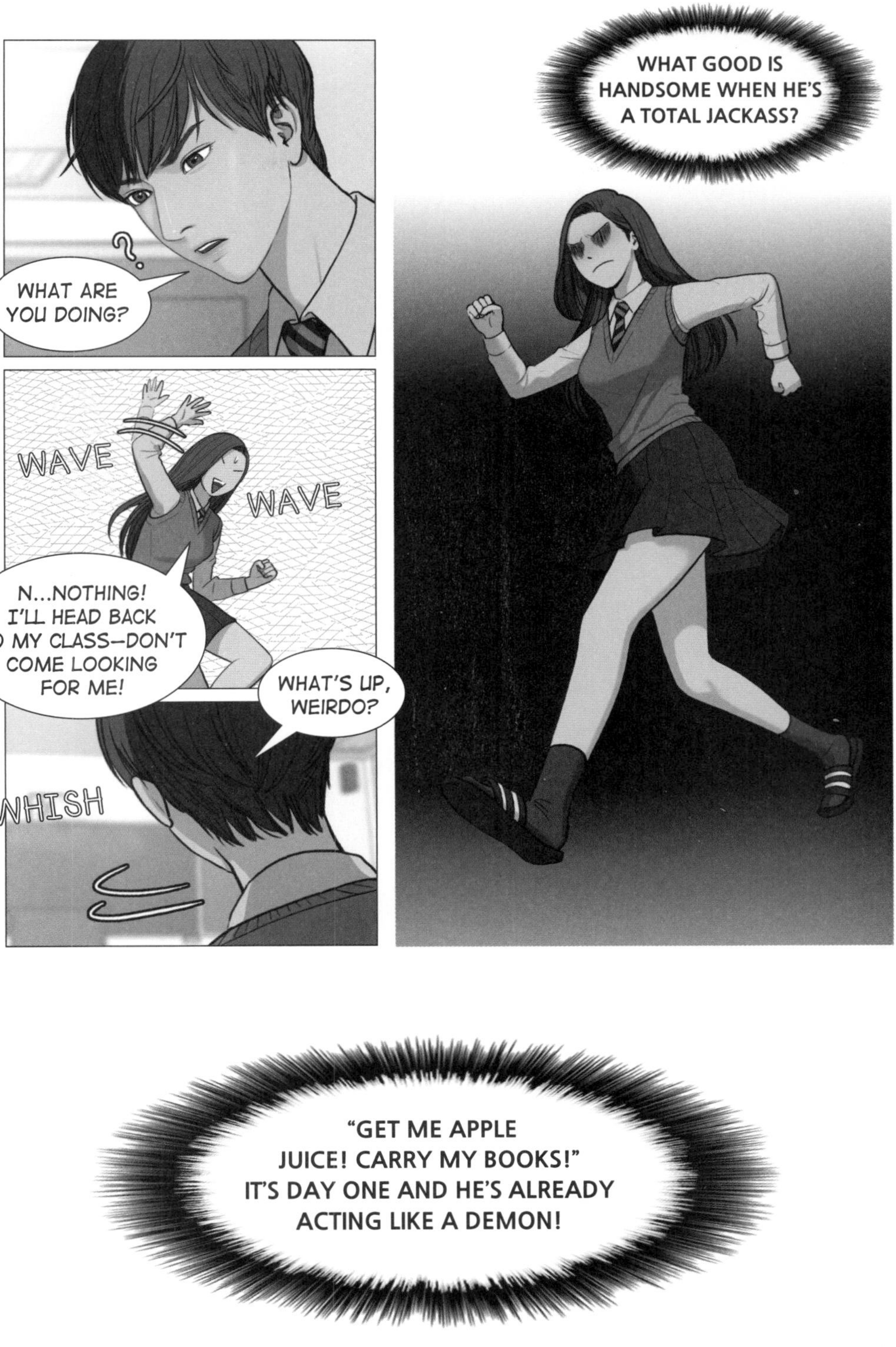

WHAT ARE YOU DOING?
WAVE
WAVE
N...NOTHING! I'LL HEAD BACK TO MY CLASS–DON'T COME LOOKING FOR ME!
WHAT'S UP, WEIRDO?
WHISH
WHAT GOOD IS HANDSOME WHEN HE'S A TOTAL JACKASS?
"GET ME APPLE JUICE! CARRY MY BOOKS!" IT'S DAY ONE AND HE'S ALREADY ACTING LIKE A DEMON!

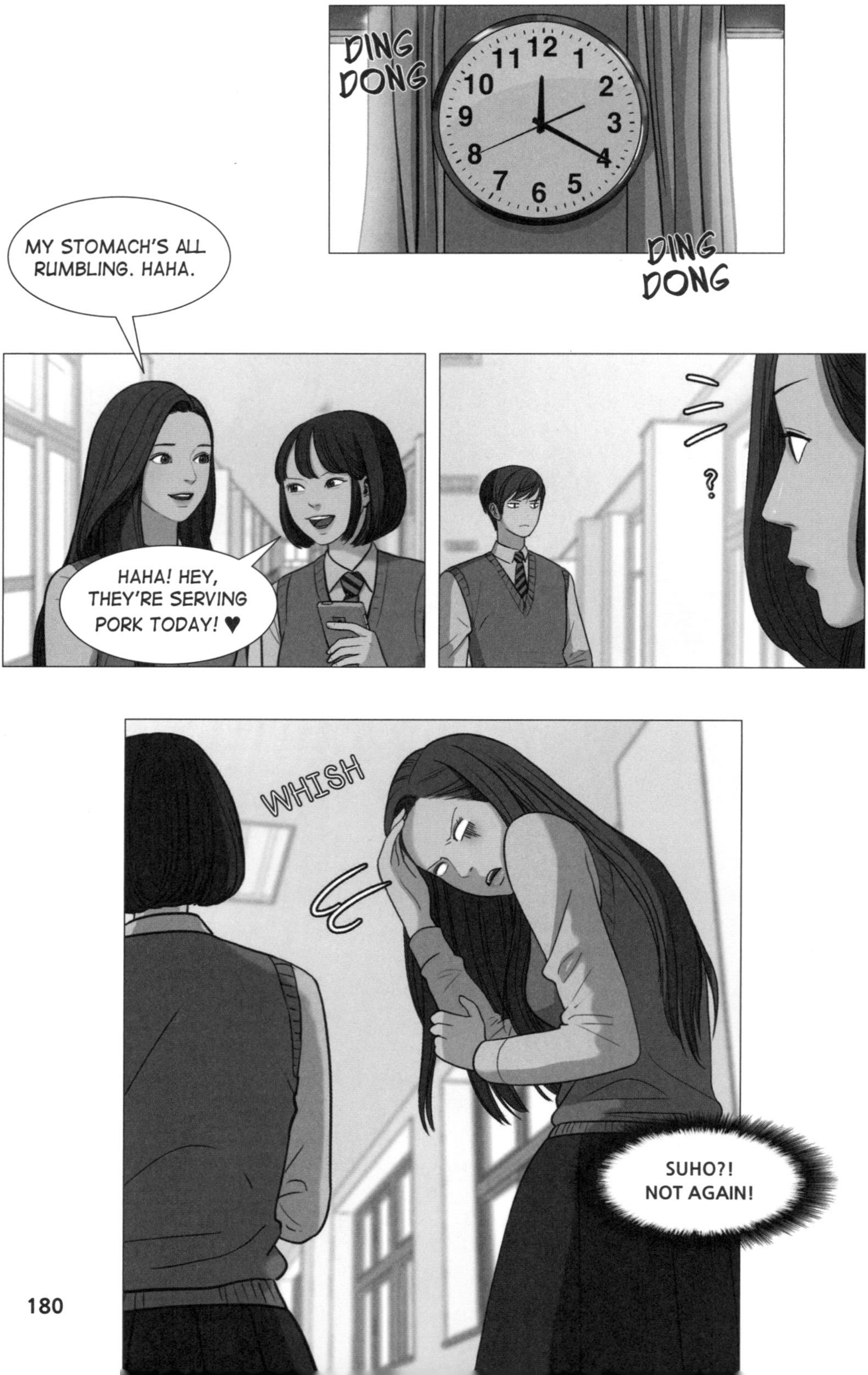
DING DONG
12 11 1 10 2 9 3 8 4 7 6 5
DING DONG
MY STOMACH'S ALL RUMBLING. HAHA.
HAHA! HEY, THEY'RE SERVING PORK TODAY! ♥
?
WHISH
SUHO?! NOT AGAIN!

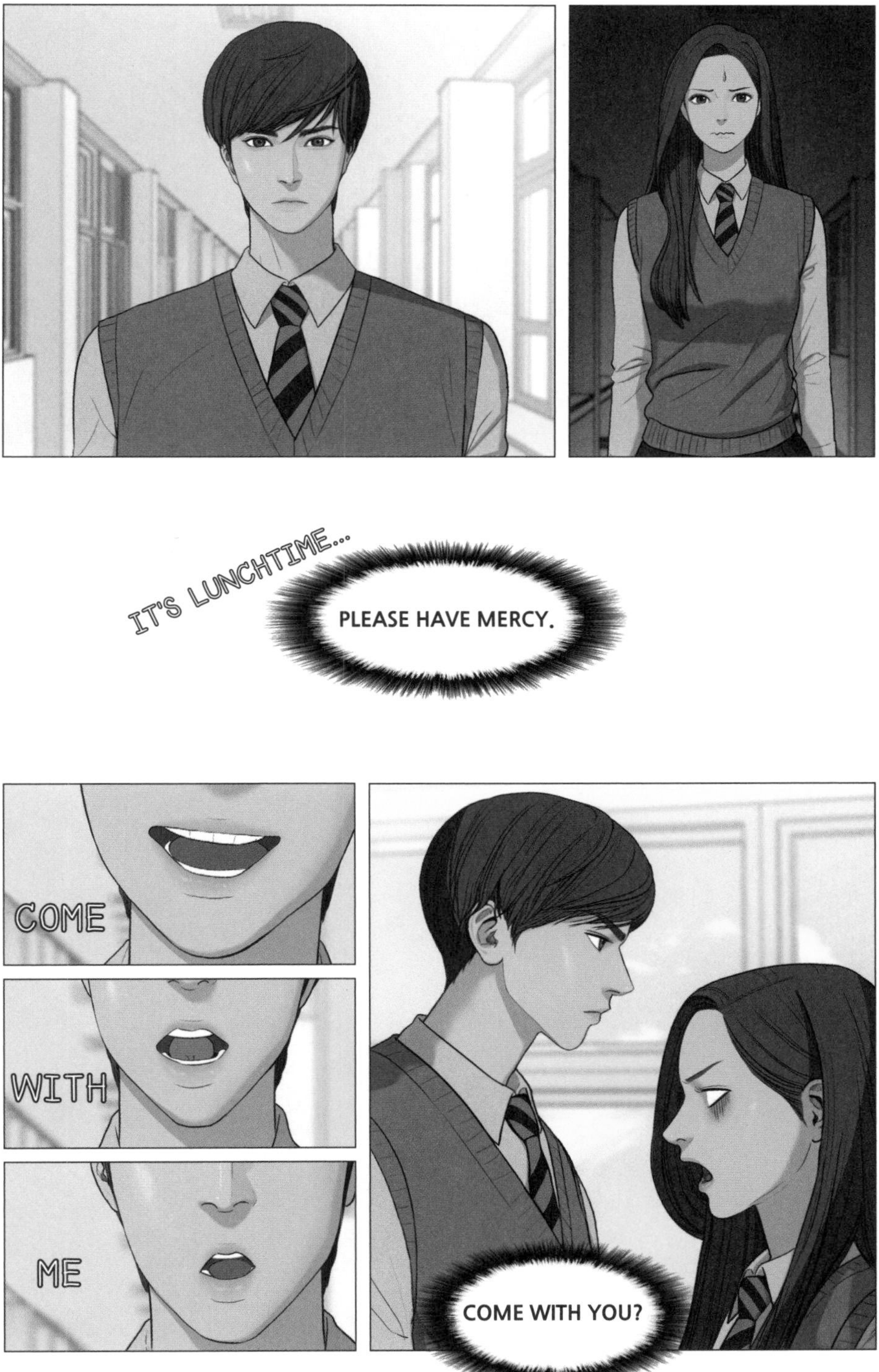
IT'S LUNCHTIME...
PLEASE HAVE MERCY.
COME
WITH
ME
COME WITH YOU?

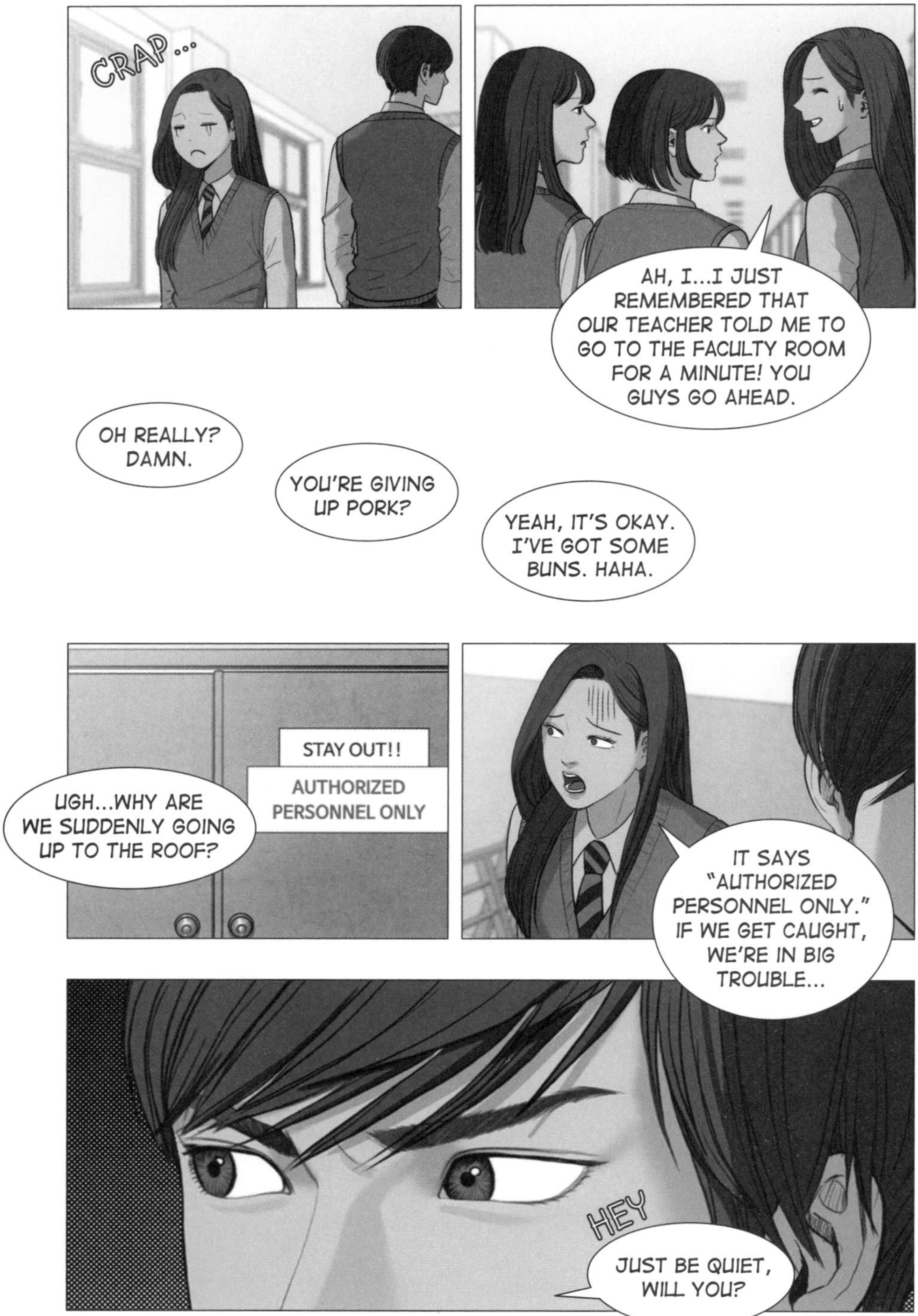
CRAP...
AH, I...I JUST REMEMBERED THAT OUR TEACHER TOLD ME TO GO TO THE FACULTY ROOM FOR A MINUTE! YOU GUYS GO AHEAD.
OH REALLY? DAMN.
YOU'RE GIVING UP PORK?
YEAH, IT'S OKAY. I'VE GOT SOME BUNS. HAHA.
STAY OUT!!
UGH...WHY ARE WE SUDDENLY GOING UP TO THE ROOF?
AUTHORIZED PERSONNEL ONLY
IT SAYS "AUTHORIZED PERSONNEL ONLY." IF WE GET CAUGHT, WE'RE IN BIG TROUBLE...
HEY
JUST BE QUIET, WILL YOU?

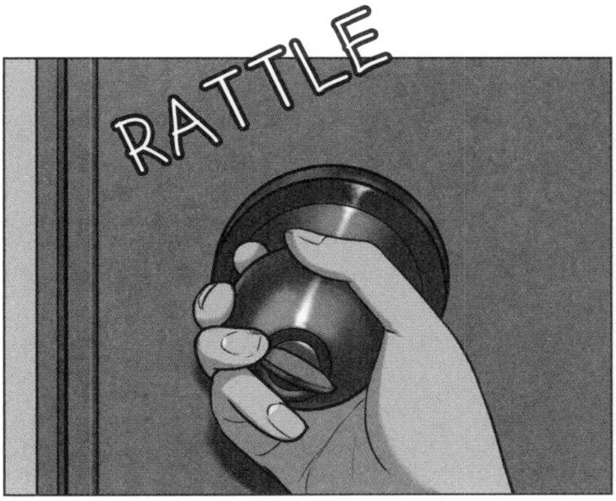
RATTLE

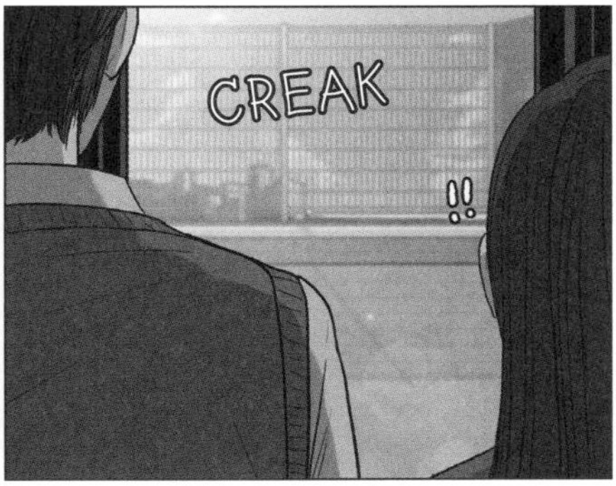
CREAK
!!

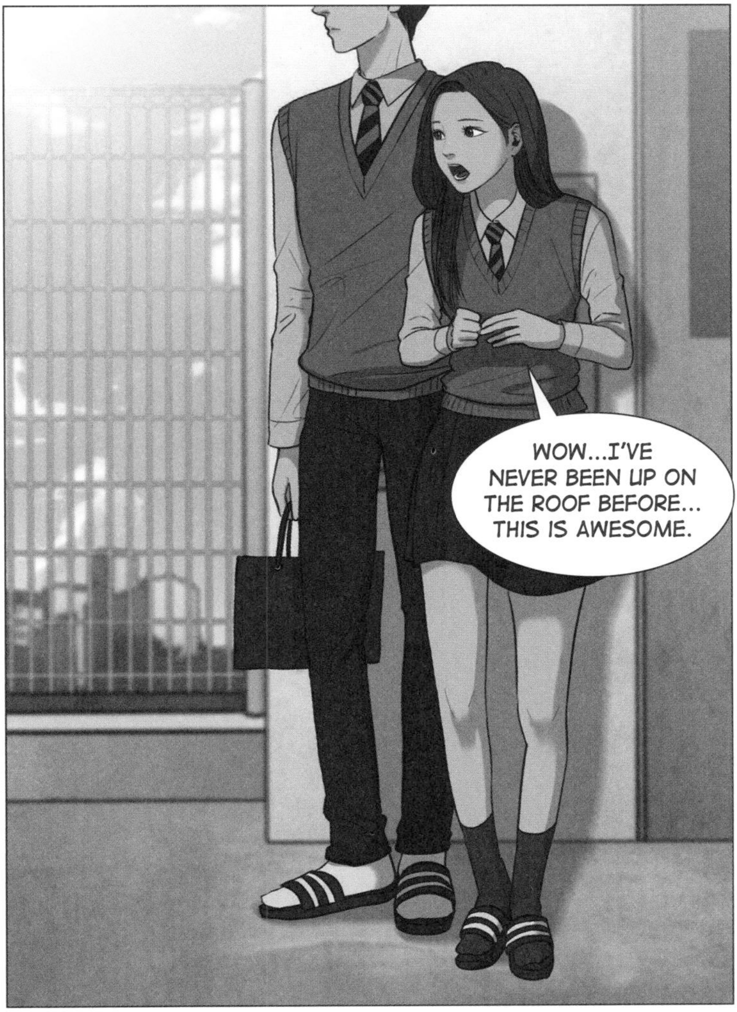
WOW...I'VE NEVER BEEN UP ON THE ROOF BEFORE... THIS IS AWESOME.

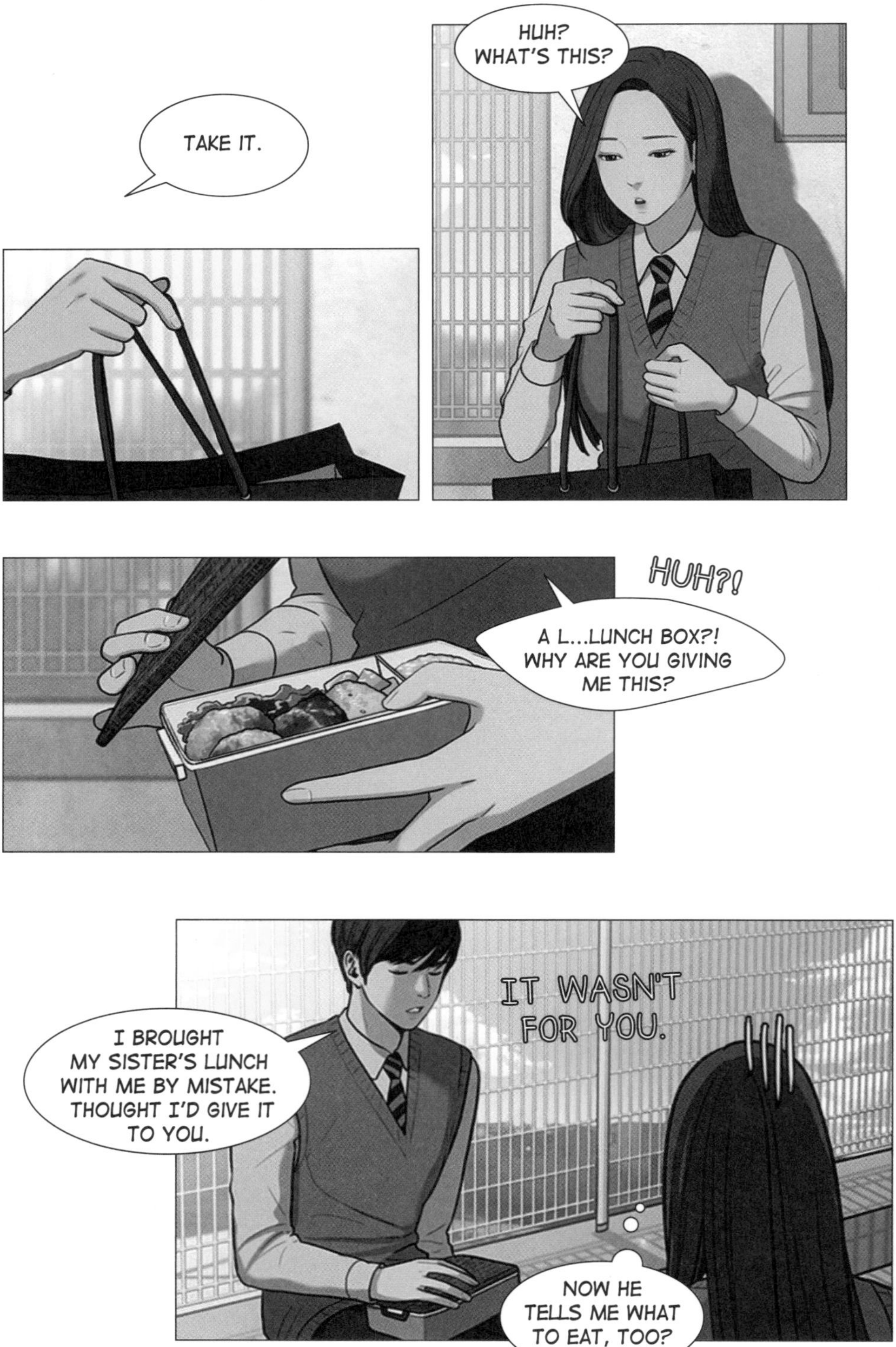
TAKE IT.
HUH? WHAT'S THIS?
HUH?!
A L...LUNCH BOX?! WHY ARE YOU GIVING ME THIS?
I BROUGHT MY SISTER'S LUNCH WITH ME BY MISTAKE. THOUGHT I'D GIVE IT TO YOU.
IT WASN'T FOR YOU.
NOW HE TELLS ME WHAT TO EAT, TOO?

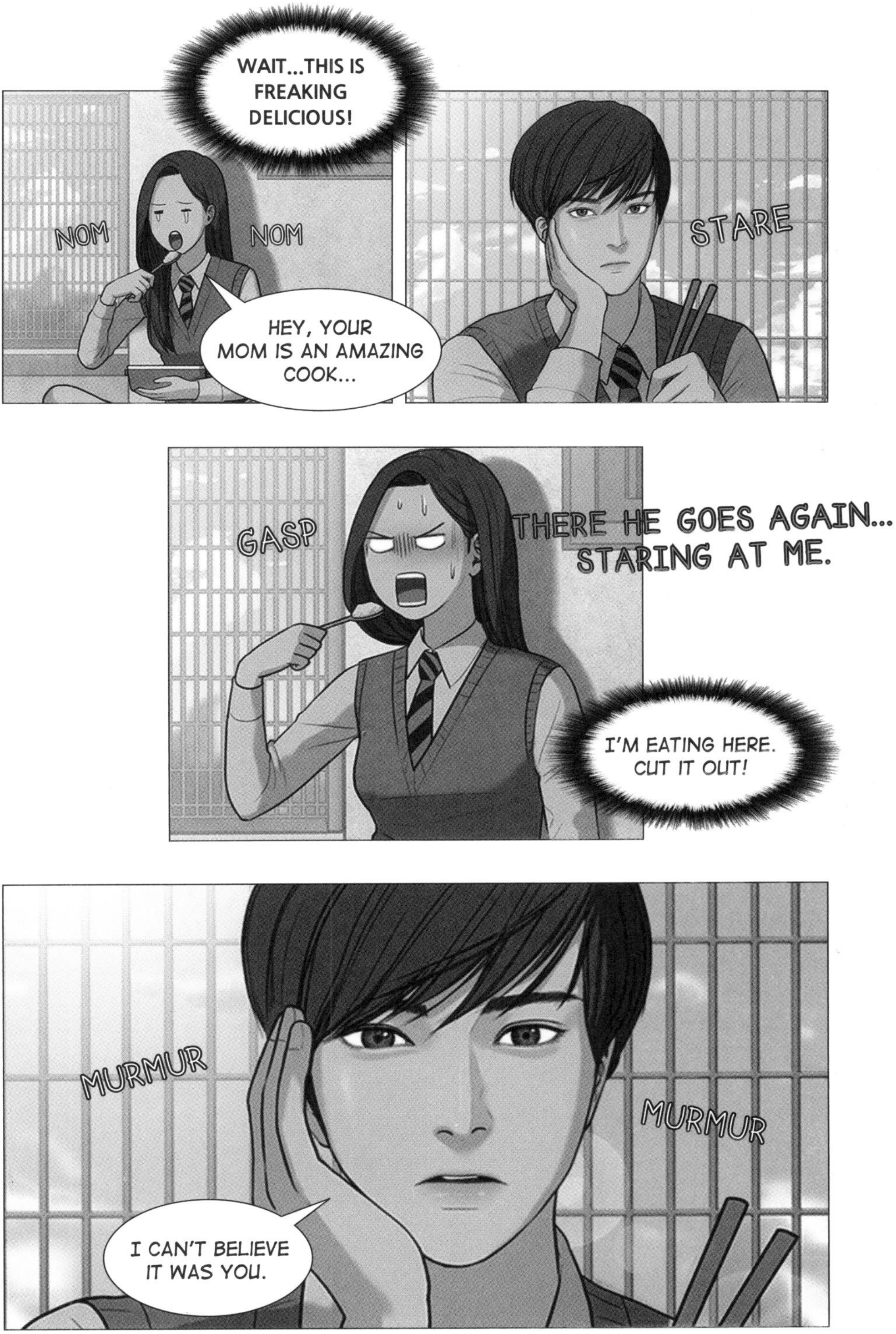
WAIT...THIS IS FREAKING DELICIOUS!
NOM
NOM
HEY, YOUR MOM IS AN AMAZING COOK...
STARE
GASP
THERE HE GOES AGAIN... STARING AT ME.
I'M EATING HERE. CUT IT OUT!
MURMUR
MURMUR
I CAN'T BELIEVE IT WAS YOU.

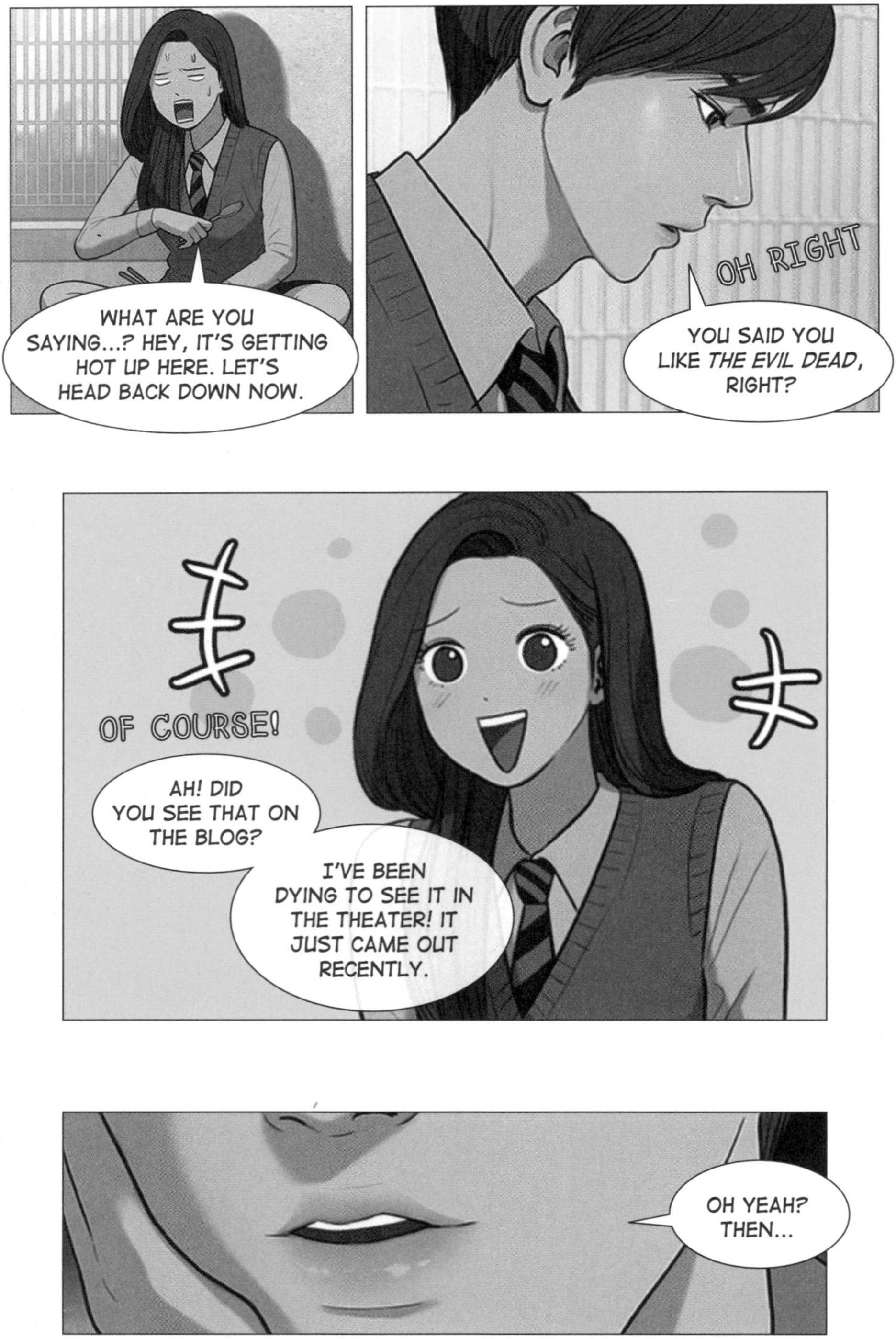
WHAT ARE YOU SAYING...? HEY, IT'S GETTING HOT UP HERE. LET'S HEAD BACK DOWN NOW.
OH RIGHT
YOU SAID YOU LIKE *THE EVIL DEAD*, RIGHT?
OF COURSE!
AH! DID YOU SEE THAT ON THE BLOG?
I'VE BEEN DYING TO SEE IT IN THE THEATER! IT JUST CAME OUT RECENTLY.
OH YEAH? THEN...

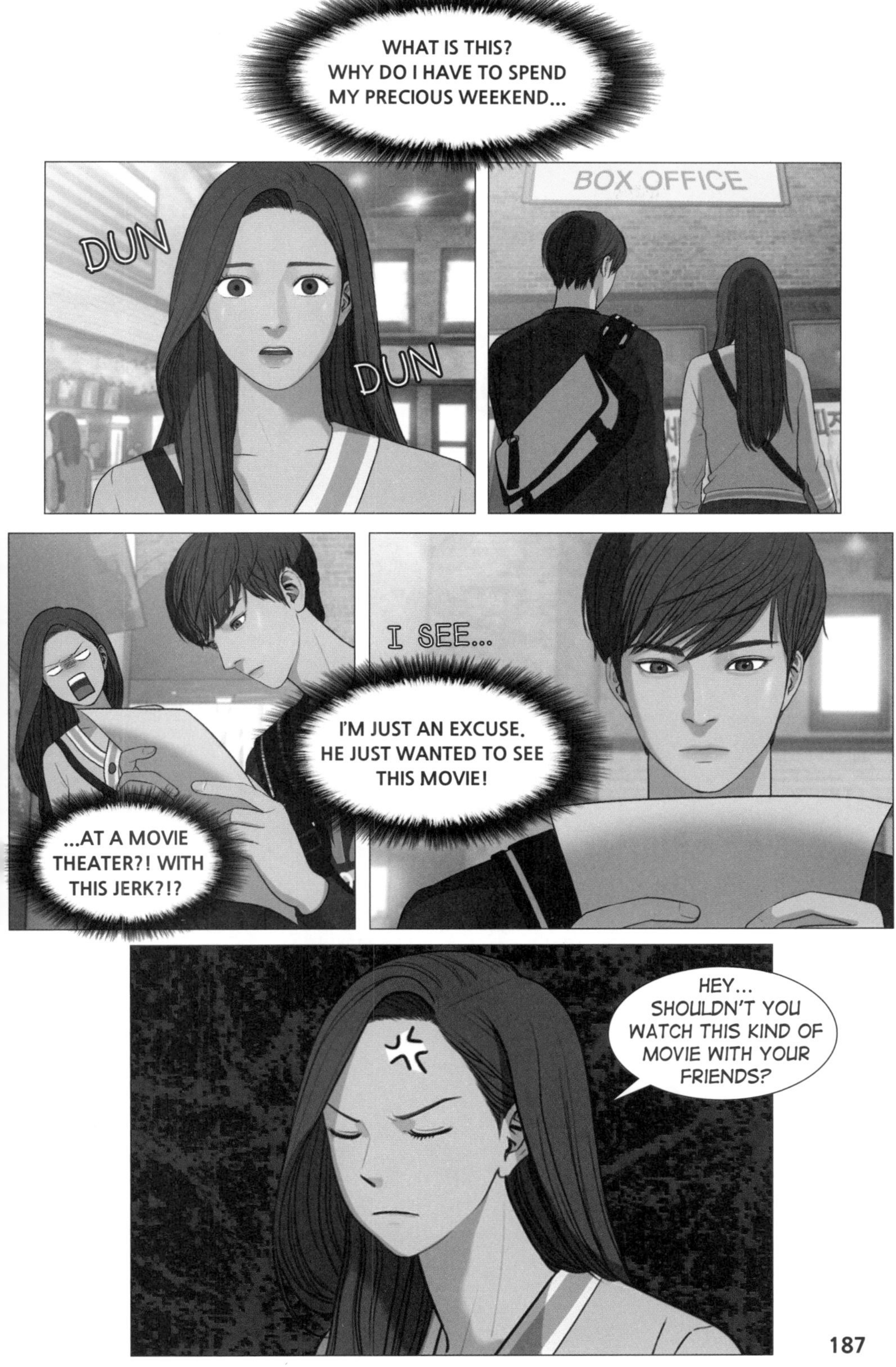
WHAT IS THIS? WHY DO I HAVE TO SPEND MY PRECIOUS WEEKEND...
DUN
DUN
BOX OFFICE
...AT A MOVIE THEATER?! WITH THIS JERK?!?
I SEE...
I'M JUST AN EXCUSE. HE JUST WANTED TO SEE THIS MOVIE!
HEY... SHOULDN'T YOU WATCH THIS KIND OF MOVIE WITH YOUR FRIENDS?

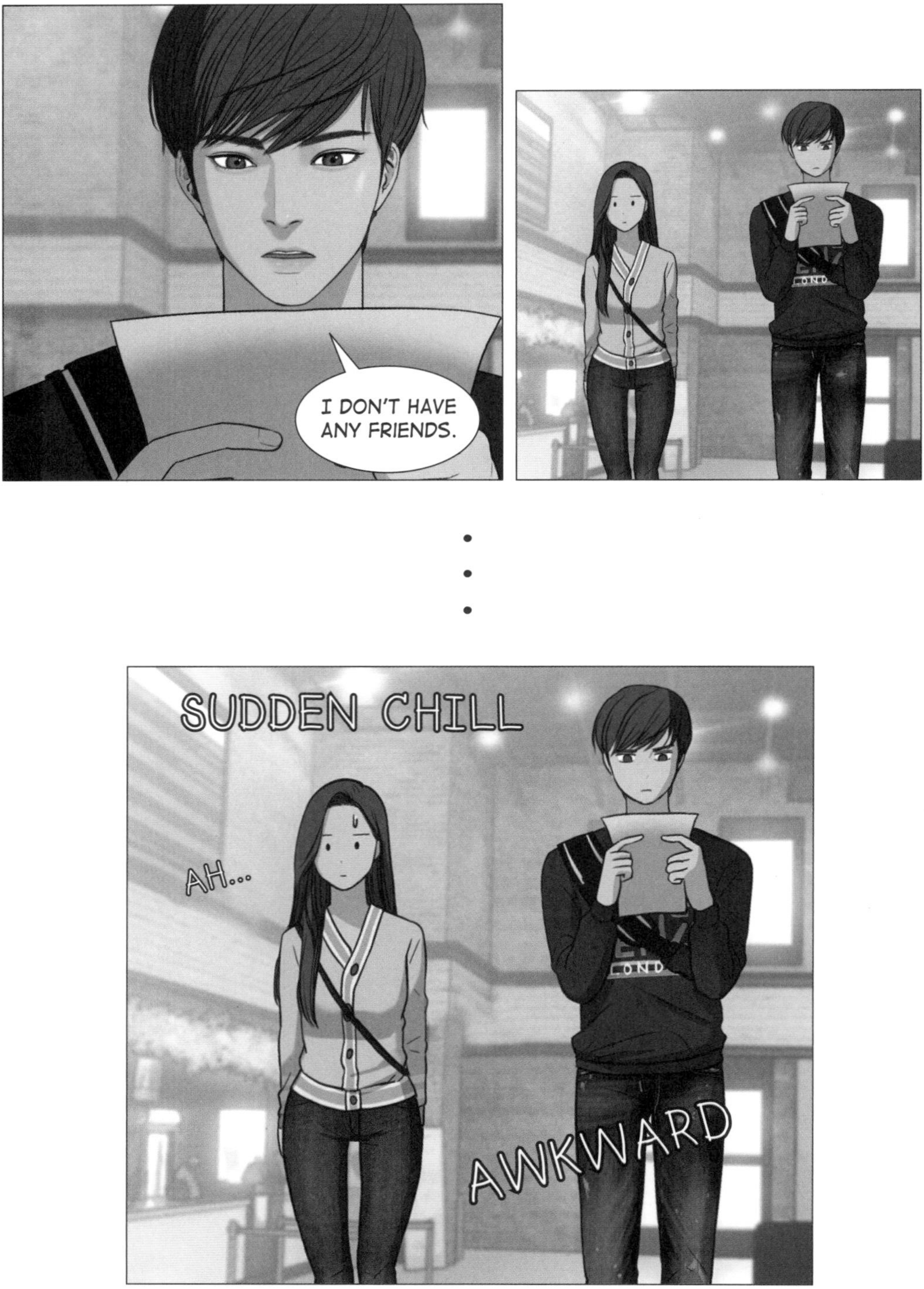
I DON'T HAVE ANY FRIENDS.
SUDDEN CHILL
AH...
AWKWARD

MAXIMUM_AWKWARDNESS.TXT

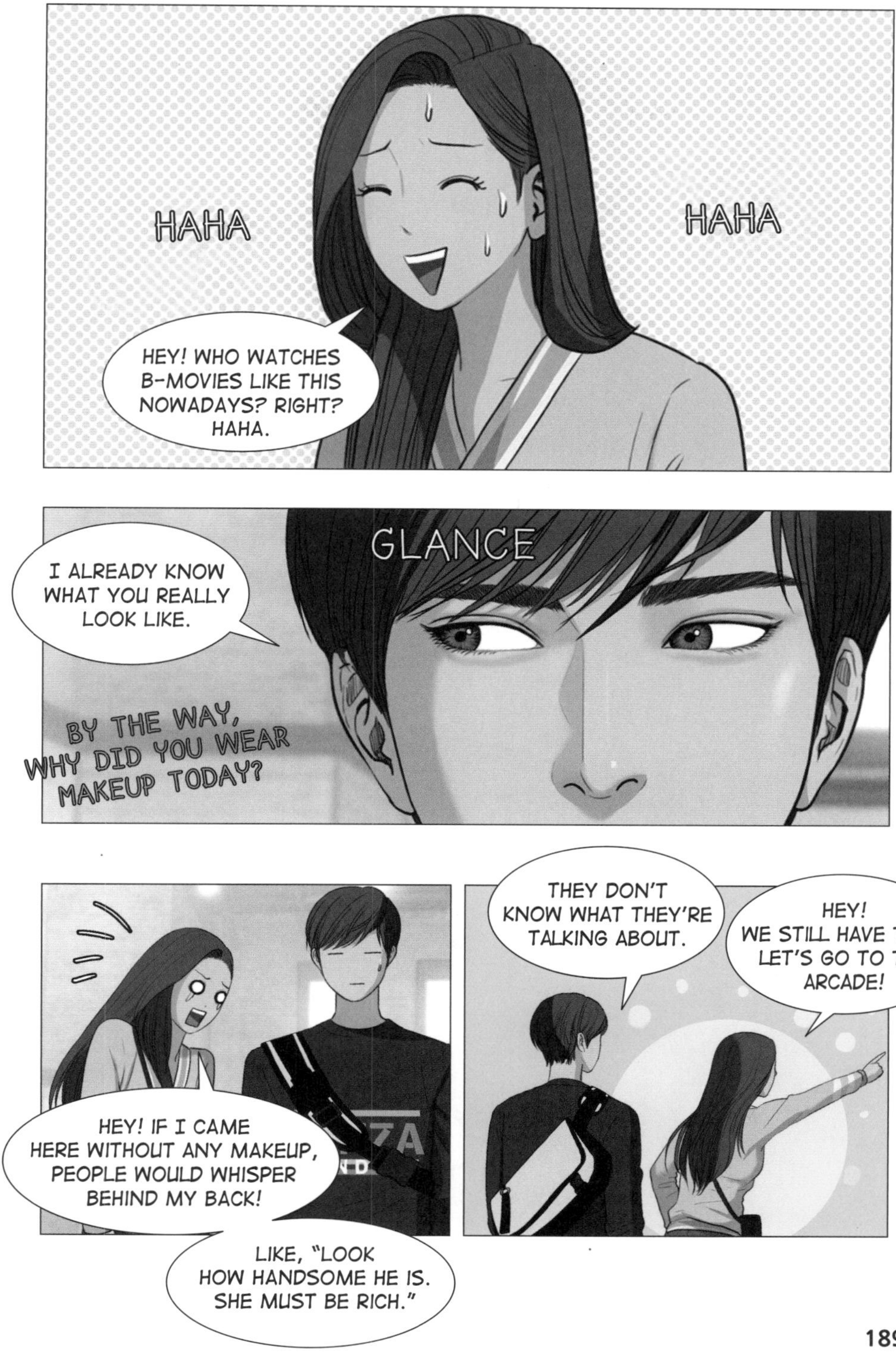
HAHA
HAHA
HEY! WHO WATCHES B-MOVIES LIKE THIS NOWADAYS? RIGHT? HAHA.
I ALREADY KNOW WHAT YOU REALLY LOOK LIKE.
GLANCE
BY THE WAY, WHY DID YOU WEAR MAKEUP TODAY?
HEY! IF I CAME HERE WITHOUT ANY MAKEUP, PEOPLE WOULD WHISPER BEHIND MY BACK!
LIKE, "LOOK HOW HANDSOME HE IS. SHE MUST BE RICH."
THEY DON'T KNOW WHAT THEY'RE TALKING ABOUT.
HEY! WE STILL HAVE TIME! LET'S GO TO THE ARCADE!

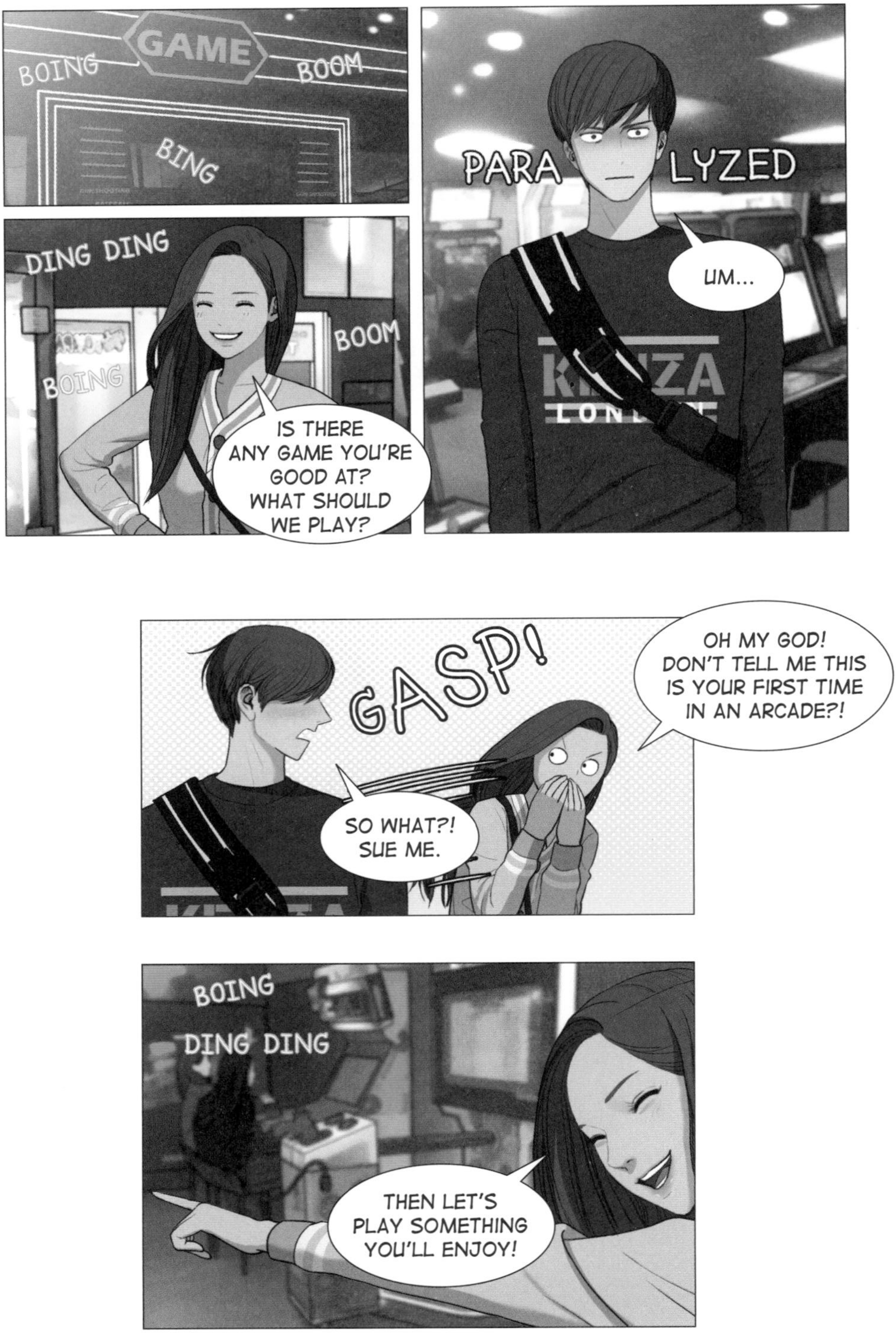
BOING
GAME
BOOM
BING
DING DING
BOOM
BOING
IS THERE ANY GAME YOU'RE GOOD AT? WHAT SHOULD WE PLAY?
PARA LYZED
UM...
GASP!
OH MY GOD! DON'T TELL ME THIS IS YOUR FIRST TIME IN AN ARCADE?!
SO WHAT?! SUE ME.
BOING
DING DING
THEN LET'S PLAY SOMETHING YOU'LL ENJOY!

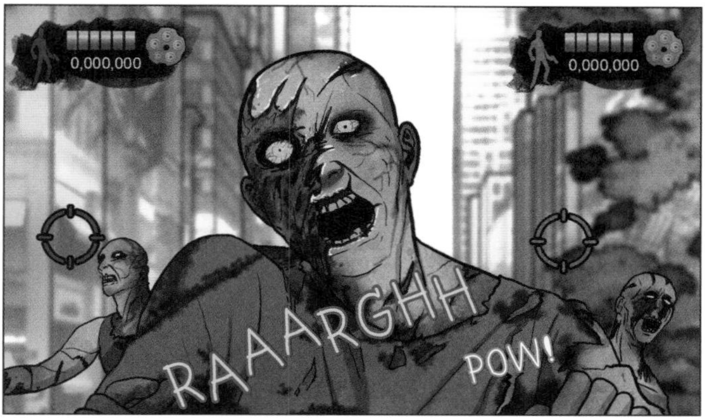
0,000,000
0,000,000
RAAARGHH
POW!

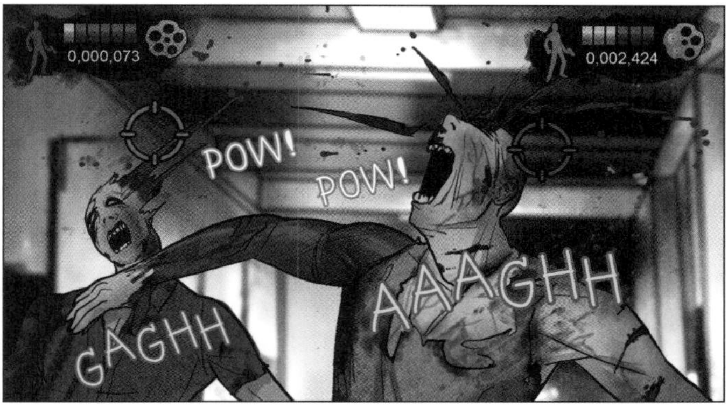
0,000,073
0,002,424
POW!
POW!
GAGHH
AAAGHH

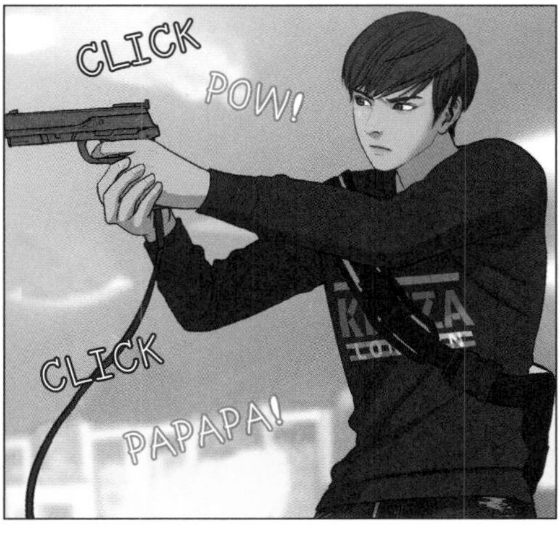
CLICK
POW!
CLICK
PAPAPA!

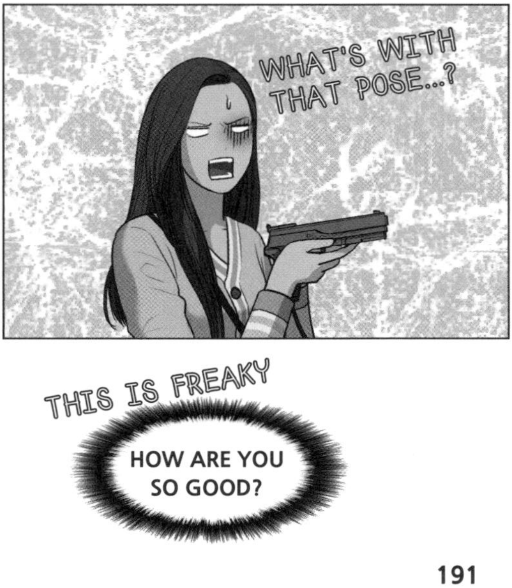
WHAT'S WITH THAT POSE...?
THIS IS FREAKY
HOW ARE YOU SO GOOD?

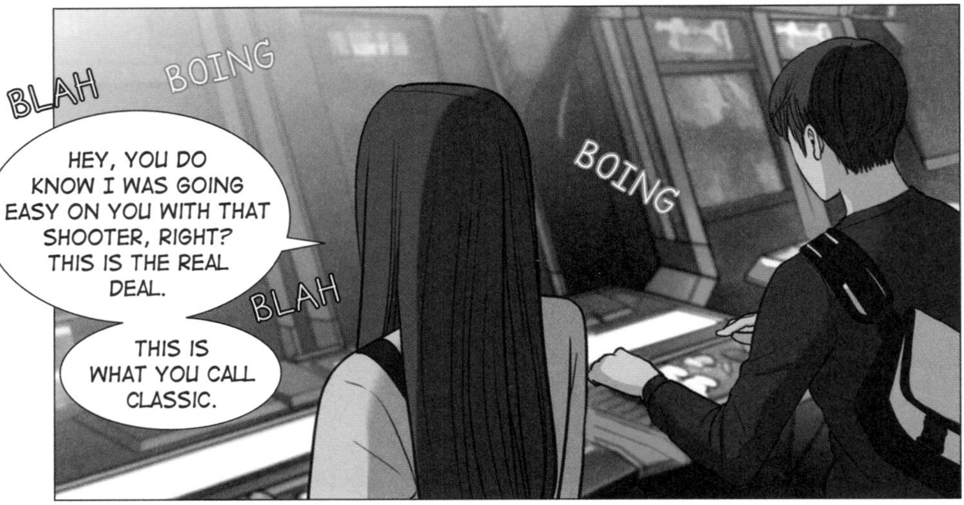
BLAH
BOING
HEY, YOU DO KNOW I WAS GOING EASY ON YOU WITH THAT SHOOTER, RIGHT? THIS IS THE REAL DEAL.
BOING
BLAH
THIS IS WHAT YOU CALL CLASSIC.

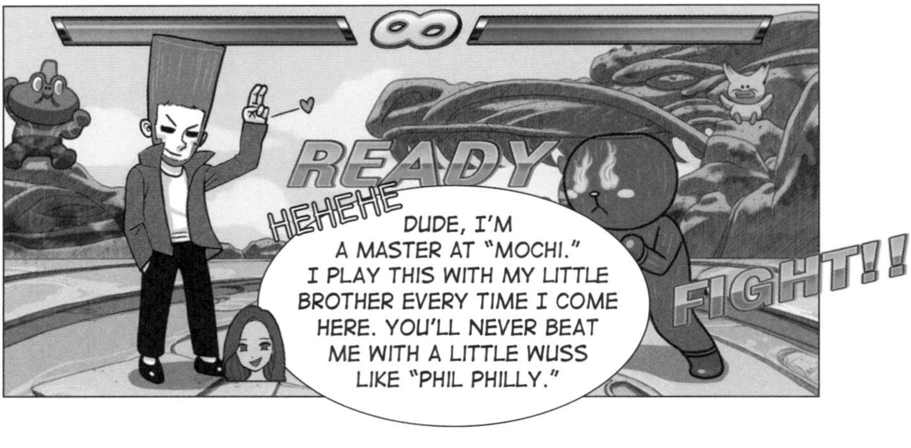
READY
HEHEHE
DUDE, I'M A MASTER AT "MOCHI." I PLAY THIS WITH MY LITTLE BROTHER EVERY TIME I COME HERE. YOU'LL NEVER BEAT ME WITH A LITTLE WUSS LIKE "PHIL PHILLY."
FIGHT!!

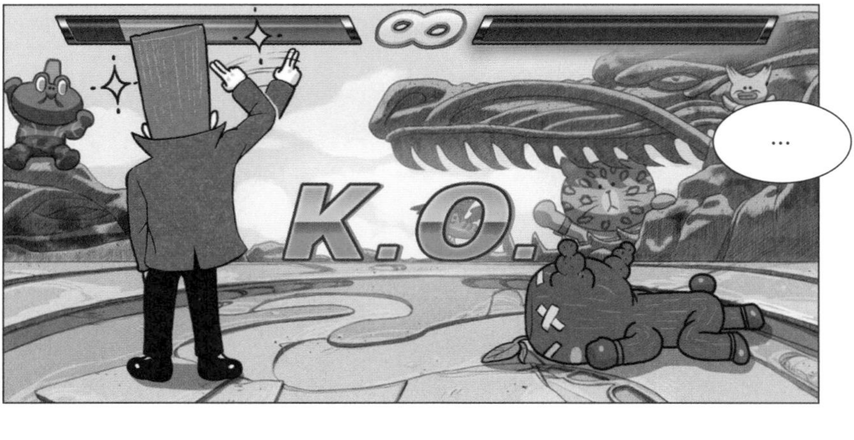
K.O.
...

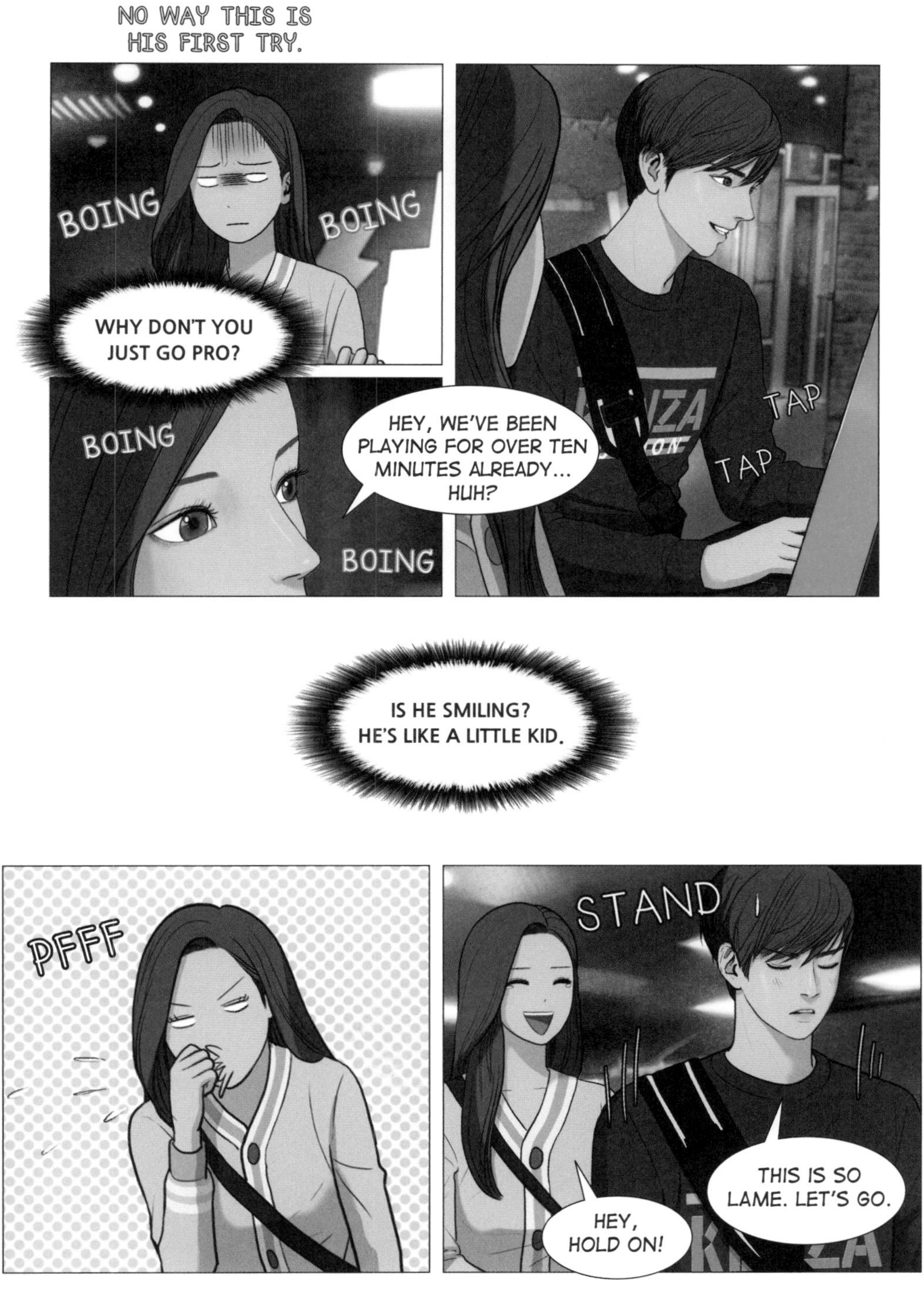
NO WAY THIS IS HIS FIRST TRY.
BOING
BOING
WHY DON'T YOU JUST GO PRO?
BOING
HEY, WE'VE BEEN PLAYING FOR OVER TEN MINUTES ALREADY... HUH?
BOING
TAP
TAP
IS HE SMILING? HE'S LIKE A LITTLE KID.
PFFF
STAND
THIS IS SO LAME. LET'S GO.
HEY, HOLD ON!

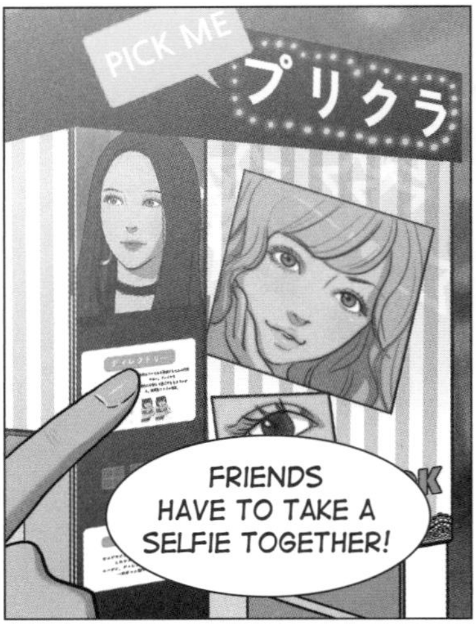
PICK ME
プリクラ
FRIENDS HAVE TO TAKE A SELFIE TOGETHER!

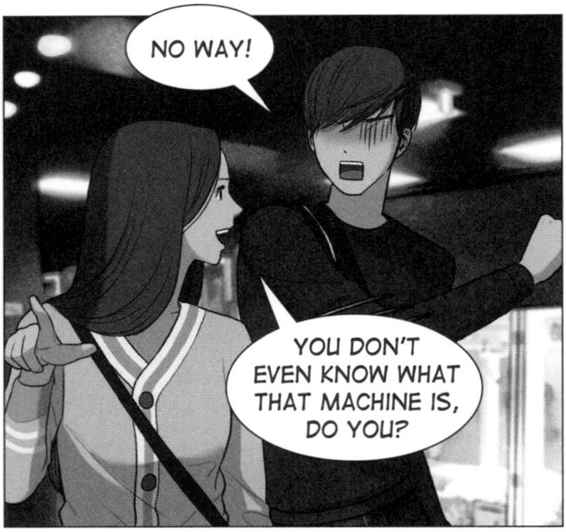
NO WAY!
YOU DON'T EVEN KNOW WHAT THAT MACHINE IS, DO YOU?

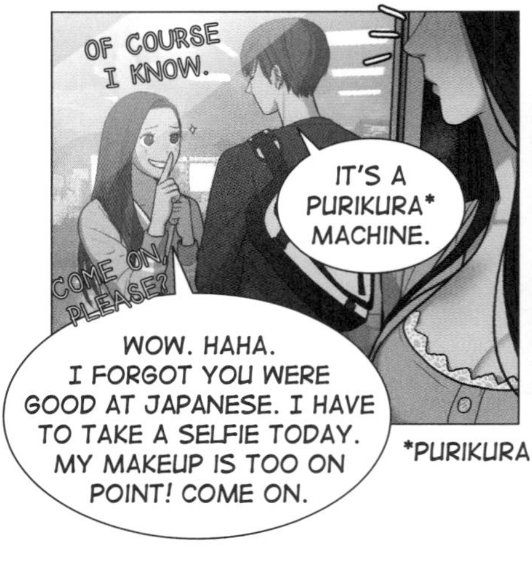
OF COURSE I KNOW.
IT'S A PURIKURA* MACHINE.
COME ON, PLEASE?
WOW. HAHA. I FORGOT YOU WERE GOOD AT JAPANESE. I HAVE TO TAKE A SELFIE TODAY. MY MAKEUP IS TOO ON POINT! COME ON.

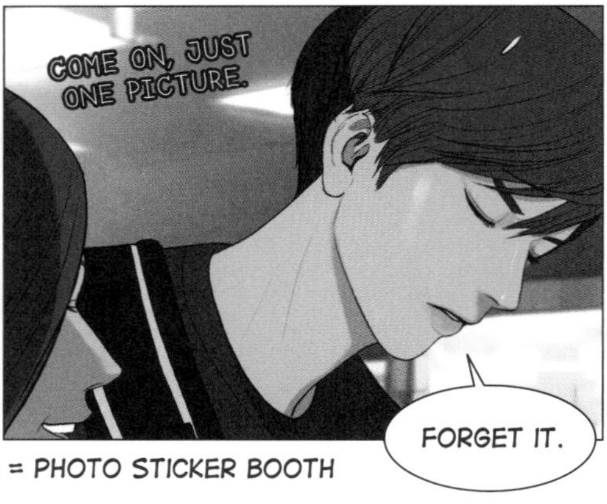
COME ON, JUST ONE PICTURE.
FORGET IT.

*PURIKURA = PHOTO STICKER BOOTH

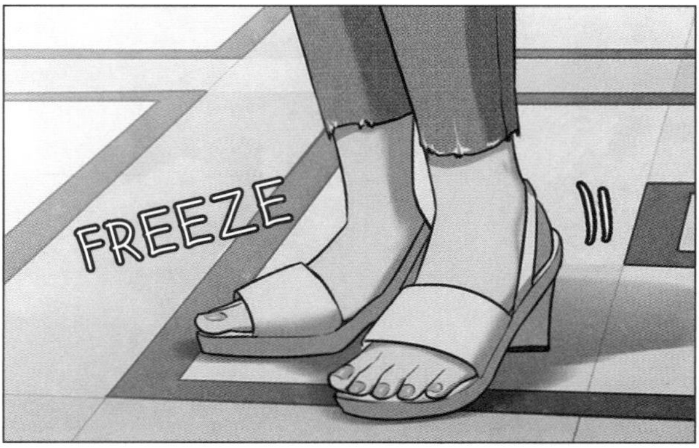
FREEZE

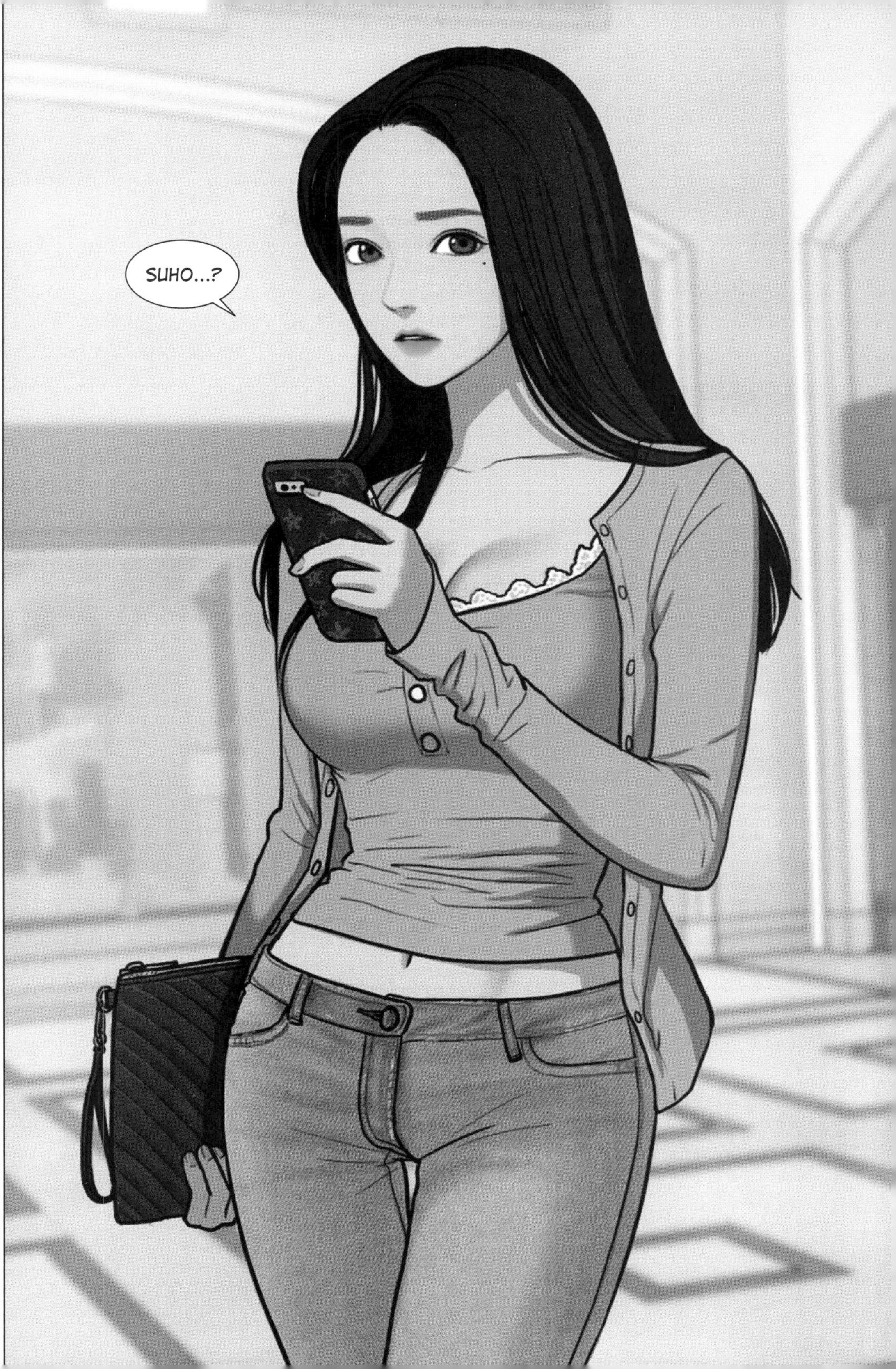
SUHO...?

Episodes
10–13

여신강림

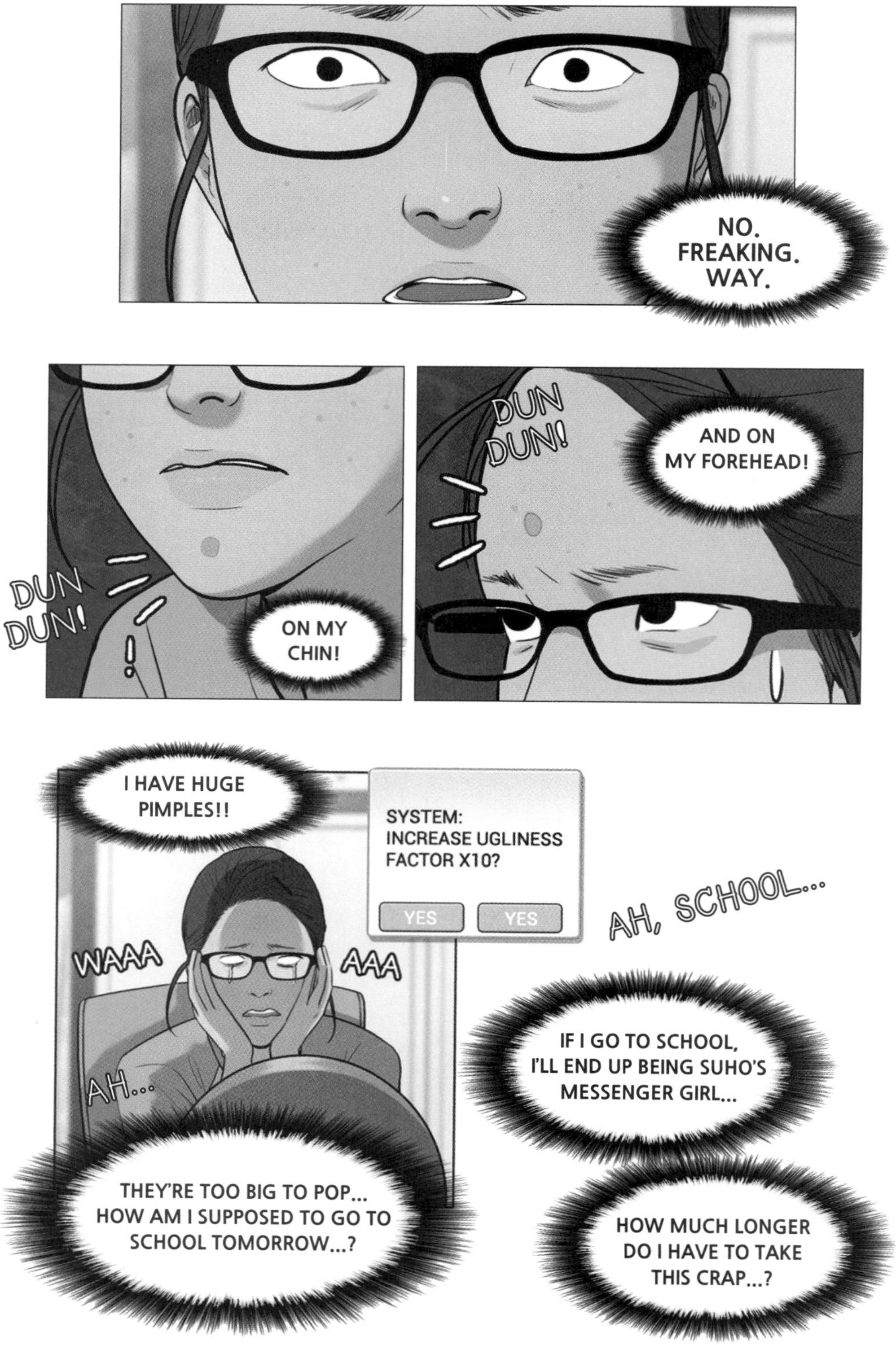
NO. FREAKING. WAY.
DUN DUN!
ON MY CHIN!
DUN DUN!
AND ON MY FOREHEAD!
I HAVE HUGE PIMPLES!!
SYSTEM: INCREASE UGLINESS FACTOR X10?
YES
YES
AH, SCHOOL...
WAAA
AAA
IF I GO TO SCHOOL, I'LL END UP BEING SUHO'S MESSENGER GIRL...
AH...
THEY'RE TOO BIG TO POP... HOW AM I SUPPOSED TO GO TO SCHOOL TOMORROW...?
HOW MUCH LONGER DO I HAVE TO TAKE THIS CRAP...?

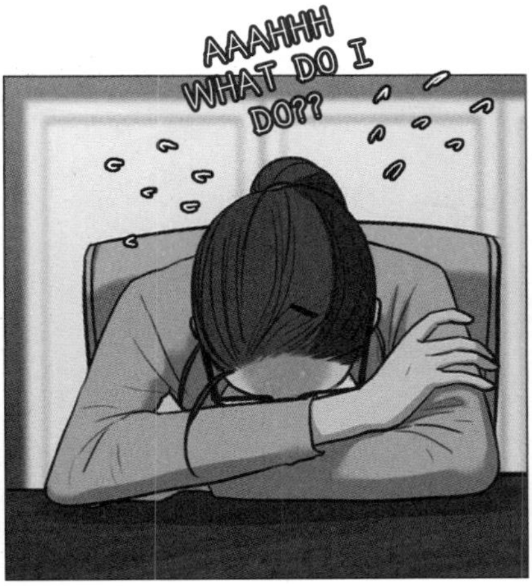
AAAHHH WHAT DO I DO??

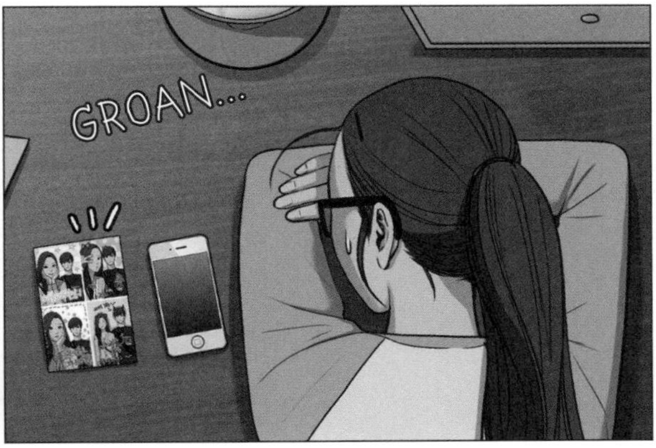
GROAN...

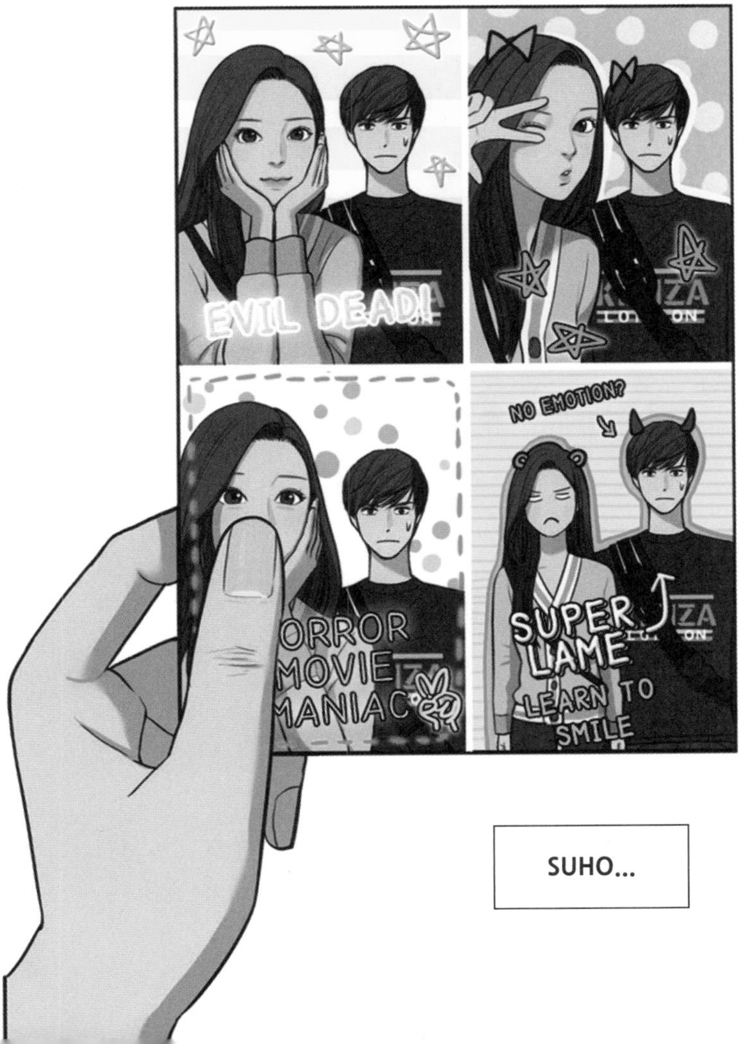
EVIL DEAD!
ORROR MOVIE MANIAC
NO EMOTION?
SUPER LAME
LEARN TO SMILE
SUHO...

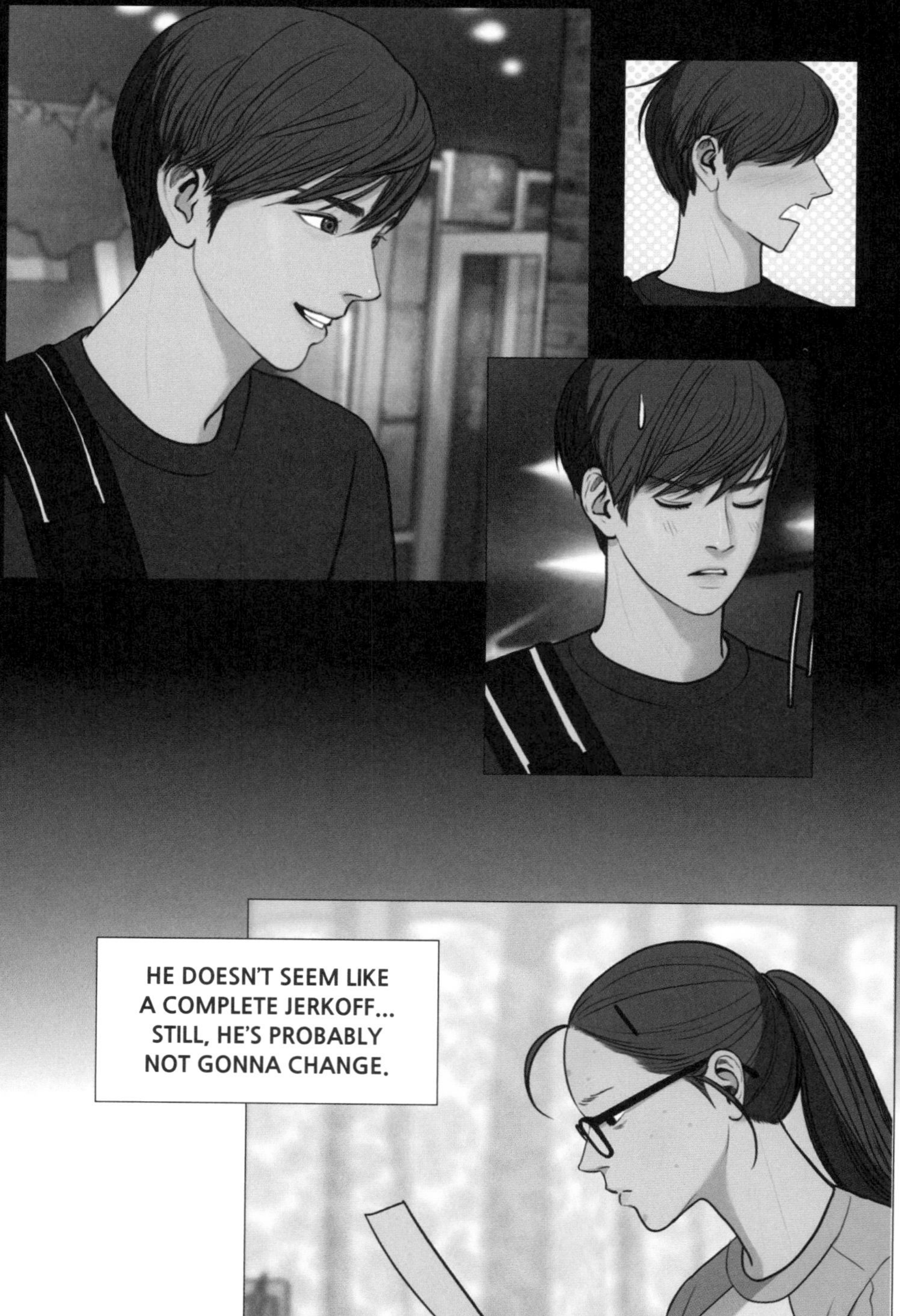
HE DOESN'T SEEM LIKE A COMPLETE JERKOFF... STILL, HE'S PROBABLY NOT GONNA CHANGE.

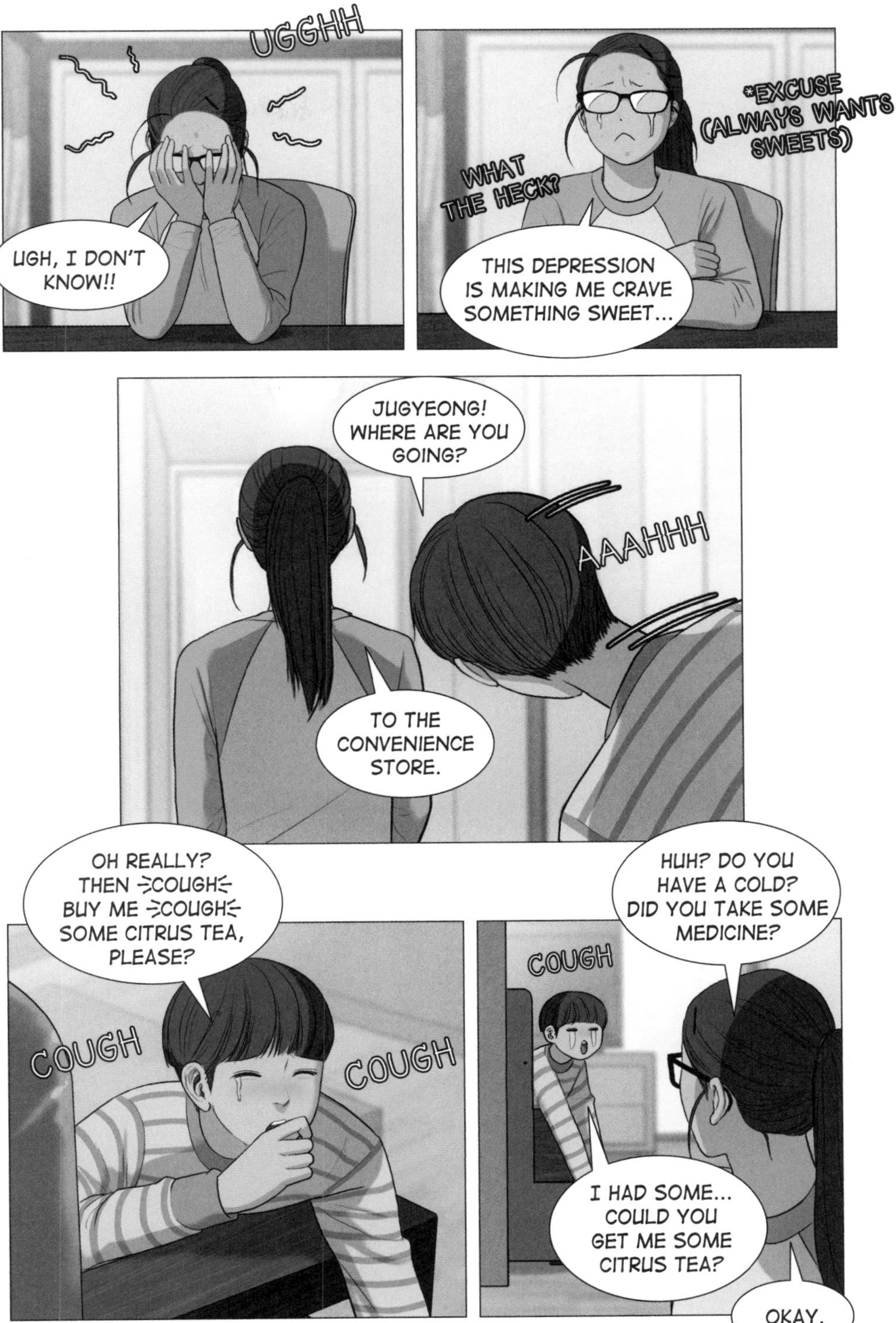
UGGHH
UGH, I DON'T KNOW!!
*EXCUSE (ALWAYS WANTS SWEETS)
WHAT THE HECK?
THIS DEPRESSION IS MAKING ME CRAVE SOMETHING SWEET...
JUGYEONG! WHERE ARE YOU GOING?
AAAHHH
TO THE CONVENIENCE STORE.
OH REALLY? THEN ⪤COUGH⪤ BUY ME ⪤COUGH⪤ SOME CITRUS TEA, PLEASE?
COUGH
COUGH
HUH? DO YOU HAVE A COLD? DID YOU TAKE SOME MEDICINE?
COUGH
I HAD SOME... COULD YOU GET ME SOME CITRUS TEA?
OKAY.

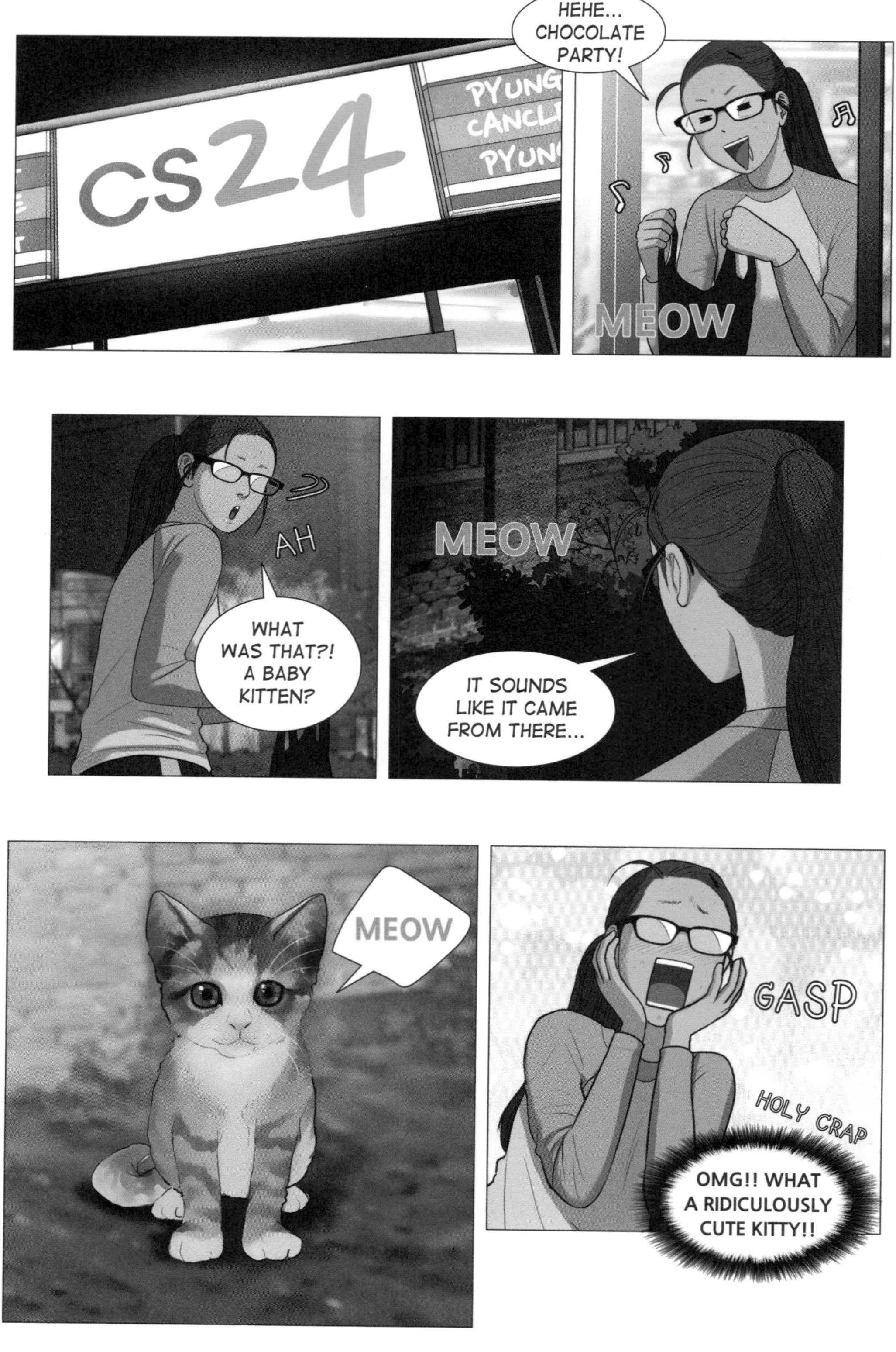
CS24
HEHE... CHOCOLATE PARTY!
MEOW
AH
WHAT WAS THAT?! A BABY KITTEN?
MEOW
IT SOUNDS LIKE IT CAME FROM THERE...
MEOW
GASP
HOLY CRAP
OMG!! WHAT A RIDICULOUSLY CUTE KITTY!!

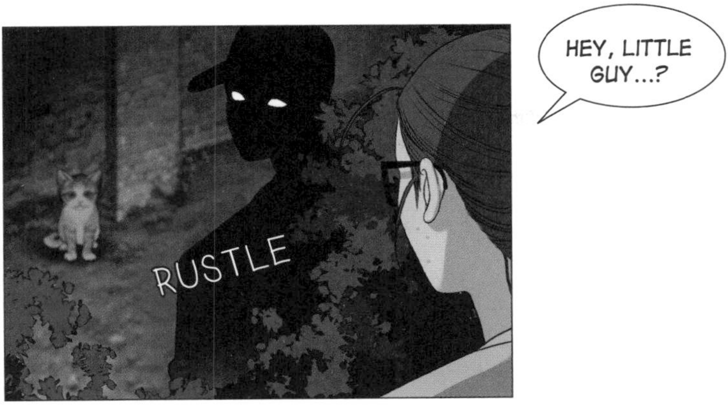
RUSTLE
HEY, LITTLE GUY...?

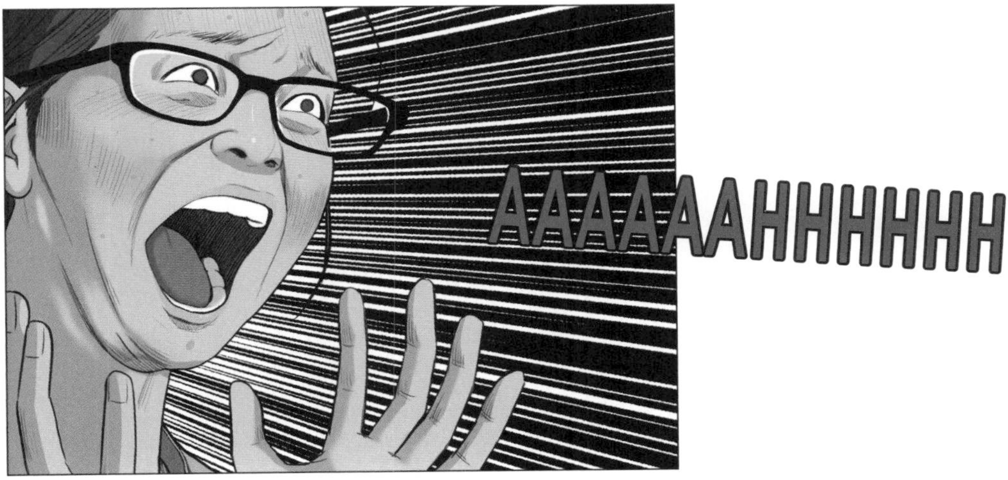
AAAAAAHHHHHH

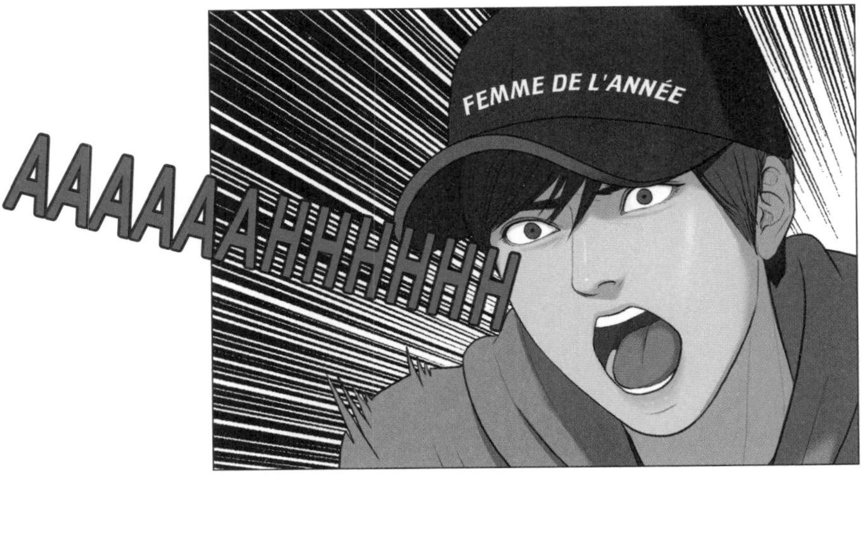
AAAAAAHHHHHH
FEMME DE L'ANNÉE

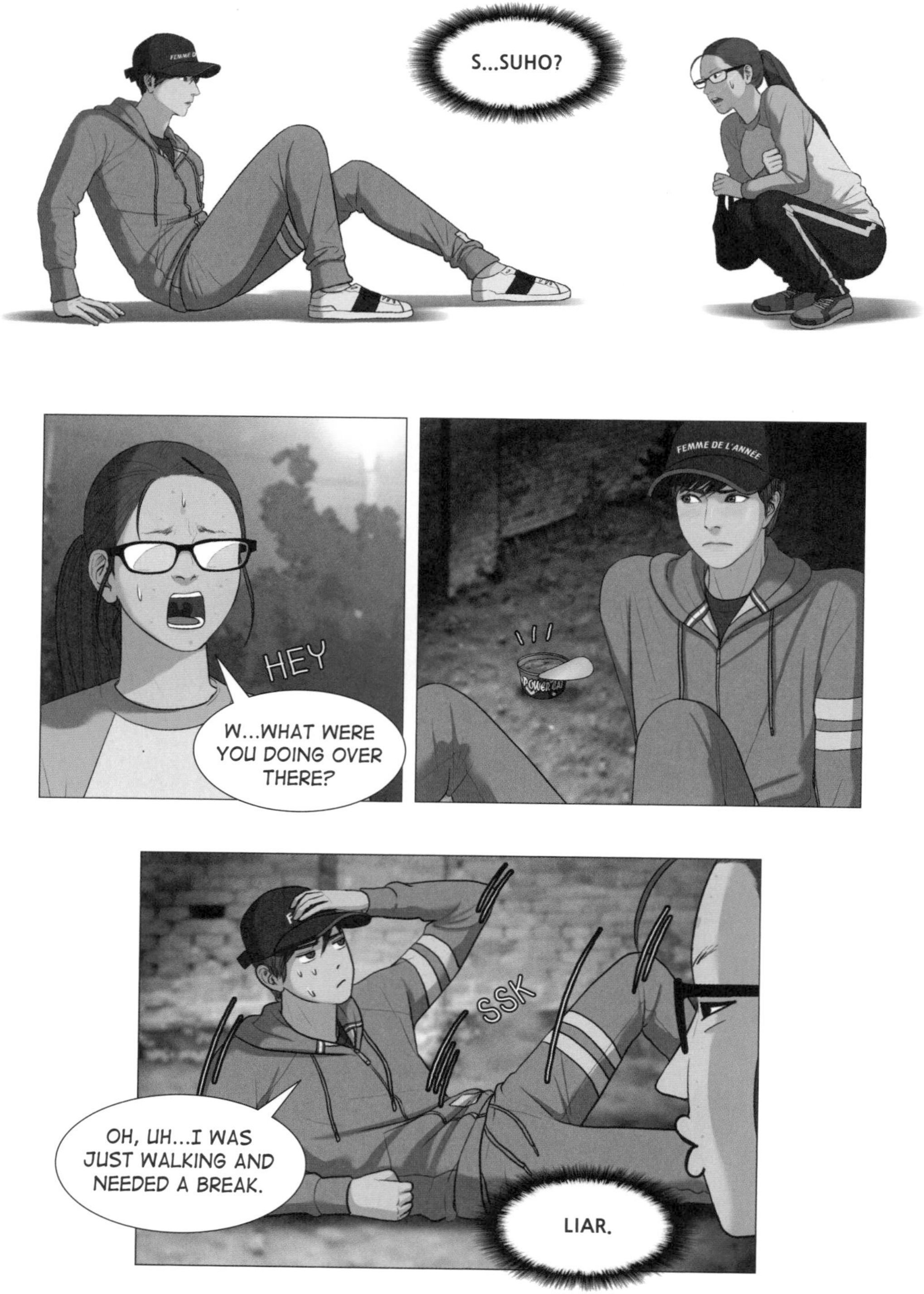
S...SUHO?
HEY
W...WHAT WERE YOU DOING OVER THERE?
FEMME DE L'ANNÉE
SSK
OH, UH...I WAS JUST WALKING AND NEEDED A BREAK.
LIAR.

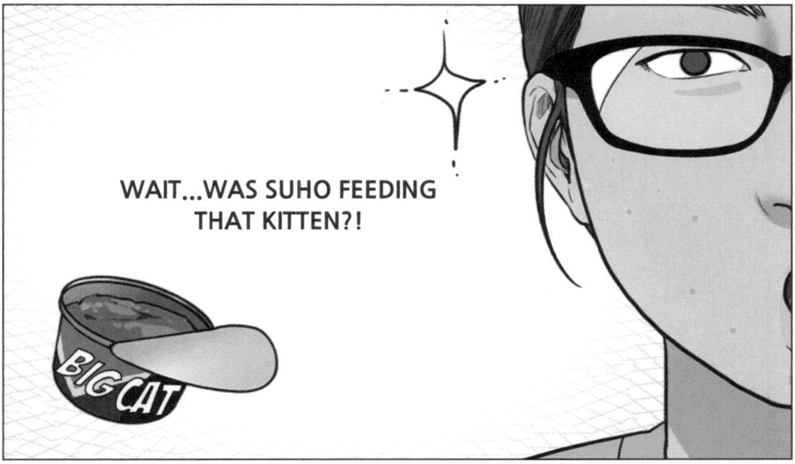
WAIT...WAS SUHO FEEDING THAT KITTEN?!
BIG CAT

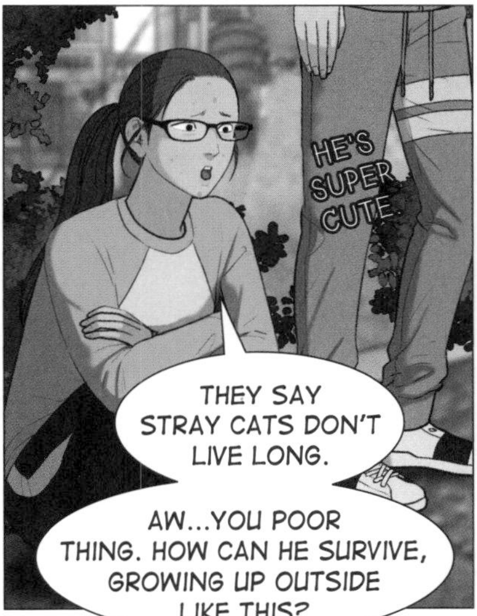
HE'S SUPER CUTE.
THEY SAY STRAY CATS DON'T LIVE LONG.
AW...YOU POOR THING. HOW CAN HE SURVIVE, GROWING UP OUTSIDE LIKE THIS?

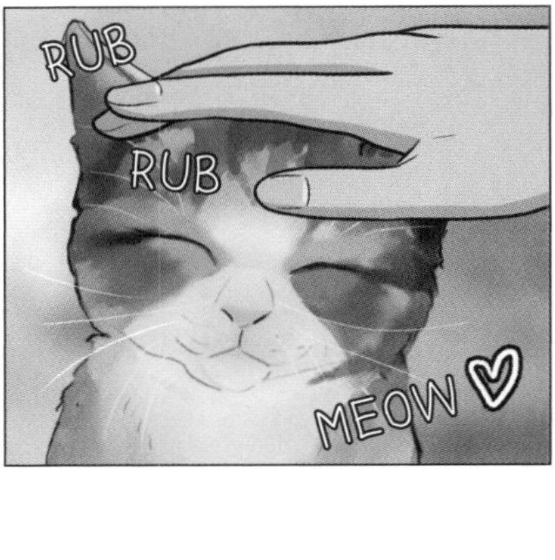
RUB
RUB
MEOW ♥

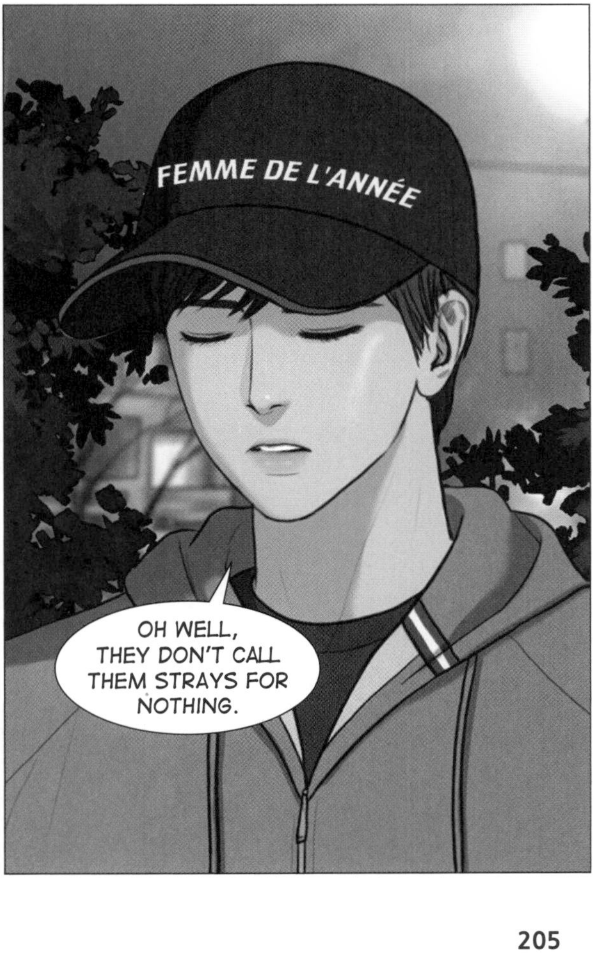
FEMME DE L'ANNÉE
OH WELL, THEY DON'T CALL THEM STRAYS FOR NOTHING.

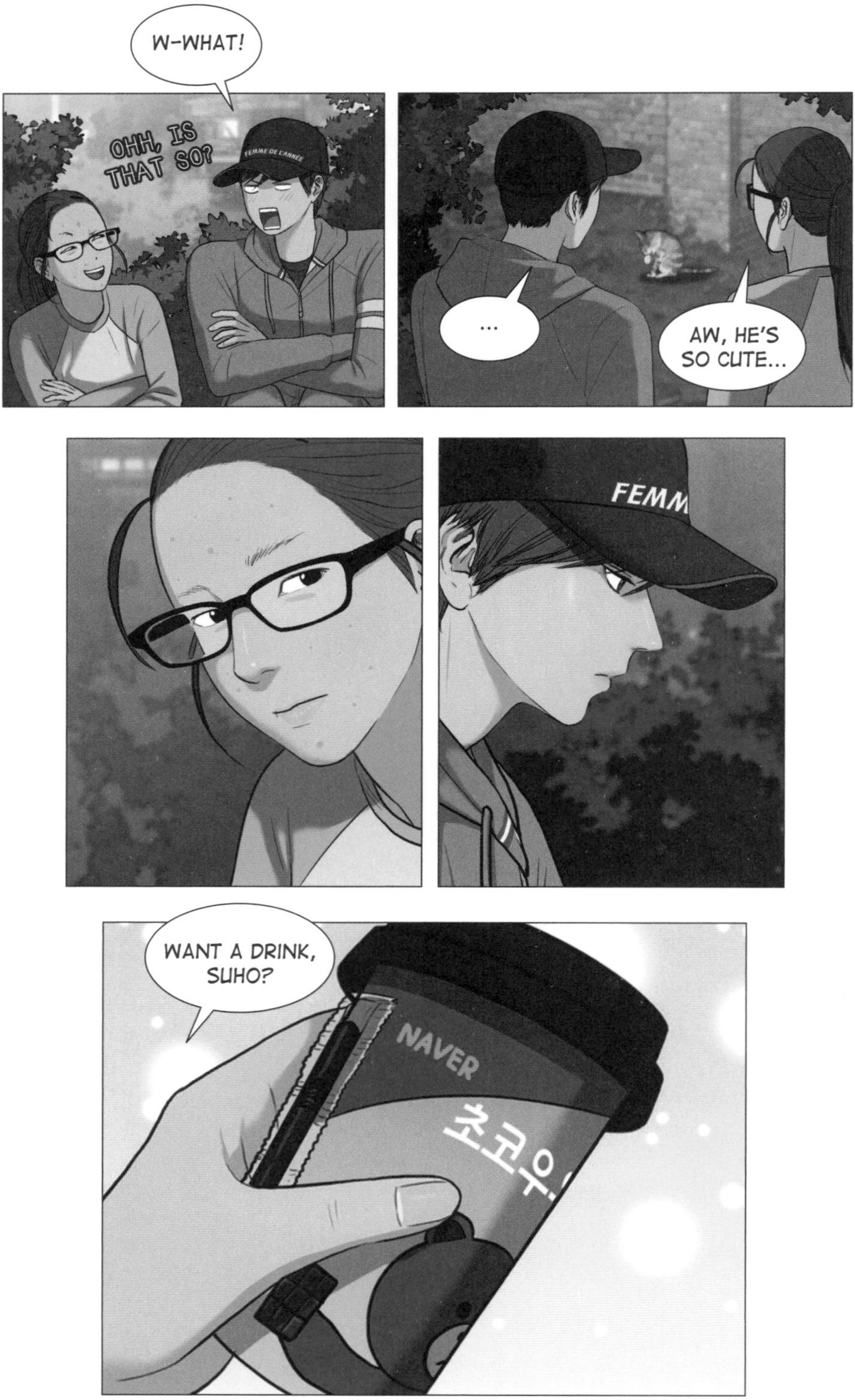
OHH, IS THAT SO?
W-WHAT!
...
AW, HE'S SO CUTE...
WANT A DRINK, SUHO?
NAVER

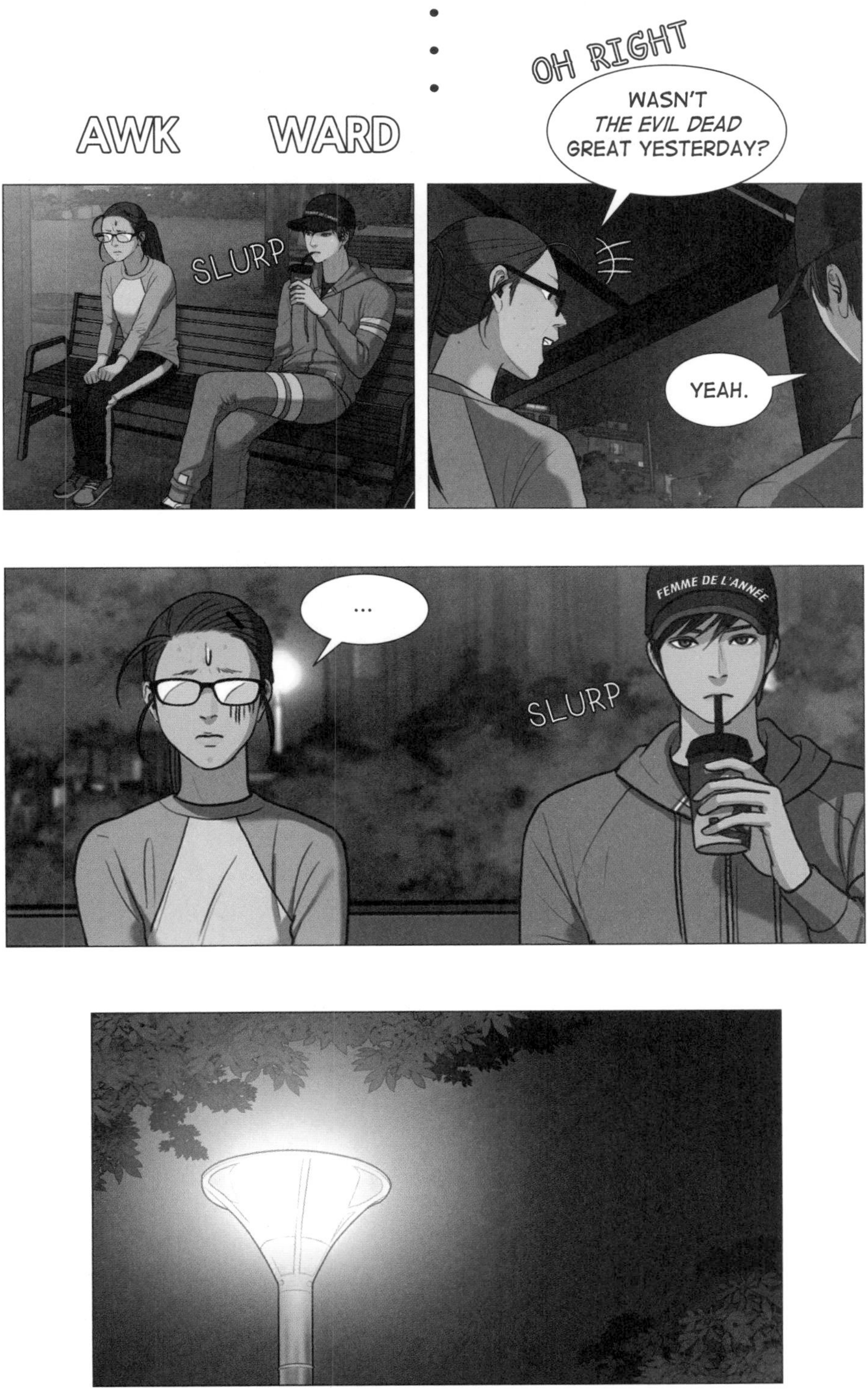
AWK WARD
SLURP
OH RIGHT
WASN'T *THE EVIL DEAD* GREAT YESTERDAY?
YEAH.
...
FEMME DE L'ANNÉE
SLURP

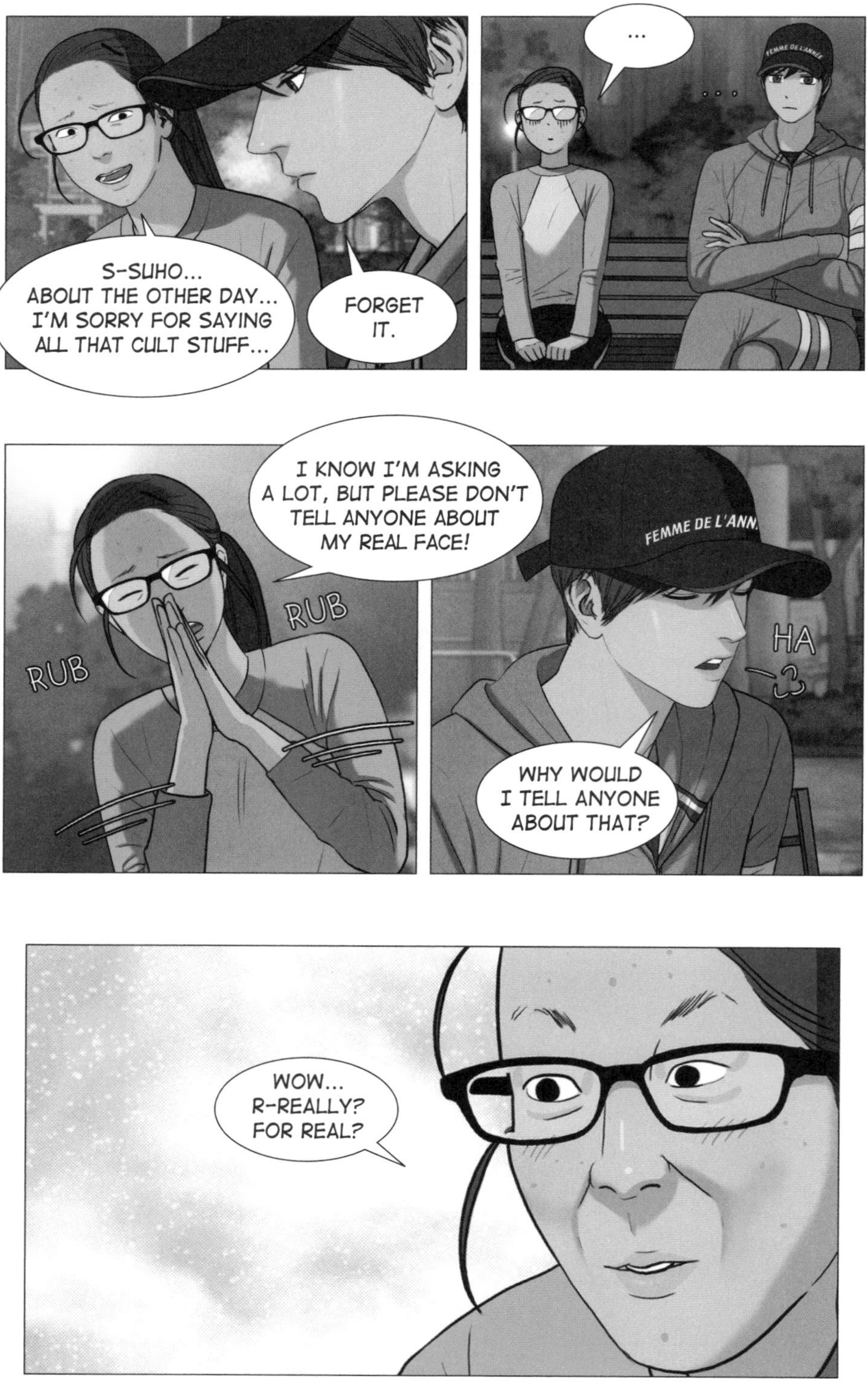
S-SUHO... ABOUT THE OTHER DAY... I'M SORRY FOR SAYING ALL THAT CULT STUFF...
FORGET IT.
...
. . .
I KNOW I'M ASKING A LOT, BUT PLEASE DON'T TELL ANYONE ABOUT MY REAL FACE!
RUB
RUB
FEMME DE L'ANN
HA
WHY WOULD I TELL ANYONE ABOUT THAT?
WOW... R-REALLY? FOR REAL?

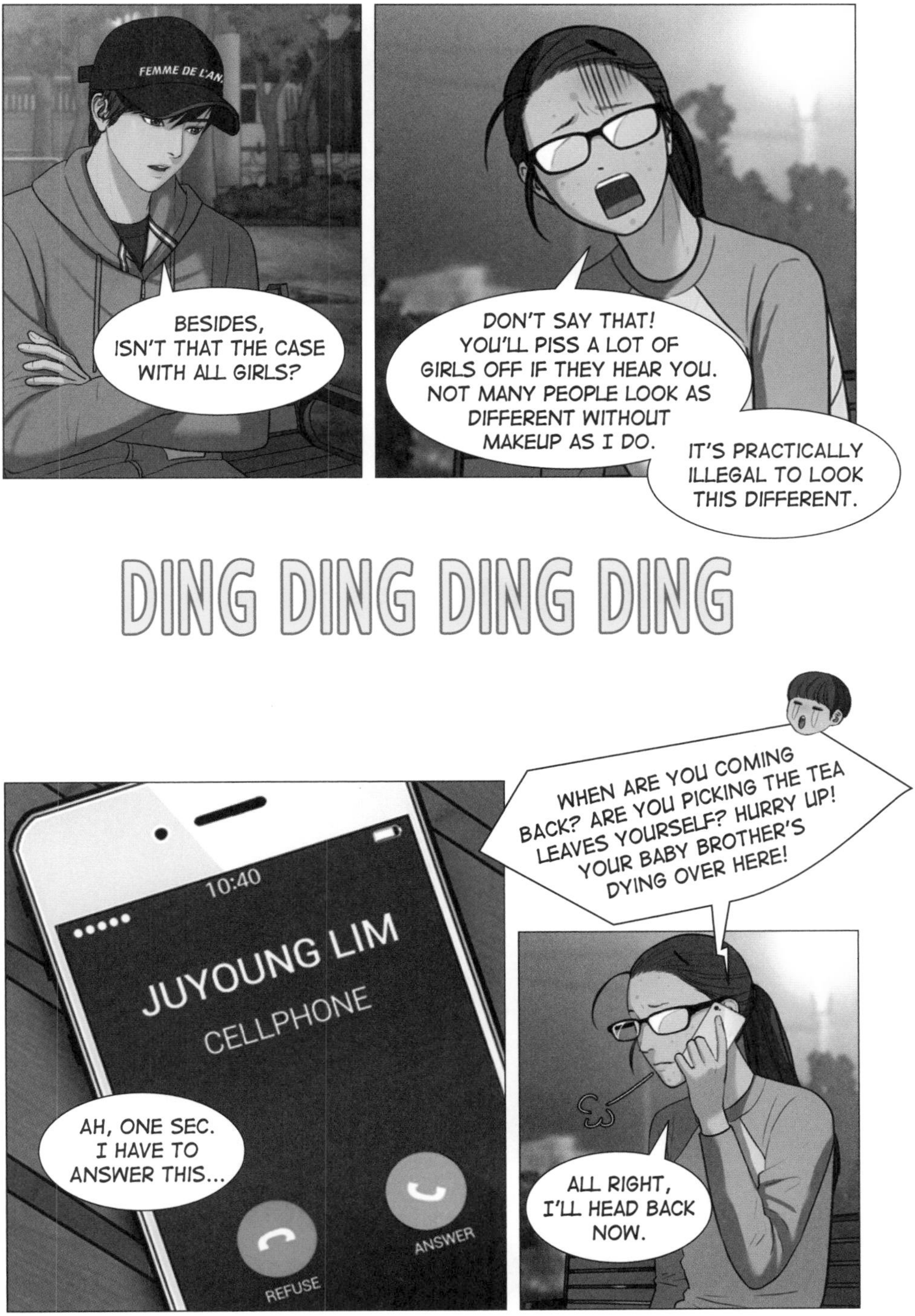
BESIDES, ISN'T THAT THE CASE WITH ALL GIRLS?
DON'T SAY THAT! YOU'LL PISS A LOT OF GIRLS OFF IF THEY HEAR YOU. NOT MANY PEOPLE LOOK AS DIFFERENT WITHOUT MAKEUP AS I DO.
IT'S PRACTICALLY ILLEGAL TO LOOK THIS DIFFERENT.
DING DING DING DING
10:40
JUYOUNG LIM
CELLPHONE
AH, ONE SEC. I HAVE TO ANSWER THIS...
ANSWER
REFUSE
WHEN ARE YOU COMING BACK? ARE YOU PICKING THE TEA LEAVES YOURSELF? HURRY UP! YOUR BABY BROTHER'S DYING OVER HERE!
ALL RIGHT, I'LL HEAD BACK NOW.

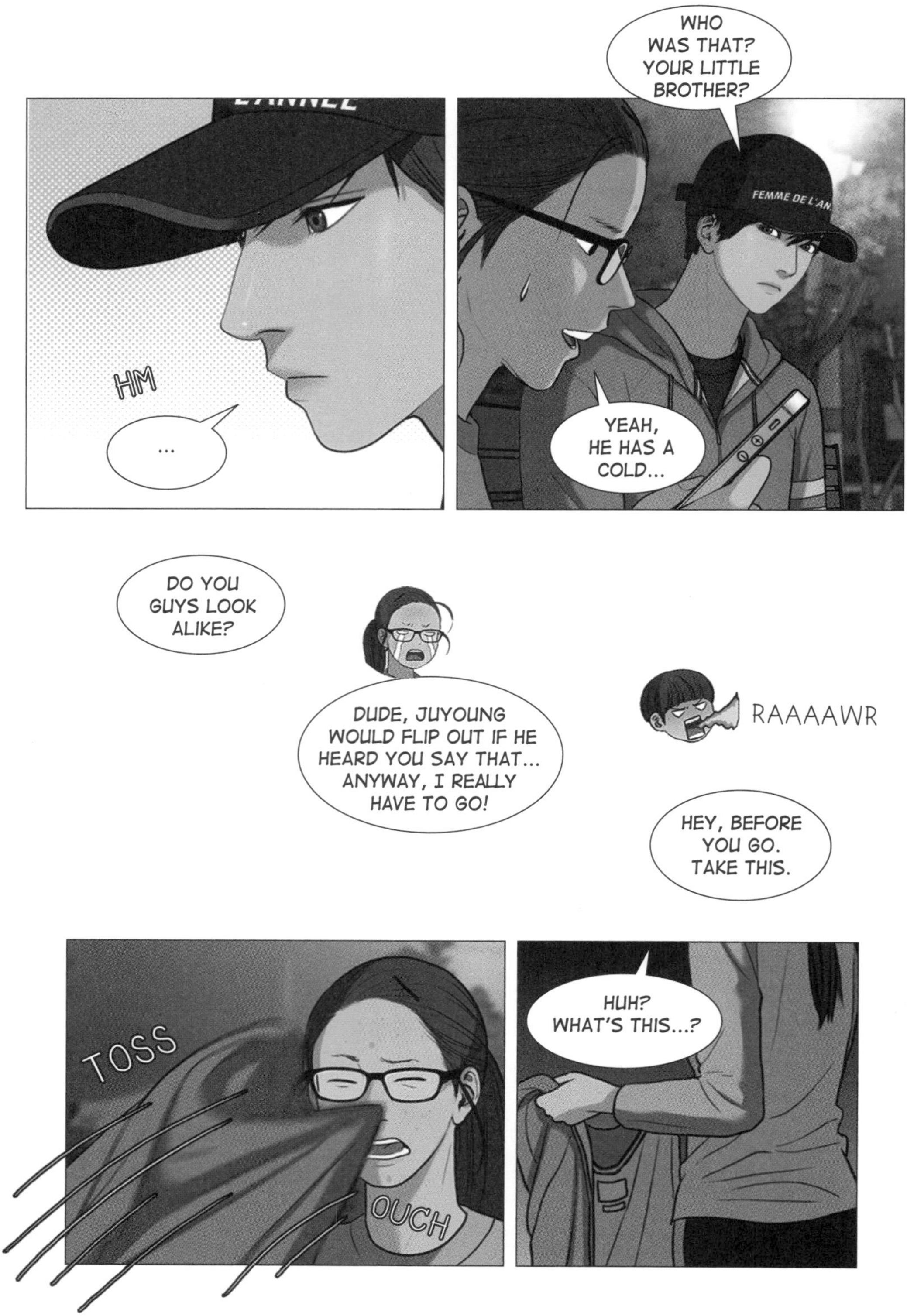
HM
...
WHO WAS THAT? YOUR LITTLE BROTHER?
FEMME DE L'AN
YEAH, HE HAS A COLD...
DO YOU GUYS LOOK ALIKE?
DUDE, JUYOUNG WOULD FLIP OUT IF HE HEARD YOU SAY THAT... ANYWAY, I REALLY HAVE TO GO!
RAAAAWR
HEY, BEFORE YOU GO. TAKE THIS.
TOSS
OUCH
HUH? WHAT'S THIS...?

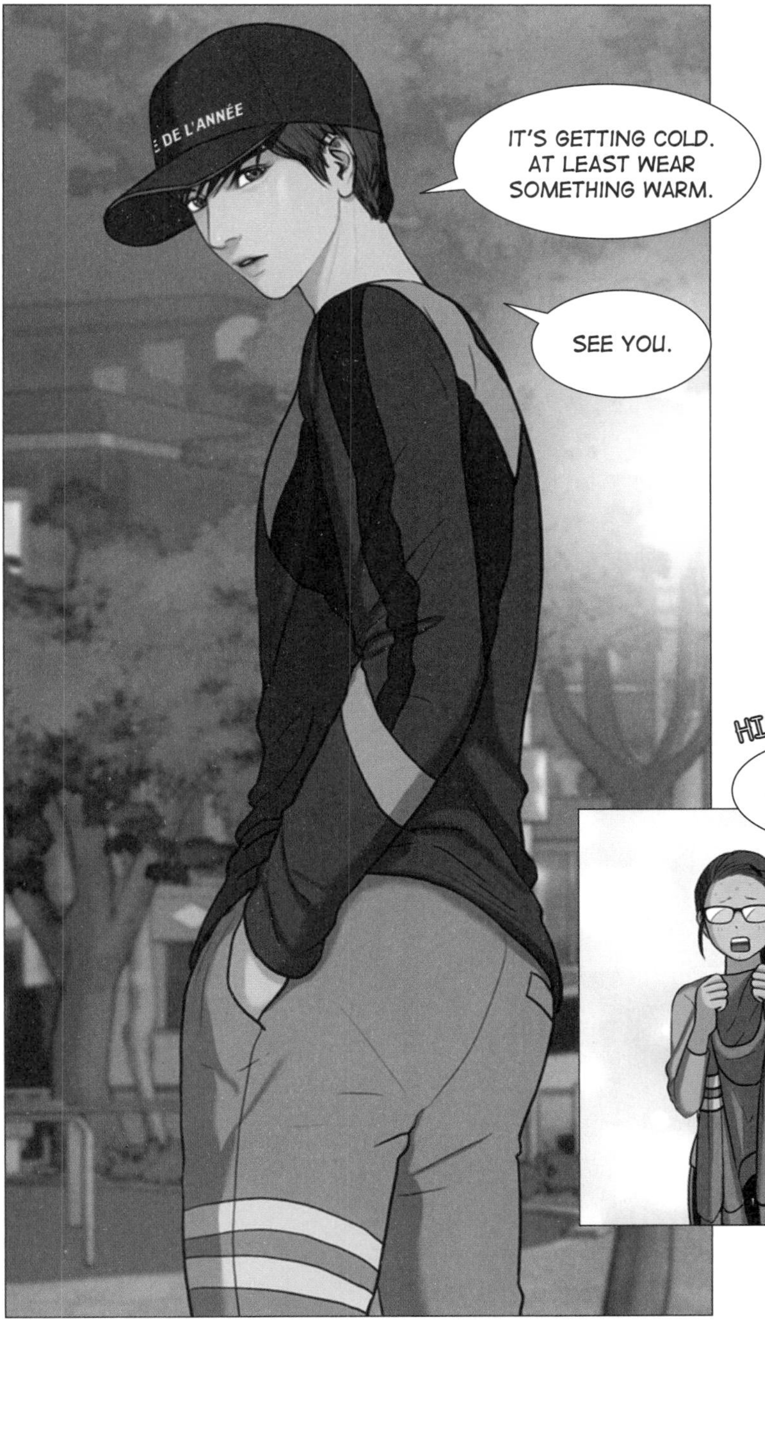
DE L'ANNÉE
IT'S GETTING COLD. AT LEAST WEAR SOMETHING WARM.
SEE YOU.
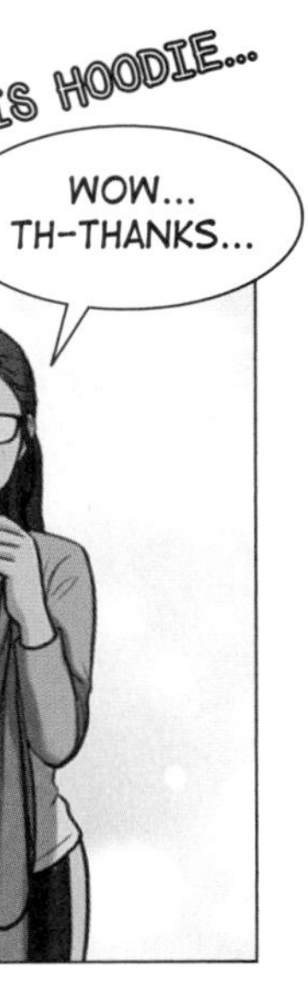
HIS HOODIE...
WOW... TH-THANKS...

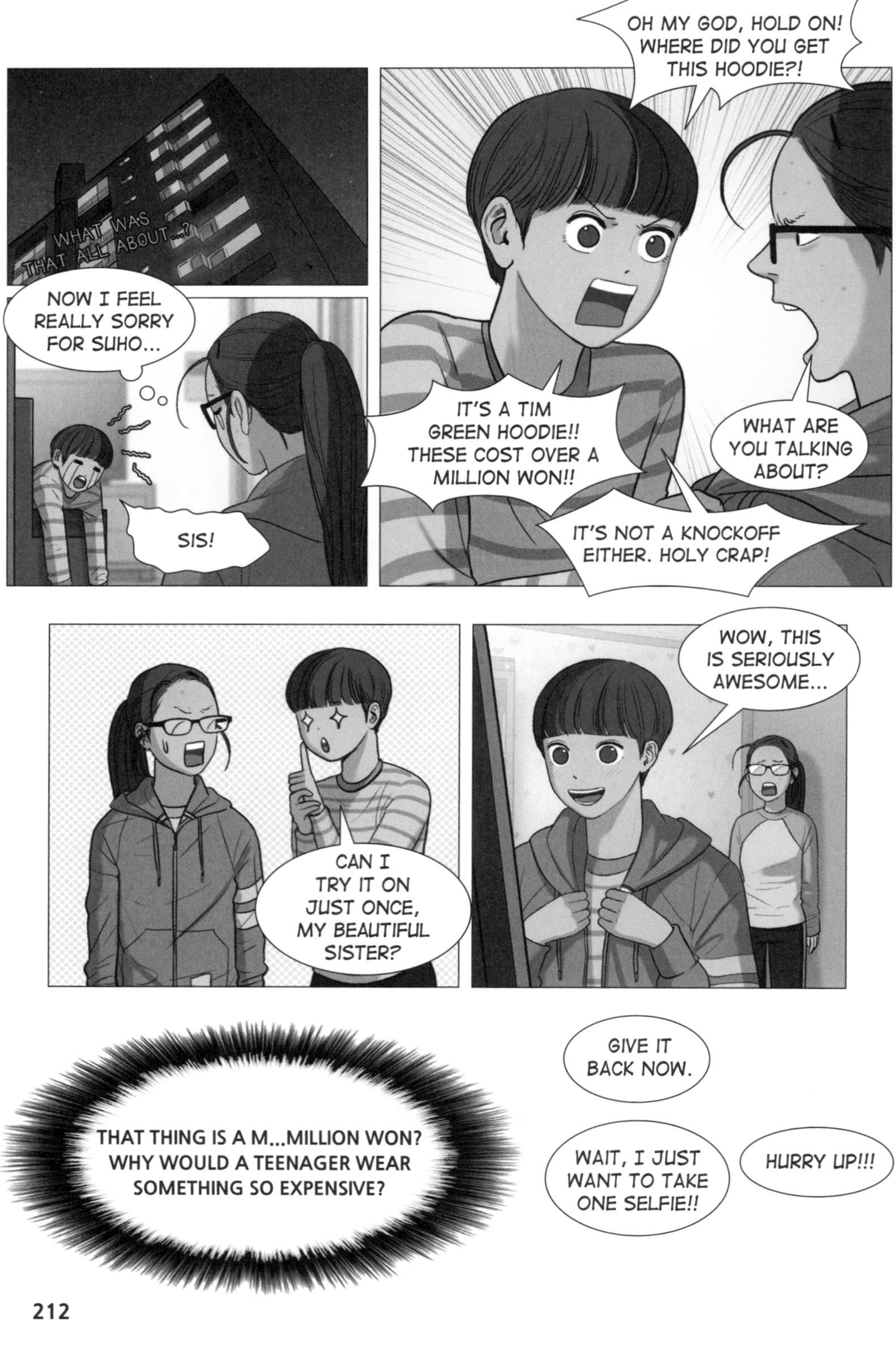
WHAT WAS THAT ALL ABOUT...?
NOW I FEEL REALLY SORRY FOR SUHO...
SIS!
OH MY GOD, HOLD ON! WHERE DID YOU GET THIS HOODIE?!
IT'S A TIM GREEN HOODIE!! THESE COST OVER A MILLION WON!!
WHAT ARE YOU TALKING ABOUT?
IT'S NOT A KNOCKOFF EITHER. HOLY CRAP!
CAN I TRY IT ON JUST ONCE, MY BEAUTIFUL SISTER?
WOW, THIS IS SERIOUSLY AWESOME...
THAT THING IS A M...MILLION WON? WHY WOULD A TEENAGER WEAR SOMETHING SO EXPENSIVE?
GIVE IT BACK NOW.
WAIT, I JUST WANT TO TAKE ONE SELFIE!!
HURRY UP!!!

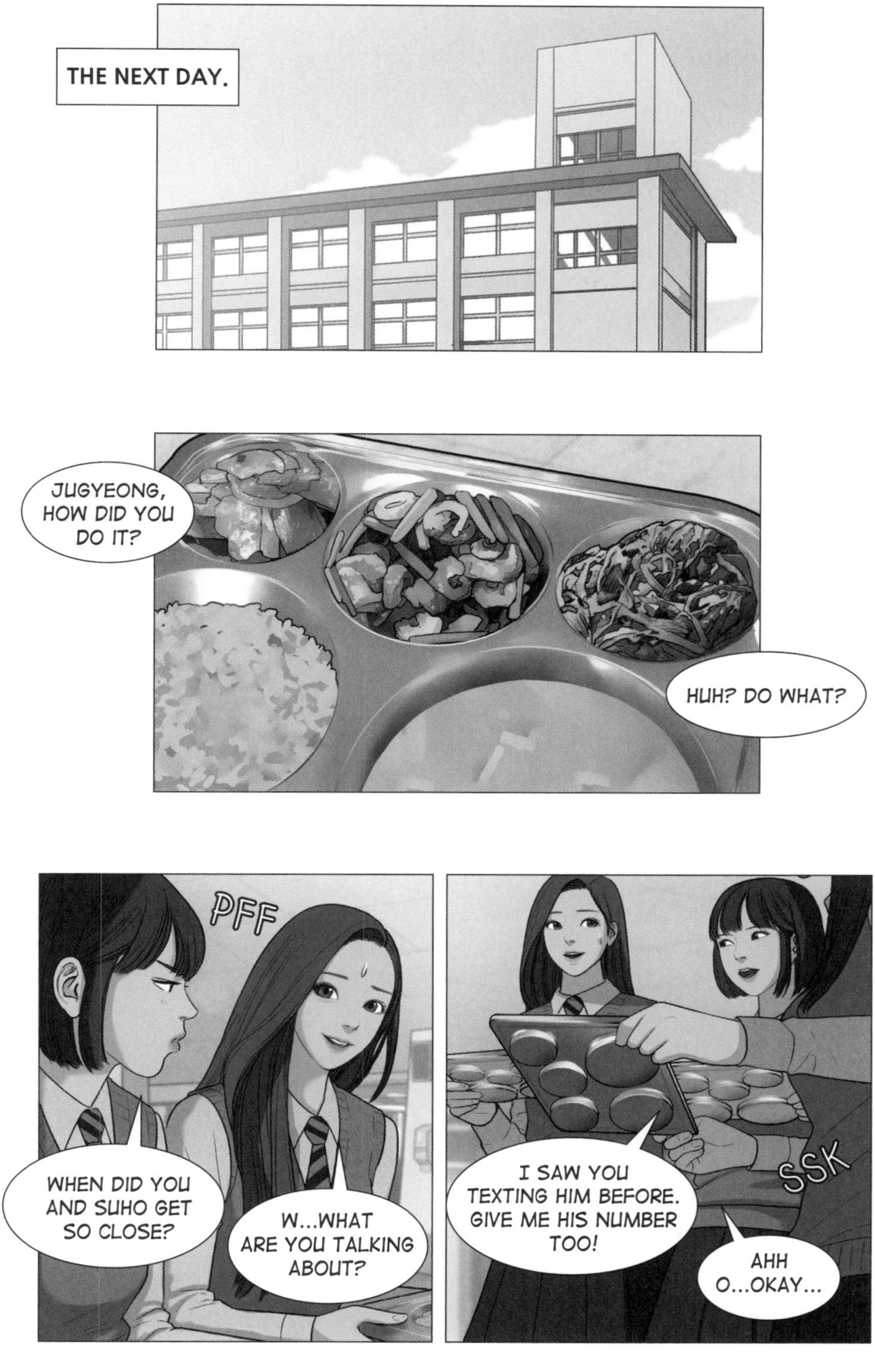
THE NEXT DAY.
JUGYEONG, HOW DID YOU DO IT?
HUH? DO WHAT?
PFF
WHEN DID YOU AND SUHO GET SO CLOSE?
W...WHAT ARE YOU TALKING ABOUT?
I SAW YOU TEXTING HIM BEFORE. GIVE ME HIS NUMBER TOO!
SSK
AHH O...OKAY...

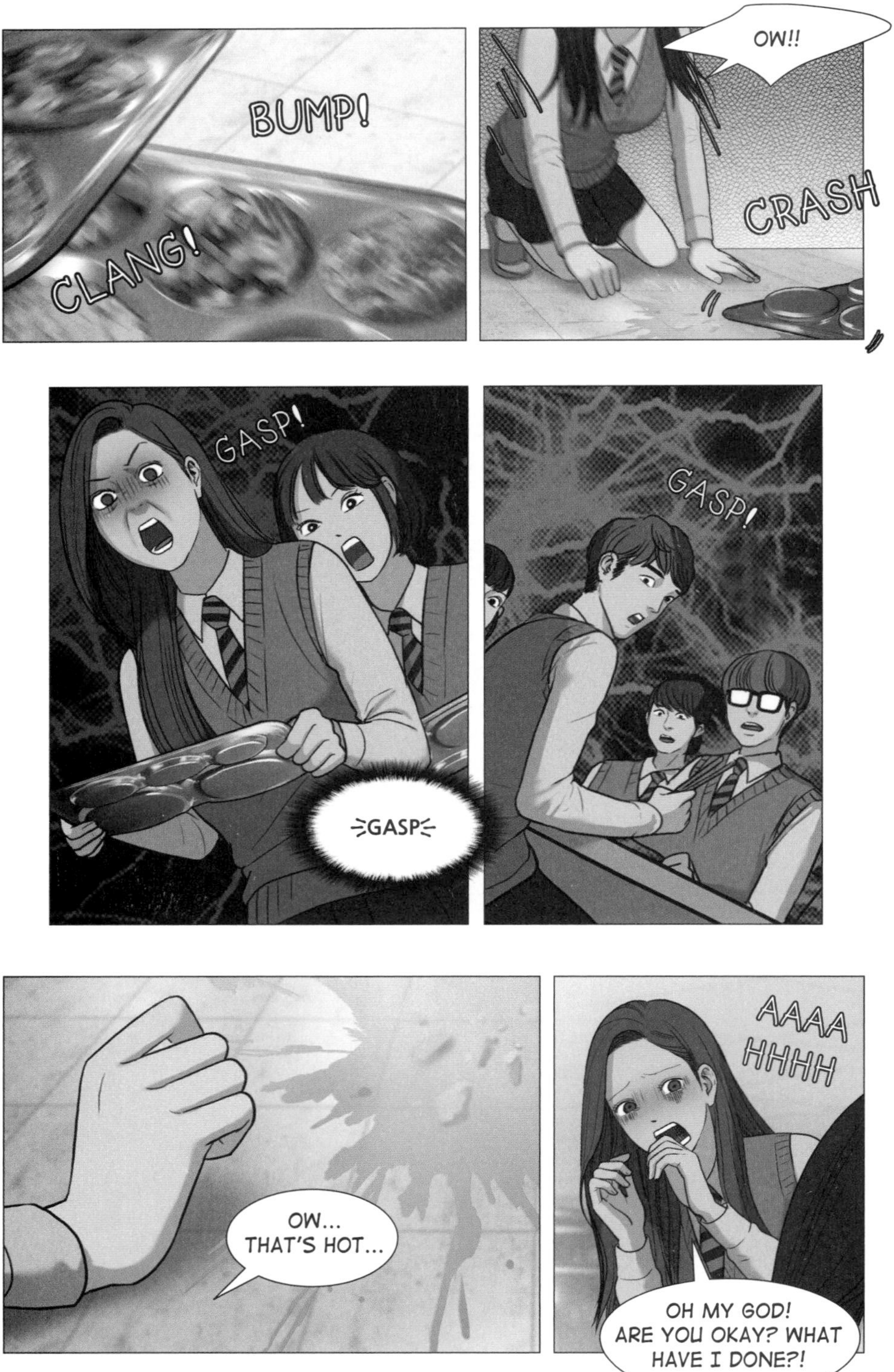
BUMP!
CLANG!
OW!!
CRASH
GASP!
GASP!
GASP
OW...
THAT'S HOT...
AAAA
HHHH
OH MY GOD!
ARE YOU OKAY? WHAT
HAVE I DONE?!

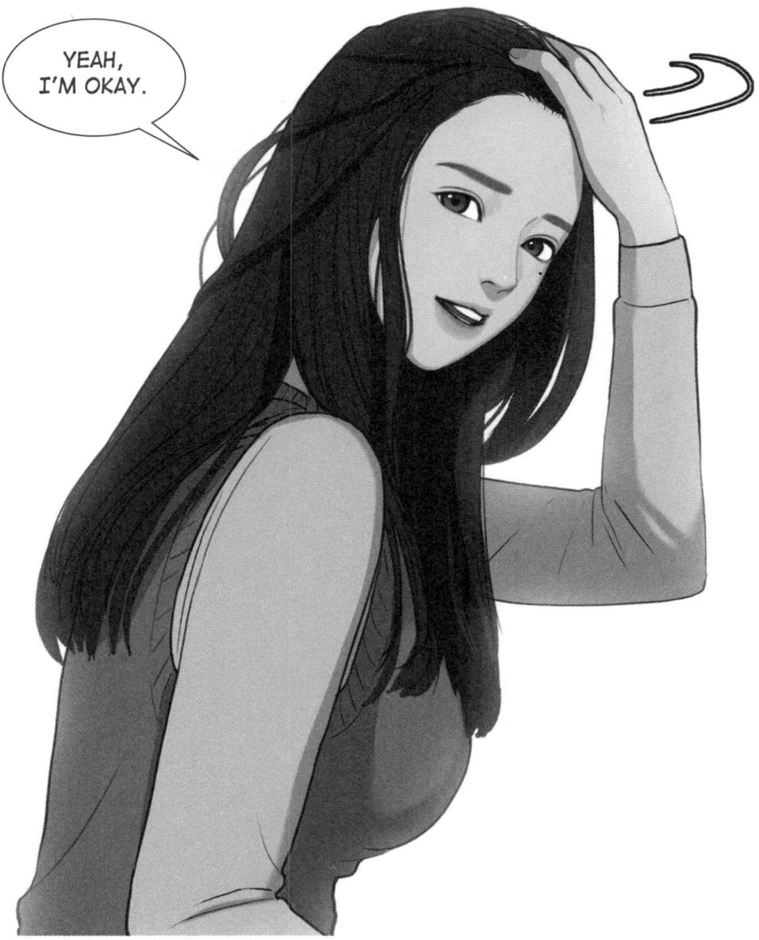
YEAH,
I'M OKAY.

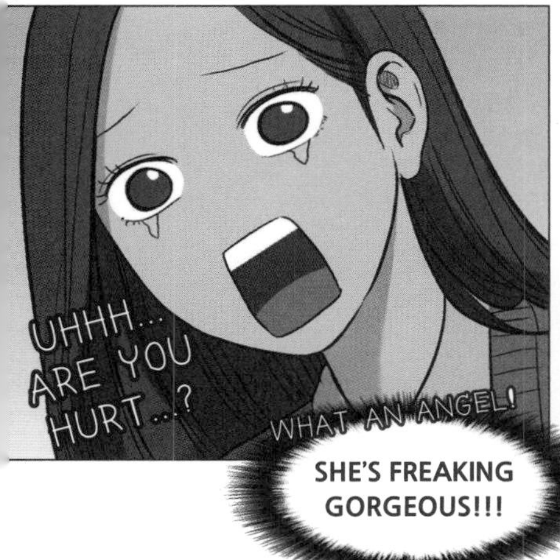
UHHH...
ARE YOU
HURT...?
WHAT AN ANGEL!
SHE'S FREAKING
GORGEOUS!!!

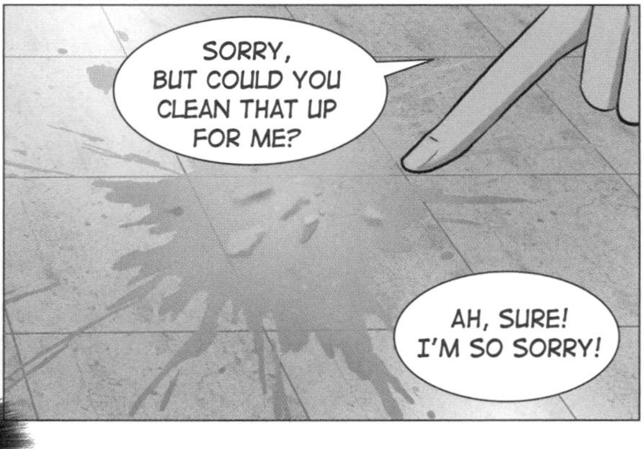
SORRY,
BUT COULD YOU
CLEAN THAT UP
FOR ME?
AH, SURE!
I'M SO SORRY!

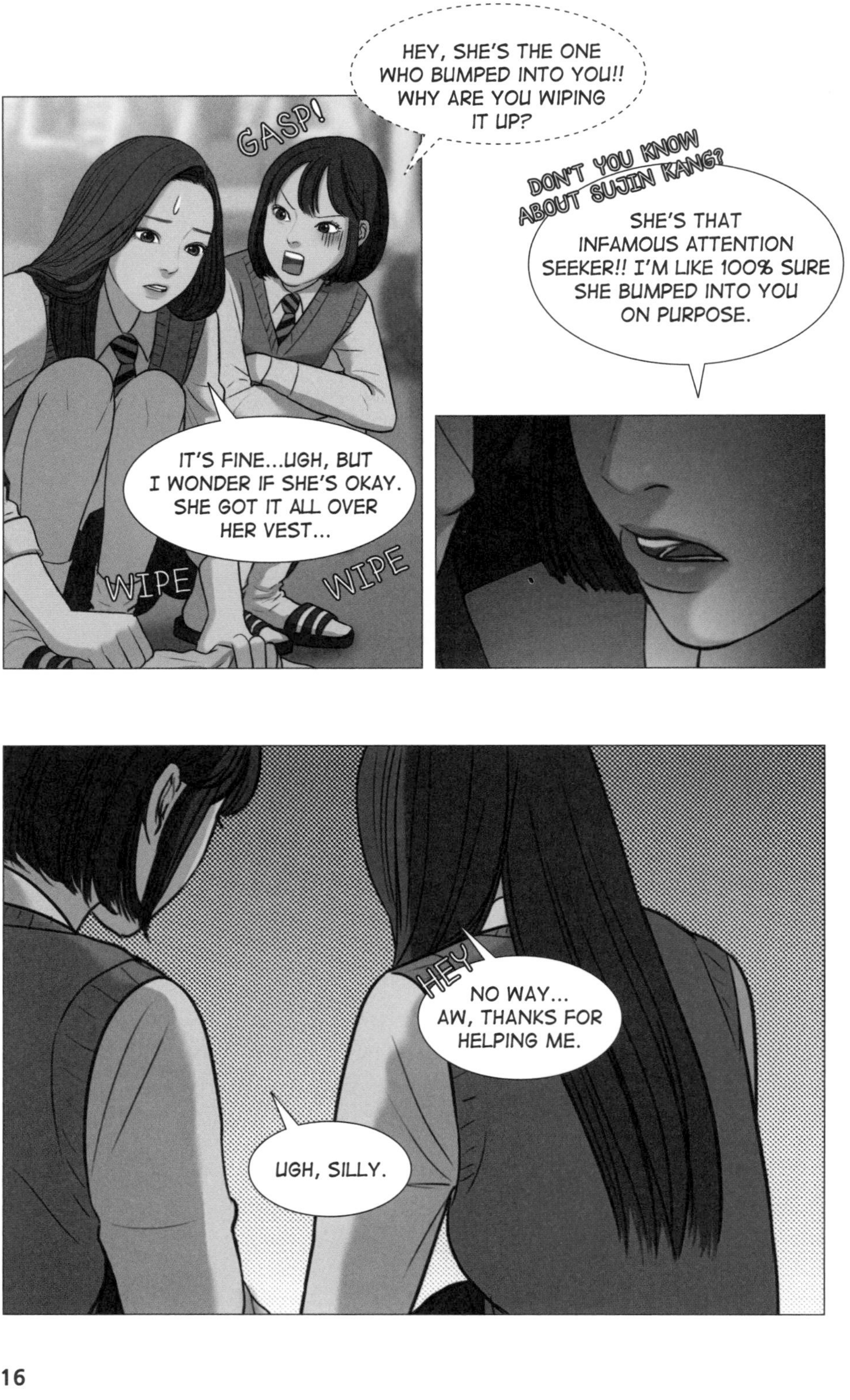
GASP!
HEY, SHE'S THE ONE WHO BUMPED INTO YOU!! WHY ARE YOU WIPING IT UP?
DON'T YOU KNOW ABOUT SUJIN KANG?
SHE'S THAT INFAMOUS ATTENTION SEEKER!! I'M LIKE 100% SURE SHE BUMPED INTO YOU ON PURPOSE.
IT'S FINE...UGH, BUT I WONDER IF SHE'S OKAY. SHE GOT IT ALL OVER HER VEST...
WIPE
WIPE
HEY
NO WAY... AW, THANKS FOR HELPING ME.
UGH, SILLY.

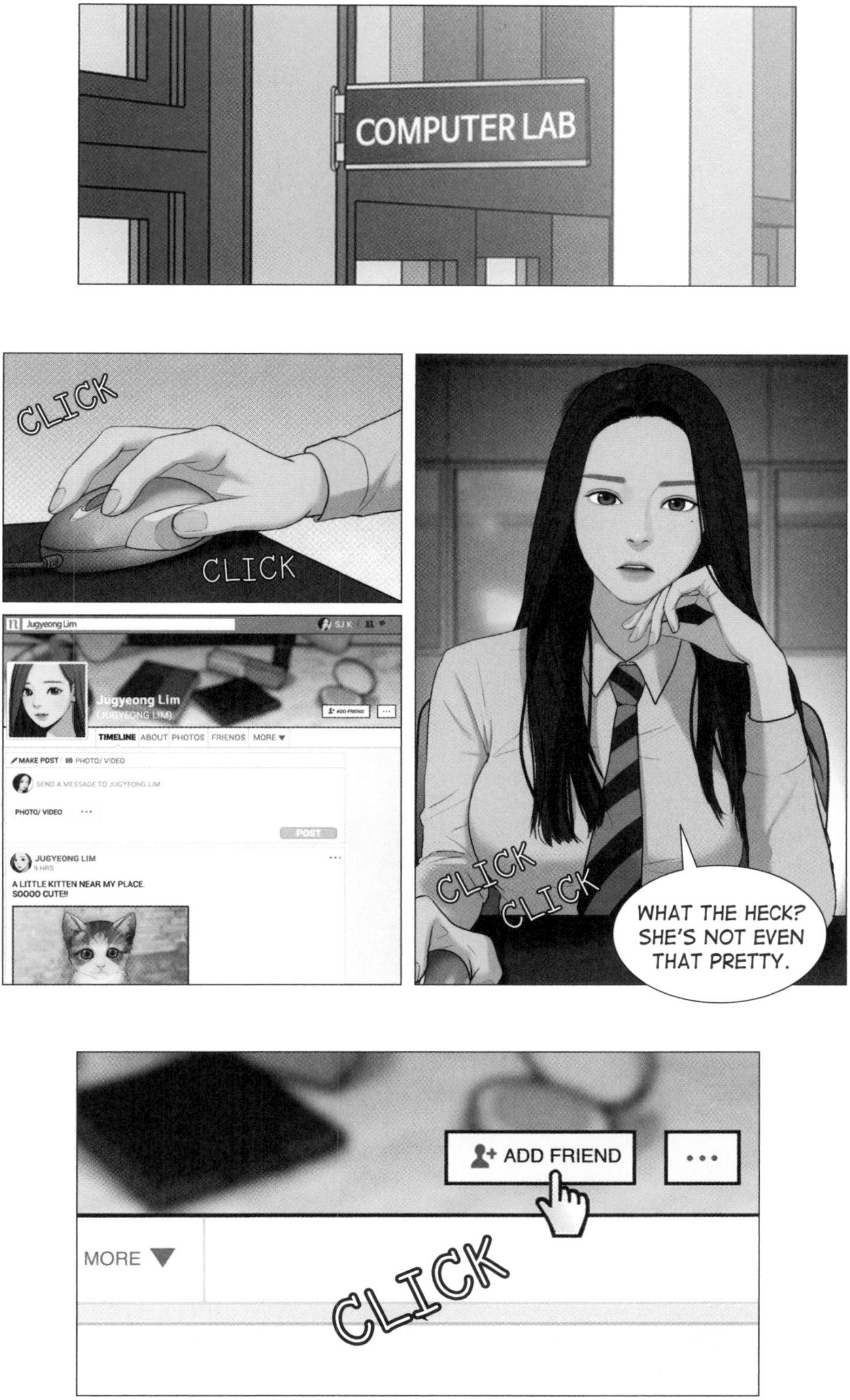
COMPUTER LAB
CLICK
CLICK
Jugyeong Lim
Jugyeong Lim
(JUGYEONG LIM)
ADD FRIEND
TIMELINE ABOUT PHOTOS FRIENDS MORE
MAKE POST PHOTO/ VIDEO
SEND A MESSAGE TO JUGYEONG LIM
PHOTO/ VIDEO
POST
JUGYEONG LIM
9 HRS
A LITTLE KITTEN NEAR MY PLACE.
SOOOO CUTE!!
CLICK
CLICK
WHAT THE HECK? SHE'S NOT EVEN THAT PRETTY.
ADD FRIEND
MORE
CLICK

SIS! I LEFT YOUR PACKAGE ON THE DESK.
OHHH! THANKS!
IT'S FINALLY HERE!!
MY SECRET WEAPON: DOUBLE-SIDED EYELID TAPE!
DUN
DUN
GONE ARE THE DAYS OF THE STICKY, MESSY DOUBLE EYELID GLUE.
WITH THIS ULTRA SLIM DOUBLE-SIDED EYELID TAPE, A NEW WORLD OF DOUBLE EYELIDS IS NOW MINE TO TAKE!!

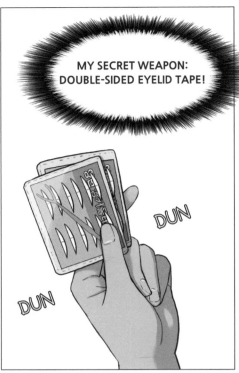

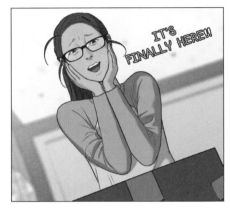

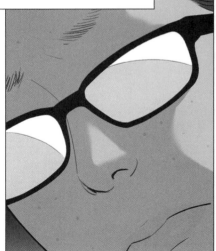

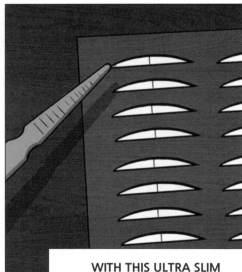

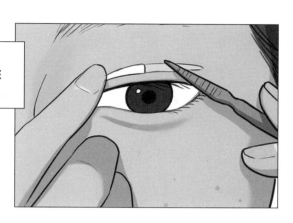

IF I JUST WIPE OFF THE
EYELID OIL AND PUT THE
TAPE ON MY EYELINE...

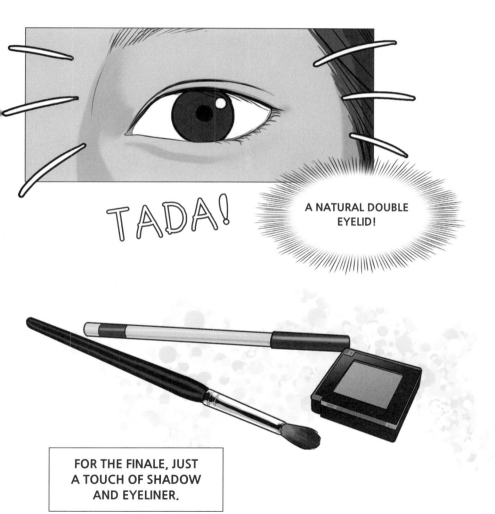

TADA!

A NATURAL DOUBLE
EYELID!

FOR THE FINALE, JUST
A TOUCH OF SHADOW
AND EYELINER.

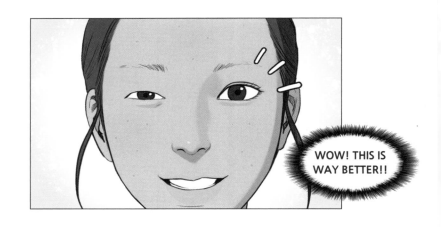

WOW! THIS IS WAY BETTER!!

TIME FOR A SELFIE.

HUH?

A FRIEND REQUEST?

WHAT THE HECK?

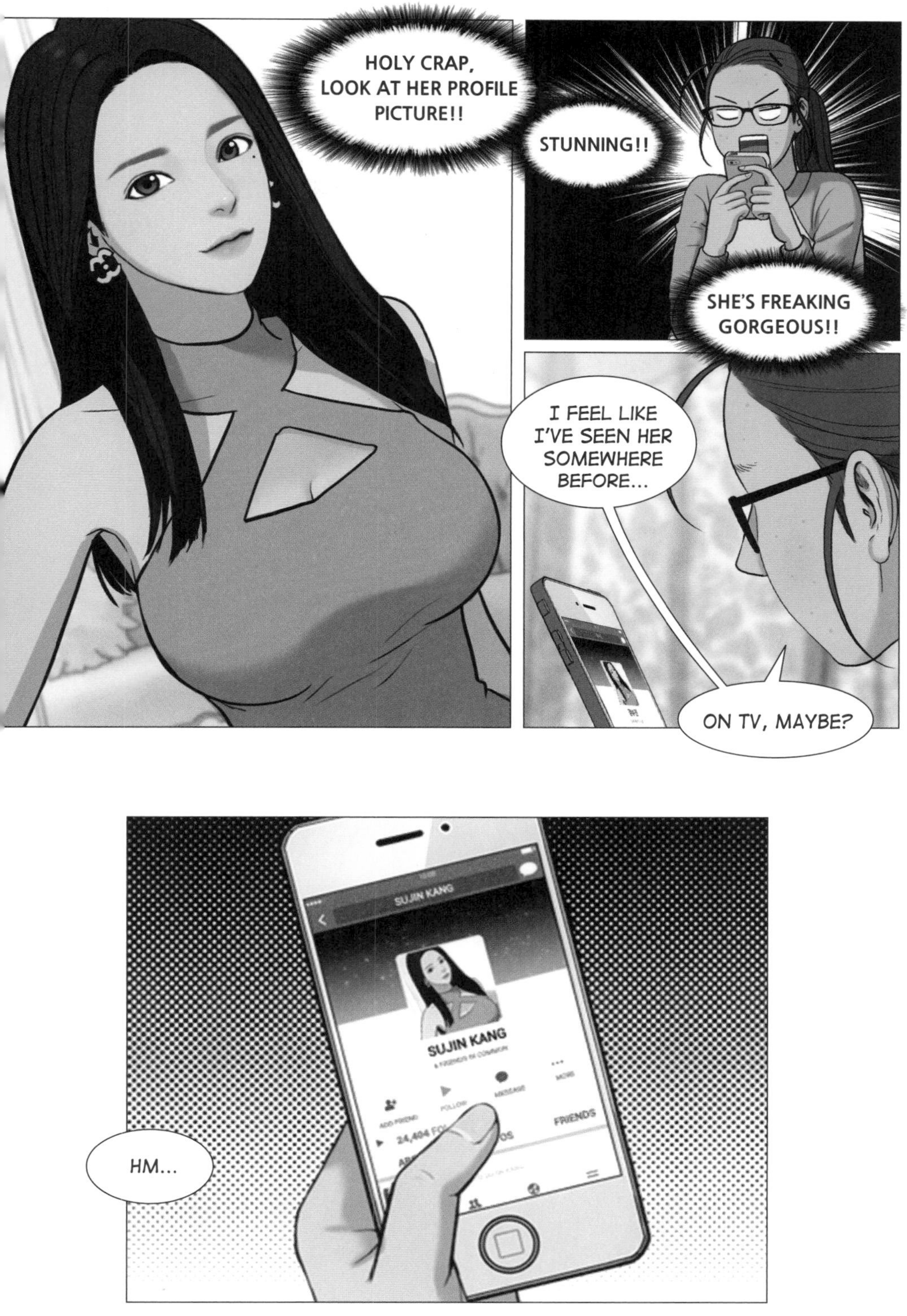
HOLY CRAP, LOOK AT HER PROFILE PICTURE!!
STUNNING!!
SHE'S FREAKING GORGEOUS!!
I FEEL LIKE I'VE SEEN HER SOMEWHERE BEFORE...
ON TV, MAYBE?
SUJIN KANG
SUJIN KANG
FRIENDS
HM...

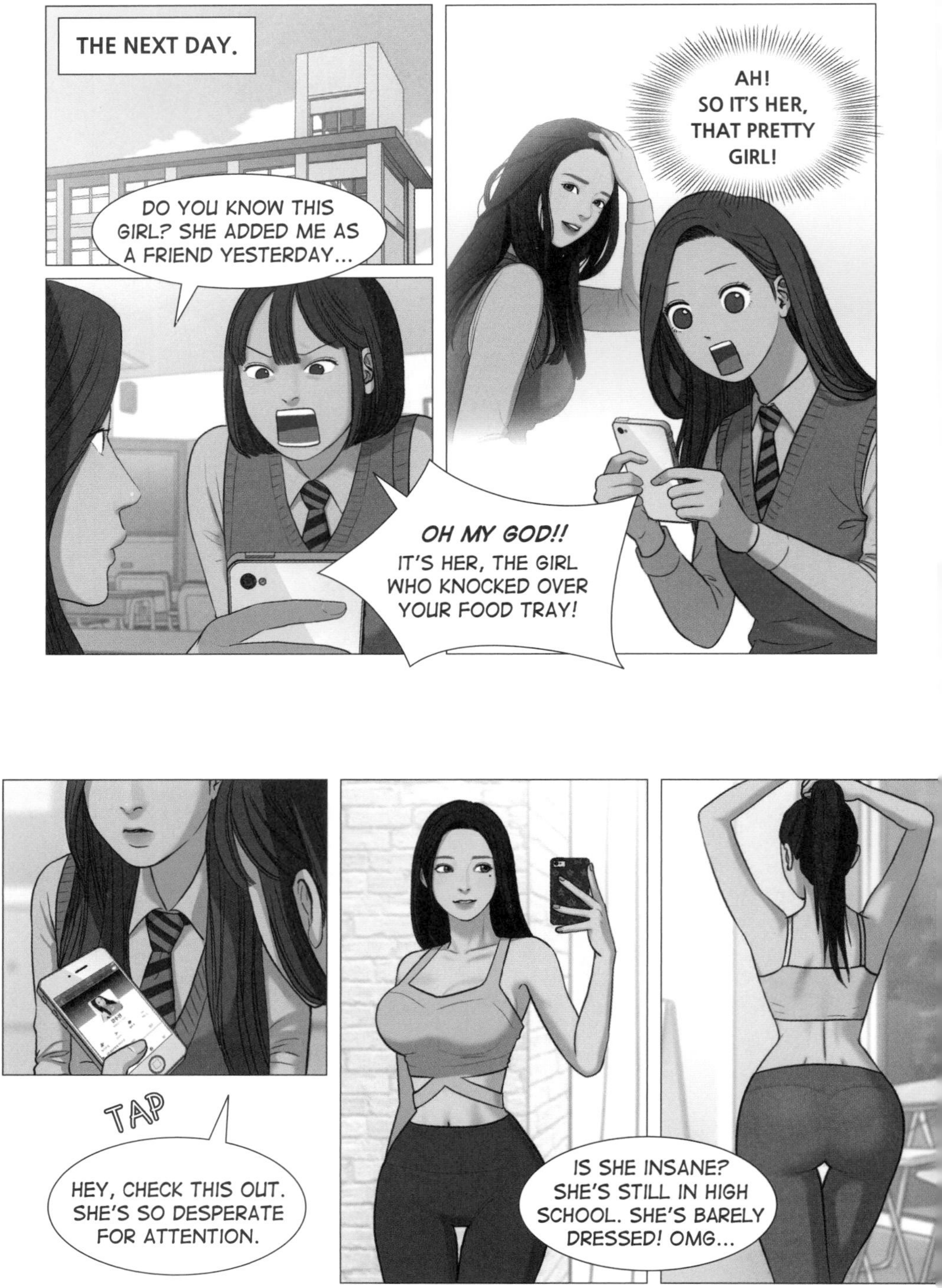
THE NEXT DAY.
DO YOU KNOW THIS GIRL? SHE ADDED ME AS A FRIEND YESTERDAY...
OH MY GOD!! IT'S HER, THE GIRL WHO KNOCKED OVER YOUR FOOD TRAY!
AH! SO IT'S HER, THAT PRETTY GIRL!
TAP
HEY, CHECK THIS OUT. SHE'S SO DESPERATE FOR ATTENTION.
IS SHE INSANE? SHE'S STILL IN HIGH SCHOOL. SHE'S BARELY DRESSED! OMG...

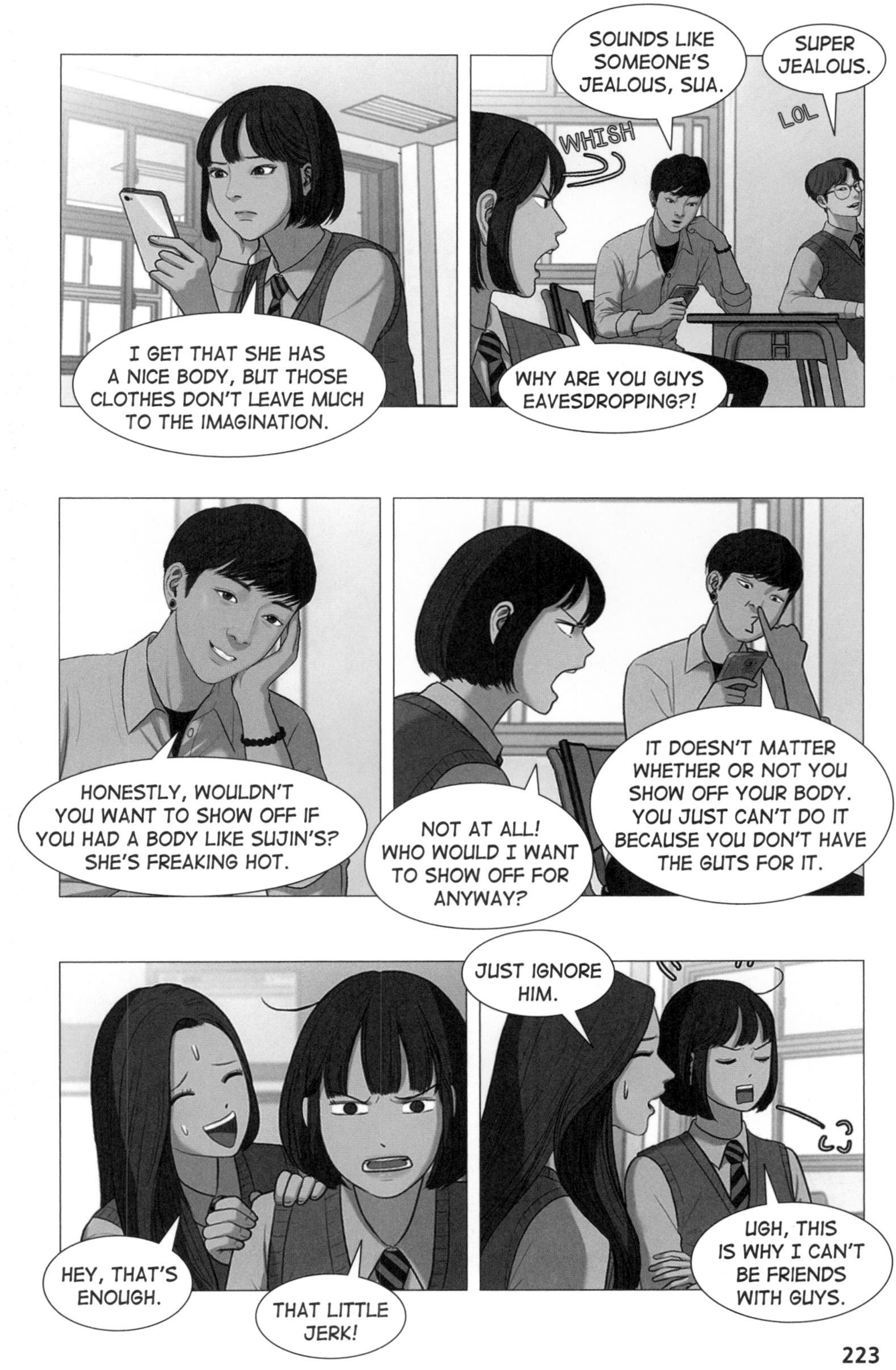
I GET THAT SHE HAS A NICE BODY, BUT THOSE CLOTHES DON'T LEAVE MUCH TO THE IMAGINATION.
SOUNDS LIKE SOMEONE'S JEALOUS, SUA.
SUPER JEALOUS.
WHISH
LOL
WHY ARE YOU GUYS EAVESDROPPING?!
HONESTLY, WOULDN'T YOU WANT TO SHOW OFF IF YOU HAD A BODY LIKE SUJIN'S? SHE'S FREAKING HOT.
NOT AT ALL! WHO WOULD I WANT TO SHOW OFF FOR ANYWAY?
IT DOESN'T MATTER WHETHER OR NOT YOU SHOW OFF YOUR BODY. YOU JUST CAN'T DO IT BECAUSE YOU DON'T HAVE THE GUTS FOR IT.
HEY, THAT'S ENOUGH.
THAT LITTLE JERK!
JUST IGNORE HIM.
UGH, THIS IS WHY I CAN'T BE FRIENDS WITH GUYS.

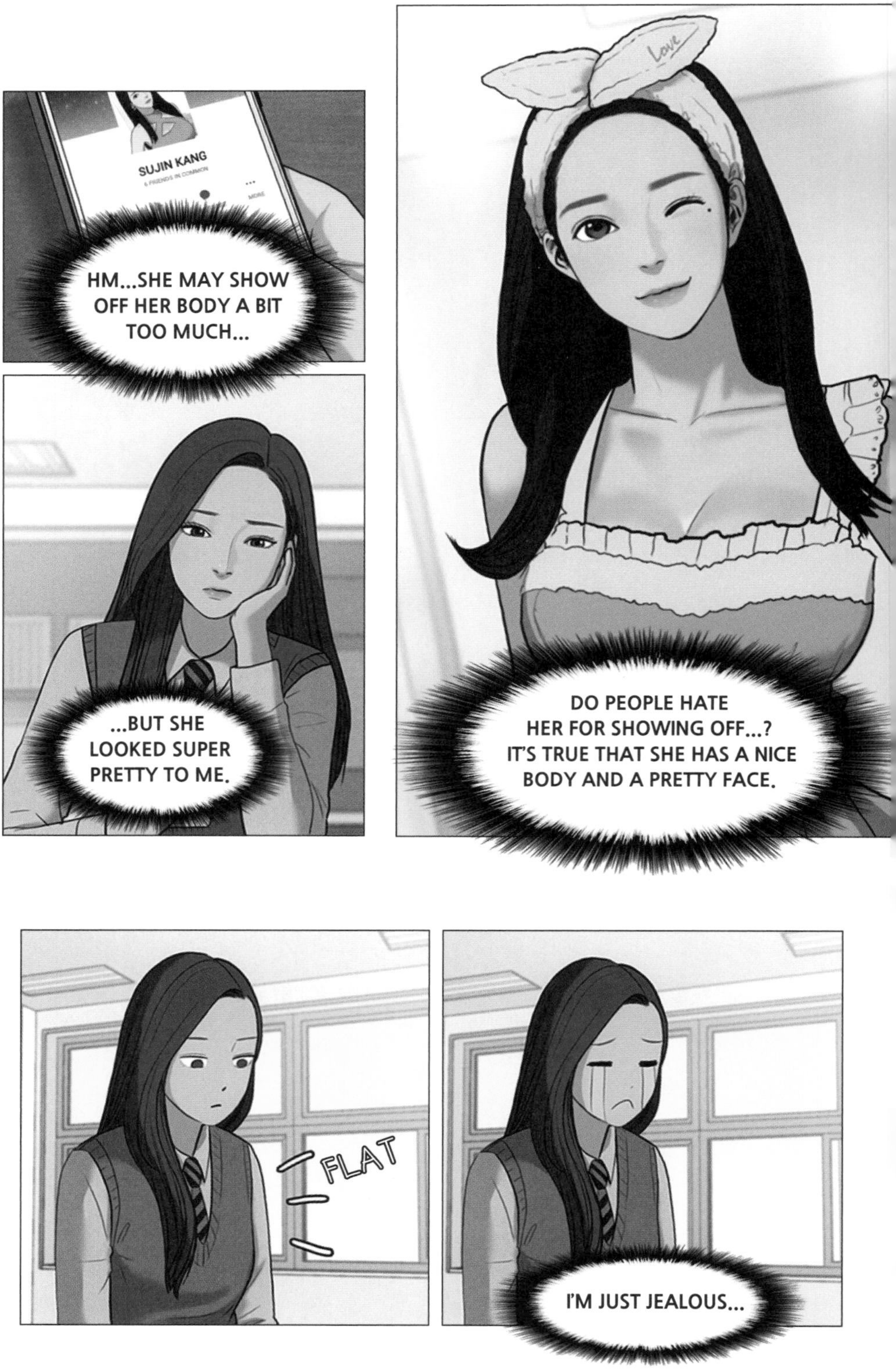
SUJIN KANG
HM...SHE MAY SHOW OFF HER BODY A BIT TOO MUCH...
...BUT SHE LOOKED SUPER PRETTY TO ME.
Love
DO PEOPLE HATE HER FOR SHOWING OFF...? IT'S TRUE THAT SHE HAS A NICE BODY AND A PRETTY FACE.
FLAT
I'M JUST JEALOUS...

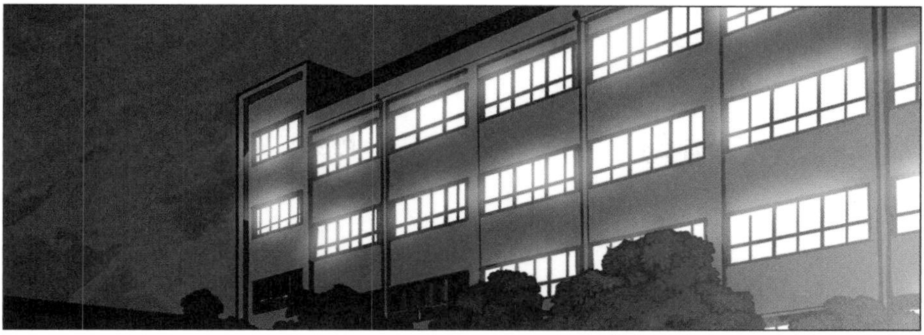

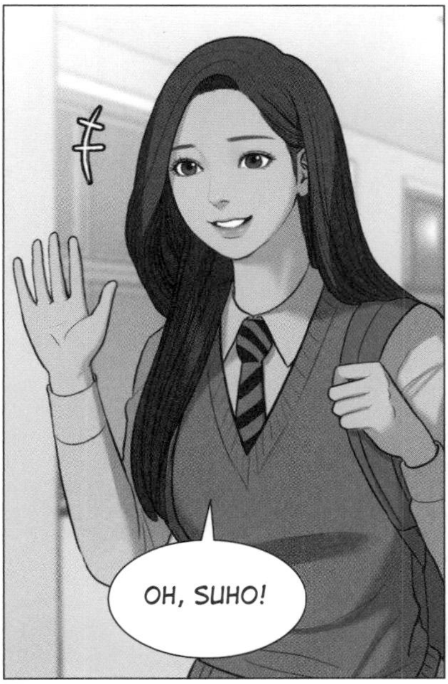
OH, SUHO!

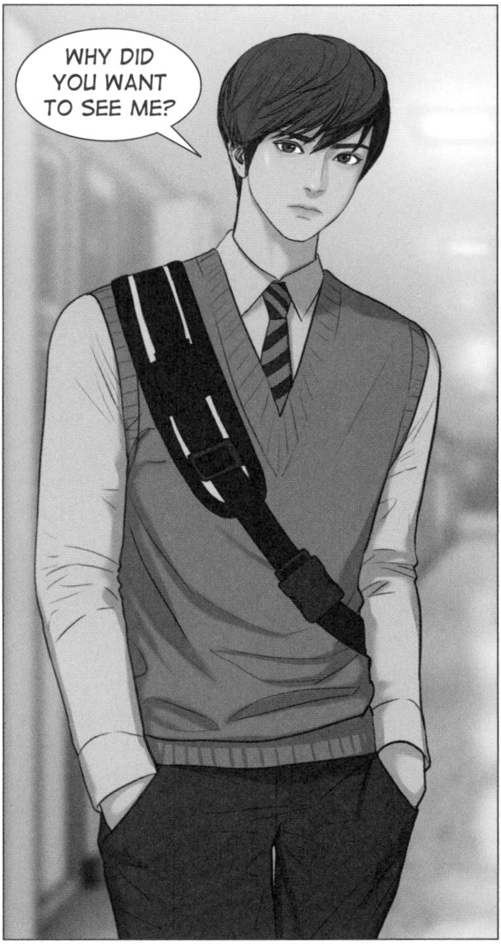
WHY DID YOU WANT TO SEE ME?

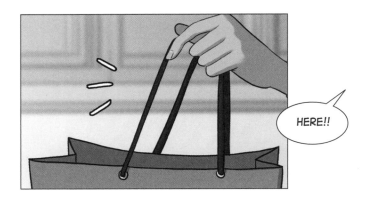

HERE!!

MY BROTHER TRIED IT ON ONCE YESTERDAY... SORRY.

AH. THE HOODIE.

OH YEAH? THEN HOW ABOUT I JUST GIVE THIS TO HIM?

≳GASP≲

WHY? TO JUYOUNG? WHY WOULD YOU GIVE HIM SOMETHING SO EXPENSIVE ?????

YOU'RE CRAZY!! NO WAY.

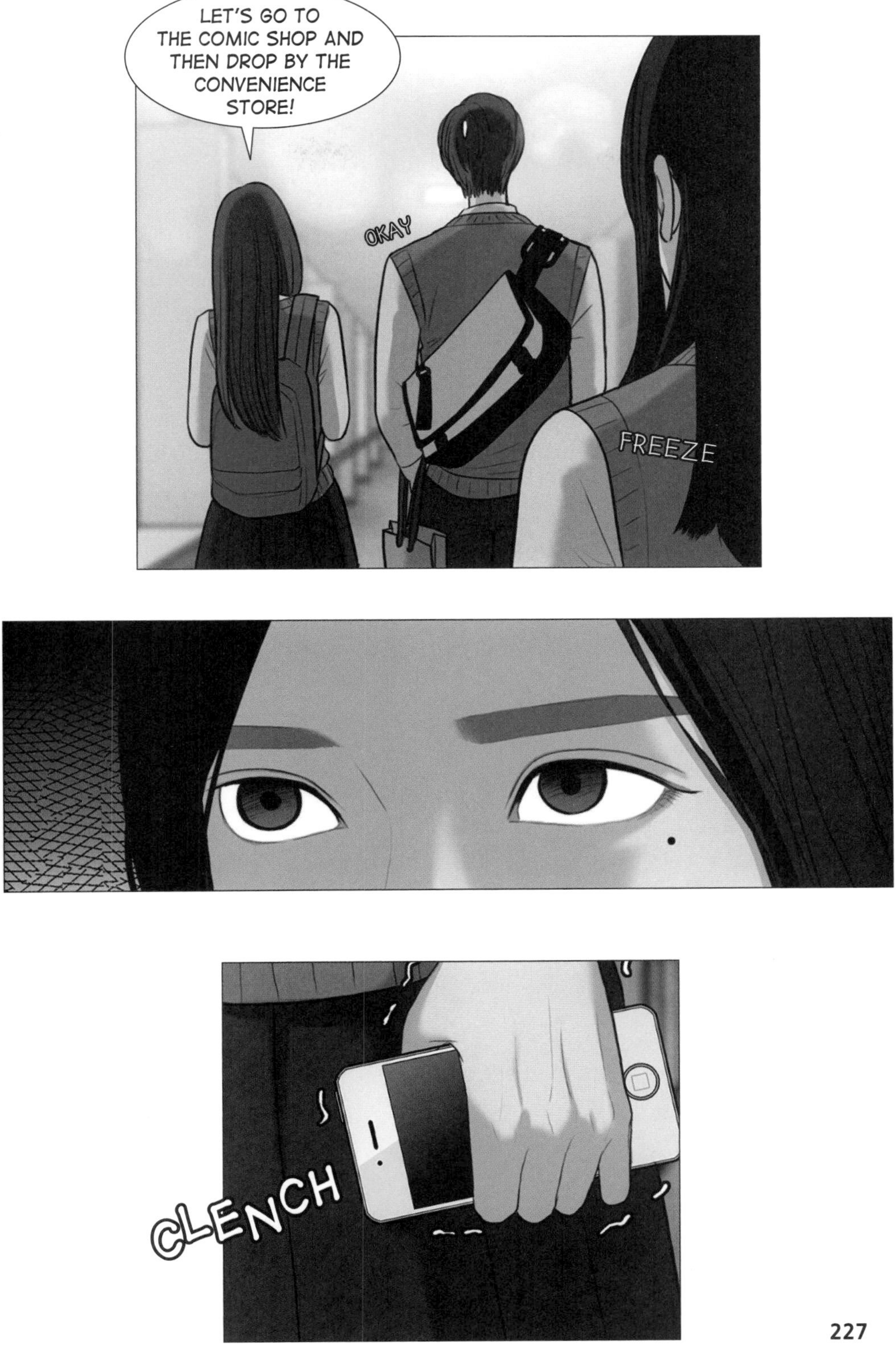
LET'S GO TO THE COMIC SHOP AND THEN DROP BY THE CONVENIENCE STORE!
OKAY
FREEZE
CLENCH

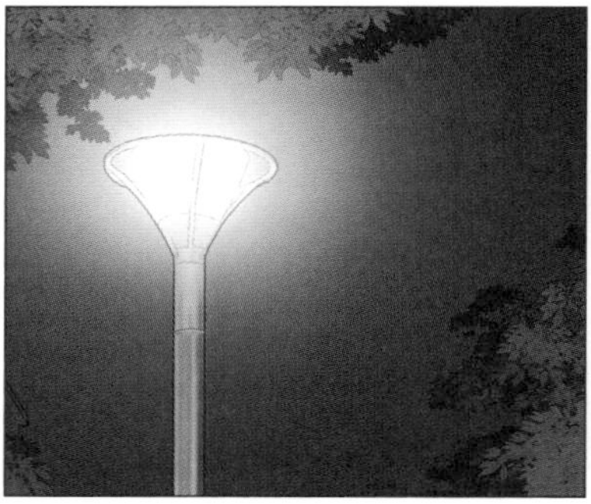

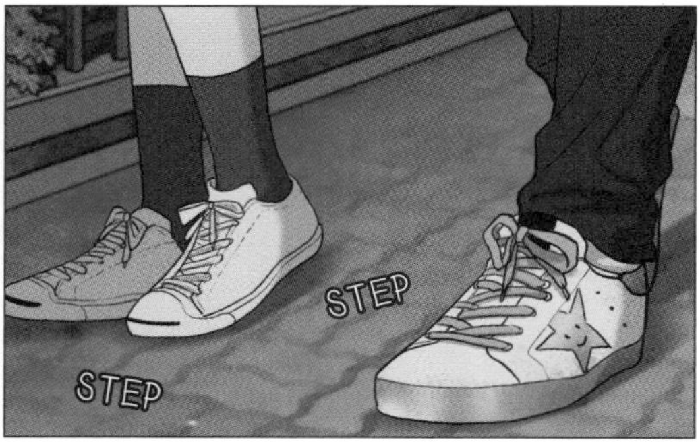
STEP
STEP

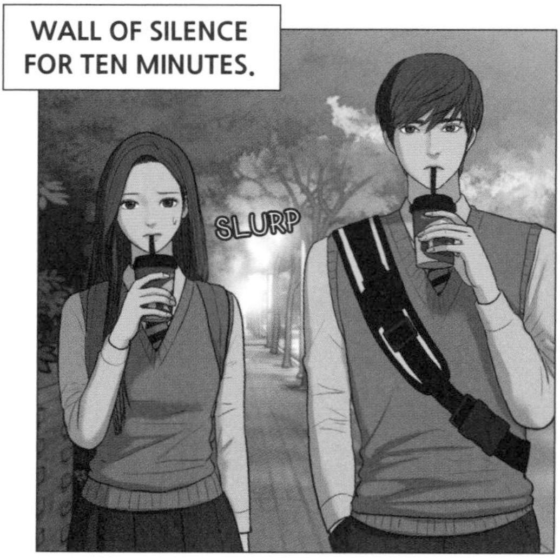
WALL OF SILENCE FOR TEN MINUTES.
SLURP

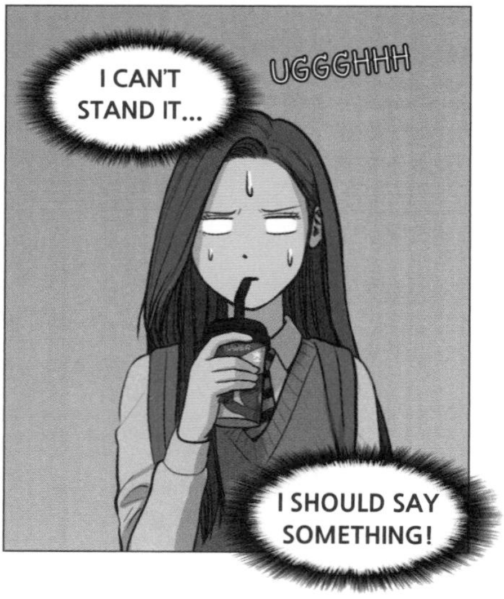
I CAN'T STAND IT...
UGGGHHH
I SHOULD SAY SOMETHING!

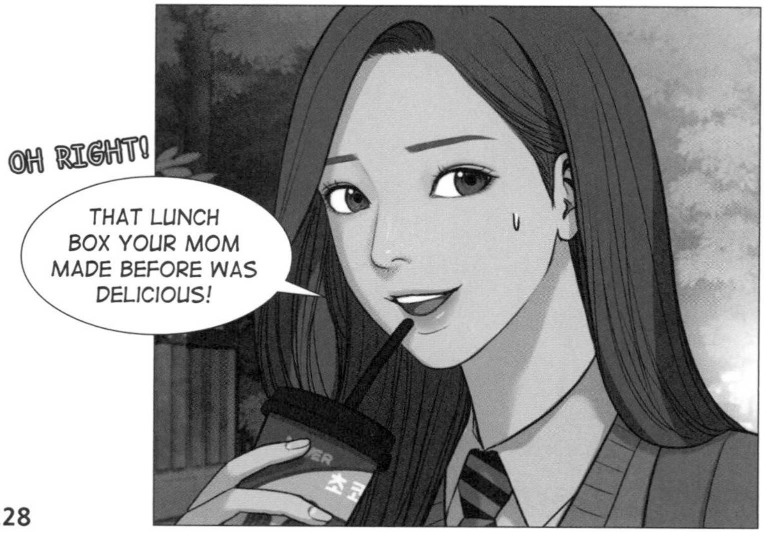
OH RIGHT!
THAT LUNCH BOX YOUR MOM MADE BEFORE WAS DELICIOUS!

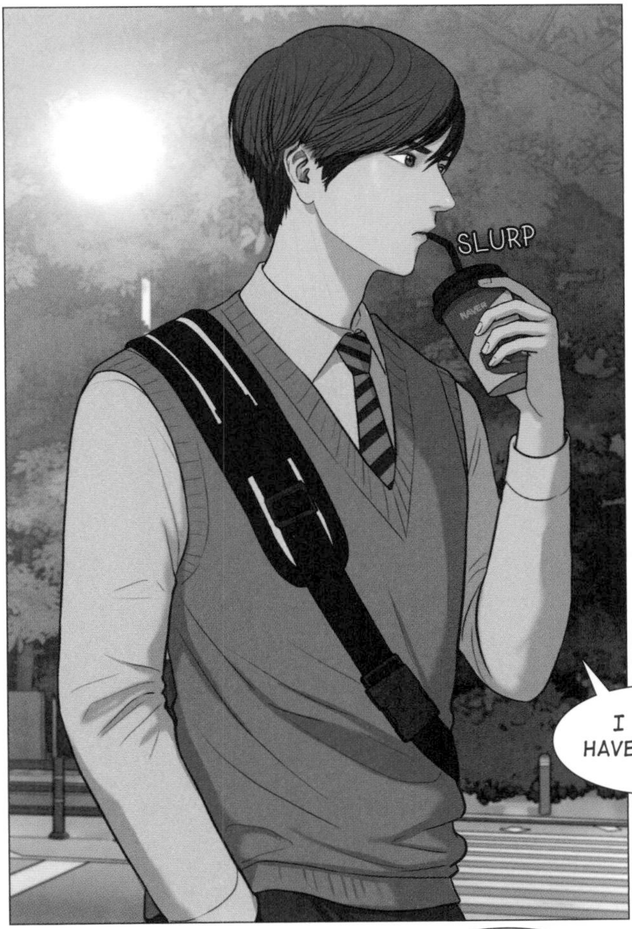
SLURP
I DON'T HAVE A MOM.

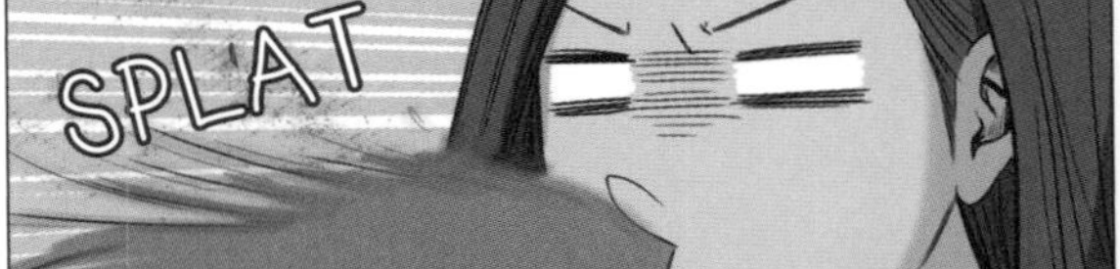
SPLAT

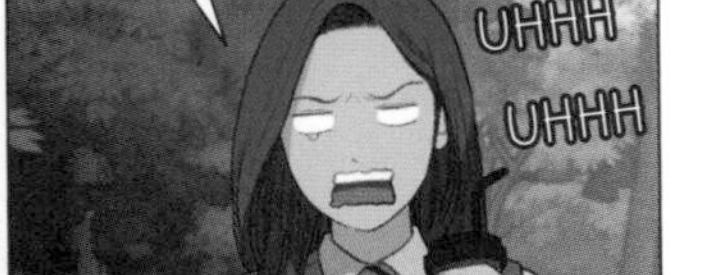
AAAHHH S...S...SORRY... SORRY TO HEAR THAT...
UHHH
UHHH
TAP
TAP

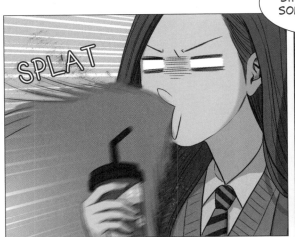

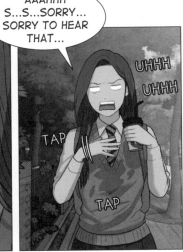

...
HERE.
PANIC
PANIC
AHH, THANKS.
UGH...
AHH...
WE'RE
ALMOST
THERE.
SEE YOU
LATER.
AND
DON'T WORRY
ABOUT IT.

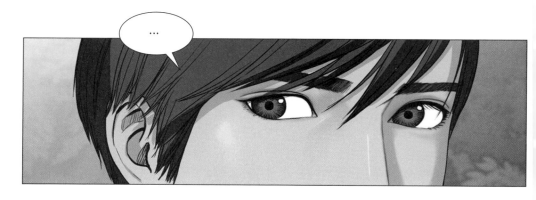

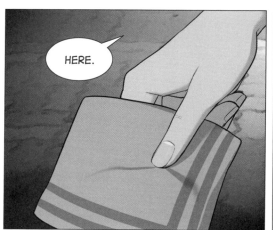

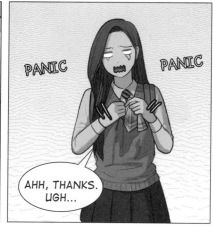

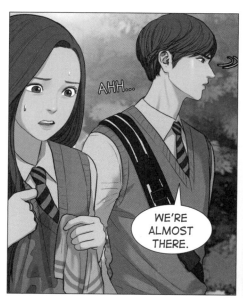

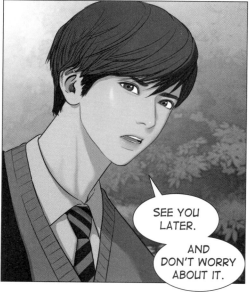

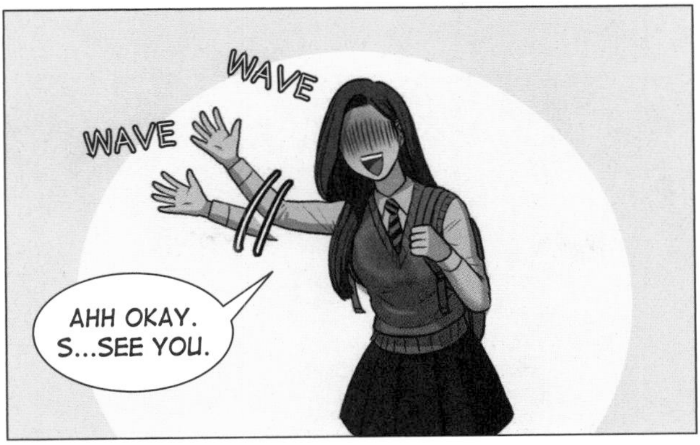
WAVE
WAVE
AHH OKAY. S...SEE YOU.

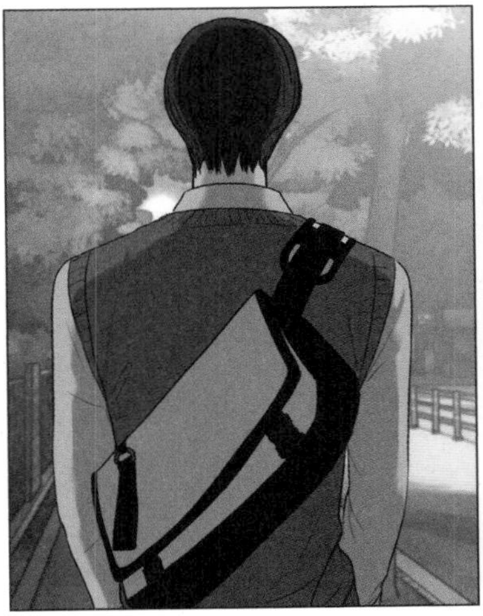

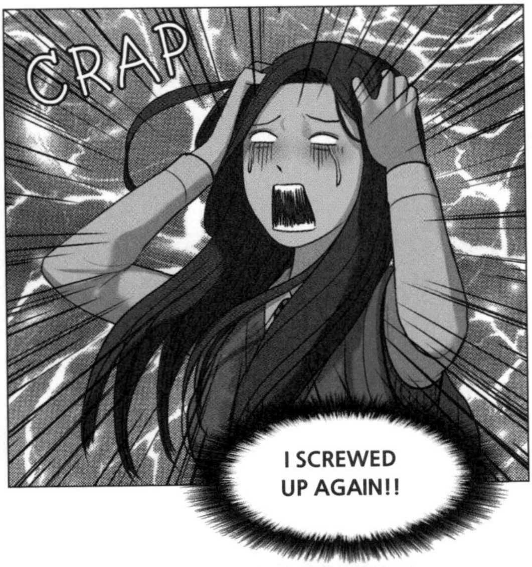
CRAP
I SCREWED UP AGAIN!!

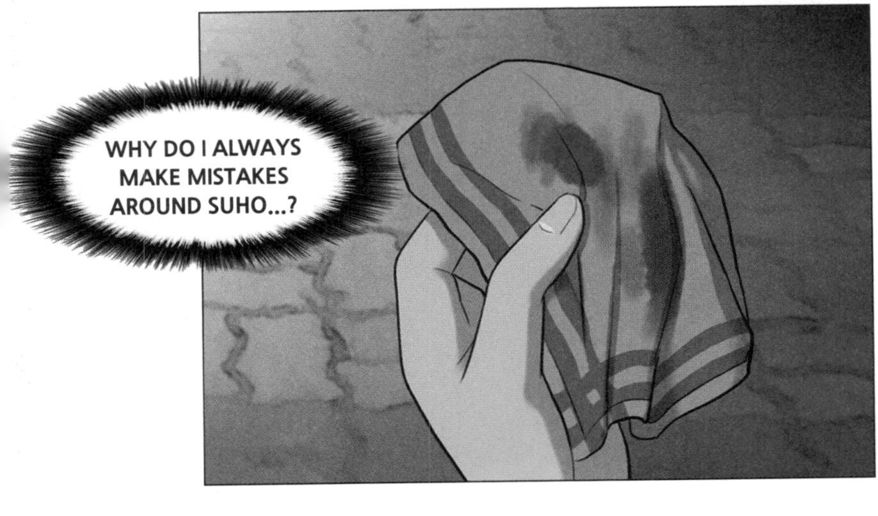
WHY DO I ALWAYS MAKE MISTAKES AROUND SUHO...?

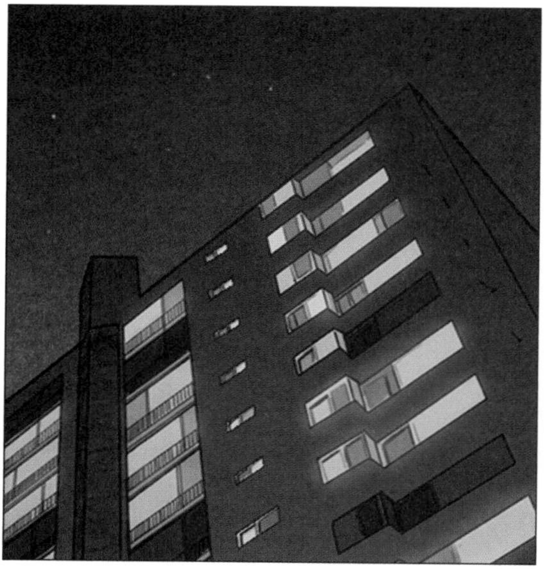

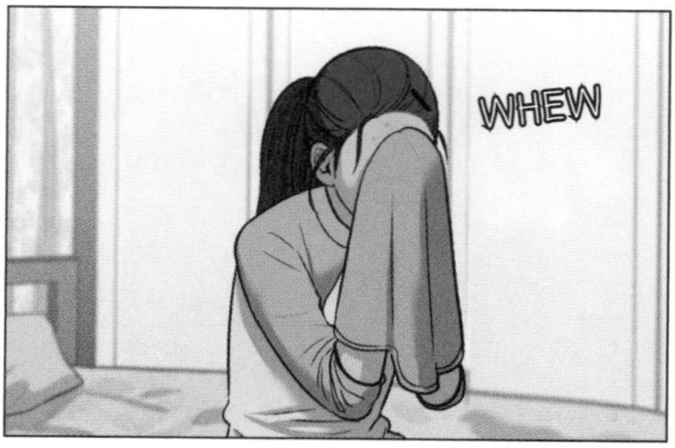
WHEW

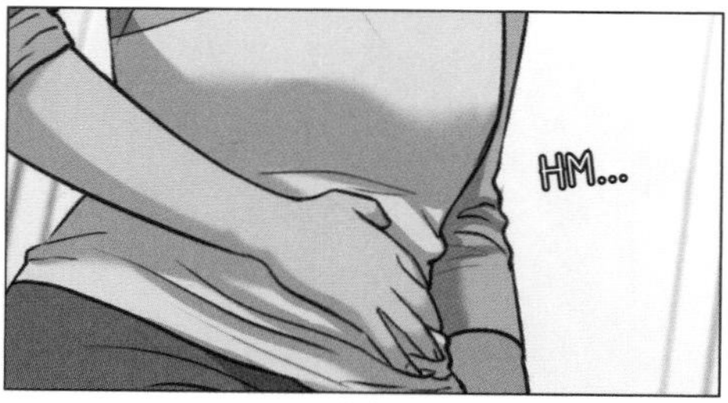
HM...

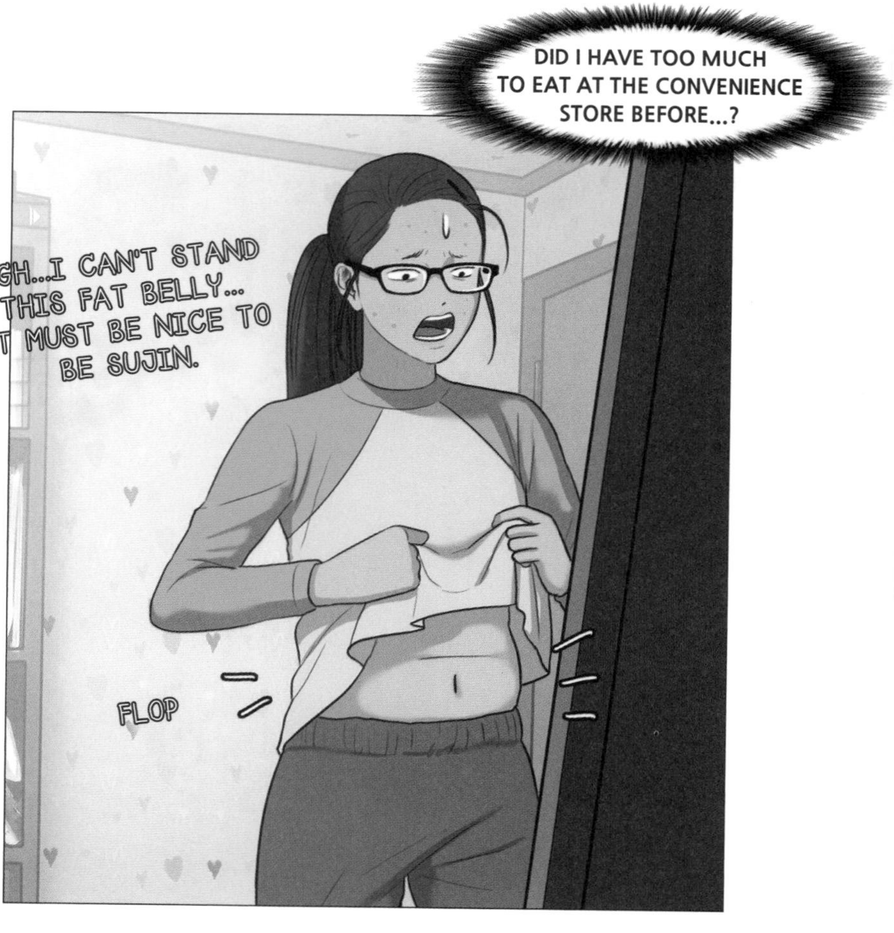
DID I HAVE TOO MUCH TO EAT AT THE CONVENIENCE STORE BEFORE...?
UGH...I CAN'T STAND THIS FAT BELLY... IT MUST BE NICE TO BE SUJIN.
FLOP

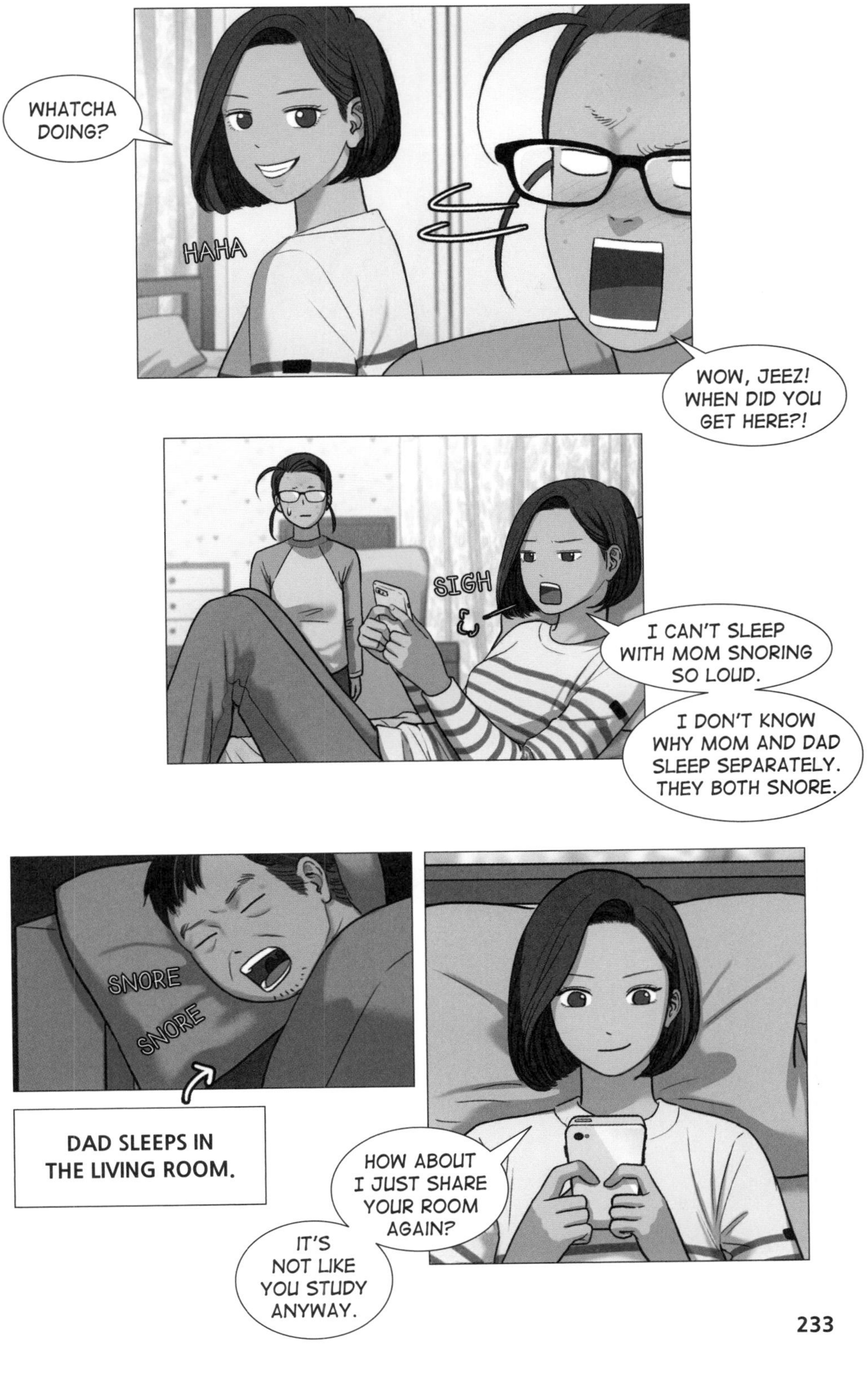
WHATCHA DOING?
HAHA
WOW, JEEZ! WHEN DID YOU GET HERE?!
SIGH
I CAN'T SLEEP WITH MOM SNORING SO LOUD.
I DON'T KNOW WHY MOM AND DAD SLEEP SEPARATELY. THEY BOTH SNORE.
SNORE
SNORE
DAD SLEEPS IN THE LIVING ROOM.
HOW ABOUT I JUST SHARE YOUR ROOM AGAIN?
IT'S NOT LIKE YOU STUDY ANYWAY.

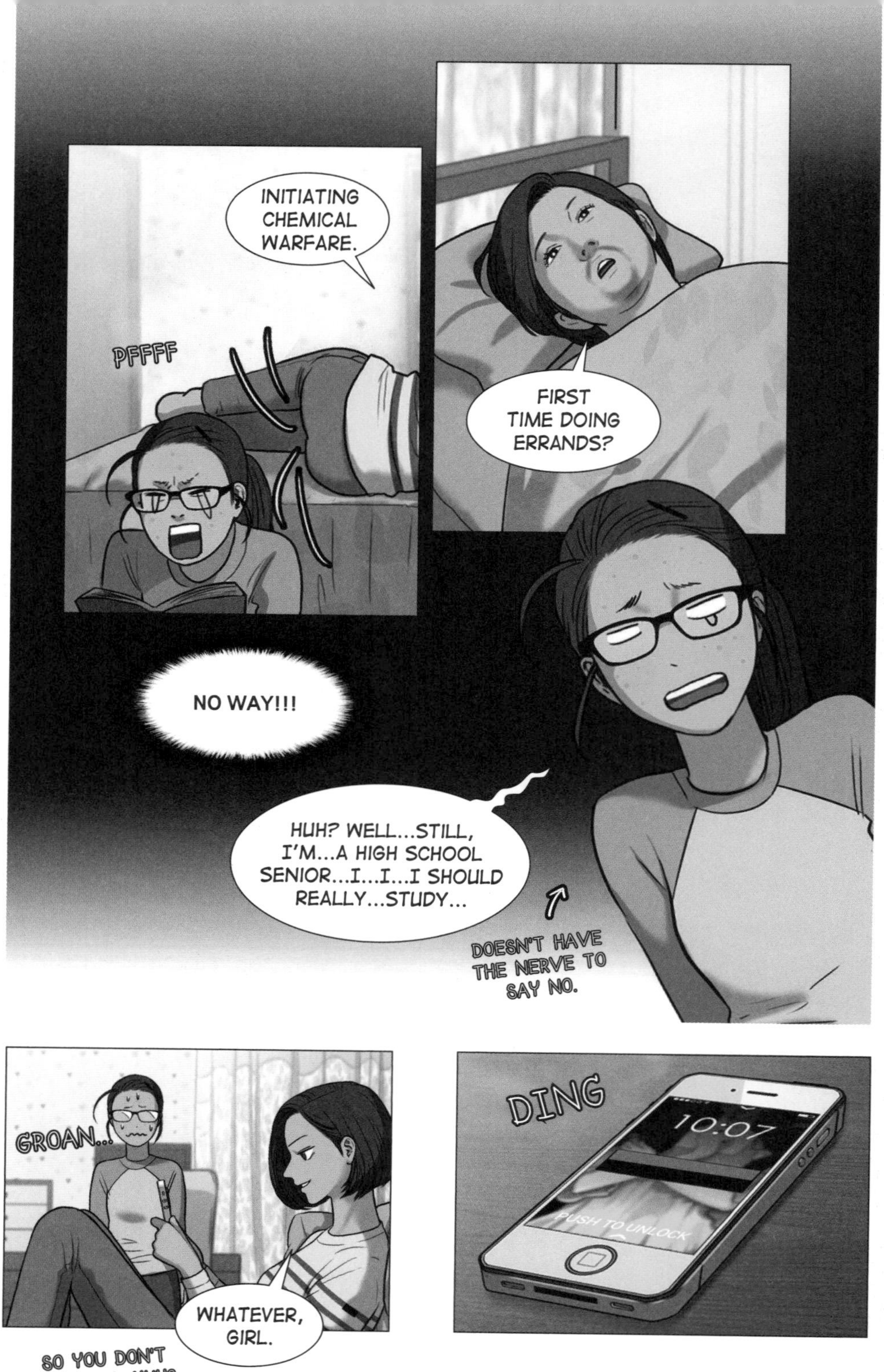
INITIATING CHEMICAL WARFARE.
PFFFF
FIRST TIME DOING ERRANDS?
NO WAY!!!
HUH? WELL...STILL, I'M...A HIGH SCHOOL SENIOR...I...I...I SHOULD REALLY...STUDY...
DOESN'T HAVE THE NERVE TO SAY NO.
GROAN...
WHATEVER, GIRL.
SO YOU DON'T WANT TO, HUH?
DING
10:07
PUSH TO UNLOCK

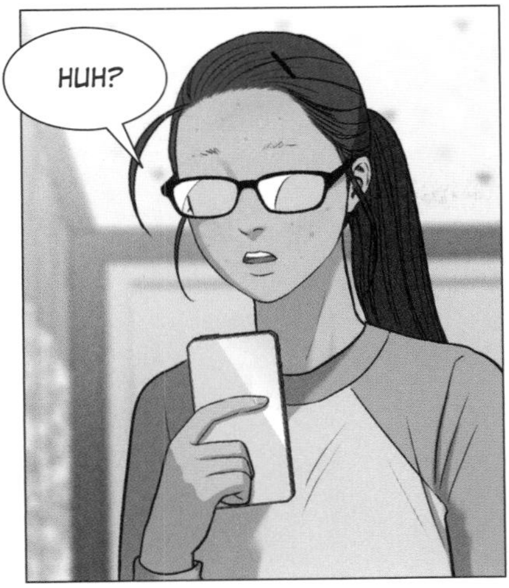
HUH?

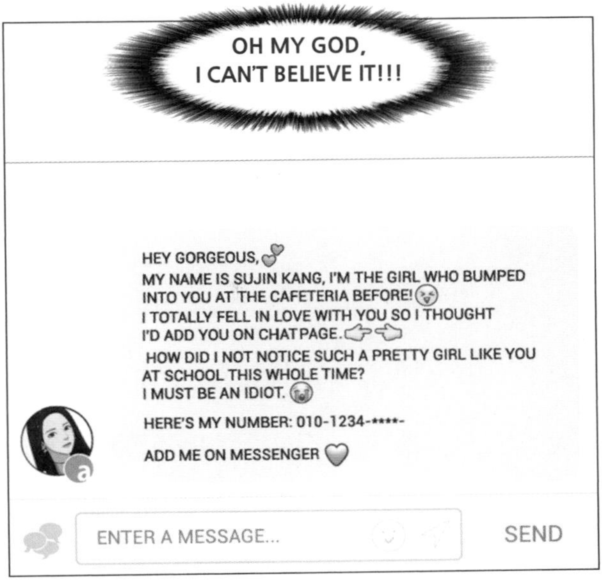
OH MY GOD,
I CAN'T BELIEVE IT!!!
HEY GORGEOUS,
MY NAME IS SUJIN KANG, I'M THE GIRL WHO BUMPED
INTO YOU AT THE CAFETERIA BEFORE!
I TOTALLY FELL IN LOVE WITH YOU SO I THOUGHT
I'D ADD YOU ON CHATPAGE.
HOW DID I NOT NOTICE SUCH A PRETTY GIRL LIKE YOU
AT SCHOOL THIS WHOLE TIME?
I MUST BE AN IDIOT.
HERE'S MY NUMBER: 010-1234-****-
ADD ME ON MESSENGER
ENTER A MESSAGE...
SEND

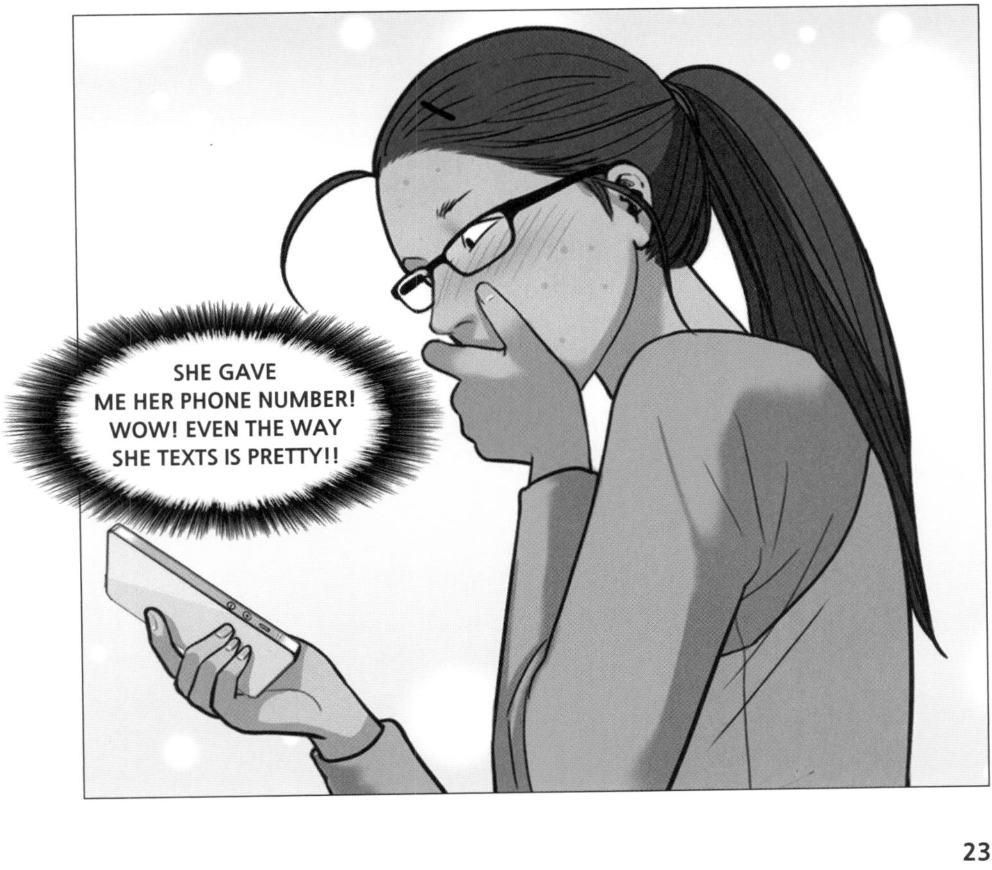
SHE GAVE
ME HER PHONE NUMBER!
WOW! EVEN THE WAY
SHE TEXTS IS PRETTY!!

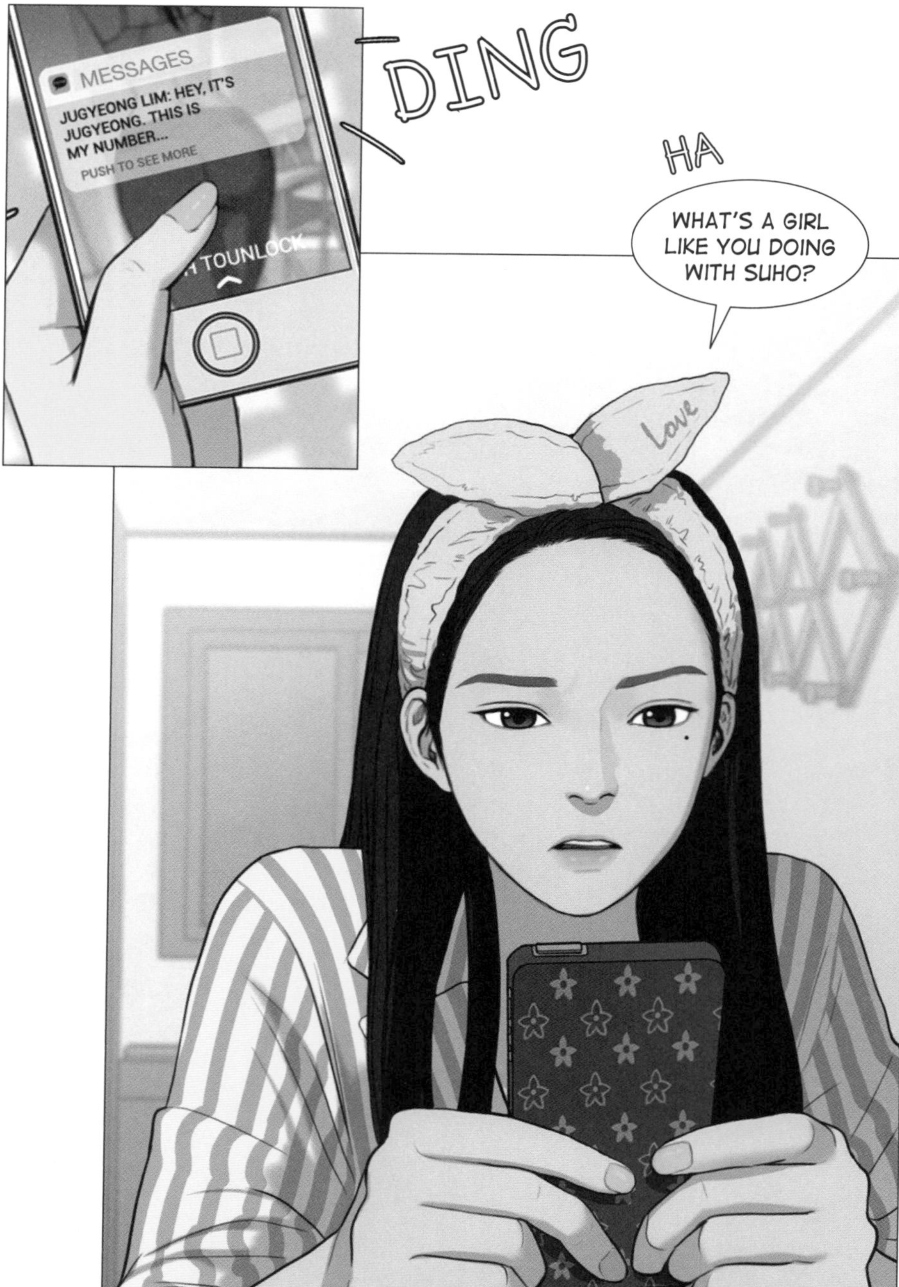
MESSAGES
JUGYEONG LIM: HEY, IT'S JUGYEONG. THIS IS MY NUMBER...
PUSH TO SEE MORE
DING
HA
WHAT'S A GIRL LIKE YOU DOING WITH SUHO?

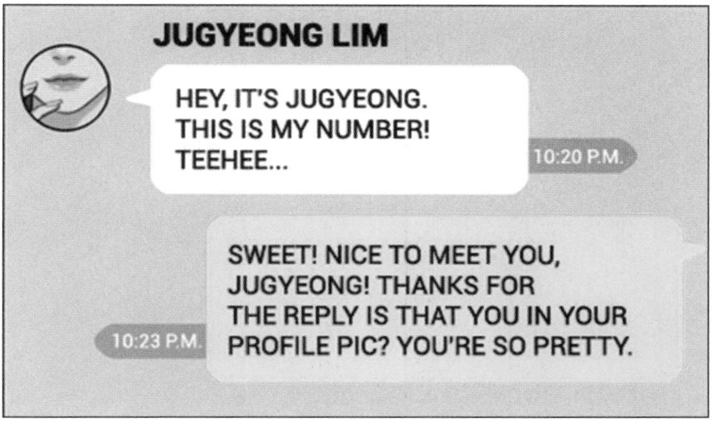
JUGYEONG LIM
HEY, IT'S JUGYEONG. THIS IS MY NUMBER! TEEHEE...
10:20 P.M.
SWEET! NICE TO MEET YOU, JUGYEONG! THANKS FOR THE REPLY IS THAT YOU IN YOUR PROFILE PIC? YOU'RE SO PRETTY.
10:23 P.M.

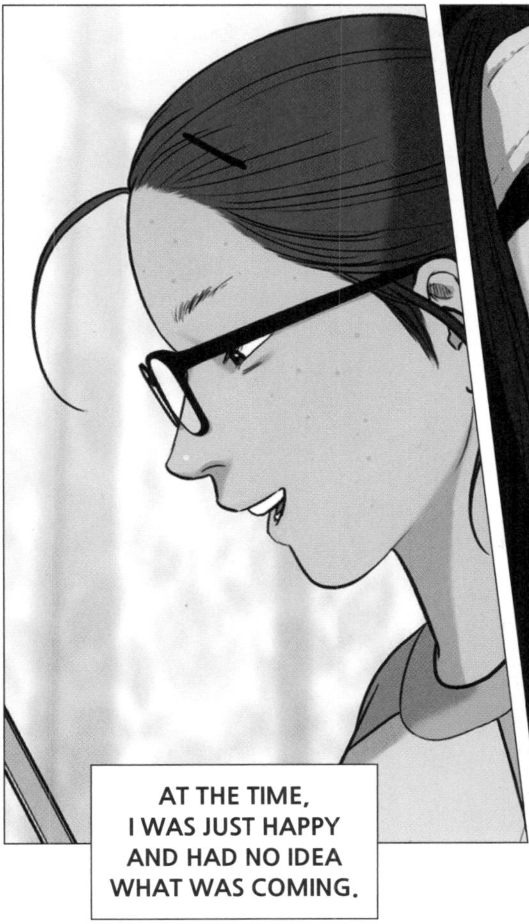
AT THE TIME, I WAS JUST HAPPY AND HAD NO IDEA WHAT WAS COMING.

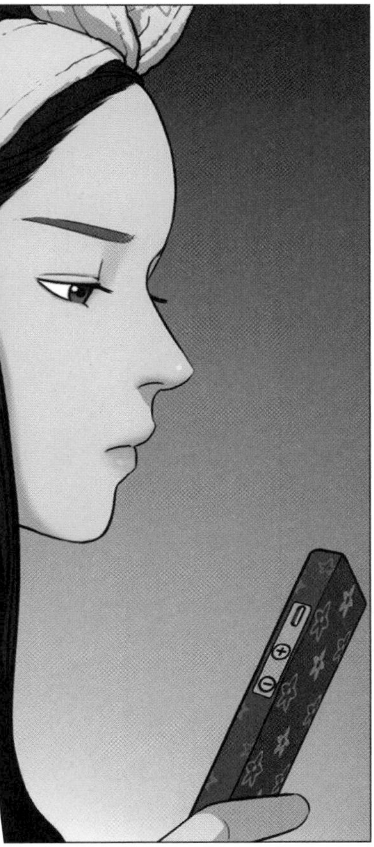

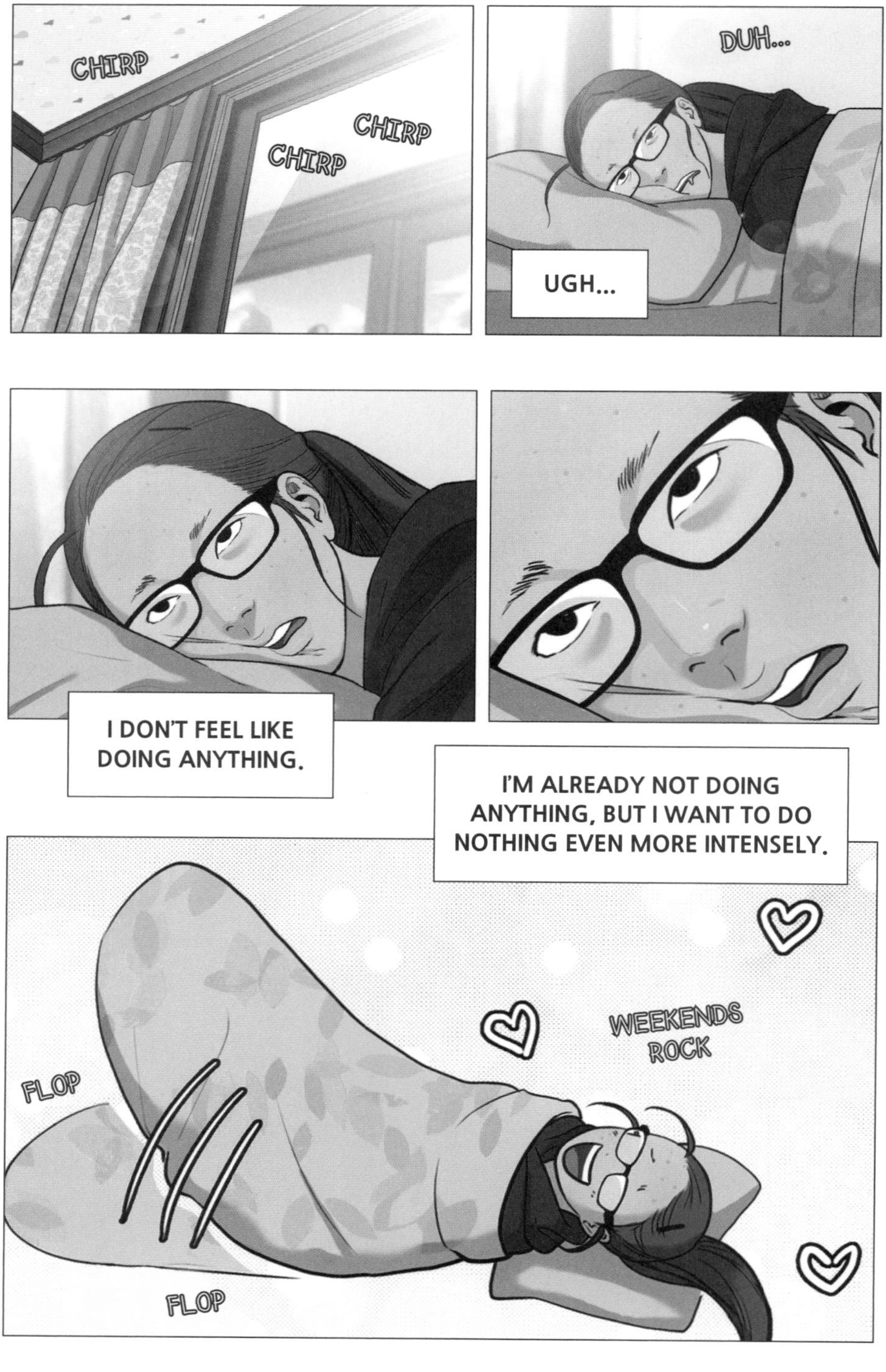
CHIRP
CHIRP
CHIRP
DUH...
UGH...
I DON'T FEEL LIKE DOING ANYTHING.
I'M ALREADY NOT DOING ANYTHING, BUT I WANT TO DO NOTHING EVEN MORE INTENSELY.
WEEKENDS ROCK
FLOP
FLOP

DING
DING

HUH?

AH, IT'S SIS.

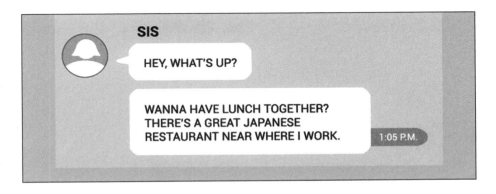

SIS

HEY, WHAT'S UP?

WANNA HAVE LUNCH TOGETHER? THERE'S A GREAT JAPANESE RESTAURANT NEAR WHERE I WORK.

1:05 P.M.

UGH, I DON'T FEEL LIKE GOING OUT NOW.

JAPANESE FOOD...

BUT

DROOL

SUSHI...

LET'S GO!!!

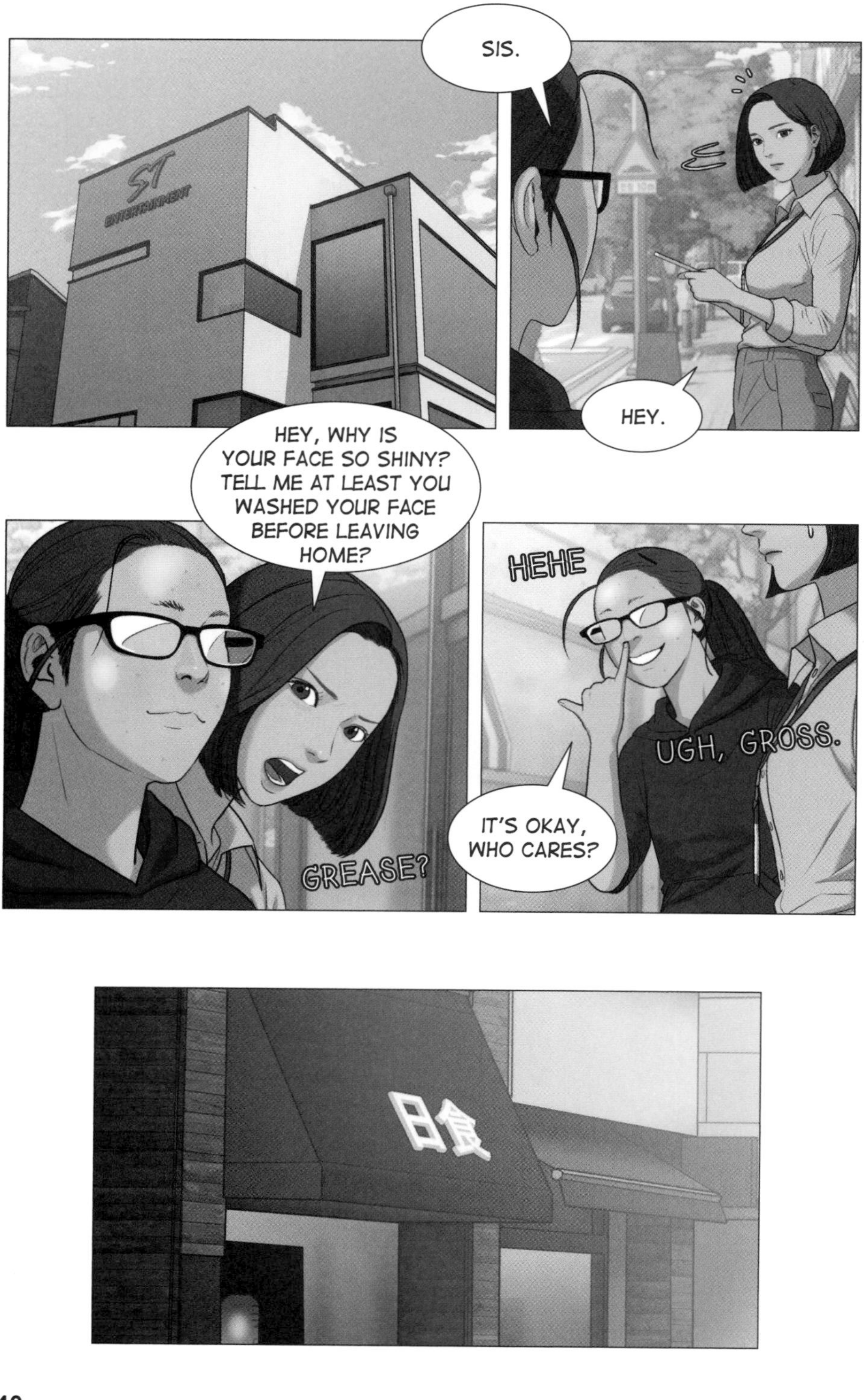
SIS.
HEY.
HEY, WHY IS YOUR FACE SO SHINY? TELL ME AT LEAST YOU WASHED YOUR FACE BEFORE LEAVING HOME?
GREASE?
HEHE
UGH, GROSS.
IT'S OKAY, WHO CARES?
日食

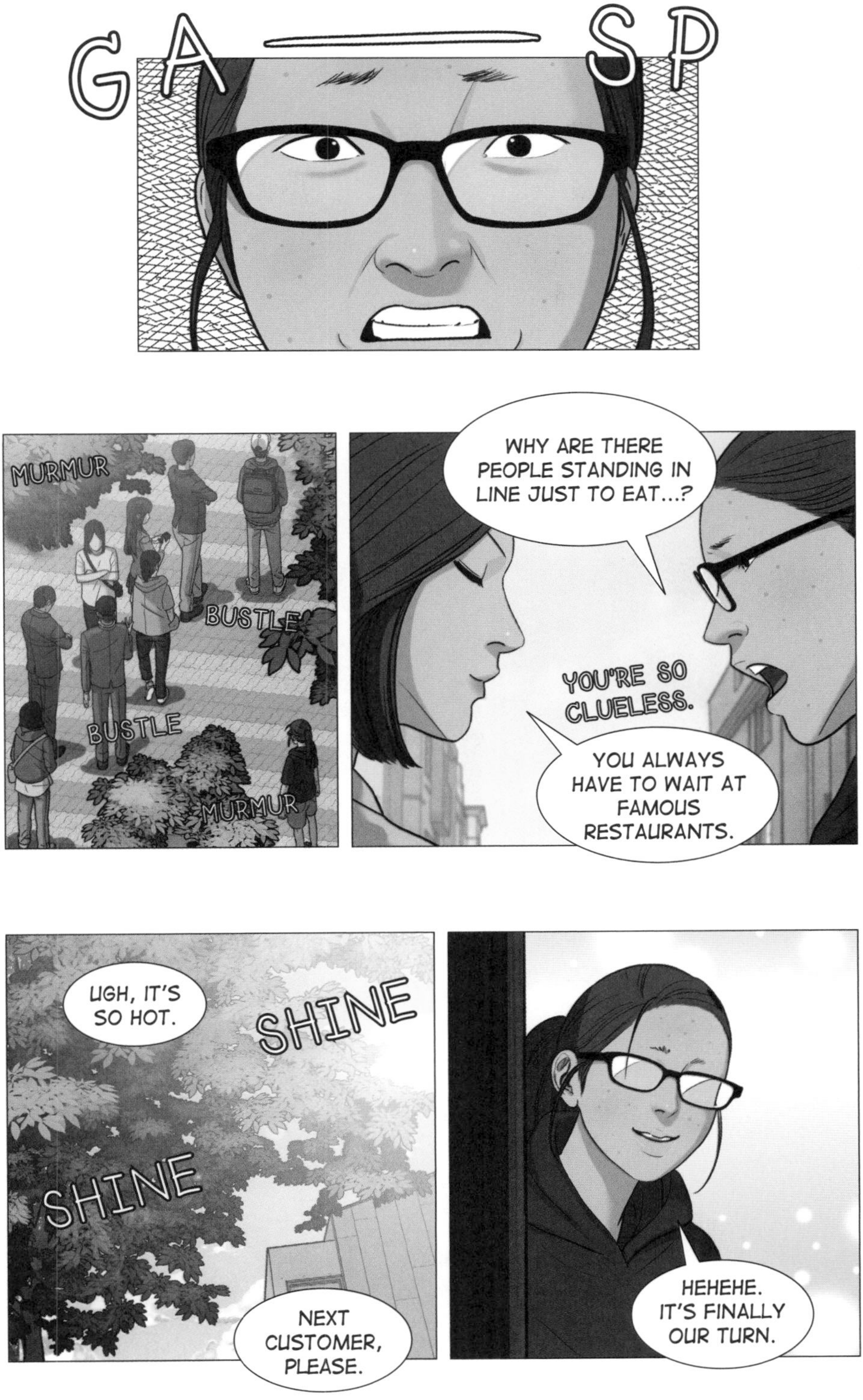
GA—SP
MURMUR
BUSTLE
BUSTLE
MURMUR
WHY ARE THERE PEOPLE STANDING IN LINE JUST TO EAT...?
YOU'RE SO CLUELESS.
YOU ALWAYS HAVE TO WAIT AT FAMOUS RESTAURANTS.
UGH, IT'S SO HOT.
SHINE
SHINE
NEXT CUSTOMER, PLEASE.
HEHEHE. IT'S FINALLY OUR TURN.

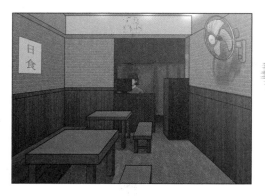

HUH...? IT'S SMALLER THAN I THOUGHT. ARE YOU SURE THIS PLACE IS FAMOUS?

WHAT DO YOU WANT TO EAT?

I'LL HAVE A KATSUDON!

OKAY, SOBA FOR ME.

EXCUSE ME, WE'RE READY TO ORDER.

CLICK

CLICK

CLICK

CLICK

CLICK

CLICK

CLICK

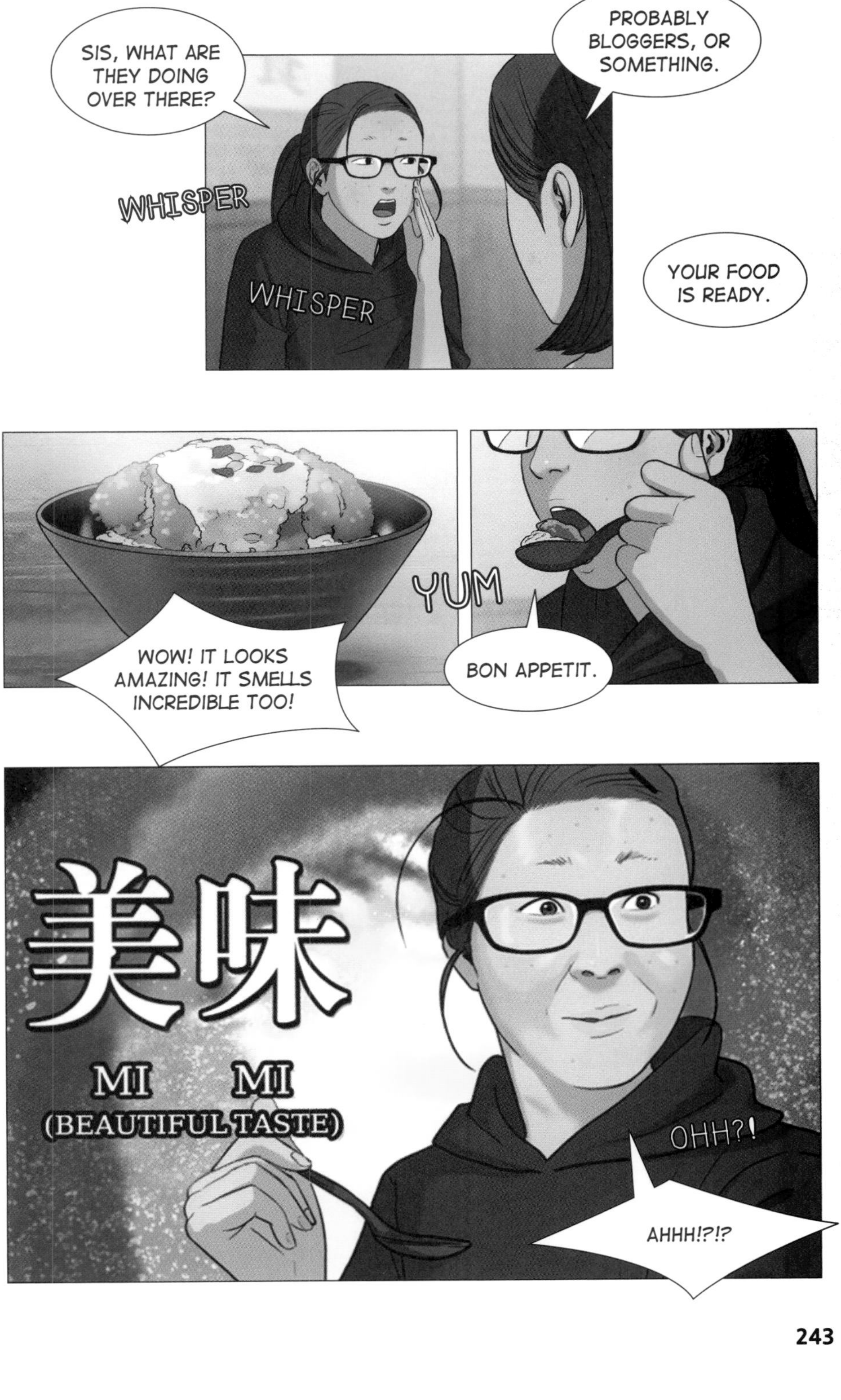
SIS, WHAT ARE THEY DOING OVER THERE?
WHISPER
WHISPER
PROBABLY BLOGGERS, OR SOMETHING.
YOUR FOOD IS READY.
WOW! IT LOOKS AMAZING! IT SMELLS INCREDIBLE TOO!
YUM
BON APPETIT.
美味
MI MI
(BEAUTIFUL TASTE)
OHH?!
AHHH!?!?

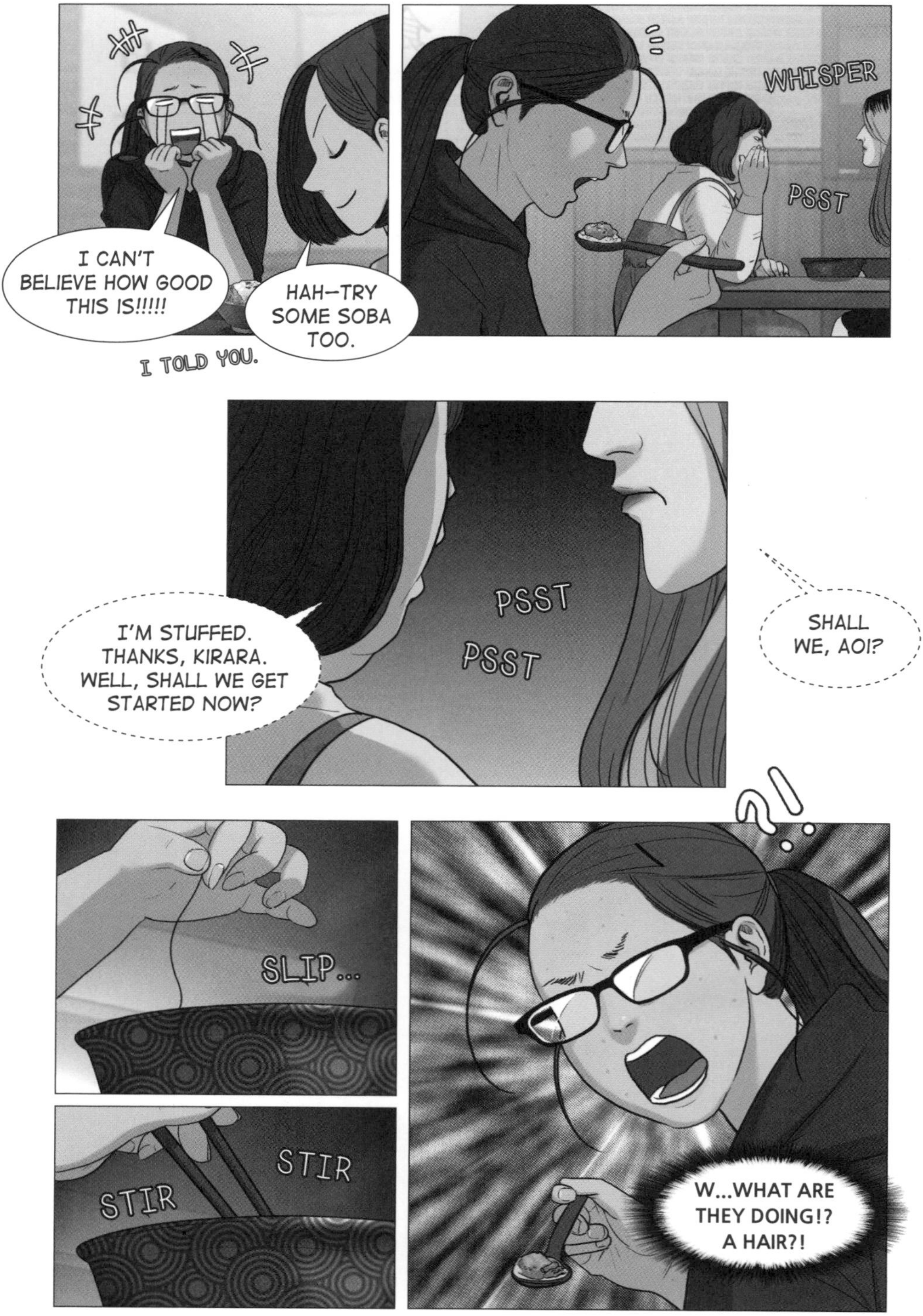
I CAN'T BELIEVE HOW GOOD THIS IS!!!!!
HAH—TRY SOME SOBA TOO.
I TOLD YOU.
WHISPER
PSST
I'M STUFFED. THANKS, KIRARA. WELL, SHALL WE GET STARTED NOW?
PSST
PSST
SHALL WE, AOI?
SLIP...
STIR
STIR
?!
W...WHAT ARE THEY DOING!? A HAIR?!

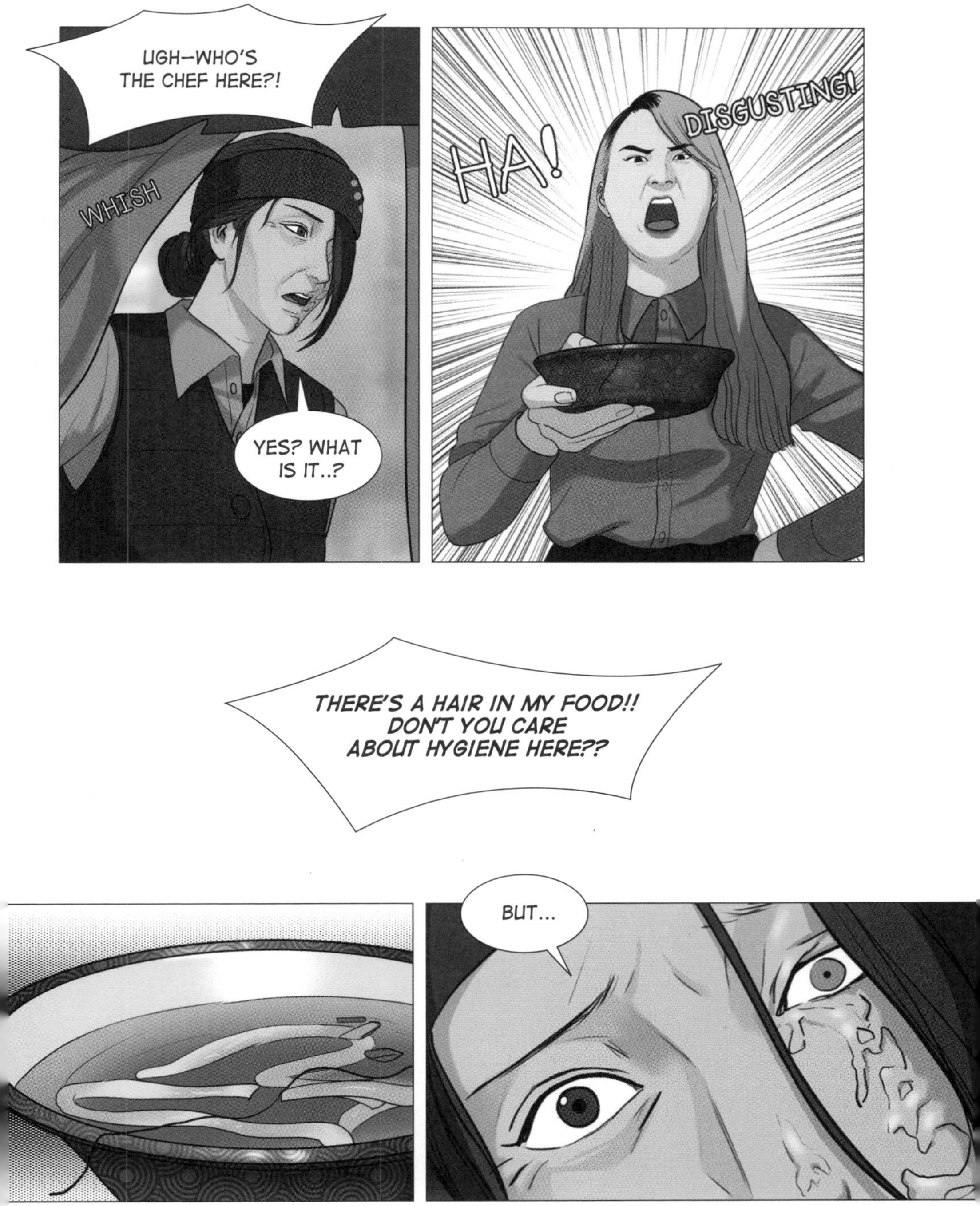
UGH—WHO'S THE CHEF HERE?!
WHISH
YES? WHAT IS IT..?
HA!
DISGUSTING!
THERE'S A HAIR IN MY FOOD!! DON'T YOU CARE ABOUT HYGIENE HERE??
BUT...

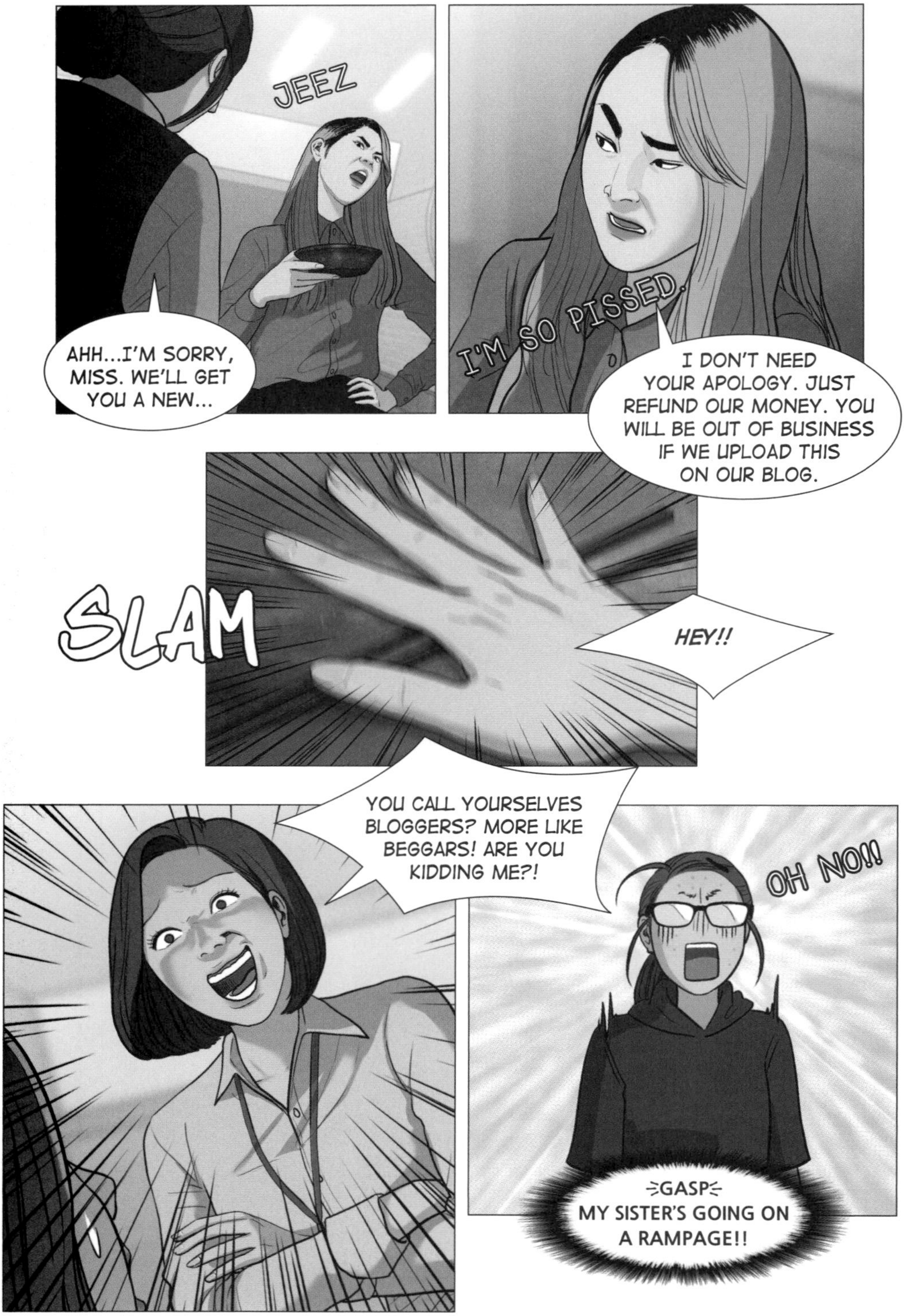
JEEZ
AHH...I'M SORRY, MISS. WE'LL GET YOU A NEW...
I'M SO PISSED.
I DON'T NEED YOUR APOLOGY. JUST REFUND OUR MONEY. YOU WILL BE OUT OF BUSINESS IF WE UPLOAD THIS ON OUR BLOG.
SLAM
HEY!!
YOU CALL YOURSELVES BLOGGERS? MORE LIKE BEGGARS! ARE YOU KIDDING ME?!
OH NO!!
GASP
MY SISTER'S GOING ON A RAMPAGE!!

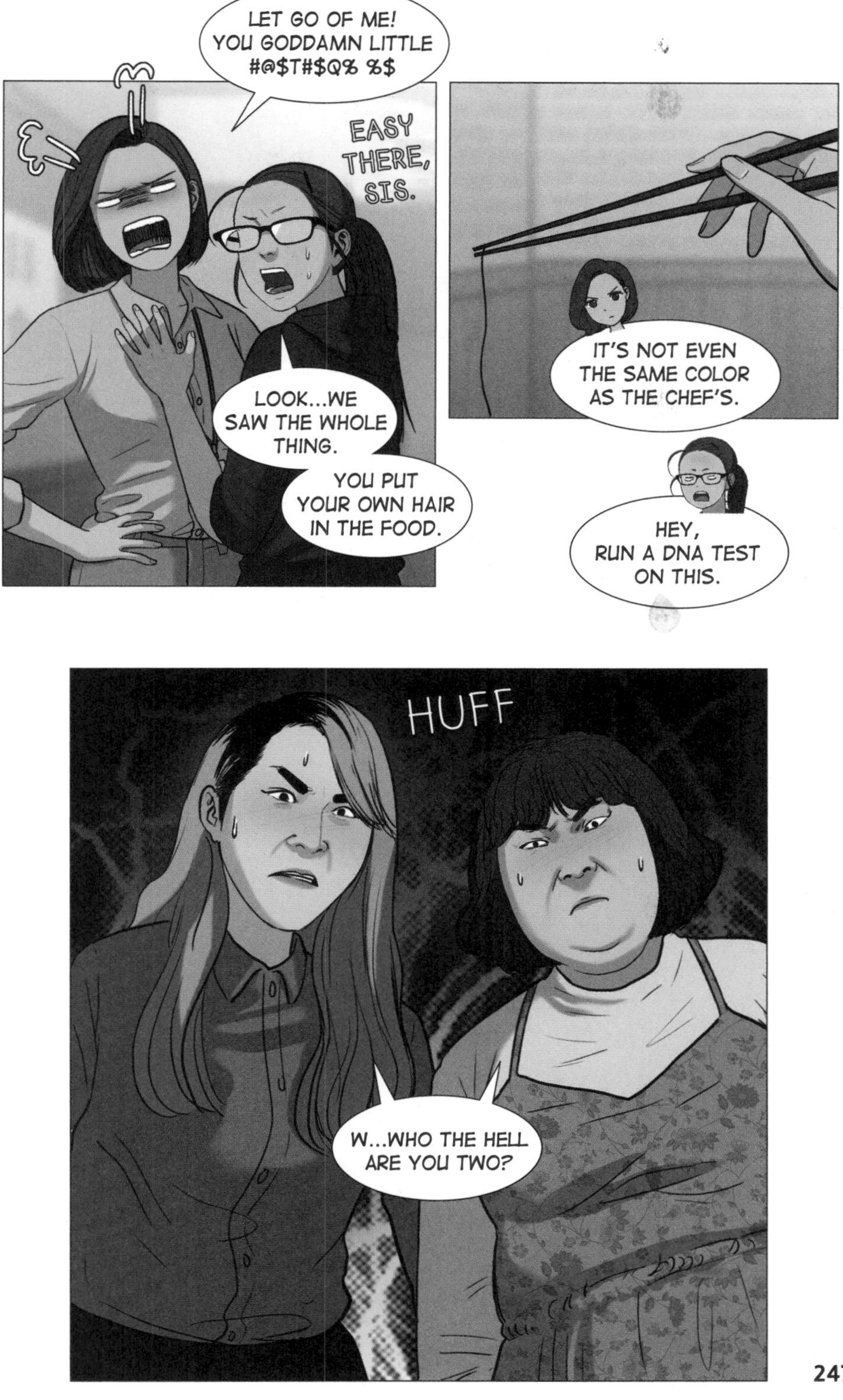
LET GO OF ME! YOU GODDAMN LITTLE #@$T#$Q% %$
EASY THERE, SIS.
LOOK...WE SAW THE WHOLE THING.
YOU PUT YOUR OWN HAIR IN THE FOOD.
IT'S NOT EVEN THE SAME COLOR AS THE CHEF'S.
HEY, RUN A DNA TEST ON THIS.
HUFF
W...WHO THE HELL ARE YOU TWO?

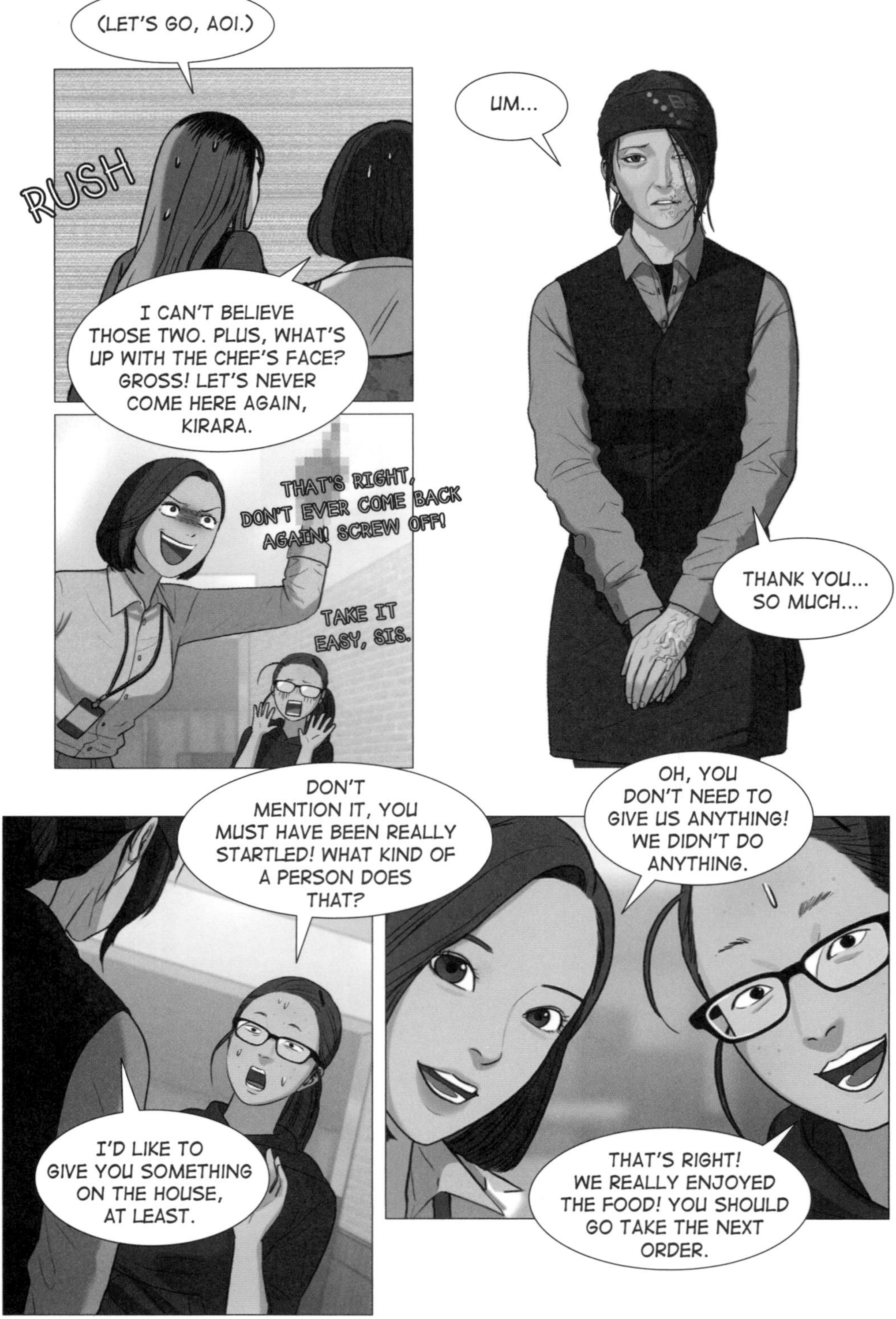
(LET'S GO, AOI.)
RUSH
I CAN'T BELIEVE THOSE TWO. PLUS, WHAT'S UP WITH THE CHEF'S FACE? GROSS! LET'S NEVER COME HERE AGAIN, KIRARA.
THAT'S RIGHT, DON'T EVER COME BACK AGAIN! SCREW OFF!
TAKE IT EASY, SIS.
UM...
THANK YOU... SO MUCH...
DON'T MENTION IT, YOU MUST HAVE BEEN REALLY STARTLED! WHAT KIND OF A PERSON DOES THAT?
I'D LIKE TO GIVE YOU SOMETHING ON THE HOUSE, AT LEAST.
OH, YOU DON'T NEED TO GIVE US ANYTHING! WE DIDN'T DO ANYTHING.
THAT'S RIGHT! WE REALLY ENJOYED THE FOOD! YOU SHOULD GO TAKE THE NEXT ORDER.

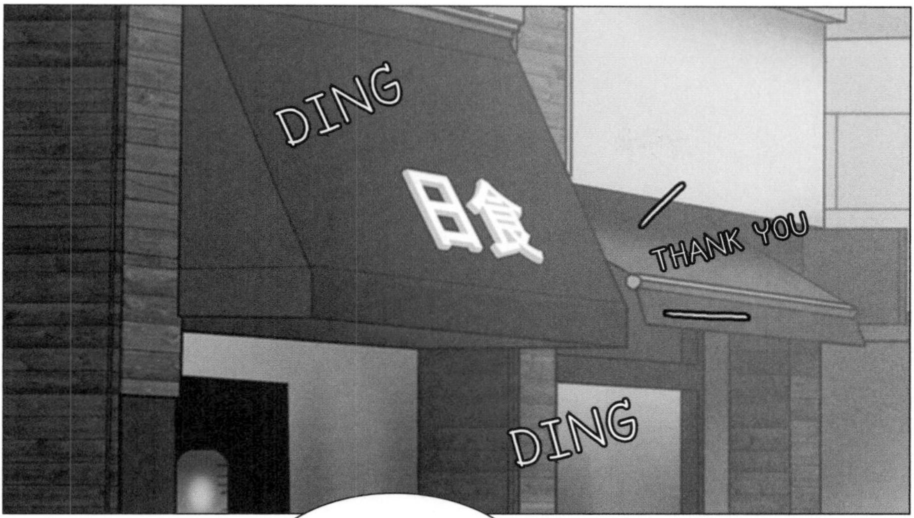
DING
日食
THANK YOU
DING

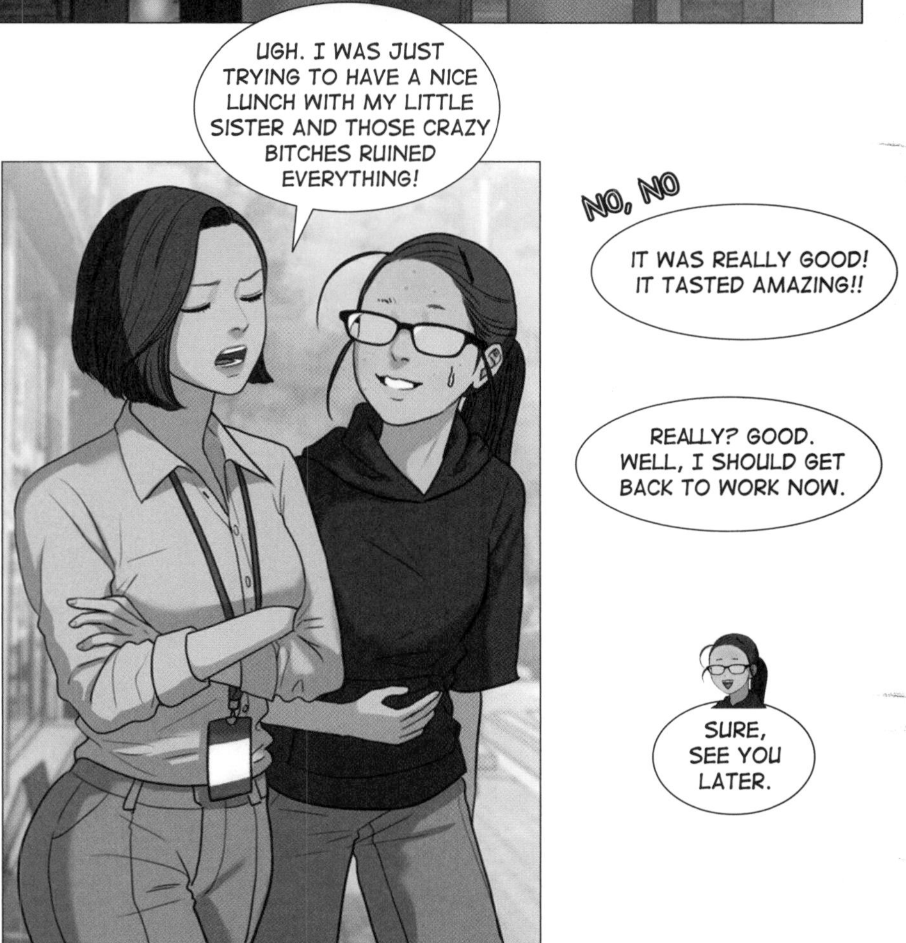
UGH. I WAS JUST TRYING TO HAVE A NICE LUNCH WITH MY LITTLE SISTER AND THOSE CRAZY BITCHES RUINED EVERYTHING!
NO, NO
IT WAS REALLY GOOD! IT TASTED AMAZING!!
REALLY? GOOD. WELL, I SHOULD GET BACK TO WORK NOW.
SURE, SEE YOU LATER.

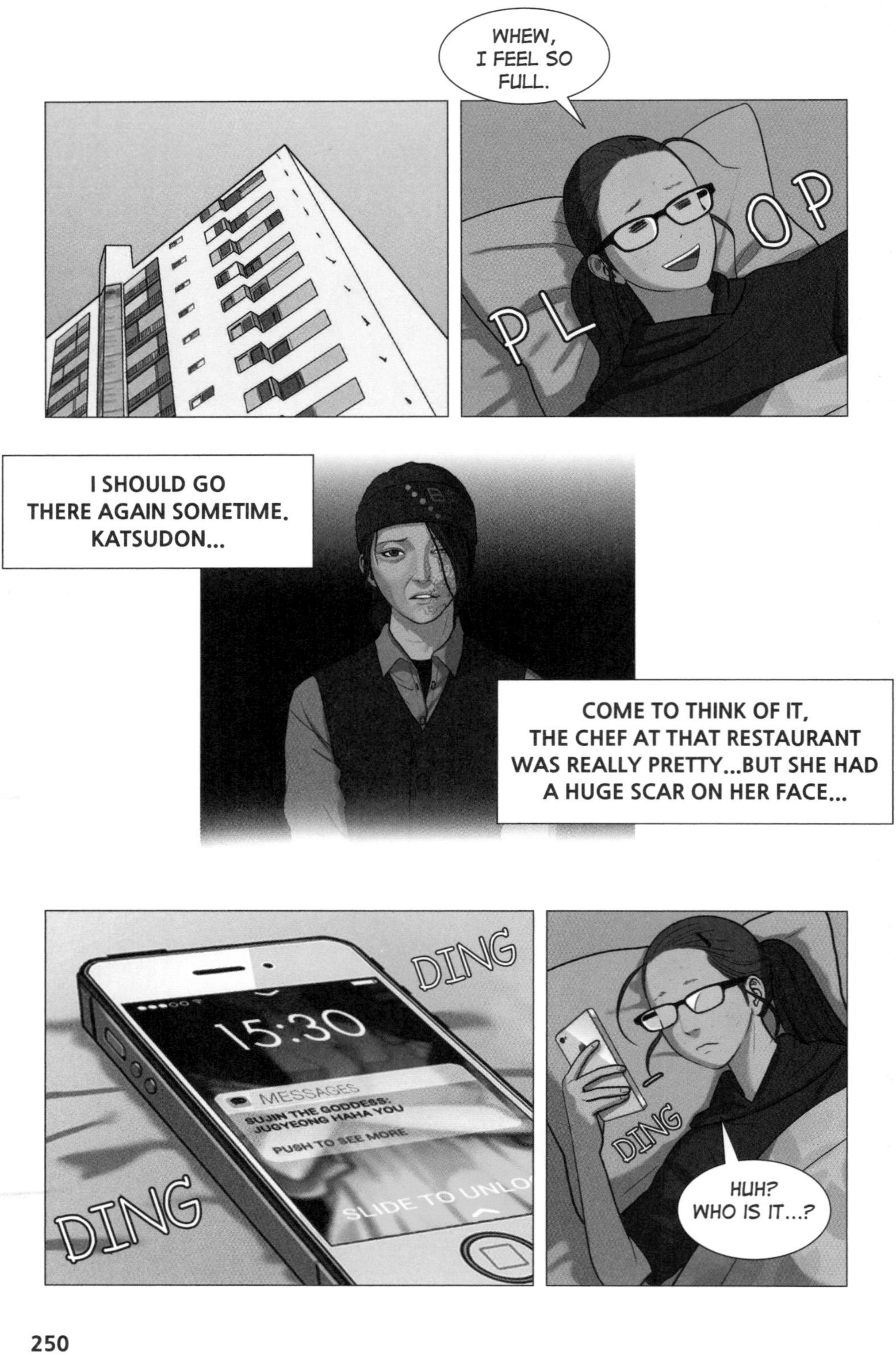
WHEW, I FEEL SO FULL.
PLOP
I SHOULD GO THERE AGAIN SOMETIME. KATSUDON...
COME TO THINK OF IT, THE CHEF AT THAT RESTAURANT WAS REALLY PRETTY...BUT SHE HAD A HUGE SCAR ON HER FACE...
DING
15:30
MESSAGES
SUJIN THE GODDESS: JUGYEONG HAHA YOU
PUSH TO SEE MORE
DING
DING-DING
HUH? WHO IS IT...?

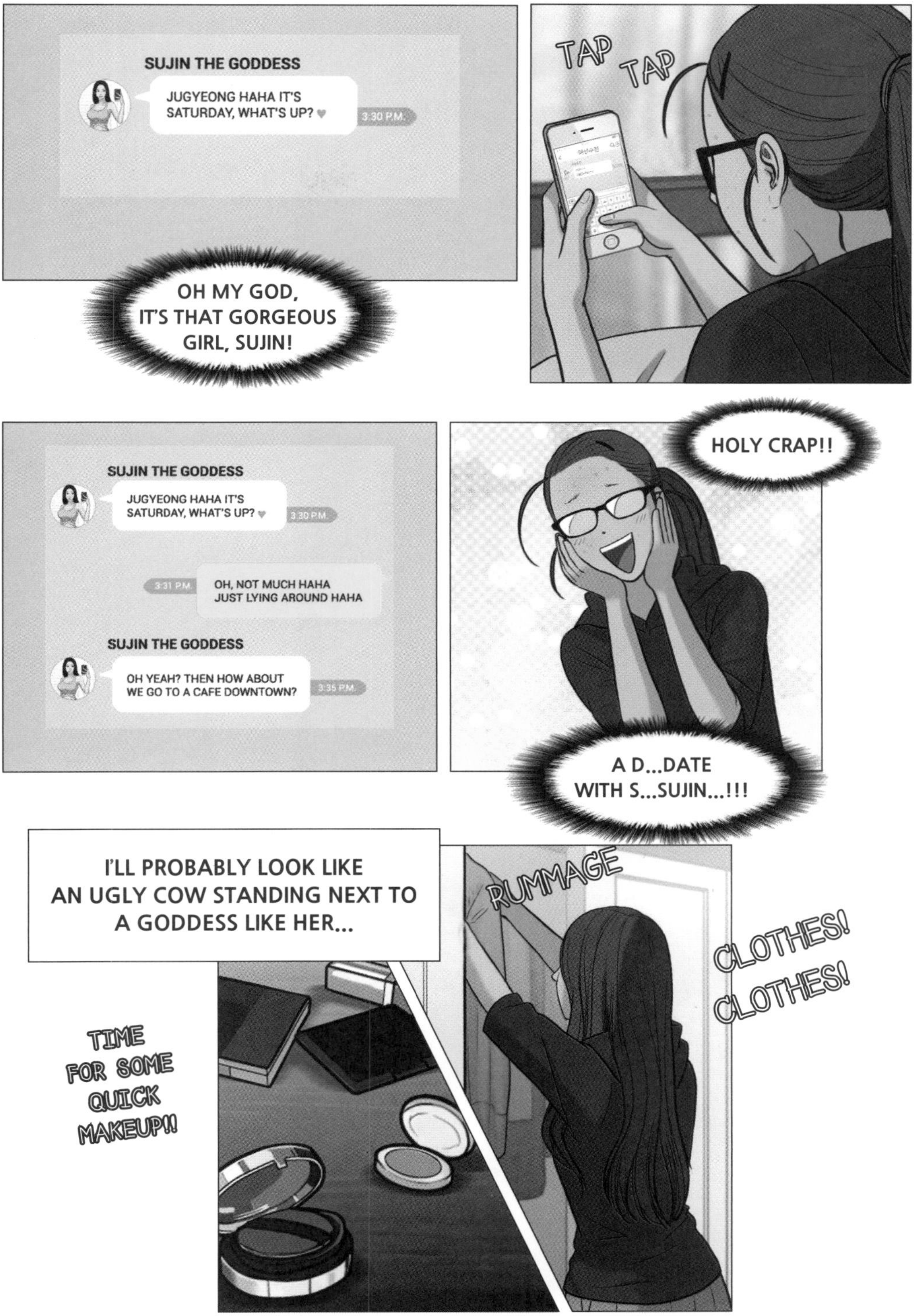
SUJIN THE GODDESS
JUGYEONG HAHA IT'S SATURDAY, WHAT'S UP? ♥
3:30 P.M.
OH MY GOD, IT'S THAT GORGEOUS GIRL, SUJIN!
TAP TAP
SUJIN THE GODDESS
JUGYEONG HAHA IT'S SATURDAY, WHAT'S UP? ♥
3:30 P.M.
3:31 P.M.
OH, NOT MUCH HAHA JUST LYING AROUND HAHA
SUJIN THE GODDESS
OH YEAH? THEN HOW ABOUT WE GO TO A CAFE DOWNTOWN?
3:35 P.M.
HOLY CRAP!!
A D...DATE WITH S...SUJIN...!!!
I'LL PROBABLY LOOK LIKE AN UGLY COW STANDING NEXT TO A GODDESS LIKE HER...
TIME FOR SOME QUICK MAKEUP!!
RUMMAGE
CLOTHES! CLOTHES!

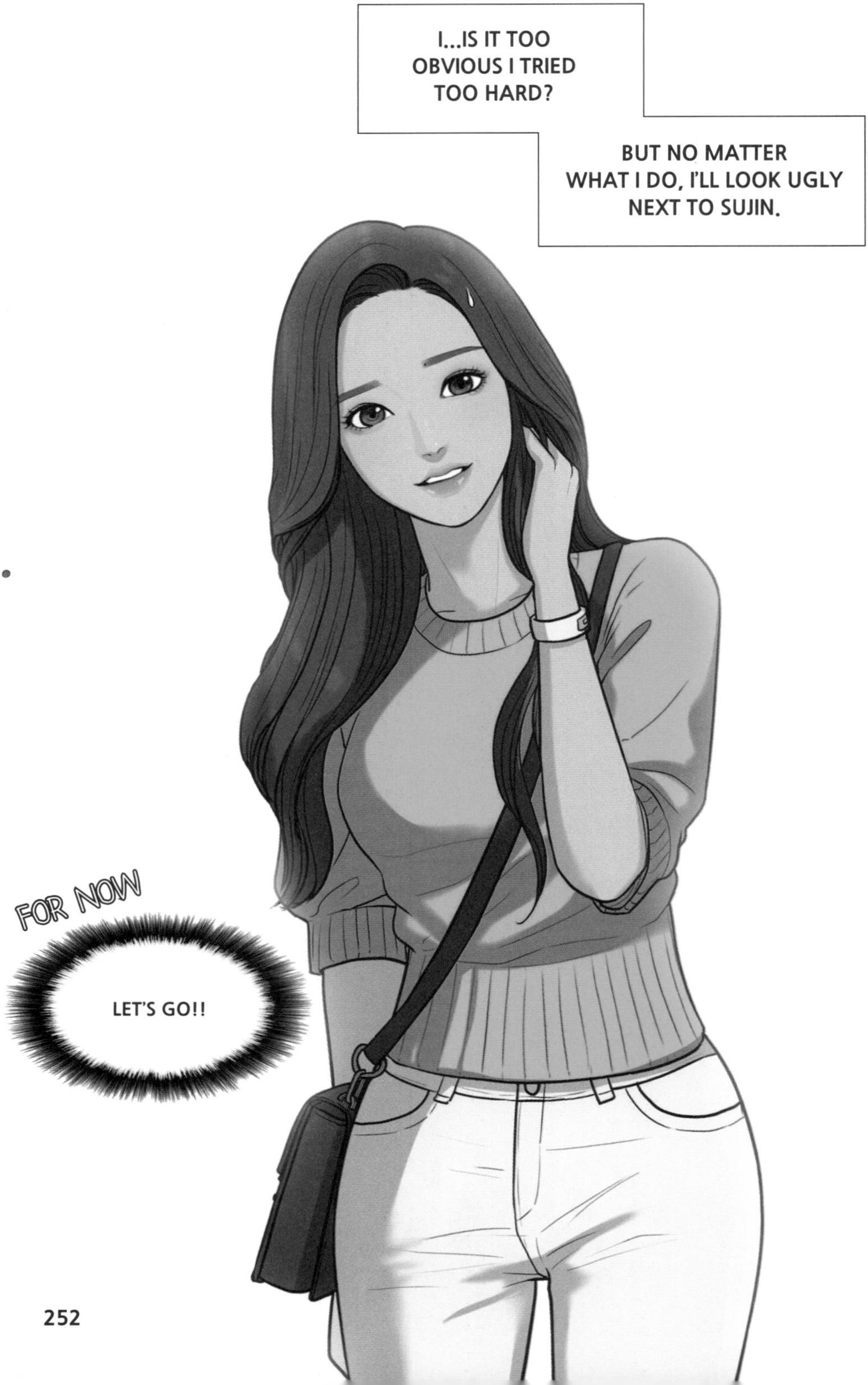
I...IS IT TOO OBVIOUS I TRIED TOO HARD?
BUT NO MATTER WHAT I DO, I'LL LOOK UGLY NEXT TO SUJIN.
FOR NOW
LET'S GO!!

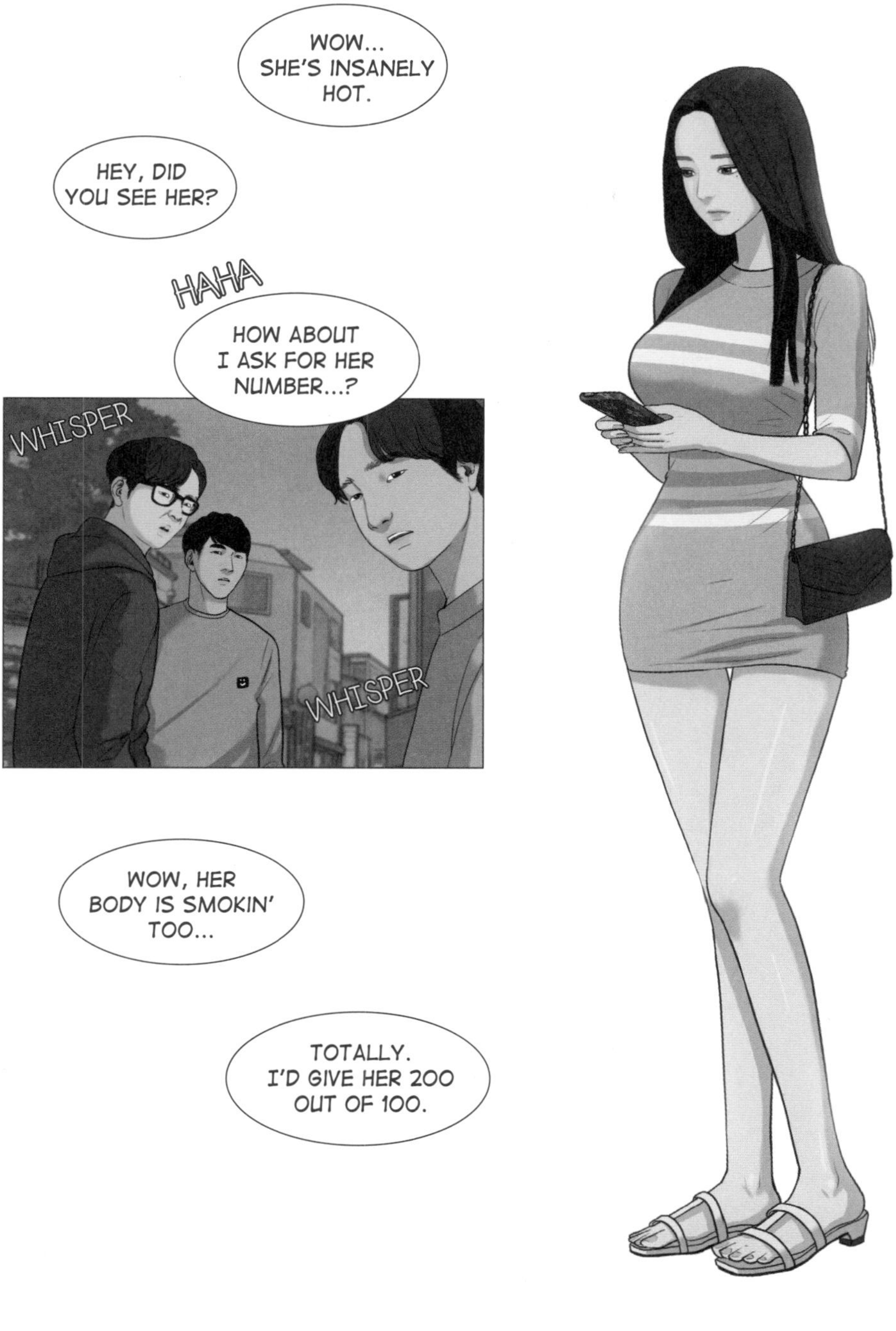
WOW... SHE'S INSANELY HOT.
HEY, DID YOU SEE HER?
HAHA
HOW ABOUT I ASK FOR HER NUMBER...?
WHISPER
WHISPER
WOW, HER BODY IS SMOKIN' TOO...
TOTALLY. I'D GIVE HER 200 OUT OF 100.

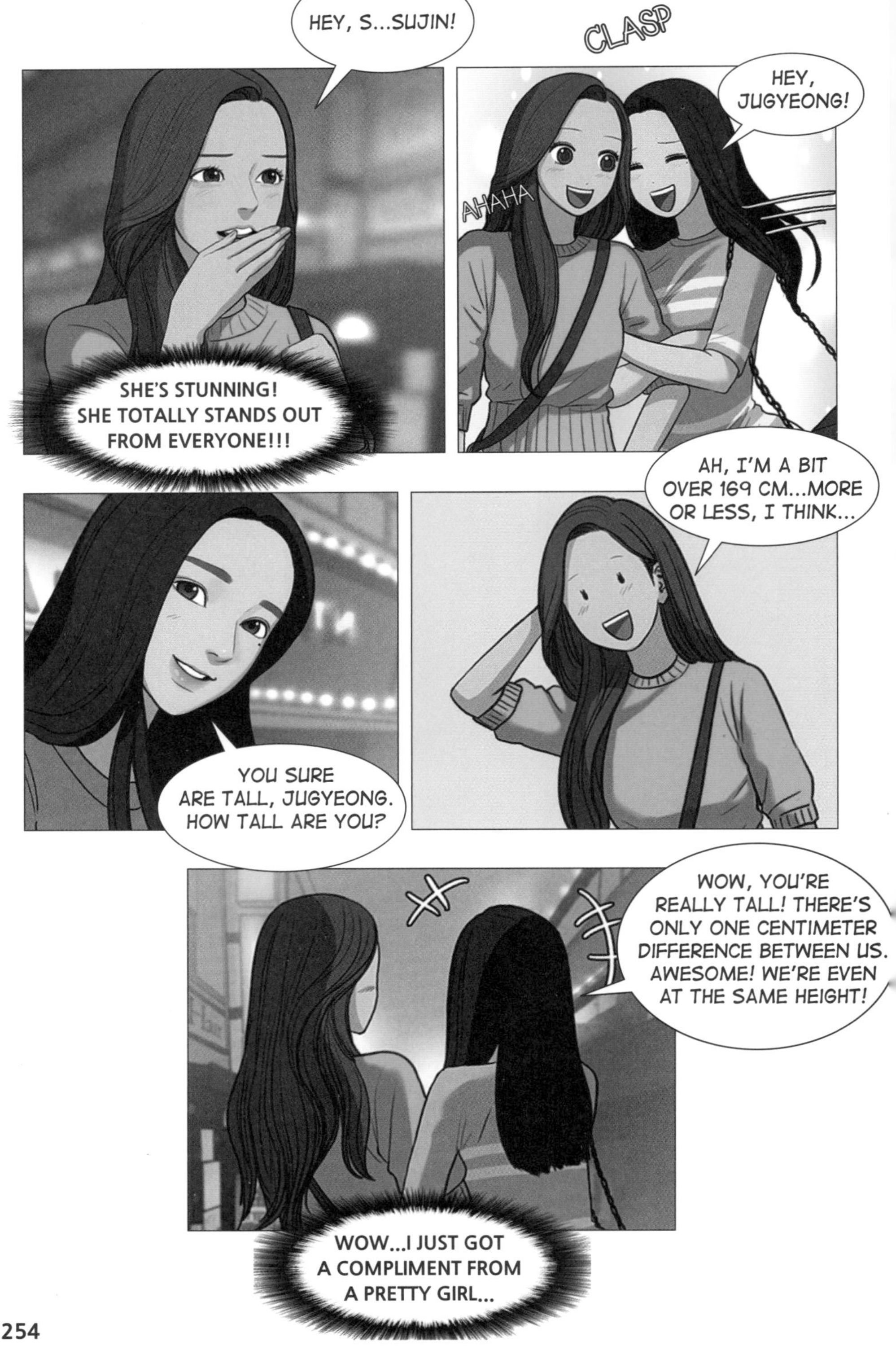
HEY, S...SUJIN!
SHE'S STUNNING! SHE TOTALLY STANDS OUT FROM EVERYONE!!!
CLASP
HEY, JUGYEONG!
AHAHA
YOU SURE ARE TALL, JUGYEONG. HOW TALL ARE YOU?
AH, I'M A BIT OVER 169 CM...MORE OR LESS, I THINK...
WOW, YOU'RE REALLY TALL! THERE'S ONLY ONE CENTIMETER DIFFERENCE BETWEEN US. AWESOME! WE'RE EVEN AT THE SAME HEIGHT!
WOW...I JUST GOT A COMPLIMENT FROM A PRETTY GIRL...

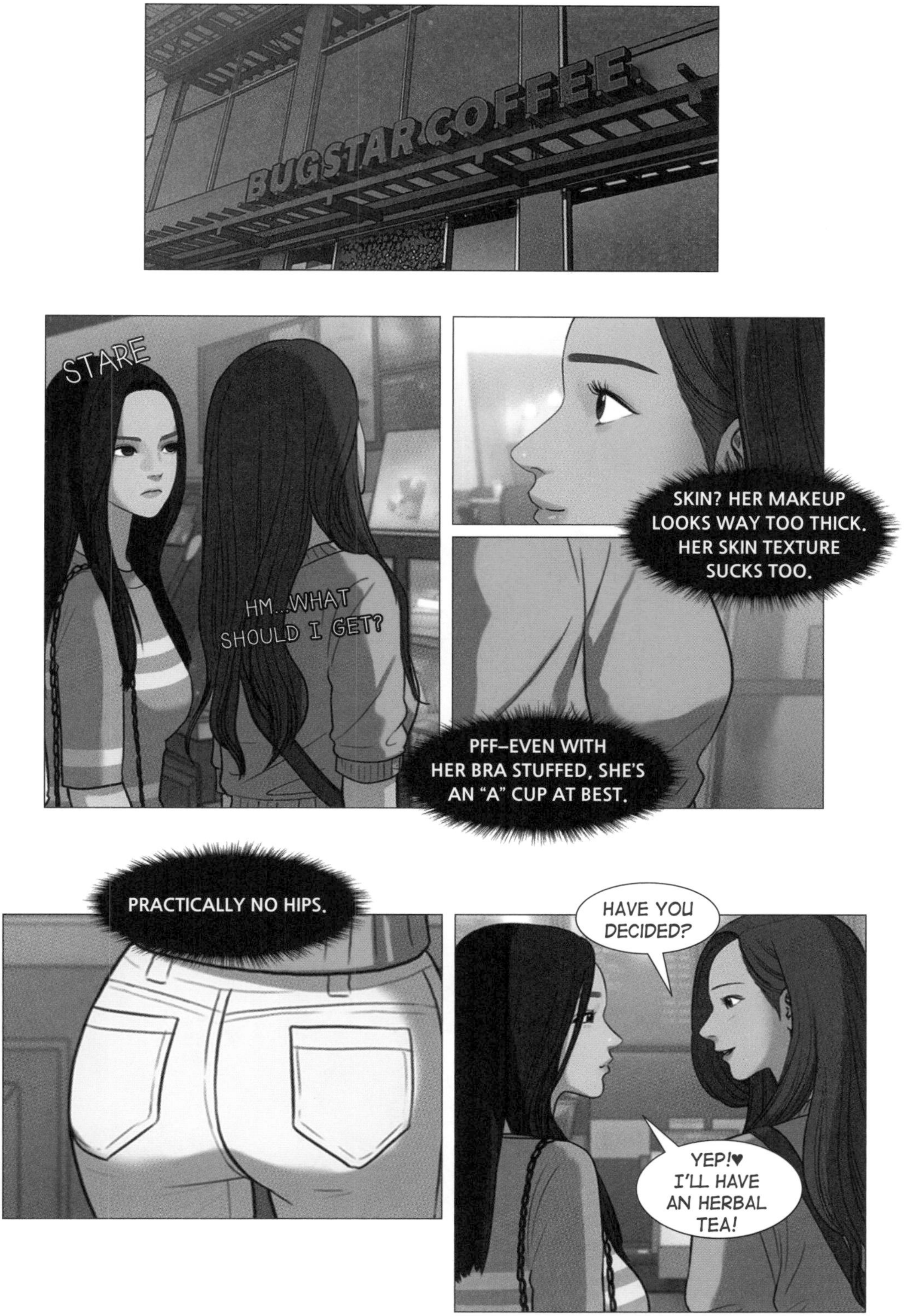
BUGSTAR COFFEE
STARE
HM...WHAT SHOULD I GET?
SKIN? HER MAKEUP LOOKS WAY TOO THICK. HER SKIN TEXTURE SUCKS TOO.
PFF–EVEN WITH HER BRA STUFFED, SHE'S AN "A" CUP AT BEST.
PRACTICALLY NO HIPS.
HAVE YOU DECIDED?
YEP!♥ I'LL HAVE AN HERBAL TEA!

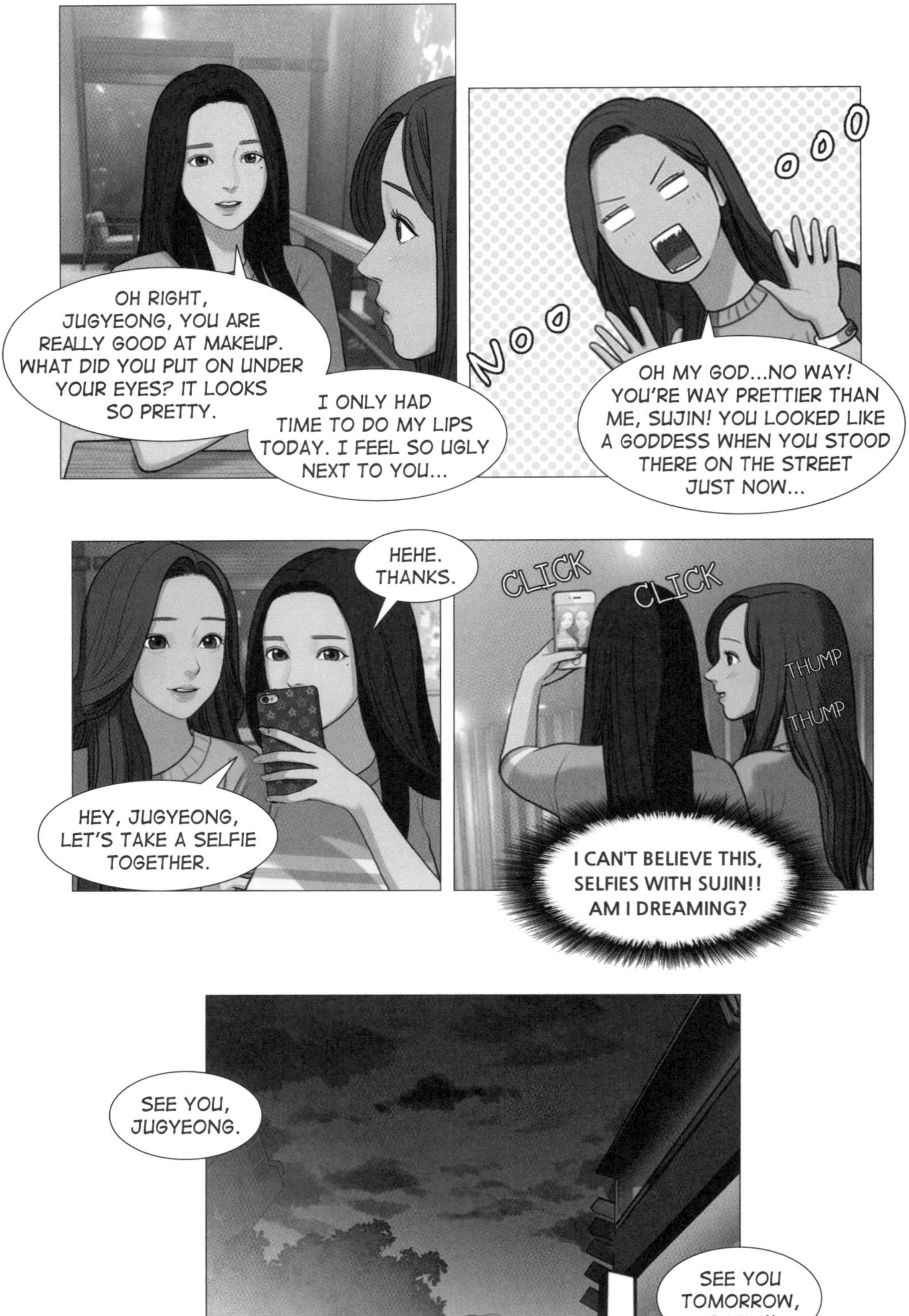
OH RIGHT, JUGYEONG, YOU ARE REALLY GOOD AT MAKEUP. WHAT DID YOU PUT ON UNDER YOUR EYES? IT LOOKS SO PRETTY.
I ONLY HAD TIME TO DO MY LIPS TODAY. I FEEL SO UGLY NEXT TO YOU...
NOOOOO
OH MY GOD...NO WAY! YOU'RE WAY PRETTIER THAN ME, SUJIN! YOU LOOKED LIKE A GODDESS WHEN YOU STOOD THERE ON THE STREET JUST NOW...
HEHE. THANKS.
HEY, JUGYEONG, LET'S TAKE A SELFIE TOGETHER.
CLICK
CLICK
THUMP
THUMP
I CAN'T BELIEVE THIS, SELFIES WITH SUJIN!! AM I DREAMING?
SEE YOU, JUGYEONG.
SEE YOU TOMORROW, SUJIN!!

HAHA I FEEL AMAZING TODAY. GETTING COMPLIMENTED BY A PRETTY GIRL...

HUH, SUA?

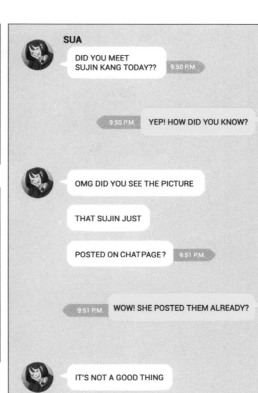

SUA

DID YOU MEET SUJIN KANG TODAY?? 9:50 P.M.

9:50 P.M. YEP! HOW DID YOU KNOW?

OMG DID YOU SEE THE PICTURE

THAT SUJIN JUST

POSTED ON CHAT PAGE? 9:51 P.M.

9:51 P.M. WOW! SHE POSTED THEM ALREADY?

IT'S NOT A GOOD THING

LOOK

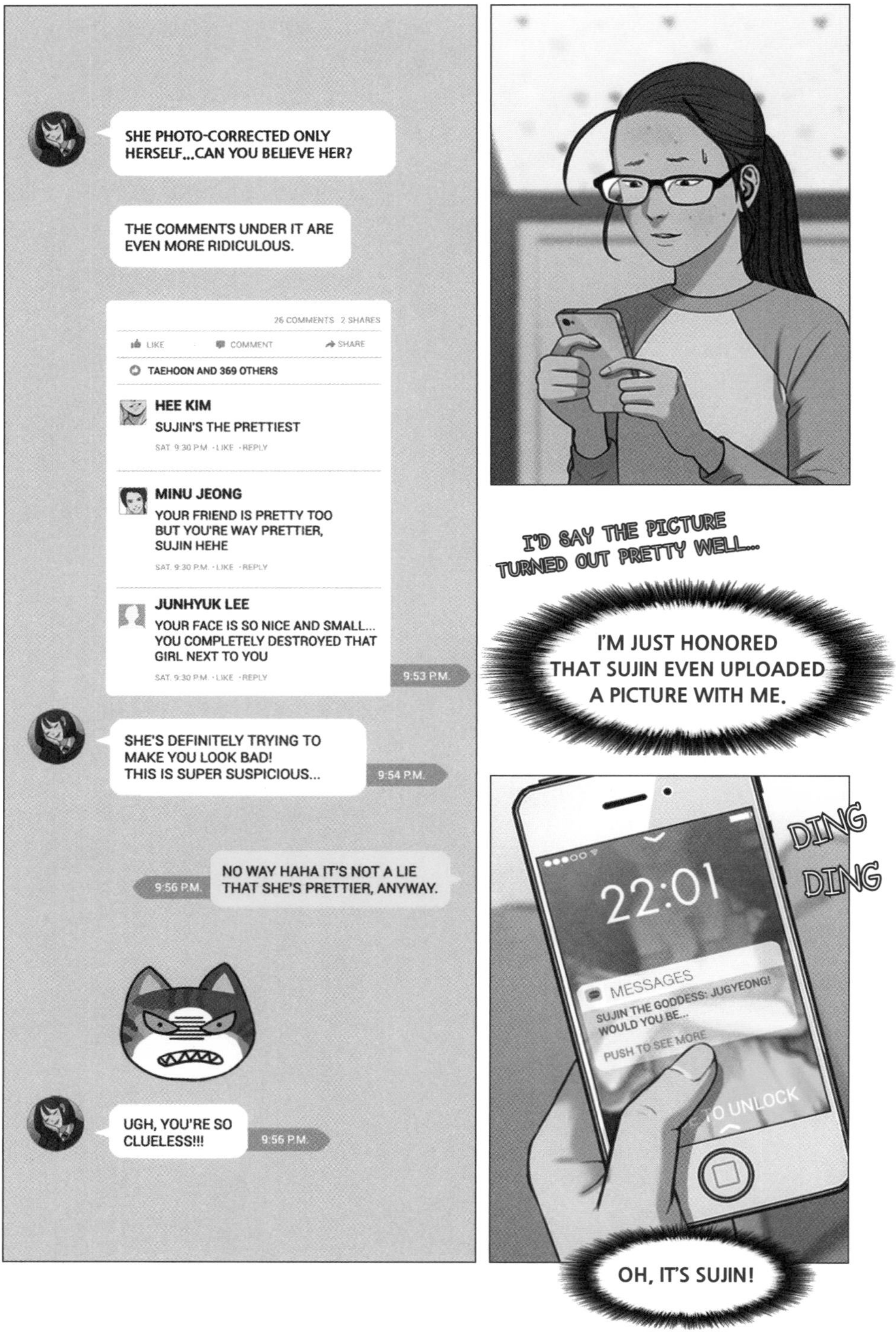
SHE PHOTO-CORRECTED ONLY HERSELF...CAN YOU BELIEVE HER?
THE COMMENTS UNDER IT ARE EVEN MORE RIDICULOUS.
26 COMMENTS 2 SHARES
LIKE
COMMENT
SHARE
TAEHOON AND 369 OTHERS
HEE KIM
SUJIN'S THE PRETTIEST
SAT. 9:30 P.M. · LIKE · REPLY
MINU JEONG
YOUR FRIEND IS PRETTY TOO BUT YOU'RE WAY PRETTIER, SUJIN HEHE
SAT. 9:30 P.M. · LIKE · REPLY
JUNHYUK LEE
YOUR FACE IS SO NICE AND SMALL... YOU COMPLETELY DESTROYED THAT GIRL NEXT TO YOU
SAT. 9:30 P.M. · LIKE · REPLY
9:53 P.M.
SHE'S DEFINITELY TRYING TO MAKE YOU LOOK BAD! THIS IS SUPER SUSPICIOUS...
9:54 P.M.
9:56 P.M.
NO WAY HAHA IT'S NOT A LIE THAT SHE'S PRETTIER, ANYWAY.
UGH, YOU'RE SO CLUELESS!!!
9:56 P.M.
I'D SAY THE PICTURE TURNED OUT PRETTY WELL...
I'M JUST HONORED THAT SUJIN EVEN UPLOADED A PICTURE WITH ME.
22:01
MESSAGES
SUJIN THE GODDESS: JUGYEONG! WOULD YOU BE...
PUSH TO SEE MORE
DING
DING
OH, IT'S SUJIN!

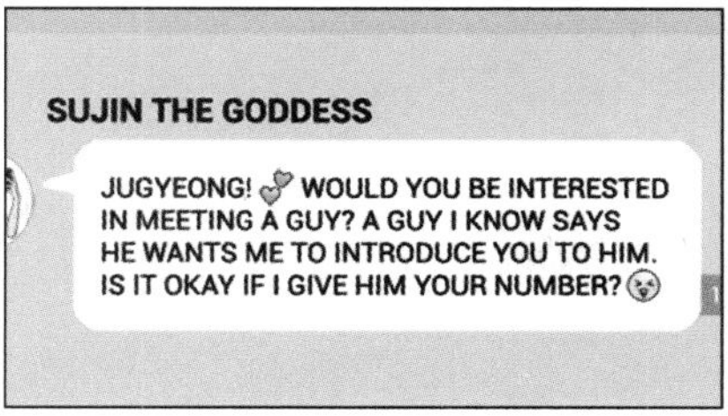
SUJIN THE GODDESS
JUGYEONG! WOULD YOU BE INTERESTED IN MEETING A GUY? A GUY I KNOW SAYS HE WANTS ME TO INTRODUCE YOU TO HIM. IS IT OKAY IF I GIVE HIM YOUR NUMBER?

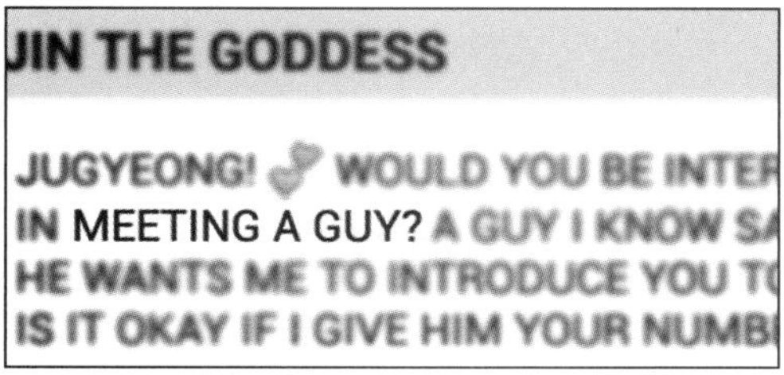
JIN THE GODDESS
JUGYEONG! WOULD YOU BE INTER
IN MEETING A GUY? A GUY I KNOW S
HE WANTS ME TO INTRODUCE YOU T
IS IT OKAY IF I GIVE HIM YOUR NUMB

* MEETING A GUY = A BLIND DATE

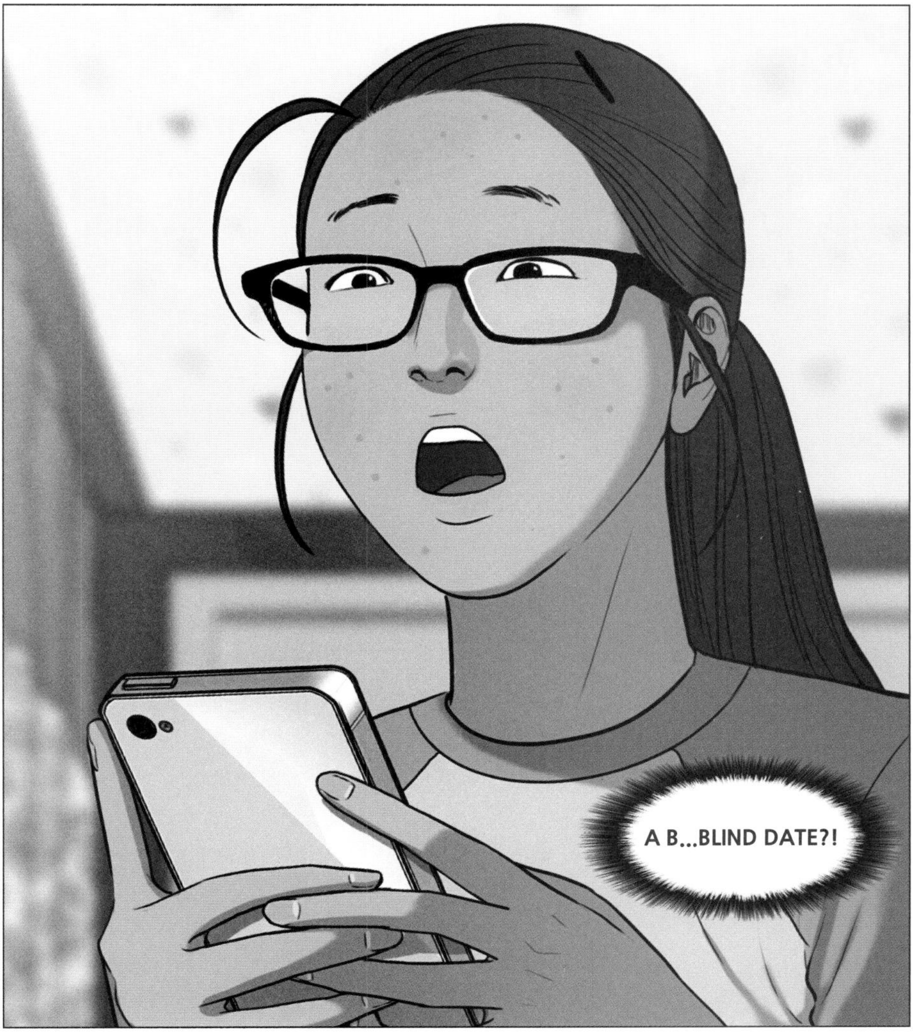
A B...BLIND DATE?!

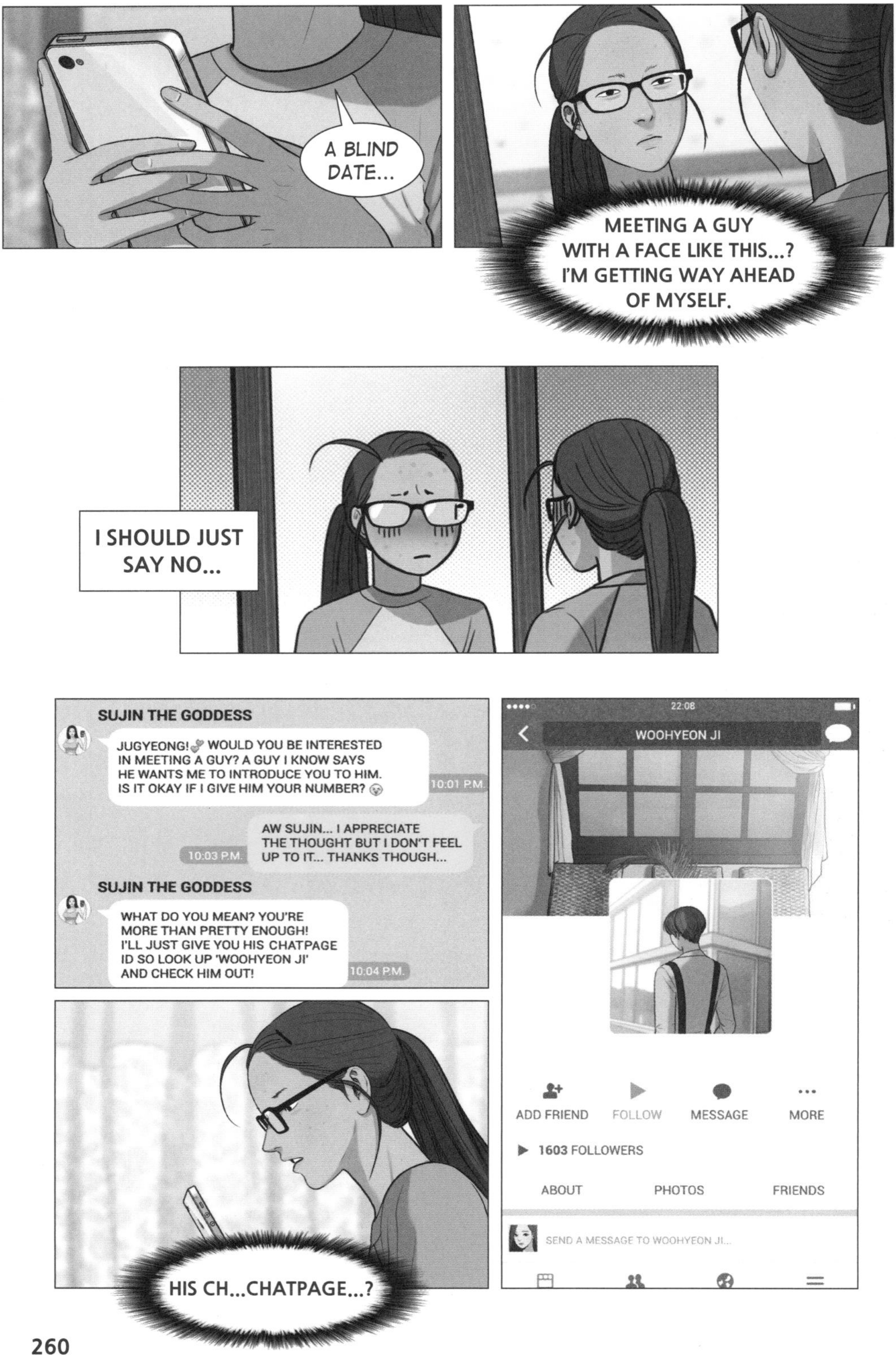
A BLIND DATE...
MEETING A GUY WITH A FACE LIKE THIS...? I'M GETTING WAY AHEAD OF MYSELF.
I SHOULD JUST SAY NO...
SUJIN THE GODDESS
JUGYEONG! WOULD YOU BE INTERESTED IN MEETING A GUY? A GUY I KNOW SAYS HE WANTS ME TO INTRODUCE YOU TO HIM. IS IT OKAY IF I GIVE HIM YOUR NUMBER?
10:01 P.M.
AW SUJIN... I APPRECIATE THE THOUGHT BUT I DON'T FEEL UP TO IT... THANKS THOUGH...
10:03 P.M.
SUJIN THE GODDESS
WHAT DO YOU MEAN? YOU'RE MORE THAN PRETTY ENOUGH! I'LL JUST GIVE YOU HIS CHATPAGE ID SO LOOK UP 'WOOHYEON JI' AND CHECK HIM OUT!
10:04 P.M.
HIS CH...CHATPAGE...?
22:08
WOOHYEON JI
ADD FRIEND
FOLLOW
MESSAGE
MORE
1603 FOLLOWERS
ABOUT
PHOTOS
FRIENDS
SEND A MESSAGE TO WOOHYEON JI...

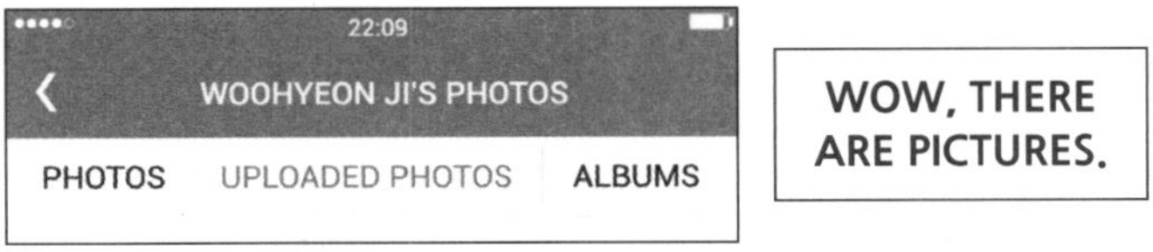
22:09
WOOHYEON JI'S PHOTOS
PHOTOS
UPLOADED PHOTOS
ALBUMS
WOW, THERE ARE PICTURES.

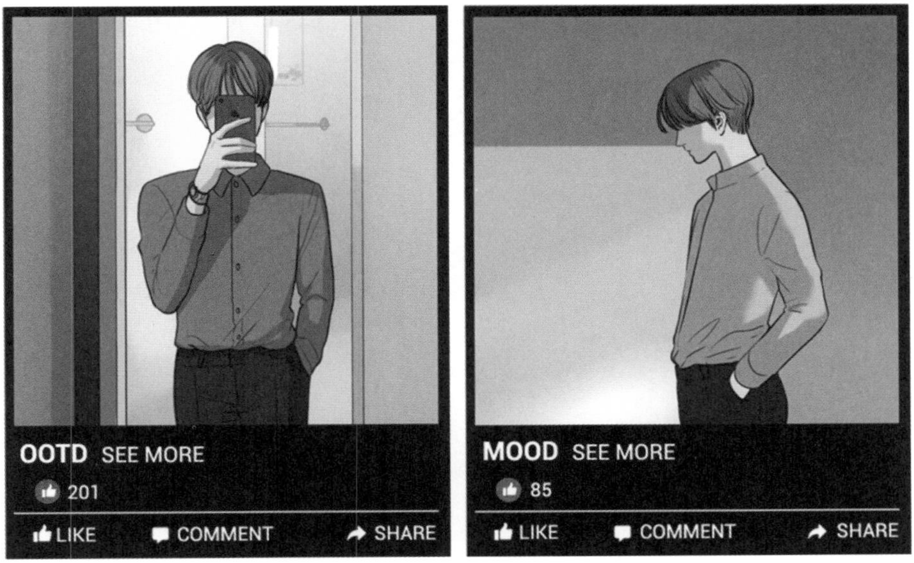
OOTD SEE MORE
201
LIKE
COMMENT
SHARE
MOOD SEE MORE
85
LIKE
COMMENT
SHARE

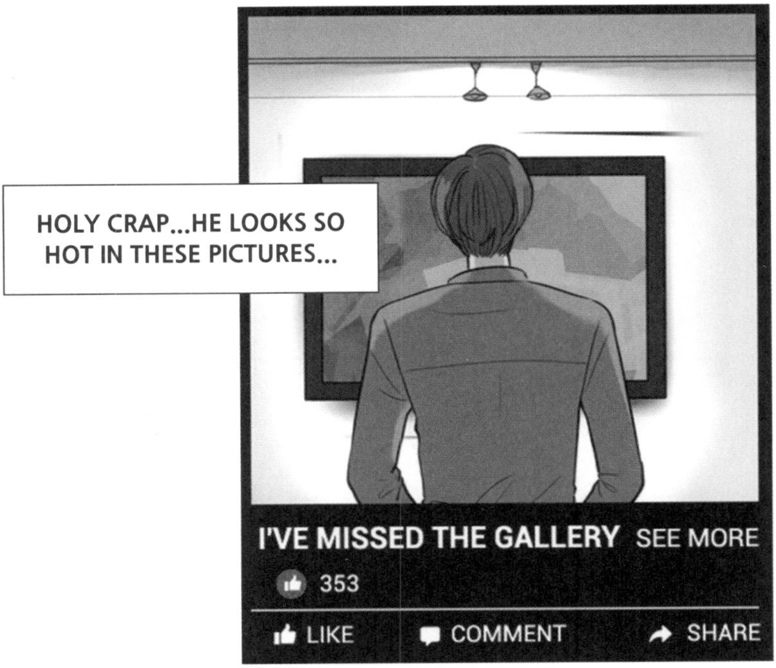
HOLY CRAP...HE LOOKS SO HOT IN THESE PICTURES...
I'VE MISSED THE GALLERY SEE MORE
353
LIKE
COMMENT
SHARE

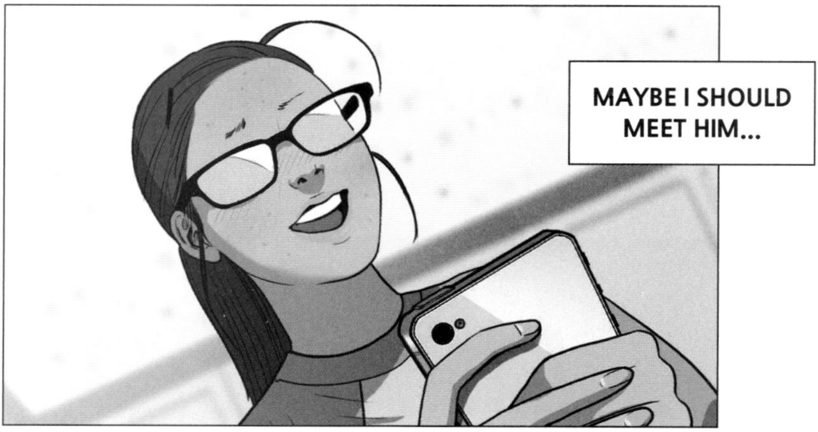
MAYBE I SHOULD MEET HIM...

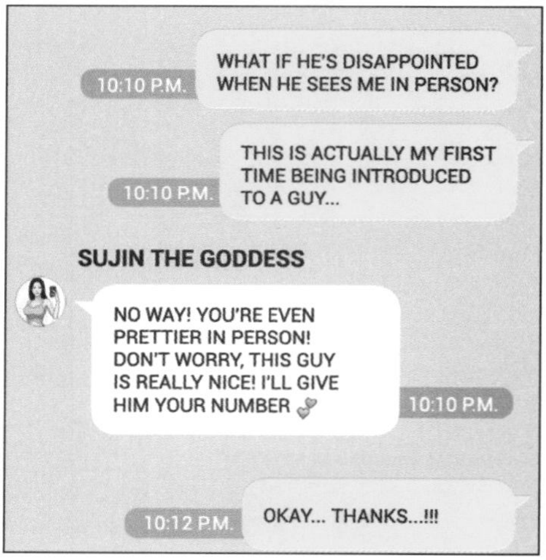
10:10 P.M.
WHAT IF HE'S DISAPPOINTED WHEN HE SEES ME IN PERSON?
10:10 P.M.
THIS IS ACTUALLY MY FIRST TIME BEING INTRODUCED TO A GUY...
SUJIN THE GODDESS
NO WAY! YOU'RE EVEN PRETTIER IN PERSON! DON'T WORRY, THIS GUY IS REALLY NICE! I'LL GIVE HIM YOUR NUMBER
10:10 P.M.
10:12 P.M.
OKAY... THANKS...!!!

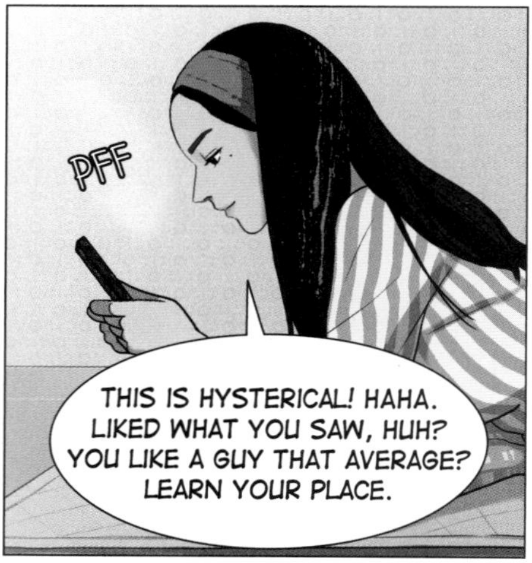
PFF
THIS IS HYSTERICAL! HAHA. LIKED WHAT YOU SAW, HUH? YOU LIKE A GUY THAT AVERAGE? LEARN YOUR PLACE.

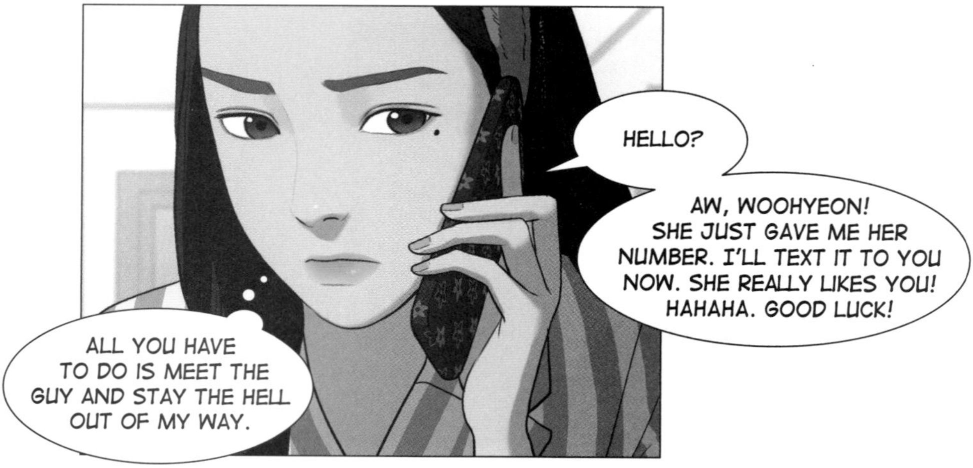
HELLO?
AW, WOOHYEON! SHE JUST GAVE ME HER NUMBER. I'LL TEXT IT TO YOU NOW. SHE REALLY LIKES YOU! HAHAHA. GOOD LUCK!
ALL YOU HAVE TO DO IS MEET THE GUY AND STAY THE HELL OUT OF MY WAY.

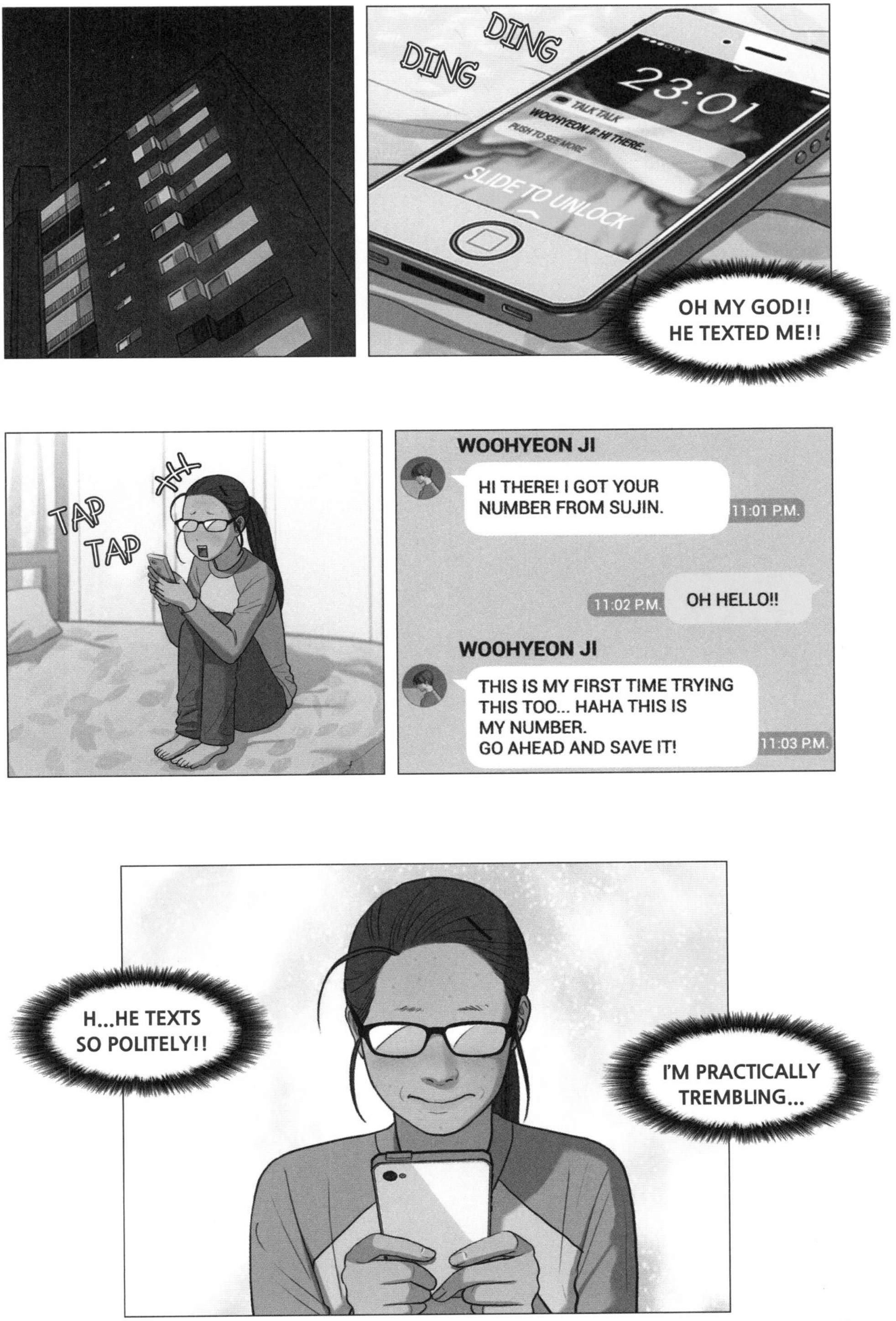
DING
DING
23:01
TALK TALK
WOOHYEON JI: HI THERE..
PUSH TO SEE MORE
SLIDE TO UNLOCK
OH MY GOD!! HE TEXTED ME!!
TAP
TAP
WOOHYEON JI
HI THERE! I GOT YOUR NUMBER FROM SUJIN.
11:01 P.M.
11:02 P.M.
OH HELLO!!
WOOHYEON JI
THIS IS MY FIRST TIME TRYING THIS TOO... HAHA THIS IS MY NUMBER. GO AHEAD AND SAVE IT!
11:03 P.M.
H...HE TEXTS SO POLITELY!!
I'M PRACTICALLY TREMBLING...

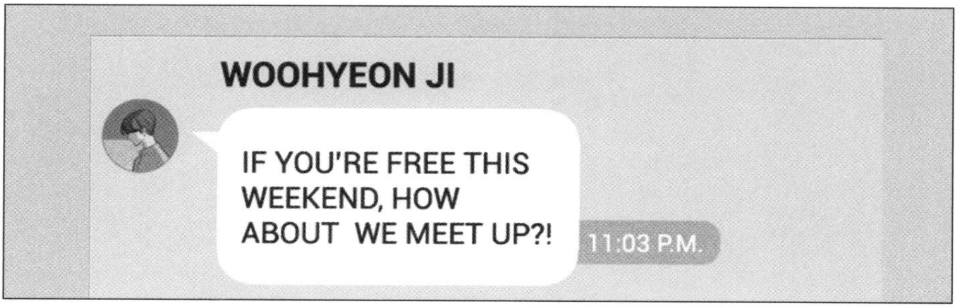
WOOHYEON JI
IF YOU'RE FREE THIS WEEKEND, HOW ABOUT WE MEET UP?!
11:03 P.M.

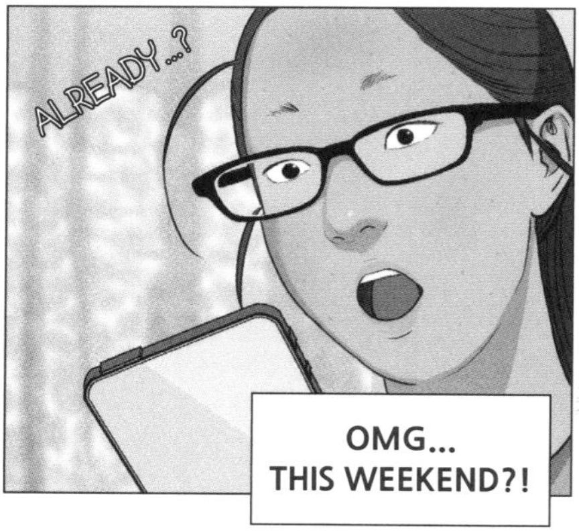
ALREADY...?
OMG... THIS WEEKEND?!

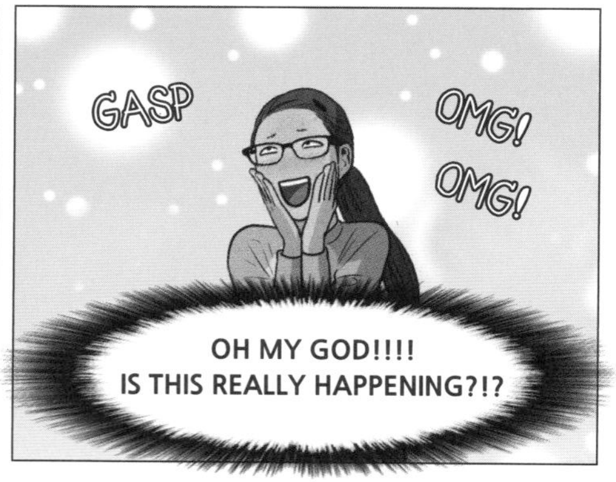
GASP
OMG!
OMG!
OH MY GOD!!!! IS THIS REALLY HAPPENING?!?

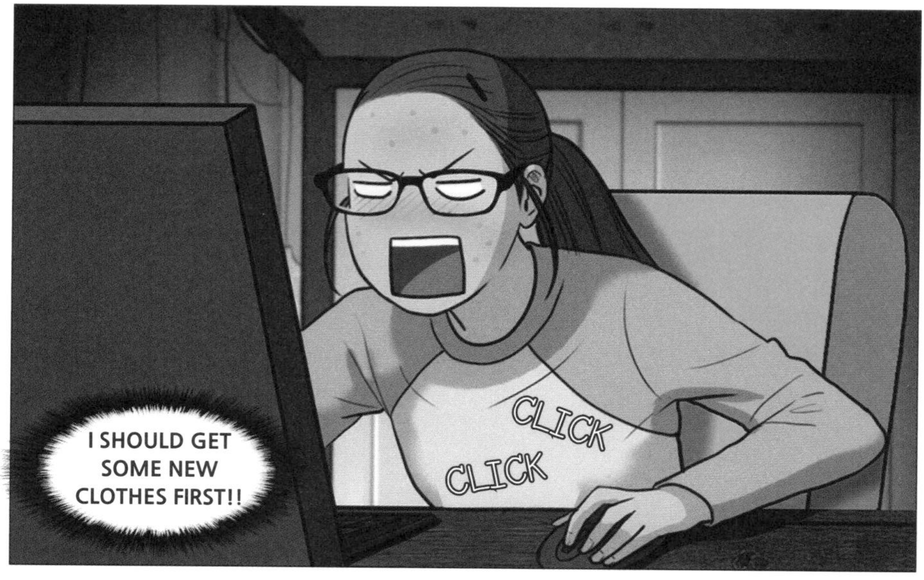
I SHOULD GET SOME NEW CLOTHES FIRST!!
CLICK
CLICK

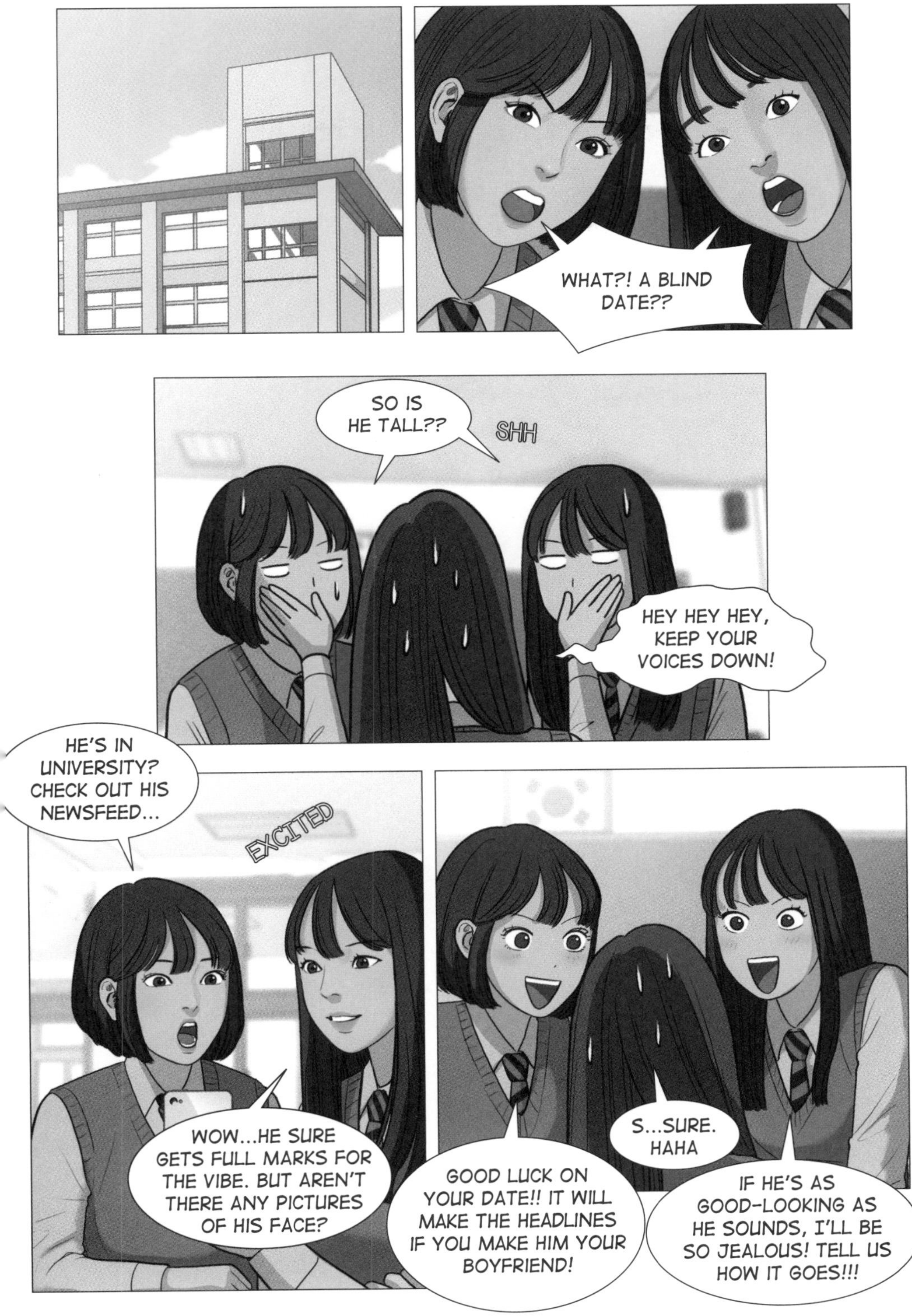
WHAT?! A BLIND DATE??
SO IS HE TALL??
SHH
HEY HEY HEY, KEEP YOUR VOICES DOWN!
HE'S IN UNIVERSITY? CHECK OUT HIS NEWSFEED...
EXCITED
WOW...HE SURE GETS FULL MARKS FOR THE VIBE. BUT AREN'T THERE ANY PICTURES OF HIS FACE?
GOOD LUCK ON YOUR DATE!! IT WILL MAKE THE HEADLINES IF YOU MAKE HIM YOUR BOYFRIEND!
S...SURE. HAHA
IF HE'S AS GOOD-LOOKING AS HE SOUNDS, I'LL BE SO JEALOUS! TELL US HOW IT GOES!!!

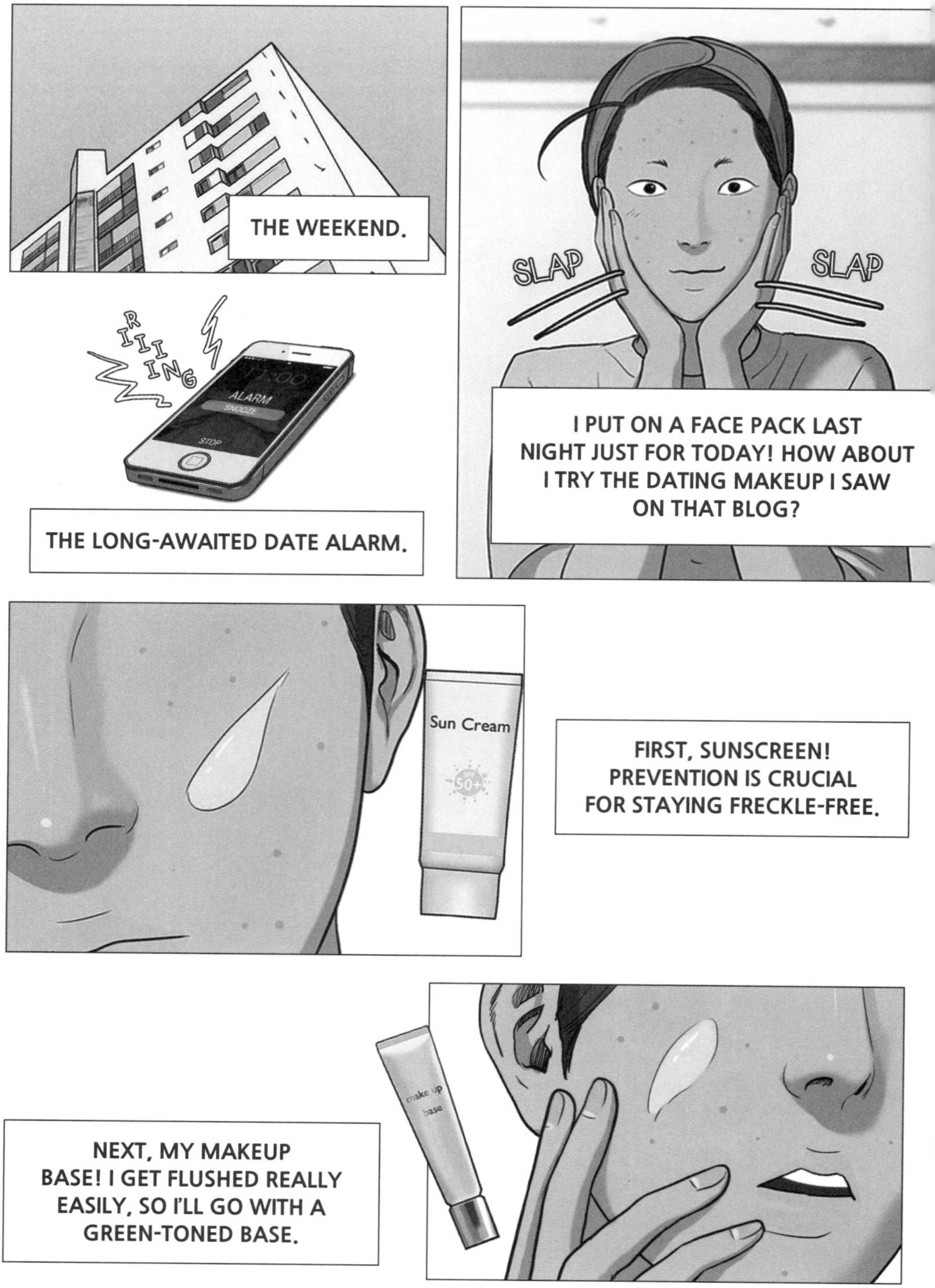
THE WEEKEND.
RIIIING
ALARM
SNOOZE
STOP
THE LONG-AWAITED DATE ALARM.
SLAP
SLAP
I PUT ON A FACE PACK LAST NIGHT JUST FOR TODAY! HOW ABOUT I TRY THE DATING MAKEUP I SAW ON THAT BLOG?
Sun Cream
SPF 50+
FIRST, SUNSCREEN! PREVENTION IS CRUCIAL FOR STAYING FRECKLE-FREE.
NEXT, MY MAKEUP BASE! I GET FLUSHED REALLY EASILY, SO I'LL GO WITH A GREEN-TONED BASE.
make up base

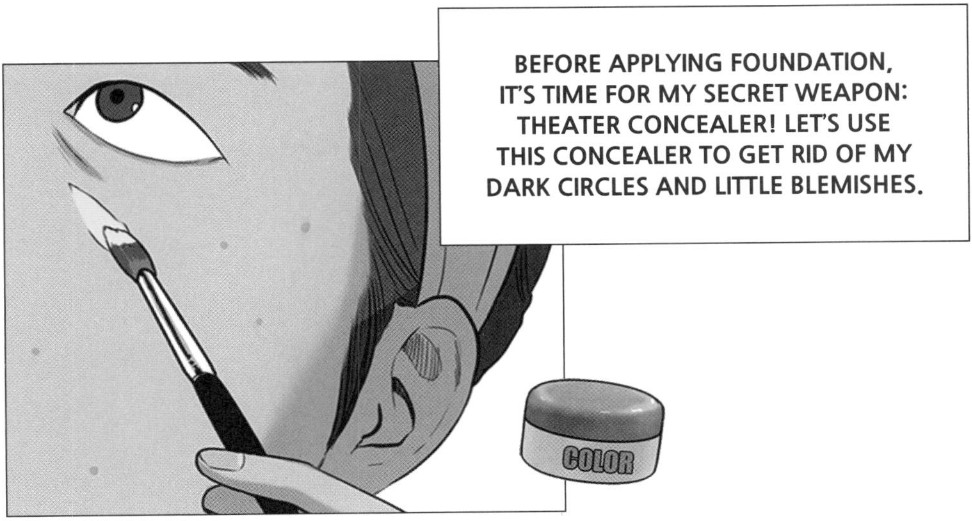
BEFORE APPLYING FOUNDATION, IT'S TIME FOR MY SECRET WEAPON: THEATER CONCEALER! LET'S USE THIS CONCEALER TO GET RID OF MY DARK CIRCLES AND LITTLE BLEMISHES.
COLOR

*THE ORDER FOR APPLYING CONCEALER DEPENDS ON YOUR PERSONAL TASTE.

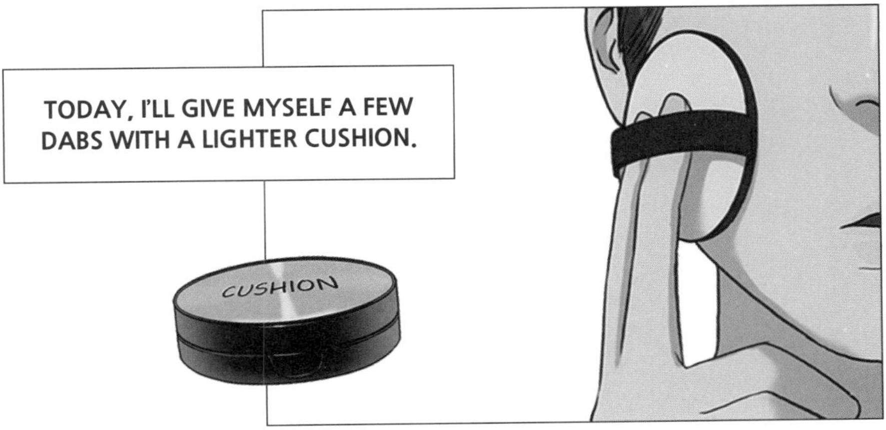
TODAY, I'LL GIVE MYSELF A FEW DABS WITH A LIGHTER CUSHION.
CUSHION

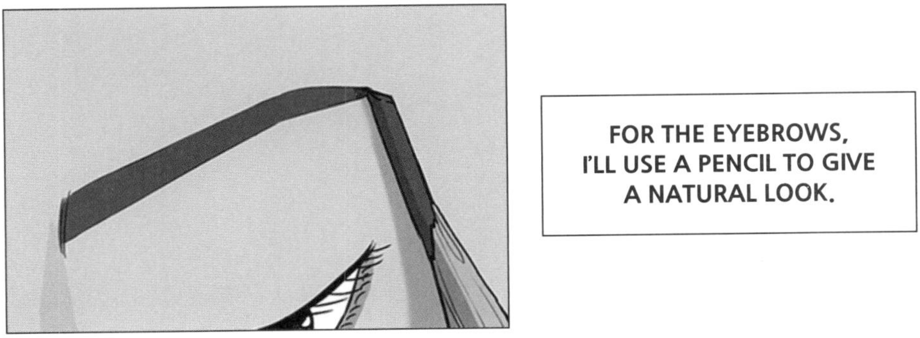
FOR THE EYEBROWS, I'LL USE A PENCIL TO GIVE A NATURAL LOOK.

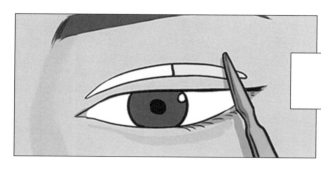

DOUBLE EYELID TAPE,
AN ABSOLUTE MUST!

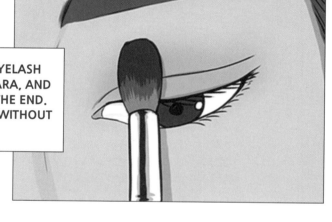

JUST A TOUCH WITH THE EYELASH
CURLER, I'LL SKIP THE MASCARA, AND
JUST A BIT OF EYELINER AT THE END.
I'LL APPLY THE EYESHADOW WITHOUT
ANY PEARL.

AS FOR THE LENSES,
I'LL USE BROWN ONES
WITH JUST THE RIGHT SIZE.

A CORAL TONE FOR THE LIPS!
A SLIGHTLY DEEPER ROSE COLOR FOR
THE INSIDE OF THE LIPS...

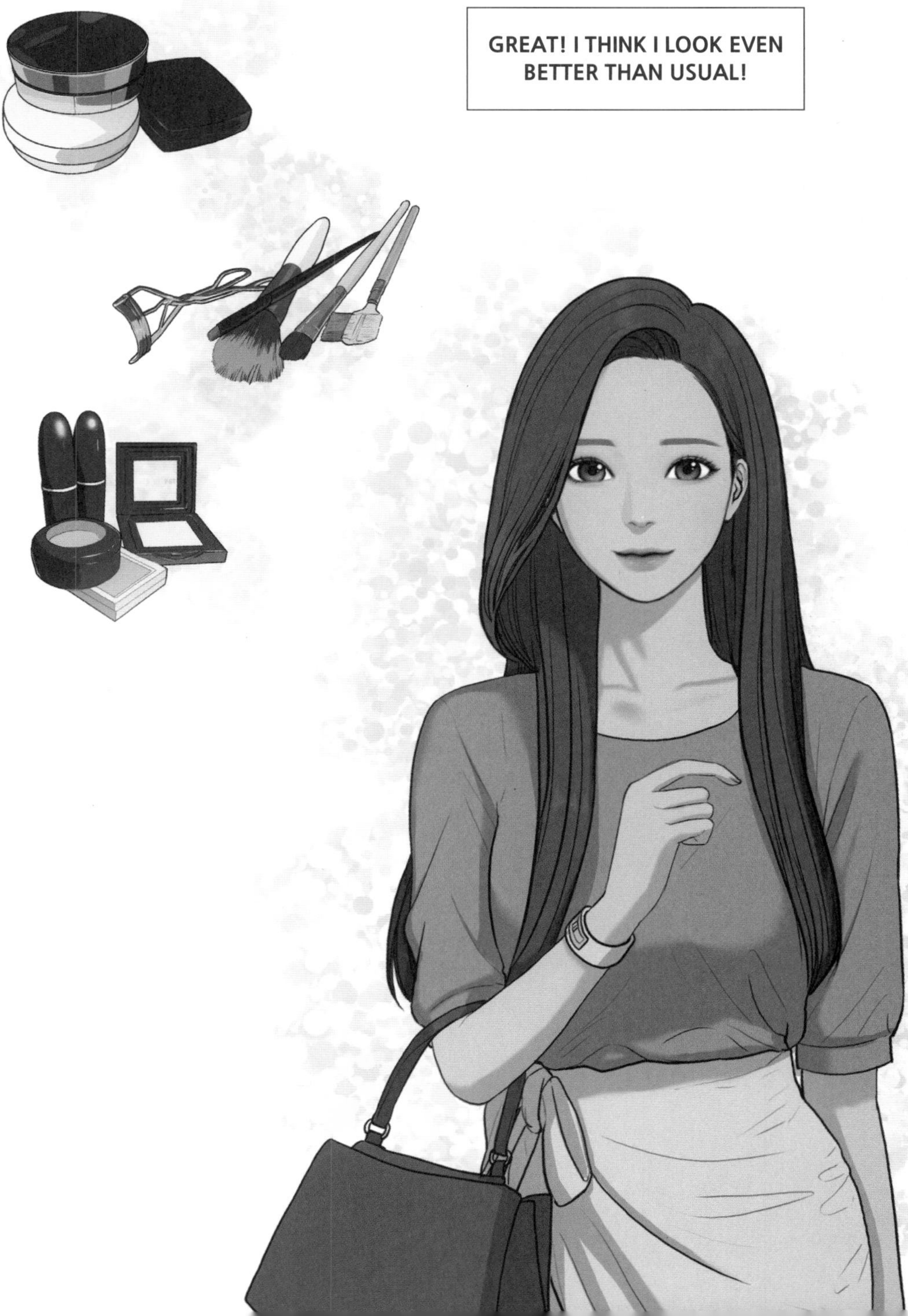
GREAT! I THINK I LOOK EVEN BETTER THAN USUAL!

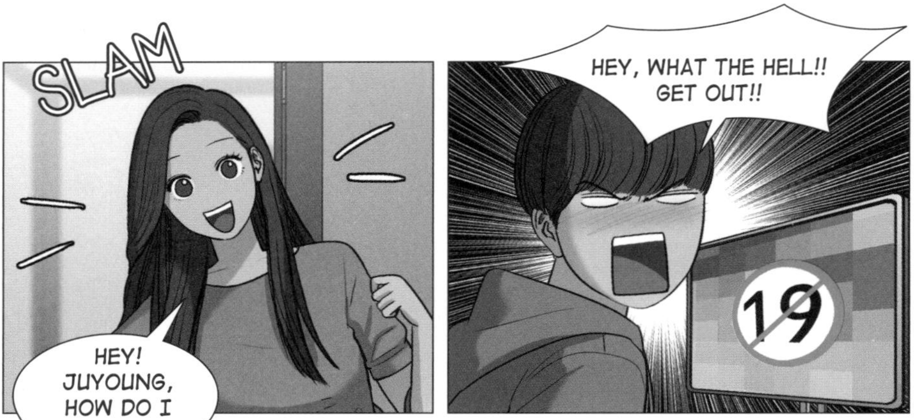
SLAM
HEY! JUYOUNG, HOW DO I LOOK?
HEY, WHAT THE HELL!! GET OUT!!
19

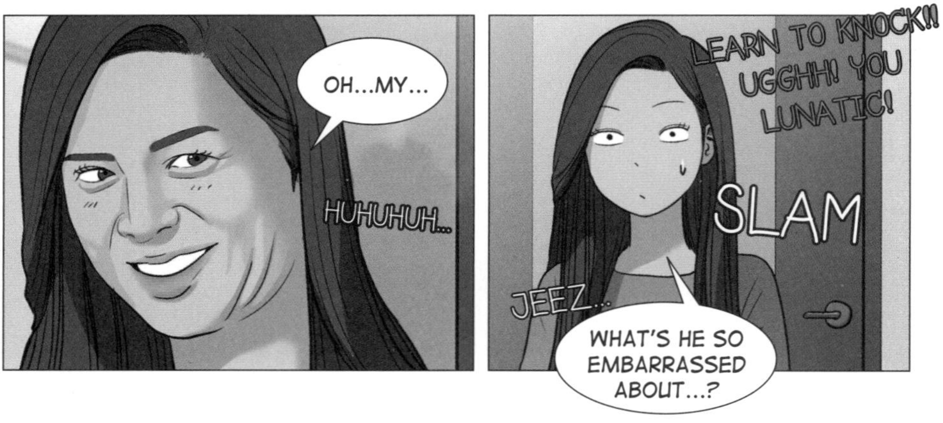
OH...MY...
HUHUHUH...
LEARN TO KNOCK!! UGGHH! YOU LUNATIC!
SLAM
JEEZ...
WHAT'S HE SO EMBARRASSED ABOUT...?

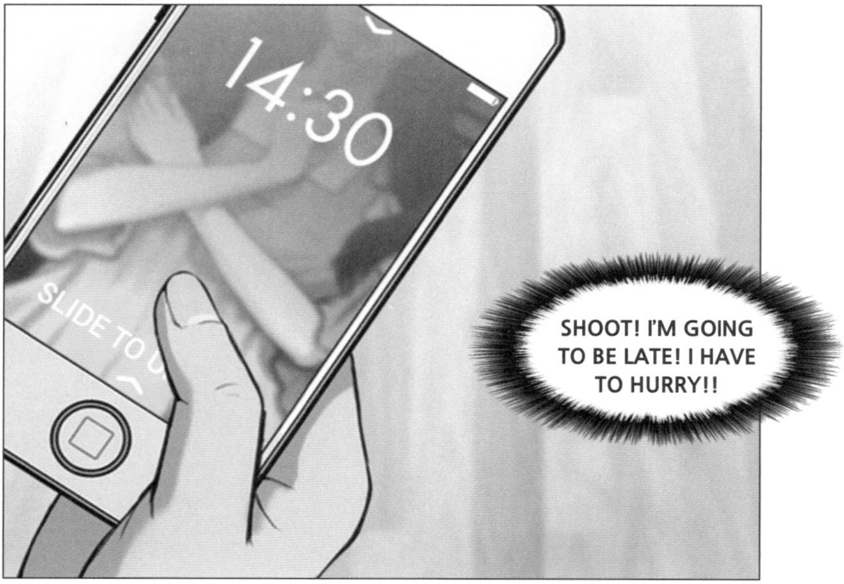
14:30
SLIDE TO U
SHOOT! I'M GOING TO BE LATE! I HAVE TO HURRY!!

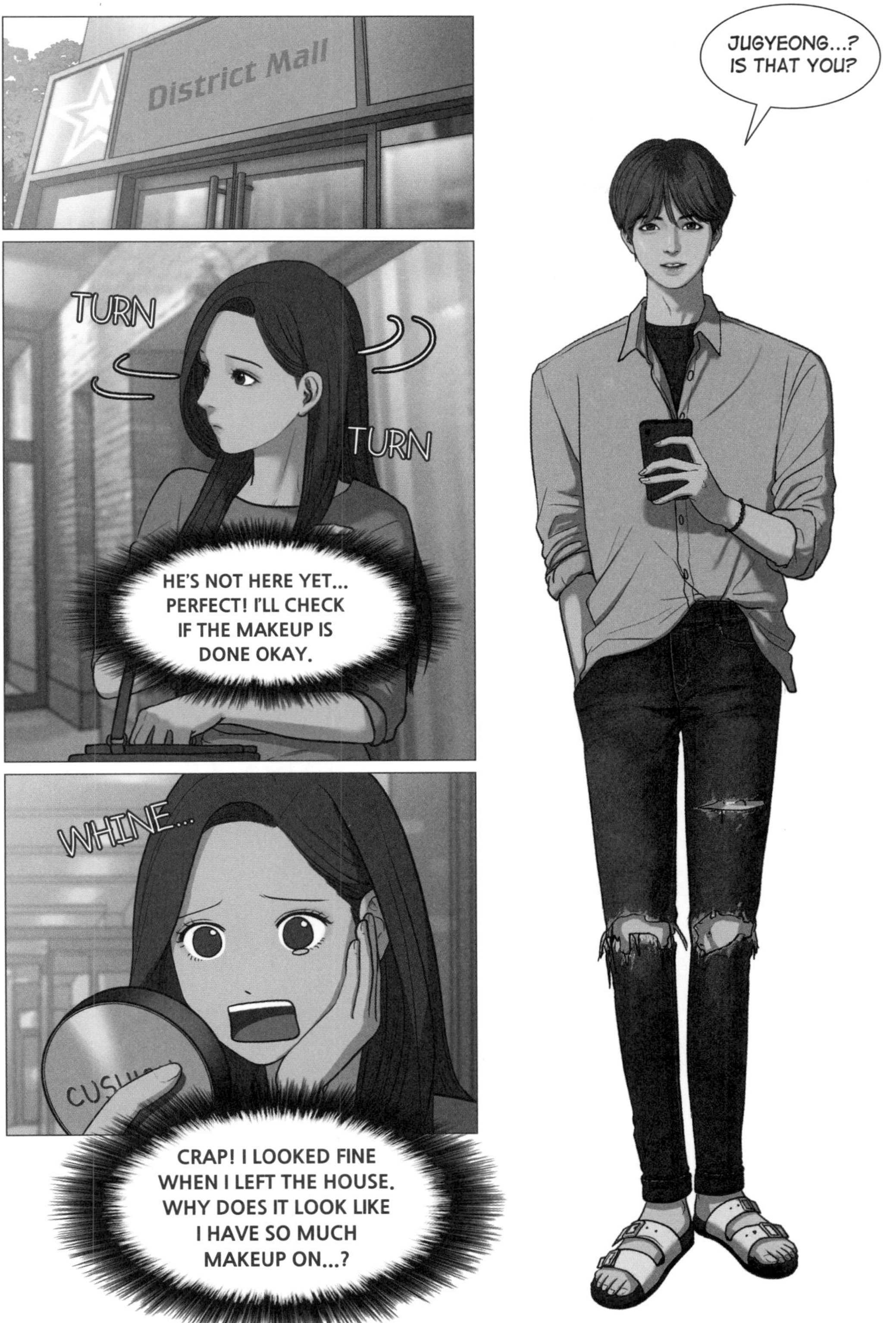
District Mall
TURN
TURN
HE'S NOT HERE YET... PERFECT! I'LL CHECK IF THE MAKEUP IS DONE OKAY.
WHINE...
CRAP! I LOOKED FINE WHEN I LEFT THE HOUSE. WHY DOES IT LOOK LIKE I HAVE SO MUCH MAKEUP ON...?
JUGYEONG...? IS THAT YOU?

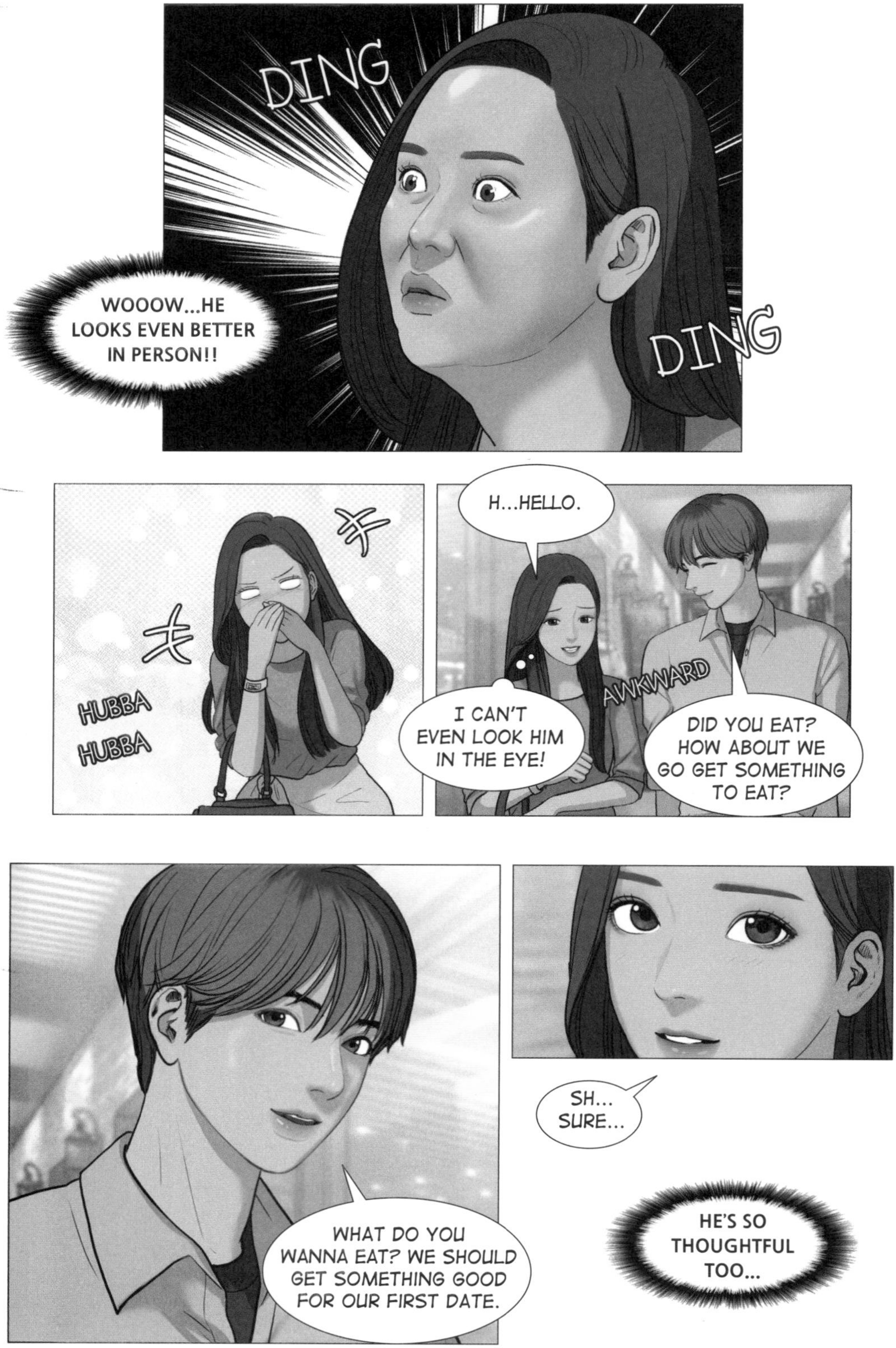
DING
WOOOW...HE LOOKS EVEN BETTER IN PERSON!!
DING
HUBBA
HUBBA
H...HELLO.
I CAN'T EVEN LOOK HIM IN THE EYE!
AWKWARD
DID YOU EAT? HOW ABOUT WE GO GET SOMETHING TO EAT?
WHAT DO YOU WANNA EAT? WE SHOULD GET SOMETHING GOOD FOR OUR FIRST DATE.
SH... SURE...
HE'S SO THOUGHTFUL TOO...

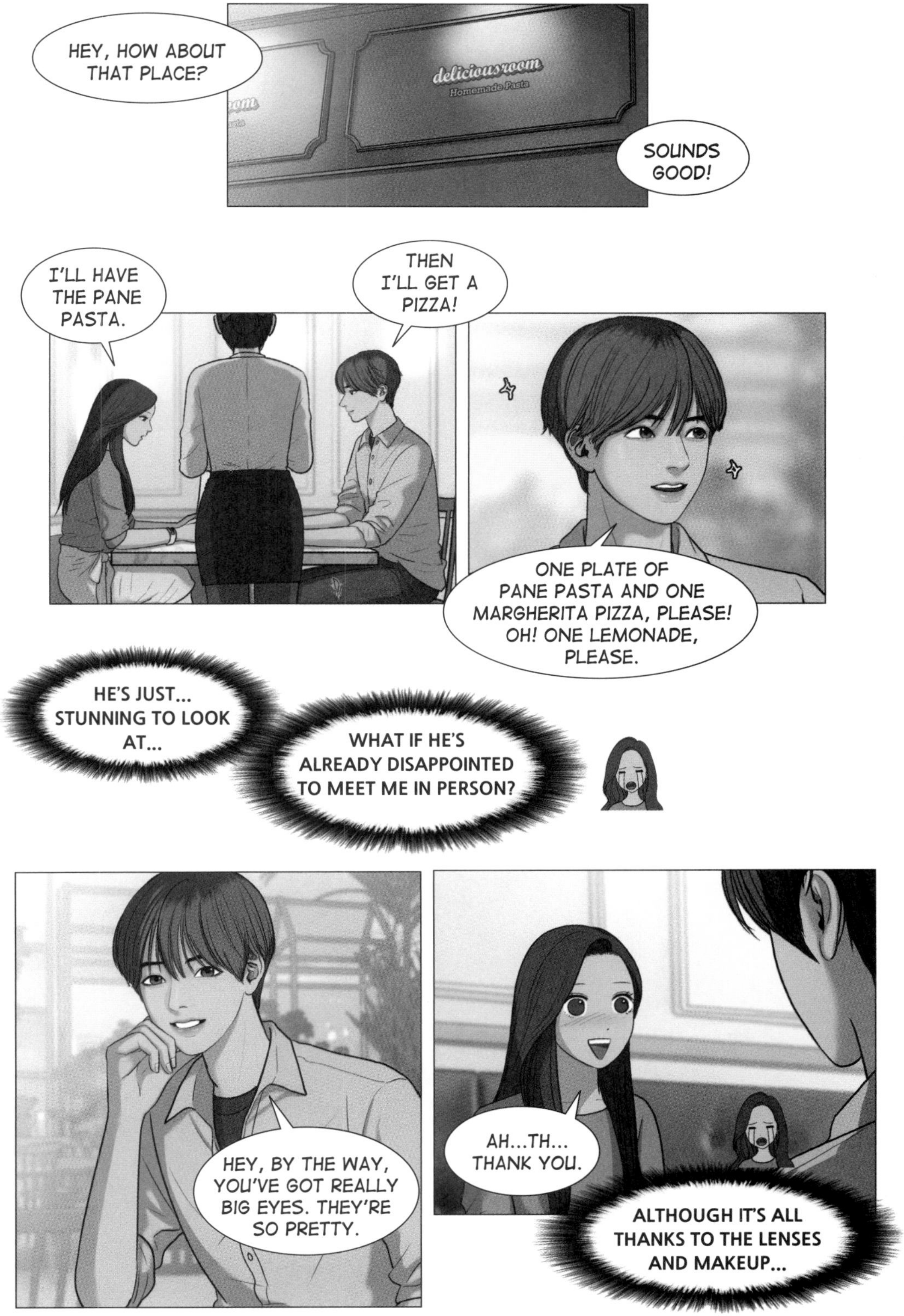
HEY, HOW ABOUT THAT PLACE?
deliciousroom
Homemade Pasta
SOUNDS GOOD!
I'LL HAVE THE PANE PASTA.
THEN I'LL GET A PIZZA!
ONE PLATE OF PANE PASTA AND ONE MARGHERITA PIZZA, PLEASE! OH! ONE LEMONADE, PLEASE.
HE'S JUST... STUNNING TO LOOK AT...
WHAT IF HE'S ALREADY DISAPPOINTED TO MEET ME IN PERSON?
HEY, BY THE WAY, YOU'VE GOT REALLY BIG EYES. THEY'RE SO PRETTY.
AH...TH... THANK YOU.
ALTHOUGH IT'S ALL THANKS TO THE LENSES AND MAKEUP...

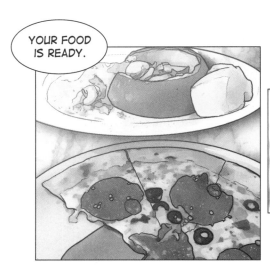

YOUR FOOD IS READY.

I'LL ROLL UP MY PASTA TODAY!

SPIN

SPIN

YUM

YUM

OMG! IT'S BEEN AGES SINCE I HAD PASTA! IT'S SO GOOD!

WHOOPS, WAS I TOO FOCUSED ON EATING?

SMILE

WANT TO TRY SOME OF MINE TOO?

HERE!

AH, TH...THANK YOU.

A CLEAN SET OF CUTLERY...

HE'S SO CONSIDERATE, TOO!

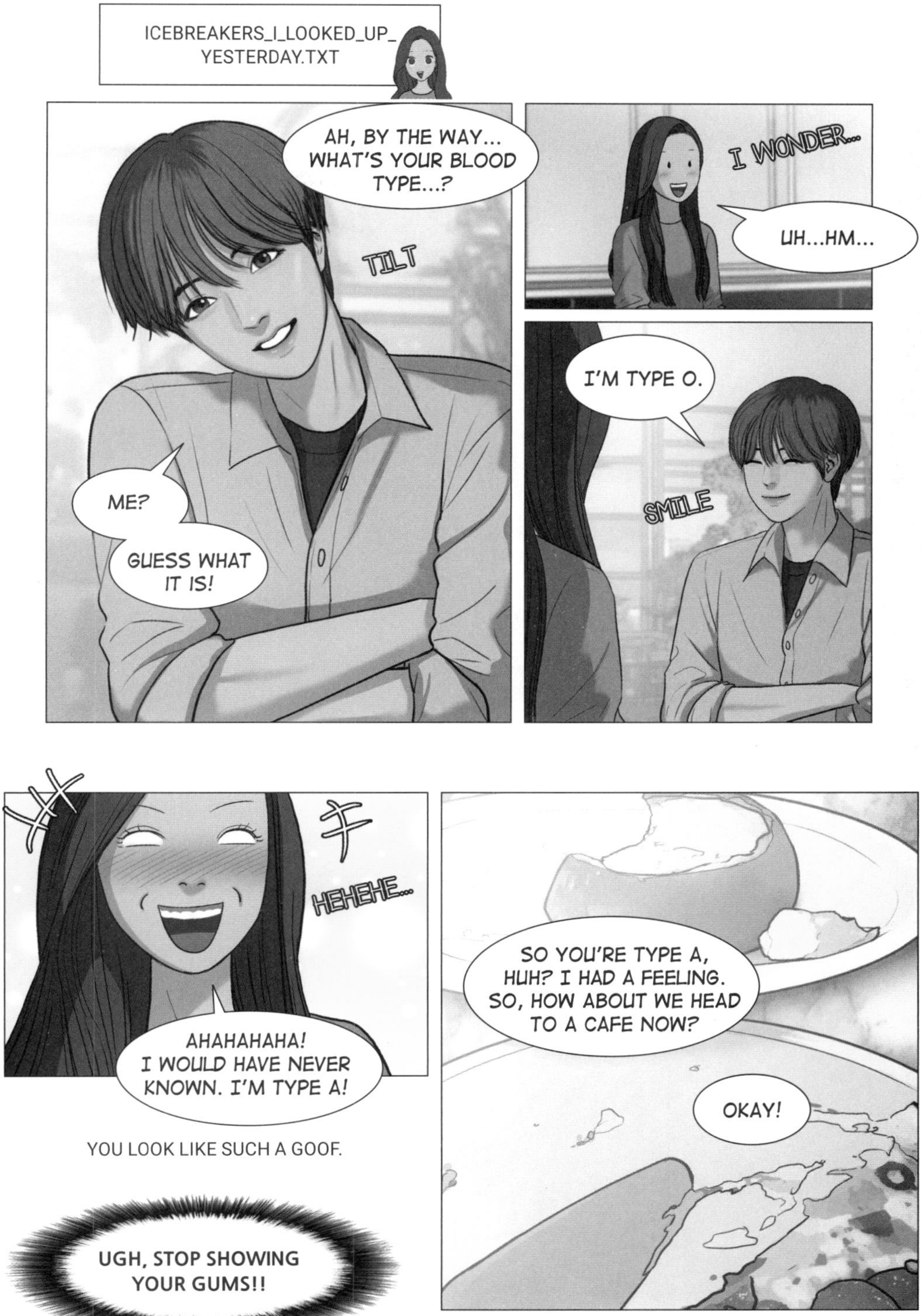
ICEBREAKERS_I_LOOKED_UP_YESTERDAY.TXT
AH, BY THE WAY... WHAT'S YOUR BLOOD TYPE...?
TILT
ME?
GUESS WHAT IT IS!
I WONDER...
UH...HM...
I'M TYPE O.
SMILE
HEHEHE...
AHAHAHAHA! I WOULD HAVE NEVER KNOWN. I'M TYPE A!
YOU LOOK LIKE SUCH A GOOF.
UGH, STOP SHOWING YOUR GUMS!!
SO YOU'RE TYPE A, HUH? I HAD A FEELING. SO, HOW ABOUT WE HEAD TO A CAFE NOW?
OKAY!

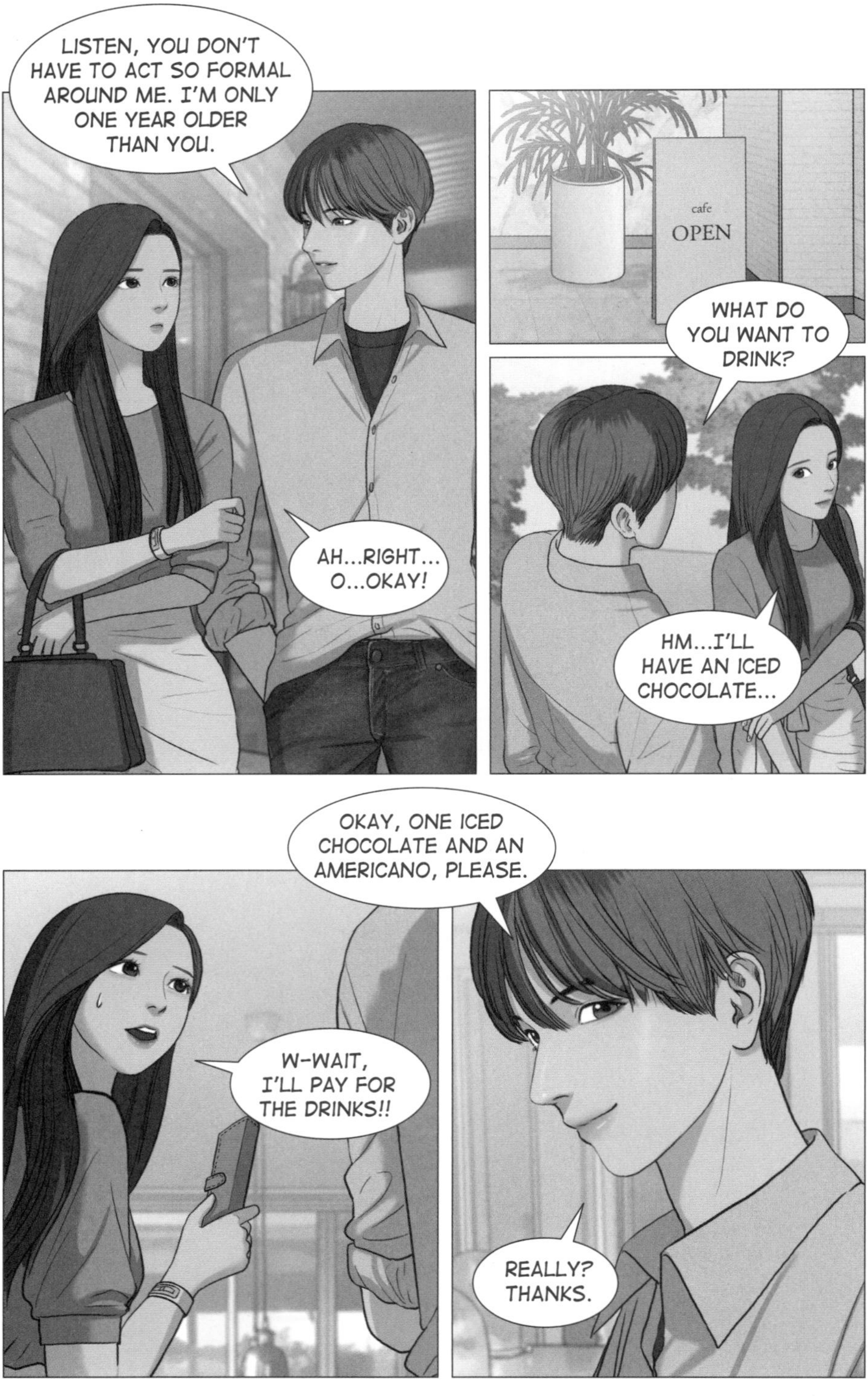
LISTEN, YOU DON'T HAVE TO ACT SO FORMAL AROUND ME. I'M ONLY ONE YEAR OLDER THAN YOU.
AH...RIGHT... O...OKAY!
cafe OPEN
WHAT DO YOU WANT TO DRINK?
HM...I'LL HAVE AN ICED CHOCOLATE...
OKAY, ONE ICED CHOCOLATE AND AN AMERICANO, PLEASE.
W-WAIT, I'LL PAY FOR THE DRINKS!!
REALLY? THANKS.

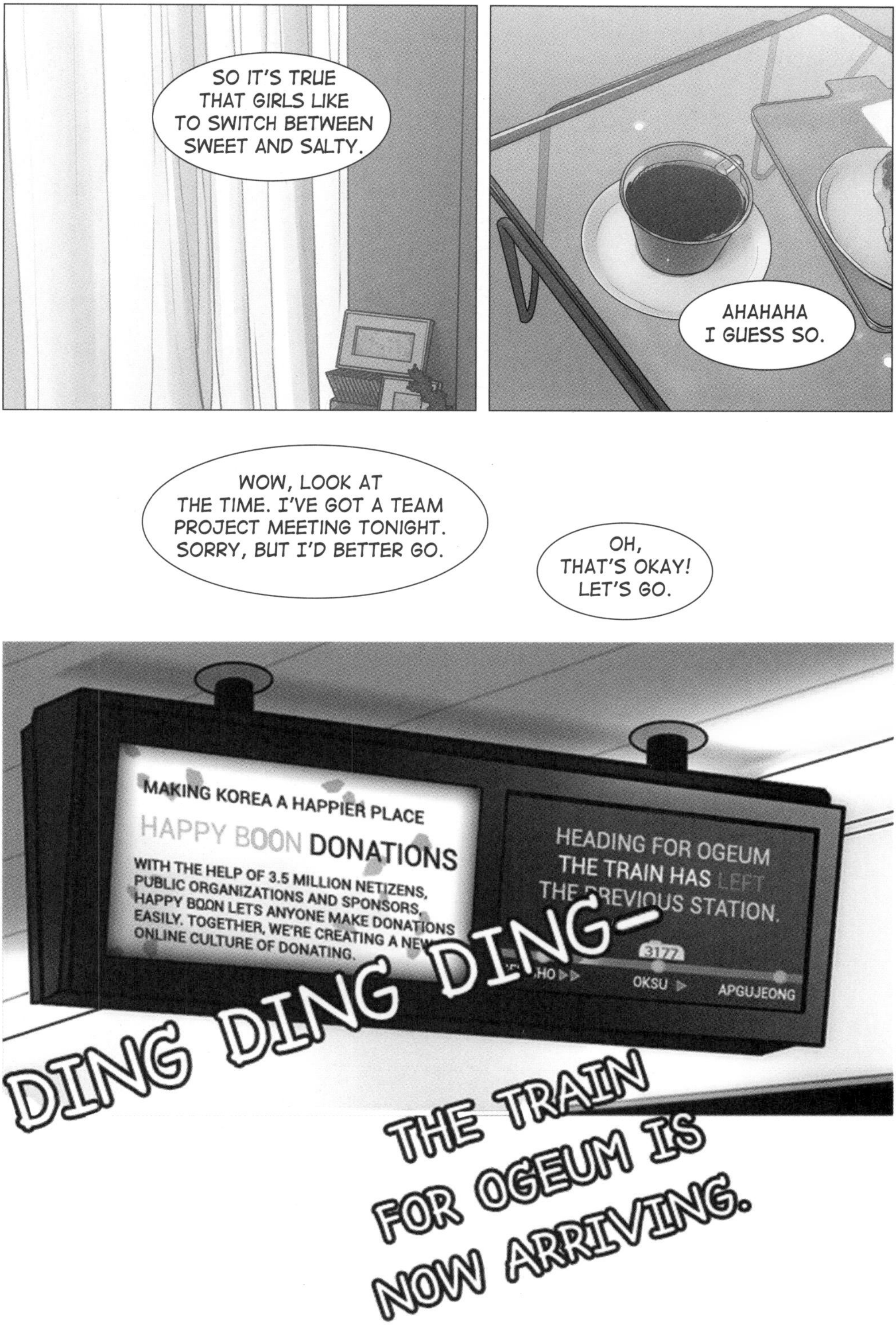
SO IT'S TRUE THAT GIRLS LIKE TO SWITCH BETWEEN SWEET AND SALTY.
AHAHAHA I GUESS SO.
WOW, LOOK AT THE TIME. I'VE GOT A TEAM PROJECT MEETING TONIGHT. SORRY, BUT I'D BETTER GO.
OH, THAT'S OKAY! LET'S GO.
MAKING KOREA A HAPPIER PLACE
HAPPY BOON DONATIONS
WITH THE HELP OF 3.5 MILLION NETIZENS, PUBLIC ORGANIZATIONS AND SPONSORS, HAPPY BOON LETS ANYONE MAKE DONATIONS EASILY. TOGETHER, WE'RE CREATING A NEW ONLINE CULTURE OF DONATING.
HEADING FOR OGEUM
THE TRAIN HAS LEFT
STATION.
3177
OKSU
APGUJEONG
DING DING DING–
THE TRAIN FOR OGEUM IS NOW ARRIVING.

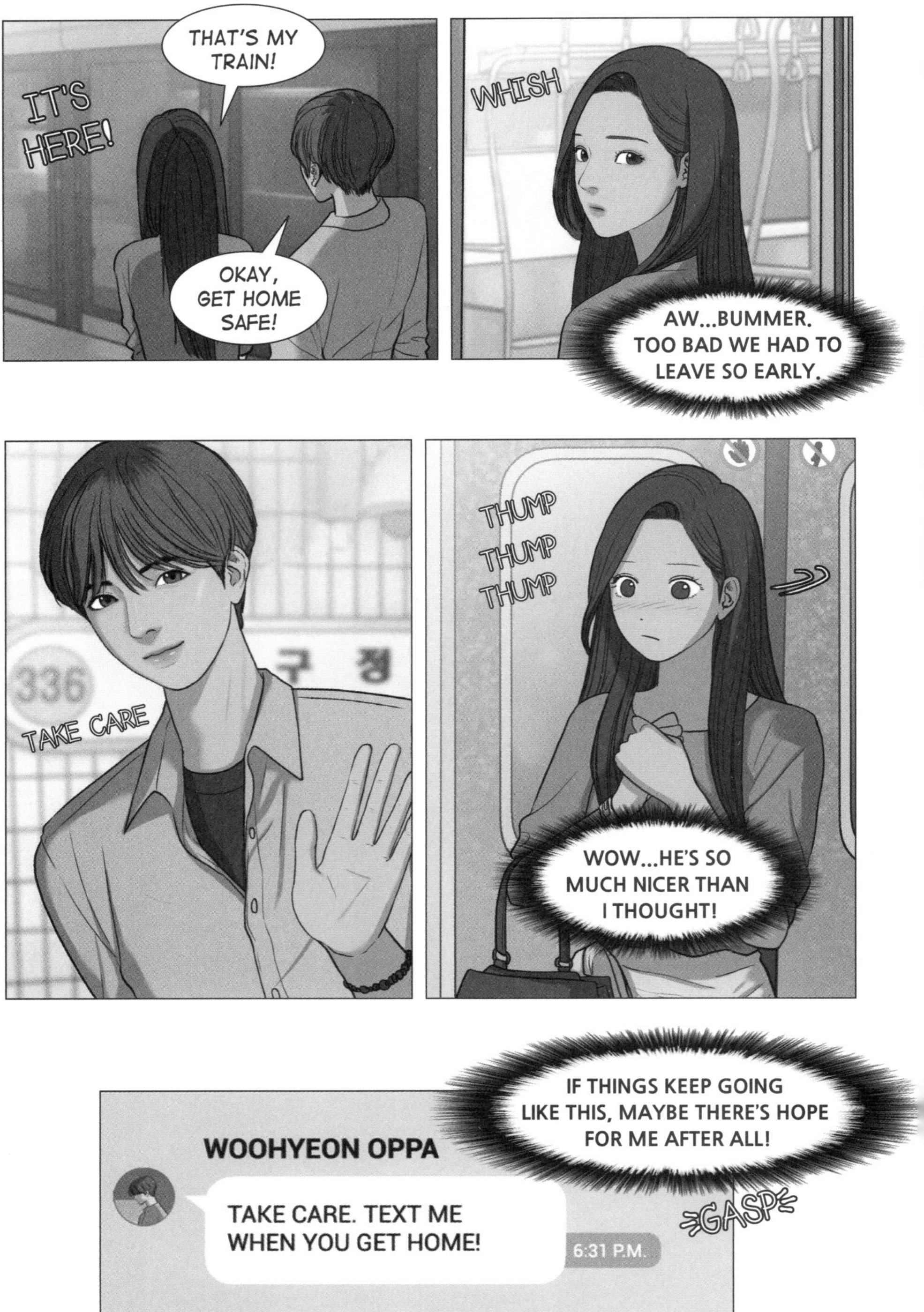
IT'S HERE!
THAT'S MY TRAIN!
OKAY, GET HOME SAFE!
WHISH
AW...BUMMER. TOO BAD WE HAD TO LEAVE SO EARLY.
336
구 정
TAKE CARE
THUMP
THUMP
THUMP
WOW...HE'S SO MUCH NICER THAN I THOUGHT!
WOOHYEON OPPA
TAKE CARE. TEXT ME WHEN YOU GET HOME!
6:31 P.M.
IF THINGS KEEP GOING LIKE THIS, MAYBE THERE'S HOPE FOR ME AFTER ALL!
GASP

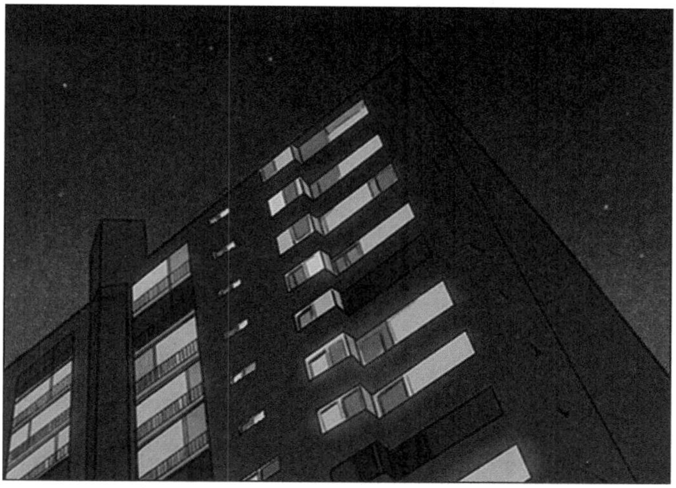

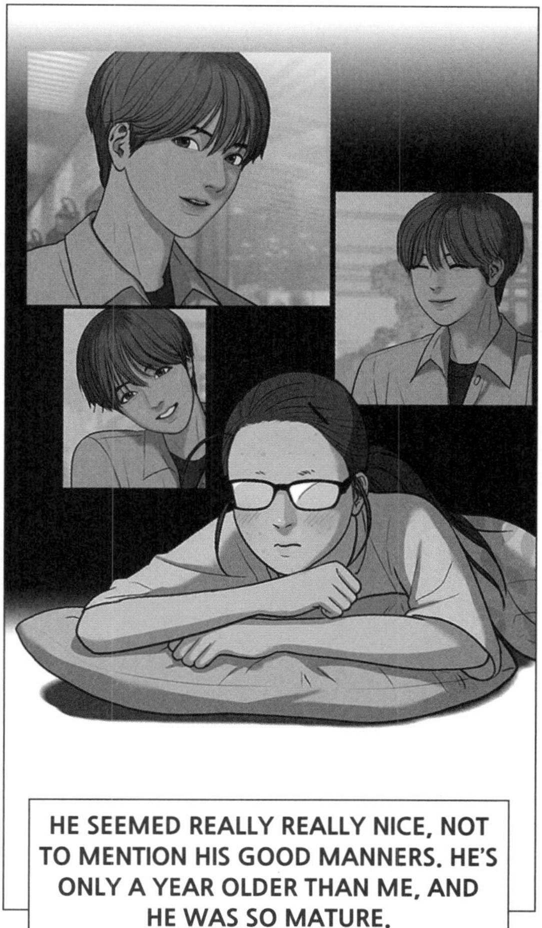
HE SEEMED REALLY REALLY NICE, NOT TO MENTION HIS GOOD MANNERS. HE'S ONLY A YEAR OLDER THAN ME, AND HE WAS SO MATURE.

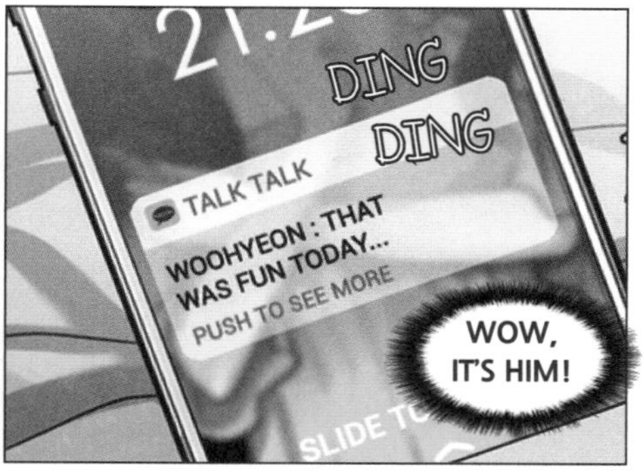
DING
DING
TALK TALK
WOOHYEON : THAT WAS FUN TODAY...
PUSH TO SEE MORE
WOW, IT'S HIM!

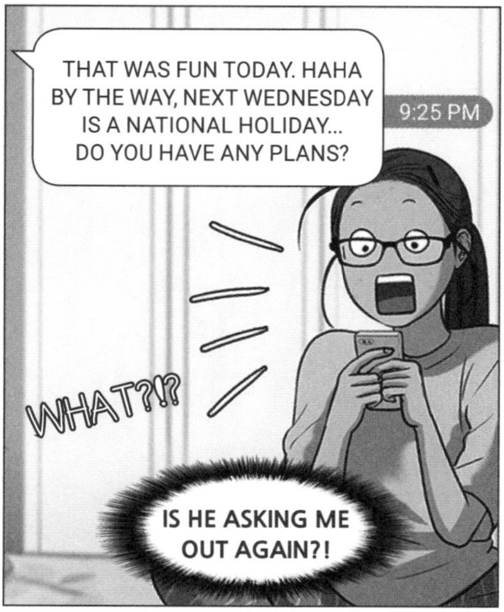
THAT WAS FUN TODAY. HAHA BY THE WAY, NEXT WEDNESDAY IS A NATIONAL HOLIDAY... DO YOU HAVE ANY PLANS?
9:25 PM
WHAT?!?
IS HE ASKING ME OUT AGAIN?!

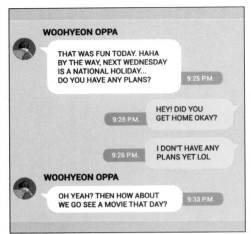

WOOHYEON OPPA

THAT WAS FUN TODAY. HAHA
BY THE WAY, NEXT WEDNESDAY
IS A NATIONAL HOLIDAY...
DO YOU HAVE ANY PLANS? — 9:25 P.M.

9:25 P.M. — HEY! DID YOU
GET HOME OKAY?

9:26 P.M. — I DON'T HAVE ANY
PLANS YET LOL

WOOHYEON OPPA

OH YEAH? THEN HOW ABOUT
WE GO SEE A MOVIE THAT DAY? — 9:33 P.M.

A MOVIE...?

REALLY...? FOR REAL...?

SERIOUSLY...?

IF HE'S ALREADY
ASKING TO MEET ME AGAIN...
THAT SURE SEEMS LIKE
A GREEN LIGHT TO ME!

WEDNESDAY.

I'M SHAKING...I EVEN PUT
ON THE LIMITED-EDITION COLORED
LENSES I'VE BEEN SAVING FOR
A SPECIAL OCCASION...

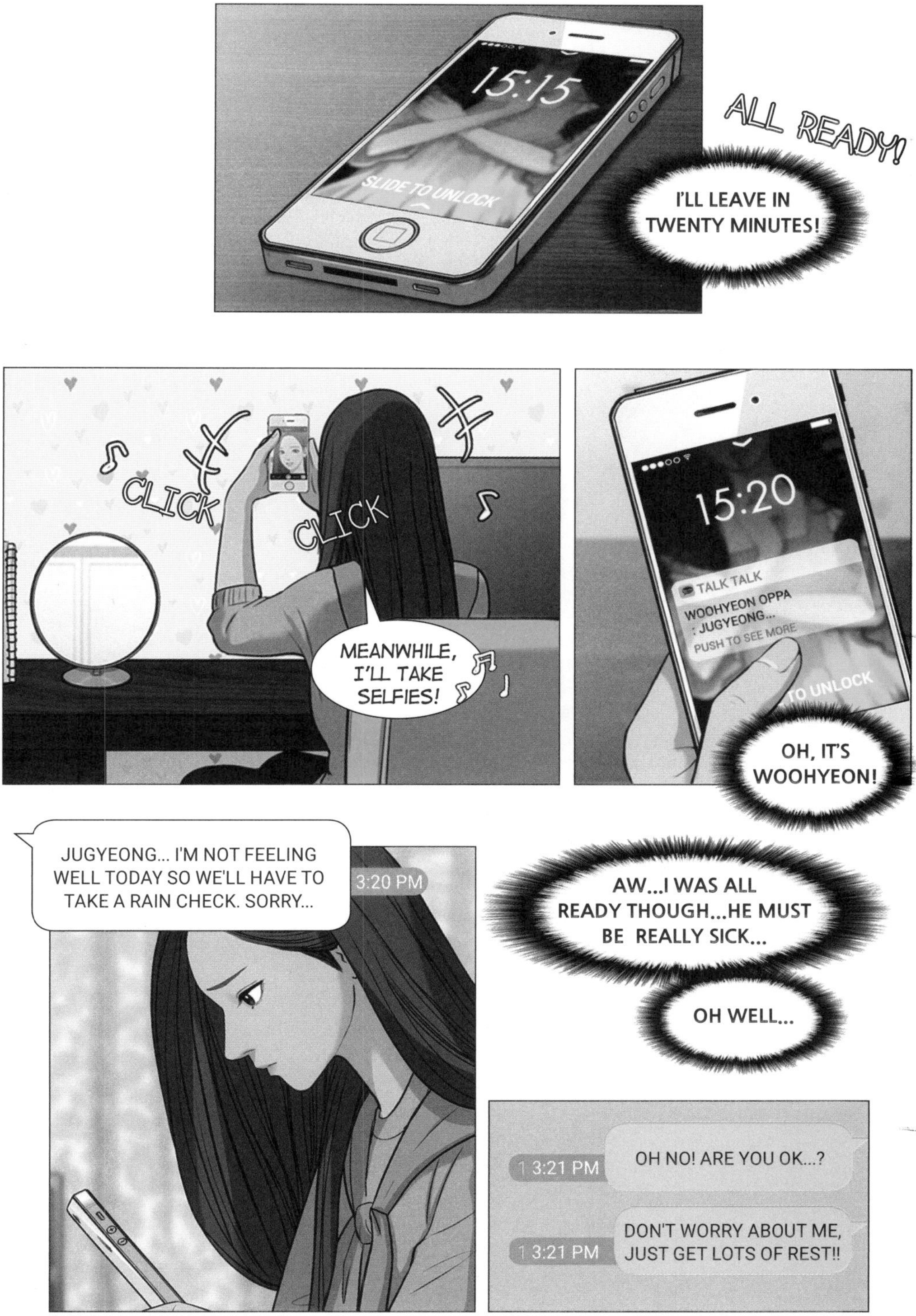
15:15
SLIDE TO UNLOCK
ALL READY!
I'LL LEAVE IN TWENTY MINUTES!
CLICK
CLICK
MEANWHILE, I'LL TAKE SELFIES!
15:20
TALK TALK
WOOHYEON OPPA
: JUGYEONG...
PUSH TO SEE MORE
TO UNLOCK
OH, IT'S WOOHYEON!
JUGYEONG... I'M NOT FEELING WELL TODAY SO WE'LL HAVE TO TAKE A RAIN CHECK. SORRY...
3:20 PM
AW...I WAS ALL READY THOUGH...HE MUST BE REALLY SICK...
OH WELL...
1 3:21 PM
OH NO! ARE YOU OK...?
1 3:21 PM
DON'T WORRY ABOUT ME, JUST GET LOTS OF REST!!

THE NEXT DAY.

SNIFFLE

SNIFFLE

JEEZ, WHAT'S WRONG WITH YOU?! DID SOMETHING HAPPEN WITH THAT GUY?

SNIFFLE

SNIFFLE

WELL...

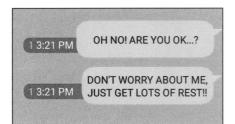

1 3:21 PM   OH NO! ARE YOU OK...?

1 3:21 PM   DON'T WORRY ABOUT ME, JUST GET LOTS OF REST!!

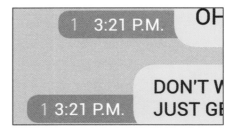

1   3:21 P.M.   OH

DON'T W

1 3:21 P.M.   JUST GI

I SENT HIM THESE MESSAGES YESTERDAY... BUT HE STILL HASN'T EVEN READ THEM...

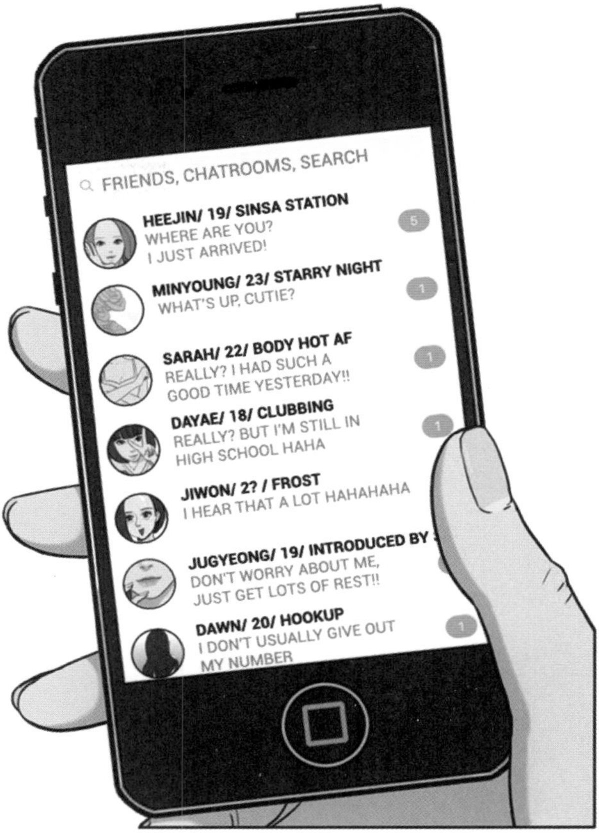
FRIENDS, CHATROOMS, SEARCH
HEEJIN/ 19/ SINSA STATION
WHERE ARE YOU?
I JUST ARRIVED!
5
MINYOUNG/ 23/ STARRY NIGHT
WHAT'S UP, CUTIE?
1
SARAH/ 22/ BODY HOT AF
REALLY? I HAD SUCH A
GOOD TIME YESTERDAY!!
1
DAYAE/ 18/ CLUBBING
REALLY? BUT I'M STILL IN
HIGH SCHOOL HAHA
1
JIWON/ 2? / FROST
I HEAR THAT A LOT HAHAHAHA
JUGYEONG/ 19/ INTRODUCED BY
DON'T WORRY ABOUT ME,
JUST GET LOTS OF REST!!
DAWN/ 20/ HOOKUP
I DON'T USUALLY GIVE OUT
MY NUMBER
1

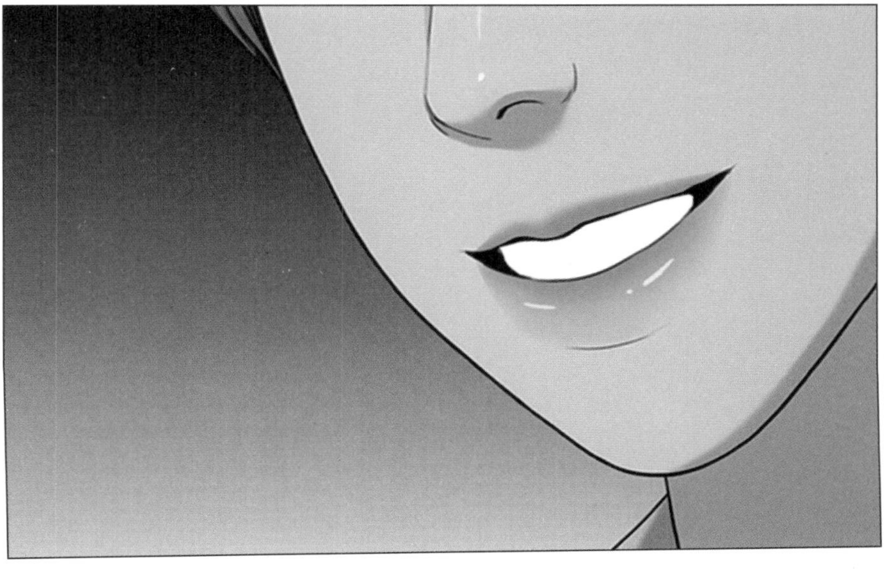

ART & STORY Yaongyi 야옹이

Kim Na-young, better known by her nom de plume, Yaongyi (야옹이, literally "meow"), is a South Korean comic artist (manhwaga), former model, and creator of *True Beauty* on WEBTOON.

Read the original
on www.WEBTOONS.com

WEBTOON
UNSCROLLED
Scrolling Not Required